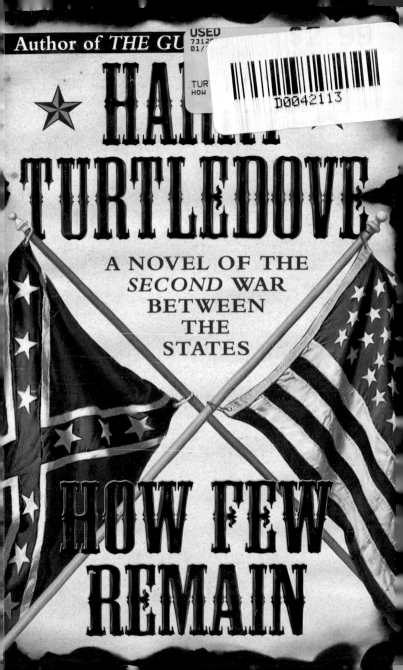

USED
7312
01/

Author of *THE GU*

HARRY TURTLEDOVE

A NOVEL OF THE *SECOND* WAR BETWEEN THE STATES

HOW FEW REMAIN

Enter the world of alternate history
and discover how things *might* have been...

Look for Harry Turtledove's newest novel—
an epic of World War I, fought on American soil!

THE GREAT WAR:
AMERICAN FRONT

Ⓑ Ⓑ
Ballantine / Del Rey /
Fawcett / Ivy

9 780345 406149

ISBN 0-345-40614-1

U.S. $7.99/Canada $9.99

50799

▷ EAN
S

"Harry Turtledove has established himself as the grand master of the alternative history form . . . *How Few Remain* is perhaps his best so far."
—POUL ANDERSON

"*How Few Remain* proves once again that Harry Turtledove is, quite simply, the best . . . and that he is getting even better. It has gripping action and real people in a history not our own; Turtledove brings off a tour de force."
—S. M. STIRLING
Author of *Drakon*

"The cast of characters is rich and wonderful and brilliantly selected to put the brightest light on what this World of If has to say to our World of Is . . . The action in the book is sweeping and exciting and opens up many wonderful cans of worms."
—GAHAN WILSON
Realms of Fantasy

"Turtledove has once again done such a masterful job of rewriting history that, after finishing this book, I had to check my copy of *USA Today* to make sure we were still one united country."
—BRYCE ZABEL
Executive Producer/Co-Creator of *Dark Skies*

"Harry Turtledove is one of the geniuses of this demanding field . . . Turtledove's latest book, *How Few Remain*, is no exception to his record of excellence."
—*Science Fiction Age*

"Displays the compelling combination of rigorous historiography and robust storytelling that readers have come to expect from Turtledove, who once again deftly integrates surprising yet believable social, economic, military, and political developments."
—*Publishers Weekly* (starred review)

By Harry Turtledove.
Published by Ballantine Books:

The Videssos Cycle:
  THE MISPLACED LEGION
  AN EMPEROR FOR THE LEGION
  THE LEGION OF VIDESSOS
  SWORDS OF THE LEGION

The Tale of Krispos:
  Book One: KRISPOS RISING
  Book Two: KRISPOS OF VIDESSOS
  Book Three: KRISPOS THE EMPEROR

The Time of Troubles Series:
  THE STOLEN THRONE
  HAMMER AND ANVIL
  THE THOUSAND CITIES
  VIDESSOS BESIEGED*

The Worldwar Series:
  WORLDWAR: IN THE BALANCE
  WORLDWAR: TILTING THE BALANCE
  WORLDWAR: UPSETTING THE BALANCE
  WORLDWAR: STRIKING THE BALANCE

NONINTERFERENCE
A WORLD OF DIFFERENCE
KALEIDOSCOPE
EARTHGRIP
DEPARTURES
THE GUNS OF THE SOUTH
THE STOLEN THRONE
HOW FEW REMAIN

*Forthcoming

Books published by The Ballantine Publishing Group
are available at quantity discounts on bulk purchases
for premium, educational, fund-raising, and special
sales use. For details, please call 1-800-733-3000.

HOW FEW REMAIN

Harry Turtledove

A Del Rey® Book
BALLANTINE BOOKS • NEW YORK

Sale of this book without a front cover may be unauthorized. If this book is coverless, it may have been reported to the publisher as "unsold or destroyed" and neither the author nor the publisher may have received payment for it.

A Del Rey® Book
Published by The Ballantine Publishing Group
Copyright © 1997 by Harry Turtledove
Map by Mapping Specialists, Ltd.

All rights reserved under International and Pan-American Copyright Conventions. Published in the United States by The Ballantine Publishing Group, a division of Random House, Inc., New York, and simultaneously in Canada by Random House of Canada Limited, Toronto.

http://www.randomhouse.com

Library of Congress Catalog Card Number: 97-97127

ISBN 0-345-40614-1

Manufactured in the United States of America

First Hardcover Edition: October 1997
First Mass Market Edition: June 1998

10 9 8 7 6 5 4 3 2 1

Now twenty years have passed away,
*   Since I here bid farewell*
To woods, and fields, and scenes of play
*   And school-mates loved so well.*

Where many were, how few remain
*   Of old familiar things!*
But seeing these to mind again
*   The lost and absent brings.*

The friends I left that parting day—
*   How changed, as time has sped!*
Young childhood grown, strong manhood gray,
*   And half of all are dead.*

—ABRAHAM LINCOLN,
"My Childhood Home I See Again"
(1846), stanzas 6–8

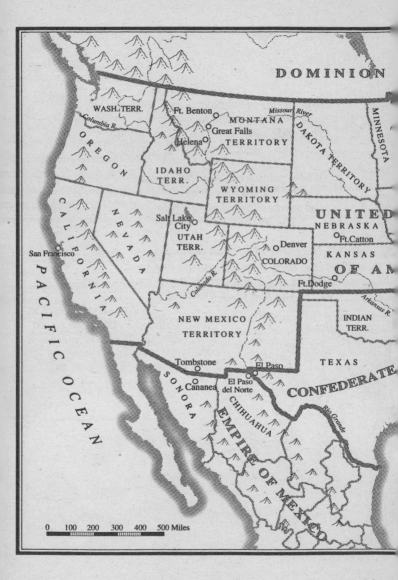

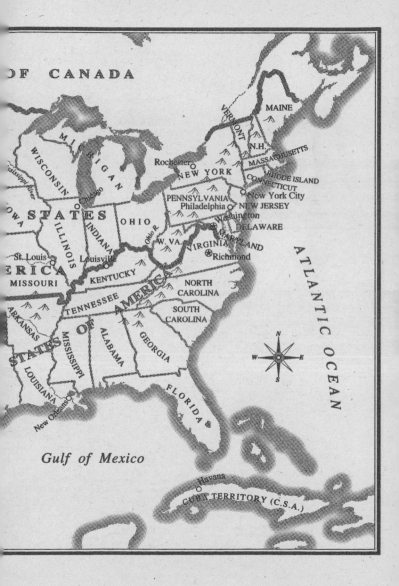

PRELUDE

1862

10 September—Outside Frederick, Maryland

The Army of Northern Virginia was breaking camp. The lean, ragged soldiers, their gray uniforms and especially their shoes much the worse for wear, began the next long tramp, this one north and west toward Hagerstown. They were profoundly—and profanely—glad to be getting away from Frederick.

"That 'Bonnie Blue Flag,' that ain't nothin' but a damn pack o' lies," a corporal announced to anyone who would listen as he slung his haversack over his shoulder.

"You'd best believe it is," one of the privates in his company agreed, pausing in the middle of the agreement to spit a brown stream of tobacco juice from the chaw that bulged out his left cheek. "This here miserable Frederick town, it ain't nothin' but a stinkin' ol' city full of damnyankees. Sons of bitches wouldn't take our money, wouldn't open up their stores so as we could get the supplies we needed, wouldn't—"

Taking a corporal's privilege, the corporal interrupted: "You can't even get into that there town without you have a letter in writin' from your officer, says you can. Otherwise, them lousy provost guards, they'd just as soon arrest you as look at you, god-damn miserable snoops. Hear them talk, you'd think we was the ones in the Yankee uniforms."

"Hell, I *am* in a Yankee uniform—Yankee trousers, anyways," the private answered. "The Northern fellow I took 'em off, he didn't need 'em no more."

The courier's horse daintily picked its way through the chaos, careful where it set its feet. The lieutenant aboard the bay gelding didn't blame the animal for that; once an army had camped in a field, it wasn't a pleasant place any more, no matter how pleasant it might have been to start out with.

They said that, once you'd been encamped for a while, you stopped noticing the stink. The lieutenant wrinkled his nose. He'd never found that to be true. Every time he breathed in, he smelled the slit trenches (and the men hadn't been all that careful about using them; this was, after all, Yankee country), horse manure, thousands of bodies that had done a heap of hard marching without baths any time lately, and the choking smoke from thousands of little fires. The good odors of cooking food, coffee, and tobacco had to fight hard to make themselves noticed against all that.

"Lieutenant!" somebody called from behind him. "Hey, Lieutenant!" The courier paid no particular attention. The Army of Northern Virginia wasn't as big as it should have been, but it was big enough to have a hell of a lot of lieutenants.

Then the call got more specific: "You there, Lieutenant, up on the bay—hold on, will you?"

The courier reined in and looked back over his shoulder. "You want me?"

"No—your cousin back in Richmond." The corporal who'd been grousing about the provost guards grinned impudently up at him. Getting men to give officers the respect their rank deserved was a battle the army hadn't won yet and wouldn't any time soon. The courier was about to tell the infantryman off when the fellow held up a fat white envelope, now somewhat stained with mud. "You dropped this, sir."

"Good God!" The courier felt woozy, light-headed. "Give it to me!"

"Here you go." The corporal handed it to him. He cocked his head to one side. "You all right, Lieutenant? You don't mind me sayin' so, you look white as a ghost, you do."

"I believe it." The lieutenant clutched the envelope as if he were a drowning man and it a plank. "Do you know what's in here?"

"Cigars, felt like," the corporal answered with the casual expertise of a man who'd done a good deal of foraging.

"Cigars it is." The courier opened the envelope and took them out. There were three, all of them nice and long and thick. He handed the corporal the biggest one. "Here—this is for you." The next went to the private with whom the fellow had been grumbling. "And this is for you." He stuck the third in his own mouth.

"Obliged, sir." The corporal walked over to the nearest fire, stuck a twig in it, and got his cigar going. He came back pugging happy clouds and leaned close to the private so he could start his. Then he came up to the courier. After he'd given him a light, he remarked, "That's good baccy, but it don't seem enough to be makin' such a much of a much over, like you was doin'."

"No?" The lieutenant's laugh was the high, sweet sound of pure relief. "Do you know what was wrapped around those cigars?"

The corporal shook his head. "Can't say as I do. Reckon you're gonna tell me, though, so that's all right."

"Oh, nothing much," the courier said, and laughed again. "Only a copy of General Lee's Special Order 191, that's all. Only the orders that say where every division in the Army of Northern Virginia's supposed to be going, and what it's supposed to do when it gets there."

The private shifted the cigar to the corner of his mouth and spoke up: "That don't sound like it'd be somethin' you'd want to lose."

"Not hardly!" The lieutenant tried to imagine what would have happened to him if General Lee found out he'd lost the order. Appalling as that notion was, an even worse one replaced it, one so horrific he said it out loud, as if to exorcise it: "If McClellan's men picked up that envelope, they'd know exactly what we aimed to do, and they'd be able to break us right up."

"Damn fine thing we got it back to you, then," the corporal said. "You hang on to it from here on out, you hear?" He touched a forefinger to the brim of his black felt hat. "And I do thank you kindly for the cigar. That was right good of you." Behind him, the private nodded.

"I'm the one who needs to thank you," the courier said. "Hell's fire, gentlemen, the Confederate States of America might have lost the whole war if you hadn't found that envelope." He waved his gratitude once more, then used the pressure of his legs and a flick of the reins to get his horse moving.

The corporal and private looked after him till he disappeared into the midst of the disorderly throng of soldiers. "Lost the whole war," the corporal echoed scornfully. "He don't think much of himself and the papers he carries, now does he?"

"Ahh, he wasn't a bad feller," the private answered. "He gave us these here cigars, an' he didn't have to do that." He tilted his head back and blew a ragged smoke ring.

1 October—Near New Cumberland, Pennsylvania

Long blond hair streaming out behind him, Captain George Armstrong Custer came galloping from General McClellan's headquarters to those of General Burnside, who commanded the Army of the Potomac's left wing. Brass Napoleons roared. Their cannonballs tore holes in the ranks of the advancing Confederates. Up ahead—up not far enough ahead—rifle muskets barked. Blackpowder smoke drifted in choking clouds, smelling of fireworks.

Custer jerked his mount to an abrupt halt by Burnside's tent. An orderly came over and held the horse's head. Custer sprang down. He ran to General Burnside, who was standing outside the tent, a telescope in his hands. "Damn it, General," Custer said, running a hand through his hair, "I've lost my *hat*."

Burnside shielded his own bald crown from the elements with a tall hat that gave him something of the look of a policeman. The whiskers sprouting luxuriantly on his cheeks and upper lip made his round face rounder yet. "I trust the nation will survive," he said. "What word from General McClellan?"

"Sir, you are to hold your position at all hazard," Custer answered.

"I shall do everything in my power." Burnside's frown deepened the dimple in his clean-shaven chin. "They are pounding us hard, though." As if to underscore his words, a Rebel shell screamed down and exploded perhaps fifty yards from the tent. Custer's horse let out a frightened whinny. It tried to rear. The orderly wouldn't let it.

"You must hold," Custer repeated. "If they get around your left, we are ruined. Also, General McClellan said, you must not fall back any farther. If Jackson's corps is able to bring its artillery to bear on the bridge over the Susquehanna, our line of retreat is cut off."

"General McClellan should have considered that before offering battle on this side of the river," Burnside said tartly.

"This is where we met the Confederates—this is where we fight them." For Custer, that was an axiom of nature.

Burnside stared gloomily at the sun. Through the clotted smoke, it looked red as blood. "Two hours till nightfall, perhaps a bit more," he said, and frowned again. "Very well, Captain. I have my orders, and shall essay to carry them out. You may assure General McClellan on that point."

"I'll do it." Custer started back toward his horse. He was about to mount when the drumroll of musketry from the battle front suddenly got louder, fiercer. "Wait," he told the orderly, his voice sharp.

Burnside was peering through the shiny, brass-cased telescope. Custer had no such aid, but did not need one, either. Men in blue were streaming back toward him. Now and then, one of them turned to fire his Springfield muzzle-loader at the foe, but most seemed intent on nothing more than getting away from the fight as fast as they could.

"What in blazes has gone wrong now?" Custer demanded of the smoky air. The whole campaign had been a nightmare, with Lee getting up through Maryland and into Pennsylvania almost before McClellan learned he'd left Virginia. Never a fast mover, Little Mac had followed as best he could—and been brought to battle here, in this less than auspicious place.

Custer vaulted lightly into the saddle. He set spurs to his horse and sent it at a fast trot, not back toward General McClellan's headquarters, but in the direction from which the retreating Federals were coming.

"Go back, sir," one of them called to him. "Ain't no more we can do here. D. H. Hill's men are over Yellow Breeches Creek and on the Susquehanna. They're a-rollin' us up."

"Then we have to drive the sons of bitches back," Custer snarled. Libbie Bacon, his fiancée, wanted him to stop swearing. He hadn't been able to make himself do it, much as he loved Libbie.

He rode forward again. A few men cheered and followed. More, though, kept right on back toward that one precious bridge.

Craack! A Minié ball zipped past him. Another cut his sleeve, so that he wondered if someone had tugged at his arm till he glanced down and saw the tear.

He yanked an Army Colt out of his holster and blazed away at the Rebels till the six-shooter was empty. He wore another, piratically thrust into the top of one of the big, floppy boots he'd taken from a Confederate cavalryman he'd captured. He emptied that pistol, too, then yanked out his saber.

The sun sparkled from the glittering steel edge. Custer urged his mount up into a caracole. He felt the perfect picture of martial splendor.

"Get out of here, you damn fool!" a grimy-faced corporal yelled. "You reckon you're gonna slaughter all them Rebs with your straight razor there?" He spat on the ground and trudged north toward the bridge.

Suddenly, Custer realized how alone he was. The horse dropped down onto all fours. Custer spurred it through and then past the soldiers from Burnside's beaten left. Behind him, Rebel yells rose like panther screams.

Rebel artillery thundered. Splashes in the Susquehanna said the guns were reaching for that one bridge offering escape from the gray-clad, barefoot fiends of the Army of Northern Virginia. Screams from the bridge said some of the guns were finding it.

As he had in front of Burnside's tent, so Custer leaped down from his horse in front of General McClellan's. Like General Burnside, Little Mac, so hopefully called the Young Napoleon, stood outside. He pointed south, toward Burnside's position. "I hear the fighting building there, Captain," he said. "I trust you conveyed to General Burnside the absolute necessity of holding in place."

"Sir, General Burnside listened, but Stonewall Jackson didn't," Custer answered. "The Rebs are on the river on this side of Yellow Breeches Creek, and I'm damned if I see anything between there and the bridge to stop 'em."

McClellan's handsome face went pale, even with that ruddy sunlight shining down on it. "It is the end, then," he said in a voice like ashes. His shoulders sagged, as if he had taken a wound. "The end, I tell you, Captain. With the Army of the Potomac whipped, who can hope to preserve the Republic intact?"

"We're not whipped yet, sir." Even in Custer's own ears, the brave words sounded hollow, impossible to believe.

"Fire!" somebody shouted off in the distance. "Jesus God, the bridge is on fire!"

"The end," McClellan said again. "The Rebs have out-numbered us from the start." Custer wondered about that, but held his peace. McClellan went on, "We are ruined, ruined, I tell you. After this defeat, England and France will surely recognize the Southern Confederacy, as they have been champing at the bit to do. Not even that buffoon in the White House, the jackass who dragged us into this war, will be able to pretend any longer that it has any hope of coming to a successful resolution."

Custer, a staunch Democrat, had if anything even less use for Abraham Lincoln than did McClellan. "If that damned Black Republican hadn't been elected, we would still be one nation, and at peace," he said.

"After the disaster his party has been to the Union, it will be a long time before another Republican is chosen to fill the White House," McClellan said. "I take some consolation in that—not much, I assure you, Captain, but some nonetheless."

Another of McClellan's officers galloped up from the north-west. "Sir," he cried, not even dismounting, "Longstreet is pounding our right with everything he has, and General Hooker—General Hooker, sir, he won't do *anything*. It's as if he's stunned by a near miss from a shell, sir, but he's not hurt."

McClellan's mouth twisted. "In his California days, Joe Hooker was the best poker player the world ever knew," he said heavily, "till it came time to raise fifty dollars. Then he'd flunk. If he flunks now—"

As it had on the left, a great burst of musketry and cannon fire told its own story. "General McClellan, sir, he just flunked," Custer said. He reloaded his pistols—not a fast business, with ball and loose powder and percussion cap for each chamber of the cylinder. After one Colt was charged, he lost patience. "By your leave, General, I'm going to the fighting before it comes to me."

"Go ahead, Captain," McClellan said. His posture said he thought all was lost. Custer thought all was lost, too. He didn't care. Fighting in a lost cause was even more splendid and glorious than battle where victory was assured. He sprang onto his horse and rode toward the loudest gunfire.

He looked back once. McClellan was staring after him, shaking his head.

☆ **I** ☆

1881

Buffalo bones littered the prairie south of Fort Dodge, Kansas. Colonel George Custer gave them only the briefest glance. They seemed as natural a part of the landscape as had the buffalo themselves a decade before. Custer had killed his share of buffalo and more. Now he was after more dangerous game.

He raised the Springfield carbine to his shoulder and fired at one of the Kiowas fleeing before him. The Indian, one of the rearmost of Satanta's raiding party, did not fall.

Custer loaded another cartridge into the carbine's breech and fired again. Again, the shot was useless. The Kiowa turned on his pony for a Parthian shot. Fire and smoke belched from the muzzle of his rifle. The bullet kicked up a puff of dust ten or fifteen yards in front of Custer.

He fired again, and so did the Kiowa. The Indian's Tredegar Works carbine, a close copy of the British Martini-Henry, had about the same performance as his own weapon. Both men missed once more. The Kiowa gave all his attention back to riding, bending low over his pony's neck and coaxing from the animal every bit of speed it had.

"They're gaining on us, the blackhearted savages!" Custer shouted to his troopers, inhibited in language by the pledge his wife, Libbie, had finally succeeded in extracting from him.

"Let me and a couple of the other boys with the fastest horses get out ahead of the troop and make 'em fight us till the rest of you can catch up," his brother suggested.

"No, Tom. Wouldn't work, I'm afraid. They wouldn't fight— they'd just scatter like a covey of quail."

"Damned cowards," Major Tom Custer growled. He was a

9

younger, less flamboyant version of his brother, but no less ferocious in the field. "They bushwhack our farmers, then they run. If they want to come up into Kansas, let 'em fight like men once they're here."

"They don't much want to fight," Custer said. "All they want to do is kill and burn and loot. That's easier, safer, and more profitable, too."

"Give me the Sioux any day, up in Minnesota and Dakota and Wyoming," Tom Custer said. "They fought hard, and only a few of them ran away into Canada once we'd licked them."

"And the Canadians disarmed the ones who did," Custer added. "I'll be—dashed if I like the Canadians, mind you, but they play the game the way it's supposed to be played."

"It's cricket," Tom said, and Custer nodded. His younger brother pointed south. "We aren't going to catch them on our side of the line, Autie."

"I can see that." George Custer scowled—at fate, not at the family nickname. After a moment, the scowl became a fierce grin. "All right, by jingo, maybe we won't catch them on our side of the line. We'll just have to catch them on theirs."

Tom looked startled. "Are you sure?"

"You'd best believe I'm sure." The excitement of the pursuit ran through Custer in a hot tide. Whatever consequences came from extending the pursuit, he'd worry about them later. Now all he wanted to do was teach the Kiowas a lesson even that sneaky old devil Satanta wouldn't forget any time soon. He shouted over to the regimental bugler: "Blow Pursuit."

"Sir?" the bugler said, as surprised as Tom Custer had been. Then he grinned. "Yes, *sir*!" He raised the bugle to his lips. The bold and martial notes rang out across the plain. The men of the Fifth Cavalry Regiment needed a moment to grasp what that call implied. Then they howled like wolves. Some of them waved their broad-brimmed black felt hats in the air.

From long experience, the Kiowas understood U.S. horn calls as well as any cavalry trooper. Their heads went up, as if they were game fearing it would be flushed from cover. *That's what they are, all right,* Custer thought.

As often happened, Tom's thoughts ran in the same track as his own. "They won't duck back into their lair this time," his younger brother said. Now that the decision was made, Tom was all for it.

They pounded past a farmhouse the Kiowas had burned in a

raid a couple of years earlier. Custer recognized those ruins; they
meant he was less than a mile from the border with the Indian
Territory. Up ahead, the Kiowas squeezed still more from their
ponies. Custer smiled savagely. That might get them over the
line, but even those tough animals would start wearing down
soon. "And then," he told the wind blowing tears from his eyes,
"then they're mine, sure as McClellan belonged to Lee twenty
years ago."

He fired again at the Kiowas, and shouted in exultation as one
of them slid from his horse's back and thudded to the ground,
where, after rolling a couple of times, he lay still. "Good shot,"
his brother said. "Hell of a good shot."

"We've got 'em now," Custer said. The first Kiowas had to be
over the line. He didn't care. "We won't let 'em get away. Every
last redskin in that band is ours." How his men cheered!

And then all of Custer's ferocious joy turned to ashes. Tom
pointed off to the east, from which direction a squadron of cavalry was approaching at a fast trot. All the Kiowas were over the
line by then. They reined in, whooping in their incomprehensible
language. They knew they were safe.

Custer knew it, too. Chasing the Kiowas into Indian Territory,
punishing them, and then riding back into Kansas with no one but
the Indians the wiser, was one thing. Doing it under the watchful
eyes of that other cavalry squadron was something else again.
Hating those horsemen, hating himself, Custer held his hand high
to halt his men. They stopped on the Kansas side of the line.

The approaching cavalrymen wore hats and blouses of a cut
not much different from those of Custer's troopers. Theirs, though,
were gray, not the various shades of blue the U.S. cavalry used.
And a couple of their officers, Custer saw, were in the new dirt-
brown uniforms the Confederate States had adopted from the
British. The limeys called that color khaki; to the Rebs, it was
butternut.

One of those Confederate officers rode toward Custer, waving
as he moved forward. Custer waved back: come ahead. The
Rebel captain proved to be a fresh-faced fellow in his twenties; he
would have been wearing short pants during the War of Secession. Seeing him made Custer feel every one of his forty-one
years.

"Good mornin' to you, Colonel," the captain drawled, nodding in a way that looked friendly enough. "You weren't planning on riding over the international border by any chance, were you?"

"If I was, you'll never prove it, Captain—" Custer tried for cool detachment. What came out was a frustrated snarl.

By the way the Confederate cavalryman smiled, he heard that frustration—heard it and relished it. He bowed in the saddle. The Rebs were always polite as cats . . . and always ready to claw, too. "I'm Jethro Weathers, Colonel," he said. "And you're right—I'll never prove it. But you and the United States would have been embarrassed if I'd come along half an hour later and found your men inside the territory of the Confederate States."

He sounded disappointed he and his troopers hadn't caught Custer *in flagrante delicto*. Custer's frustration boiled into fury: "If your government would keep those murdering redskinned savages on your side of the border, we wouldn't want to go over yonder"—he waved south, into Indian Territory—"and give 'em what they deserve."

"Why, Colonel," Captain Weathers said, amusement in his voice, "I have no proof at all those Kiowas ever entered the territory of the United States. As far as I can see, you were leading an unprovoked punitive expedition into a foreign country. Richmond would see things the same way, I'm sure. So would London. So would Paris."

Tom Custer spoke up: "There's a dead Kiowa, maybe half a mile north of here."

That didn't faze Weathers a bit: "For all I know, you've already been into the Confederate States, murdered the poor fellow, and then hauled him back into the USA to justify raiding Confederate soil."

A flush spread up Custer's face; his ears went hot at the sheer effrontery of that. "You—dashed Rebs will pay one day for giving the redskins guns and letting them come up and raid white men's farms whenever it strikes their fancy."

"This is our territory, Colonel," Captain Weathers said, amused no more. "We shall defend it against the incursion of a foreign power—by which I mean the United States. And you have no call—none, sir, none whatever—to get up on your high horse and tell me what my country ought and ought not to be doing, especially since the United States harbor swarms of Comanches in New Mexico and turn them loose against west Texas whenever it strikes your fancy."

"We didn't start that until those outrages in Kansas grew too oppressive to ignore," Custer answered. "Why, on this very raid—this raid you have the gall to deny—the savages made two white women minister to their animal lusts, then cut their throats and worked other dreadful indignities upon their bare and abused bodies."

"You think the Comanches don't do that in Texas?" Captain Weathers returned. "And the way I heard it, Colonel, they started doing it there first."

Custer scowled. "We killed off the buffalo to deny the Kiowas a livelihood, and you gave them cattle to take up the slack."

"The Comanches are herding cattle these days, too." Weathers made as if to go back to his troopers, who waited inside Confederate territory. "I see no point to continuing this discussion. Good day, sir."

"Wait," Custer said, and the Confederate captain, polite still, waited. Breathing heavily, Custer went on, "When our two nations separated, I had a great deal of sympathy and friendship for many of the men who found high rank in the Army of the Confederate States. I hoped and believed that, even though we were two, we could share this continent in peace."

"And so we have," Jethro Weathers said. "There is no war between my country and yours, Colonel."

"Not now," Custer agreed. "Not yet. But you will force one upon us if you continue with this arrogant policy of yours here in the West. The irritations will grow too great, and then—"

"Don't speak to me of arrogance," Weathers broke in. "Don't speak to me of irritation, not when you Yankees have finally gone and put another one of those God-damned Black Republicans in the White House."

"Blaine's only been in office a month, but he's already shown he's not nearly so bad as Lincoln was," Custer answered, "and he's not your business anyhow, any more than Longstreet's ours."

"Blaine talks big," the Confederate captain answered. "People who talk big get to thinking they can act big. You talked about war, Colonel. If your James G. Blaine thinks you Yankees can lick us now when you couldn't do it twenty years ago, he'd better think twice. And if you think you can ride over the line into Indian Territory whenever it strikes your fancy, you'd better think twice, too, Colonel."

When Weathers moved to ride back to his squadron this time,

Custer said not a word. He stared after the Indians whom Weathers' timely arrival had saved. His right hand folded into a fist inside its leather gauntlet. He pounded it down on his thigh, hard, once, twice, three times. His lips shaped a silent word. It might have been *dash*. It might not.

As the train rattled west through the darkness over the Colorado prairie, the porter came down the aisle of the Pullman car. "Make you bed up, sir?" he asked in English with some foreign accent: Russian, maybe, or Yiddish.

Abraham Lincoln looked up from the speech he'd been writing. Slowly, deliberately, he capped his pen and put it in his pocket. "Yes, thank you," he said. He rose slowly and deliberately, too, but his lumbago gave a twinge even so. As best he could, he ignored the pain. It came with being an old man.

Moving with swift efficiency, the porter let down the hinged seat back, laid a mattress on the bed thus created, and made it up in the blink of an eye. "Here you are, sir," he said, drawing the curtain around the berth to give Lincoln the chance to change into his nightshirt in something close to privacy.

"I thank you," Lincoln said, and tipped him a dime. The porter pocketed it with a polite word of thanks and went on to prepare the next berth. Looking down at the bed, Lincoln let out a rueful chuckle. The Pullman attendant had been too efficient. Lincoln bent down and undid the sheet and blanket at the foot of the mattress. Pullman berths weren't made for men of his inches. He put on his nightclothes, got into bed, and turned off the gas lamp by which he had been writing.

The rattling, jouncing ride and the thin, lumpy mattress bothered him only a little. He was used to them, and he remembered worse. When he'd gone from Illinois to Washington after being elected president, Pullmans hadn't been invented. He'd traveled the whole way sitting upright in a hard seat. And when, four years later, the voters had turned him out of office for failing to hold the Union together, he'd gone back to Illinois the same way.

Ridden out of town on the rails, he thought, and laughed a little. He twisted, trying to find a position somewhere close to comfortable. If a spring didn't dig into the small of his back, another one poked him in the shoulder. That was how life worked: if you gained somewhere, you lost somewhere else.

He twisted again. There—that was better. He'd had a lot of

experience on the railroads, these sixteen years since failing of reelection. "Once you get the taste for politics," he murmured in the darkness, "everything else is tame."

He'd thought he would quietly return to the law career he'd left to go to the White House. And so he had, for a little while. But the appetite for struggle at the highest level he'd got in Washington had stayed with him. Afterwards, legal briefs and pleadings weren't enough to satisfy.

He yawned, then grimaced. The way the Democrats had fawned on the Southern Confederacy grated on him, too. And so he'd started speechifying, all across the country, doing what he could to make people see that, even if the war was lost, the struggle continued. "I always was good on the stump," he muttered. "I even did some good, I daresay."

Some good. The United States had eventually emancipated the thousands of slaves still living within their borders. The Confederate States held their millions in bondage to this day. And a lot of Republicans, nowadays, sounded more and more like Democrats in their efforts to put the party's sorry past behind them and get themselves elected. A lot of Republicans, these days, didn't want the albatross of Lincoln around their necks.

He yawned again, twisted one more time, and fell asleep, only to be rudely awakened half an hour later when the train hissed and screeched to a stop at some tiny prairie town. He was used to that, too, even if he couldn't do anything about it. Before long, he was asleep once more.

He woke again, some time in the middle of the night. This time, he swung down out of his berth. Once a man got past his Biblical threescore-and-ten, his flesh reminded him of its imperfections more often than it had in his younger days.

Sliding the curtain aside, he walked down the aisle of the sleeper car, past the snores and grunts coming from behind other curtains, to the washroom at the far end of the car. He used the necessary, then pumped the handle of the tin sink to get himself a glass of water. He drank it down, wiped his chin on the sleeve of his nightshirt, and set the glass by the sink for the next man who would want it.

Up the aisle he came. Someone was getting down from an upper berth, and almost stepped on his toes. "Careful, friend," Lincoln said quietly. The man's face went through two separate stages of surprise: first that he hadn't seen anyone nearby, and then at whose feet he'd almost abused.

"Damned old Black Republican fool," he said, also in a near-whisper: he was polite to his fellow passengers, if not to the former president. Without giving Lincoln a chance to reply, he stalked down the aisle.

Lincoln shrugged and finished the short journey back to his own berth. That sort of thing happened to him at least once on every train he took. Had he let it bother him, he would have had to give up politics and become as much a hermit as Robinson Crusoe.

He got back into bed. The upper berth above his was empty. He sighed as he struggled for comfort again. Mary had been difficult all the years of their marriage, and especially in the years since he'd left the White House, but he missed her all the same. He'd got over the typhoid they'd caught in St. Louis four or five years before. She hadn't.

The next thing he knew, daylight was stealing through the curtains. His back ached a little, but he'd had a pretty good night—better than most he spent rolling from one town to the next, that was certain.

He got dressed, used the necessary again, and was back in his berth when the day porter came by. "And the top o' the mornin' to you, sir," he said. Lincoln had no trouble placing *his* accent. "Will you be wanting a proper seat the now, 'stead o' your bedding and all?"

"That I will." A natural mimic, Lincoln needed an effort of will not to copy the porter's brogue. After he tipped the fellow, he asked, "How much longer until we get into Denver?"

"Nobbut another two, three hours," the porter answered. Lincoln sighed; he was supposed to have arrived at sunrise, not mid-morning. Well, no doubt the people waiting for him knew of the distant relationship between scheduled and actual arrival times.

"Time enough for breakfast, then," he said.

"Indeed and there is, sir, and to spare," the porter agreed.

Lincoln went back to the dining car. He did appreciate the bellows arrangements the railroads were using between carriages these days. Going from car to car on a jolting train had been a dangerous business even a handful of years before. More than a few people had slipped and fallen to their death, and a cinder in the eye or a face full of soot was only to be expected.

After ham and eggs and rolls and coffee, the world looked a more cheerful place. He was leaving behind the prairie now, going up toward the mountains. The locomotive labored over the upgrades and then, as if relieved, sped down the other side of each rise. Watching trees and boulders flying past was exhilarating, even if Lincoln knew how many accidents happened on such downgrades.

At last, nearer three hours late than two, the train pulled into Denver. The depot was small and dilapidated. A broad stretch of empty ground on the other side of the tracks would, Lincoln had heard, be a fancy new station one day. At the moment, and for the foreseeable future, it was just empty ground. Wildflowers and weeds splashed it with color.

"Denver!" the conductor shouted, as he had for every hamlet along the way to the biggest city in the heart of the West. "All out for Denver!"

Lincoln put his speech in a leather valise, got up, grabbed his bulky carpetbag, and made his way out of the Pullman car. After a couple of days on the train, solid ground felt shaky under his feet, as it was said to do for sailors just off their ships. He set his stovepipe firmly on his head and looked around.

Amid the usual scenes on a railway-station platform—families greeting loved ones with cries of joy, bankers greeting capitalists with louder (if perhaps less sincere) cries of joy—Lincoln spotted a couple of rugged fellows who had the look of miners dressed up in their best, and probably only, suits. Even before they started moving purposefully through the crowd toward him, he had them pegged for the men he was to meet.

"Mr. McMahan and Mr. Cavanaugh, I presume?" he said, setting down the carpetbag so he could extend his right hand.

"That's right, Mr. Lincoln," said one of them, who wore a ginger-colored mustache. "I'm Joe McMahan; you can call Cavanaugh here Fred." His grip was hard and firm.

"Long as you don't call me late to supper," Cavanaugh said agreeably. He was a couple of inches taller than McMahan, with a scar on his chin that looked as if it had come from a knife fight. Both men were altogether unselfconscious about the revolvers on their right hips. Lincoln had been in the West a good many times, and was used to that.

"Come on, sir," McMahan said. "Here, let me take that." He picked up the carpetbag. "We'll get you to the hotel, let you freshen up some and get yourself a tad more shut-eye, too, if that's what you want. These here trains, they're all very fine, but a body can't hardly sleep on 'em."

"They're better than they used to be," Lincoln said. "I was thinking that last night, when the porter made up my berth. But you're right—they're not all they might be."

"Come on, then," McMahan repeated. "Amos has the buggy waiting for us."

As they walked out of the station, they passed a beggar, a middle-aged fellow with a gray-streaked beard who had both legs gone above the knee. Lincoln fumbled in his pockets till he found a quarter, which he tossed into the tin cup on the floor beside the man.

"I thank you for your kind—" the beggar began in a singsong way. Then his eyes—eyes that had seen a lot of pain, and, by the rheumy look in them, a lot of whiskey, too—widened as he recognized his benefactor. He reached into the cup, took out the quarter, and threw it at Lincoln. It hit him in the chest and fell to the ground with a clink. "God damn you, you son of a bitch, I don't want any charity from *you*," the legless man snarled. "Wasn't for you, I'd be up and walking, not living out my days like this."

Fred Cavanaugh took Lincoln by the arm and hurried him along. "Don't take no notice of Teddy there," he said, the beggar's curses following them. "He gets some popskull in him, he don't know what the hell he's talkin' about."

"Oh, he knows well enough." Lincoln's mouth was a tight, hard line. "I've heard that tune before, many times. The men who suffered so much in the War of Secession blame me for it. They have the right, I think. I blame myself, too, though that's little enough consolation for them."

Amos, the buggy driver, was cut from the same mold as Cavanaugh and McMahan. The horses clopped up the street. Mud kicked up from their hooves and the wheels of the buggy. For all the wealth that had come out of the mines nearby, Denver boasted not a single paved road. Streams of water ran in the gutters. Trees shaded the residential blocks. Most of the houses—and the public buildings, too—were of either bright red brick or the local yellow stone, which gave the town a pleasingly colorful look.

Miners in collarless shirts and blue-dyed dungarees mingled

on the streets with businessmen who would not have been out of place in Chicago or New York. No, after a moment, Lincoln revised that opinion: some of the businessmen went armed, too.

When he remarked on that, Joe McMahan's mouth twisted in bitterness. "A man has more'n what he deserves and don't see fit to share it with his pals who ain't got so much, Mr. Lincoln, he's a fool if he don't reckon they're liable to try and equalize the wealth whether he likes it or not."

"True enough," Lincoln said. "So true, it may tear our country apart again one day. Slave labor comes in more forms than that which still persists in the Confederate States."

Amos shifted a wad of tobacco into his cheek, spat, and said, "Damn straight it does. That's why we brung you out here—to talk about that."

"I know." Lincoln went back to watching the street scenes. Miner, merchant, banker—you could tell so much about a man's class and wealth by how he dressed. Women were sometimes harder to gauge. Who was poor and who was not gave him no trouble. But if a woman dressed as if she'd come from the pages of *Leslie's Illustrated Weekly* but painted her face like a strumpet, was she a strumpet or the wife of some newly rich mining nabob? In Denver, that was less obvious than it would have been farther east, where cosmetics were *prima facie* evidence a woman was fast. The rules were different here, and no wonder, for a woman could go—and several had gone—straight from strumpet to nabob's wife.

In its ornate pretentiousness, the Hôtel Métropole matched anything anywhere in the country. "Here you go, Mr. Lincoln," Fred Cavanaugh said. "You'll be right comfortable here, get yourself all good and ready for your speech tonight. You'd best believe a lot of folks want to hear what you've got to say about labor nowadays."

"Hear me they shall," Lincoln said. "What they do if they hear where I'm staying, though, may be something else again. Are they not liable to take me for one of the exploiters over whom they are concerned?"

"Mr. Lincoln, you won't find anybody in Colorado got a thing to say against living soft," Cavanaugh answered. "What riles folks is grinding other men's noses in the dirt to let a few live soft."

"I understand the distinction," Lincoln said. "As you remind me, the essential point is that so many in the United States, like virtually all the whites in the Confederacy, do not."

The Hôtel Métropole met every reasonable standard for soft living, and most of the unreasonable ones as well. After a hot bath in a galvanized tub at the end of the hall, after a couple of fried pork chops for lunch, Lincoln would have been happy enough to stretch out on the bed for a couple of hours, even if he would have had to sleep diagonally to keep from kicking the footboard. But the speech came first.

He was still polishing it, having altogether forgotten about supper, when Joe McMahan knocked on the door. "Come on, Mr. Lincoln," he said. "We've got ourselves a full house for you tonight."

The hall was not so elegant as the opera house near the Hôtel Métropole. It was, in fact, a dance hall with a podium hastily plunked by one wall. But, as McMahan had said, it was packed. From long practice guessing crowds, Lincoln figured more than a thousand men—miners and refinery workers, most of them, and farmers, with here and there a shopkeeper to leaven the mix— stood shoulder-to-shoulder, elbow-to-elbow, to hear what he had to say.

They cheered loud and long when McMahan introduced him. Most of them were young. Young men thought of him as labor's friend in a land where capital was king. Older men, like the beggar in the railway depot, still damned him for fighting, and most of all for losing, the War of Secession. *I'd have been a hero if I won,* he thought. *And I'd have been a housewife, or more likely a homely old maid, if I'd been born a woman. So what?*

He put on his spectacles and glanced down at the notes he'd written on the train and in the hotel. "A generation ago," he began, "I said a house divided against itself, half slave and half free, could not stand. And it did not stand, though its breaking was not in the manner I should have desired." He never made any bones about the past. It was there. Everyone knew it.

"The Confederate States continue all slave to this day," he said. "How the financiers in London and Paris smile on their plantations, their railroads, their ironworks! How capital floods into their land! And how much of it, my friends, how much drips down from the eaves of the rich men's mansions to water the shacks where the Negroes live, scarcely better off than the brute beasts beside which they labor in the fields? You know the answer as well as I."

"To hell with the damn niggers," somebody called from the audience. "Talk about the white man!" Cries of agreement rose.

Lincoln held up a hand. "I am talking about the white man," he said. "You cannot part nor separate the two, not in the Southern Confederacy. For if the white laborer there dare go to his boss and speak the truth, which is that he has not got enough to live on, the boss will tell him, 'Live on it and like it, or I'll put a Negro in your place and you can learn to live on nothing.'

"And what of our United States, which were, if nothing else, left all free when the Rebels departed from the Union?" Lincoln went on. "Are we—are you—all free now? Do we—do you—enjoy the great and glorious blessings of liberty the Founding Fathers fondly imagined would be the birthright of every citizen of our Republic?

"Or are we returning to the unhappy condition in which we found ourselves in the years before the War of Secession? Do not our capitalists in New York, in Chicago, yes, and in Denver, look longingly at their Confederate brethren in Richmond, in Atlanta, in new and brawling Birmingham, and wish they could do as do those brethren?

"Are we not once more becoming a nation half slave, half free, my friends? Does not the capitalist eat bread gained by the sweat of *your* brows, as the slavemaster does by virtue—and there's a word turned on its ear!—of the labor of his Negroes?" Lincoln had to stop then, for the shouts that rose up were fierce and angry.

"You know your state, your condition," he continued when he could. "You know I tell you nothing but the truth. Time was in this country when a man would be hired labor one year, his own man the next, and hiring laborers to work for him the year after that. Such days, I fear, are over and done. On the railroads, in the mines, in the factories, one man's a magnate, and the rest toil for him. If you go to your boss and tell him you have not got enough to live on, the boss will tell you, 'Live on it and like it, or I'll put a Chinaman or an Italian or a Jew in your place and you can learn to live on nothing.' "

A low murmur came from his audience, more frightening in its way than the fury they had shown before. Fury didn't last. Now Lincoln was making them think. Thought was slower than anger to flower into action, but it was a hardy perennial. It did not bloom and die.

"What do we do about it, Abe?" shouted a miner still grimy from his long day of labor far below ground.

"What do we do?" Lincoln repeated. "The Democrats had their day, and a long day it was, from my time up until President Blaine's inauguration last month. Did they do a thing, a single solitary thing, to help the lot of the working man?" He smiled at the cries of *No!* before going on, "And Blaine, too, though the good Lord knows I wish him well, has railroad money in his pockets. How much labor can hope for from him, I do not know.

"But I know this, my friends: when the United States were a house divided before, they were divided, and did divide, along lines of geography. No such choice avails us now. The capitalists cannot secede as the slavemasters did. If we are not satisfied with our government and the way it treats its citizens, we have the revolutionary right and duty to overthrow it and substitute one that suits us better, as our forefathers did in the days of George III."

That brought a storm of applause. Men stomped on the floor, so that it shook under Lincoln's feet. Someone fired a pistol in the air, deafeningly loud in the closed hall. Lincoln held up both hands. Slowly, slowly, quiet crawled back. Into it, he said, "I do not advocate revolution. I pray it shall not be necessary. But if the old order will not yield to justice, it shall be swept aside. I do not threaten, any more than a man who says he sees a tornado coming. Folks can take shelter from it, or they can run out and play in it. That is up to them. You, friends, you are a tornado. What happens next is up to the capitalists." He stepped away from the podium.

Joe McMahan pumped his hand. "That was powerful stuff, Mr. Lincoln," he said. "Powerful stuff, yes indeed."

"For which I thank you," Lincoln said, raising his voice to be heard through the storm of noise that went on and on.

"Ask you something, Mr. Lincoln?" McMahan said. Lincoln nodded. McMahan leaned closer, so only the former president would hear. "You ever come across the writings of a fellow named Marx, Mr. Lincoln? Karl Marx?"

Lincoln smiled. "As a matter of fact, I have."

"Sam!" Clay Herndon spoke sharply. "Sam, you're woolgathering again."

"The devil I am," Samuel Clemens replied, though his friend's comment did return his attention to the cramped office of the *San Francisco Morning Call.* "I was trying to come up with something for tomorrow's editorial, and I'm dry as the desert between the Great Salt Lake and Virginia City. I hate writing editorials, do you know that?"

"You have mentioned it a time or two." Now Herndon's voice was sly. That suited the reporter's face: he looked as if he had a fox for his maternal grandmother. His features were sharp and clever, his green eyes studied everything and respected nothing, and his rusty hair only added to the impression. Grinning, he sank his barb: "Or a hundred times or two."

"Still true," Clemens snapped, running a hand through his own unruly mop of red-brown hair. "Do you have any notion of the strain on a man's constitution, having to come up with so many column inches every day on demand?—and always something new, regardless of whether there's anything new to write about. If I had my Tennessee lands—"

Herndon rolled his eyes. "For God's sake, Sam, give me the lecture on editorials if you must, but spare me the Tennessee lands. They're stale as salt beef shipped round the Horn."

"You're a scoffer, that's what you are—nothing but a scoffer," Clemens said, half amused but still half annoyed, too. "Forty thousand acres of fine land, with God only knows how much timber and coal and iron, and maybe gold and silver, too, and all of it in my family."

"It's in another country these days," Clay Herndon reminded him. "The Confederate States have been a going concern for a long time now."

"Yes, a long time ago, and in another country—and besides, the wench is dead," Clemens said, scratching his mustache.

Herndon gave him a quizzical look. However clever the reporter was, he wouldn't have known Marlowe from a marlinspike. "The way you do go on," he said. "Let's us go on over to Martin's and get some dinner."

"Now you're talking." Clemens rose from his chair with enthusiasm and stuck his hat on his head. "Any excuse not to work is good enough for me. Weren't for this"—he patted the battered copy of the *American Cyclopedia* on his desk with a touch as tender as a lover's for his beloved—"I don't know how I'd ever manage to come out for something or against something every day of the year. As if any man needs so blamed many opinions, or has any business holding them! Wasting my sweetness on the morning air, that's what I'm doing."

Herndon pulled out his pocket watch. "As of right now, you're wasting your sweetness on the afternoon air, and you have been for the past ten minutes. Now let's get moving, before we can't find a place to sit down at Martin's."

Clemens followed his friend out onto the street. It was an April midday in San Francisco: not too warm, not too cold, the sun shining down from a clear but hazy sky. It might as easily have been August or November or February. To Clemens, who had grown up with real seasons, always seeming not far from spring remained strange after almost twenty years.

When he remarked on that, Herndon snorted. "You don't like it, go down to Fresno. It's always July there, and a desert July at that."

With a lamb chop, fried potatoes, and a shot of whiskey in front of Sam Clemens, life improved. He knocked back the shot and ordered another. When it came, he knocked it back, too, with the sour toast, "Here's to hard work every day."

Clay Herndon snorted again. "I've heard that one almost as often as the Tennessee lands, Sam. What the devil would you be doing if you weren't running the *Morning Call*?"

"Damned if I know," Clemens answered. "Writing stories, maybe, and broke. But who has time? When the big panic of '63 hit after we lost the war and hung on and on and on, the whole world turned upside down. I was damn lucky to have any sort of position, and I knew it. So I hung on like a limpet on a harbor rock. If I ever get ahead of the game—" He laughed. "About as likely as the Mormons giving up their extra wives, I expect."

Herndon had a couple of shots of whiskey in him, too. "Suppose you weren't a newspaperman? What would you do then?"

"I've tried mining—I was almost rich once, which is every bit as fine as almost being in love—and I was a Mississippi River pilot. If I wanted to take that up again, I'd have to take Confederate citizenship with it."

"Why not?" Herndon said. "Then you could have yourself another go at those Tennessee lands."

"No, thank you." Briefly, Clemens had served in a Confederate regiment operating—or rather, bungling—in Missouri, which remained one of the United States, not least because most Confederate troops there had been similarly inept. He didn't admit to that; few in the USA who had ever had anything to do with the other side admitted it these days. After a moment, he went on. "Their record isn't what you'd call good—more like what you'd call a skunk at a picnic."

Herndon laughed. "You do come up with 'em, Sam. Got to hand it to you. Maybe you ought to try writing yourself a book after all. People would buy it, I expect."

"Maybe," Clemens said, which meant *no*. "Don't see a lot of authors living off the fat of the land, do you? Besides, it may have taken me a while to cipher out what steady work was about, but I've got it down solid now. I lived on promises when I was a miner. I was a boy then, pretty much. I'm not a boy any more."

"All right, all right." Herndon held up a placatory hand. He looked at his plate, as if astonished the beefsteak he'd ordered had disappeared. His shot glass was empty, too. "You want one more for the road?"

"Not if I intend to get any work done this afternoon. You want to listen to me snore at my desk, that's another matter." Clemens got to his feet. He set a quarter and a small, shiny gold dollar on the table. Herndon laid down a dollar and a half. They left Martin's—a splendid place, for anyone who could afford to eat there—and walked back to the *Morning Call* office.

Edgar Leary, one of the junior reporters, waved a flimsy sheet of telegraph paper in their faces when they got in. He was almost hopping with excitement. "Look at this! Look at this!" He had crumbs in his sparse black beard; he brought his dinner to the *Morning Call* in a sack. "Didn't come in five minutes ago, or I'm a Chinaman."

"If you'll stop fanning me with it, I will have a look," Clemens said. When Leary still waved the wire around, Sam snatched it out of his hand. "Give me that, dammit." He turned it right side up and read it. The more he read, the higher his bushy eyebrows climbed. Once he'd finished, he passed it to Clay Herndon, saying, "Looks like I've got something for the editorial after all."

Herndon quickly skimmed the telegraphic report. His lips shaped a soundless whistle. "This here is more than something to feed you an editorial, Sam. This here could be trouble."

"Don't I know it," Clemens said. "But I can't do the first thing about the trouble, and I can do something about the editorial. So I'll do that, and I'll let the rest of the world get into trouble. You ever notice how it's real good about taking care of that whether anybody wants it to or not?"

He pulled a cigar from a waistcoat pocket, bit off the end, scraped a match against the sole of his shoe, lighted the cigar, and tossed the match into a shiny brass cuspidor stained here and there with errant expectorations. Then he went over to his desk and pulled out the *George F. Cram Atlas of the World*. He flipped through it till he found the page he needed.

His finger traced a line. Herndon and Leary were looking over his shoulder, one to the right, the other to the left. Herndon whistled again. "This is going to be big trouble," he said. "Bigger than I thought."

"That's a fact." Clemens slammed the atlas closed with a noise like a rifle shot. Behind him, Edgar Leary jumped. "Hell of a big mess." He spoke with somber anticipation. "But I don't have to worry about what I'm going to write this afternoon, so I'm as happy as Peeping Tom in Honolulu, if half of what they say about the Sandwich Islands is true."

He inked a pen and began to write.

If the wires are not liars—and of course experience has made us all familiar with Messrs. Western and Union's solemn vow that only the truth shall be permitted to pass over their telegraphic lines, and with the vigilance with which they guard them from every falsehood; of course experience has done such a thing, we say, for under our grand and glorious Constitution anyone may say what he pleases—if this is so, then it seems that His Mexican Majesty Maximilian has been persuaded to sell his northwestern provinces of Chihuahua and Sonora to the Confederate States for the sum of three millions of dollars.

This is remarkable news on several counts, which is how lawyers speak of indictments. First and foremost, superficially, is the feeling of astonishment arising in the bosoms of those who are familiar in the least with the aforesaid provinces at learning that anyone, save possibly Old Scratch in contemplation of expanding the infernal regions due to present overcrowding, should want to purchase them at any price, let alone for such a munificent sum.

But, as the fellow said after sitting on a needle, there is more to this than meets the eye. Consider, friends. Mexico's principal export, aside from the Mexicans whose charm pervades our Golden State, is, not to put too fine a point on it—that being the needle's business, after all—debt. She owes money to Britain, she owes money to France, she owes money to Germany, she owes money to Russia—no mean feat, that—and she is prevented from owing money to the Kingdom of Poland only by that Kingdom's extinction before she was born.

Being a weak country in debt to a strong one—or to a slew of strong ones—is in these enlightened times the quickest recipe known for making gunboats flock like buzzards to one's shores, as the Turkish khedives will assure Maximilian if only he will ask them. Time was when the United States held up the Monroe Doctrine to shield the Americas from European monarchs, bill collectors, and other riffraff, but the Doctrine these days is as dead as its maker, shot through the heart in the War of Secession.

So the Empire of Mexico needs cash on hand if it is to go on being the Empire of Mexico, or at least the abridged edition thereof. Thus from Maximilian's point of view the sale of Chihuahua and Sonora makes a deal of sense, but he is apparently going ahead and doing it anyhow. The question remaining before the house is why the Confederate States would want to buy the two provinces, no matter how avidly he might want to sell them.

Owning Texas, the Confederacy would already seem to have in its possession a sufficiency—indeed, even an oversupply—of hot, worthless land for the next hundred years. Sonora, though, has one virtue Texas lacks—not that having a virtue Texas lacks is in itself any great marvel—it touches on the Gulf of California, while Chihuahua connects it to the rest of the CSA. With these new acquisitions, the Confederate States would extend, like the USA, from sea to shining sea, and, even more to the point, run a railroad from the same to the shining same. Is that worth three millions of dollars? Pete Longstreet seems to think so.

Yet to be seen is how the new administration in Washington will view this transaction. There can be no doubt that any of the previous governments—if by that the reader will forgive our stretching a point—would do no more than passively acquiesce to the sale, in much the same manner as the bull acquiesces to the knife that makes him into a steer. Richmond, London, Paris, and Ottawa form a formidable stall in which the United States are held.

But will James G. Blaine, having been elected on a platform that consisted largely of snorting and pawing the ground, now have to show the world it was nothing but humbug and hokum? Even if it was humbug and hokum, will he dare admit it, knowing that if he should confess to weakness, even weakness genuinely and manifestly in existence, he will become a laughingstock and an object of contempt not only in foreign capitals but in the eyes of the exasperated millions who sent him to the White House to make America strong and proud again and will with equal avidity send him home with a tin can tied to his tail if he bollixes the job?

Our view of the matter is that caution is likelier to be necessary than to be, while our hope is that, for once, our well-known editorial omniscience is found wanting.

Sighing, Clemens set down the pen and shook his wrist to get the cramp out of it. "I want to buy me one of those type-writing machines they're starting to sell," he said.

"Good idea," Clay Herndon said. "They can't weigh much more than a hundred pounds. Just the thing to take along to listen to the mayor, or to cover a fire: that'd be even better."

"They're the coming thing, so you can laugh all you like," Clemens told him. "Besides, if I had one, the compositors would be able to read the copy I give 'em."

"Now you're talking—that's a whole different business." Herndon got up from his desk and ambled over to Sam. "I never have any trouble—well, never much—reading your writing. You were really scratching away there. What did you come up with?"

Wordlessly, Clemens passed him the sheets. Herndon had a lot of political savvy, or maybe just a keen eye for where the bodies were buried—assuming those two didn't amount to the same thing. If he was thinking along the same lines as Clemens . . .

He didn't say anything till he was through. Then, with a slow nod, he handed the editorial back. "That's strong stuff," he said, "but you're spot on. When I first saw the wire, I thought about the ports on the Pacific, but I didn't worry about the railroad the Rebs'll need to do anything with the ports they get."

"What about Blaine?" Sam asked.

"I'm with you there, too," Herndon answered. "If he lies down for this, nobody will take him seriously afterwards. But I'm damned if I know how much he can do to stop it. What do you think's going to happen, Sam?"

"Me?" Clemens said. "I think there's going to be a war."

General Thomas Jackson left his War Department office in Mechanic's Hall, mounted his horse, and rode east past Capitol Square toward the president's residence on Shockoe Hill—some from his generation still thought of it as the Confederate White House, though younger men tried to forget the CSA had ever been connected to the USA. Richmond brawled around him. Coaches clattered over cobblestones, Negro footmen in fancy livery standing stiff as statues at their rear. Teamsters driving wagons filled with grain or iron or tobacco or cotton cursed the men who drove the coaches for refusing to yield the right of way. On the sidewalk, lawyers and sawyers and ladies with slaves holding parasols to shield their delicate complexions from the springtime sun danced an elaborate minuet of precedence.

A middle-aged fellow who walked with a limp tipped his homburg in Jackson's direction and called out, "Stonewall!"

Jackson gravely returned the salutation. It rang out again, shortly thereafter. Again, he touched a hand to the brim of his own hat. Somber pride filled him. Not only his peers but also the common people remembered and appreciated what he'd done in the War of Secession. In a world where memory was fleeting and gratitude even more so, that was no small thing.

An iron fence surrounded the grounds of the presidential mansion. At the gateway, guards in the fancy new butternut uniforms stiffened to attention. "General Jackson, sir!" they exclaimed in unison. Their salutes were as identical as if they'd been manufactured in succession at the same stamping mill.

Conscientiously, Jackson returned the salutes. No doubt the guards were good soldiers, and would fight bravely if the need ever came. When he measured them against the scrawny wildcats he'd led during the War of Secession, though, he found them wanting. He was honest enough to wonder whether the fault lay in them or in himself. He'd turned fifty-seven earlier in the year, and the past had a way of looking better and the present worse the older he got.

He rode up to the entrance to the president's home. A couple of slaves hurried forward. One of them held his horse's head while he dismounted, then tied the animal to a cast-iron hitching post in front of the building. Jackson tossed him a five-cent piece. The slave caught the tiny silver coin out of the air with a word of thanks.

Tied close by was the two-horse team of a landau with which he was not familiar. The driver, a white man, sat in the carriage reading a newspaper and waiting for his master to emerge. That he was white gave Jackson a clue about who his passenger might be, especially when coupled with the unfamiliar carriage.

And, sure enough, out of the president's residence came John Hay, looking stylish if a little funereal in a black sack suit. The new minister from the United States was a strikingly handsome man of about fifty, his brown hair and beard frosted with gray. His nod was stiff, tightly controlled. "Good day, General," he said, voice polite but frosty.

"Your Excellency," Jackson said in much the same tones. As a young man, Hay had served as Abe Lincoln's secretary. That in itself made him an object of suspicion in the Confederate States, but it also made him one of the few Republicans with any executive experience whatever. Jackson hoped the latter was the reason U.S. President Blaine had appointed him minister to the CSA. If not, the appointment came perilously close to an insult.

Hay had bushy, expressive eyebrows. They twitched now. He said, "I should not be surprised, General Jackson, if we were seeing President Longstreet on the same business."

"Oh? What business is that?" Jackson thought Hay likely right, but had no intention of showing it. The less the enemy—and anyone in Richmond who did not think the United States an enemy was a fool—knew, the better.

"You know perfectly well what business," Hay returned, now with a touch of asperity: "the business of Chihuahua and Sonora."

He was, of course, correct: an enemy he might be, and a Black Republican (synonymous terms, as far as the Confederacy was concerned), but not a fool. Jackson said, "I cannot see how a private transaction between the Empire of Mexico and the Confederate States of America becomes a matter about which the United States need concern themselves."

"Don't be disingenuous," Hay said sharply. "President Longstreet spent the last two hours soft-soaping me, and I'm tired of it. If you don't see how adding several hundred miles to our common border concerns us, sir, then you don't deserve those wreathed stars on your collar." Giving Jackson no chance to reply, he climbed up into the landau. The Negro who had helped the Confederate general undid the horses. The driver set down his paper and flicked the reins. Iron tires clattering, the wagon rolled away.

Jackson did not turn his head to watch it go. Diplomacy was not his concern, not directly: he dealt only with its failures. Back straight, stride steady, he walked up the stairs into the presidential mansion.

G. Moxley Sorrel, Longstreet's chief of staff, greeted him just inside the door. "Good morning, General Jackson," he said, his tone almost as wary as Hay's had been.

"Good morning." Jackson tried to keep all expression from his own voice.

"The president will see you in a moment." Sorrel put what Jackson reckoned undue stress on the second word. The chief of staff had served Longstreet since the early days of the War of Secession, and had served through the time when Longstreet and Jackson, as corps commanders under Lee, were to some degree rivals as well as comrades. Over the years, Jackson had seen that Longstreet never forgot a rivalry—and what Longstreet remembered, Moxley Sorrel remembered, too.

Having little small talk in him, Jackson simply stood silent till Sorrel led him into President Longstreet's office. "Mr. President," Jackson said then, saluting.

"Sit down, General; sit down, please." James Longstreet waved him into an overstuffed armchair upholstered in flowered maroon velvet. Despite the soft cushions, Jackson sat as rigidly erect as if on a stool. Longstreet was used to that, and did not remark on it. He did ask, "Shall I have a nigger fetch you some coffee?"

"No, thank you, sir." As was his way, Jackson came straight to the point: "I met Mr. Hay as I was arriving here. If his manner be of any moment, the United States will take a hard line toward our new Mexican acquisitions."

"I believe you are correct in that," Longstreet answered. He scratched his chin. His salt-and-pepper beard spilled halfway down his chest. He was a few years older than Jackson. Though he had put on more flesh than the general-in-chief of the Confederate States, he also remained strong and vigorous. "The Black Republicans continue to resent us merely for existing; that we thrive is a burr under their tails. I wish Tilden had been reelected—he would have raised no unseemly fuss. But the world is as we find it, not as we wish it."

"The world is as God wills." Jackson declared what was to him obvious.

"Of course—but understanding His will is our province," Longstreet said. That could have been contradiction in the guise of agreement, at which the president was adept. Before Jackson could be sure, Longstreet went on, "And Chihuahua and Sonora are *our* provinces, by God, and by God we shall keep them whether the United States approve or not."

"Very good, Mr. President!" Having no compromise in his own soul, Jackson admired steadfastness in others.

"I have also sent communications to this effect to our friends in London and Paris," Longstreet said.

"That was excellently done, I am sure," Jackson said. "Their assistance was welcome during the War of Secession, and I trust they shall be as eager to see the United States taken down a peg now as they were then."

"General, their assistance during the war was more than merely necessary," Longstreet said heavily. "It was the *sine qua non* without which the Confederate States should not be a free and independent republic today."

Jackson frowned. "I don't know about that, Your Excellency. I am of the opinion that the Army of Northern Virginia had a certain small something to do with that independence." He paused a moment, a *tableau vivant* of animated thought. "The battle of Camp Hill for some reason comes to mind."

Longstreet smiled at Jackson's seldom-shown playfulness. "Camp Hill was necessary, General, necessary, but, I believe, not sufficient. Without the brave work our soldiers did, England and France should never have been in position to recognize our independence and force acceptance of that independence on the Lincoln regime."

"Which is what I said, is it not?" Jackson rumbled.

But the president of the CSA shook his head. "No, not quite. You will remember, sir, I had rather more to do with the military commissioners of the United States than did you as we hammered out the terms under which each side should withdraw from the territory of the other."

"Yes, I remember that," Jackson said. "I never claimed to be any sort of diplomatist, and General Lee was not one to assign a man to a place in which he did not fit." Jackson saw that as a small barb aimed at Longstreet, who was so slippery, he might have ended up a Black Republican had he lived in the United States rather than the Confederacy. Being slippery, though, Longstreet probably took it as a compliment. Jackson asked the next question: "What of it, sir?"

"This of it: every last Yankee officer with whom I spoke swore up and down on a stack of Bibles as tall as he was that Lincoln never would have given up the fight if he'd only been fighting against us," Longstreet said. "The man was a fanatic—still is a fanatic, going up and down in the USA like Satan in the book of Job, stirring up trouble wherever he travels. The only thing that convinced him the United States were licked—the *only* thing, General—was the intervention of England and France on our behalf. Absent that, he aimed to keep on no matter what we did."

"He would have done better had he had generals as convinced of the righteousness of his cause as he was himself," Jackson remarked. "As well for us he did not."

"As well for us indeed." Longstreet nodded his big, leonine head. "That, however, is not the point. The point is that the English and French, by virtue of the service they rendered us, and by virtue of the services they may render us in the future, have a strong and definite claim upon our attention."

"Wait." Jackson had not lied when he said he was no diplomat; he needed a while to fathom matters that were immediately obvious to a man like Longstreet. But, as in his days of teaching optics, acoustics, and astronomy at the Virginia Military Institute, unrelenting study let him work out what he did not grasp at once. "You are saying, Your Excellency, are you not, that we are still beholden to our allies and must take their wishes into account in formulating our policy?"

"Yes, I am saying that. I wish I weren't, but I am," Longstreet replied. Jackson started to say something; the president held up a hand to stop him. "Now you wait, sir, until you have answered this question: does the prospect of taking on the United States over the Mexican provinces alone and unaided have any great appeal to you?"

"It could be done," Jackson said at once.

"I do not deny that for an instant, but it is not the question I put to you," Longstreet said. "What I asked was, has the prospect any great appeal to you? Would you sooner we war against the USA by ourselves, or in the company of two leading European powers?"

"The latter, certainly," Jackson admitted. "The United States have always outweighed us. We have more men and far more factories now than I ever dreamt we should, but they continue to outweigh us. If ever they found leaders and morale to match their resources, they would become a formidable foe."

"This is also my view of the situation." Longstreet drummed his fingers on the desk in front of him. "And Blaine, like Lincoln, has no sense of moderation when it comes to our country. If he so chooses, as I think he may, he can whip them up into a frenzy against us in short order. This concerns me. What also concerns me is the price London and Paris have put on a renewal of their alliance with us. The necessity for weighing one of those concerns against the other is the reason I asked to see you here today."

"A price for continued friendship? What price could the British and French require for doing what is obviously in their interest anyhow?" By asking the question, he proved his want of diplomacy to Longstreet and, a moment later, to himself. "Oh," he said. "They intend to try to lever us into abandoning our peculiar institution."

"There you have it, sure enough," Longstreet agreed. "Both the British and French ministers make it abundantly clear that their governments shall not aid us in any prospective struggle against the United States unless we agree in advance to undertake emancipation no later than a year after the end of hostilities. They are acting in concert on this matter, and appear firmly determined to follow their words with deeds, or rather, with the lack of deeds we should otherwise expect."

"Let them," Jackson growled, as angry as if Britain and France were enemies, not the best friends the Confederate States had. "Let them. We'll whip the Yankees, and after that we'll do whatever else needs doing, too."

"I assure you, General, I admire your spirit from the bottom of my heart," Longstreet said. "If we are assured of success in a conflict against the USA over Chihuahua and Sonora, please tell me so, and tell me plainly."

Jackson hesitated—and was lost. "In war, Your Excellency, especially war against a larger power, nothing is assured, as I said before. I am confident, however, that God, having given us this land of ours to do with as we will, does not intend to withdraw His gift from our hands."

"That, I fear, is not enough." Longstreet let out a long sigh. "You have no conception, General, to what degree slavery has become an albatross round our necks in all our intercourse, diplomatic and commercial, with foreign powers. The explanations, the difficulties, the resentments grow worse year by year. We and the Empire of Brazil are the only remaining slaveholding nations, and even the Brazilians have begun a program of gradual emancipation for the Negroes they hold in servitude."

"Mr. President, if we are *right*, what foreigners have to say about us matters not at all, and I believe we *are* right," Jackson said stubbornly. "I believe, as I have always believed, that God Himself ordained our system as the best one practicable for the relationship between the white and Negro races. Changing it now at foreigners' insistence would be as much a betrayal as changing it at the Black Republicans' insistence twenty years ago."

"I understand this perspective, General, and, believe me, I am personally in sympathy with it," Longstreet said. When a politician, which was what the president of the CSA had long since become, said he was personally in sympathy with something, Jackson had learned, he meant the opposite. And, sure enough, Longstreet went on, "Other considerations, however, compel me to take a broader view of the question."

"What circumstances could possibly be more important than acting in accordance with God's will as we understand it?" Jackson demanded.

"Being certain we do understand it," Longstreet answered. "If we fight the United States alone and are defeated, is it not likely that the victors would seek to impose emancipation and even, to the degree they can effect it, Negro dominance upon us, to weaken us as much as possible?"

Jackson grunted. He had never considered the aftermath of a Confederate defeat. Victory was the only consideration that had ever crossed his mind. Reluctantly, he gave President Longstreet credit for subtlety.

Longstreet said, "Can we successfully fight the United States without their coasts being blockaded, a task far beyond the power of our navy alone? Can we fight them without pressure from Canada to make them divide their forces and efforts instead of concentrating solely against us? If you tell me we are as certain, or even nearly as certain, of success without our friends as with them, defying their wishes makes better sense."

"I think, as I have said, we can win without them," Jackson said, but he was too honest not to add, "With them, though, the odds improve."

"My thought exactly," Longstreet said, beaming, jollying him toward acquiescence. "And if we emancipate the Negro *de jure* of our own free will, we shall surely be spared the difficulties that would ensue if, as the result of some misfortune, we were compelled to emancipate him *de facto*."

There was some truth—perhaps a lot of truth—in that. Jackson had to recognize it. Longstreet made him think of a fast-talking hoaxer, selling Florida seaside real estate under water twenty-two hours out of every twenty-four. But the president had been elected to make decisions of this sort. "I am a soldier, Your Excellency," Jackson said. "If this be your decision, I shall of course conduct myself in conformity to it."

☆ II ☆

Theodore Roosevelt looked over his ranch with considerable satisfaction. *Ranch* was the western word, of course, borrowed from the Spanish; back in New York State, it would have been a farm.

He sucked in a deep breath of the sweet, pure air of Montana Territory. "Like wine in the lungs," he said. "No coal smoke, no city stinks, nothing but pure, wholesome, delicious oxygen." He'd been a scrawny weakling when he came out to the West a couple of years before, an old man inside though he'd scarcely passed his twentieth birthday. Now, though older by the calendar, he felt years—decades—younger inside. Strenuous labor, that was the trick.

One of the hands, a grizzled ex-miner who possessed but did not rejoice in the name of Philander Snow, cocked an eyebrow at that. "Oxy-what, boss?" he asked.

"Oxygen, Phil," Roosevelt repeated. "Oxygen. What we breathe. What makes lamps burn. What, without which, life would be impossible."

"I thought that was whiskey, or maybe women, depending," Snow said. "More women in the Territory than there used to be, and nowadays I can't do as much with 'em. Ain't that the way it goes?" He spat a mournful stream of tobacco juice onto the ground.

Roosevelt laughed, but quickly sobered. His education made him stick out in these parts. He had trouble talking with his hands, with his fellow ranchers, and even with the townsfolk in Helena about anything past superficialities. Sometimes he felt more nearly an exile than an emigrant from his old way of life. The closest civilized conversation was down in Cheyenne, or maybe even Denver.

But then Philander Snow remarked, "It'll be lambing time any day now," and thoughts of the work at hand replaced those having to do with combustion and metabolism.

Off in the distance, the sheep cropped the new spring grass. The ranch had several hundred head, and a couple of hundred cattle to go with them. Along with the fields of wheat and barley and the vegetable plot near the ranch house, Roosevelt produced all the food he needed, and had a tidy surplus to sell. "Self-sufficiency," he declared. "Every man's dream—and, by jingo, I've got it! Lord of the manor, that's what I am."

"Ain't nothin' wrong with your manners, boss," Snow said, spitting again. "Oh, you was kind of fancified and dudish when you first got here, I reckon, but you've done settled in nice as you please."

"For which I do thank you, Phil, most sincerely." As he had many times in the past, Roosevelt reflected that, while both he and his hands used English, they did not speak the same language.

"This here's a nice spread you got," Snow said. "Not so small you can't do all sorts of things with it, not so big you got to have your own army before you can get any work done. Down in Texas, I hear tell, they got ranches big as a whole county, do nothin' on 'em but raise cows. Pack of damn foolishness, anybody wants to know." Another stream of brown landed wetly in the dust.

"You get no arguments from me." Roosevelt looked south, as if, someone having mentioned Texas, he could see it from here. "Do you know, it broke my father's heart when the United States lost the War of Secession, but I'd say we're just as well rid of those Rebels. They'd bring their ways of doing things—everything larger than life, as you say—up here if we were still part of the same nation."

"They'd bring their niggers, too." One more expectoration gave Philander Snow's opinion of that. "Far as I'm concerned, the Rebs are welcome to 'em. This here's a white man's country, nothin' else but."

"I agree with you once again," Roosevelt said. "The United States are better off without any great presence of the dusky race in our midst. Were it not for the Negro, I doubt we and our former compatriots should ever have come to blows."

"Likely tell, us and the Rebs wouldn't have fought a war, neither," Snow observed. Roosevelt's metal framed spectacles and the mustache he was assiduously cultivating helped keep his face from showing what he thought. After a moment, the ranch hand went on, "And now it looks like we're goin' to fight them sons of bitches again."

"And bully for Blaine, I say!" Roosevelt clenched his fists. "Lord knows I have no use for the Republican Party except in that it wants us to take a strong line with our neighbors, but that, these days, is an enormous exception."

"You damn straight it is, boss," Philander Snow said with a vehement nod. "Them Rebs, they been rubbin' our noses in the dirt since we lost the war, and them Easterners, they just smile and take it and say *thank you* meek and mild as you please. Hope to Jesus they get around to lettin' Montana into the Union one day soon, so as I can vote for people who'll show a little backbone. Not even a lot, mind you—a little'd be plenty to make the Rebels climb down off their high horse, you ask me."

"I think you're dead right, Phil, but the Confederates aren't the only ones we have to worry about, not here in Montana they're not." Where Theodore Roosevelt had looked south toward Texas, he now turned north. "Here near Helena, we're only a couple of hundred miles away from the Canadian border."

"I've met me some Canucks," Snow said. "They ain't the worst people you'd ever want to know. But Canada ain't free and independent, not all the way it ain't. The limeys, they do whatever they please there."

"They certainly do," Roosevelt agreed, "and they're able to do it, too, since their transcontinental railroad went through about the time I came to Montana. The only reason they had for building that railroad—the *only* reason, I say, Phil—is to shuttle British soldiers along the frontier to those places where they might prove most advantageous."

"And where they'll do the most good, too," Snow said.

Roosevelt smiled. His hired hand had no idea what was funny. He didn't explain he had no desire to make the older man feel foolish. Instead, he came round to the other subject uppermost on his mind: "And now the Confederates, not content with battening on our weakness these past twenty years, have sunk their fangs into the Empire of Mexico as well."

"By what the papers were saying last time you went into town, President Blaine ain't gonna take that layin' down," Snow said.

"He'd better not. If he does, the whole country lies down with him. He wasn't elected to play the coward, which is what I've been saying." Resolution crystallized in Roosevelt. When he made up his mind, he made it up in a hurry, and all the way. "Harness the team to the Handbasket, Phil. I'm going into town to find out what the latest news is. If there's war, sure as the sun comes up tomorrow we'll have hordes of redcoats pouring over the border. By jingo, I wish the telegraph line reached all the way out here. I want to know what's going on out in the bigger world."

If Philander Snow cared about the wider world, he concealed it very well. He might have been—he probably had been—a rough character once, but work on the farm and the occasional spree in Helena satisfied him now. "Give me just a few minutes, boss, and I'll take care of it." He spat and chuckled and spat again. "You're a hell of a funny fellow, boss, when you take it in your mind to be."

Roosevelt went back into the ranch house for his Winchester. The ranch lay about ten miles north of Helena, in a little valley whose surrounding hills protected it from the worst of the winter blizzards. He was more worried about bears than bandits or hostile Indians, but you never could tell. He took a box of .45 caliber cartridges along with the rifle.

Snow brought the buggy out of the barn almost as quickly as he'd promised. "Here you go," he said, climbing down from the driver's bench so Roosevelt could get aboard. "To Helena Handbasket," he said, and chuckled again. "You struck the mother lode when you came up with that one, sure as hell."

"Glad you like it." Roosevelt liked it, too. He stowed the rifle where he could grab it in a hurry if he had to, flicked the reins, and got the horses going toward Helena.

He reached the territorial capital a couple of hours later. Farms much like his own covered most of the flat land, with stretches of forest between them. Here and there, on the higher ground, were shafts and timbers from mines hopeful prospectors had begun. Most of them were years abandoned. Most of the prospectors, like Philander Snow, were making their living in some different line of work these days.

Helena sat in a valley of its own. Some of the log cabins of the earliest settlers, those who'd come just after the end of the War of Secession, still stood down near the bottom of the valley, by the tributary of the Prickly Pear that had made people pause hereabouts in the first place. Newer, finer homes climbed the hills to either side.

Down on Broadway, as Roosevelt drove the wagon toward the newspaper office, he felt himself returned to a cosmopolitan city, even if not to a sophisticated one. Here riding beside him was a bearded prospector leading a pack mule. The fellow still hoped to strike it rich, as did some of his comrades. Every once in a while, those hopes came true. Mines near Helena, and newer ones by Wickes to the south and Marysville to the west, had made millionaires—but only a handful.

A Chinaman in a conical straw hat walked by, carrying two crates hanging from a pole over his right shoulder. Roosevelt approved of Chinese industriousness, but wouldn't have minded seeing all the Celestials gone from the West. *They don't fit in,* he thought: *too different from Americans.*

Solomon Katz ran a drugstore near the office of the *Helena Gazette*; Sam Houlihan ran the hardware store next door, and Otto Burmeister the bakery next to that. Among Helena's ten or twelve thousand people, there were members of every nation ever to set foot on the North American continent.

And, trotting up the street on their ponies, a couple of the original inhabitants of the continent came toward Roosevelt. One of the Sioux wore the buckskin tunic and trousers traditional to his people, the other blue denim trousers and a calico shirt. Idly, Roosevelt wondered what Helena—a medium-sized town at best, but a larger assemblage of people than their tribe had ever managed—seemed like to them.

He shrugged. In the larger scheme of things, their opinion counted for very little. As if to take their minds off the defeat the United States had suffered at the hands of the Confederacy, and also spurred by the Sioux uprisings in Minnesota, the USA had thrown swarms of soldiers across the prairie, subduing the aborigines by numbers and firepower even if not with any great military skill. These days, the Indians could only stand and watch as the lands that had been theirs served the purposes of a stronger race.

Roosevelt looked for the Indians to head into one of the saloons sprouting like mushrooms along Broadway. Instead, they tied up their horses in front of Houlihan's establishment and went in there. Roosevelt's head bobbed up and down in approval: Indians who needed hammers or saw blades or a keg of nails were Indians on the way to civilization. He'd heard the Lord's Prayer had been translated into Sioux, which he also took for a good sign.

The *Gazette* had a copy of the front page of the day's edition displayed under glass in front of the office. A small crowd of people stared at it. Roosevelt worked his way through the crowd till he could read the headlines. REBEL INTRANSIGENCE, shouted one. BLAINE TAKES FIRM LINE ON CONFEDERATE LAND GRAB, said another. ENGLAND WARNS USA NOT TO MEDDLE, declared a third.

"England, she has no right to make such a warning," said one of the men in front of Roosevelt. He had a guttural accent; *warning* came out *varning*. Roosevelt's big head nodded vehemently— even a German immigrant could see the nose in front of his face.

He wondered if Blaine would see it or back down, spineless as the Democrats who'd run the country since Lincoln was so unceremoniously shown the door after the war against secession turned out to be the War of Secession. By that second headline, the president seemed to be doing what the people had elected him to do, for which Roosevelt thanked God.

Behind Roosevelt, the crowd parted as if it were the Red Sea and Moses had come. But it wasn't Moses, it was a fierce-looking fellow with a bushy white mustache and chin beard who wore a banker's somber black suit.

"Mornin', Mr. Cruse," a grocer said respectfully. "Good day, sir," one of the men who worked at the livery stable added, tipping his straw hat. "How's the boy, Tommy?" said a miner who matched Cruse in years but not in affluence.

"Mornin' to you all," Cruse said, affable enough and to spare. A few years earlier, he'd been poorer than the miner who'd greeted him. Roosevelt doubted whether any bank in Montana Territory would have lent him more than fifty dollars. But he'd made his strike, which was rare, and he'd sold it for every penny it was worth, which was rarer. These days, he didn't need to borrow money from a bank, for he owned one. He was one of the handful of men throughout the West who'd gone at a single bound from prospector to capitalist.

He'd dealt squarely with people when he was poor, and he kept on dealing squarely with them now that he was rich. Had he wanted to be territorial governor, he could have been. He'd never given any sign of being interested in the job.

Like everyone else, Roosevelt gave way for him. It was a gesture of respect for the man's achievement, not one of servility. Roosevelt had money of his own, New York money, infinitely older and infinitely more stable than that grubbed from the ground here in the wild territories.

"Good morning, Mr. Roosevelt," Cruse said, nodding to him. The self-made millionaire respected those who gave him his due and no more.

"Good morning to you, Mr. Cruse," Roosevelt answered, hoping he would be as vigorous as the ex-miner when he got old. He pointed toward the front page of the *Helena Gazette*. "What do you think we ought to do, sir, about the Confederates' land grab?"

"Let me see the latest before I answer." Unlike so many of his comrades, Thomas Cruse would not leap blind. He stood well back from the newspaper under glass, studying the headlines. The crowd of men who had also been reading them waited, silent, for his considered opinion. Once he was done, he spoke with due deliberation: "I think we ought to continue on the course we've taken up till now. I see no other we can choose."

"My exact thought, Mr. Cruse," Roosevelt agreed enthusiastically. "But if the Confederates and the British—and the French who prop up Maximilian—also continue on their course . . ."

"Then we lick 'em," Tom Cruse said in a loud, harsh voice. The crowd in front of the newspaper office erupted in cheers. Theodore Roosevelt joined them. Cruse could speak for all of Montana Territory. The miner turned banker had certainly spoken for him.

General James Ewell Brown Stuart's way had always been to lead from the front. As commander of the Confederate States Department of the Trans-Mississippi, he might have made his headquarters in Houston or Austin, as several of his predecessors had done. Instead, ever since being promoted to the position two years earlier, he'd based himself in the miserable village of El Paso, as far west as he could go while staying in the CSA.

Peering north and west along the Rio Grande—swollen, at the moment, with spring runoff and very different from the sleepy stream it would be soon—Jeb Stuart looked into the USA. That proximity to the rival nation made El Paso important as a Confederate outpost, and was the reason he'd brought his headquarters hither.

But El Paso had been a place of significance before an international border sprang up between Texas and New Mexico

Territory, between CSA and USA. It and its sister town on the other side of the Rio Grande, Paso del Norte, had stood on opposite sides of the border first between Mexico and the USA and then between Mexico and the CSA. The pass the names of the two towns commemorated was one of the lowest and broadest through the Rockies, a gateway between east and west travelers had been using for centuries.

Stuart looked across the Rio Grande to Paso del Norte. Not quite twenty years earlier, the national border between Texas and New Mexico had gone up. (It would have gone up farther west and north, but the Confederate invasion of New Mexico, mounted without adequate manpower or supplies, had failed.) Now, as soon as Stuart got the telegram for which he was waiting, the border on the Rio Grande would cease to be.

His aide-de-camp, a burly major named Horatio Sellers, came walking up to the edge of the river to stand alongside him. Sweat streaked Sellers' ruddy face. Dust didn't scuff up under his boots, as it would in a few weeks, but the heat was already irksome, and gave every promise of becoming appalling.

Sellers peered across into what remained for the moment the territory of the Empire of Mexico. Paso del Norte was larger than its Confederate counterpart, but no more prepossessing. A couple of cathedrals reared above the mud-brick buildings that made up most of the town. The flat roofs of those buildings made the place look as if the sun had pounded it down from greater prominence.

Sellers said, "We're giving Maximilian three million in gold and silver for those two provinces? Three *million*? Sir, you ask me, we ought to get change back from fifty cents."

"Nobody asked you, Major," Stuart answered. "Nobody asked me, either. That doesn't matter. If we're ordered—when we're ordered—to take possession of the provinces for the Confederacy, that's what we'll do. That's all we can do."

"Yes, sir," his aide-de-camp answered resignedly.

"Look on the bright side," Stuart said. "We've got the Yankees hopping around like fleas on a hot griddle. That's worthwhile all by itself, if you ask me." He grinned. "Of course, Longstreet didn't ask me, any more than he asked you."

Sellers remained gloomy, which was in good accord with his nature. "Two provinces full of desert and Indians and Mexicans, and we're supposed to turn them into Confederate states, sir? It'll be a lot of work, I can tell you that. Christ, Negro servitude is illegal south of the border."

"Well, if the border moves south, our laws move with it," Stuart answered. "I expect we'll manage well enough there." He chuckled. "I'll bet Stonewall wishes he were here instead of me. He liked Mexico when he fought there for the USA—he even learned to speak Spanish. But he's stuck in Richmond, and that's about as far from El Paso as you can be and still stay in the Confederate States."

"Sir," Sellers persisted, exactly as if Jeb Stuart could do something about the situation, "supposing we do annex Sonora and Chihuahua. How the devil are we supposed to defend them from the USA? New Mexico Territory and California have a lot longer stretch of border with 'em than Texas does, and the Yankees have a railroad down there, so they can ship in troops faster than we can hope to manage it. What are we going to do?"

"Whatever it takes, and whatever we have to do," Stuart said, though he recognized the answer as imperfectly satisfactory. "I'll tell you this much, Major, and you can mark my words: once those provinces are in our hands, we *will* have a railroad through to the Pacific inside of five years. We aren't like Maximilian's pack of do-nothings down in Mexico City. When the Anglo-Saxon race sets its mind to do something, that thing gets done."

"Of course, sir." Major Sellers was as smugly confident of the superiority of his own people as was Stuart. After a moment, he added, "We'll need a railroad more than the greasers would have, too. We'll use it for trade, the same as they would have done, but we'll use it against the United States, too, and they never would have bothered with that."

Stuart nodded. "Can't say you're wrong there. If Mexico ever got into a brawl with the USA, first thing she'd do would be to pull out of that part of the country and see whether a Yankee army was still worth anything once it got done slogging its way through the desert."

"No, sir." Sellers shook his head. "The first thing Maximilian would do would be to scream for us to help. The second thing he'd do would be to pull out of Sonora and Chihuahua."

"You're likely to be right about that, too," Stewart said. The sound of boots clumping on the dirt made him turn his head. An orderly was coming up, a telegram clenched in his right fist.

"Well, well." One of Stuart's thick eyebrows rose. "What have we here?"

"Wire for you, sir," said the orderly, a youngster named Withers. "From Richmond."

"I hadn't really expected them to wire me from Washington, D.C.," Stuart answered. Major Sellers snorted. Withers looked blank; he didn't get the joke. With a small mental sigh, Stuart read the telegram. That eyebrow climbed higher and higher as he did. "Well, well," he said again.

"Sir?" Sellers said.

Stuart realized *well, well* was something less than informative. "We are ordered by General Jackson to assemble two regiments of cavalry and two batteries of artillery at Presidio, and also to assemble five regiments of cavalry, half a dozen batteries, and three regiments of infantry here at El Paso, the said concentrations to be completed no later than May 16." The date amused him. Most officers would surely have chosen the fifteenth. But that was a Sunday, and Jackson had always been averse to doing anything not vitally necessary on the Sabbath.

Sellers whistled softly. "It's going to happen, then."

"I would say that appears very likely, Major," Stuart agreed. "Presidio is on the road to the town of Chihuahua, the capital of Chihuahua province, which we would naturally have to occupy upon annexation. And of the larger force to be assembled here, I presume some will go to Hermosillo, the capital of Sonora province—which I suppose will become Sonora Territory—and some will defend El Paso against whatever moves the United States may make in response to our actions."

"We'll have to post guards all along the railroad." Now Major Sellers looked north. The Texas–New Mexico frontier and the Rio Grande pinched El Paso off at the end of a long, narrow neck of Confederate territory, through which the Texas Western Railroad necessarily ran. Small parties of raiders could do a lot of damage along that line.

"Once the annexation goes through, we won't have any trouble moving south of the Rio Grande. We'll have more depth in which to operate," Stuart said. That was true, but it wasn't so useful as it might have been, and he knew as much. No railroad to El Paso ran through Chihuahua province; movement would have to be by horseback and wagon. He sighed, folded the telegram, and put it in the breast pocket of his butternut tunic: he was not a man to wear an old-style uniform once the new one had been authorized. "Have to go back to my office and see what I can move, and from which places."

The longer he studied the map, the less happy he got. To carry out General Jackson's orders, he would have to pull troops from as far away as Arkansas, and that would result in weakening a different frontier with the USA. He would also have to call down the Fifth Cavalry and to denude the rest of the garrisons protecting west Texas from the Comanche raiders who took refuge in New Mexico Territory. If the Yankees turned the Comanches loose, there was liable to be hell to pay among the ranchers and farmers in that part of the country.

But there would certainly be hell to pay if he did not obey Jackson's order in every particular. Old Stonewall had sacked one of his officers during the war for failing to deliver an ordered attack even though the fellow had learned he was outnumbered much worse than Jackson thought he was. Jackson did not, would not, take no for an answer.

By the time Stuart was done drafting telegrams, he had shifted troops all over the landscape. He took the text of the wires over to the telegraph office, listened to the first couple of them clicking their way east, and then went off to watch the cavalry regiment regularly stationed at El Paso go through its morning exercises.

Troops began arriving a couple of days later. So did cars filled with hardtack, cornmeal, beans, and salt pork for the men, and with oats and hay for the horses and other animals. Every time he looked across the river into Chihuahua province, he wondered how he could keep his soldiers supplied there. He also sent out orders accumulating wagons at El Paso. If he didn't bring food and munitions with him, he suspected he'd have none.

No troop movements on this scale had been seen in the Trans-Mississippi since the end of the war, not even during the great Comanche outbreak of 1874. Some officers had been rusticating in their fortresses since Lincoln abandoned the struggle to keep the Confederacy from gaining its independence. All things considered, they did a good job of shaking off the cobwebs and going from garrison soldiering to something approaching field service.

By the tenth of May, Stuart was convinced he would have all his troops in place before the deadline General Jackson had sent him. On that day, a messenger came galloping into El Paso. "Sir," he said when he came before Stuart, "Sir, Lieutenant Colonel

Foulke has crossed the border from Las Cruces under flag of truce and wants to speak with you."

"Has he?" Stuart thought fast. There were any number of places where the Yankees could have sneaked an observer over the border to keep an eye on the one railroad into El Paso; spotting troop trains would have given them a good notion of the force he had at his disposal. But what the United States knew and what they officially knew were different things. "I want his party stopped four or five miles outside of town. I'll ride out and confer with him there. Hop to it, Sergeant. I don't want him in El Paso."

"Yes, sir." The noncommissioned officer who'd brought him the news hurried away to head off the U.S. officer.

Stuart followed at a pace only a little more leisurely. Accompanied by Major Sellers and enough troopers to give the idea that he was someone of consequence, he rode up the dirt track that led northwest toward New Mexico.

He met Lieutenant Colonel Foulke's party nearer three miles outside El Paso than five. One of Foulke's aides was peering toward the Confederate garrison town with a telescope he folded up and put away when Stuart and his retinue came into sight. He could have done it sooner without Stuart's seeing it. That he'd waited meant he wanted Stuart to know the Yankees had him under observation.

"Wait here," Stuart told the troopers when they drew close to the U.S. soldiers. "They didn't come here to start a fight, not under flag of truce." He and his aide-de-camp rode on toward the men in blue.

Lieutenant Colonel Foulke and the officer who'd been using the telescope imitated his practice, so that the four leaders met between their small commands. "A very good morning to you, General," Foulke said politely; seeing his baby-smooth skin and coal-black mustache reminded Stuart he himself would be fifty soon.

He didn't let himself dwell on that. "The same to you, Lieutenant Colonel," he answered. "I hope you will not mind my asking the purpose of your visit to the Confederacy here."

"By no means, sir." Hearing the polite phrase in Foulke's Yankee accent—New York, Stuart thought—was strange. The U.S. officer went on, "I have been instructed by the secretary of war, Mr. Harrison, and by the general-in-chief of the United States Army to inform you personally that the United States will view with great concern any movement of Confederate forces into the territory of the Empire of Mexico."

"I would point out to you, sir, that, when and if the purchase arrangements between Mexico and the Confederacy are completed, the provinces of Chihuahua and Sonora shall no longer be the territory of the Empire of Mexico, but rather that of the Confederate States of America." Stuart's smile looked ingratiating, but was anything but. "Surely, Bill—"

"William," Foulke said. "I prefer William. William Dudley Foulke, sir, at your service."

"Beg your pardon, William," Stuart said easily, wondering what such a pompous little fellow was doing so far out West. "As I was saying, surely the United States cannot be thinking of forbidding the Confederate States from moving their forces from one part of their own territory to another."

William Dudley Foulke took a deep breath. "I am requested and required to inform you, General, as the government of the United States has informed President Longstreet in Richmond, that the United States consider the sale of Sonora and Chihuahua to be made under duress, and therefore to be invalid and of no consequence."

"Oh, they do, do they?" Stuart had understood that to be the position of the United States, but had never heard it explicitly till now. The way it was stated . . . "William, I assure you I mean no offense by this, but you talk more like a lawyer than a soldier."

Foulke smiled: he was amused, not angry. "I considered a career in the law in my early days, General Stuart. In the aftermath of the War of Secession, I determined that I could better use my talents in the service of my country as a soldier than as a jurist. As I am of Quaker stock, my family was distressed at my choice, but here I am today."

"Here you are," Stuart agreed. "And since you are here, Lieutenant Colonel Foulke, I have to tell you that the view of the Confederate States is that, if the sale of Sonora and Chihuahua be completed, those two provinces become territory belonging to the Confederate States of America, to be administered and garrisoned at the sole discretion of the government of the CSA. In plain English, sir, once they're ours, we'll do with them as we please."

"In plain English, sir, the United States do not aim to let themselves be outflanked on the south," Foulke said. "The United States do not aim to let the Confederacy take advantage of a weak neighbor, as you did when you bullied Cuba out of Spain a few years ago. I expect you will wire a report of this meeting back to Richmond. Rest assured that I am telling you nothing different from what Minister Hay is telling President Longstreet there, or for that matter what President Blaine is telling Minister Benjamin in Washington."

Major Horatio Sellers spoke up: "You Yankees keep barking that way, Lieutenant Colonel, you're going to have to show whether you've got any bite to go with it."

Foulke flushed: with his fine, fair skin, the darkening was quite noticeable. But his voice was cool as he replied, "Major, if your nation persists in its unwise course, you will feel our teeth, I assure you."

"The United States have already felt our teeth, sir," Jeb Stuart said. "It has been a while, I admit; perhaps you've forgotten. If you have, we are prepared to remind you. And, I will point out, we have good friends, which is more than the United States can say."

Lieutenant Colonel Foulke shrugged. "Sir, I have delivered to you the message with which I was charged. I personally have no great use for war, nor does any man, nor any nation, of sense. But you are to know that the United States are firmly resolved in this matter. Good day." Without waiting for a reply, he and the captain with him rode back toward their men.

Stuart watched until all the Yankees started riding off in the direction of New Mexico. When he'd been Foulke's age—Lord, when he'd been even younger—he'd loved nothing better than riding to war. Now that he had sons of his own growing to manhood, he was no longer so sure.

He turned to Major Sellers. "The next time we see that Yankee, it will be on the battlefield."

His aide-de-camp gave a sharp, short nod. "Good," he said.

Colonel Alfred von Schlieffen had heard that the British government designated diplomatic service in Washington, D.C., a hardship position on account of the abominable climate of the capital of the United States. He didn't know for a fact that that was true. If it wasn't, though, it should have been. The weather had already got hotter and muggier than it ever did in Berlin, and May was only a bit more than half done. Kaiser Wilhelm I's military attaché in the United States ran a finger under the tight collar of his blue Prussian uniform to try to let in some air. That helped little, if at all.

Sweating, Schlieffen stepped onto the black cast-iron balcony outside his office. He startled a pigeon on the rail. It flew away, wings flapping noisily. Schlieffen reckoned that a victory of sorts. Too many pigeon droppings streaked the dark red brick of the German ministry.

Against the humidity and heat, though, he won nothing. No breeze stirred the air; it was as hot outside as back in the office. Horses and buggies and wagons rattled up and down Massachusetts Avenue. The street was paved with bricks, so they didn't raise great choking clouds of dust as they might have done, but the racket of iron-shod hooves and iron tires on the paving was terrible.

That racket drove whatever thoughts Schlieffen had had clean out of his head. For a man so intensely intellectual, that could not be borne. He went back inside, closing the French doors behind him. As the air was so still, he made the office no hotter, and, since they were almost all glass, he hardly made it dimmer.

Above his desk hung three framed portraits. A Catholic might have thought them images of a secular Trinity. That had never occurred to Schlieffen, a devout Hutterite. To him, they were merely the most important men in his life: ascetic-looking Field Marshal von Moltke, whose victories over Denmark, Austria, and France had made Prussian-led Germany a nation; plump, imperious Chancellor von Bismarck, whose diplomacy had made von Moltke's victories possible; and, above them both, the Kaiser, bald now, his fringe of hair, mustache, and fuzzy side whiskers white, his chest full of well-earned medals, for he had been a formidable soldier in his own right before succeeding his brother as King of Prussia.

Whenever Schlieffen thought of the Kaiser's soldierly career, he could only marvel, for Wilhelm had first seen action in the Prussian puppet forces that fought under Napoleon's command when the century was young. "How many men still living can say that?" Schlieffen murmured. And afterwards, Wilhelm had helped guide Prussia's rise to greatness, had known when to urge his brother to decline the throne of a united Germany after the revolutions of 1848, and had known when to accept it himself a generation later.

From the Kaiser's portrait, Schlieffen's eyes fell briefly to the small photograph of a pretty young woman on his desk: the one bit of sentiment he permitted himself in a room otherwise utterly businesslike. Anna had been his cousin as well as, for four wonderful years, his wife. In the nine years since her death in childbed, he'd found it easier to care for the ideal of Germany than for any merely human being.

He inked his pen and wrote the last few sentences of the report he'd been working on. After scrawling his signature at the bottom, he checked his pocket watch: a few minutes past ten. He had a ten-thirty appointment at the War Department.

Precise as always, he signed the daybook in the front hall, noting his departure time to the minute. The guards outside the door saluted as he left the embassy. He punctiliously returned the courtesy.

He walked half a block southeast on Massachusetts, then turned right onto Vermont, which cut diagonally across Washington's square grid and led straight toward the White House and the War Department building just west of it. Civilians waved to him, mistaking his light blue uniform for one belonging to the U.S. Army. He'd had U.S. soldiers make the same mistake and salute him.

He ignored the misdirected greetings, as he ignored most human contact. Then a fat man on a pony that didn't seem up to bearing his weight recognized the uniform for what it was. "Hurrah for the Kaiser!" the fellow called, and tipped his hat. Schlieffen acknowledged that with a polite nod. The Kaiser was popular in the United States, not least because his army had beaten the French.

Newsboys hawked papers on every corner. Headlines screamed of coming war. Schlieffen's glance lifted toward the Arlington Heights on the far side of the Potomac. Buildings screened most of his view of them, but he knew they were there. He also knew the Confederate States had guns mounted on them, and on other high ground along the southern bank of the river. If war came, Washington would suffer.

More soldiers were on the streets than usual, but not many more. Unlike Germany, the United States had no conscription law, relying instead on volunteers to fill out the relatively small professional army once war was declared. That struck Schlieffen as the next thing to insane, even if the Confederacy used the same system. *Mobs*, he thought scornfully. *Mobs with rifles, that's what they'll be.*

Harry Turtledove   53

The War Department was a four-story brick building with a two-story entranceway fronted by half a dozen columns. To Schlieffen's way of thinking, it would have been adequate for a provincial town, but hardly for a national capital. The Americans had talked for years of building something finer: talked, but spent no money. Still, the soldiers on duty at the entrance were almost as well drilled as the guards in front of the German embassy.

"Yes, Colonel," one of them said. "The general is expecting you, so you just follow Willie here. He'll take you to him."

"Thank you," Schlieffen said. The soldier named Willie led him up to the third-floor office where the general-in-chief of the U.S. Army carried out his duties. *"Guten Tag, Herr Oberst,"* said the general's adjutant, a bright young captain named Saul Berryman.

"Guten Tag," Schlieffen answered, and then, as he usually did, fell back into English: "How are you today, Captain?"

"Ganz gut, danke. Und Sie?" Berryman kept up the German for the same reason Schlieffen spoke English—neither was so fluent speaking the other's language as he would have liked, and both enjoyed the chance to practice. *"Der General wird Sie sofort sehen."*

"I am glad he will see me at once," Schlieffen said. "He must be very busy, with the crisis in your country."

"Ja, er ist." Just then, the general opened the door to the outer room where Berryman worked. Seeing him, his adjutant returned to English himself: "Go ahead, Colonel."

"Yes, always good to see you, Colonel," Major General William Rosecrans echoed. "Come right in."

"Thank you," Schlieffen said, and took a chair across the desk from Rosecrans. The military attaché's nostrils twitched. He'd smelled whiskey on Rosecrans before, but surely at a time like this— He gave a mental shrug.

"Good to see you," Rosecrans repeated, as if he'd forgotten he'd said it the first time. He was somewhere in his early sixties, with graying hair, a fairly neat graying beard, and a nose with a formidable hook in it. His color was very good, but the whiskey might have had something to do with that. He looked shrewd, but, Schlieffen judged, wasn't truly intelligent; he owed his position mostly to having come out of the War of Secession less disgraced than any other prominent U.S. commander.

"General, I am here to present my respects, and also to convey to you the friendly good wishes of my sovereign, the Kaiser," Schlieffen said.

"Of your suffering Kaiser?" Rosecrans said. "I hope he gets better, with all my heart I do. Germany has always been a country friendly to us, and we're damned glad of that, believe me, considering the way so many of the other countries in Europe treat us."

Schlieffen gave him a sharp look, or as sharp a look as could come from the military attaché's nondescript, rather pinched features. Rosecrans showed not the slightest hint of embarrassment, nor even that he noticed the glare. Schlieffen concluded the fault lay in his own accented English, which Rosecrans must have innocently misunderstood. Having concluded that, the colonel dismissed the matter from his mind. If no insult had been offered, he could not take offense.

"I would be grateful, General, if you could make arrangements so that, in the event of war between the United States and the Confederate States, you might transport me to one of your armies so that I can observe the fighting and report on it to my government," he said.

"Well, if the war's not over and done with before you catch up to it, I expect we'll be able to do that," Rosecrans said. "You'll have to move sharp, though, because we ought to lick the Rebs in jig time, or Bob's your uncle."

Although Schlieffen knew he was missing some of that—the English spoken in the United States at times seemed only distantly related to what he'd learned back in Germany—the root meaning remained pretty clear. "You believe you will win so quickly and easily, then?" He did his best to keep the surprise he felt out of his voice.

"Don't you?" Rosecrans made no effort to hide his own amazement. Very few Americans, as far as Schlieffen could see, had even the least skill in disguising their thoughts and feelings: indeed, they took an odd sort of pride in wearing them on their sleeves. When Schlieffen didn't answer right away, Rosecrans repeated, "Don't you, sir? The plain fact of the matter is, they're afraid. It's plain in everything they do."

"I am nothing more than an ignorant stranger in your country," Schlieffen said, a stratagem that had often given him good results. "Would you be so kind as to explain to me why you think this is so?"

Rosecrans swelled with self-importance. "It strikes me as an obvious fact, Colonel. The government of the United States told Richmond in no uncertain terms that there would be hell to pay if a single Confederate soldier crossed over the Rio Grande. Not a one of 'em has done it. Q.E.D."

"Is it not possible that the Confederate soldiers have not yet moved only because their own preparations remain incomplete?" Schlieffen asked.

"Possible, but not likely," Rosecrans said. "They put a large force of regulars into El Paso a couple of weeks ago—that was before we warned 'em we wouldn't stand for any funny business in Chihuahua and Sonora. And since that day, Colonel, since that day, not a one of the stinking sons of bitches has dared stir his nose out of their barracks. If that doesn't say they're afraid of us, I'd like to know what it does say."

Schlieffen thought he'd already told General Rosecrans what it said. To the American, evidently, *preparations* meant nothing more than moving troops from one place to another. Schlieffen wondered if his own English was at fault again. He didn't think so. The problem lay in the way Rosecrans—and, presumably, President Blaine—saw the world.

"If you fight the Confederate States, General, will you fight them alone?" Schlieffen tried to put the concept in a new way, since the first one had met no success.

"Of course we'll fight 'em alone," Rosecrans exclaimed. "They're the ones who suck up to foreigners, not us." That he was speaking with a foreigner did not cross his mind. His voice took on a petulant tone, almost a whine, that Schlieffen had heard before from other U.S. officers: "If England and France hadn't stabbed us in the back during the War of Secession, we'd've licked the Confederates then, and we wouldn't have to be worrying about this nonsense now."

"That may be true." Schlieffen felt something close to despair. Rosecrans was not a stupid man; Schlieffen had seen as much. But it was hard to tell whether he was more naive than ignorant or the other way round. "Could your diplomacy not try to keep Great Britain and France from doing in this war what they did in the last, or even more than they did in the last?"

"That's not my department," Rosecrans said flatly. "If they stay out, they stay out. If they come in, I suppose we'll deal with 'em. Stabbed in the back," he muttered again.

"You have, I trust, made plans for fighting the Confederate

States by themselves, for fighting them and Great Britain, for fighting them and France, and for fighting them and both Great Britain and France?" Schlieffen said.

Rosecrans gaped at him. After coughing a couple of times, the American general-in-chief said, "We'll hit the Rebs a couple of hard licks, then we'll chase 'em, depending on where they try to run. Whatever they try themselves, we'll beat that back, and . . . Are you all right, Colonel?"

"Yes, thank you," Schlieffen answered after a moment. He was briefly ashamed of his own coughing fit—was he an American, to reveal everything that was in his mind? But Rosecrans apparently saw nothing more than that he'd swallowed wrong. As gently as he could, Schlieffen went on, "We have developed in advance more elaborate plans of battle, General. They served us well against the Austrians and later against the French."

"I did enjoy watching the froggies get their ears pinned back," Rosecrans agreed. "But, Colonel, you don't understand." He spoke with great earnestness: Americans weren't always right, any more than anyone else was, but they were always sure of themselves. "Can't just go and plan things here, the way you do on your side of the Atlantic. The land's too big here, and there aren't enough people to fill it up. Too much room to maneuver, if you know what I mean, and that's hell on plans."

He had a point—no, he had part of a point. "We face the same difficulty when we think of war with Russia," Schlieffen said. "There is in Russia even more space than you have here, though I admit Russia has also more men. But this does not keep us from developing plans. If we can force the foe to respond to what our forces do, the game is ours."

"Maybe," Rosecrans said. "And maybe you're smarter than the Russians you'd be fighting, too. The next general who's smarter than Stonewall Jackson hasn't come down the pike yet, seems to me."

"I do not follow this," Schlieffen said, but then, all at once, he did. His own ancestors must have gone off to fight Napoleon with that same mixture of arrogance and dread. Comparing a backwoods Confederate general to the great Bonaparte, though, struck him as absurd—until he considered that Rosecrans and his ilk were hardly a match for Scharnhorst, Gneisenau, and Blücher.

"But we will lick 'em." Suddenly, Rosecrans was full of bluff confidence again. "We outweigh 'em two to one, near enough, and that's plenty to make any general look smarter than he really is—even an old ne'er-do-well like me." The grin he sent Schlieffen had a self-deprecating charm to which the German military attaché could not help responding.

And Rosecrans was right. An army with twice the men and guns of its foe went into a war with an enormous advantage. As Voltaire had said, God was always for the big battalions. Even Frederick the Great, facing odds like those, had been at the end of his tether during the Seven Years' War till the opportune death of the Tsarina and her abrupt replacement by a successor who favored the Prussian king made Russia drop out of the war.

"I repeat the question I asked before," Schlieffen said again: "What will you do if England or France or both of them at once should enter the war on the side of the Confederate States?"

"The best we can," Rosecrans answered. *Brave,* Schlieffen thought, *but not helpful.* But then the American Army commander looked sly. "Between you, me, and the wall, Colonel, I don't think it's going to happen. The reports we're getting from London and Paris say both governments over there are sick to death of the Confederacy keeping niggers as slaves, and they won't lift a finger unless the Rebs say they'll turn 'em loose. Now I ask you, sir, what are the odds of that? Biggest reason they fought the war was on account of they were afraid the United States government would make 'em do something like that. If they wouldn't do it for their own kith and kin, why do you think the stubborn bastards'll do it for a pack of foreigners?"

"This may be an important point," Schlieffen said. It was, at any rate, a point interesting enough for him to take it up with Minister von Schlözer when he got back to the brick pile on Massachusetts Avenue. He concerned himself with politics as little as he could. Political considerations could of course affect military ones, but the latter were all that fell within his purview. Civilians set policy. He made sure the armed forces could do what the leaders required of them.

Rosecrans said, "If you'll excuse me, Colonel, I do have a deal to see to here, just on the off chance the Confederates get frisky after all."

"I understand." Schlieffen rose. So did Rosecrans, who came around the desk to shake hands with him again. "One more question, General?" the attaché asked. "In case of war, you are rather vulnerable to the foe while here in Washington. What would the signal be for shifting your headquarters up to Philadelphia, which is less likely to come under attack?"

"It had better not," Rosecrans exclaimed. "Soon as the first shell falls, we all pack up stakes and head north. Everything will go smooth as clockwork, I promise you. We aren't fools, Colonel. We know the Rebs will shell this place."

"Very good," Schlieffen said. As he left the War Department, he wondered whether both of Rosecrans' last two sentences were true.

Black smoke—and showers of sparks—pouring from her twin stacks, the *Liberty Bell* steamed down the Mississippi toward St. Louis. When he'd boarded the sternwheeler in Clinton, Illinois, Frederick Douglass had taken her name as a good omen. With every mile closer to the Confederate States he drew, though, his doubts increased.

He stood on the upper deck, watching farms and little towns flow past. He was the only Negro on the upper deck, the deck that housed cabin passengers. That did not surprise him. But for one of the men who fed wood to the fire under the *Liberty Bell*'s boiler, he was the only Negro aboard the steamboat. He was used to that, too. Over the years since the War of Secession, he'd grown very used to being alone.

"Look," somebody not far away said. "Look at the nigger in the fancy suit."

Douglass turned. He was, he knew, an impressive man, with handsome features whose leonine aspect was enhanced by his silvery beard and mane of hair. That silver, and his slow, deliberate motions, told of his age. He thought he was sixty-four, but might as easily have been sixty-three or sixty-five. Having been born into slavery on Maryland's Eastern Shore, he had, to put it mildly, not been encouraged to enquire into the details of his arrival on the scene.

Two young white men, both dressed like drummers or cheap confidence men (there sometimes being little difference between the two trades) were gaping at him, their pale eyes wide. "May I help you gentlemen?" he asked, letting only a little irony seep into his deep, rich voice.

Despite his formidable presence, despite the rumbles of oratorical thunder audible in even his briefest, most commonplace utterances, the whites were unabashed. "It's all right, it's all right," one of them said, as if soothing a restive child—or a restive horse. "Dick here and me, we're from St. Paul, and ain't neither one of us ever got a good look at a nigger before."

"I can see as much," Douglass said. "I also discern that you have never had occasion to learn how to speak to a Negro, either."

That went right past the two men from St. Paul. They kept on staring, as if he were a caged monkey in a zoo. He'd had that feeling too many times in his life already. Seeing they *would* be rude, no matter how unintentionally, he turned his back, set both hands on the rail, and peered out over the Mississippi once more.

Ain't neither one of us ever got a good look at a nigger before. His fingers clamped down on the white-painted cast iron with painful force. He'd heard that, or variations on it, hundreds of times since the war.

He let out a long sigh punctuated by a couple of short coughs. Before the Southern states left the Union to form their own nation, he had been a spokesman for one man in eight in the United States. Now, ninety percent of the Negroes on the North American continent resided in a foreign country, and most of the white citizens of the USA were just as glad it was so. They might have been gladder yet had the figure been one hundred percent. As often as not, they blamed the relative handful of blacks left in the United States for the breakup of the nation.

And if a Negro, tormented beyond endurance, tried to flee from, say, Confederate Kentucky across the Ohio into the United States and freedom, how was he greeted? With congratulations for his love of liberty and a hearty welcome to a better land? Douglass' laugh was sour. If a U.S. Navy gunboat didn't sink his little skiff or raft in midstream, white men with guns and dogs would hunt him down and ship him back over the river to the CSA. Why not? As an inhabitant of a different nation, he had no claim on the United States.

Douglass laughed again—better that than weeping. Before the war, the Fugitive Slave Act had been a stench in the nostrils of most Northerners. Now, though the law was no longer on the book, slavery having at last become extinct in the USA, fugitive slaves found less sympathy than they had a generation earlier. Did calling them foreigners make such a difference? Evidently.

Not wanting to know whether the two white men had finished their examination of him or whether others, equally curious and equally rude, had taken their place, Douglass looked ahead. The dark cloud of smoke and haze blowing west across the Mississippi was not a reflection of his mood. It was a reflection of the soft coal St. Louis, like so many Western cities, burned to heat its homes, cook its food, and power the engines of its factories. The *Liberty Bell* would be landing before long.

Past the northern suburb of Baden steamed the sternwheeler. Over there, black roustabouts carried cargo off barges and small steamers. Douglass warmed to see men of his own color once more, even if those men were doing labor of a sort their brethren still in bondage might have performed at lonely little landing stations along the Confederate-held reaches of the southern Mississippi.

Then across the water came the ingenious curses of the white men who bossed those roustabouts. Douglass' mouth tightened into a thin, hard line. He'd had curses like those fall on his own head back in the days when he was property, before he became a human being of his own. He'd also known the lash then. That, at least, these bosses, unlike the overseers still plying their trade in the CSA, were forbidden. Perhaps the prohibition made their curses sharper.

Other Negroes floated on the Mississippi in rowboats. Douglass watched one of them draw a fish into his boat: the day's supper, or part of it. Blacks and whites both plied larger skiffs, in which they went after the driftwood that always fouled the river. They would not make much money from their gleanings, but none of them, it was likely, would ever make, or expect to make, much money till the end of his days.

St. Louis sprawled for miles along the riverbank. The riverbank had long been its *raison d'être*. On the Mississippi, close to the joining of that river with the Missouri and not too far above the joining with the Ohio, it was at the center of a commerce stretching from Minnesota to New Orleans, from the Appalachians to the Rockies. Railroads had only added to its importance. Smoke belching from the stack of its locomotive, a loaded train chugged north. The engineer blew a long blast on his whistle, apparently from nothing more than high spirits.

Not even the rupture of the Union had for long interrupted St. Louis' riverine commerce. Many of the steamers chained up at the landing-stages along the stone-fronted levee—no regular wharves here, not with the Mississippi's level liable to fluctuate so drastically—were Confederate boats, with names like *Vicks-*

burg Belle, *New Orleans Lightning*, and *Albert Sidney Johnston*.
The Stars and Bars fluttered proudly at their sterns. As they had in
the days before the war, they carried tobacco and cotton and rice
and indigo up the river, trading them sometimes for wheat and
corn, sometimes for iron ore, and sometimes for the products into
which that ore was eventually made. The Confederate States had
their own factories these days (some of them, to Douglass' unending mortification, with Negro slaves as labor), but their demand remained greater than their own industry could meet.

Names were not the only way to tell Confederate steamboats
from their U.S. counterparts. None of the boats from the United
States posted armed guards on deck to keep parts of their crews
from escaping. The welcome newly fled blacks would receive in
St. Louis was no warmer than anywhere else in the United States,
but that did not keep some from trying their luck.

To Douglass' mingled pride and chagrin, the *Liberty Bell*
pulled in alongside one of those Confederate boats, an immense
sidewheeler emblazoned with the name *N.B. Forrest*. The escaped
slave wondered how his brethren still trapped felt about sailing in
a vessel named for a dealer in human flesh who had also proved a
successful officer in the war.

One of the guards aboard the *Forrest*, looking over to watch
the *Liberty Bell* tie up at the landing-stage, saw Douglass standing at the upper-deck rail. He gaped at the spectacle of a colored
man there rather than on the main deck, where the poor and the
engine crew spread their blankets. Douglass sent an unpleasant
smile his way. The guard was close enough to recognize it as unpleasant. He scowled back, then spat a brown stream of tobacco
juice into the equally brown Mississippi.

Berthed on the opposite side of the *Liberty Bell* from the Confederate steamboat was the USS *Shiloh*, one of a number of river
monitors that made St. Louis their home port. The gunboat's dark
iron armor plating and starkly functional design made a sharp
contrast to the *N.B. Forrest*'s gaudy paint and gilding and gloriously rococo woodwork.

Among the crowd waiting at the top of the gently sloping levee
for the *Liberty Bell* to disembark her passengers was a small
knot of black men in clothes much like Douglass': undoubtedly
the clergymen he was to meet. He hurried back to his cabin to
retrieve his carpetbags. He carried them to the gangplank himself. Though porters—immigrants from Eastern Europe, many of

them—were eager enough to assist the whites traveling with him, they were more often than not reluctant to serve a Negro. *How quickly they learn the ways of the land to which they came seeking freedom,* Douglass thought with a bitterness now dull with scar tissue but no less true and real on account of that.

The ministers, by contrast, were eager to relieve him of his burdens. "Thank you, Deacon Younger," he said as he shook hands with them. "Thank you, Mr. Towler. Good to see you gentlemen—and you, too, of course, Mr. Bass; I don't mean to forget you—again. It's been four or five years since I last had the pleasure, has it not?"

"Fo' years, Mistuh Douglass," Deacon Daniel Younger answered. "It sho' enough is a pleasure to set eyes on you again, suh, I tell you truthfully." Like his colleagues, Younger was a man of education. He wrote well, as Douglass knew. His grammar and vocabulary were first rate. But he, like Towler and Bass, retained most of the intonations of slavery in his speech.

Douglass' own Negro accent was much less pronounced; as a boy, he'd learned white ways of speaking from his master's daughter. Over the years, he had seen many times how that made people both white and black take him more seriously. He found it useful and unfortunate at the same time.

"Come on to the carriage wid us," Washington Towler said. "We'll take you over to the Planter's Hotel on Fo'th Street. They know you're a-comin', and they will be ready fo' you." By that, he meant the hotel wouldn't make a fuss about having a Negro use one of its rooms for a few days. Douglass, of course, was not just any Negro, either, but as close to a famous Negro as the United States boasted.

The Reverend Henry Bass drove the buggy. He was younger than his two colleagues, both of whom were not far from Douglass' age. He said, "Don't know what all the excitement of the past few weeks will do to your crowds, Mistuh Douglass. What has yo' experience been in the other towns where you were?"

"It would be hard to state a general rule," Douglass answered. "Some people—by which I mean white people, of course—"

"Oh, of course," Bass said. He and the other two ministers rolled their eyes at the never-ending indignities of living on sufferance.

"Some people, I say," Douglass resumed, "take the threat of renewed war as a chance to punish the Confederate States, which works to our advantage. Others, though, continue to make the

Negro the scapegoat for the dissolution of the Union, and because of that discount every word I say."

"You will see a deal o' dat last here, I am afraid." Deacon Daniel Younger's broad shoulders—the man was built like a barrel—moved up and down as he sighed. "During the war, there were plenty who fought"—he pronounced it *fit*, as did many, black and white, in the West and in the CSA—"to make Missouri a Confederate state. They have made up their minds to be part o' de Union now, but they are still not easy about it."

"I remember how Kentucky fell after Lincoln pulled troops east—too little, too late—to try to halt Lee's army," Douglass said. "I remember the talk about partitioning Missouri, too, on the order of what was done with Virginia and West Virginia. I thank God you were preserved entire for the United States."

"We praise Him every day," Washington Towler said. "Without His help, we should still be slaves ourselves." Henry Bass pulled up in front of the Planter's Hotel. Towler pointed to the entrance. "They bought and sold us, Mr. Douglass, right there, even in the days after the war, till emancipation finally became de law of de land."

The Planter's Hotel had a Southern look to it even now. Its arches were of a style old-fashioned in the USA, incised into the façade rather than raised in relief from it. Some of the men going in and out wore the white linen suiting common in the warm, muggy South, too, and spoke with drawls: traders up from New Orleans and Memphis, Douglass supposed. They stared at his companions and him as if a nightmare had come to life before their eyes—and so, Douglass hoped, one had.

He took his bags and went into the hotel. As he had on the steamboat, he carried them himself. Maybe the white porters assumed that, despite his clothes, he was a servant. Or maybe, and more likely, they just refused to lower themselves, as they saw it, by serving one of the Negroes who had served their kind for so many long, sorrowful years.

"I am Frederick Douglass," he said when he reached the front desk. "A room has been reserved in my name."

He waited for the clerk to shuffle through papers. The fellow lifted up his eyes now and again to stare at Douglass' dark countenance. What followed was as inevitable as night following day. "I'm sorry, s—" The clerk could not bring himself to say *sir* to a Negro. He started again: "I'm sorry, but I don't find that reservation."

"Young man," Douglass said coldly, "if you do not find it by the time I count ten, I promise you this hotel will be a stench in the nostrils of the entire United States by a week from Tuesday, when my next newspaper column goes out over the wires. Your superiors will not thank you for that. I commence: one, two, three . . ."

How the clerk stared! And how quickly the missing reservation appeared, as if by magic. Thoroughly cowed, the clerk even browbeat a white bellboy into taking Douglass' carpetbags from him and carrying them to the room. It was one of the smaller, darker rooms in the hotel, but Douglass had expected nothing better than that. Daniel Younger and his friends had probably been able to book no better.

After supper—which he ate at a table surrounded by empty ones—Henry Bass came by to take him to the Merchants' Exchange, where he would speak. St. Louis was a handsome city of gray limestone and a sandstone almost as red as brick, though soot dimmed its color on many buildings. The Merchants' Exchange proved to take up the whole block between Chestnut and Pine on Third Street. "We've got plenty of room for a good house, Mr. Douglass," Bass said. "President Tilden was nominated in the Grand Hall back in '76, he was."

But, when Douglass went into the hall, he was sadly disappointed. Plainly, every Negro in and around St. Louis who could afford a ticket was there. Somber-suited black men and their wives in fancy dresses filled to overflowing the seats allotted to them. Douglass had long prided himself, though, on his reputation for being able to speak to whites as well as blacks. Tonight, it failed him. The bright gaslights shone down on great empty rows of chairs, with here and there a clump of people.

He went ahead with his address; as a professional, he had no other choice. He sounded his familiar themes: tolerance, education, enlightenment, progress, the appropriateness of giving all their due for what they could do, not for the color of their skins. He drew rapturous applause from the Negroes in the hall, and got a polite hearing from the whites.

It could have been worse. He knew that. He'd started riots with his speeches now and again, sometimes meaning to, sometimes not. Tonight, he would have welcomed a riot in place of the near-indifference his white audience showed him. When U.S. whites had nothing else on their minds, they were sometimes willing to listen to tales of the Negro's plight and ways by which it might be alleviated. When they were distracted, they might as well have forgotten the USA still held any Negroes.

Once it was finally over, he stood down from the podium. To his surprise, one of the people who came up to speak with him was a gray-bearded white man, a former Army officer whom Douglass, after a bit, recognized from years gone by. "You must not take it to heart, sir," he said with touching sincerity. "Do remember, our present concern over the Confederate States is also, in its way, concern for your people."

Douglass smelled liquor on his breath. *No wonder he is so sincere,* the Negro thought. *And no wonder he is a soldier no more, despite having won a couple of battles against the Rebels.* By his rather worn suit, the fellow had made no great success of civilian life. *Liquor again.* But he had done his best to be kind on a dismal evening, and he did have a point of sorts. Exercising forbearance, Douglass said, "Thank you, General Grant."

"Salt Lake City!" the conductor shouted. "All out for Salt Lake City!" The train gave a convulsive jerk—*like a man letting out his last breath,* Abraham Lincoln thought—and came to a stop.

Wearily, Lincoln heaved himself up out of his seat and grabbed his valise and carpetbag. After speaking in Denver and Colorado Springs, in Greeley and Pueblo, in Cañon City and Grand Junction, leaving Colorado and coming into Utah Territory was almost like entering a foreign country.

That impression was strengthened when he got out of the Pullman car. An eastbound train was loading as his was unloading. Most of the men filing aboard wore the blue tunics and trousers and black felt hats of the U.S. Army, and were burdened with the impedimenta of the soldier's trade. As the crisis with the Confederate States worsened, the regulars were being called to the threatened frontiers.

A crowd of men, women, and children cheered the soldiers' departure. At most train stations, as Lincoln had seen during the war, the soldiers would have responded, waving their hats and calling out to the pretty girls. Not here, not now. Every cheer they heard seemed to make them glummer, or perhaps cheerful in a different way. "Jesus," one of them said loudly to a friend, "will I be glad to get out of this God-damned place."

"Sad, isn't it?" said a little man who appeared at Lincoln's elbow while the former president was watching the troops embark. "They aren't cheering to wish the men good luck if they have to fight the Rebs. They're cheering because those fellows are getting out of *here,* and they hope they won't come back."

"I had the same impression myself, Mister . . . ?" Lincoln hesitated.

"I'm the chap who's supposed to meet you here, Mr. Lincoln:

66

Gabriel Hamilton, at your service." Despite his small size—
Lincoln towered over him—Hamilton had a jaunty manner and a
way of raising one eyebrow just a little to suggest he was hard to
impress. After shaking hands, he went on, "Call me Gabe, if you
please, sir. All my Gentile friends do."

"Your—Gentile friends?" Lincoln wondered if he'd heard correctly. His ears, these days, weren't what they had been. Gabe
Hamilton had neither a Hebraic name nor Hebraic features.

The little man laughed out loud. "If you're not a Mormon in
Salt Lake City, Mr. Lincoln, you're a Gentile. Aaron Rothman
runs a dry-goods shop down the street from me. Here, he's a
Gentile."

"And what is his opinion of his . . . unusual status?" Lincoln
asked.

"He thinks it's funny as blazes, matter of fact," Hamilton
answered. "He's a pretty good egg, Rothman is. But Presbyte-
rians like me, Catholics, Baptists, Jews, what have you—in Utah
Territory, we're all outsiders looking in. We hang together better
than we would if that weren't so, I expect."

"If you don't hang together, you will hang separately?" Lincoln suggested.

Hamilton took that for his wit rather than Ben Franklin's and
laughed again, uproariously this time. "You're a sharp man, Mr.
Lincoln. I'm glad we've got you out here, for a fact, I am. You'll
buck up the miners and the other working folks, and you'll make
the bosses think twice about what they're doing, and those are
both good things. Come on back to my buggy, sir, and I'll take
you to your hotel."

"Thank you." Lincoln followed his guide away from the train.
Soldiers were still boarding the one bound for the East. The local
crowd was still applauding their departure, too. "Those would be
Mormons, I suppose?"

"That they would." Now Gabriel Hamilton sounded more than
a little grim. "I tell you frankly, Mr. Lincoln, the rest of us in town
are nervous about it. Without soldiers here, God only knows
what's liable to happen. God and John Taylor, I suppose. The
Mormons think that's the same thing. Gentiles, though, will tell
you different."

"You're referring to Brigham Young's successor?" Lincoln
said as Hamilton took his luggage from him and loaded it onto

the buggy. "Young was an uncrowned king here during my administration."

"And up till the day he died, four years ago," Hamilton agreed. "And do you know what? I think he loved every minute of it." He untied the horses from the rail and clambered into the carriage, nimble as a monkey. "Mr. Taylor's got the same power, but not the same bulge, if you know what I mean."

"I do indeed." Law and politics had both shown Lincoln that, of two men with the same nominal authority, one was liable to be able to do much more than the other if their force of character differed. "So Taylor is King Log instead of King Stork, eh?"

"Wouldn't go so far as that. He's quieter about what he does, that's all. You settled there?" At Lincoln's nod, Hamilton clucked to the horses, flicked the reins, and got the carriage going. After a little while, he continued, "The Mormons still listen to him, I'll tell you that." He sounded mournful: a man relating a fact he wished a falsehood. "You won't have many of them coming to your speech tomorrow night, I'm afraid."

"That's a pity," Lincoln said. "From what I've read of Utah, and from what you've told me, they are the ones who most need to hear it."

As in Denver, the streets in Salt Lake City were all of dirt. Dust rose from the horses' hooves and from the wheels of the carriage. Though traffic was not heavy, a lot of dust hung in the air. But the water that ran over the pebbles in the gutter looked bright and clean enough to drink, and Lincoln saw a couple of women in calico dresses and sunbonnets dipping it up in pails, so he supposed it was used for that purpose.

Trees—poplar, mulberry, locust, maple—grew alongside those gutters, and their branches, green and leafy with the fresh growth of spring, spread above the streets, shielding them from the full force of the sun. The prospect was attractive, especially when compared to either the flat, dull towns of the prairie or the stony gulches in which most Rocky Mountain cities were set.

"Where's the Great Salt Lake?" Lincoln asked, suddenly realizing he could not see the natural feature for which the city was named.

Hamilton pointed west. "It's almost twenty miles from here. There's a little excursion train that'll take you there if you want to see it. Don't drink the water if you do go; it'll burn you up from the inside out."

"I've seen if from the train several times, on my way out to California," Lincoln said. "I have no desire for a closer acquaintance—it's only that I haven't been in, as opposed to through, Salt Lake City till now, and so missed it."

A few of the houses were log cabins that took Lincoln back to the long-vanished days of his own youth. More were of creamy gray-brown adobe bricks, some stuccoed over and whitewashed or painted, others left their natural shade. Newer homes might have been transplanted straight from the East. Almost all of them—cabins, low adobes, and modern clapboards and fired-brick houses—were surrounded by riots of trees and shrubs and climbing vines and flowers, making a spectacle all the more impressive when measured against the bleak, brown Wasatch Mountains just east of town.

Some of those adobe houses, despite being of a single story, nevertheless had a great many rooms, with several wings spreading out from what had begun as small, simple dwellings. Pointing to one of those, Gabe Hamilton said, "You see a place like that, Mr. Lincoln, and you can bet a polygamist lives there. He'll take the center for himself and give each wife and her brats a wing."

"How many Mormons are polygamists, truly?" Lincoln asked. "They write all sorts of things in the Eastern papers."

"They say all sorts of things here, too," Hamilton answered. "The truth is devilish hard to find, and they don't keep any public records of marriages past the first, which makes it harder yet. I'd say it's about one in ten, if that, but the polygamists have influence beyond their numbers. If you're going to support more than one wife and family, you need more than the common run of money, you see."

"Oh, yes," Lincoln said. "A case similar to that of slaveholders in the Confederate States. And those not in the elite group will some of them aspire to join it over the course of time, and thus support it even without presently enjoying its benefits."

"Benefits?" Gabe Hamilton let out a derisive guffaw. "Have you ever *seen* most of these Mormon women, Mr. Lincoln? You ask me—not that anybody did—taking 'em is an act of charity."

Like the residential blocks, the central business district of Salt Lake City boasted avenues lined with trees. The buildings back of those trees were modern enough, and included several fine-looking hotels. Ahead loomed what looked like an enormous Gothic cathedral, about three fourths of the way to completion.

"That would be the famous Mormon Temple?" Lincoln asked, pointing.

"That's right." Hamilton nodded. "And that long dome there—the one that'd look handsomer if the wall and the trees didn't hide its lines—that's the Tabernacle, where they worship. They don't think small, do they?"

"No," Lincoln allowed. "Many things may be said of them, but not thinking small."

From the window of his hotel room, Lincoln could look out at the Tabernacle and the Temple. On scaffolding that seemed hardly thicker than cobwebs, men tiny as ants against the granite bulk of the latter labored to bring Brigham Young's grandiose vision one day closer to completion.

Lincoln had just finished unpacking when someone knocked on the door. When he opened it, he found a handsome young man in a dignified suit standing in the hallway. "Mr. Lincoln, President Taylor presents his compliments, and hopes you will be free to take supper with him this evening at seven o'clock," the youngster said. "If that is convenient to you, sir, I will come by with a carriage at about half past six, to convey you to his home."

"President Taylor?" For a moment, the only president by that name who came to Lincoln's mind was Zachary, now thirty years dead. Then he remembered where he was. "The head of your church, you mean?"

"Yes, sir, of course." The emissary had probably learned of Zachary Taylor in school, but John Taylor was the living reality for him.

"Tell him I thank him for the invitation, and I shall be pleased to see him at the hour he named." For the life of him, Lincoln could not see why the spiritual leader of the Latter-Day Saints wanted to meet with him, but what he did not show to the young messenger, that worthy would not guess. And his own ignorance and curiosity would be relieved soon enough.

As promised, the bright young man came by the hotel in a handsome buggy at six-thirty. The journey to John Taylor's home took a little less than half an hour. The home itself, or at least the central portion of it, would not have looked out of place in Chicago or Pittsburgh: it was a two-story building, brilliantly white-washed, with a slate roof. Added to that central portion, though, were enough wings for several butterflies, each, no doubt, housing a separate portion of the Mormon president's extended and extensive family. Poplars, maples, and grapevines surrounded the house, and ivy climbed up the front wall.

When Lincoln knocked at the front door, a man of about his own age opened it. "Come in, sir," he said in an accent that showed he'd been born in England. "I am John Taylor; it is a pleasure to meet you." His hair, his eyebrows, and the beard growing along the angle of his jaw and under his chin were all snowy white. He habitually pursed his lips, which made his mouth look narrow and bloodless; his deep-set eyes, very blue, seemed to have seen more sorrows than joys. Lincoln understood that. He would have said the same of himself.

He looked around with no small curiosity. The central portion of the house seemed no more unusual within than without: the furniture was comfortable without being lavish; bookshelves lined many walls; the knickknacks and gewgaws on tables, the pictures on the walls, were the sort any minister might have had.

Nor was the dining room in any way strange. As Lincoln sat down, Taylor said, "I fear I can offer you only water or milk with your meal, for I have no tea or coffee or liquor in the house."

"Water will do," Lincoln said.

They talked of small things during supper. Taylor did not offer to introduce the girl—she was about sixteen—who brought bread and butter and beefsteaks and potatoes and squash in from the kitchen. Maybe she was a servant. Maybe she was a daughter. She didn't look much like him, but she might have favored her mother. Maybe she was a wife. Lincoln did his best to put that unappealing thought (not that the girl herself was unappealing, in spite of what Gabe Hamilton had said about Mormon women) out of his mind.

After she had cleared away the last of the dishes, the Mormon president said, "When you next communicate with President Blaine, sir, I hope you will convey to him that the line the U.S. government has taken here makes it more difficult than it might otherwise be for us to support that government with our full power in the event of a collision with the Confederate States."

"I have no notion when I shall be in touch with Mr. Blaine again," Lincoln answered truthfully.

John Taylor coughed. "Please, sir, I know you may not love the faith I follow, but that I follow it does not make me a child or a fool. Can it be a coincidence that the one former Republican president of the United States comes to Deseret—Utah, if you'd rather—at the same time as the present Republican president is leading the country toward war with the CSA? For what other purpose could you be here than to examine our loyalty in the event of a conflict?"

"I was invited here to speak to the working men of this Territory on ways in which they can hope to better their lot," Lincoln said, again truthfully.

"A plausible pretext, I don't deny," Taylor said, seeming intent on finding deviousness whether it was there or not. "The timing, however, makes me doubt it conveys the whole story of your visit. Be that as it may, do please tell President Blaine that, since he seems to be continuing the longstanding U.S. policy of attempting to suppress our institutions, some of our number wonder if continued allegiance to the United States be worth the cost. All we have ever sought is to be left alone, to practice our own ways as we think best."

"If you will recall, President Taylor, that was also the rallying cry of the Confederate States during the war," Lincoln answered. "Your people were loyal then—conspicuously loyal. I note also, whether you care to believe it or not, that I have no influence to speak of on President Blaine." Once again, that was true. Blaine did his best not to remember that he and Lincoln were members of the same party.

"Come, come." Having dismissed the truth with two words, Taylor went back to the point he had been making before: "Unlike the case of the Confederacy, our practices have the consent of all those involved in them. We seek to impose them on no one, but the United States have continually labored to subvert them, the more so since the railroads have brought such an influx of Gentiles into our homeland. Do you wonder at our resentment, sir?"

Lincoln thought again of that young girl. *Could* she have been a wife? Taylor's public face was the image of decorum. What did he do in private, in this great rambling boardinghouse of a home? That question, and others like it, echoed through the minds of ordinary Americans when they thought of Mormonism.

He shrugged. In any case, it was an irrelevance. "If you like, President Taylor, I shall pass on to President Blaine what you say. I fear I cannot promise that he will take any special notice of it. As I told you, I am not a man he is in the habit of heeding."

"He would be well advised to do so in this instance," John

Taylor said. "We left the United States once, to come here to Utah. The borders of the USA then followed us west. We cannot emigrate again, not physically, yet we must be able to practice our religion unimpeded." The light from the kerosene lamps filled his face with harsh shadows.

"I very much hope that is not a threat, sir," Lincoln said.

The sockets of Taylor's eyes were shrouded in darkness. "So do I," he said. "So do I."

"General Stuart! General Stuart! Telegram from Richmond, General Stuart!" At a dead run, a messenger came from the telegraph office, waving the flimsy sheet of paper that bore the message.

"Thank you, Bryce." From the runner's tone, Stuart guessed what the telegram said before he read it. When he did, he nodded to himself. The day had come later than it should have, but was at last at hand.

Major Horatio Sellers came up to Stuart. "Is it what we've been hoping it will be, sir?" he asked eagerly.

"That's exactly what it is, Major," Stuart answered. "We are to enter and occupy the Mexican provinces of Chihuahua and Sonora, the movement to proceed on the outline already at hand and to commence at sunrise on Tuesday, the fourteenth of June."

"Three days from now," his aide-de-camp said, his voice thoughtful. A satisfied expression made his heavy features seem almost benignant. "We'll have no trouble meeting that deadline, since we've been ready to go for most of the past month."

"Anyone wants to know my view of the matter, we should have moved the day we had the troops in place," Stuart said. "We've wasted all this time trying to keep the damnyankees sweet about what we're doing, but when you come right down to it, what we do in our own territory—which this is now—and in our relations with the Empire of Mexico is our business and nobody else's."

Sellers looked north and west, toward Las Cruces, across the international border in New Mexico Territory. "What do you suppose Lieutenant Colonel Foulke would have to say about that?" he said, and then changed verb tenses: "What do you suppose Lieutenant Colonel Foulke *will* have to say about that?"

"Did I not make myself clear, Major?" Stuart said. "I don't care what Foulke or any other Yankee has to say about what we do on our territory. And if the United States choose to resent our actions with weapons in hand, they are welcome to make the effort, but I doubt they will have a friendly reception here or any-where else along our common frontier."

"Sir, do you really think they would be stupid enough to fight a war with us over this?" Sellers asked. "Don't they know we could lick 'em by ourselves, but odds are we won't have to?"

"We walked away from the United States the last time they put a Black Republican in the White House, and they fought to try to hold us to an allegiance we could stand no more," Stuart answered. "Now they have another Republican president, and there's every sign they're feeling frisky again. I hope they act sen-sibly; having seen one war, I don't care to see another one. But their politicians haven't seen the elephant—all they've done is talk about it. They'd be wiser if they knew more." He shrugged. "Be that as it may, we have our orders, and we are going to carry them out. Go issue the commands that will get the occupation forces ready to commence their movements at the required time, and also the orders for the infantry and artillery that will stay behind to defend El Paso in case the United States do decide to be foolish."

"Yes, sir." Sellers started to hurry away.

"Wait," Stuart said. His aide-de-camp paused and looked back. The commander of the Military District of the Trans-Mississippi grinned at him. "However this works out, Major, it's going to be fun."

Sunday evening, Stuart was summoned to the bridge spanning the Rio Grande. At its midpoint, precisely at the border between the Confederate States and the Empire of Mexico, stood Colonel Enrique Gutierrez, commander of the Mexican garrison in Paso del Norte. His uniform, of the French pattern Maximilian's men favored, was far brighter and shinier than the plain butternut Stuart wore.

Gutierrez, a lean, saturnine man, spoke good English, which was fortunate, because Stuart had only a handful of words of Spanish. "I have just received word, General, that the arrange-ments long under discussion are now complete," the Mexican colonel said. "Accordingly, on the day following tomorrow my men shall withdraw from these provinces."

"That is when we intend to enter Chihuahua and Sonora, yes," Stuart said. "I am glad the news has reached you from Mexico

City. We do not want to come as invaders; the Confederate States are pleased at the good relations we enjoy with the Empire of Mexico." Given the muddle in which Maximilian's government commonly found itself, for Gutierrez to have been only thirty-six hours late in getting the word showed uncommon efficiency.

"I am glad of this," Gutierrez said politely. He didn't show whatever he was thinking. He was, Stuart knew, a pretty fair soldier, and couldn't have been happy to serve a regime so feckless that it had to sell off pieces of the country to pay its bills. After a moment, he went on, "I have a question: as we move back toward territory that will remain under our control, shall we also take with us the city guards who maintain order in the streets?"

"No," Stuart said. "My orders are to class them as police—as officers of the civilian government—not as soldiers. They will go right on doing their jobs until and unless our own government makes changes hereabouts."

"Muy bien." Gutierrez nodded. He took a deep breath. "Speaking for myself, General Stuart, and as a man, I will say that I would sooner see these provinces pass to the Confederate States, which paid before occupying them, than to the United States, which invaded my country and only then paid."

Stuart thought it wiser not to mention that Stonewall Jackson and some other veterans in Confederate service had fought for the USA during the Mexican War. "Thank you," seemed safer. Colonel Gutierrez snapped off a salute, spun on his heel, and walked back toward the fort he would control for another day and a half.

That Tuesday morning, like most June days in El Paso, dawned bright and clear and hot. As soon as the sun rose, Jeb Stuart led his infantry and cavalry and rumbling cannons toward and then onto the bridge. He did not stop at the midpoint, but kept going till his horse's hooves thudded on the gray-brown dirt at the southern end: Chihuahua was now as much Confederate soil as was Texas.

A red, white, and green Mexican flag still flew on a pole at the southern end of the bridge. Colonel Gutierrez waited there with a last squad of soldiers in ornate uniforms. Politely, Stuart took off his hat and saluted the Mexican flag. Honor satisfied, Gutierrez barked orders in Spanish. Two of his men ran the flag down the pole for the last time and reverently folded it.

At Stuart's command, a couple of Confederate soldiers raised the Stars and Bars over Paso del Norte and, by extension, over all of Chihuahua and Sonora. Polite as a priest, Colonel Gutierrez saluted the new flag as General Stuart had saluted the old. If the Mexican colonel's eyes were unusually bright and moist, Stuart had no intention of remarking on it.

From Paso del Norte, the road ran almost due west, bending only slightly toward the south as it took advantage of the break in the mountains. That meant it stayed close to the border with the United States. Stuart didn't care for the course the geography dictated. Neither did Major Sellers. "All I can say, sir," he remarked, "is that it's a good thing New Mexico Territory is just about as empty as Chihuahua here."

"I agree, Major," Stuart said. "The logistics are poor for both sides in this part of the world." As he had when first learning he would have to move troops into this newly Confederate territory, he sighed. "If General Sibley had been able to keep his men in food and munitions during the war, New Mexico would be ours now, and our worries would be gone—or, at least, farther north."

The country west of the mountains was even more unabashedly desert than that to the east. Saguaro cactuses stood close by the road and far away, their cigar-shaped bodies and angular, sometimes upthrust arms putting Stuart in mind of giant green men surprised by bandits. The Fifth Cavalry Regiment seemed peculiarly at home in that harsh terrain, even if it did have to travel a bit apart from the rest. It was most often known as the Fifth Camelry, being mounted on ships of the desert rather than horses. Jefferson Davis had introduced camels to the Southwest as U.S. secretary of war before the War of Secession. The Fifth, at first stocked with beasts captured wild in the desert, had done good work against the Comanches, showing up in places its troopers could never have reached on horseback.

Here and there, wherever there was water, tiny towns punctuated the route: Janos; Agua Prieta right across the border from the equally sleepy hamlet of Douglas, New Mexico; Cananea; Imuris. At Imuris, Stuart detached one regiment of infantry and one of cavalry and ordered them south to Hermosillo. To the cavalry commander, Colonel L. Tiernan Brien, who was senior to the infantry regiment's colonel, he said, "The occupation being peaceful thus far, I am not sending so large a force to the interior of this province as originally contemplated. I expect you to split off what part of it you deem necessary for garrisoning Guaymas on the coast and send that portion of your forces there."

"Yes, sir," Brien said. He had served under Stuart since the war, having led a regiment of state troops in the Pennsylvania campaign. "If the Mexicans do choose to give us trouble, though, we probably won't be able to do much about it, especially if you're keeping all the artillery for yourself."

"I understand that, Colonel," Stuart answered. "It is, I believe, a good gamble. Colonel Gutierrez may not have loved what his government did, but he accepted it like a soldier and a man. By all the signs, the same will hold true in Hermosillo and Guaymas as well. The Mexicans in these little villages haven't tried to resist us in any way; all they've done is stare."

"Well, the camels likely have something to do with that, but it's true enough, heaven knows," Brien said. He waved out over the barren landscape. "If you keep most of your men so far forward, sir, will you be able to provision them?"

"I certainly hope so," Stuart said. "I'm given to understand Hermosillo is in the center of a farming district. Whatever supplies you can send north will be welcome, the more so if the route west from El Paso is . . . interrupted."

"Yes, sir," Tiernan Brien said again. Most of two decades of garrison duty had laid a heavy patina of routine over the dashing young trooper he'd once been, but, like a lot of the other veteran officers in Stuart's force, he was starting to shine up once more. "By your dispositions, sir, you really do think the Yankees will try to make good on their bluster."

"No, Colonel, truth to tell, I don't," Stuart answered. "But I am going to act as if I did. If the United States are foolish enough to contest this annexation, my judgment is that they pose a greater threat to us than any disaffected Mexicans. That being so, I intend to keep the bulk of my forces where they can best respond to any moves by the USA." He grinned. "My dispositions reflect my disposition, which is cautious."

Colonel Brien smiled, showing teeth stained brown by the plug of tobacco that swelled one cheek. "Beg your pardon, sir, but we've been soldiering together for a long time, and I don't reckon cautious is a word I'd put together with your name up till now."

"Maybe I'm getting old," Stuart said. Then he grinned again, and barked a couple of times. "Or maybe I'm learning a new trick."

"Now you're talking, sir," Tiernan Brien said enthusiastically.

"Wake up, Sam." Alexandra Clemens nudged her husband, then nudged him harder when he didn't move. "It's half past seven."

Reluctantly, Samuel Clemens pried his eyes open. His nostrils twitched. "You're an angel in human form, my dear. I say that, you understand, only because you've already got the coffee boiling."

"You'd throw me in the street if I didn't." Alexandra owned—and honed—a wit that could rival her husband's, and wasn't shy about using it. It was all the more effective because she looked so mild and innocent: wide, fair face; blue eyes mild as milk till the devil came out in them; golden hair that, let down for the night, spilled over her shoulders and onto her white nightdress so that, but for wings, she really did have something of an angelic aspect at the moment.

When Sam, still in his own nightshirt, came downstairs for that coffee, his son Orion leaped into his lap and almost made the cup and contents end up there, too. Not a thing angelic about Orion; sometimes all that kept Sam from strangling him was remembering he'd been even worse at the same age. "Why aren't you busy getting ready for school?" Sam demanded.

Orion withered him with a glance. " 'Cause it's closed for the summer," he said triumphantly.

"I know that," his father answered. "But if you were, you'd be out of my hair." With six-year-old gusto, Orion stuck out his tongue.

Ophelia, who was four, came into the dining room a little later: of the family, she was fondest of sleeping late. She looked like her mother, with a child's sweetness thrown in for good measure. Walking up to her father, she took his big hands in her little ones and said, "Hello, you old goat."

"Hello, yourself," Sam said gravely. However much Ophelia looked like Alexandra, she behaved more like Orion, which horrified her mother and—most of the time—amused her father. "If you live, you'll go far, my dear." Sam tousled her golden curls, then added, in meditative tones, "Of course, the penitentiary is pretty far from here."

Ophelia, for once, missed the joke. So did Orion. Alexandra, who didn't, sent her husband a severe look he ignored.

Sometimes getting out of the house on Turk Street and heading over to the *Morning Call* offices on Market felt more like escape than anything else. Despite going uphill and down, Sam enjoyed the walk. Going uphill was harder work for heavily laden horses. Teamsters' whips cracked over and sometimes on the backs of the straining beasts. Then, brakes squealing on the wagons they pulled, the horses had to ease the loads downhill.

Fifteen minutes after kissing his wife good-bye, Clemens walked into the office. When he got there, Clay Herndon leaped at him with almost as much terrifying enthusiasm as Orion had shown. Herndon, though, had an excuse any newspaperman would have forgiven: the telegram he waved in Clemens' face. "You've got to see this!" he shouted.

"How can I argue with logic like that?" Sam took the thin sheet of paper and rapidly read through it. When he was done, he nodded a couple of times, then said, "A lot of people must be surprised today: everybody who didn't think Blaine knew a four-syllable word, for instance."

"If he only knows one, he picked the right one to know," retorted Herndon, a resolute Republican. "I'd say it gives us the headline for the next edition, wouldn't you?"

" 'Ultimatum'?" Clemens said. "Now that you mention it, yes. If ever a word screamed for seventy-two-point type, that's the one." He took off his derby and hung it on the hat tree just inside the door. As soon as he got to his desk, he slid off his jacket and draped it over the back of his chair. Then he removed the studs from his cuffs, put them in a vest pocket, and rolled up his sleeves.

"Ready to give it a go, are you?" Herndon said.

His tone was mildly mocking, but Sam ignored that. "You bet I am," he said. "Give me that wire again, will you? I want to make sure I have everything right." He paused to light a cigar, then reread the telegram. "Always a good day when the editorial comes up and whimpers in your face, begging to be set at liberty."

"If you say so, Sam," Herndon replied. "Makes me glad I'm nothing but a humble scribe."

"Get over to City Hall, scribe," Clemens said. "Get the mayor's reaction. In other words, give me the statement that goes with this." He donned an expression somewhere between dumbfound- ment and congenital idiocy. The *San Francisco Morning Call* did not love Mayor Adolph Sutro. It was mutual.

Herndon struck a pose that might have been a politician on the stump or a man waiting with concentrated urgency to use the privy. " 'I am opposed with every fiber of my being to the war that may come, and I expect us to gain great and glorious triumph in it,' " he declaimed. "There. Now I don't need to make the trip."

Sam blew cigar smoke at him. "Go on, get out of here. His Honor might have got up on the wrong side of the bed this morning, and if he did he'll say he's all for the war but calculates we'll take a licking. God forbid we should misquote him. He wouldn't notice, since he can't remember on Tuesday what he said the Friday before—figures that's the papers' job—but some of his friends—well, cronies; a creature like that's not likely to have friends—just might."

Snickering, Herndon grabbed his hat, slung his jacket over his shoulder—it was another of those seasonless San Francisco days, not quite warm, not quite cool—and departed. Clemens drew on the cigar again, absentmindedly tapped its ash into a brass tray, and set it back in the corner of his mouth. He knew he was liable to forget about it once he started writing.

Pen scraped across paper.

President Blaine has told the nation and the world that, if the Con- federate States do not withdraw their soldiers—soldiers they deployed without the consent of the United States, and against the express wishes of the same—from the provinces of Chihuahua and Sonora within ten days, he will ask Congress to declare a state of war in existence between the United States and the Con- federate States.

He fails to include the Empire of Mexico in his ultimatum, which is no doubt only an oversight on his part. After all, leaving the disputed provinces out of the bargain, the United States do still abut Maximilian's dominions where our Upper California touches his Lower, whose cactuses are every bit as dire a threat to the United States as any now sprouted in Sonora.

As noted before in this space, acquiring Sonora and Chihuahua represents—or, at least, may represent in the future—a new ac- cess of strength for the Confederate Sates, as did their purchase of Cuba a few years ago, a purchase to which the United States consented without a murmur. But we were then under a Democratic administration, and a Congress likewise Democratic: a party whose attitude toward the Confederacy has always been that the blamed thing would not be there if anybody had listened to them in the beginning and patted the then-Southern states on the head and told them what good boys they were until they eventually believed it and went to sleep in place of seceding, and has dealt with them since the War of Secession as if they were so many percussion caps filled with fulminate, and liable to explode if stepped on or dropped.

By contrast, the Confederate States are to the Republican Party—the phrase "a nigger in the woodpile" is tempting, but no; we shall refrain—an illegitimate child in the family of nations, and so to be deprived of plum pudding every Christmas Eve. Well, the illegitimate child is now above eighteen years of age, and a d—d big b—d, now suddenly the bigger by two provinces gulped down in lieu of the plums once denied it. No wonder, then, that President Blaine is in the way of seeing things red.

The question before the house, however, is—or rather, ought to be, the failure to understand the difference between the two being one of the chief causes of boiler explosions, marital discord, and drawing in the hope of filling an inside straight—not whether the United States have the right to be displeased at the transaction just concluded between the Confederacy and Mexico, but whether the transaction presents them with a legitimate *casus belli*. This we beg leave to doubt. The suspicion lingers that, had the United States offered a brass spittoon and a couple of candles' value above the price the Confederacy agreed to pay him, the Stars and Stripes would now be flying above Chihuahua and Sonora—and maybe even above the dangerous cacti of Lower California as well—and there would be a great wailing and gnashing of teeth from Richmond, with every politician in Washington sitting back as sleek and contented as the dog that stole the leg of lamb out of the roasting pan.

For better or worse—more like, for better *and* worse—Maximilian's sale of Sonora and Chihuahua strikes us as having been peaceful and voluntary enough to keep anyone sniffing around the deal from gagging at the smell, which in to-day's diplomacy marks it as something of a prodigy. We find it dashed uncomfortable to share a continent with a people who did not care to share a country with us, but we had best get used to it, because the Confederate States show no signs of packing up and moving to the mountains of Thibet. While we may regret the sale, we have not the right to seek to reverse it by force of arms. We may have been outsmarted, but we were not insulted, and being outsmarted is not reason enough to go to war—if it were, the poor suffering world should never have known its few brief—too brief!—moments when the bullets were not flying somewhere.

He had hardly laid down his pen before Clay Herndon came back into the office, slamming the door behind him. "Sam, have you got whatever you're going to say ready to set in type?" he demanded. "News of the ultimatum is already on the street. If we don't get into print in a hurry, it'll outstrip us. The *Alta Californian* is beating the war drum, loud as it can." He threw himself into his chair and began to write furiously.

"Yes, I'm ready." Clemens exhibited the sheets he'd just finished. "What did the mayor say?"

"Sutro?" Herndon didn't look up from his scribbles. "The way he talks, we'll be in Richmond tomorrow, Atlanta the day after, and New Orleans the day after that. Huzzah for our side!" He sounded imperfectly delighted with the mayor's view of the world.

"You were a Blaine man last November, Clay," Sam reminded him. "Why aren't you over at the *Californian*, banging the war drum yourself?"

"Me? I'd love to take the Rebs down a peg," Herndon said, "but Blaine's going at it like a bull in a china shop, trying to make up for eighteen years in a couple of months. There." He threw down the pen and thrust paper at Clemens. "Here's mine. Let's see what you wrote."

Sam scrawled a few changes on Herndon's copy; Herndon used adverbs the way a bad cook used spices—on the theory that, if a few were good, more were better. In spite of that, he said, "Good story." It convicted Sutro of being a pompous fool with his own words, the best way to do it.

"Thanks. You could have said 'a plague on both your houses' and let it go at that," Herndon said. "I'm glad you didn't, though. This is more fun."

The door flew open. Edgar Leary rushed in. Somebody had knocked a big dent in his hat, which he hadn't noticed yet. "They're hanging Longstreet in effigy at the corner of Market and Geary," the youngster said breathlessly. Then he took off the derby, and exclaimed in dismay. "The whole town's going crazy." He held out the hat as if it were evidence.

"Write the piece. Write it fast," Sam said. He took the pages of his editorial back from Herndon. "Sounds like they're not going to listen to me again." He sighed. "Why am I not surprised?"

Outside, somebody emptied a six-shooter, the cartridges going off in quick succession. Sam hoped whoever it was, was shooting in the air.

Newsboys on Richmond street corners waved copies of the *Whig* and the *Examiner*, the *Dispatch* and the *Enquirer* and the *Sentinel*, in the air. They were doing a roaring trade; lawyers and mechanics, ministers and farmers, drummers and teamsters and even the occasional colored man who had his letters crowded round them and shoved pennies at them.

Whichever paper the boy on any one corner touted, the main headline was the same: "Ultimatum runs out today!" After that, imagination ran riot: "President Longstreet to answer latest Yankee outrage!" "Navy said ready to put to sea!" "Navy said to be already at sea!" "Troop movements in Kentucky!" "Yankees said to be concentrating in Missouri!" And one word, like a drumbeat: "War!" "War!" "War!"

General Thomas Jackson, whose business was war, rode through the clamor as if through rain or snow or shellfire or any other minor distraction. "We'll whip 'em, won't we, Stonewall?" a fat man in a butcher's bloodstained apron shouted to him.

"We are not at war with the United States, nor have the United States declared war against us," Jackson answered. He'd said the same thing any number of times since leaving the War Department for yet another journey to the presidential residence. "I hope they do not. Peace is too precious to be casually discarded like an outgrown suit of clothes."

That wasn't what the butcher wanted to hear. "We'll whip 'em!"

Jackson guided his horse past the fat man without saying anything more. He got asked the same question, or a variant upon it, three more times in the next half block. He gave the same answer each time, and began to wish he hadn't started answering at all.

The crush of people thinned as he rode up Shockoe Hill, away from Capitol Square and the center of town. Jackson let out a small, involuntary sigh of relief: he did not care for being trapped in crowds, and was often happiest when most solitary. Duty, however, came above happiness. Duty came above everything.

One of the sentries who saluted him said, "Reckon we'll lick them damnyankees good—ain't that right, sir?"

To a soldier, Jackson spoke a bit more openly than to a civilian on the street who might, for all he knew, have been a U.S. spy: "If we have to fight them, Corporal, rest assured we shall beat them."

U.S. Minister John Hay's landau was tied up in front of the residence. Hay, these days, visited Longstreet as often as Jackson did, and on related business: if the minister's talks with the Confederate president succeeded, Longstreet and Jackson would no longer need to confer so much. Hay's driver sat waiting patiently for his principal, reading a copy of the *Richmond Whig*. He nodded to Jackson, then went back to the paper.

Moxley Sorrel escorted Jackson to the waiting room outside Longstreet's office. "Mr. Hay has come to obtain the president's reply to the ultimatum," the chief of staff said in a near whisper.

"There can be only one response to that piece of impertinence," Jackson growled. Sorrel nodded. The two men did not love each other, but both saw the interests of the Confederate States in the same light.

Jackson started to say something more, but the door to President Longstreet's office came open. Out stalked John Hay, his handsome face set and hard. Jackson rose politely to greet him. Hay gave a cold half bow. "Sir, I am forced to the conclusion that your president is more inclined to hear your counsel than mine." Moxley Sorrel came over to lead him out to the door. He shook off the chief of staff. "No thank you, sir. I can find my own way." Off he went. Had he owned a tail, it would have bristled.

"Come in, General," President Longstreet called through the open door.

"Thank you, Your Excellency," Jackson said. He closed the door after himself, then sat down, stiff as usual, in the chair to which Longstreet waved him. "By that, sir, am I to gather that you have told the United States they have no business meddling in our internal affairs?"

James Longstreet nodded. He looked pleased with himself. "You are to gather precisely that, General. Had I told him anything else, I have no doubt I should be impeached, convicted, and removed from office by this time next week—and I would vote for my own conviction, too. And I in turn gather that we are in full readiness to meet any emergency that may arise?"

He asked the same question every time he saw Jackson. As always, the general-in-chief of the Confederate Army nodded. "Yes, Mr. President, all regular units are deployed close to the U.S. frontier save those engaged in occupying our new provinces, and General Stuart has done more than anticipate along those lines himself." He briefly summarized Stuart's deployment for Longstreet, who nodded, and then continued, "And we are ready to accept, clothe, arm, train, and deploy volunteers as that may become necessary."

"I fear it will come to that," Longstreet said. "I do not fear the result, you understand, only its being required of us."

"Yes, Your Excellency. I understand." Jackson glanced toward the map on the wall to his right. "As soon as the wires inform our forces that the United States have been so misguided as to declare war on us, we shall strike them a blow that—"

"Wait," President Longstreet said, and Jackson obediently halted. Longstreet looked over at the map, too. "General, I must make one thing clear beyond any possibility of misunderstanding: regardless of the existence of a declaration of war on the part of the United States, they, not we, must strike the first blow in the ensuing conflict. Must, I say, sir. *Must.*"

Jackson's eyebrows shot upwards. "Mr. President, do I have to remind you how rash it is to yield the enemy the initiative, even for a moment? Had General Lee been content to stand on the defensive, I fear we should have been defeated in the War of Secession." To cap his point, he essayed a small joke: "Were this one of the United States, sir, you might even find yourself a Republican these days."

"From which fate, God deliver me," Longstreet said. "General Jackson, I do not deny for a moment the general applicability of the rule you state. But other factors militate against it in this particular instance. Do you remember how artfully Abe Lincoln maneuvered us into firing the first shots at Fort Sumter, thereby putting us in the wrong in the eyes of the world?"

"It came right in the end," Jackson said.

"So it did, but it made our task more difficult." Longstreet plucked at his beard. "I want us to appear unmistakably as the wronged party in the eyes of the world over this affair, General. Is that sufficiently clear, or must I explain myself further?"

Instead of asking for further explanation, Jackson went into one of his intense studies. He was unsure how long he remained in it: not too long, for President Longstreet didn't seem annoyed. "I believe I understand, sir. You particularly desire us to appear the wronged party in the eyes of Britain and France."

"Just so." Longstreet nodded. "We must show them we have done everything in our power to remain at peace with the United States, and that the United States thrust war on us nonetheless."

Jackson made a sour face. "This despite Britain's having sent soldiers to Canada to reinforce the Dominion's own army? This despite France's having pledged support for Maximilian, who is her creature? This despite both nations' having moved naval forces in both the Atlantic and Pacific to stations from which they might more readily confront the United States? This despite its being in the obvious interest of both Britain and France to take the USA down a peg? This despite most of the money Maximilian receives from the sale of Chihuahua and Sonora's going straight to the bankers in London and Paris? All these things are true, and yet we are still required not merely to show ourselves wronged, but to show ourselves blatantly wronged? Forgive me, Your Excellency, but I have trouble seeing any justice there."

"Objectively speaking, General, so do I," Longstreet said. "The problem we face—and an all but insuperable problem it has shown itself to be—is that Britain and France do not and cannot view support for us as objectively as we should like. If they *can* find a reason not to move in concert with us, they *will* find it and take advantage of it."

"They are our allies," Jackson said. "They have been our allies. They gain by remaining our allies. Why would they be so foolish?"

Longstreet looked at him without replying. It was almost a pitying look, the sort of look a mathematics instructor gave a scholar who could not for the life of him prove the Pythagorean theorem. It was a look that said, *This is why I am the president of the Confederate States and you remain nothing more than a soldier.* Jackson had never wanted to be anything more than a soldier. As a soldier, he could remain an honest man, and a godly one. He was unsure how much either word applied to James Longstreet these days. Longstreet, odds were, would die wealthy. What would become of him after that was another question.

And getting that sort of look from anyone, godly or not,

rankled. The look said all the pieces lay in front of him, if only he would see them. After a moment, he did. "They deprecate property in Negro slaves to that great a degree, sir?"

"They do," Longstreet said. "They have my pledge to move an amendment to the Constitution requiring manumission and to support the amendment and as far as possible to anticipate it through legislative and executive action—and still they hesitate, not believing I can accomplish what I have promised."

Jackson, who did not think it should be accomplished, said, "I do not see you manumitting your own slaves, Mr. President."

Now Longstreet's look was a frank and unmistakable glare. Jackson bore up under it, as he had borne up under worse, and from men he reckoned better. He realized, belatedly, that he had been less than diplomatic. That did not bother him, either: he *was* less than diplomatic. But then Longstreet said, "General, on the successful conclusion of this war, I intend to set at liberty all of the Negroes now my property. I shall at that time urge other members of the executive branch of the government as a whole to do likewise, and hope my example will be emulated by private citizens as well."

"You are in earnest in this matter, sir," Jackson said in no small surprise.

"I am," Longstreet said. "I can look ahead and see the twentieth century, with machines performing much of the labor now done by swarms of niggers. What will those swarms do then? Work in factories at no wages, and depress the wages of white men? Become a drain on their present owners' purses? If we do not keep abreast of the times, they will smash us into the dust. And yet I see you have trouble believing me, and so do the illustrious ministers and governments of our allies. Thus our need to be irrefutably in the right in our dispute with the USA."

"Very well, sir," Jackson said. "You have made both the issues involved here and your own resolve pertaining to them clearer in my mind than had previously been the case. It shall, of course, be as you say. Until the Yankees are the first to cry haro, we shall not let slip the dogs of war."

"By Godfrey, General, I didn't know they had you teaching English literature there at the Virginia Military Institute," Longstreet exclaimed. Both men laughed, more at ease with each other than they usually were. Jackson rose to go. Longstreet rose with him, came round the desk, and clapped him on the shoulder. "Wait," the president told him. "Wait until the Yankees hit us first—and then hit 'em hard."

Jackson's pale eyes glowed. "Yes, *sir*!"

On the parade ground at Fort Dodge, Kansas, Colonel George Custer walked curiously around the two newfangled weapons that had just arrived. "I've heard of these Gatling guns before," he remarked to his brother, "but I've never set eyes on one till now. The way I hear it, Gatling invented them about the time the . . . dashed Rebs were getting up into Pennsylvania, and he's been trying to sell them to the Army ever since. I wonder if I ought to be glad he finally turned the trick."

Major Tom Custer was giving the guns a dubious once-over, too. "Looks like a Springfield was unfaithful with a cannon, and then went and had sextuplets."

"I thought I was the writer in the family," Custer said with jealousy mostly mock. The description fit. Six rifle-caliber barrels were mounted in a long brass body on a carriage that could have carried a field piece. A separate ammunition limber like that which went with a field piece accompanied the Gatling, too. A crew of five served the weapons. Custer rounded on the artillery sergeant in charge of one gun. "*How* many rounds a minute do you say this thing can spit, Buckley?"

"Sir, when everything is going the way it ought to, about two hundred," the sergeant answered.

"When everything is going the way it ought to," Custer echoed. "And how often is that?" He didn't really want an answer. Scowling, he went on, "Too many gadgets in the world already, if anyone wants to know. We should still be fighting with sabers— then we could tell who the real men are."

His brother pointed to the blockhouses at each corner of the fort. "If we mount these opposite each other, Autie, we could rake the plain around the fort if the Kiowas come calling—or if the Confederates do."

"Maybe," Custer said. Fort Dodge was on highest alert, awaiting a report that President Blaine's declaration of war on the CSA had passed both houses of Congress. Custer scowled. "Wouldn't put it past either the redskins or the Rebs to sneak up here and do us dirt while we're still supposed to be at peace."

Sergeant Buckley said, "Sir, give me good horses for my teams and I'll keep up with any cavalry you like. That's what these guns are for."

"I'll believe it when I see it," Custer said, careless of wounding the Gatling gunner's pride. "For now, we'll leave these white elephants right where they are. Maybe we'll come up with a notion for getting some good out of them." By the way he spoke, he didn't believe it for a minute.

Sentries paced the walkways on the walls of Fort Dodge, dull routine most days but vitally urgent now. They stared out over the prairie in all four directions. If those on the south-facing wall were particularly alert, Custer did not see how he could blame them. He worried, though he did his best not to show it. Against the Kiowas, the fort would stand forever. What a battery of Confederate horse artillery might do to the walls, though, was something else again.

He stalked back toward his quarters. He had a suite of rooms in Fort Dodge, where his troopers made do with a footlocker and a straw tick on an iron bed with wooden slats in the barracks. From the walls of his parlors, the heads of a buffalo, two antelopes, and a coyote stared at him with glass eyes. He'd shot all the animals and mounted all the heads, too; practice had made him a fine taxidermist.

A raccoon stared at him from the back of the sofa. It was holding an egg in its handlike paws. The cook, a redheaded Irish girl named Sal, came running in from the kitchen and glared first at the animal and then at Custer. "That is the thievingest creature I've ever seen, and why you keep it I cannot be guessing," she snapped.

"Stonewall? He's a fine fellow." Custer's voice held more indulgence then he commonly showed his men. He'd raised the raccoon from an orphaned pup, and it had been with him longer than Sal. He couldn't keep cooks. They kept marrying soldiers or local civilians—and, if they were pretty, as Sal was, Libbie made a point of introducing them to every male around. Custer was friendly toward women other than his wife. Libbie sometimes thought he was too friendly.

Drawn by Sal's complaint about the coon, she came out of the bedroom: a short, plump, dark-eyed woman close to Custer's age. No matter how friendly he was to other women—and he was as friendly as he could get away with—he loved her unreservedly.

Now she advanced on the raccoon. "Give me the egg, Stone-wall," she said, in tones that might have sent a regiment into battle. She was as firm of will as her husband; he sometimes wondered uneasily if she wasn't the smarter of the two of them.

Stonewall, however, instead of surrendering the egg, devoured it. Sal cursed the animal with fury and fluency. Custer laughed at the raccoon and at the cook both. Libbie scowled impartially at beast, servant, and husband. She did not care to have her will thwarted, even by a raccoon.

"Get back to work, Sal," she snapped. Still muttering, the Irish girl returned to the kitchen. Custer watched her hips work as she walked. Libbie watched him watching. "Have to find her a man," she muttered.

"What's that, dear?" Custer asked, recalled to himself.

"Nothing at all, Autie," his wife answered sweetly. "What do you think of those new guns that came in earlier this morning?"

"Not much," he said, and was about to go into detail—Libbie loved details of any sort—when an orderly burst into his quarters and thrust a telegram at him. He unfolded it and read it out loud: " 'As of this date, state of war exists between United States, Confederate States. Prosecute with all vigor. Victory shall be ours. Rosecrans.' " He let out a war whoop a Kiowa would have been proud to claim, then ran out into the parade ground, shouting for the trumpeters to blow Assembly. The men rushed to form up from their drills and fatigues, excitement on their faces—most of them guessed what the unusual summons meant.

When Custer read the telegram to the assembled force, the men cheered. Loudest were the shouts from the officers and the veteran sergeants and corporals: men who remembered the War of Secession and wanted revenge for it. "We'll kick the Rebs from here to the Rio Grande!" Tom Custer yelled. Then he remembered the annexation of Sonora and Chihuahua that had brought on the war. "And after that, we'll kick 'em another fifty miles!"

"That's right!" Custer said. "Nobody casts scorn on the United States of America! Nobody, do you hear me? I've waited almost twenty years for this moment to come, and at last it's here." His voice quivered with emotion. More cheers rose. "For now, dismissed. Soon, we start getting our own back."

Buzzing with talk, the men returned to their duties. Tom walked up to his brother. "Autie," he said, "I've got an idea how to get some real use out of those Gatling guns. If it's war, all the better."

Custer sent the weapons a mistrustful look. "I don't think they're good for much, myself. If you want to try to convince me I'm wrong, go ahead."

Tom talked for ten minutes straight, illustrating his scheme with gestures and with sketches in the dust of the parade ground. Finishing, he said, "And, of course, I'll command the party. It's my notion; my neck is the one that should be on the line."

He spoke altogether matter-of-factly. George Custer, as brave a man as any, recognized a braver in his brother. He said, "No, I'll lead it. I won't send someone out with an untried weapon while I stay home safe. Lieutenant Colonel Crowninshield will do a perfectly fine job commanding the regiment while I'm gone. We'll leave at sunrise tomorrow."

Tom Custer's grin was enormous. "Yes, sir, Autie, sir!"

"Pick a dozen men to go with us," Custer said. "Oh, and make certain those guns have good horses pulling them, and the limbers, too. We'll see how they do as they head down toward the border. If they can't keep up, they're useless."

He briefed Casper Crowninshield on the patrols he wanted set out while he was away. The regiment's second-in-command looked horrified when he outlined what he would be doing, but said very little. Either Custer would come back trailing clouds of glory, or he wouldn't come back at all. No matter which, carping wouldn't matter.

Custer, his brother, a dozen picked cavalry troopers, and the two Gatling guns and their crews rode out of Fort Dodge before the sun was up. As the fort shrank behind him, Custer laughed for joy. "No need to worry about that blasted international border, not any more," he said.

"That's right," his brother said exuberantly. "Only thing we need to worry about is running into a Rebel patrol coming to kick us in the slats before we can get down into Indian Territory."

Custer and one of the troopers rode out ahead as scouts to make sure that didn't happen. Without false modesty, Custer was sure he could outride any of his companions except perhaps his brother. When they thought he couldn't hear, the men of the regiment called him Hard Ass. It didn't anger him; it made him proud. He glanced back over his shoulder at the Gatling guns.

They were slowing the party, but not by much. Sergeant Buckley had had a good notion of what he was talking about.

On over the Kansas prairie he rode. Here and there, farmhouses poked up from the flat terrain. Some were dugouts, with only chimneys and stovepipes above ground. Some were of sod blocks, some of wood, some—the most prosperous—of brick. Sod or wood or brick, all had something of a fortress look to them—squat and low, with small windows. In country vulnerable to Indian raids, that was safe and smart.

They camped on the prairie that night, boiling coffee, frying salt pork, and then frying soaked hardtack biscuits sprinkled with brown sugar in the grease from the meat. An occasional firefly winked to light, then out. Off in the distance, an owl hooted. Custer rolled himself in his blanket, stared up at the stars sprinkled like powdered sugar across the sky, and fell asleep almost at once.

It was still dark when he woke, but twilight was turning the eastern horizon gray. He shook his brother. "Wake up, lazybones!" Tom groaned and thrashed. Custer laughed. He'd scored himself a point.

They passed into Indian Territory—into Confederate territory—a little before noon. Custer let Sergeant Buckley and the Gatling guns catch up to him. "You pick your spot," he said. "You best know the requirements and capabilities of your weapons." The artillery sergeant nodded. Custer hoped the Gatlings *were* capable.

Toward evening, Buckley chose a gently rising little hillock with a commanding view in all directions. The party camped there for the night. When morning came, the Gatling crews stayed behind. Custer, his brother, and the cavalry troopers went out looking for streams, and for the Kiowas' villages they were likely to—were hoping to—find along such waterways.

They found cattle first. The Indians herded cattle these days, instead of hunting the nearly vanished buffalo. "At them!" Custer shouted. At them they went, whooping and waving their hats and shooting their carbines in the air. The cattle bellowed in terror and stampeded. Custer whooped again, in sheer small-boy delight at having made an enormous confused mess.

A bullet made dirt spurt up, not too far from him. It hadn't come from any of his own men, but from one of the Kiowas who'd been tending the herd. Custer fired back, and missed—good shooting from horseback was next to impossible. He waved his men forward against the Indian herders. The outnumbered Kiowas fled. Their ponies, tails bound up in bright cloth, bounded over the prairie.

Custer knew they were leading him and his cavalrymen toward more of their comrades. He followed as eagerly as the Indians could have wanted. If he didn't stir up the hornets' nest, he wasn't doing his job.

His brother pointed off to the northwest. There, down by the bed of a creek, stood the big village to which the herders belonged. Tom Custer rode straight for it, hard as he could go. The rest of the cavalrymen, George Custer among them, pounded after him. "Stay away from the horses!" Custer shouted. "We don't want to stampede the horses." If they stampeded the horses, the Kiowas wouldn't be able to come after them. That was the idea. Custer hoped it was a good idea. One way or the other, the Gatlings would answer that.

Tom Custer rode right down what did duty for the village's main street, past dogs and children and squaws who all ran like the devil to get out of the way. Again, Custer followed his brother, past hide teepees painted with bears and bear tracks, past screaming women, past an old man who fired a pistol at him and missed from a range where he shouldn't have missed a mouse, let alone a man.

Out the other side of the village galloped the cavalrymen. Custer knew they'd just done a very Indian sort of thing: a wild dash that couldn't help but singe the Kiowas' pride. Behind him, warriors were rushing to their ponies. He fired a couple of rounds at them so they wouldn't get the idea they were doing exactly what he wanted.

He waved his little troop back to the east, toward the hill on which the Gatlings waited. If he couldn't retrace his way across the plain, he and his men were dead. Somewhere between fifty and a hundred Kiowas were on their trail. The Indians had fresher horses and, thanks to the Confederates, rifles as good as his own.

"This is the one part of the business I don't fancy," Tom Custer said: "I don't like running, even for pretend."

In the chase, one of the cavalrymen slid out of the saddle. Another trooper's horse went down, which meant the soldier was a dead man shortly thereafter. The cavalrymen, firing over their shoulders, hit two or three Indians and two or three horses.

After a couple of hours of hard riding one of the troopers

pointed northeast. "There, sir!" Sure enough, there atop the little hill waited the two Gatling guns and their crews. Custer spurred toward them. The Kiowas came on after his men, shouting in high excitement. They saw the soldiers on the low hillock, too, but they also saw they still greatly outnumbered their foes.

The artillerymen at the Gatlings waved the troopers on. "At the crest of the hill, dismount as if for a last stand," Custer called to his riders. Maybe it would *be* a last stand. The Kiowas were close behind. Up the hill thundered the horses. Custer did his best to stay out of the Gatlings' line of fire, in case they opened up too soon. He reined his blowing, lathered mount to a halt and sprang down. A bullet snapped past him. He shouted to the gunners: "It's your show now, boys!"

Sergeant Buckley and the crew chief of the other Gatling, Sergeant Neufeld, swung the guns so they bore on the Kiowas. Then they began working the cranks at the rear of the weapons. The barrels revolved. As each one fired, it went around till another cartridge from the brass drum magazine atop the Gatling gun was chambered and discharged.

The noise was astonishing, like an enormous sheet of sailcloth being torn in two. The smoke from the black-powder rounds built a fogbank around the top of the hill. As a magazine went dry, the gun crews took it off and replaced it with a full one. When a barrel jammed, that gun went silent for a moment to clear a cartridge or clean away the worst of the fouling. But, for the most part, Buckley and Neufeld cranked and cranked and cranked.

Custer peered through the drifted smoke. The Kiowas might have run headlong into a stone fence. They'd been in easy range before the Gatlings opened up, and they hadn't had a prayer. More than half their band, more than half the horses, lay still and dead in front of the two guns. The rest were riding off as fast as they could go. They were brave, but they hadn't been ready for what they'd just come up against. "God bless my soul," Custer said softly.

Sergeant Neufeld was also looking out through the smoke, but to the east. "Sir," he called to Custer, "more riders. They look like Rebs, not Indians."

"Let 'em come, Sergeant." Custer's voice was gay. From no confidence in the Gatlings, he'd swung to the other extreme. "Plenty for everyone, isn't there?"

And the Confederates came. In their shoes, Custer would have done likewise. They had a company's worth of men. A couple of dozen Yankees on a no-account hilltop? Get rid of 'em and start the war in style. If the Rebels noticed the dead Kiowas, they paid them no heed.

They should have. As they came galloping toward Custer's little detachment, the Gatlings began their deadly ripping noise again. Troopers and horses went down as if scythed. Custer and his companions added the fire of their carbines to the mechanical murder the Gatling guns dealt out. Like the Kiowas, the Confederates, meeting weapons they hadn't imagined, broke and ran.

Custer walked over to Neufeld and slapped him on the back. Then he did the same with Buckley. "This may not be sporting," he said, "but it's no humbug."

☆ **IV** ☆

Alfred von Schlieffen rode toward the Long Bridge, the most important bridge from Washington, D.C., down into Confederate Virginia. He had no trouble making his way south from the German ministry: many, though far from all, of Washington's civilians had fled north when war broke out, and so traffic was less oppressive than it would have been before the crisis.

Boys still hawked newspapers on the street. From their frantic shouts, some U.S. officer named Custard—Schlieffen didn't think that could be right, but it was what he kept hearing—had single-handedly massacred a division of Confederates and a whole tribe of Indians somewhere out beyond the Mississippi. In a leap of logic that escaped the German military attaché, the war was as a result supposed to be as good as won.

As yet, the war had not made an appearance around Washington. The Confederate States could have pounded the capital of the United States to bits, but had not fired a shot hereabouts. Neither had local U.S. forces; despite big talk, President Blaine was proving more circumspect when it came to action.

But the Confederates had let it be known they were sending an officer across the Long Bridge under flag of truce at noon today. Schlieffen noticed he was not the only military attaché heading toward the bridge. He nodded to Major Ferdinand Foch, his French opposite number. The Frenchman coolly returned the courtesy; like Schlieffen, he had fought in the Franco-Prussian War. Schlieffen wondered how long Foch would be welcome here.

The British military attaché was not in evidence, but before long his assistant, a captain still on the eager side of thirty, rode up alongside Major Foch and began trying to converse with him in French. Unfortunately, the Englishman knew less of the language than he thought. The pauses in the conversation grew longer and longer.

"Get out of our country, you damned redcoat!" somebody shouted at the assistant military attaché, who was indeed decked out in his dress reds. He tipped his hat to the heckler. Schlieffen nodded slightly, admiring his panache if not his skill with languages.

Almost but not quite in a group—Schlieffen hung back—the three foreign officers rode south through the Agricultural Grounds west of the Smithsonian Institute, then west along Maryland Avenue toward the Long Bridge. Now Schlieffen could see the positions of the Confederate guns trained on the capital of the United States. He had also seen, in amongst the trees, U.S. guns ready to reply. More U.S. guns were positioned on the high ground north and west of the city, and elsewhere around it. If the Confederates tried to seize Washington, those guns could make it an expensive business.

At the U.S. end of the Long Bridge waited Captain Saul Berryman—General Rosecrans' adjutant—a few soldiers, and Hannibal Hamlin, the U.S. secretary of state. In his black suit, the jacket unbuttoned in the humid heat to expose a large expanse of white shirtfront, Hamlin resembled nothing so much as a roly-poly old penguin.

Captain Berryman nodded to Schlieffen as he dismounted. He did his best to pretend the British and French military representatives, servants of unfriendly powers, did not exist. They took up positions where they could see and remain inconspicuous.

Church bells on both sides of the Potomac began announcing noon. As they did so, a Confederate officer on a black horse rode north over the Long Bridge carrying a small white flag. As he drew near, Schlieffen saw by the red trim on his uniform that he was an artilleryman. "I am Colonel William Elliott," he announced, "and I bear a proposal from President Longstreet and General Jackson seeking to avoid the needless effusion of blood."

Captain Berryman and Secretary Hamlin introduced themselves. Hamlin said, "Say what you will, Colonel. The United States do not and shall not condemn unheard any such proposal." Hamlin's accent was different from Elliott's, almost as different as a Bavarian's from a Berliner's: like President Blaine, the secretary of state came from Maine, as far from the border of the Confederacy as any place in the eastern USA.

"Thank you, sir," Elliott said. "Believing it obvious, then, that the United States cannot hope to defend Washington, D.C., against the sanguinary bombardment the Confederate States have it within their power to unleash at any time, the president and the general-in-chief ask in the name of humanity that you declare Washington an open city and permit its peaceable occupation by Confederate forces. Otherwise, they cannot answer for what will ensue."

"I can speak to that," Captain Berryman said quickly, almost treading on the heels of Elliott's last words. "General Rosecrans has ordered me to reject categorically any such proposal. If you want Washington, Colonel, you are going to have to fight for it, and that's flat."

"I am sorry to hear you say that, Captain," Colonel Elliott said. "I had hoped to be able to avoid visiting destruction on this lovely city."

"You'd hoped to get it for nothing," Berryman replied. "I'm sorry to disappoint you, but that's not going to happen."

"Colonel," the British captain said, "do please remember that legations of powers friendly to your nation are located within this city." With his upper-class accent, he swallowed more syllables than the U.S. secretary of state and the Confederate colonel put together.

"We shall make every effort to strike only military targets," Elliott said.

Hannibal Hamlin said, "In any case, this is irrelevant. Due to the outrageous and unacceptable nature of the notes President Blaine received this morning from the ministers of Great Britain and France, the government of the United States is declaring all diplomatic personnel of those two nations to be *personae non gratae* in this country; arrangements to return the lot of you to your own nations are already under way."

"As a neutral power, the German Empire may be well suited to arrange those transfers in both directions," Schlieffen said.

"Thank you, sir," Hamlin answered. "I believe one of my assistants has an appointment with the German minister to discuss that very arrangement." Schlieffen inclined his head. He had exceeded his authority by making the suggestion, but you never could tell what the Americans might overlook.

"This is your final reply, Captain?" William Elliott asked. When Berryman nodded, the Confederate artillery officer rode back toward his own country. As soon as he was off the Long Bridge,

Berryman walked over to a telegraph clicker Schlieffen hadn't noticed and rapidly tapped out a message.

A couple of minutes later, an explosion smote the air. Flame and a great cloud of black smoke sprang from the U.S. half of the Long Bridge, which crashed down into the Potomac. Moments after that, other explosions rang out to the east and west, no doubt severing the rest of the bridges linking the USA and CSA.

"We've already burned our bridges behind us," Captain Berryman said with a jaunty smile. "Now we're blowing them up in front of us. Captain, Major"—he spoke to the British and French officers—"I request and require you to return to your ministries at once, that you may be evacuated with your fellow nationals. My men will accompany you to see that this is done. Colonel Schlieffen, I impose no such order on you, but you might be wise to return to the German ministry anyhow. Surely the Confederates will not make it a target."

"No doubt you are right," Schlieffen said. He clambered up onto his horse and rode back toward the red brick building on Massachusetts Avenue. The Prussian Army had shelled and starved Paris into submission. Then he had been on the giving end of the bombardment. Now he might learn what he had given out.

A column of wagons heading east along G Street held him up. U.S. cavalrymen guarding them made sure they had the right of way. General Rosecrans rode in a buggy near the head of the column: heading for the train station, no doubt. Had the Confederate gunners chosen that moment to open up, they could have beheaded the U.S. Army. Whether or not that would have made it stupider than it was already, Schlieffen was not prepared to say.

A couple of blocks after that, as he was about to urge his horse up into a canter, a little girl of six or seven darted into the street in front of him. He brought the horse to a halt before any harm was done. The girl's mother hauled her back and spanked her, saying, "Be careful, Nellie! Watch where you're going!"

"I'm sorry, Ma," the girl blubbered. Schlieffen sympathized with her—she reminded him of his own daughters back in Germany—but only to a point. She had to learn discipline.

As soon as he did get back to the ministry, he asked to see Kurd von Schlözer. The minister had served in Washington since Germany united under Wilhelm I, and understood the United States far better than Schlieffen did. "Very unfortunate," Schlözer said now, running a hand over his glistening bald pate. "The Americans have a gift for antagonizing all their neighbors, and they have chosen this moment to exercise it. I urged restraint on them, but they would not listen. They never listen."

"I have seen the same thing," Schlieffen answered. "As you say, unfortunate. Not the slightest notion of forethought."

"And because they are so stubborn, they find themselves encircled," the German minister said. "They do not have a Bismarck, who has kept French jealousy from wrapping Germany in similar cords."

"Captain Berryman this morning spoke of notes from England and France to the government of the United States," Schlieffen said. "Have they declared war?"

"Not in so many words," Schlözer told him. "They demanded the United States cease all military action against the Confederate States within twelve hours, on pain of war."

Schlieffen weighed in his mind the forces on either side. "The United States might be wiser to accede to this demand."

"They will not." Sadly, Schlözer shook his head. "President Blaine sees that the United States are larger and richer than the Confederate States, and that is all he sees. No European powers have fought in North America since England and the United States had a brush during the Napoleonic Wars. Blaine, I fear, does not fully understand what he is getting into."

"I think you are right, Your Excellency," Schlieffen said. "General Rosecrans called the notes outrageous. And Rosecrans himself, when I spoke with him before, had made no preparations for war against Britain and France, even knowing such was not only possible but likely."

"Americans insist on improvising, as if the spur of the moment will itself impel them to find the right answer." Kurd von Schlözer sighed, like a judge about to pronounce sentence, and a harsh sentence at that, on a likable rogue. "Until they learn to think before they act, they will not be taken seriously on the stage of the world. Please furnish me by tonight with a written report on what you saw and heard at the Long Bridge, so that I may cable it to Berlin."

"Yes, Your Excellency." Schlieffen went up to his stuffy office and drafted the report. After giving it to the minister's secretary, he went back up and studied for a while the Confederate General Lee's move up into Pennsylvania, the stroke that had won the

War of Secession for the CSA. Lee had faced inferior opposition, no doubt of that, but the move, an indirect rather than a direct threat to Washington, showed considerable strategic insight. The North Americans were raw, but not all of them were stupid.

Schlieffen expected the Confederate guns to open up on Washington at any moment, but they stayed quiet. *Inefficient,* he thought, but then checked himself. Maybe the Confederate States were waiting for their allies formally to join the war before commencing offensive action of their own: again, not the worst strategic notion. He went to bed still wondering, and did so with a perfectly clear conscience. If anything happened, he would know about it.

Dawn was breaking when the bombardment began. Schlieffen sprang out of bed, threw on his uniform, and hurried up to the roof of the ministry. Other buildings around it were of similar height, impeding his view, but he saw more there than he could have anywhere else—and his ears told him some of what he could not see.

Great clouds of smoke rose from the south and the southwest, from the Confederate batteries on the Arlington Heights and elsewhere along the Potomac. U.S. guns were answering, too: not only the big cannon in the fortresses that had surrounded Washington since the War of Secession but also field guns in the city itself and down by the river. Shells made freight-train noises through the air.

He judged the weight of fire to be about equal. If anything, the USA might have held a slight edge: so his ears said, at any rate. But what did it matter? The U.S. guns could chew up Confederate emplacements in Virginia, but nothing more. Meanwhile, though, the Confederate cannon still in the fight were wrecking the capital of the United States.

He heard only artillery—no rifle fire. That meant the Confederate States weren't trying to throw infantry across the Potomac. Had he been in charge in Richmond, he would have held back, too: with the small professional army that was all the Confederates had in the field at the moment, they would have taken casualties they could not afford. Shelling Washington was in any case a largely symbolic act, for which artillery more than sufficed.

It was also a destructive act. Schlieffen watched Confederate shells exploding around some of the fortresses in the hills back of the city. He also heard them landing to the south and the southeast, around the White House, with the War Department next door to it, and the U.S. Capitol. Smoke rose from both directions. Schlieffen went downstairs for a moment, returning with a pair of field glasses. Peering southeast through them, he nodded to himself. Not all of those shells over there were coming down near the Capitol. Others, farther away, pounded the Navy Yard by the eastern branch of the Potomac.

In the streets, panic reigned. People who hadn't fled the city were all trying to leave at once now. Schlieffen hoped the little girl his horse had almost run over was safe. A fire engine, bell clanging, did its valiant best to force its way through the crush. Its valiant best wasn't nearly good enough.

An errant Confederate shell landed less than a block away from the German ministry. It started a fire. The fire engine could not get to that one, either. The firemen cursed as their big horses went forward by inches. Schlieffen breathed in gunpowder smoke like a man gauging the bouquet of a new bottle of wine. After a moment, he shrugged. Too soon to judge the quality of the vintage yet, but it was a war.

The *Queen of the Ohio* steamed up the river for which she had been named. Frederick Douglass impatiently paced her deck. She'd had a disgracefully long layover in Evansville taking on wood, and she'd been bucking the current ever since Cairo. He didn't want to be late for his speaking engagement in Cincinnati.

"I should have taken the train," he muttered. But he shook his massive head. Whenever he traveled to a city on the northern bank of the Ohio, he went by steamboat. That way, standing by the port or starboard rail—depending on whether he was going downstream or up—he could look into Confederate Kentucky.

The green, gently rolling land looked no different from that on the Ohio side of the river. The shadow lying over it, unlike the one over smoky St. Louis, was not real. To Douglass, that made the shadow no less palpable, no less oppressive. On the southern bank of the river, millions of his brethren suffered in bondage—and most of his own countrymen did their best to pretend those suffering millions did not exist.

Not far away from Douglass, a white man and his wife were staring into Kentucky, too. He warmed to the worried expressions on their faces. Not all U.S. whites ignored the plight of the Negro in the Confederate States. Then the woman said, "Jack, are you sure it's safe to travel on the Ohio with the war on?"

"Safe as houses, sweetheart," Jack said reassuringly, and patted the woman's hand. He was wearing a flashy brown-and-white checked suit and a derby with a feather in the hatband: someone who wanted to impress the ignorant with an importance he didn't really possess, Douglass guessed. He was certainly doing his best to impress his wife. In a loud, pompous voice, he went on, "If the Rebs were going to make a real fight, they'd have done it by now. You ask me, they don't have the stomach for it. Last night, we got past Louisville all right, didn't we? And look how that Custer chewed them up out west. Was it Texas or the Indian Territory? I misremember."

They had got past Louisville and the Falls of the Ohio without trouble, true enough. One reason they'd got past without trouble was that they'd used the canal on the Indiana side of the river, the one painfully excavated through solid rock after the war, not the Louisville and Portland Canal in Confederate Kentucky. Douglass understood that, even if Jack didn't.

The *Queen of the Ohio* rounded a bend in the river just past Madison, Indiana. Jack's wife pointed to the riverbank on the Kentucky side. "Those are guns," she said.

Guns they were indeed. Douglass recognized them: four twelve-pounder Napoleons, leftovers from the war. As guns went these days, they weren't anything special. Neither were the troops who manned them. By their ill-fitting gray uniforms, they were Kentucky militiamen, not Confederate regulars at all.

Antique cannon, amateur soldiers—an armored gunboat would have slaughtered the men and wrecked the guns in a matter of minutes. The *Queen of the Ohio* was anything but a gunboat.

"You! Yankee boat! Surrender!" one of the Kentuckians shouted across the water—the sidewheeler flew a large U.S. flag. "Come aground on this here bank. We got to search you to make sure you ain't carrying troops, and then you're a prize of war."

Frederick Douglass quickly went down to the main deck and toward the steamboat's bow. If he had to swim for it, he didn't want to have to swim around the boat before striking out for the northern bank of the Ohio. Nothing could have induced him to stay aboard if the boat grounded itself in Confederate territory. If those militiamen caught him, they would sell him into slavery.

He'd been free for more than forty years, all his adult life. He was ready to die trying to stay free before going back into bondage.

"Surrender!" the militiaman shouted again. When the *Queen of the Ohio* kept steaming along, the fellow turned to his battery and waved. The gun crews had been standing around watching the sidewheeler. Now one crew sprang into action.

"Are they going to shoot at us?" an unshaven desk passenger in dirty overalls asked.

"They can't," his equally grubby female companion answered. "They wouldn't."

The Napoleon roared. Flame and smoke belched from its muzzle. The cannonball splashed into the river in front of the steamboat. The gun rolled backwards with the recoil. The artillerymen began reloading. The other three crews were serving their pieces, too.

"That one was a warning," the Kentuckian shouted to the *Queen of the Ohio*. "Surrender or we blow y'all out of the water."

Passengers cried out in alarm and dismay. From the pilothouse up above came an order delivered with such furious vehemence that it cut through the rising din: "Tie down the safety valves and pour on the ether! Get us the hell out of here!"

An order like that meant the steamboat was liable to explode even if the boiler didn't take a hit from the Confederate guns. Douglass couldn't have cared less. He clapped his hands together, applauding the captain's good sense: surrender, for him, was unthinkable. The sooner they got out of range of those Napoleons, the better.

The rest of the battery opened up on the sidewheeler, in earnest this time. One ball whizzed over her, a clean miss. Another went into the river just short of her, throwing water up onto Douglass and the other passengers standing nearby. The third carried away the top couple of feet of one smokestack. The Rebels jumped up and down as if they'd sunk the *Queen of the Ohio*. Their commander's furious yells set them to swabbing out and reloading again.

"My God!" Jack's groans from above reached Douglass' ears. "What do we do?"

"I think we'd better get down onto the main deck," his wife answered—she, evidently, had sense enough for both of them. "If the boat catches fire, we'll have to go into the river."

Passengers by the score flooded out of the steamboat's cabins and salons, down the stairs, and onto the main deck. Some went to starboard, to stare across the river at the militiamen shooting at them. Some ran to port, as if they were assured of safety because they couldn't see the Confederate guns from there.

Those guns proved any such safety illusory a moment later. A ball slammed into the *Queen of the Ohio*'s superstructure and tore through the boat's timbers as if they were made of pasteboard. A fusillade of screams—some women's, some men's—from the port side said the ball had torn through one of the passengers, too.

"Dear sweet Jesus!" somebody shouted. "If we take a hit in the boiler, this whole damn boat'll go up like it was filled with powder."

That had already occurred to Douglass. He wondered if it had occurred to the Confederate gunners, too. Maybe, to them, it was all good fun, like boys gigging frogs. But the frogs died in earnest—and so would a couple of hundred civilians, if the Rebs chanced to make a lucky, or rather an unlucky, shot . . . or if, in their exertions to flee the battery, the crew overstrained the boiler and it went up without being hit.

On the heels of that thought came another, even worse. "How many guns await us around the *next* bend of the river?" the Negro orator asked the heavens.

"Shut your mouth, you damn nigger," snapped a white woman who looked like somebody's maiden aunt. Douglass fell silent, but that didn't matter. If one battery of guns was out along the Ohio, scores would be—U.S. guns as well as C.S., he supposed, but the Confederate cannon were the ones that worried him.

Boom! Wham! A cannonball slammed into the steamboat's starboard paddlewheel. Wood splinters flew. One of them stabbed a man, who shrieked like a damned soul. The wheel kept turning, though now it put Douglass in mind of a man smiling with a missing tooth.

Under his feet, the *Queen of the Ohio* quivered like a racehorse suddenly given the whip. She fairly leaped forward in the water. Great gouts of smoke and sparks poured from her newly uneven stacks. The riverbank seemed almost a blur, such was the side-wheeler's speed.

But the boat's fastest clip was a pathetic creep when measured against the speed of a twelve-pound iron ball. More splashes around the *Queen of the Ohio* said the crews firing at her were not masters of their trade. But more crashes and screams said they didn't need to be masters to score hits. "Have we got a doctor on board?" somebody shouted.

Then another shout rose, far more terrible: "Fire!" Not all the smoke shrouding the steamboat was coming from the stacks, not any more. She was built of wood and bore many coats of paint. One of those hits from hot iron might have ignited her. Or a cannonball might have spilled the coals from a stove in the galley or broken a kerosene lamp or ... When he thought about it, Douglass realized how many unpleasant possibilities there were.

"Buckets!" somebody shouted. "The pump!" someone else yelled. Douglass hadn't known the boat carried a pump, but it was irrelevant, anyhow. Peering back, he saw the whole stern of the *Queen of the Ohio* engulfed in flames. A glance told him no one would be able to put out that fire.

A glance must have told the steamboat captain the same thing. The *Queen of the Ohio* turned hard to port, making straight for the U.S. bank of the river. A steward shouted, "Brace yourselves, folks! We're going to ground, and we're going to ground hard. Soon as we do, everybody off by the bow. Gentlemen, help the ladies, please." He might have been talking about dance figures, not a matter of life and death.

The *Queen of the Ohio* ran aground with force surely great enough to tear the bottom out of her—not that that mattered at the moment. Douglass had been grasping a pillar. The impact tore his grip loose. He landed on one ham, hard. Scrambling to his feet, he struggled toward the rail. A drop of about ten feet separated the deck from the muddy riverbank.

"May I assist you, ma'am?" he asked the woman closest to him: the sour spinster who'd cursed him for daring to suggest the Confederates might have more guns along the Ohio than this one battery.

She climbed over the rail, nimble despite her long skirt and petticoats, and jumped down on her own without even bothering to give him a no. *A woman of strong convictions,* he thought. Others were not so fussy about letting him take their pale hands in his dark ones and letting him put his black arms around their waists to help them down to safety. Some of them even thanked him.

After a while, the white man next to him said, "Well, Sambo, I reckon it's about time we light out for the tall timber ourselves." Douglass didn't think the fellow intended to offend; he likely would have called someone from the Emerald Isle *Mick* or a Jew *Abe* in the same way—classification, not insult.

Whatever the case there, he was right. Despite the best efforts of the men fighting the flames, they were racing forward. The crackling roar dinned in Douglass' ears; he could feel the heat on his skin and through his clothes. A hot cinder landed on the back of his hand. With an oath, he brushed it away.

He looked around to make sure no women were left on the sidewheeler. He saw none. When he looked back, the man who'd called him Sambo had already gone over the rail. Other men shoved forward, intent on doing the same. Douglass decided he could honorably leave. He swung over the rail, sat on the very edge of the bow, and jumped.

He landed heavily in the mud, going down to one knee and fetching up against someone who'd abandoned the *Queen of the Ohio* a moment before. "I beg your pardon, sir," he said, picking up his hat.

"Don't mention it," the man said. "God damn those cursed Rebels to hell!" As if to punctuate his words, another cannonball screamed past.

A man landed right behind Douglass, staggered, and trod on his toes. He didn't bother to excuse himself. Douglass said, "Perhaps we should get clear of this vicinity, to let those escaping the steamboat more readily descend in safety."

No one argued with him, which was a pleasant novelty. Limping a little, he walked away from the sidewheeler. He didn't look back. All he had left here were the clothes on his back, and they were muddy and torn. He'd had no more when he fled his master, and then he'd had nothing more anywhere. Now he was comfortably well off, and only a telegram away from being able to draw on his resources.

"Rebs must've thought the boat was a troopship," somebody not far from him said. That made a certain amount of sense; the U.S. and the C.S. both moved soldiers by steamboat.

"Maybe they're just a filthy pack of stinking bastards," somebody else said savagely. To Douglass, that made sense, too, a lot of sense: he was always ready to believe the worst of the Confederate States.

"Whatever they are, the whole Ohio's gonna be shut down as tight as a man's bowels with an opium plug up his ass," the first man said. That was crude, but true without any doubt whatsoever: if one side started shooting at steamboats, the other surely would.

And one other thing was also true without any doubt whatsoever: he was going to be very, very late to Cincinnati.

The Handbasket rattled toward Helena. "*Get* up, there!" Theodore Roosevelt called to the horses. They snorted resentfully as he flicked the reins and cracked the whip above their backs. Not only was he making them go faster than they usually did on a trip to town, they were pulling a heavier load.

From the back of the wagon, Esau Hunt said, "Easy, boss, easy. Slow down. We'll get there quick enough, any which way." The other five farmhands who sprawled in the back with him loudly agreed. Only Philander Snow had chosen to stay back at the ranch, and he'd already seen the elephant. The rest of the hands, like Hunt, like Roosevelt himself, were young men one and all.

"I'm not going to slow down for anything—not for one single thing, do you hear me?" Roosevelt declared. "Our country needs us, and I intend to meet the call, and to meet it as quickly as I possibly can."

"Can't meet it if you drive us off the road into a ditch," said Charlie Dunnigan, another hand.

Roosevelt didn't answer. He didn't slow down, either. When he conceived in his own mind that something needed doing, he went and did it, and he didn't waste time about it, either. He came up on another wagon heading toward Helena—but not fast enough to suit him. He didn't have much room between the road and the trees alongside it there, but he pulled out and passed, leaving the other driver to eat his dust. The fellow shouted angrily. Roosevelt waved his hat in a derisive salute.

"That's showing him, boss!" Hunt exclaimed. Roosevelt grinned, though he didn't turn back to show the hand he was pleased. Straightforward action, that was the ticket. People who accomplished anything in this world grabbed with both hands. If you didn't, you got left behind with your face dusty.

This time, Roosevelt steered away from the *Gazette* office when he got into Helena, heading toward the territorial capitol, farther south and east. "I only hope they still have slots open for us," he said, for about the dozenth time since setting out. Then he went on, again for the dozenth time, "By thunder, if they haven't got any, we'll make our own, that's what we'll do."

"Doesn't look packed to the rafters, anyway," Dunnigan remarked.

Sure enough, Roosevelt had no trouble hitching the buggy close to the capitol. He saw no line snaking out of the small stone building, either. "Is patriotism dead everywhere in the country, save my ranch alone?" he demanded, not of the farmhands but perhaps of God.

He leaped out of the wagon, tied up the horses, and led his men toward the capitol. As they charged up the steps, a man he knew came out: Jeremiah Paxton, a neighbor. "I know what you're here for, Roosevelt," he said: "the same thing I was, or I'm a Chinaman. You ain't gonna have any better luck'n I did, neither."

"What do you mean?" Roosevelt asked.

All Paxton said after that was "You'll find out." He spat into the dirt, then strode over to his horse, untied it from the rail, swung up onto it, and rode back toward his ranch. His stiff back radiated disgust with the world.

"Follow me!" Theodore Roosevelt said. He led his men up the steps to the capitol as if they were charging to the crest of an enemy-held hill. Stopping the first person he saw inside who looked as if he belonged there, he asked, "Where in blue blazes do I find the volunteer office hereabouts?"

"Third door on the left-hand side," the man answered. "But I have to tell you—"

Roosevelt pushed past him, as he'd pushed past the slow wagon. He opened the third door on the left-hand side, which was indeed emblazoned U.S. MILITIA, with an obviously new addition below: & VOLUNTEERS.

Inside the little office sat two clerks. The brass nameplate on the closer one's desk proclaimed him to be Jasper St. John. "Good day to you, Mr. St. John," Roosevelt boomed. "These gentlemen and I are here to offer our services to the U.S. Volunteers. High time we taught our high-handed neighbors not to get gay with the United States of America."

Jasper St. John did not look like a clerk. Except for spectacles much like Roosevelt's, he looked like a barroom brawler. His voice was a bass rumble: "We aren't accepting applications right now."

"What?" Roosevelt dug a finger in his ear, as if to assure himself he was hearing correctly. "You're not taking volunteers? Why the devil aren't you?"

"We haven't got any orders to do it," St. John returned stolidly.

"Good God in the foothills!" Now Roosevelt clapped a dramatic hand to his forehead. "We're at war with the Confederate States—by what I've heard, they're shooting up everything that moves on the rivers—we're at war with England and France, and, for good measure, we're at war with the Dominion of Canada. Have we declared war on ourselves, too? Is that why we don't want volunteers?"

"In the Montana Territory, volunteers are only being accepted at U.S. Army posts," Jasper St. John said. "This is by order of the secretary of war, as received here when war was declared against the Confederate States."

Roosevelt felt ready to explode. "But there aren't any forts within fifty miles of Helena!" he shouted.

"I understand that." St. John was as unmoving as a hilltop fortress. "I can only follow the orders I was given. You are not the first patriotic citizen I've had to turn away, believe me."

"Mr. St. John, sir, use your reason," Roosevelt said, doing his best to keep a rein on his temper. "That order may possibly have made some sense when we were at war with only the Confederate States. I do not say it did; I deny it did; but it is a point on which reasonable men might differ. I understand that we are a long way from the Southern Confederacy here in Montana. But good God in the foothills, Mr. St. John"—he was shouting again; not for the life of him could he keep from shouting again—"that's Canada right up over the border there! Has anyone back in Washington bothered to look at a map since England and the Dominion declared war on us? If they put a proper army over the border, the handful of regular troops we have in the Territory won't be able to stop them. They'll hardly be able to slow them down."

"Let us suppose, for the sake of argument, that I accept you and your friends here as U.S. Volunteers, Mister . . . ?" St. John paused.

"Roosevelt. Theodore Roosevelt. Now you're talking, sir!" Roosevelt said enthusiastically.

But the clerk shook his head. "No, not yet," he said. "I'm just beginning. If I do that, you still will not *be* U.S. Volunteers, because I have no authority to make you such. And, as soon as the people above me find out I have done it, they will give me the sack for exceeding what authority I do have. You will be no better off, and I will be worse. Do you see my trouble now?"

"I see it, all right," Roosevelt said, breathing hard. "The trouble is, you're one hidebound paper-shuffler in a regime full of petty paper-shufflers. If your sort is the best this nation can afford to send out to the Territories, we *deserve* to lose this war. A stronger and more able race will supplant us here, as surely as we have supplanted the savage red man."

Roosevelt's farmhands burst into cheers. Jasper St. John remained unmoved. "That's very pretty, Mr. Roosevelt," he said, and paused to spit, almost accurately, at the cuspidor next to the desk of the other clerk, who, with his papers, seemed oblivious to the argument. "It's very pretty," St. John repeated. "You could run for the Territorial Legislature on it, no two ways about that. But it cuts no ice with me. I have not the power to do what you want. Good day." He inked the pen that had been lying on his desk, ready to go back to his own bureaucratic minutiae.

"God damn it, you stupid fool, I am trying to help my country!" Roosevelt yelled.

Slowly, St. John put down the pen. Slowly, he got to his feet. He was half a head taller than Roosevelt, and looked half again as wide through the shoulders. "And I," he said pointedly, "am tired of being shouted at. No matter how much you want to help your country, I am not authorized to help you do it."

Regardless of his size, Roosevelt was about to punch him in the nose. He would have felt the same had he been in the office alone; that he had his men with him never entered his mind. But something else did, so the punch remained unthrown. "Then I'll raise my own troops!" he exclaimed. "Roosevelt's Unauthorized Regiment, that's what I'll call 'em!"

His men pounded him on the back and shouted themselves hoarse. "Do whatever you please," Jasper St. John said. "Do it somewhere else."

"Come on, boys," Roosevelt said. "We'll show him not everybody in Montana Territory is stuck in the mud."

As they left the Territorial capitol, Roosevelt's mind whirled with plans. If he was going to recruit the Unauthorized Regiment, he would have to wire back to New York for money: the ranch, though profitable, didn't make nearly enough to support a project of that size. He didn't think he would have to arm the men he raised, not with Winchesters as common as weeds out here. A Winchester didn't have the range or stopping power of an Army Springfield, but, with their tubular magazines, Winchesters put more bullets in the air than single-shot Springfields. The regiment could take its chances there.

He would have to feed and shelter the men till such time as the Unauthorized Regiment really did pass under U.S. control. And not men alone—"We'll be a cavalry regiment, of course," he said, as if he'd known as much all along. "No use pounding along wearing out boot leather."

"That's it, boss," Esau Hunt said. "First class all the way, that's how the Unauthorized Regiment goes."

The nucleus and, at the moment, the entire membership of Roosevelt's Unauthorized Regiment piled into Roosevelt's Ranch Wagon (he was, he knew, thinking in capital letters). He drove over to the *Gazette* office, more sedately now than before: the horses hadn't had a chance to cool down fully during his brief, unfortunate visit to the capitol.

At the newspaper, he bought a large advertisement seeking recruits for the unit he was forming. "Roosevelt's Unauthorized Regiment?" said the printer who took down the text he dictated. "I know they aren't accepting volunteers—I tried—but this here—"

"May light a fire under them," Roosevelt interrupted. "And even if it doesn't, I'll still have the troops to present to the U.S. Army. I'll also want you to print up some handbills with the same information as goes into this advertisement. Can you hire someone to paste them up here in town?"

"Sure can," the printer said, "but it'll cost you two dollars extra per five hundred."

"I'll take a thousand," Roosevelt declared. "I don't want a man to be able to walk down any street in Helena without seeing one of them."

"A thousand should do it," the man in the ink-stained apron said, nodding. "That'll be ten dollars for the advertisement, eight for the handbills—we'll print from the same type, so I'll cut you a break on that; would be ten otherwise—and four more to paper the town with 'em. Comes to twenty-two altogether . . . Colonel."

Roosevelt had already tossed a double eagle and two big silver cartwheels onto the counter when that registered. "By jingo!" he said softly. If he was raising the regiment, he *would* be its colonel. That was how things had worked in the War of Secession, and the rules hadn't changed since.

He stood straighter and pushed out his chest. Though he'd never fired a shot at anything more dangerous than a coyote, suddenly he felt as one with Washington and Napoleon and Zachary Taylor: a leader of men, a conqueror. This was what he was meant to do with his life. He could feel it in his marrow.

He'd already felt a couple of other callings—writer, rancher—in his marrow during his twenty-two years on earth, but so what? He'd obviously been mistaken then. He wasn't mistaken now. He couldn't be mistaken now.

"Let's find a saloon, boys," he said. In Helena, that was harder than finding air to breathe, but not much. He had his choice, only a few doors away from the *Gazette*. He and the farmhands strode into the Silver Spoon. "Drinks on me!" he yelled, which made him friends in a hurry. "Let me tell you about Roosevelt's Un-authorized Regiment, gents, if you'll be so kind." His new friends listened. Why not? He was buying.

Up in Front Royal, Virginia, far to the northwest of Richmond, General Thomas Jackson felt like a man released from prison. Once real fighting started, he'd taken advantage of it to escape from the capitol to the front line. President Longstreet hadn't liked that decision, not even a little.

Jackson smiled at the memory of how disingenuous he'd been. "But, Your Excellency," he'd said, "surely the telegraph can bring me the same intelligence in the field as it can far behind the lines here. It can also convey to me any instructions you have as to the prosecution of the war. And I shall gain the important advantage of viewing some segments of the action at first hand."

"You don't fool me a bit," Longstreet had answered. "You want to get out from under my thumb, and you want to get back into a camp."

Having been a garrison soldier for more years than he cared to recall, Jackson had picked up a certain measure of guile. "Mr. President, my desires, whatever they may be"—he was not about to admit that Longstreet had hit the nail on the head—"are of no importance. All that matters is the country's need. Can you deny my proposal possesses military merit?"

Try as he would, Old Pete Longstreet hadn't been able to deny it. And so Jackson was encamped just north of Front Royal, in charge of a Confederate force that had fallen back in the face of the larger Yankee army that had come out of West Virginia and Maryland and was now occupying Winchester, near the head of the Shenandoah Valley.

More than the Confederate defenders had fallen back. Half the civilian population—half the white civilian population, at any rate—had fled Winchester before the invaders. Their tents and lean-tos were scattered promiscuously over the ground around the neat rows of gray and butternut canvas that marked the Confederate bivouac.

Jackson did not like having to deal with civilians. They clogged the roads, and they were eating up a good part of the supplies that should have gone to his men. And they possessed not the slightest clue about discipline or order. He feared lest they infect his troops with their chaotic stridency.

He also did not like his position. Front Royal sat at the confluence of two branches of the Shenandoah. An enterprising U.S. commander could move artillery to the high ground on either side of the town, much as Jackson himself had done against the United States during the War of Secession. Fortunately, the Yankees seemed so impressed with having taken Winchester as to have no notion of trying anything more at the moment.

That let Jackson enjoy the luxury of sitting on the top rail of a fence outside Front Royal and sucking on a lemon while he contemplated ways and means of doing unto the Yankees before they did unto him. It also let a plump, middle-aged civilian in a cutaway coat and a stovepipe hat—a gentleman who, if he was half so important as he thought himself to be, was a very important fellow indeed—come up to him and say, "See here, General, you simply must do something about the outrageous, illegal, and immoral way the damnyankees are confiscating our property. The first thing they did, sir, the very first thing, on marching into our fair city, was to proclaim the liberation of every last nigger in Winchester. Outrageous, I say!"

"I agree with you," Jackson said. "They weren't so blatant about it in the last war, but we had much property stolen then in the fashion you describe."

"Well, sir, what do you propose to do about it?" the refugee from Winchester demanded. "I've lost thousands thanks to their thieving ways, thousands, I tell you!"

"How much do you suppose the nation has lost?" Jackson asked. The important—or, at least, self-important—man stared at him. As the general had thought, concern for the nation had never entered his mind. He cared only for himself. Jackson went on, "The best remedy I can conceive, sir, is retaking Winchester from

the United States. Then their actions are no longer of any consequence to us."

That wasn't strictly true, as he knew. Negroes who had been
told they were free would believe it. They might try to escape to
the USA—though the Yankees were anything but eager to have
them there. If returned to bondage, they would surely prove frac-
tious and unruly. President Longstreet, Jackson reflected unhappily, might well have known what he was about when he proposed
manumission.

"What the devil are you doing perched there chawing on that
damn thing"—the man in the stovepipe hat pointed to the lemon
Jackson was holding—"when you could be liberating the city?"

"Contemplating the best way *to* liberate it." Deliberately, Jackson
began sucking on the lemon again. The plump man went right on
expostulating. Jackson used the lemon as an excuse not to say
another word. He looked through the fellow from Winchester, not
at him. The man took a long time to get the message, but finally
did. He went away, muttering dark things under his breath.

An orderly trotted up. Jackson did acknowledge his existence.
"Telegram for you, sir," the soldier said, and handed him the
sheet.

Jackson rapidly read through it. "A brigade of volunteer infantry on its way up here, eh?" he said. That would better than
double his force. He liked what he'd seen of the volunteer regiments in Richmond before leaving for the action: they had a solid
leavening of men in their late thirties and early forties, War of
Secession veterans, to help show the younger men what soldiering was about. "That's good. That's very good."

Then, abruptly, he stared through the orderly—not with inten-
tional rudeness, as he had with the plump man, but because his
mind was for the moment elsewhere. Still clutching the telegram,
he went back to the two-story brick house that served him as
headquarters—and also as home for his family.

His son Jonathan was outside, playing with a dog. At fifteen,
Jonathan was just too young to go to war, and wild with frustration because of it. "What's up, sir?" he called. Jackson did not
answer him. Jackson hardly heard him. Jonathan shrugged and
threw the stick again; he'd seen his father like that many times
before. The general went inside.

Several young officers in the parlor sprang to stiff attention.
They were not studying the map spread over the table there: they

had been chatting with his pretty daughter, Julia, who was—where did the time go?—heading toward nineteen. Under his gaze, the officers soon found urgent reasons to go elsewhere. "Father!" Julia said reproachfully: she enjoyed the attention.

She got no more answer than had her brother, and flounced off in some dudgeon. Jackson never noticed. He studied the map for a while, traced a railroad line with his finger, and finally grunted in satisfaction. His wife had come into the parlor to see why Julia had left so abruptly. He walked past Anna without seeing her, either.

Only when he got to the telegraphy office did he recover the power of speech. "Send a wire at once to Rectorstown," he told the operator before whom he stood. "The troops en route hither must disembark from their trains there, on the eastern side of the Blue Ridge Mountains." He continued with a detailed stream of orders, which the telegrapher wrote down. At last, he finished: " 'The utmost celerity must be employed, to reach point named by time required.' Now read that back to me, young man, if you'd be so kind."

"Yes, sir," the telegrapher said, and did.

Jackson nodded his thanks and left. The headquarters of Colonel Skidmore Harris, who had been in command in the northern Shenandoah Valley till Jackson arrived, were next door. Harris was a stringy, middle-aged Georgian who had commanded a regiment in Longstreet's corps during the war. Without preamble, Jackson told him, "Colonel, I have taken away from this army the brigade of volunteer troops bound this way from Richmond."

Harris' pipe sent up smoke signals. "I'm sure you have good reason for doing that, sir," he said, his tone suggesting Longstreet would hear about it in a red-hot minute if anything went wrong.

"I do." Jackson went over to the map Harris had nailed up to a wall and did some explaining. When he was through, he asked, "Is everything now perfectly clear to you, Colonel?"

"Yes, sir." Harris puffed on the pipe. "If the Yankees don't take the bait, though—"

"Then the bait will take them," Jackson said. "We shall advance at first light tomorrow, Colonel. Prepare your troops for it. I desire divine services to be held in each regiment this evening, that the men may assure themselves the Almighty favors our just cause. Have you any questions on what is required of you?"

"No, sir." In meditative tones, Colonel Harris went on, "Now we get to see how the new loose-order tactics work out in action."

"Yes." Jackson was curious about that himself. Firing lines with men standing elbow to elbow and blazing away at their foes had taken gruesome casualties from the rifled muzzle-loaders of the War of Secession. Against breechloaders, which fired so much faster, and against improved artillery, they looked to be suicidal. On paper, the system the Confederate Army had developed to replace close-order drill in the face of the enemy looked good. Jackson knew wars were not fought on paper. Had they been, General McClellan would have been the greatest commander of all time. "Dawn tomorrow," the general-in-chief reminded Skidmore Harris. He left before the colonel could reply.

That evening, as the soldiers prayed with their chaplains, Jackson prayed with his family. "Lord," he declared on bended knee, "into Thy hands I commend myself absolutely, trusting that Thou grantest victory to those who find favor in Thine eyes. Thy will be done." He murmured a favorite hymn: "Show pity, Lord. Oh, Lord, forgive!"

He slept in his uniform, as had been his habit during the War of Secession. Anna woke him at half-past three. *"Gracias, señora,"* he said. His wife smiled in the darkness. He put on the oversized boots he favored, jammed on his slouch hat, and went off to war without another word.

Long columns of men in new butternut uniforms and old-fashioned gray ones were already on the move north before the sun crawled over the Blue Ridge Mountains. Winchester was about twenty miles from Front Royal, the Yankee lines a few miles south of the town they'd taken. If not for those lines, he could have been in Winchester before sundown. He hoped to be there by then despite them.

One advantage of the early start was getting as far as possible before the full muggy heat of the day developed. Even on horseback, Jackson felt it. Sweat cut rills through the dust on the faces of the marching men. Dust hung in the air, too. It made gray uniforms look brown, but also let the Yankees, if they were alert, know his forces were advancing on them.

The men rested for ten minutes every hour, their weapons stacked. Otherwise, they marched. Field guns and their ammunition limbers rattled along between infantry companies. At a little past twelve, the soldiers paused to eat salt pork and corn bread and to fill their canteens from the small streams near which they rested. After precisely an hour, they headed north again.

Just after they'd moved out, a messenger galloped up to Jackson from Front Royal and pressed a telegram into his hand. He read it, permitted himself a rare smile, and then rode over to Colonel Skidmore Harris. "The volunteers, Colonel, are threatening Winchester from the east, by way of both Ashby's Gap and Snicker's Gap," he said. "They report considerable and increasing resistance in their front, which means the U.S. commander in Winchester has surely pulled men from in front of us in order to contest their advance. Having done that, he will find some difficulty in also contesting ours."

Colonel Harris tilted back his head and blew a large, excellent smoke ring. "I'd say that's about right, sir. They don't have all *that* many more men than this army does—not enough to turn two ways at once and take on two forces our size."

Had Jackson been in Winchester with a force not greatly inferior to the one attacking him, he would not have retreated in the first place. But that was water over the dam now. "Onward," he said.

U.S. forces had dug a line of firing pits about half a mile south of Kernstown, a few miles below Winchester. Jackson smiled again, this time savagely. In the War of Secession, the Yankees had thrown him back from Kernstown. He'd waited more than nineteen years to pay them back, but the hour was at hand.

Their guns opened on his troops at a range of better than a mile and a half. His artillery swung off the roads and went into battery in the fields to reply. At the same time, his infantry deployed from column into line, moving with the drilled smoothness that showed how many times the regulars had bored themselves carrying out the maneuver on the practice field.

The line wasn't much thicker than a skirmish line had been during the War of Secession. To a veteran of that war, it looked gossamer thin—until one noticed how many rounds the men were firing as they advanced, and how thick the black-powder smoke swirled around them. A division of soldiers in the earlier war would have shown no more firepower than this light brigade.

But the Yankees had breechloaders, too; their Springfields were a match for the Confederate Tredegars. Their commanding officer had left no more than a regiment and a half behind. Even so, Jackson feared for the first few minutes of the fight that the

Yankees, with the advantages of position and cover the defender enjoyed, would beat him at Kernstown again.

His men had less practice at advancing by rushes and supporting one another with fire than at close-order drill and at shifting into the looser formations from which they could attack. The galling enemy resistance served to concentrate their minds on the task at hand better than weeks of exercises might have done.

After close to an hour's fighting, the first Confederate soldiers leaped down into the Yankee field works off to Jackson's left. That let them pour enfilading fire along the length of the U.S. line. Once the position began to unravel, it soon disintegrated. U.S. soldiers in dark blue emerged from their trenches and fled back toward Kernstown. Confederate small arms and artillery took a heavy toll on them. More Yankees threw down their rifles and threw up their hands in surrender. Guarded by jubilant Rebels, they shambled back toward the rear.

"We have a victory, sir," Colonel Harris said.

Jackson fixed him with a coldly burning gaze. "We have the beginnings of a victory, Colonel. I want the pursuit pressed to the limit. I want those Yankees chased out of Kernstown, out of Winchester, and back to Harper's Ferry and Martinsburg. I want them chased across the Potomac—that part of West Virginia should never have been allowed to leave the state of Virginia—but I am not certain we can bring that off in this assault. Still, if we put enough fear in the U.S. forces, they will skedaddle. We'll see how far they run."

Harris stared at him. "You don't want to just lick the damn-yankees, sir," he said, as if a lamp had suddenly been lighted in his head. "You want to wipe 'em clean off the slate."

"Why, of course." Jackson stared back, astonished the other officer should aim at anything less. "If they face us, the volunteer brigade will take them in the flank. If they face the volunteers, we shall take them in the flank. If they seek to face both forces at once, we shall defeat them in detail. Now let the thing be pressed."

Pressed it was. The U.S. troops retreated straight through Kernstown; the locals clapped their hands when Jackson rode through the hamlet. The Yankees tried to make a stand at Winchester, but pulled out just before sunset. The racket of rifle fire coming from the east said the volunteers were at hand.

Their commander, a bespectacled fellow named Jenkins, rode

up to Jackson in the middle of a wildly cheering crowd in Winchester (though Jackson saw not a single colored person on the streets). "What do you want us to do now, sir?" he asked. "We've about marched our legs off, but—"

"Your men won't fall over yet," Jackson said. "We head north, as long as there is light. As soon as it grows light in the morning, we go on. Our task is to drive the foe from our soil, and I do not intend to rest until that is accomplished." He drew his sword and pointed with it; dramatic gestures were all swords were good for these days, but dramatic gestures were not to be despised.

Jenkins looked as astonished as Colonel Harris had south of Kernstown, and then as exalted. He turned to his troops and cried, "You hear that, boys? You see that? Old Stonewall wants us to help him run the damnyankees clean out of Virginia. I know you're worn down to nubs, but are you game?"

The volunteers howled like catamounts. The veterans of the War of Secession had already taught their younger comrades the fierce notes of the Rebel yell. Jackson waved his hat to thank the men for their show of spirit, then pointed with the sword once more. Through the shrill yells, he spoke one word: "Onward."

There were, Abraham Lincoln reflected, undoubtedly worse places in which to be stranded than Salt Lake City. Technically, *stranded* was the wrong word. He'd had several speaking engagements canceled because of the outbreak of war, and had decided to stay where he was till more came along. The Mormons who made up the majority of the population were unfailingly polite and considerate to him. Whatever he thought of their religious beliefs, they were decent enough and to spare.

Even so, he felt more at home among the Gentiles, the miners and merchants and bureaucrats who leavened the town and surrounding countryside. Most of them, especially the officials, were Democrats, but that still left them closer to his way of looking at the world than were the Mormons, who thought in terms of religion first and politics only afterwards.

"They wish we'd all go away," Gabe Hamilton said at breakfast one morning at his hotel. "They wish we'd never come in the first place, matter of fact." He popped a piece of bacon into his mouth, then turned to the waiter, whom he knew. "Isn't that right, Heber?"

"I'm sorry, Mr. Hamilton; I wasn't listening," Heber said blandly. "Can I get you and Mr. Lincoln more coffee?"

"Yes, thanks," Hamilton told him, whereupon he went away. Sighing, the sharp little Gentile spoke to Lincoln: "What do you want to lay that every word he wasn't listening to goes straight into John Taylor's ear before the clocks chime noon?"

"I don't know what Mr. Taylor is in the habit of doing of a morning," Lincoln answered. "That aside, I'd say you're likely right."

"Or which of his wives he's in the habit of doing it to, do you mean?" Hamilton said, winking. Mormon polygamy roused some people to moral outrage. It roused others to dirty jokes. So far as Lincoln could tell, it left no one not a member of the Church of Jesus Christ of the Latter-Day Saints indifferent.

He said, "I am glad to have had the chance and taken the opportunity to have learned more about other aspects of the Mormons' way of life while here. I did not know, for instance, that they formerly practiced what might be described as a communistic system during their earlier years in Utah."

"You mean the Deseret Store?" Hamilton waited for Lincoln to nod, then went on, "I'd call it syndicalism myself. People brought their tithes to the store, and it sold what they brought to whoever needed it. The church—and that meant the government—kept some of the profit, too. Brigham Young didn't die poor, Mr. Lincoln, I'll tell you that. I expect you've seen the Lion House?"

"The long, long building where he housed his wives? One could hardly come to Salt Lake City and not see it." Lincoln paused to eat a couple of bites of tasty ham. "I do thank you, by the way, Mr. Hamilton, for arranging lectures hereabouts to tide me over and help keep me going until other engagements come through."

"Think nothing of it, sir, nothing at all," Hamilton replied. "You're educating the workers about labor and capital, and you're educating everybody else about the war. I can't think of anybody who'd know more about it who doesn't wear stars on his shoulders."

"The proper relation of labor to capital has concerned me since before the War of Secession," Lincoln said, "nor has defining and, if need be, regulating it grown less urgent since the war. The Mormons seem to employ the strictures of religion to lessen its harshness, but I do not think that a solution capable of wider application. The Mormons are the godly, pious folk we profess ourselves to be."

"That's a fact." Gabe Hamilton's eyes twinkled. "They won't skin each other, exploit each other, the way capitalists do—or the way they do with Gentiles, come to that. What they skin each other out of is wives."

He couldn't leave that alone. Few of the Gentiles who lived in Utah Territory *could* leave it alone, from what Lincoln had seen. That was why Utah had several times failed of admission to the Union as a state. Although the Book of Mormon spoke against it, the Latter-Day Saints would not renounce polygamy, while those outside their church could not countenance it.

After looking around to make sure Heber the waiter was out of earshot, Hamilton said, "I'm just glad the Confederates have even less use for the Mormons than we do. If they didn't, Utah would rise up right in the middle of this war, and that's a fact."

Remembering some of the things John Taylor had said at their supper meeting, Lincoln replied, "Don't be too sure they won't rise up on their own, taking advantage of our distraction with the CSA and with the European powers. I think President Blaine was shortsighted to pull the soldiers out of Fort Douglas here."

He didn't care whether or not Heber took his words to John Taylor. He rather hoped the waiter would, to let the Mormon president know someone wondered about his intentions. He did not mention that he also found Blaine shortsighted for involving the USA with England and France. In his administration, he'd done everything he could to keep the European powers out of the struggle against the Confederacy. *Everything he could* had not included enough victories to keep the Confederate States from bludgeoning their way to independence.

"I'd be glad to have some bluecoats around myself, I'll tell you that," Gabe Hamilton said. "Sometimes I thought they were the only thing keeping the Mormons from riding roughshod over us."

"They've behaved themselves well thus far," Lincoln said. Later—not much later—he would remember the optimistic sound of that.

"So they have," Hamilton said grudgingly, as if he were talking about a spell of good weather in late fall: something pleasant but unlikely to last. Remembering Brigham Young's loyalty during the War of Secession, Lincoln dared hope the Gentile was worrying over nothing.

After breakfast, Lincoln said, "Mr. Hamilton, would you be kind enough to drive me to the Western Union office? I want to send my son a wire."

"I'd be happy to, sir," Hamilton said. "What's your son do, if you don't mind my asking?"

"Robert? He's a lawyer in Chicago—a lawyer for the Pullman Company, as a matter of fact." Lincoln's long, lugubrious face got longer and glummer. "And he doesn't approve of his old pa's politics, not even a little he doesn't." His expression lightened, just a bit. "We don't let that come between us, though, not for family things. We aren't so foolish as USA and CSA, you see."

Hamilton chuckled appreciatively. "I like that—though the Rebs wouldn't. To hear them talk, they're as old as we are, and the only tie is that they decided to stay in the same house with us for a while before they moved on to a place of their own."

"I prefer to think of it as knocking down half our house, and using its floors and walls to build their own." A rueful smile creased Lincoln's face. "Of course, the Confederate States don't care what I think." As he rose from the table, he stuck up a forefinger in self-correction. "No, that's not quite so."

"Really?" Gabriel Hamilton raised an eyebrow. "I didn't reckon you'd have to qualify that statement in any way, shape, form, color, or size."

"Color is the proper term," Lincoln said. "I have heard that certain of my writings are popular with the handful of educated Negroes in the Confederacy, their race's labor being exploited even more ruthlessly—or perhaps just more openly—than any in the United States."

"Isn't that interesting?" Hamilton said. "How do they get hold of your speeches and articles and books, do you suppose?"

"Unofficially," Lincoln answered, picking up his stovepipe hat and going outside. "I am given to understand that my works are on the *Index Expurgatorum* for Negroes in the CSA, along with those of Marx and Engels and other European Socialists. I hope you will forgive my taking a certain amount of pride in the company in which they place me." He climbed up into Hamilton's carriage.

"You deserve to be there." Hamilton unhitched the horses and got into the carriage himself. "Won't be but a couple of minutes," he said, flicking the reins. "We're just four or five blocks away."

Lincoln coughed a couple of times at the dust the carriage—

and all the other buggies and wagons and horses on the street—kicked up. It tasted of alkali on his tongue. Dust was the biggest nuisance Salt Lake City had.

"You can drop me off, if you want to go on about your own business," he told Hamilton when they got to the telegraph office. "I expect I can find my way back to the hotel without too much trouble."

"It's no bother for me, Mr. Lincoln." Hamilton guided the horses toward a hitching post. As he got down to tie them, he frowned. "The doors to the office should be open. Maybe they've got them shut to try and keep the dust out, but that's a fight they lose before it's started."

"Is that a notice tacked to the door frame?" Lincoln walked over to the Western Union office and read the handwritten words: " 'All lines out of Utah Territory are down at the present time. We hope to be able to start sending telegrams to the rest of the USA again soon. We regret any inconvenience this may cause.' " The former president took off his hat and scratched his head. "What in the dickens could make all the telegraph lines from here—north, south, east, and west—go haywire at the same time?"

"Not *what*, Mr. Lincoln." Gabriel Hamilton sounded thoroughly grim. "The right question is *who*: *who* could make all those telegraph lines go haywire at the same time?" He looked around as he had back in the hotel dining room, as if expecting to find Heber the waiter lurking behind a cottonwood tree. "As for what the right answer is, I give you one guess."

Lincoln turned his head in the direction of the enormous granite bulk of the rising Temple. "Why would John Taylor—why would the Mormons—want to shut down telegraphy between Utah and the rest of the country?"

"Because they're up to something that won't stand the light of day," Hamilton suggested at once. "I couldn't begin to tell you what that might be, but I'll bet it's nothing *I* want."

"They'd be very foolish to try that," Lincoln said. "The United States may be distracted by this war, but not so distracted as to be incapable of dealing with a rebellion here." He clicked his tongue between his teeth. "Like South Carolina, Utah is too large to be an insane asylum and too small to make a nation, and, unlike South Carolina, lacks other nearby states full of zanies to join her in her madness."

A man on a horse came trotting up. He dismounted and hurried toward the closed door in front of which Lincoln was standing. "Sorry, pal," Gabe Hamilton called to him. "Office is closed. You can't send a wire."

"But I have to," the man exclaimed. "I was supposed to be on the train for San Francisco, and it couldn't leave the station. There's some sort of break in the tracks west of here—and, from what I heard people talking about, there's one to the east, too."

"Uh-*huh*," Hamilton said, as if the fellow had proved an obscure point. "And one to the north and one to the south somewhere, too. What a surprise, eh, Mr. Lincoln?"

All at once, Lincoln didn't feel stranded in Salt Lake City any more. He felt trapped.

☆ V ☆

Jeb Stuart led his troopers north out of Sonora and into New Mexico Territory. Now that the United States and Confederate States were at war, his opinion was that the best way to keep the USA from invading the new Confederate acquisitions was to make U.S. forces defend their own land.

He'd managed to stay in touch with Richmond through a spider-web of telegraph wires across the Sonoran and Chihuahuan desert back to Texas. He reckoned that a mixed blessing, as it deprived him of fully independent command. But he had heard not a word of reproof from the War Department on his plan to move into the United States.

"Not likely that you would, is it, sir?" Major Horatio Sellers said.

"With Stonewall Jackson heading up the Army, do you mean?" Stuart said with a grin. "You're right about that, Major, no doubt about it. Stonewall will never quarrel with a man who goes toward the enemy."

"That's what I meant, all right." Stuart's aide-de-camp checked his map. "Sir, are we going to strike Tombstone or Contention City?"

"Contention City," Stuart said at once. "That's where the stamping mills and refineries are for the ore, and that's what we want. Where the mines are doesn't matter; what comes out of them is what counts. You think we won't get a pat on the back if we bring home a few tons of refined gold and silver ore?"

"Just might," Sellers said dryly.

It wasn't *might*. Both men knew as much. The Confederate States were shorter than they cared to be on precious metals. The United States had far more in the way of mineral wealth, which helped keep their currency sound. The CSA relied on commerce to bring in most of their gold and silver. Well, this was commerce, too, commerce of a different and ancient sort.

A scout came galloping back to Stuart. "Sir, looks like the damnyankees have some soldiers in that there Contention City," he reported. "Can't rightly tell how many—don't look like a whole lot, but they won't be showin' all the cards they've got, neither."

The way he spoke gave Stuart an idea. He turned to his aide-de-camp. "Major Sellers, will you be so kind as to ride into Contention City under flag of truce and ask the Yankee commander to ride back here for a parley with me? You won't get back before nightfall, I expect, but that's all right. It's better than all right, as a matter of fact. Tell him I desire to prevent any useless bloodshed on his part, and so will not fall upon him with the overwhelming force at my disposal."

"Yes, sir; I'll tell him," Major Sellers said obediently. He looked around at the cavalry riding with Stuart; they'd left the infantry behind for the dash up into the United States. "Begging your pardon, if he's got more than a couple of companies entrenched around that town, this *isn't* an overwhelming force."

"Not now, it isn't." Stuart's voice was light and gay. "It will be by tonight, when everyone joins us. Just you make certain you don't bring the Yankee commander back here till after full dark. Ten o'clock will be perfect."

"Yes, sir," Sellers said again, still obedient but very puzzled. He knew as well as Stuart—maybe better than Stuart—no other Confederate soldiers would or could join them, not for the next several days. He was scratching his head as he rode north after the scout.

Stuart shouted orders to his trumpeter, who blew Halt. The cavalry troopers reined in, as bemused as Major Sellers: they'd been pushing hard toward their goal, and couldn't imagine why their commander was stopping them in the middle of this godforsaken desert. Their confusion only increased when Stuart said, "We'll make camp here, boys."

He gave more orders after that. By the time he was through, the troopers, confused no more, fell to with a will. One of them said, "Any day we get to knock off early is a good day by me." As the work progressed, they discovered they hadn't knocked off early after all. They kept at it, though, fired by the same enthusiasm as had filled Stuart when the idea came to him.

He sent scouts out well in front of his force, so they could intercept Major Sellers and the U.S. commander (if he chose to come; if he didn't, a lot of work was being wasted) well before they reached the camp. Instead of pitching his own tent near the center of the encampment, as he usually did, he had it set at the northern edge, and made sure the scouts knew as much.

As the sun went down, the men lighted their fires. Sagebrush and greasewood, the staples of campfires farther north, weren't so common here, but the troopers had scoured the desert roundabout for what they could find, and had also cut down a good many of the cottonwoods and mesquite trees growing alongside the San Pedro River. At this season of the year, the San Pedro was as thin and lethargic a stream as the Rio Grande, but it kept the trees alive.

Firelight gleamed off cannons, reflected palely from tent canvas, and showed row on row of tethered horses and camels, the latter being closer to Stuart's shelter. Men lined up to get their tin plates filled from the pots hanging over cookfires, and carried beans and salt pork and hardtack back toward their tents with every sign of satisfaction. Halting in mid-afternoon had let the cooks do a proper job of boiling the beans, instead of serving them up as hard little bullets as they so often did.

At five past ten, a scout led Major Horatio Sellers and an officer dressed in the dark blue wool of the U.S. Army up to Jeb Stuart. "General," Sellers said, "allow me to present to you Lieutenant Colonel Theron Winship, commander of the U.S. forces in Contention City."

"Very pleased to make your acquaintance," Stuart said politely, shaking hands with the U.S. officer, a sun-browned fellow in his early forties with a neat blond beard. Stuart waved to the fires and tents behind him. "I have no doubt of the courage of your soldiers, sir, but, as you see, we are present in such force as to make any resistance on your part not only foolish but suicidal."

Winship turned and stared. Not far away, a camel brayed, a hideous, almost unearthly sound. Winship's eyes swung to the beast and fixed on it for close to half a minute. Then he surveyed the camp again. "General," he said at last, his voice hoarse, "had anyone told me you had even a brigade here, I'd have called him a liar to his face. How the devil you managed to move a whole goddamn division so far and so fast is beyond me. My hat's off to you, sir." Fitting action to word, he removed the broad-brimmed black felt from his head.

"I wouldn't have believed it myself," Major Sellers said solemnly. Stuart was about to kick him in the shins when he redeemed himself by adding, "But the general can do just about anything he sets his mind to."

"I've seen that," Winship said, his voice gloomy. "I was in the Army of the Potomac when he rode all the way around us during the Seven Days." Turning to Stuart, he asked, "What are your terms for the surrender of my force, sir?"

"About what you'd expect: men to stack arms and yield up all ammunition. You and your officers may keep your sidearms."

"Very well." Theron Winship looked at the acres of campfires, at the men moving from one to another, at the rows of tents, at the rows of animals—with another lingering glance of disbelief at the camels—and at the ranked field guns stretching back toward and into the night. "Under the circumstances, that's generous enough. I accept."

"Excellent," Stuart said briskly. "Major Sellers will accompany you back to Contention City, to make sure you are complying with the terms. We'll see you by eight tomorrow morning. Be ready to travel then."

They shook hands again. Horatio Sellers looked back toward Stuart. Stuart kept his face bland as grits without butter. With a grunt, Sellers and Lieutenant Colonel Winship rode north toward the Yankee garrison. When Stuart announced to his men that the U.S. officer had surrendered, their cheers and Rebel yells split the night.

As soon as it was light enough to travel, they rode up the San Pedro to Contention City. They reached the refining town before Stuart had said they would. He was glad to see the Yankee troops hadn't burned any of the stamping mills or refineries. He hadn't mentioned that when discussing the surrender with Lieutenant Colonel Winship, for fear of putting ideas in his head.

Winship had his men drawn up in formation, waiting for the Confederates. He had eight companies of infantry there, and a battery of field guns. Fighting from cover, he could have put up a formidable resistance.

When Stuart came up to him, the U.S. officer looked puzzled. "Where are the rest of your men, sir?" he asked. "Have you detached them for duty elsewhere, having obtained my capitulation?"

Stuart knew he should have answered *yes* to that, to increase Winship's confusion. But he couldn't resist the temptation to tell the truth: "Lieutenant Colonel, this is my entire force."

Winship needed a moment to take that in. When he did, he went purple under his coat of tan. "Why, you God-damned son of a bitch!" he shouted, which made his own men stare at him. "You hoaxed me. If I'd known this was all the men you had, I'd've fought—and I'd've whipped you, too."

"I doubt it," Stuart said, on the whole truthfully; Winship could have hurt him, but he didn't think the U.S. officer could have kept him out of Contention City if he had a mind to break in. He grinned at the furious Winship. "It doesn't matter anyhow, not now it doesn't. You're under my guns, sir."

"You hoaxed me," Winship repeated, as if ruses of war were not permitted. "Let me unstack my guns, General, and fight it out. Fair is fair, and this isn't. You got my surrender under false pretenses."

"Yes, and I'm going to keep it, too," Stuart said cheerfully. "My men worked long and hard to set up that camp and all those fires last night. If you think I'm going to waste what they did, Lieutenant Colonel, you can think again."

"It isn't right," Winship insisted. He kept staring at the Confederate soldiers who were taking charge of his men, as if still convinced there should have been five times as many of them as there were. His company officers, on the other hand, were looking at him. Jeb Stuart would not have been happy, were he on the receiving end of those looks.

More of his troopers, including a couple who knew a good deal about mining, went into the refining works. They came out with enormous smiles on their faces. "General, we're going to make us a hell of a lot of money on this little visit," one of them called to Stuart.

"Load up some wagons, then," Stuart answered. He detailed guards to try to make sure the profits accrued to the Confederate States rather than to individual soldiers.

"What are you going to do with us?" Theron Winship asked.

It was a good question. Most of the defenders of Contention City were infantrymen. They would have as hard a time keeping up with his troopers as his own foot soldiers would have done. Reluctantly, he decided he had to take them down into Sonora even so. "If I parole you, you'll still be able to fight Indians and free up other men to fight us," he told Winship. "You'll come along south with us, and probably sit out the rest of the war in Hermosillo."

If that prospect appealed to the U.S. officer, he concealed it very well. "General, you've just made a hash of my military career," he said bitterly.

"That's too bad," Stuart answered. "If things had gone the other way, though, you would have made a hash of mine. Since those are my only two choices, I know which one I'd pick if I had my druthers. And since I do—"

Since he did, his soldiers methodically plundered the mineral wealth of Contention City, then set fire to the stamping mills and refineries. With great clouds of black smoke rising behind them, they started south down the San Pedro River toward the border between New Mexico Territory and Sonora.

They didn't push the pace now, not with prisoners marching on foot and the sun blazing down from the sky. Even as things were, men and animals suffered from the heat. It wasn't nearly so humid as it would have been back in New Orleans or Richmond, but it was fifteen degrees or so hotter than it would have been back East, which rendered the advantage meaningless.

To Stuart's disappointment, they didn't reach the deceitfully oversized camp with which he'd fooled Theron Winship before darkness forced a halt to the day's travel. The Confederate commander was proud of his work, and wanted to show it to Winship in detail. Whether the man he'd gulled would have appreciated it never crossed his mind.

Stuart had already fallen asleep when Major Sellers came into his tent and shook him back to consciousness. "Sorry to bother you, sir," he said while Stuart groaned and sat up on his folding bed, "but there's some Indians out there want to have a powwow with you."

"Scouts bring 'em in?" Stuart asked, pulling on his boots.

"Uh, no, sir," his aide-de-camp answered. "One second they weren't anywhere around. Next thing anybody knew, they were right in front of your tent. They could have come in if they'd had a mind to. They said they've been watching us all day, and we never set eyes on them once."

"They're good at that," Stuart remarked. He stepped out into the night. Sure enough, half a dozen Indians stood there waiting, some with U.S. Springfields, the rest carrying Winchesters. The oldest of them, a stocky fellow in his late fifties or early sixties, let loose with a stream of Spanish. Stuart, unfortunately, knew none.

One of the younger Indians, who had a look of the older, saw that and translated: "My father likes the way you tricked the bluecoats. He wants to fight the bluecoats at your side. He has been fighting them alone too long." More talk from the old man, this time in his own gurgling tongue. Again, the younger one spoke for him: "He wants—sanctuary, is that the word?—for his band of the *Dineh*, the Apaches, you would say, in Sonora, like the Confederacy gives to the tribes in the Indian Territory who fight against the USA. When Sonora belonged to Mexico, the bluecoats would chase us over the border. The Confederate States are strong, and will not let that happen. We will fight for you because of this."

"Does he?" Stuart said. "Will you?" Whoever the old Indian was, he had an astute understanding of the way the Confederacy dealt with the Indian tribes along the U.S. border. If he had any power, he might make a useful ally. Even if he was only a bandit chief, his men would make useful scouts. Stuart spoke carefully to the younger Indian: "Tell your father I thank him. Tell him that because I am new in this country, I do not recognize him by sight no matter how famous he may be, but perhaps I will know his name if he gives it to me."

The younger Indian spoke in Apache. When he fell silent, his father nodded to Stuart, then pointed to his own chest. "Geronimo," he said.

Riding over the prairie somewhere between Wichita and the border with the Indian Territory and the Confederacy, Colonel George Custer was in a foul mood. "I have the Thanks of Congress back in my quarters at Fort Dodge," he said to his brother, "there up on the wall where everyone can see it. And what is it for, I ask you?" He answered his own question: "For going after the enemy and hitting him a good lick. It was your idea, I know, but I'm the one with the eagles on my shoulders, so the scroll came to me."

"Don't fret yourself about that, Autie," Tom Custer said. He was not and never had been jealous of his older brother. "Plenty of chances for glory to come our way."

"Not when we're doing what we're doing," Custer ground out. "The Rebs poked at Wichita once, so we have to gallop back and forth to make sure they don't do it again. I tell you, it makes us look like a prizefighter covering up where he got hit last instead of doing any punching himself. And for what? For Wichita?" He clapped a hand to his forehead in florid disbelief.

"It's not much of a town," Tom agreed.

"Not much of a town?" Custer said. "Not much of a town? If it weren't on the railroad, it wouldn't have any reason for existing. Oh, the Rebs shipped a few cows through there ten years ago, when they were still pretending to be nice fellows, but they gave that up a good while ago. Now it just sits there, bleaching in the sun like any old bones. And we have to defend it?" He rolled his eyes.

"We have to defend the railroad line and the telegraph, too," Tom said.

Custer sighed. His brother had advanced the one irrefutable argument. Without the railroads and the talking wire, travel and information in the United States would move as slowly as they had in the days of the Roman Empire. Even bereft of the Confederate States, the United States were too vast to let Roman methods work.

"Trouble is," Custer said, "if we try to defend the whole line of the railroad, that ties up so many men, we can't do much else in these parts."

"I know," Tom answered. "If it's any consolation to you, Autie, the Rebs have exactly the same problem in Texas."

"The only way I want the Rebs to have my problems is for them to have problems I give 'em," Custer said, which made his brother laugh. "I don't want any problems myself, and they're welcome to as many I don't have as they like."

He waved back toward the two Gatling guns, which weren't having any trouble keeping up with his troopers. The men weren't going flat out, of course, and he'd taken pains to make sure the Gatlings had fine horses pulling them. Tom understood his gesture perfectly, saying, "Yes, that's the kind of problem the Rebels should have, all right. Those guns mowed them down same as they did to the Kiowas."

One of Custer's men let out a yell. The colonel's first glance was to the south—were they about to collide with the Confederates? He looked around for a rise on which to site the Gatling guns. What had worked once would probably work twice.

But he saw no Rebel horsemen, nor Indians, either. More troopers were calling out now, and some of them pointing north. Custer spied a courier riding hard for the regiment. He waved to the bugler, who blew Halt. The men reined in. A couple of them took advantage of the stop by getting out their tobacco pouches and rolling cigarettes.

Bringing his lathered horse to a halt, the courier thrust an envelope at Custer. "Urgent, sir," he said, saluting. "From Brigadier General Pope, up at Fort Catton."

Custer stared at him. "Good God," he said. "That's all the way up in Nebraska." The troopers close enough to have heard him started buzzing with speculation. He didn't blame them. Why the devil was General Pope reaching down to the border with the CSA?

Only one way to find out. Custer tore the envelope open and read the orders it contained. When he was done, he read them again. They still said the same thing, no matter how hard a time he had believing it. "What's the news, Autie?" Tom Custer demanded impatiently.

"We—the whole regiment, including the Gatlings—are ordered to report to Fort Catton as expeditiously as possible." Custer knew he sounded numb. He couldn't help it. In the slang of the War of Secession, this was a big thing, and no mistake. "A regiment of volunteer cavalry will take over patrolling here in southern Kansas."

"Fort Catton? On the Platte?" Tom sounded as bewildered as his brother felt. "It's a couple of hundred miles from here, and a couple of hundred miles from any fighting, too. Why don't they send the volunteers there?"

"I don't know. It says we'll get further orders when we arrive." Custer pointed to the courier. "You there, Corporal—do you know anything more about this?"

"No, sir," the horseman answered: a simple but uninformative reply.

"What in the blue blazes does General Pope want with me?" Custer muttered. He wondered if it dated back to his service on

McClellan's staff during the War of Secession. Pope and Little Mac had been fierce rivals then. After Lee whipped Pope at Second Manassas, Lincoln had relegated Pope to fighting Indians in the West, and he'd been here ever since. Of course, a little later on Lee had whipped McClellan even worse up at Camp Hill. That relegated the whole war to the ash heap, so Pope was in a sense already vindicated.

"We'll have to find out when we get there, that's all," Tom said. He worried less about Army politics than his brother did. If it was a legal order, he would obey it, and that was that.

And it was a legal order. No questions there. Custer muttered again, this time something Libbie would not have approved of. But Libbie was in Fort Dodge. Who could guess when he would have the pleasure of sleeping in the same bed with her again? He raised his voice and called out to his troopers: "We are ordered to Fort Catton, men, and to leave the defense of the plains to others." Through the surprised exclamations the horsemen sent up, he went on, "We are ordered to reach the fort as quickly as we can. By the speed with which we arrive, I want to show General Pope what sort of men he is getting when he calls upon the Fifth Regiment." The troopers raised a cheer and set out to the north with a will. Not all of them were disappointed to ride away from the dangers of combat.

Fort Catton lay by the confluence of the North Platte and South Platte, across the river from the Union Pacific tracks. From southern Kansas, Custer and his command reached it in a week. The pace told on the men—and even more on the horses. Had Custer had to go much farther, he could not have pressed so hard. But the surprise the sentries at the fort showed when he and the regiment arrived made up for a lot of weariness and discomfort.

He found himself ushered immediately into Brigadier General Pope's office. Pope was a handsome man of about sixty, who wore his hair long—though not so long as Custer did—and had a fine silver beard. "I am altogether delighted to see you here so promptly, Colonel," he said in a deep, rumbling voice; he'd had a reputation for bombast during the War of Secession, and hadn't changed since.

"Reporting as ordered, sir," Custer said. "The orders you sent me said I would receiver further information on coming here."

"And so you shall," Pope declared. "Colonel, President Blaine has named me military governor of Utah Territory. The Mormons there are this far—*this* far, Colonel"—he held thumb and forefinger together so they almost touched—"from open revolt against the authority of the United States. They have cut off rail service through the Territory, and telegraphy as well. I am charged with restoring them to their allegiance to the USA by any means necessary, and I intend to do exactly that."

"Yes, sir. I see, sir." Custer hadn't heard anything about what the Mormons were up to, but he'd been in the field and then on a forced march. "Trying to take advantage of our being busy elsewhere, are they? A coward's trick, sir, if you care anything for my opinion."

"That is my precise view of the situation, Colonel," Pope said, beaming. "I aim to bring them to heel and to keep them from perpetrating any such outrage in the future. We've tolerated their evil sensuality far too long, and what is our reward? Disloyalty. Well, thanks to it, they have placed themselves beyond the pale. I am assured on highest authority that whatever I do will be accepted, as long as they are reduced to obedience."

"Very good, sir." Custer breathed a silent sigh of relief that arguments left over from the War of Secession were not what had brought him here. Now to find out what had: "How does my regiment fit into your plan, sir?"

"I am assembling an army with which to occupy the Territory, especially the essential rail lines," Pope said. Custer remembered his own recent thoughts on the importance of railroads. Pope went on, "You and your men have already shown you can do good work, and, as regulars, are more reliable than volunteer units. And I have noted your success with the Gatling gun. I aim to overawe the Mormons, to demonstrate how futile any resistance to my might must be. Many of them, no doubt, have rifles. But they have no artillery to speak of, and they have no Gatlings. Once they see the destructive power of these weapons, they will be less inclined to try anything rash, and more likely to suffer if they do."

"Yes, sir!" Custer said enthusiastically. He hesitated, then asked, "And if they persist in their foolishness, sir? If they attempt to resist us by force of arms?"

"If they are so stupid, Colonel, then we wipe them off the face of the earth." Pope sounded as if he looked forward to such a result. "That's what we've done with the savages who presumed to challenge our expansion over the western plains, and that's what we'll do with the Mormons. If they resist us, they deserve destruction even more than the redskins, for they are not primitive by nature, but rather men of our own stock corrupted by a wicked, perverse, and licentious doctrine."

"Yes, sir," Custer said again. Having come out of McClellan's camp, with the natural bias of Little Mac's staff officers against the Young Napoleon's rivals, he had never imagined John Pope to be a man of such obvious and evident good sense. "If they transgress against the moral code universally recognized as correct and legitimate, on their heads be it."

"Well said." Pope was studying Custer with some of the same surprise with which Custer had eyed him. After coughing once or twice, the brigadier general said, "I hope you will forgive my saying this, Colonel, but I had not expected us to see so many things in so nearly the same light."

"If the general will pardon me, sir, neither had I," Custer answered. "I suspect we are both bound by the prejudices of the past." Impulsively, Custer thrust out his hand. Pope clasped it. Custer went on, "The only enemies I recognize as such—the only enemies I have ever recognized as such—are the enemies of the United States of America."

"I think we shall work very well together, then, for my attitude is the same in every particular," Pope said. His smile, which showed a couple of missing teeth, was not altogether pleasant. "Do you know who happens to be in Salt Lake City at the moment, Colonel?" When Custer shook his head, Pope took no small pleasure in enlightening him: "Abraham Lincoln. I have it on good authority from the War Department."

"Is he, by thunder?" Custer said. "Well, there's the first good reason I've heard yet for letting the Mormons go their own way."

John Pope stared at him, then threw back his head and roared Jovian laughter. "That's good, Colonel; that's very good indeed. It hadn't occurred to me, but I suppose it's true that those who were of General McClellan's party have as much cause to deprecate the capacity of our former chief executive as I do myself." Plainly, he'd forgotten nothing over the years: neither his rivalry with McClellan nor his humiliation at being so ignominiously sent to the sidelines after failing against Lee and Jackson.

Custer said, "Sir, I don't know of any U.S. officer serving during the War of Secession who does not have good cause to deprecate the capacity of Honest Abe, such as it is. I do know that the only good thing I've had to say about the Republican Party in all the years since is that they've finally given us the chance to have another go at the Confederate States—and now the Mormons are trying to interfere with that."

This time, Pope reached out to shake Custer's hand. "Colonel, whatever hard feelings may have existed between us in the past, I am suddenly certain we shall work together very well indeed." Custer beamed at him. He was suddenly certain of the same thing. Pope took a bottle and a couple of glasses from a desk drawer. He poured amber liquid into the glasses, then passed one to Custer. "Down with the Mormons, and with Abe Lincoln, too!"

"I'm normally teetotal, General, but how can I resist a toast like that?" Custer drank the whiskey. It burned his throat; he'd drunk hardly at all since the War of Secession. Manfully, he didn't cough. In his stomach, it was warm.

Philadelphia struck Alfred von Schlieffen as being a real city, a city with past, present, and future. Washington, D.C., had always given him the impression of existing in a world of its own, slightly skewed from the rest of the planet. Because it had sprung *ex nihilo* from the wilderness by government fiat, it lacked many of the irregularities and imperfections that made cities interesting and different from one another. And, existing as it had for a generation under the guns of the Confederate States, Washington had also felt impermanent, as if it was liable to be smashed to bits at any moment.

"And so it has been," Schlieffen murmured. Some of the staff of the German ministry remained behind in Washington; the Confederates had not tried to occupy it, and their bombardment was desultory these days. Schlieffen and Kurd von Schlözer had come north, though, the military attaché to maintain his connections in the War Department, the minister to offer whatever services in the cause of peace he could to President Blaine and to represent the interests of Great Britain (though not those of France) with the U.S. government.

Grudgingly, Schlieffen conceded that the War Department's move from Washington up to Philadelphia had gone more smoothly than he'd expected. "But," he said to the German minister after the two of them had settled into offices at the headquarters of the German consul in Philadelphia (a prominent sausage merchant), "but, I say, Your Excellency, they were madmen—madmen, I tell you—to delay so long. One well-placed Confederate shell and the United States would have had no War Department left."

"I am not saying you are mistaken, Colonel Schlieffen." Schlözer paused to make a production of lighting a large, smelly cigar—the larger and smellier the cigar, the better he liked it. "I am asking whether it would have made much difference in the way the United States are conducting the war if they were suddenly bereft of this department."

Seeing General Rosecrans leaving Washington, Schlieffen had wondered the same thing. Now he considered the question objectively, as he had been trained to do while serving on the General Staff. "Do you know, Your Excellency, it is very possible that you are right. The general-in-chief has not the competence to serve in his capacity."

"That is your judgment to make, Colonel, but it is not precisely what I meant in any case." Kurd von Schlözer blew a meditative and rather lopsided smoke ring. "The individual American, or the small group of Americans, has far more ingenuity and initiative than the individual German or small group of Germans. But we are much better at harnessing many small groups to work together for a common purpose. The Americans might be better off without anyone trying to impose order on them, for they do not take to it well."

"You have said several things on this order," Schlieffen replied thoughtfully. "If you are correct, this country must be doomed to anarchy before too long. I would call that a pity, the Americans' situation on this continent having so much in common with our own in Europe."

"If they would set their house in order, they might make valuable allies," Schlözer agreed. "They might make allies of sorts in any case, but they would be worth more if they regimented themselves better."

"This is true of anyone," Schlieffen said, as if quoting God's law from Deuteronomy. Trying to be charitable, he went on, "Even we Prussians needed to put our house in order after Napoleon defeated us."

"Defeat is often a salutary lesson," Schlözer said, nodding. "Of course, a generation ago, the United States were defeated in the War of Secession, and seem to have learned little from that. They made an even greater point of antagonizing Britain and France this time than in the previous war."

"I wonder what the Confederate States have learned," Schlieffen said. "They are full of Americans, too."

"They have learned at least one thing the United States have not," the German minister replied. He waited for Schlieffen to make a polite interrogative noise, then went on, "They have learned to make alliances, and to make those alliances last. The folk of the United States are so cross-grained, this seems not to have occurred to them, and that the Confederate States can do it is certainly part of the resentment the United States bear against them."

"Foolishness," Schlieffen said, like a man judging the antics of a neighbor who, while a good enough fellow, could not keep from getting drunk three nights a week. "If the United States are not strong enough to do as they desire by themselves, they need allies of their own."

"The last allies they had were France and Spain, in their war of rebellion against Britain," Schlözer said. "Since then, they have lost the knack for making them. They lived alone behind the Atlantic, and, like a woodcutter alone in the forest, forgot how to make friends with others. Now, with the Confederate States bringing alliances to the American continent, the United States need to relearn the arts of diplomacy." He sighed. "They have not yet taken this lesson to heart."

"If they learn the lessons of war well enough, the lessons of diplomacy matter less," Schlieffen said. One corner of his mouth twitched, a gesture of irony as dramatic as any he permitted himself. "They have, unfortunately, shown no great aptitude for the lessons of war, either."

"It is a pity," Kurd von Schlözer said.

"Also a pity that I have not yet been permitted to observe any of the war save the Confederate bombardment of Washington, and that observation was not thanks to the good offices of the government of the United States," Schlieffen said.

"As you requested, Colonel, I have laid on the carriage for you today, so that you may go down to the War Department and protest once more," Schlözer said.

"For this I thank you very much," Schlieffen said. "It is important that I do observe and report my findings to the Fatherland. Weapons have advanced considerably since we fought the French. As with the late war between the Russians and the Turks, what we learn here will apply to any future conflicts of ours. The Russians and Turks were less than strategically astute, I must say, and so are the USA and CSA, but still—"

"I have in the past heard you speak well of Confederate strategy and tactics," Schlözer said.

"Compared to those of the United States, yes," Schlieffen said. "Compared to ours, no." And then, because he was a judicious man, he added, "On the whole, no. Some of what they do shows a certain amount of insight, I admit."

He took his leave of the German minister of the United States and went downstairs, where the carriage was indeed waiting for him. Gustav Kleinvogel's sausage factory, and, therefore, the German consulate, and, therefore, for the time being, the German ministry, were in the appropriately named Germantown district, north of Philadelphia's city center. It was also appropriate, Schlieffen thought as he got into the carriage, for politics and sausage making to be so inextricably mixed. As Bismarck had observed, in neither did it pay to examine too closely the ingredients that went into the final product.

Washington's reason for being was—or perhaps had been—government. Philadelphia had been a thriving port and industrial center for many years before the results of the War of Secession forced big chunks of the government of the United States to move north, away from the muzzles of Confederate cannon. Factories belched black smoke into the air. So did the stacks of steamships and trains bringing raw materials into the city and taking away finished goods. Schlieffen looked on the smoke with approval, as a sign of modernity.

In Philadelphia, the War Department operated out of a building of muddy-brown brick northwest of Franklin Square. It was, Schlieffen thought, an even homelier edifice than the one next to the White House in Washington. He was of the opinion that the military should have the finest headquarters possible, to hearten the men who protected the nation. The view of the United States seemed to be that the military, like any other arm of the government, rated only the cheapest headquarters possible.

The sentries at the entrance were not so well trained as those with whom he had dealt in Washington. That his uniform was close to the shade of theirs convinced them he was no Confederate, but they had not the slightest clue as to what a military attaché was, what he did, or what his privileges were. He had to grow quite severe before one of them would take a message announcing his presence up to General Rosecrans' office. The fellow returned looking flabbergasted at bearing the news that Rosecrans would see Schlieffen at once.

A different sentry escorted him up to the office of the general-in-chief. In the outer office, he traded English for Captain Berryman's German. He listened to the bright young adjutant with only half an ear, for in the inner office General Rosecrans was bellowing, "Yes, Mr. President . . . I'll try and take care of it, Your Excellency . . . Yes, of course." That left Schlieffen puzzled, for he could not hear President Blaine at all, and the chief executive of the United States did not have a reputation for being soft-spoken—on the contrary.

Presently, Rosecrans came out into the antechamber. Looking harassed, he said, "Captain, I am convinced the telephone is an invention of the devil, inflicted upon us poor soldiers so politicians can harangue us at any hour of the day or night, without even the pause for thought sending a telegram affords." That off his chest, he deigned to notice Schlieffen. "Come in, Colonel, come in," he said, invitingly standing aside from the doorway. "Believe me, it will be a pleasure to talk with a man who knows what he's talking about. Have you got telephones in Germany, Colonel?"

"I believe we are beginning to use them, yes," Schlieffen said, eyeing with interest the wooden box and small attached speaking trumpet bolted to the wall by Rosecrans' desk.

"Invention of the devil," Rosecrans repeated. "Nothing but trouble." He waved his visitor to a chair, then asked, "And what can I do for you today besides complain about inventors who should have been strangled in the cradle? Bell's a Canadian, which probably explains a good deal."

It explained nothing to Schlieffen. Since it didn't, he came straight to the point: "As I asked in Washington, General, I should like to get a close view of the fighting in this war. Perhaps you will be so kind as to authorize my travel for this purpose to the headquarters of one of your armies in the field."

"Very well, Colonel; I can do that." Rosecrans had made promises before. Schlieffen was about to ask him to be more specific when he did so unasked: "We are going to take Louisville away from the Rebs. How would you like to watch us while we're doing that?"

Schlieffen glanced at the map hanging by the telephone. "You will send me to the province of Indiana? The state, I should say—excuse me. You plan on crossing the Ohio River to make your assault? Yes, I should be most interested in seeing that." If France ever mounted an invasion of Germany, she would have to cross the Rhine. Seeing how the United States attempted a river crossing in the face of opposition would tell Schlieffen something of what the French might try; seeing how the Confederates defended the province—no, the state—of Kentucky would also be informative.

"Well, that's easy enough, isn't it?" Rosecrans reached into his desk for stationery and with his own hand wrote the authorization Schlieffen needed. "Nice to know *something* is easy, by thunder. The Rebs aren't—I'm finding that out. But you hang onto that sheet there, and I'll send a telegram letting 'em know you're on the way."

"Thank you very much," Schlieffen said, and then, sympathetically, "A pity your arms did not have better luck in Virginia."

Rosecrans flushed. "They have Stonewall, dammit," he muttered. He had an ugly expression on his face, to go with the ugly color he'd turned. Austrian generals—and Prussian generals, too—must have talked that way about Bonaparte. Austrian generals—and French generals, too—must have talked that way about Moltke.

Sympathetically still, Schlieffen said, "As you have said to me, your land is wide. General Jackson cannot be everywhere at once, cannot take charge of all the battles your two countries are fighting."

"Thank God for that," Rosecrans said. The telephone on the wall clanged, like a trolley using its bell to warn traffic at a corner. Rosecrans went over to it. He listened, then shouted, "Hello again, Mr. President." That hunted look came back onto his face. Schlieffen left before the general had to order him out. As he walked down the hall toward the stairs, he heard Rosecrans still shouting behind him. All at once, he hoped the General Staff back home in Berlin did without this newfangled invention.

* * *

"Come on!" Samuel Clemens fussed like a mother hen. "Come on, everyone. We've no time to waste, not a single, solitary minute."

Alexandra Clemens set her hands on her hips. "Sam, if you'll look around, you'll see that you're the only one here who isn't ready for the picnic."

"Well, what has that got to do with the price of persimmons?" Sam demanded. "Pshaw! If you hadn't stolen my jacket, I'd have it on by now."

His wife didn't know anything about persimmons: she was that rarity, a native San Franciscan, having been born a little more than a year after the gold rush started Americans flooding into California. She did, however, know where his jacket was: "It's hanging on the chair behind you there, Sam, where you put it when you looked under the bed for your shoes."

"And I found them, too, didn't I?" Clemens said, as if in triumph. He put on the white linen jacket, jammed a hat down over his ears, and handed Alexandra a sunbonnet. "There! All ready. Now we'd better see what mischief the children have got into since you started hiding things from me."

Ignoring that sally, Alexandra Clemens said, "They *are* being quiet downstairs, aren't they?" She swept out of the bedroom in a rustle of skirts. "What *are* they doing?" Sam hurried after her.

The quiet broke even as they hurried—broke into shouts from both Orion and Ophelia, a growl from Sutro the dog, and a series of yowls and hisses from Virginia the cat. Virginia shot by at a speed that would have done credit to a Nevada jackrabbit, then vanished under the sofa in lieu of diving into a hole in the ground.

"She scratched me!" Ophelia said. "Bad kitty!"

Sam examined the damage, which was superficial. "The next question before the house, young lady, is why she scratched you."

Ophelia stood mute. Orion, either more naive or less sure of how much his parents had seen, said, "We weren't really trying to feed Ginny to Sutro, Pa. It just looked that way, honest Injun."

"Did it?" Sam said. Departure for the picnic was briefly delayed for reasons having nothing to do with missing clothes. When Orion and Ophelia climbed up into the family buggy, they took their seats with considerable caution. Above their heads, Sam and Alexandra looked into each other's eyes. That might have been a mistake. They both had all they could do to keep from laughing.

The horse went down a couple of blocks to Fulton, and then west to Golden Gate Park, a narrow rectangle of land south of the Richmond district. Much of it was sand dunes and scrubby grass. Here and there, where irrigation and better soil had been brought in, real grass grew and young, hopeful trees sprouted.

Sam tethered the horse to an oak that had advanced further beyond saplinghood than most. He gave it a long lead, so it could crop the grass and, thus distracted, not interfere with the family's enjoyment of a Sunday afternoon. Having explained this to his wife, he added, "Don't you wish we could do the same with the children?"

"Not more than half a dozen times a day," Alexandra answered. "Not usually, anyhow." She spread a blanket on the grass, then set the picnic hamper upon it. Ham sandwiches and fried shrimp from a Chinese café and hard-boiled eggs—not the elderly sort the Chinese esteemed—and a homemade peach pie and cream puffs from an Italian bakery and lemonade were enough to keep the children from running wild for a while, and gave them sufficient ballast once they were through to slow them down for a while.

"Ha! First match!" Sam said proudly once he got his cigar going. That proved what a fine, mild day it was. The wind blew off the Pacific, as it almost always did, but only gently. "It's not strong enough to lift sand today, let alone dogs, trees, houses, or one of Mayor Sutro's public proclamations," he added. "Of course, they call *that* kind of wind a cyclone."

"*I* call that kind of wind an editorial," Alexandra said, which made him mime being cut to the quick.

Other picnicking families dotted the grass of the park. Children ran and played and got into fights. Boys barked their bare knees. Somebody who'd brought a bottle of something that wasn't lemonade started singing loudly and badly. Sam lay back, watched the gulls wheeling through the blue sky, and declared, "I refuse to let myself despair on account of God's creation being imperfect to the extent of one noisy drunk."

Alexandra reached out and ruffled his hair. "I'm sure He could have done a much better job if only He'd listened to you."

"It's so nice to know, my dear, that we can stay together when they start burning freethinkers," he said, quite without irony. "And to think that, if I'd left San Francisco, I never would have met you. I didn't intend to settle down here, not for good." He started another cigar, also on the first match. "But it has turned out to be good, I'd say."

Before Alexandra could answer—if she was going to answer with anything more than a smile—the breeze brought a thin series of cries from the west: "Hut! Hut! Hut hut hut!"

"Hear that?" Orion said to Ophelia, who nodded. "You know what it is?" She shook her head. He was jumping up and down with excitement. "That's soldiers, that's what it is!" He ran off, legs pumping. His little sister followed a moment later, slower both because she was younger and because her dress dragged the ground, but determined even so.

Samuel Clemens got to his feet. "Those *are* soldiers, of sorts," he said; he knew the sounds of drill when he heard them. "I'd forgotten they were teaching the volunteers to walk—I beg your pardon, to march—in the park. I think I'll have a look at them myself. After all, they may be protecting us one day soon—and if that notion doesn't frighten you, for heaven's sake why not?"

"Go ahead," Alexandra said. "I'll stay here and make sure things don't take a mind to wander off by themselves."

Only a couple of low swells of ground had hidden the volunteer troops from Sam. There on the grass, surrounded by admirers, a company raggedly marched and countermarched. Seeing them took Clemens back across the years to his own brief service as a Confederate volunteer. They looked just the way his comrades had: like men who wanted to be soldiers but didn't have it down yet.

About half of them wore Army blouses. About half wore Army trousers. Only a few wore both. The rest of the clothes were a motley mixture of civilian styles. A few carried Army Springfields. Rather more had Winchesters, probably their own weapons. Many still shouldered boards in place of rifles.

"Left!" shouted the sergeant drilling them, a grizzled veteran no doubt from the Presidio. A majority of them did start out with the left foot. He cursed the rest with fury enough to make women flee, small boys cheer, and Clemens smile reminiscently. No, sergeants hadn't changed a bit.

Somebody called, "What the devil good are you people if you can't get to where the shooting's at because the Mormons have the railroad blocked?"

One of the volunteers took the board off his shoulder and thrust with it as if it were a bayoneted Springfield. "We ain't afraid o' no Mormons," he declared, "nor their wives, neither. They send us east, we'll clean them bastards out and then go on and slaughter the Rebs." Spectators burst into applause.

The drill sergeant was less impressed. "Pay attention to what I tell you, Henry, you goddamn stupid jackass," he bellowed. "Forget about these, these, these—*civilians*." He could have cursed for a day and a half without venting more scorn than he packed into the single word. Still in stentorian tones, he went on, "How do you know that nosy bastard isn't a Confederate spy?"

"I am not!" the man so described said indignantly.

"I'm sorry, Sergeant," Henry said. "I didn't think."

"Of course you didn't think," the sergeant snarled. "You've got your brains in your backside, and you blow 'em out every time you go to the latrine. And you're not sorry yet. You haven't even started being sorry yet. But you will be, oh yes you will." He spoke in somber anticipation of disaster still ahead for the unfortunate volunteer private. "Hut! Hut! Hut hut hut!"

A small hand tugged at Sam's trouser leg. Face shining, Orion looked up at him. "I wanna be a soldier, Pa, and have a gun. Can I be a soldier when I get big?"

Before Clemens could answer that, Ophelia, who'd tagged after her brother, shook her head so vehemently that golden curls flew out from under the edge of her bonnet. "Not me," she said, and folded her arms across her chest as if things were already settled. "I want to be a *sergeant*."

Sam threw back his head and shouted laughter. He picked up Ophelia, spun her through the air till she squealed, then set her back on the ground. "I think you'll do it, too, little one—either that or wife, which is the same job except you don't get to wear stripes on your sleeve."

"What about me, Pa?" Orion jumped up and down. "Pa, what about me?"

"Well, what about you?" Clemens spun his son around and around, too. By the time he put Orion down, the boy was too dizzy to walk, and had had all thoughts of soldiering whirled out of his head. Sam hoped they wouldn't come back. Having been a small boy himself, he knew what a forlorn hope that was.

When Orion was steady on his pins, Sam took both children

back to Alexandra. As if by magic, she produced two more cream puffs. That partially reconciled Ophelia and Orion to going home.

Alexandra was putting the picnic hamper back in the buggy and Sam folding the blanket so he could lay it on top of the hamper when a great roar, like a rifle shot magnified a hundred-fold, smote the air. Even the gulls in the sky went silent for a moment, then screeched their anger at being frightened so.

Ophelia squealed. Orion jumped. "Good heavens!" Alexandra said. "What was that?"

"One of the big guns up at the Presidio," Sam answered. "They've had guns there since this place belonged to Spain—never mind Mexico. I don't think any of them have ever shot at anything." Another roar, identical to the first, disturbed the tranquility of Golden Gate Park—and of the rest of San Francisco, and, no doubt, of a good stretch of surrounding landscape as well. Sam thoughtfully peered northward. "Sounds like they're getting ready to, though, doesn't it?"

"Golly!" Orion said. "It'd be fun to shoot one of those." This time, Ophelia agreed with her brother.

"How much fun do you think it would be to have somebody shooting one at you?" Sam asked. His children stared at him. That side of war meant nothing to them. It seldom meant anything to anyone till the first bullet flew past him.

The coast-defense guns kept firing as Sam drove home. "By the sound of them," Alexandra said, "they think we're going to be attacked tomorrow."

"Whatever else may happen in this curious world of ours, my dear, I don't expect the Confederate Navy to come steaming into San Francisco Bay tomorrow, flags flying and guns blazing." Sam winked at his wife. "Nor the day after, either."

"Well, no," Alexandra said. "Hardly." Another gun boomed. "I suppose they have to practice, the same as the soldiers you were watching."

"If they're no better at their jobs than those poor lugs, the Indians could paddle a fleet of birchbark canoes into the Bay and devastate the city." Sam held up a forefinger. "I exaggerate: a *flotilla* of canoes." That made Alexandra laugh, which was what he'd had in mind.

When they got back to the house on Turk Street, Ophelia and Orion ran themselves and the pets ragged. Watching them, listening to them, Sam wondered where they came by the energy;

even though they'd torn up Golden Gate Park all afternoon, they were still going strong. But, by the time he and Alexandra went through the house lighting the gas lamps, the children were fading. They went to bed with much less fuss than they usually put up, and fell asleep almost at once. Ophelia snored, but then Ophelia always snored.

Once things had been quiet for a while, Alexandra said, "Shall we go to bed, too?" By her tone of voice, she didn't mean, *Shall we go to sleep?*

"Yes, let's." Sam sounded casual, or thought he sounded casual, but the alacrity with which he leaped up and turned off the lamps they'd lighted not long before surely gave him away.

He turned off the bedroom lamp, too, before he and his wife undressed and lay down together. A thin stripe of moonlight came in through the window, just enough to make Alexandra's body, warm and soft in his arms, a more perfect mystery than complete darkness would have done.

She sighed and murmured when he kissed her, when he fondled her breasts and brought his mouth down to them, when his hand found the dampness at the joining of her thighs. As always, her excitement excited and embarrassed him at the same time. Doctors swore on a stack of Bibles that most women knew little or nothing of sexual pleasure, and did not care to make its acquaintance. But then, considering the track record doctors had elsewhere, how much did that prove?

With Alexandra, it proved very little. "Come on, Sam," she whispered after a while, and took him in hand to leave no doubt as to her meaning. Her legs drifted farther apart. He poised himself between them and guided himself into her. Her breath sighed out. When their lips met, she kissed him as she did at no other time. She worked with him while their pleasure built, and moaned and gasped and called his name when she reached the peak. Her nails were claws in his back, urging him on till he exploded a moment later.

When he would have flopped limply down onto her as if she were a feather bed, she poked him in the ribs. "Terrible woman," he said, and rolled off. It was mostly but not entirely a joke; the delight he took with her sometimes seemed scandalous, married though they were. If she felt any similar compunctions, she'd never once shown it.

They used the chamber pot under the bed and got into their

nightclothes in the dark. "Good night, dear," Alexandra said, her voice blurry.

"Good night," Sam answered, and kissed her. "Work tomorrow." In its own way, that was a curse as vile as any the foul-mouthed sergeant had used in Golden Gate Park.

Reveille blared from the bugler's horn. Theodore Roosevelt bounded out of his cot and groped for the spectacles on the stool next to it. "Half past five!" he exclaimed as he threw on his uniform: an obliging tailor in Helena had fitted him out. "What a wonderful time to be alive!"

He rushed from his tent into the cool sunshine of early morning. The ranch house stood, comfortable and reassuring, less than a hundred feet away. Roosevelt was glad to have an excuse to avoid comfort. Were comfort all he wanted, he could have stayed in New York State. When the men of Roosevelt's Unauthorized Regiment lived under canvas, their equally unauthorized colonel would not sleep in an ordinary bed with a roof over his head.

The men of the Unauthorized Regiment lived under a great variety of canvas. Some slept in tents that dated back to the War of Secession. Some, prospectors who'd heard of the Regiment when they came into Helena or another nearby town, had brought the tents in which they'd sheltered out in the wilderness. There were even a few who shared buffalo-hide teepees that might easily have belonged to the Sioux.

They came tumbling out now, routed by the strident notes of the morning call. The only thing uniform about their shirts and trousers and hats was a lack of uniformity. Some of them had one article or another of military clothing. Some were veterans, while others had acquired the gear from soldiers either leaving the service or selling it on the sly. Most, though, wore civilian clothes of varying degrees of quality and decrepitude. The variety in hats was particularly astonishing.

Whatever else the men had on, though, each of them wore a red bandanna tied around his left upper arm. That was the mark of the Unauthorized Regiment, and the men had already made it a mark to respect in every saloon within a day's ride of Roosevelt's ranch. Several loudmouths were nursing injuries of various sorts for having failed to respect it. No one was dead because of that, and, by now, odds were no one would be: roughnecks had learned the men of the Regiment looked after one another like brothers, and that a challenge to one was a challenge to all.

"Fall in by troops for roll call!" Roosevelt shouted. The men were already doing precisely that. They'd picked up the routine of military life in a hurry. Some, of course, had known it before, either half a lifetime earlier in the War of Secession or in the more recent campaigns against the Plains Indians. Their example rubbed off on the new volunteers—and on Roosevelt, who had everything he knew about running a regiment from tactical manuals by Hardee (even if he was a Rebel) and Upton. "Fall in for roll call!" he yelled again.

"Listen to the old man," one of the Unauthorized troopers said to a friend, who laughed and nodded. Roosevelt grinned from ear to ear. Both men were close to twice his age. That they granted him an informal title of respect usually given to an officer who *was* well up in years showed he'd won their respect as a commander: so he assured himself, anyhow.

Troop officers and noncoms—elected by their comrades, as had been done in volunteer regiments during the War of Secession—went through the men. They brought Roosevelt the returns: half a dozen sick, three absent without leave. "They're probably hung over in Helena, sir," one of the captains said.

"So they are," Roosevelt said grimly. "They'll be even sorrier than that when they turn up wagging their tails behind them, too." The manuals stressed an officer's need to be strict in the way he dealt with his men. The manuals, of course, were written for regulars; volunteers needed a lighter touch. Roosevelt's own inclination was to keep a light rein on his troopers as long as they went in the direction in which he wanted to guide them, but to land on them hard when they strayed from the straight and narrow.

After roll call, the bracing smell of brewing coffee filled the air as the men lined up for mess call. Along with the coffee, the cooks served up beans and salt pork, hardtack, bread, and rolls, and oatmeal. The road between Helena and Roosevelt's ranch was getting deep new ruts in it from supply wagons rattling back and forth. His bank account back in New York was getting deep new ruts in it, too. He noted that without worrying about it unduly; the country came first.

From breakfast, the troopers went to tend their horses. Along with beans and other provender for men, those wagons brought in hay by the ton, and oats to go with it. No one within a couple of miles downwind of the ranch could have had the slightest doubt that a great many horses were dwelling there. Flies got bad when the weather warmed up, but they hadn't started buzzing yet.

Philander Snow came up to Roosevelt; to Roosevelt's disappointment, he still showed no interest in joining the Regiment. Working in the fields and with the livestock—what the troopers hadn't eaten of it—contented him. Pausing now to spit, he observed, "One thing's plain as day, boss—you ain't gonna need to go out and buy manure for about the next hundred years."

"That's a fact, Phil," Roosevelt allowed. "A regiment's worth of horses leaves a lot on the ground, don't they?" A regiment's worth of cavalrymen left a lot on the ground, too. They'd already had to dig a couple of new sets of slit trenches. Roosevelt didn't want those too close to the creek or the well. That way lay sickness; the Roman legionaries had known as much. If typhoid—or, worse, cholera—broke out, he'd be down to half a regiment in nothing flat.

The first wagon of the day came rattling up from Helena a little past eight in the morning. Roosevelt's quartermaster sergeant, a skinny little fellow name Shadrach Perkins who was a storekeeper down in Wickes, took charge of the sacks of beans and crates of hardtack it contained. The teamster who'd driven the wagon to the ranch handed Roosevelt a copy of the *Helena Gazette*. "Hot off the press, Colonel," he said.

"Good," Roosevelt answered, and tossed him a ten-cent tip. Since the supply wagons had started coming up from Helena every day, he was far less cut off from the world than he had been before. Now, instead of waiting a week or two between looks at a newspaper, he got word of what was going on as fast as the telegraph brought it into town and the typesetters turned it into words on paper.

What Roosevelt read now made him paw the ground like one stallion challenging another over a mare. He felt that full of rage, too. "Richardson!" he roared. "Get your damn bugle, Richardson!" He fumed until the trumpeter came dashing up, horn in hand, then snapped, "Blow Assembly."

"All right, Colonel," Richardson answered. "What's up and gone south on us now?" Roosevelt glared at him till he raised the bugle to his lips and blasted out the call.

Men came running; a summons during morning fatigues was out of the ordinary and therefore a good bet to be interesting and maybe even important. The troopers buzzed with talk until Roosevelt strode out before them, *Helena Gazette* clenched in his left fist. "Do you men know—do you men have any idea—what the Confederate States, the English, and the French have had the infernal impudence to do?" he demanded.

"Reckon you're gonna tell us, ain't you, Colonel?" a trooper said.

Roosevelt ignored the distraction, which, for a man of his temperament, wasn't easy. But fury still consumed him. "They have had the gall, the nerve, to declare a blockade against the coasts and harbors of the United States of America—against *our* coasts and harbors, gentlemen, saying we have not got the right to conduct our own commerce." He squeezed the *Gazette* in his fist and waved it about, as if it were the criminal rather than the messenger. "Shall this great nation let such an insult stand?"

"No!" shouted the cavalry troopers, who were about as far from any coast as men in the United States could be.

"You're right, boys!" Roosevelt agreed. "We won't let it stand. By jingo, we *can't* let it stand. These vile foreign dogs will see they're barking at the wrong hound if they think they can impose themselves on the United States that way. We'll lick 'em back to their kennels with their tails between their legs."

By the time he was done whipping up the men, they were ready to ride for the Canadian border and shoot everybody they could catch who followed Queen Victoria instead of President Blaine. By the time he was done whipping himself up, he was ready to lead them over the border. He needed a distinct effort of will to remember his Regiment was still Unauthorized. If they went over the border, it wouldn't be war; it would be a filibustering expedition, and the enemy would be within his rights to treat them as bandits. He sighed. He hated having to remember such fine distinctions.

"Let's ride," he shouted. "To horse and let's ride! We cannot fight the backstabbing Englishman and complacent Canuck, not yet, not until we are formally invested with the mantle of the government of the United States. But we can ready ourselves so that, when the investiture comes—as it certainly shall—we'll be ready to do our all for the land we hold dear."

It wasn't what he'd planned to do with the day. It also wasn't the first time his impetuosity had run away with him. He knew himself well enough to be sure it wouldn't be the last time his

impetuosity ran away with him. The tide of cheers the men un-
leashed made breaking routine seem worthwhile.

Almost as fast as he would have liked, Roosevelt's Unauthorized Regiment was mounted and pounding north along the road
in a long, sinewy column of fours. They thundered past wagons
and buggies and lone horsemen who stared and stared at the
power Roosevelt had assembled and now controlled. Those stares
left him happier than the whiskey that flowed like water in the
Montana mining towns. Anyone could get a drink of whiskey.
Only a few men, special men, *great* men, attracted the awe the
Regiment gained for him.

"Heavens above, this is bully!" he cried in a great voice. Just
then, he would gladly have kept riding all the way to Canada. He
would gladly have kept riding all the way through Canada. With
the men he had at his back, he was sure he could do it.

Prudence prevailed, though. Montana Territory was as yet
thinly settled; finding open land on which the Regiment could
practice its evolutions was only a matter of riding out past the
little farms and herds of livestock that clung close to running
water. Once out on the prairie, the horsemen went through the
tedious but vital business of shifting from column into line, of
moving by the left flank and the right, and also, much to Roosevelt's delight, of charging straight at an unfortunately imaginary enemy.

But, because Roosevelt had read the latest tactical manuals,
the Unauthorized Regiment also practiced fighting as dragoons:
mounted infantry. With some of their number left behind to hold
horses, the rest tramped in skirmish lines through the grass and
brush. The troops' captains had to rotate the job of horse-holder
through their units, because everyone wanted to go forward and
no one was keen to be left behind.

As the afternoon wore along, Roosevelt came to another of his
snap decisions. "We'll sleep here in the open tonight, men," he
announced. "We need to be hardened, to ready ourselves against
the rigors of the field."

Some of the men—the lazy ones who hadn't bothered packing hardtack and salt pork in their knapsacks, unless Roosevelt
missed his guess—grumbled at that, but their comrades' jeers
squelched them. The soldiers (so Roosevelt insisted on thinking
of them, though they remained Unauthorized despite telegrams to

the War Department in Philadelphia) were getting the idea that they had to be prepared when they took the field.

"You never know what may happen," Roosevelt said. "You simply never know." He was looking north, toward Canada.

☆ VI ☆

Anna Douglass shook her finger at her husband. "You ain't never gonna ride on no steamboats no more," she said severely, as if to an errant child. "Never, do you hear me?"

"Yes, dear, I do," Frederick Douglass answered, his voice dutiful. "I am not traveling anywhere for the time being. I'll stay here in Rochester with you."

"That's not what I mean," his wife said in tones that brooked no argument. "Sooner or later, out you'll go again—but not by steamboat. Promise me, Frederick, as one Christian to another."

"I promise," Douglass said. These days, he refused Anna nothing she asked. Her health was visibly failing, while he remained robust. He let out a small sigh. He'd never meant to eclipse her, to have her live her life in his shadow, but that was how things had happened. In the beginning, she'd been above him: when they first came to know each other, back in Baltimore almost half a century earlier, she had been free while he still toiled in bondage. After his escape, he'd sent for her, and she'd come. In all the years since then, she'd given him a comfortable home from which he was too much absent and a fine family he'd had too small a part in raising. And now she got feebler by the day. He sighed again. There was nothing he could say, nothing he could do. It was years—decades—too late to say or do anything.

"Don't you worry about me," she said, picking a thought from his mind as a cunning thief might pick a wallet from a pocket. "I'll be fine. Whatever happens, the Lord will provide. But whatever happens, I don't want you ridin' on no steamboats."

"I already promised once," Douglass said. "The vow will not be made twice as strong by my repeating it."

"You just remember, that's all," Anna said, and hobbled back toward the kitchen, leaning heavily on her stick. Rheumatism made her joints ache.

Douglass knew he should have been writing, transmuting his few minutes of fear aboard the *Queen of the Ohio* into prose that would galvanize men both black and white to the effort needed to overthrow the Confederate States and thereby ameliorate the plight of the millions of Negroes still enslaved. His first pieces, which had talked of his own fear of reenslavement if the steamboat went aground on Confederate soil, had won wide notice and praise. The newspapers and magazines eagerly awaited more, and had made it plain they would pay well.

But, at the moment, the urge to write was not upon him. He shook his head and grimaced wryly. As a veteran newspaperman, he knew you wrote when you had to write, not when the Muse sprinkled fairy dust in your hair and tapped you with a magic wand. He also knew he didn't *have* to write quite yet. Instead of going upstairs to his study, he walked outside.

Out on the street, the grandson of one of his neighbors was trying to stay upright on an ordinary. The huge front wheel of the bicycle was almost as tall as its rider. As he pedaled along on a wavering course, he waved proudly to Douglass.

Douglass waved back. He'd lived in Rochester for almost thirty-five years, long enough for most people to have come to take him for granted in spite of his color. These days, the city did not separate Negroes by race on trolleys or omnibuses or in places accommodating the public. It hadn't been that way when Douglass first came to upstate New York. He knew no small pride in having had a lot to do with the changes over the years.

"Look out, Daniel!" he called, just too late. The ordinary went into a pothole and fell over, dashing its rider to the street from a considerable height. The boy picked himself up, picked up the bicycle, and sturdily clambered aboard once more. *You fall down till you do it right,* Douglass thought with an approving nod. *That's the only way to learn.*

Aside from a couple of church steeples, the biggest buildings on the skyline were boxy flour mills. Grain came into Rochester from all the surrounding countryside—the Genesee Valley held some of the finest farmland in the United States—and went out again by way of the Erie Canal, the railroads, and the Great Lakes. From his home, which stood near the crest of a small hill, Douglass could look out across the city to the gray-blue waters of

Lake Ontario. But for those waters' being fresh, he might have been looking out at the sea.

As always, barges and small steamers glided slowly across the lake. Pillars of smoke rose from their stacks, as they did from the stacks of Rochester's factories. The air, though, was far better than that in St. Louis or other western towns, for the coal burned here was of higher grade than what they used along the Mississippi.

Several unusually large plumes of smoke out on the lake caught Douglass' eye. The vessels from which those plumes sprang were also unusually large, and appeared to be moving together. They made Rochester seem more like a seaside town than ever; when he'd been in Boston and New York, he'd often watched flotillas of Navy ships steaming into port in tight formation like these.

No sooner had that thought crossed his mind than fresh clouds of smoke billowed from the ships. Douglass was seeing them from a long way off. For a moment, he wondered whether their boilers had burst. Then the roars, which took some little time to cross that distance, reached his ears. He froze in place, the ice of remembered terror shooting up his back. He'd heard explosions of that sort not long before, coming from the southern bank of the Ohio.

"Dear God," he groaned, "those are naval ships, all right, but they don't belong to the U.S. Navy."

Like foxes in a henhouse, the British warships (or would they be Canadian? Douglass worried little about such niceties, and suspected no one else worried any more), having fired warning shots to let the numerous grain- and flour-haulers know what they were, sent motor launches off to those closest to them. One of those steamers, instead of receiving the boarding party, tried to flee into the harbor. The cannon boomed again, sounding angry this time. The steamer exploded, a thunderclap to dwarf the roar of the guns.

"What's that?" Daniel exclaimed, awe on his face at the blast of noise.

Douglass wasn't sure the boy was talking to him. He answered anyhow: "That," he said in his most impressive and mournful tones, "that is war."

A noise—a small noise—behind him made him turn. "Frederick, what the devil is going on?" his wife demanded sharply.

"The enemy"—that covered both England and Canada—"is attacking our shipping in the lake," he replied. He hung his head, close to tears. "The British people once helped so much in the fight against slavery, and now they stand allied to it. There are times when I think my life's struggle has been in vain."

"You can only keep on," Anna answered. That closely paralleled his own thought about Daniel's effort to master the ordinary, so closely that he had to nod. But, while his intellect agreed, his heart misgave him.

Cannon boomed from the shore. From the War of 1812 to the War of Secession, the Great Lakes had seen half a century of peace. In the embittered aftermath of the latter war, though, both the USA and the British and Canadians had built up fleets on these waters and fortified their lakeshore towns, each side mistrusting the other. Few people in Rochester thought much of its shore defenses. The government had not had a lot of money to spend in the tight times after the war, and had had so many places to spend it . . .

In hardly more than the twinkling of an eye, the locals' worries proved justified. The warships turned their fire against the guns that had presumed to engage them. Puffs of smoke rose along the shore as their shells smashed into the emplacements of those guns—and against whatever buildings happened to be close by.

One by one, the cannon defending Rochester fell silent. The guns from the ships kept pounding the waterfront anyhow, as if to punish the city for having the effrontery to resist.

"What are they doing?" Anna Douglass said, her voice not far from a moan.

"Beating us," her husband answered. "Few here ever truly believed we should have to go to war against the British Empire. It would appear they took the possibility of war against us rather more seriously."

"What right have they got to shoot at us like this here?" Anna asked. "We folk here in Rochester, we never done them any harm."

The short answer was, *They're strong enough to do it.* Trying to be judicious, Douglass steered clear of the short answer. "They declared a blockade against our ports," he said. "When they did it, no one thought—no one here thought, certainly—that they meant anything beyond our ports on the Atlantic and the Pacific.

But this is a port, and so are Buffalo, and Cleveland, and Duluth. In a blockade, they may close our ports if they can close them."

Here at Rochester, at least, the enemy could. The warships methodically pounded the waterfront to bits. Neither the quays nor the vessels tied up at them could withstand the shells. Smoke climbed into a sky now rapidly darkening from the great profusion of fumes rising to block the rays of the sun. Not all of the smoke, nor even the greatest part of it, came from the gunpowder that propelled the shells and burst inside them. Douglass could see the fierce yellow-orange of fire crawling along piers and over barges.

A few stubborn guns still fired at the enemy vessels. Contemptuously, the warships ignored them. After the first steamer out on Lake Ontario was blown to bits, none of the others tried to make a break for it. They sat very still in the water, waiting to be boarded. Then, one after another, they steamed off. A couple of the warships shepherded them on their way.

"Northwest," Frederick Douglass said. "Toward Toronto, I suppose. Prizes of war."

He sighed again. Back before the War of Secession, as Rochester stationmaster for the Underground Railroad, he'd sent plenty of escaped Negroes to Toronto, to put them forever beyond the reach of recapture. He'd even sent on a few after the war, though the Underground Railroad had withered and died in the bitterness following the U.S. defeat. And now Britain and Canada stood against the USA and with the land from which those Negroes had escaped, and from which so many millions more still longed to escape.

But only a couple of the warships were departing. The rest cruised back and forth, either out of range of the few surviving shore guns or still not thinking their fire worth noticing. With them out there, Rochester's harbor was effectually closed. They proved that bare minutes later, halting an inbound steamer. It soon headed off in the direction of Toronto, likely with a prize crew on board to make sure it got there.

"Blockade, without a doubt," Frederick Douglass said. "Now we pay the price for not having paid the price since the War of Secession."

"Terrible thing," his wife said. "Now I see for my own self what those Rebels did when they shot up your steamboat. You are *never* going to set foot in one of those contraptions again, not while I live and breathe you won't. You done gave me your promise, Frederick, and I expect you to keep it."

The gunners who'd set the *Queen of the Ohio* ablaze were amateurs with obsolete guns. Real artillerymen with modern breech-loading field guns would never have let the sidewheeler escape. "You know I keep my promises," Douglass said. "I'll keep this one, the same as any other."

All that day and into the night, the Rochester wharves burned.

Superficially, everything in Salt Lake City was normal. So far as Abraham Lincoln could divine, everything from Provo in the south to Ogden in the north was superficially normal. The Mormons went on about their business as they always did, pretending to the best of their ability that the world beyond the fertile ground between the Wasatch Mountains on the one hand and the Great Salt Lake and Utah Lake on the other did not exist. The Gentile minority also tried to pretend it was not cut off from the outside world, a pretense that grew more nervous as day followed day with no trains going into or out of Utah, with no telegrams connecting the Territory to the rest of the nation of which it was a part.

As if to emphasize that Utah had not followed the Confederate States into secession from the USA, the Stars and Stripes still flew from the Council House: the ugly little building near Temple Square wherein the Territorial Legislature and governor did their jobs. But the legislature, though in session, had no quorum. The Mormons who made up a majority of its membership were staying home.

The flag still flew above Fort Douglas, too. But the only soldiers in the fort were Utah volunteers: Mormons, in other words. In the Mexican War, the Mormon Legion had fought on the American side. In what was being called the Second Mexican War, the Mormons were playing their cards closer to the vest.

Lincoln, these days, was a guest in Gabriel Hamilton's home, the bill he was running up at the Walker House having grown too steep for Hamilton and the other activists who'd invited him to Salt Lake City to go on paying it. Had he been able to send a wire out of Utah, he could have drawn on his own funds. As things were, he depended on the charity of others.

That galled him. At breakfast one morning, he said, "I hope

you're keeping a tab for all this, Gabe, because I intend paying you back every penny of it when I get the chance."

Both Hamilton and his wife, a plump, pretty blonde named Juliette, shook their heads. "Don't you worry about a thing, Mr. Lincoln," Hamilton said. "None of this here is your fault, and you aren't liable for it."

Lincoln gave him a severe look. "I've been paying my own way in the world since I was knee-high to a grasshopper, and since I haven't been knee-high to anything excepting possibly a giraffe for upwards of sixty years"—to show what he meant, he rose from his chair and extended himself up to his full angular height, towering over Gabe and Juliette—"it's not a habit I feel easy about breaking."

"Think of it as visiting with friends who are glad to have you, then," Hamilton said.

"That's right." Juliette nodded emphatically. "Have some more griddle cakes. We'll put some meat on those bones of yours yet, see if we don't."

"No one's done that my whole life through, either," Lincoln said, "and I expect that means it can't be done. But I will have some more, because they're very fine, and I'll thank you to pass the molasses, too."

"My guess is, you don't mind my saying so, Mr. Lincoln, you haven't had a holiday since you once started in to work," Gabriel Hamilton said, "and you're all at sixes and sevens on account of you don't know what to do with yourself when you're not hard at it."

"Oh, I've had a holiday, all right," Lincoln said, stabbing at a piece of ham with unnecessary violence. "It took me a couple of years to be up and doing after the people turned me out of the White House. I wanted nothing to do even with my wife, God rest her soul, let alone with the world."

"That's not the same thing—not the same thing at all," Juliette said, speaking ahead of her husband. "No one could blame you for being sad then. You did the best you could, but it didn't work."

"You're kind to an old man," Lincoln said. Juliette Hamilton would have been a girl of perhaps ten when the War of Secession ended: too young to have been consumed by the political passions of the day. Looking back, Lincoln thought the whole nation had gone into a funk when the Confederate States made good their independence. Mary had tried to drag him out of his gloom by main force. Maybe, in the end, she'd even succeeded. In the meantime, he'd never come so close to laying violent hands on a woman.

"You don't act old, Mr. Lincoln," Gabe Hamilton said. That was a perceptive comment, perceptive enough to make the former president incline his head in gratitude. Most people would thoughtlessly have said, *You aren't old, Mr. Lincoln,* no matter how obvious a lie it was. Hamilton went on, "There aren't enough people half your age, sir, who have such a progressive view of what labor in this country needs to do to make its voice felt."

"I think—I've always thought—it's wrong for one man to say to another, 'You bake the bread by the sweat of your brow, and I'll eat it,'" Lincoln answered. "That's plain common sense; whoever wrote the fable of the little red hen knew as much."

To his surprise, two tears ran down Juliette's cheeks. "That was Harriet's favorite fairy tale," she said, dabbing at her eyes with her apron. "We lost her to diphtheria when she was four, and we haven't been able to have another."

"A lot of diphtheria in this town," Gabe Hamilton said, as if by thinking of the disease he did not have to think of his dead child. "I wish they knew what causes it."

"Yes. I grieve with you." Lincoln had lost his young son, Tad, not long after losing the War of Secession. One pain piled on the other had been almost too much to bear.

"That isn't what we were talking about, though," Juliette said, determined to be gay. "We were talking about your holiday, and how it's high time you had a proper one after working so hard for so long."

"Well, I have it," Lincoln said. "I might not have wanted it much, but here it is. You finally even put me on the little train over to the Great Salt Lake, which is an extraordinary place indeed if it will bear up this bony old carcass, as it most assuredly did. In any proper, self-respecting water, I sink like a stone."

"Everything in Utah is contrary," Gabe said, to which Lincoln could only nod.

He said, "I expected the other shoe to drop by now, and the Mormons to declare themselves out of the Union if that was what they had in mind when they cut themselves off from the rest of the states."

"That was what I thought they'd do, too," Hamilton said. "Maybe they haven't the nerve for it, when push comes to shove."

"On brief acquaintance, I would say the Mormons' nerve suffices for almost anything," Lincoln answered. "Did you see the notice in the *Bee* for the ball tomorrow night at the Social Hall? Ten dollars for a gentleman and one wife, with all wives after the first in at two dollars a head." Polygamy had captured his attention in the same way it did the attention of the Utah Gentiles.

"Those affairs were commoner in Brigham Young's day than they are now," Hamilton said. "And the price is pretty dear there: my guess is, they're raising money for guns or lawyers or maybe both. I don't think they'll up and secede, not now I don't; they've waited too long. If I'm reading John Taylor right, he's trying for Utah's admission as a state on his terms—he'll promise to let the flag fly if Washington leaves polygamy alone and lets him keep out the Gentiles so they can't ever outvote the Mormons here. In the United States but not of them, you might say."

"They would use the same sorts of laws to keep out certain white men that some states now employ to exclude Negroes, you mean," Lincoln said. "I might almost be tempted to favor their effort along those lines, if for no other reason than to see that entire class of legislation, which has long outlived its usefulness, cast down."

"I'm only guessing, mind you," Hamilton said. "Do you want me to take you to the Tabernacle Sunday, to hear what the Mormon leaders tell their flock?"

"I'd be very interested to hear that, and to see it, too," Lincoln answered. "How easy are they about having Gentiles come in and watch them at worship? Can we do it without causing a ruction?"

"Won't be any trouble at all," Gabe assured him. "Anyone can go into the Tabernacle: they reckon some of the folks who come to watch end up converting, and they're right, too. When the Temple's built, now, that'll be sacred ground, I hear, with no Gentiles allowed inside."

"If you're sure it would be no trouble, then," Lincoln said. "I don't want to keep you from your own devotions."

"Oh, you don't need to fret about that," Juliette assured him. "They don't start their services till two in the afternoon, to let people come into Salt Lake City from their farms and from the little towns roundabout."

"We'll do it," Gabe Hamilton declared, as decisive as a rail-road president ordaining higher freight rates.

Do it they did. Lincoln spent that Sunday morning by himself, reading *Pilgrim's Progress*. Though he believed in God and reck-oned himself a Christian, he'd been disappointed by too many preachers who smugly accepted things as they were to attend church regularly. Walking through the wilderness of the world with Bunyan suited him better: he'd known the valley of Hu-miliation, and many times had to fight his way out of the slough named Despond.

Gabe and Juliette came back from church a little before noon and, with Lincoln, ate a hasty dinner of sausage and bread, washed down with coffee. When they finished, Gabe asked, "Are you ready, sir?"

"I reckon I am," Lincoln said. "Do we need to leave so early?"

He soon discovered they did. As Juliette had said, people came from a long way outside of Salt Lake City to attend the service. A great many people from within the city came to attend the ser-vice, too. The streets around Temple Square were a sea of car-riages, wagons, horses, mules, and people on foot. The Hamiltons had to tie up their buggy a couple of blocks off and, with Lincoln, make their slow way through the press toward the Tabernacle. In most towns, Lincoln would have worried more about leaving the horse and carriage so far from where he was going, but Salt Lake City, save for a small number of hoodlums, seemed an exception-ally law-abiding place.

Lincoln's height and familiar face made some people stop and stare and others draw away to give him and his companions room to advance past the granite blocks awaiting inclusion in the Temple. The net result was that he, Gabe, and Juliette got into the Tabernacle about as fast as they would have had he been incon-spicuous and anonymous.

The Tabernacle seemed large from the outside. From the inside, with one great hall covered by the overarching white-washed roof (the latter decorated with evergreen and with paper flowers), it was truly enormous. "You could have taken the crowds in both the buildings where I was nominated for president and lost them inside here," Lincoln said. "How many does this place hold, anyhow?"

"Twelve, thirteen thousand, something like that," Gabe Hamilton answered. Women predominated in the center of the church, while men made up the majority in the side aisles. Hamilton led his wife and Lincoln up into the gallery rather than down onto the floor, explaining, "If you like, we can sit down front, but they'll aim some of the preaching straight at us."

"I've had enough preaching aimed straight at me, thanks," Lincoln said, at which Hamilton chuckled. Lincoln went on, "If you don't mind, let's find one seat on the aisle, so I can stretch out these long legs of mine." Once seated, he looked around with a lively curiosity. The Tabernacle seemed to be soaking up people as a thirsty towel soaks up water. Many paused to drink from the huge cask of water by one door, dipping it up with the tin cups provided for the purpose.

At the front of the Tabernacle sat the choir, men on one side, women on the other. When the great organ began to play, Gabe Hamilton took his watch from his pocket. "That's two o'clock, on the dot," he said, adjusting the timepiece.

A lay brother in a sack suit announced a hymn. He stood a long way off, but Lincoln could hear him clearly: the acoustics of the building were very good. He prepared to add his own voice to those of the folk around him, but the audience did not sing, leaving that to the choir. He'd heard the choir was so fine, you could listen to it once and die happy. He didn't find it so; *good but not grand* was his mental verdict. The organ accompanying the singers was something else again—as mighty an instrument, and as well played, as he'd ever heard.

Hymn succeeded hymn, all performed by the choir and that formidable organ. Once they were done, another layman-priest— a businessman in everyday life, by his clothes—offered a long prayer. Many of the references, presumably drawn from the Book of Mormon, were unfamiliar to Lincoln, but the prayer's moral tone would not have been out of place in any church he had ever visited.

Another choral hymn followed, this one longer than any that had gone before. While it went on, eight bishops of the church cut sliced loaves of bread into morsels for communion. Attendants took the morsels on trays and passed them out to the audience.

While they were doing so, an elderly man took his place behind the pulpit. Lincoln did not recognize his appearance, not at the distance from which he saw him, but stiffened when the man began to speak: he knew John Taylor's voice.

"I wish to read a couple of verses from the twenty-first chapter of the book of Revelations, and to talk about them with you," Taylor said. "St. John the Divine begins the chapter as follows: 'I saw a new heaven and a new earth: for the first heaven and the first earth were passed away, and there was no more sea. And I John saw the holy city, new Jerusalem, coming down from God out of heaven, prepared as a bride adorned for her husband.'

"My friends, my brethren, have we not here the new Jerusalem? Have we not been tested in the fire of persecution, and assayed as pure metal?" Lincoln found it interesting that he should use a figure drawn from mining. He could not linger on it, for Taylor was continuing: "Has God not given us this land, the new Jerusalem, to use and to shape according to our desire and to His? Have we not richly adorned our Deseret, which was empty when we came to it?"

In many churches, the congregation would have shouted out agreement. Here they sat quiet as the communion morsels came to them row by row. President Taylor went on, "By the first heaven and the first earth I take John to mean the requirements forced upon us up to this time by the government of the United States, requirements violating the freedom of religion guaranteed to all by the first amendment to the Constitution. These infringements on our liberty shall not stand, for now we enter into the new heaven and the new earth. The sea of tears which was our lot shall pass away, and exist no more, as John clearly states.

"In the new heaven and the new earth we are creating, we shall be free to worship and to live as we reckon best and most fitting, and no one shall have the power to abridge our rights in any way. For the United States are undergoing their own apocalypse now; if they choose not to treat us as we deserve, they shall be given over to that old serpent, called the Devil, and Satan, which deceiveth the whole world. Washington is bombarded. Babylon is fallen, is fallen, that great city."

Lincoln turned to Gabe Hamilton. "It seems you were right," he murmured.

"It does, doesn't it?" the activist answered. "I tell you the truth, sir: I'd sooner have been wrong."

The attendants with the trays of communion bread took a long time to reach the gallery. When at last they got to Lincoln's row, he passed the tray on without taking a morsel. He wanted no part of the communion being celebrated in the Tabernacle.

* * *

George Custer sat up straighter in his seat as the train wheezed to a halt west of the little town of Wahsatch, Utah. The satiny plush upholstery and soft padding made sitting straight require an effort of will: the leading officers in John Pope's hastily improvised army rode in the comfort of a deluxe Pullman car, while the soldiers they commanded were packed like sardines into the cramped and battered confines of cars commandeered from emigrant trains.

"Let me see the map, would you, Tom?" Custer said. His brother, who had the seat on the aisle beside him, handed him the folded sheet. He unfolded it, traced with his finger the route they'd taken thus far, and grunted. "Next would be Castle Rock, and then the bridge over Echo Creek."

"*Would be* is right," Tom Custer said. "Next is the place where the Mormons have blocked the tracks." He sounded quiveringly eager to go to war, even if it was against citizens of his own country.

As soon as the train had come to a complete stop, Brigadier General John Pope rose from his seat and addressed his officers in the grandiloquent tones he commonly used: "Gentlemen, we now have the privilege and the opportunity of restoring the refractory Territory of Utah to its proper allegiance to the United States of America. I suggest that we now disembark to examine the damage and vandalism the Mormons have inflicted upon the tracks in their illegal and improper effort to separate themselves from our great country."

"That'll give us the privilege and opportunity of getting shot if the damned Mormons decide they don't care to return to their proper allegiance," Tom Custer whispered to his brother. But he was one of the first men to rise and head out of the car.

George Custer was on his brother's heels. It had been hot and stuffy and close in the Pullman car, the air so full of tobacco smoke that Custer might as well have been puffing a cigar himself. Outside, it was hot and dry: gray rocks and roan mixed together. The breeze smelled spicily of sagebrush and tasted of alkali.

Colonel John Duane, the chief Army engineer attached to Pope's command, walked along the tracks till there were no more tracks. Custer trailed along with him. The two men had known each other a long time, both having served in McClellan's headquarters during the War of Secession. Duane had been thin and scholarly looking then, and still was; the only difference in him Custer could see was that his mustache and the hair at his temples had gone gray. After peering west for a couple of minutes, he spoke in tones of professional admiration: "Well, well. They didn't do things by halves, did they?"

"Not a bit of it," Custer agreed. From perhaps a hundred yards west of where the locomotive had stopped, the tracks of the Union Pacific quite simply ceased to exist. The rails were gone. So were the cross ties that anchored them in place. In case that hadn't been enough to get across the impression that the Mormons did not want people traveling through Utah, they had also dug a series of deep ditches across the roadbed to make repairing it as hard as possible.

John Pope came up to examine the damage. "They'll pay for this," he ground out, "every last penny's worth of it." He started walking west, paralleling what had been the line of the track.

"Where are you going, sir?" Custer called.

"I am going to find some Mormons," General Pope replied. "I am going to tell the first one I do find that if any further destruction of the railroad takes place, their heads and the heads of their leaders shall answer for it." He stumped on. No one had ever impugned his courage, not even at McClellan's headquarters.

Custer glanced back over his shoulder. His brother and the other regimental officers were already taking charge of getting men and horses off the train and readying them for whatever lay ahead. Properly, he should have supervised the job. But danger drew him. So did the chance to make an impression on his commanding officer. "I'm with you, sir!" he exclaimed, and hurried after Pope.

Sweat ran down his face. When he reached up to wipe it away from his eyes, his hand slid across the skin of his forehead as if it had soapsuds on it. He nodded to himself. The dust was alkaline, sure enough.

Pope glanced over to him as he caught up. "Misery loves company—is that it, Colonel?" he asked, skirting yet another ditch.

"It's a nice day for a walk," Custer answered with a shrug. The Mormons could have posted sharpshooters anywhere in this boulder-strewn landscape. Custer looked neither right nor left. If they had, they had. Custer and Pope strolled along as casually as if they were in New York's Central Park. Pointing ahead to a small collection of ramshackle buildings, Custer said, "I do believe that's Castle Rock."

"I do believe you're right," Pope said. "With any luck at all, we'll find some Mormon bigwigs there. If they haven't been waiting for me or somebody like me to show up, I miss my guess."

He'd missed plenty of guesses against Lee and Jackson. Against the Mormons, he was spot on. A small party came out of Castle Rock behind a flag of truce. Pope stopped and let them approach. Custer perforce stopped with him. Along with the standard bearer, the Mormon party included a couple of tough-looking youngsters carrying Winchesters and an old man whose unkempt white beard spilled halfway down his chest.

The old-timer stepped out in front of the others and walked up to Pope and Custer. Nodding to them, he said, "Gentlemen, I am Orson Pratt, one of the apostles of the Church of Jesus Christ of the Latter-Day Saints. I can treat with you."

"I am Brigadier General John Pope of the United States Army, Mr. Pratt," Pope said, not offering to shake hands, "and with me here is Colonel Custer of the Fifth Cavalry. President Blaine has appointed me military governor of the Utah Territory and charged me with bringing this Territory into full obedience to all the laws of the United States. That is exactly what I intend to do, and that is exactly what I shall do." He pointed back toward the train. "I have with me a force I believe adequate to ensure obedience, and can summon more men at need."

One of the rifle-toting young Mormons said, "They'll be sorry if they try it."

"You'll be sorrier if you get in our way," Custer snapped, angry at the fellow's arrogance. Pope nodded, as if Custer had simply got the words out before he could.

Orson Pratt held up a hand. "I would sooner negotiate than quarrel." His heavy features turned severe. "I will note, however, that your high-handed attitude, General, is a symptom of the prejudice of the government of the United States that has brought us to this pass."

"Obedience to the laws of the United States is not negotiable," Pope replied. "As military governor of a territory judged to be in rebellion against U.S. authority, I have powers far beyond those of any civil official. The fewer of those powers you require me to use, the happier you and your people will be. Remember, a great many back East would be as glad to see you wiped off the face of the earth."

Pratt's countenance darkened with anger. "We are not without strength, General. If you seek to impose yourself upon us by force—"

"We'll do exactly that," Pope declared. "You have not the slightest notion of what you're up against, Mr. Pratt. This would not be a war of bushwhackers against riflemen. We have the power to smash your troops and smash your towns, sir, and the will to use it if provoked."

"Talk is cheap," Pratt's bodyguard jeered.

Pope turned on his heel. "Come with me," he said. "You have my word you'll be allowed to return here whenever you like. If, however, you judge I am lying about the force at my disposal, I feel myself obliged to disabuse you of your misapprehension." Without looking to see whether he was being followed, he started back toward the troop train. Custer fell in behind him. Pope's bombast had its uses. Pratt and his companions tagged along, as the general must have known they would.

Had Custer been in charge of the Mormons who had chosen to defy the authority of the United States, he would have attacked the troop train with everything he had the minute it came within range of his weapons. That the Mormons had failed to do so struck him as cowardice, and as a confession of their guilty consciences. That they might have worried about the consequences of such a precipitate assault never entered his mind, as he rarely worried about consequences himself.

They would not have the chance to attack now. Infantrymen and Custer's cavalry had already formed a defensive perimeter. The foot soldiers were methodically scraping out firing pits in the rocky ground. Some of them had trowel-shaped bayonets that doubled as entrenching tools. The others used conventional bayonets and whatever other tools they happened to have.

A battery of artillery had come off the freight cars. The breechloading field pieces were drawn up in a line facing south; sunlight gleamed from the bright steel of their barrels. Next to them stood the two Gatling guns attached to Custer's regiment. Sergeants Buckley and Neufeld and their crews looked ready and alert.

Orson Pratt was a hard man to impress. "I knew you had soldiers here, General," he said tartly. "I didn't have to walk all that way in the hot sun to see as much."

Pope remained unfazed. "No one who has not seen modern weapons demonstrated has an accurate understanding of their destructive power. You say you are prepared to prevent us from advancing to Salt Lake City. Perhaps you are in fact less prepared than you fondly believe." He raised his voice and spoke to the artillerymen: "Each piece, six rounds, bearing due south, range three thousand yards."

The soldiers with red trim and chevrons on their uniforms sprang into action. Inside of two minutes, each cannon had roared half a dozen times. Choking clouds of black-powder smoke rose. Through them, Custer watched three dozen shells slam into the desert hillside almost two miles away. They threw up smoke and dust, too, all of it coming from a surprisingly small area: Pope had evidently picked his best gunners for the demonstration. Custer hoped it impressed Orson Pratt. It certainly impressed him. Artillery played only a small role in Indian fighting on the plains. The art had come a long way since the War of Secession.

After the guns fell silent, General Pope said, "That is by no means their extreme range. I could be bombarding Castle Rock now. If I have to fight my way to Salt Lake City, I can bombard it at ranges from which you could not hope to reply."

Pratt looked as if he'd just cracked a rotten egg. "That is an uncivilized way to make war, sir," he said.

"It's also deuced effective," Pope answered. "I have been charged with returning Utah to obedience by whatever means prove necessary. President Blaine cares only about results, not about methods. No one outside Utah will care about methods, either."

That made the Mormon apostle look even less happy. The mouthier of his two bodyguards spoke up: "You can't knock everything down with your guns there. What happens when we come at you man-to-man?"

"I was hoping someone would ask me that," Pope said with a nasty smile. He turned to Custer and gave a half bow. "Colonel, the Gatlings being under your command, would you be so kind as to do the honors?"

"My pleasure, sir," Custer replied, saluting. "Will two magazines per gun suffice?" At John Pope's nod, Custer raised his voice: "Soldiers positioned in front of the Gatling guns, please take yourself out of harm's way." Bluecoats in dust-streaked uniforms hastily abandoned the pits and trenches they'd dug for themselves. Custer nodded to the Gatlings' crew chiefs. "Sergeants, two magazines from each weapon, if you please."

Buckley and Neufeld snapped out orders. Their commands were tiny, but they led them with confidence and skill. As each sergeant cranked his weapon, the barrels revolved, spitting bullets at the astonishing rate in which Custer had delighted down in the Indian Territory. The pauses while full magazines replaced empty ones were barely perceptible.

Silence slammed down after each Gatling went through its second magazine. Into it, Custer addressed the bodyguard with the Winchester: "If you want to charge into that, friend, make sure you tell your mother and your wives good-bye first."

John Pope nodded to Orson Pratt in a friendly-seeming way. "As you see, we are fully prepared to crush without mercy any resistance your people may be rash enough to offer, and have with us the means to do precisely that." He didn't mention that the two Gatling guns the Mormons had seen were the only two he had with him. He did such a good job of not mentioning it, Custer was glad he didn't play poker against him. As if every other freight car were full of Gatlings, Pope went on, "I will have your answer now, Mr. Pratt: either that, or I shall commence operations against your forces immediately you have returned to them."

Under that beard, Pratt's jaw worked. The Mormon apostle looked a good deal like an angry prophet. He also, Custer realized with a small chill, looked a good deal like an older, fleshier version of John Brown. But, where John Brown had had no give in him whatever, Pratt's eyes kept sliding to the field guns and especially to the Gatlings. "You drive a hard bargain, General," he said at last, each word dragged from him.

"I am not here to bargain." Pope drew himself up straight. "I am here to rule. Either peacefully yield your usurped authority to me and accept whatever penalties I see fit to impose on your misguided people or chance the hazards of war. Those are your only choices."

"You would hold our people hostage—" Pratt began.

"You are holding the United States of America hostage," Pope broke in. He drew his sword. To Custer's surprise, he found something to do with it besides making a dramatic gesture, or rather, he found a new sort of dramatic gesture to make: he drew a ring around Orson Pratt in the dirt. "As the Roman told the

Greek king's envoy, say yes or no before you step out of the circle."

Pratt understood the allusion. He also understood that, like the Seleucids when measured against Rome's might, he had no choice. "I yield, sir," he said. "Under compulsion, I yield. Let me go back to Castle Rock, and I will wire President Taylor to that effect. God will judge you for what you do in Utah, General Pope."

"So will the president," Pope replied. "I worry more about him."

Custer clapped his hands together. "Very good, sir!" he said. Pope beamed. Custer nodded to himself. You couldn't go far wrong praising your commander.

General Thomas Jackson paced in the antechamber outside President Longstreet's office like a wolf confined for too long in a cage too small for it. After watching him for a few minutes, G. Moxley Sorrel said, "Please be at ease, General. The president will see you soon, I assure you."

"No doubt. No doubt." Jackson didn't sit. He didn't even slow down. "I should not be here at all. I should be in the field, where I belong."

"Being summoned to confer with your chief executive is not an insult, sir," Sorrel said. "On the contrary: it is a signal honor, a mark of the president's confidence in you and in your judgment."

As far as Jackson was concerned, Longstreet showed confidence in only one person's judgment: his own, a confidence Jackson reckoned exaggerated. To the president's chief of staff, he replied, "I am not insulted, Mr. Sorrel. I am delayed. Who knows what the Yankees may be doing whilst I fritter my time away in useless consultation?"

The door to Longstreet's office came open. The French minister, a dapper little man who looked like a druggist, strode out, bowed to Jackson, and hurried away. President Longstreet followed him. "You think I'm wasting your precious time, do you?" he said.

"Of course I do, Your Excellency," Jackson said: when asked a direct question, he was never one to back away from a direct answer. Moxley Sorrel, whose principal function, so far as Jackson could see, was shielding President Longstreet from unpleasantness of any sort, looked horrified.

Longstreet himself, however, merely nodded, as if he'd expected nothing different. "Well, come on in, General, and we'll talk about it."

"Yes, Mr. President," Jackson said: he might have been restive, but he understood perfectly well that the president of the Confederate States was his superior. Inside Longstreet's office, he took his usual stiff seat in a chair not really designed to accommodate such a posture.

Longstreet picked up a pen and pointed it at him as if it were the bayonet on the end of a Tredegar. "I know what you're thinking," the president said. "You're thinking what a blasted nuisance it is to have a president who's also a soldier, and that I wouldn't be such an interfering old buzzard if I were a civilian."

"Your Excellency, if this was not a thought that crossed your mind a great many times during the administration of President Davis, I should be astonished," Jackson said.

"Touché," Longstreet said with a laugh, and then, "You see how having Monsieur Méline here just before you has had its influence on me."

Again, Jackson was frank to the point of bluntness: "Very little influences you, Mr. President, when you do not care to let yourself be influenced."

Longstreet started to reply to that, but checked himself. Setting down the pen, he made a steeple of the fingertips of both hands. "Do you know, General, you can at times be alarmingly perceptive," he remarked. "Perhaps it is as well that you never took any great interest in politics."

"As well for me, certainly," Jackson agreed, "and, I have no doubt, also for our nation."

Longstreet surprised him by being frank in turn (any frankness from Longstreet surprised him): "By the first part of which you mean you'd sooner see others do the dirty work, so as not to tarnish your own moral perfection." He held up a hand—he used them expressively, as a politician should. "Never mind. What I'm driving at is that you chafe under me for exactly the opposite reason I—and so many others—chafed under Jeff Davis."

Jackson realized he would have to examine, and if necessary root out, what looked like a stain of hypocrisy on his own soul. But that had to wait. Duty first. Always duty first. "I beg your pardon, Mr. President, but I do not see the distinction you are drawing."

"No?" President Longstreet sounded amused. "I'll spell it out for you. President Davis interfered with the way his commanders fought the War of Secession because he thought he was a better general than they were. I am interfering in the way you fight this war because I think I am a better politician than you are."

"I would not presume to argue that, despite your intimations to the contrary a moment ago," Jackson replied.

"All right, then," Longstreet said. "Believe me, General, I would constrain you less if I did not have to worry more about keeping our allies satisfied with the manner in which we conduct the war."

"It is war," Jackson said simply. "We must conduct so as best and most expeditiously to defeat the enemy."

"How best to defeat the United States and how to defeat them most expeditiously may not be one and the same," Longstreet said. "This is one reason I ordered you not to go on and attack Harper's Ferry after beating the Yankees at Winchester."

"Mr. President, I do not understand." Jackson knew no better way to express the frustration he felt at having to abandon an assault he was certain would have been successful.

"I know you don't. That is why I called you back to Richmond." Longstreet pointed to the map on the wall. "Suppose we win an overwhelming victory in this war, which God grant. Can we hope to overrun and conquer the United States?"

Jackson didn't need to look at the map. "Of course not, sir."

"Good." The president of the CSA nodded approval. "There you have the first point: any success we win must of necessity be limited in scope. After it, we still face United States larger and stronger than ourselves." He cocked his head to one side, awaiting Jackson's response. Reluctantly, Jackson nodded in turn. The president proceeded, like a teacher taking a scholar through the steps of a geometric proof: "It therefore follows, does it not, that we should be wise to maintain and cultivate our alliance with the powers whose intervention was essential in securing our independence a generation ago?"

Like a scholar who did not grasp the proof, Jackson said, "I fail to see how the one follows from the other."

"I thought not—another reason to call you away from the front." Longstreet seemed willing, even eager, to go through the proof the long way where the short way had failed. "The key to your understanding, General, is that, in the eyes of our allies, we are engaged in a defensive struggle. The United States declared war against us, not the other way round. The United States first took offensive action, sending their cavalry down into the Indian Territory. That justified our responding."

"You don't win a war by merely responding, Mr. President." Jackson was as unyielding as the stone wall that had given him his lasting nickname.

"We aren't *merely* responding," Longstreet said. "General Stuart has stung the Yankees down in the New Mexico Territory, and our raids into Kansas have been effective in keeping the USA off balance there—and the United States have pulled regular troops from that front to bring in Mormons in Utah back under their thumb."

"Ah—the Mormons." Jackson leaned forward. "Had we anything to do with their . . . timely disaffection?" That sort of inspired chicanery, sowing trouble in the Yankees' rear, was what he would have expected from Longstreet.

"I despise the Mormons, General, and I thank heaven every day that we have only a handful of them in the Confederacy," the president said.

For a moment, Jackson thought Longstreet had denied abetting the unrest in Utah Territory. Then he realized the president of the CSA had done no such thing. He suspected he'd got all the answer he was going to get, too. No point to pursuing it further; he returned to the main subject at hand: "What we've given the United States are pinpricks, fleabites. We need to hit them hard enough to let them know they're hurt."

"I will not strike them blows that, in my judgment, would cause Britain and France to conclude they are being used as instruments of our aggrandizement rather than protectors of our legitimate rights," Longstreet said. "I will not. If that makes the war more difficult, so be it. My firm view is that, in the long run, we shall be better for it."

Jackson got to his feet. "If I cannot prosecute the war to the utmost, Your Excellency, I hope you will accept my resignation."

"Oh, sit down, Tom. Don't be a stiff-necked fool," Longstreet said testily. Surprised, Jackson did sit. The president went on, "Even if I tie one hand behind your back, I need you. You're the best I've got. That's all the more true *because* I tie one hand behind your back. I'm not the only one who needs you. The country does."

Jackson saw that Longstreet deserved his place in the executive mansion. The president knew precisely which levers to pull to return a recalcitrant general to obedience. Maybe that meant he knew which levers to pull to keep Britain and France on good terms with the Confederate States, and maybe it meant he correctly gauged how important the alliance was. If all that was so . . .

"For the sake of the nation we both serve, I retract what I just said." Jackson spoke firmly. Through his life, he'd seldom had to backtrack. When he found the need, he was as unflinching in meeting it as with any other tactical necessity.

"Did you say something, General?" Longstreet brought a hand to his ear. "I'm an old man. I must be getting deaf, because I didn't hear a word."

That drew a chuckle from Jackson. Longstreet was smoother than Jackson had ever wanted to be, and crookeder than Jackson ever wanted to be, too. But he'd found a way out of a situation from which the general-in-chief would have been too stubborn to retreat unaided. He deserved credit for that.

"Very well, then." Jackson gave him credit by proceeding from the point of their disagreement as if he had in fact agreed. "Recognizing that we cannot hope to conquer the United States, how are we to secure victory over them?"

"By demonstrating to them that they cannot hope to conquer us," President Longstreet answered. "The way you ran them out of Winchester was first-rate, General. That is how we won the War of Secession, after all."

"Our armies were in Pennsylvania when we won the War of Secession," Jackson pointed out.

"True," Longstreet said, "but we were compelled to invade their territory then, for they had gained several lodgments in ours: along the Carolina coast, in Virginia, and in the West. That is not the case now. Our navy is far more able to defend our shores than was so then, and we have our allies to assist us. We stand in firm control on our side of the Potomac, and have punished Washington for the effrontery of the United States. And Kentucky and the line of the Ohio River are now ours, where we had to gain that line by force of arms during the previous war. The United States have not got the initiative, nor shall they gain it."

"Hard to be assured of that while we stand on the defensive," Jackson said.

Longstreet shrugged his broad shoulders. "Modern weaponry favors the defensive, at least on land. Having seen the fighting at first hand, do you deny it?"

"No, sir," Jackson said. "Harder now to break a strongly held defensive position than it was in the War of Secession, and it wasn't easy then. As my written report states, a bare regiment of entrenched Yankees fought manfully against my brigade south of Kernstown, though eventually being overcome by superior force."

"Well, then," Longstreet said, as if everything were settled, "is it not more profitable to strike where we and our allies are strong, as in the recent bombardments of U.S. towns on the shores of the Great Lakes, and to let the Yankees beat their heads against the wall coming at us?"

"But the trouble is—" Jackson realized he could not oppose the president of the Confederate States with anything resembling a logical argument. He gave him an emotional one instead: "The trouble is, Your Excellency, I want to hit them a good lick."

"That should not be impossible, even standing on the defensive." Longstreet looked over to the map again. "As you no doubt know, they appear to be massing troops in Indiana opposite Louisville. Would it make you happy if I sent you to Kentucky to supervise the defense of the city?"

Jackson knew Longstreet was offering him a bribe. If he did as the president desired, he would in essence forfeit the right to express his disagreement with present Confederate policy— especially as he would be an instrument of making that policy succeed. Longstreet was a subtle man, but not so subtle as to be able to disguise what he was about here. Understanding what Longstreet was about, though, did not make Jackson able to resist the temptation set before him. Leaning forward in his chair, he said, "Yes, Mr. President!"

Major Horatio Sellers came up to Jeb Stuart while the general commanding the Military District of the Trans-Mississippi was engaged in the unmilitary but nevertheless important task of making sure no scorpions had crawled into his boots during the night. Once satisfied on that score, Stuart said, "And what can I do for you this morning, Major?"

Sellers' heavy features were not made for expressing joy under the best of circumstances. Since traveling along the border between Sonora and New Mexico Territory was hardly the best of circumstances, Stuart supposed his aide-de-camp could hardly be blamed for looking grim. Sellers said, "Sir, how far are we going to trust these Apache devils, anyhow? I keep having the feeling that one fine morning we're going to wake up with our throats cut, if you know what I mean."

"I may," Stuart answered. "I just may. But before I answer that, let me ask you a few questions of my own." Since he was the general, the major inclined his head in agreement. Stuart began: "Are these Apache devils the best guides and scouts we could have, or not?"

"Oh, yes, sir," Sellers said. "Not a doubt about that. They know every cactus in this whole damn desert by its first name. They know where the Yankees are, where they were, and where they'll turn up day after tomorrow. If I hadn't seen it so often by now, I wouldn't believe it. It's almost uncanny, like a nigger *gris-gris* woman down in New Orleans."

"If Geronimo understood that, he'd thank you for it—from everything I've been able to figure out, he's as much a medicine man as a chief," Stuart said. "It's neither here nor there, though." The general paused to pull on one of his scorpion-free boots before continuing the catechism: "Do these Apache devils hate the Yankees and the Mexicans both?"

"I hope to spit, they do," Major Sellers exclaimed. "Can't say I much blame 'em, either, if you look at things from their side of the mirror. The only reason they can't figure out which bunch to hate worse is that the damnyankees and the Mexicans have both been doing their damnedest to massacre 'em."

"Which means they've got good, solid reasons to be loyal to the Confederate States, doesn't it, Major?" Stuart said.

"When you put it like that, yes, sir, I suppose it does." Major Sellers neither looked nor sounded happy. "The only thing I hope, sir, is that we don't end up sorry we ever trusted them."

Jeb Stuart was pulling on the other boot when his aide-de-camp said that. He stopped with it halfway up his calf. Both eyebrows rose. "Good God, Major, you'd have to send me to an idiots' asylum if I trusted them once they were out of my sight. They're as dangerous as . . . as scorpions." He finished putting on the boot. "If they weren't, how could so few of them have given so many U.S. soldiers and so many Mexicans so much trouble for so long?"

"Sir?" Now Sellers wore a new expression: confusion. "In that case, why have we given them all Tredegars?"

"So they can shoot them at the Yankees, of course," Stuart replied. "They will do that. As you said yourself, they have good reason to do that."

"Well, yes, sir," Major Sellers said. "But once Sonora is ours, won't they find reasons to shoot them at us?"

"I hope not. I hope that, once Sonora is ours, they'll go shoot up New Mexico when they're feeling frisky," Stuart said. "But it's a chance I'm willing to take, for now. If they decided to start raiding our supply line instead of working with us, life could get lively faster than we really wanted, couldn't it?"

He watched Sellers think that over. He watched Sellers look as unhappy as he had while making the same consideration. "Sir, we need that railroad from El Paso," his aide-de-camp said.

"So we do," Stuart said. "Unfortunately, it's not built yet. If the war with the United States isn't over by the time it is built, things will have gone a great deal worse than I hope. Once the war is over and the railroad built, I expect we'll be able to deal with any trouble a few hundred redskins cause. Until then, we'll use them to our best advantage. Since that's also to their advantage, I don't see how they can fail to make us useful tools for the time being."

His aide-de-camp's face cleared. "Well, that's all right, then," Major Sellers said with some relief. "As long as you're thinking of them as cat's-paws and not as genuine allies, everything's fine. After all, sir, it's not as if they're white men."

"No, it's not," Stuart agreed. "Of course, even if we are white men, that doesn't stop our allies from using us as cat's-paws against the USA. After all, it's not as if we were Europeans."

That sailed past Horatio Sellers. Sellers was a detail man, which made him a devil of an aide-de-camp. He wasn't so good at fitting details inside the frame of a larger picture. Some aides-de-camp used their posts at the side of high-ranking officers to gain high rank themselves. Sellers would likely be a major till he retired, if he lived to retirement.

Every man is good at—and good for—something, Stuart thought. Without Major Sellers, the thin Confederate force operating on the U.S. border would have been far less effective than it was. Without him, too, Stuart would have overlooked any number of things to worry about, some of which probably would have proved important. If Horatio Sellers didn't think something was worth worrying about, it wasn't.

Stuart pulled aside the tent flap and went outside. The day was bright and clear and hot. But for occasional storms that blew up from the south, every summer's day hereabouts was bright and clear and hot. Stuart thought he could see forever. Water seemed to shimmer in the middle distance. He'd warned his men about chasing mirages.

A roadrunner skittered past with a horned toad's tail sticking out of its beak. It gave Stuart a wary glance, as if afraid he might try to steal its breakfast. When he just stood there, it ran off to where it could dine in privacy.

Geronimo and the young son who translated for him approached Stuart. "Good day to you, General," said the young man, whose name was Chappo. His accent might almost have come from New England. Stuart didn't know if the sounds of the Apache language made it seem that way, or if Chappo had learned the language from somebody from the northeastern United States. Either way, he found it funny. Also funny was the spectacle of a couple of Indians carrying Confederate Army—issue tin plates full of beans (they carefully picked out the salt pork, which they didn't like) and tin cups full of coffee, both of which (except for the pork) they thought highly.

"Good day to you, Chappo," Stuart answered gravely, "and to your father."

Chappo spoke in the Apache language. Geronimo answered. His voice was on the mushy side, for he was missing quite a few teeth, which also gave the lower part of his face the pinched-in look often thought of as characteristic of witches. Stuart wondered if that had helped give him reputation among the Apaches. That story they told about his making the daylight hold off for two or three hours so they could escape from a raid . . . No Christian man would believe it, but they did.

"I think you can take Tucson, if you want it," he said now, through his son.

"Do you?" If the old Indian had been looking for a way to grab Stuart's attention, he'd found one. With Tucson in Confederate hands, Yankee control over all of western New Mexico Territory south of it would wither. The catch, of course, was that taking it would be anything but easy. Keeping it would be harder still, since it lay on the Southern Pacific line. Stuart had thought it beyond his slender means.

He studied Geronimo with the same sort of cautious gaze the roadrunner had given him. Geronimo might be a savage, but he was a long, long way from a fool. He might well hope U.S. and C.S. troops would engage in a struggle that depleted forces from both sides, leaving no white soldiers to protect the area from the Apaches.

With something approaching the truth, the general commanding the Trans-Mississippi said, "I don't think we are strong enough to do that, even with the help of the brave Apaches. I wish I did, but I don't."

When Geronimo had that translated for him, he spoke for some time. Chappo had to hold up a hand so he would stop and let the interpreter do his job. "My father says he would not tell this plan to any other man. He thinks you can make it go, though. He says that, if you fooled the bluecoats so well once, you can do it again, and he will help."

"Tell him to go on." Stuart did his best to keep his voice and face impassive. He could read nothing on Geronimo's weathered features. He might have been back in one of the endless card games with which U.S. Army soldiers out West had made time pass before the War of Secession. How big a bluff was Geronimo running? Stuart realized he'd have to see more of the Indian's hand to tell.

Through Chappo, the Apache chief did go on: "With these new rifles you gave us, we will go on the warpath. We will go up toward Tucson. We will be loud. We will be noisy. The bluecoats will have to see us."

Stuart had no trouble understanding what that meant. The Apaches would hit farmers and herders and miners between the international border and Tucson. Livestock would vanish. Men the Indians caught would die. Women would probably suffer a fate worse than death, and then die, too.

He'd been talking with Major Sellers about how good it would be for the redskins to keep the USA too busy chasing them to trouble Sonora and Chihuahua. Now he had to contemplate what those cold-blooded words meant. He hadn't fought like that during the War of Secession. Not even the damnyankees had fought like that then.

But he hadn't given the Apaches Bible tracts. He'd given them

guns, lots of guns. "Ask your father what happens then," he told
Chappo.

Geronimo answered in detail. He'd thought this through. Stuart had seen how the fellow who proposed an idea usually had the
edge on the fellow who was hearing it for the first time. That still
held true, he discovered, when the fellow doing the proposing
was an Indian who didn't know how to write his name.

Chappo said, "My father says we can do one thing or the other
thing. One thing is, when the bluecoats chase us, we can go up
into the mountains and pretend to be rocks and trees. While they
look for us, you go behind them and into Tucson."

Stuart studied Geronimo with surprise and considerable admiration. Had the Apache had a proper military education, he might
have been sitting in General Jackson's office in Richmond. But
Stuart said, "For that plan to work, we have to depend on the Yankees' commander in Tucson being stupid. By now, he's probably
heard the Apaches and the Confederates are friends. He will not
forget about us while he goes chasing after you."

Once Chappo translated that, Geronimo looked at Stuart for a
moment before going on. His expression didn't change, but
Stuart had the strong feeling that he'd just impressed Geronimo
the same way Geronimo had impressed him. He should have
been angry that a savage presumed to judge him in that fashion.
He wasn't. Geronimo had earned his respect. He was glad he'd
managed to earn Geronimo's.

The Apache chieftain said, "The other plan is, we war toward
Tucson. The bluecoats chase us. We do not go into the mountains.
We lead them to an ambush you set with your men and your guns.
This does not give you Tucson. It gives you the men who hold
Tucson. Is it enough?"

"Hmm," Stuart said, and then again: "Hmm." He hadn't expected a savage to presume to propose a plan of campaign. Nor
had he expected the plan to be so tempting once the savage did
presume to propose it.

Geronimo said, "For a long time, I have fought the bluecoats
and the Mexicans hard, even when I had little. Now you Confederates are on my side, and, with you to help, I can strike a great
blow."

"All right—we'll try it," Stuart said, coming to an abrupt decision. Even before Chappo translated, Geronimo caught the tone

of his answer and smiled the broadest smile Stuart had seen from him. Stuart smiled back, and clasped his hand. Once the damn-yankees were licked and the CSA got Sonora and Chihuahua fully under control, the Confederates would have much, and the Apaches little. *One step at a time,* Stuart thought.

☆ VII ☆

Sitting as it did at the corner of Larkin and McAllister in Yerba Buena Park, the San Francisco City Hall was only a few blocks from the offices of the *Morning Call*. Samuel Clemens looked up from the sentence he was writing—*level of bungling last seen when Lot's wife was turned to a pillar of salt and not a single foolish soul thought to carry her along regardless, to sell for a shekel the half-pound*—and spoke to Clay Herndon: "Mayor Sutro's giving a speech in half an hour. Why don't you amble on over there and find out what the old whale's spouting this time?"

"Do I have to, Sam?" Herndon asked in mournful tones. "I've covered him the last three times he's shot off his mouth, and if four in a row isn't cruel and unusual punishment, I don't know what is. Besides, I'm about three-quarters of the way through this story you said you wanted today, and it's going pretty well. I hate to waste a couple of hours listening to His Honor gab, and then come back and find I've forgotten half the good lines I figured on using."

"Which story is that?" Clemens asked. "There were a couple of them, if I recall."

"The one about the defenses of San Francisco Bay," the reporter answered. "I finally talked Colonel Sherman into giving me an interview yesterday, and I went out to Alcatraz and talked with the garrison commander there, too, so I've got the straight dope, all right. 'Muzzle-loading rifled cannon'—it's almost as bad as 'she sells seashells by the seashore,' isn't it?"

"And their shells may be even more dangerous than seashells, not that we've seen any proof of that," Clemens said. "Well, you're right—I do want that piece, as fast as you can turn it out, so I won't inflict our magnificent mayor on you this morning." He took another look at the editorial he was working on. It was, by something approaching a miracle, for the day after tomorrow, not tomorrow. He got up from his desk. "I'll cover the speech myself. By the way things are going, I'm bound to have more of our blunders to write about by the time I have to give this to the typesetters."

"I didn't want you to have to go and do that," Clay Herndon exclaimed. "I just meant for you to send Leary or one of the other cubs."

"Don't fret yourself about it." Sam threw on his houndstooth coat. As if he were a gentleman of fashion, he buttoned only the top button. As he set his straw hat at a jaunty angle on his head, he went on, "If I go to City Hall, I'm halfway home. You can't tell me Sutro won't talk till noon, or maybe one o'clock. Whenever he finally decides to shut up, I can walk over for dinner and surprise Alexandra."

"Thanks, Sam," Herndon said. "You're a good boss to work for; you remember what it was like when you were just an ordinary working fellow yourself."

"Get that story about the seashells on Alcatraz done." Clemens patted his pockets to make sure he had an adequate supply of both pencils and cigars. Satisfied, he grabbed a notebook and headed out the door.

The weather was fine for wearing a mostly unbuttoned coat. The breeze ruffled the flags that, in a display of patriotic fervor, flew from what seemed like every other building and from every trolley and cable-car stop. Despite the admission of several territories as new states since the War of Secession, the flags sported fewer stars than they had before the war. President Tilden had finally ordered the stars representing states now Confederate removed from the banner, which was, Clemens remained convinced, one reason Blaine beat him.

Sam walked southwest down Market to McAllister, and then west along the latter street to the City Hall, a fine building of composite neoclassical style. He waved to a couple of other reporters who were also coming to hear Mayor Sutro's latest pronouncement.

"Good God in the foothills, Sam, the *Call* must really have its claws out if you're covering this in person," said Monte Jesperson, who wrote for the *Alta Californian*. His paper was as staunchly pro-Sutro as the *Morning Call* was anti-.

"Not quite so bad as that, Three-Card," Clemens returned.

Regardless of editorial policy, newspapermen got on well with one another. "Only reason I'm here is that Clay's in the middle of a story he needs to get done quick as he can."

"Ah, I've got you." When Jesperson nodded, his flabby jowls and several chins bobbed up and down. His sack suit had to have been cut from the bones of a great many herrings to fit round his bulk. He stood aside to let Sam go into City Hall ahead of him; the doors weren't wide enough to let them go in side by side.

Noting the rich furnishings, the marble floors, the fancy paintings on the walls, the general profusion of velvet and gilt and elaborately carved walnut and mahogany, Sam said, "I wonder how much stuck to whose pockets when they were running up this place."

Monte Jesperson's sniff was like that of a bloodhound taking a scent. "Ah, that'd be worth knowing, wouldn't it?" he said. "If there be any bodies buried, nobody's ever dug 'em up."

"That's the truth." Clemens cocked his head to one side, listening to Jesperson with a reporter's attentive ear. "So you're one of the ones who still say 'if there be,' are you, Three-Card? I know the fancy grammarians like it better, but 'if there are' has always been good enough for me."

"I'm an old man." Jesperson ran a pudgy finger along the gray walrus mustache he wore. "The things the modern generation does to the English language are a shame and a disgrace, nothing less. Not you, Sam—you've got some bite to you, under that cloak of foolishness you like to wear—but a lot of the pups nowadays wouldn't know a subjunctive if it kicked 'em in the shins. Comes of not learning Latin, I expect."

Sam's own acquaintance with Latin was distinctly of the nodding variety. Not without relief, he let one of Mayor Sutro's flunkies lead him to the hall where Sutro stood poised behind a podium, ready to give forth with deathless prose. It was, in Clemens' opinion, deathless because it had never come to life.

He sometimes thought Sutro looked as if he'd never come to life, either. The mayor of San Francisco was pale and plump, with a brown mustache Jesperson's could have swallowed whole. His eyes, dark lumps in a doughy face, resolutely refused to show any luster. That he wore a suit he might have stolen from an undertaker did not enliven his person.

Along with the reporters, clerks and lawyers helped fill the room. So did some of Adolph Sutro's friends, most of them as dreary as the mayor. Sutro said, "Thank you for coming here today, gentlemen." He looked down at the podium, on which surely reposed his speech, nicely written out. Having grown up with politicians who memorized two-hour addresses and were venomously deadly in repartee, Clemens found that all the more dismaying.

"I have called and gathered you here together today," Sutro droned, "for the purpose of delivering a warning pertaining to spies and to matters relating to espionage." *I want to warn you about spies,* Sam translated mentally. He'd edited a lot of bad prose in his time, but little to compare to this. A cleaver wasn't enough to cut the fat from the mayor's speeches; a two-man ripsaw might possibly have done the job.

"In particular this morning, I address my remarks to the noble gentlemen belonging to the Fourth Estate, irregardless of whether or not they and I have previous to this time been in agreement with each other on the concerns concerning our city and our state and the United States," Sutro continued. He doubtless thought of that *irregardless* as a polished touch, and either hadn't noticed *concerns concerning* or labored under the delusion that it improved the product. With a distinct effort of will, Clemens lowered the flame under his critical boiler. Taking notes on Sutro's speeches was easier because they were so padded and repetitious.

The mayor said, "It is up to you and your responsibility to disseminate to the many who depend on you the vital necessity of being as alert and aware as it is possible to be to the dangers posed by spying and the measures to be taken in order that those dangers are to be reduced to as small an extent as may be. Now, then, these dangers are— Yes, Mr. Clemens?"

Sam's hand had shot into the air. He couldn't help himself. In his most innocent voice, he asked, "Mayor, can you please tell me how a danger, which is abstract, can have an extent, which is physical?"

Sutro coughed. "This danger is not abstract. It is real. Perhaps we can hold the rest of the questions until the completion of my address. Now, then, as I was saying—"

Invincible dunderhead, Clemens scrawled in his notebook. He glanced over at Monte Jesperson, who would not meet his eye. No matter what Jesperson thought, though, the *Alta Californian* would make Mayor Sutro sound like a statesman when its next edition came out.

To Sam, he sounded like a lunatic. His speech went on for as long as the newspaperman had expected it would, but furnished only a couple of pages' worth of notes. The gist of it was that Sutro had a bee in his bonnet about spies, because Confederates, Canadians, and Englishmen all spoke English—"in the same way and manner that we do ourselves," the mayor said. Sam was confidently certain many of them spoke it better than Adolph Sutro did, not that that made any enormous compliment.

Still . . . *Mayor Sutro has a point,* Sam wrote. Then he added, *He was not wearing his hat, which let him show the world exactly where he has it.* The mayor's idea was that, since enemy spies didn't give themselves away by how they talked, everyone should report everything (that wasn't quite how he phrased it, but it was what he meant) to the police and to the military authorities, so everybody who said anything could be locked up and the keys either thrown away or filed in the mayor's office, which made them even more certain never to be seen again.

When the speech was finally over, Clemens asked, "Once the entire population of the city is incarcerated, Your Honor, from which states do you plan on importing loyal citizens to take its place?"

"I doubt it will come to that," Sutro answered primly. "Next question, please." Sam sighed. He should have known better. He had known better, in fact, but hadn't wanted to admit it to himself. If U.S. Navy ships were armored against shells as the mayor was against sarcasm, they'd prove unsinkable.

Sam did find one serious question to ask: "Have you reviewed this plan with the chief of police and with the military authorities?"

"Why, no," the mayor said, "but I have the utmost confidence they will show themselves to be as zealous in the pursuit of the sneaking spies who have done so much damage to our cause"—another statement, Clemens thought, that would have been all the better for proof—"as I am myself, and will profit from the assistance of our fine and upstanding vigilant citizens."

"*I* have the utmost confidence," Sam said as the reporters headed out of City Hall, "that every low-down skunk with a grudge against his neighbor is going to call him a Rebel spy."

"We'll catch some real spies, thanks to this," Monte Jesperson said: faint praise for the speech, but praise.

It made Clemens furious. "Oh, no doubt we will—but how the devil will we be able to tell which ones they are, when we've arrested their bartenders and blacksmiths and druggists along with 'em? And what about the Constitution, where it says you can't arrest a man on nothing better than somebody's say-so?"

Jesperson's shoulders moved up and down. "It's wartime. You do what you have to do, then pick up the pieces afterwards."

"Three-Card, the very first war this country ever fought was against people who said things like that," Sam answered.

Jesperson only shrugged again. Instead of staying to make an argument out of it, he waddled off toward the *Alta Californian*'s office on California Street. If he wrote fast enough, the last couple of editions of his paper would have a no doubt carefully polished version of Mayor Sutro's speech in them, along with an editorial giving half a dozen good reasons for treating San Franciscans like Confederate slaves or Russian peasants.

"Because some petty tyrants are tired of being petty," Clemens muttered under his breath.

He went back to his house almost at a run, hoping Alexandra would be able to lift him out of his evil mood. Part of it lifted at the delighted reception his children gave him: he didn't usually come home in the middle of the day. His own delight at seeing them was somewhat tempered when his wife told him Ophelia had broken a vase not fifteen minutes before.

"It wasn't *my* fault," Ophelia said in tones of virtue impugned. Sam, who had heard such tones before, raised an eyebrow and waited. His daughter went on, "I never would have done it if Orion hadn't ducked when I threw the doll at him."

"Is the world ready?" Sam asked Alexandra.

"I don't know," his wife answered. "If it's not, though, it had better be."

Along with boiled beef and horseradish, that sage comment helped persuade him the world was likely to be able to muddle on a bit longer in spite of Mayor Sutro's aggressive idiocy. He was glad to discover Alexandra disliked Sutro's plan as much as he did.

The dog, hearing everyone saying Sutro over and over, decided people were talking about him. He walked up to Sam and put his head and front paws on his lap. Clemens scratched his ears, which was what he'd had in mind. "Ah, you poor pup," Sam said. "I thought I was insulting the mayor when I gave you your name, and here all the time I was insulting you."

* * *

At the Rochester train station, Frederick Douglass embraced his wife and son. "Now don't you worry about me for even a minute," he said. "This will be how I always wanted to enter the Confederate States: with banners flying and guns blazing and a great army leading the way."

"You make sure you let the army lead the way," Anna Douglass said. "Don't go any place where them Rebels can shoot at you."

"Seeing that the invasion is not yet launched, that's hardly a concern," Douglass answered. "I am delighted that General Willcox recalled the plight of the colored man and wanted one of our race present to witness the U.S. return to Kentucky."

His son, Lewis, embraced him. "Don't just *be* a witness, Father. Bear witness for the world."

"I'll do that. I'll do exactly that." A shouted *All aboard!* from the conductor punctuated Douglass' promise. He climbed up onto the train and took his seat. If the white man next to him was dismayed to have a Negro traveling companion, he was polite enough not to show it, more than which Douglass could not ask.

Going from Rochester to Louisville (or rather, to the Indiana towns across the Ohio from Louisville) took two days. The polite white man left the train at Fort Wayne, to be replaced by a fellow who stared at Douglass in a marked manner and kept sniffing, as if to say the Negro had not bathed as recently as he might have done. Since no one in the car was fresh by then, and since several people apparently had not bathed since the start of the year, Douglass felt he was being unduly singled out. But, as the man from Fort Wayne took things no further than that, Douglass ignored him. He'd known worse.

New Albany, Clarksville, and Jeffersonville, Indiana, had been trading partners with Louisville. They'd sent U.S. manufactured goods into the Confederate States in exchange for tobacco and whiskey and fine Kentucky horseflesh. With the Ohio closed to shipping, with bridges blown up, with cannon barking at one another, they could have had the look of western mining towns after the veins that spawned them had run dry.

Instead, they boomed as never before. The reason was easy to understand: tent cities bigger than any of them filled the countryside beyond the reach of Confederate guns. The U.S. Army was there in numbers not seen since the War of Secession, and bought everything the Rebels would have and more besides.

A driver was supposed to be waiting for Douglass when he got off the train. He stood on the platform, looking around. No driver was in evidence, and it wasn't likely that the man had gone off with some other elderly colored gentleman by mistake. Douglass sighed. Brigadier General Willcox or one of his officers had managed to make a hash of things.

That meant hiring a cab. The first driver Douglass approached shifted a wad of tobacco deep into his cheek so he could growl, "I don't take niggers." Southern Indiana had never been territory friendly to the cause of abolition, and till the war began the locals had probably associated more with the Confederates across the river than with their more enlightened countrymen from other regions of the USA. The second cab driver Douglass approached dismissed him as curtly as had the first.

He finally found a man willing to take him—for a ten-dollar fare. "That's robbery!" he burst out.

"That's business," the fellow returned. "Uncle, ain't many folks round here who'd drive you for any money."

Douglass had already seen as much. *Uncle* was one of the less malicious things whites called blacks: not a compliment, certainly, but an improvement over a lot of choices the driver might have made. "Ten dollars it is," the Negro said, and hoped the man wouldn't try to hold him up for twenty when they got to Willcox's headquarters.

The cab had to pick its way down little paths that had never been meant to take much traffic but were now choked with wagon trains bringing the army the munitions it would need to fight and the food it needed till such time as it did go into battle. The dust was overpowering. Above the rattle of wagon wheels, the driver said, "By the time we get there, pal, we'll be the same color."

If he was exaggerating, he wasn't exaggerating by much. Was that the solution to the problem of white and black in the USA—and, for that matter, in the CSA? Put everybody behind a dozen wagons on a dusty road on a dry summer's day? Douglass wished things could have been so simple.

He soon discovered he could tell which regiments were Regular Army and which volunteers before he saw the banners identifying them. The regulars knew what they were doing. Everything was neat, everything just so. Even the dust around regular regiments seemed less, as if it were afraid to come up lest some officer give it fatigue duty for untidiness.

Volunteer encampments straggled more. The men themselves straggled more, too, and slouched more, as if some of the iron in the regulars' backbones had been omitted from theirs. They looked like what they were: men unsure how to be soldiers but called upon to play the role. A lot of them had been called upon; their regiments far outnumbered those of the long-service professionals who filled the ranks in time of peace. A large part of the volunteer strength of the Army was concentrated here for the blow against Louisville.

"All right, Uncle." The driver halted the cab. "Ten dollars, like I said." Douglass paid without a murmur, relieved he'd kept to the price he'd set at the station. The driver hauled his trunk down from the roof of the cab, nodded in a friendly enough way, and headed back to town. Douglass guessed he would have gouged a white man almost as badly. That made the orator and writer feel a little better.

General Willcox was supposed to know he was coming. When he strode up to the tent with the general's one-star flag flying in front of it, he discovered the sentries had not been informed. "You want to see the *general*?" one of them said, gray eyes widening. He turned to his companion. "Eb, this here dusty old nigger wants to see the general."

Both soldiers guffawed. Eb said, "Yeah, but does the general want to see this here dusty old nigger?" They thought that was funny, too.

"I am Frederick Douglass," Douglass ground out in icy fury. "I was asked to come here to write the story of this army and its assault on Louisville. The story I have in mind to write at the moment will not cast the two of you in the best of light, of that you have my assurance."

His tone worked the wonder his appearance had failed to effect: the sentries began to treat him like a man, not like a Negro. The one who wasn't Eb disappeared into the tent, to return with a spruce young captain. "Mr. Douglass!" the officer said with a broad smile. "So good to meet you. I'm Oliver Richardson, General Willcox's adjutant." He shook hands with Douglass with every sign of pleasure. "I trust you had no difficulty finding the headquarters?"

"Finding them—no," Douglass said. Whatever else he might

have added, he kept to himself. For all he knew, his difficulties might lie at Richardson's feet. He'd met plenty of white men who were friendly to his face and called him a nigger the minute he turned his back.

"Let me take you in to see the general, Mr. Douglass," Richardson said. "I'm sure the men will carry your trunk there to the tent where you are to be quartered."

"Sir, there ain't no such tent," the sentry who wasn't Eb said, "on account of we didn't know this here ... fellow was a-comin'."

"Set one up, then," Richardson snapped. An instant later, he was all affability again. "Come with me, Mr. Douglass."

Douglass came. He found Brigadier General Orlando Willcox slogging down a mountain of papers, a scene he remembered from visiting headquarters during the War of Secession. He wondered how generals ever got to fight; they seemed too busy filling out forms and writing reports to have the time for it.

Willcox was a roly-poly man six or eight years younger than Douglass, with a high forehead that looked higher because his hair had retreated from so much of it. "Mr. Douglass!" he exclaimed, putting down his pen with every sign of delight. "God be praised that you have been able to join us before the commencement of the great struggle."

"I had worried about that, yes," Douglass said, "knowing how celerity is so vital a constituent of the military art."

"We are less hasty than we might have been under other circumstances, there being so many volunteers to weave into the fabric of the Regular Army," Willcox said. "But the mingling of warp and weft proceeds well, and I still have every confidence that the good Lord will grant our arms and our righteous cause the victory they deserve."

"May it be so," Douglass agreed. "If, however, you will forgive my speaking on a matter where I am the rankest amateur and you learned in every aspect, much the same sort of talk was heard in General McClellan's headquarters during the War of Secession. The Lord is, as the saying has it, in the habit of helping them that help themselves."

Captain Richardson sent Douglass a venomous glance that made him suddenly surer than he had been where his difficulties in making arrangements had arisen. General Willcox did not see that glance; he was answering, "I forgive you readily, as it is my

Christian duty to do. But if you knew how many hours I have spent on my knees in prayer, beseeching God to grant me the answers to the riddles of this campaign, you would be more certain I am acting rightly."

Douglass had nothing against the power of prayer: on the contrary. He did wish, though, that General Willcox also spoke of how many hours he'd spent studying maps, examining the enemy's positions on the far side of the Ohio, and sending over spies to examine them close up.

"The event will prove my strategy," Willcox declared.

"Very well, sir," Douglass replied. As he'd said, he was no soldier himself. And Orlando Willcox was certain to be right . . . one way or the other.

Philander Snow leaned out to spit over the side of the Handbasket. "Six days on the road!" he said. "Reckon my backside's as petrified as some of the bones them perfessers dig out of the ground."

"If my hindquarters were that petrified," Theodore Roosevelt said, "I wouldn't be able to feel them, and I most assuredly can. But six days of hard riding would have left us just as worn, and we can carry more supplies in the wagon. Besides, Fort Benton can't be much farther, not when we passed through Great Falls day before yesterday."

"If it *was* much further, I expect I'd be too crippled-up to walk *a*-tall by the time we got there," Snow said.

"If the mountain won't come to Mohammed, Mohammed has to go to the mountain," Roosevelt said. He saw at once that his traveling companion had not the slightest idea what he was talking about. Suppressing a sigh, he made himself what he thought was remorselessly clear: "If forts are the only places in Montana Territory where volunteers may be enrolled into the U.S. Army, then I needs must go to a fort to remove the unfortunate adjective from Roosevelt's Unauthorized Regiment."

"Yeah, and all your toy soldiers'll be a real part of the Army then, too," Snow said, which made Roosevelt swallow another sigh. The ranch hands were good men, honest men, true men: he'd seen as much many times. Just as many times, though, he'd tried to hold any sort of intelligent conversation with one of them, and just as many times he'd failed.

With or without intelligent conversation, he and Phil Snow

rattled northeast close by the north bank of the Missouri River, on toward Fort Benton. They'd followed the river all the way from the farm; except for enormously overdeveloping the buttocks and every single circumadjacent nerve, the trip was easy.

Snow pointed ahead. "Smoke on the horizon, boss. If that don't mean we're about there, I'll swallow my chaw."

"What would happen if you did?" Roosevelt asked, as usual curious about everything.

"I'd sick my guts up, and pretty damn quick, too," Snow said, expectorating for emphasis. "I done it once, when I got throwed off a horse." His tone turned mournful: "It ain't somethin' you want to do twice."

As he must have known, he didn't have to make good on his promise. Inside of half an hour, the Handbasket rolled into Fort Benton. A considerable town had grown up around the fort, which lay as far west along the Missouri as even the shallowest-draft steamboat could reach. *The same thing happened around the legionary camps in the days of the Roman Empire,* Roosevelt thought. He glanced over to Philander Snow and shook his head. Snow's many admirable qualities did not include an interest in ancient history. Roosevelt kept the thought to himself.

Snow was glancing around, too, into the back of the wagon. "You gonna put on your fancy uniform, boss?" he asked. "Hope it ain't got too wrinkled from sittin' there bundled up this past week."

"I think I'll be smarter leaving it bundled up," Roosevelt answered. "By what I heard in Great Falls, this Henry Welton in command of the Seventh Infantry is only a lieutenant colonel himself. I don't want to go in there looking as if I'm claiming to be his superior officer."

"That's clever. That's right clever." Philander Snow shifted the reins to his left hand so he could slap the other down on his thigh. "You don't mind my sayin' so, you're wasting your time runnin' a ranch. You ought to be in politics."

"The thought has crossed my mind," Roosevelt admitted. "If I hadn't decided to come out here, I might have run for the Assembly back in New York. I'll tell you this much—we need to see some changes made, and that's a fact. If the people who are running things now won't make 'em, we need to throw the rascals out and put in some people who will."

Snow brought the wagon to a stop across the street from the

timber gate and adobe walls of Fort Benton. Perhaps not coinci-
dentally, he brought it to a stop directly in front of a saloon. "You
won't need me to go in and talk with this lieutenant colonel,
whatever his name was, will you, boss?"

"No, I don't suppose I will." Roosevelt stuck out his lower jaw
and looked fierce. "But I will need you in some sort of state to
travel when I come out again. Have a few drinks. Enjoy yourself.
But if I have to pour you into the wagon, you will regret it, and
not only on account of your hangover."

"I'll be good," Snow said. "Don't really fancy the notion of
heading back toward the ranch with my head poundin' like a
stamping mill." Next to that prospect, nothing Roosevelt threatened could put fear in him.

But he hurried into the saloon with such alacrity that Roosevelt
clicked his tongue between his teeth. Then he shrugged. He'd see
when he came out of Fort Benton.

"Mornin' to you," the sentry at the gate said when he approached. "State your business, if you please." The soldier did
not stand aside.

"I wish to speak with Lieutenant Colonel Welton," Roosevelt
answered. "I have assembled a body of volunteer troops to offer
to the U.S. Army."

"How big a body of troops?" the sentry asked, unimpressed.
"You got five men? Ten? Fifteen, even? Dribs and drabs is what
we're gettin', and they're hell to put together."

Roosevelt's chest inflated with pride. "My friend," he boomed,
"I have a complete and entire regiment of cavalry, ready for
action. Your colonel has only to give us our orders, and we shall
ride!"

He had the satisfaction of watching the sentry drop his rifle and
catch it before it hit the ground. He had the further satisfaction of
watching everyone within earshot—and he hadn't tried to keep
his voice down: far from it—turn and stare at him. Had the sentry
had a plug of tobacco rather than a pipe in his mouth, he might
have swallowed it. As things were, he needed a couple of tries
before he managed to say, "You're that Roseyfelt fellow down by
Helena, fry me for bacon if you ain't. Heard about you a couple-
three days ago, but I didn't believe a word of it."

"Believe it," Roosevelt said proudly. "It's true."

The sentry did. "Bert!" he called to a soldier within. "Hey, you,
Bert! Come take Mr. Roseyfelt here to the old man's office. He's

the one that's fitted out a cavalry regiment by his lonesome." Bert exclaimed in astonishment. The sentry now seemed to believe he'd invented Roosevelt, saying, "It's a fact. You go right on in, Mr. Roseyfelt. I can't leave my post, but Bert there'll take care of you."

"Thank you." Roosevelt strode into Fort Benton. He wouldn't have wanted to try bombarding the place; the walls had to be thirty feet thick. Two bastions at diagonal corners further strengthened the fort. All the buildings faced inward, having the outer wall as their back.

Bert led Roosevelt across the parade ground to the regimental commandant's office. Through the window, Roosevelt saw a man busily wading through paperwork. He understood that more vividly than he would have a few weeks before; regimental command, even of the as yet Unauthorized Regiment, involved more attention to detail and less glory than he would have dreamt.

When Bert announced him, Lieutenant Colonel Welton set down his pen and stared in astonishment. "*You're* the Roosevelt we heard about?" The officer rose from behind his battered desk. "Good God, sir, I mean no offense, but I believe my son is older than you are."

"It's possible, Lieutenant Colonel," Roosevelt admitted. Henry Welton was about forty-five—twice his own age, more or less—with red-gold hair going gray and a formidable mustache. His grip as they shook hands was odd; he was missing the last two joints of his right middle finger. Once the polite greetings were out of the way, Roosevelt went on, "No one else down toward Helena was doing the job, sir, so I resolved to undertake it myself."

"That's—most commendable, Mr. Roosevelt. A whole regiment? By God, that's amazing." Welton still sounded flummoxed. "Please, sir, sit down." His gray gaze speared Roosevelt as he grew more alert. "I'll bet you call yourself a colonel, too, don't you?"

"Well—yes." Roosevelt was suddenly very glad he'd left the uniform in the wagon. The man with whom he was speaking looked to be a veteran of the War of Secession, and had earned regimental command with years of patient service. Next to that, having the wealth to outfit a unit all at once seemed a tawdry way to gain such a post. Unwontedly humble, Roosevelt went on, "I would not presume to claim rank superior to yours if and when we are accepted into the service of the United States."

"Ah, that. Yes." Welton shook his head. "I never thought I'd have to worry about taking in a whole regiment at a gulp. You've had 'em gathered together for a bit now, too, if what I hear is anywhere close to straight. I bet they're eating you out of house and home."

"As a matter of fact, they are." Roosevelt leaned forward in his chair. "That's not the reason I ask you to accept them, though." He pointed north, toward Canada. "What lies between this fortress and the Canadian border but miles of empty land? Would you not like to have a regiment of mounted men patrolling that land, guarding against attack from the treacherous British Empire and perhaps taking the war into Canadian soil?"

"If the regiment is worth having, I'd like that very much," Welton answered. "If they're a pack of cutthroats, or if they're fair-weather soldiers who look pretty on parade but won't fight, I want no part of 'em." He leaned forward in turn. "What precisely have you got down there by Helena, Mr. Roosevelt?"

For the next hour, the Regular Army officer subjected Roosevelt to a searching interrogation on every aspect of the Unauthorized Regiment, from recruitment to sanitation to discipline to weapons to medicine to tactics. Roosevelt thanked his lucky stars he had done such a careful job of keeping records. Without them, he would never have been able to respond to the barrage of questions.

"Why Winchesters?" Henry Welton snapped at one point.

"Two reasons," Roosevelt answered. "One, I could gain uniformity of weapons for my men with them but not with Springfields, which are far less common among the volunteers. And two, mounted men being widely spaced in combat, rapidity of fire struck me as a vitally important consideration."

He waited to see how Welton would respond to that. The officer's next question was about something else altogether, which, Roosevelt hoped, meant the reply had satisfied him.

At last, the commander of the Seventh Infantry set both hands down flat on the desk. After staring down at them for a few seconds, he said, "Well, Mr. Roosevelt, I had trouble believing it when I heard about it, and I had a damn sight lot more trouble believing it when I saw you're still wet behind the ears. But, unless you've got P. T. Barnum for your adjutant, I'd say you've done a hell of a job—a *hell* of a job, sir. I saw damn few volunteer regiments twenty years ago that could hold a candle to yours. And you're telling me you had no soldierly experience before you decided to organize this regiment?"

"That's right," Roosevelt said. "I've always strongly believed, though, that a man can do whatever he sets his mind to do."

"I already told you once, I wouldn't have believed it," Welton said. "Where did you learn what you need to know about being a colonel?"

"From books—where else? I am a quick study."

"Quick study be damned." Henry Welton gave Roosevelt a very odd look. "Do you have any notion how rare it is for any man, let alone a pup like you, to read something and then up and do it, just like that?" He held up the hand with the mutilated finger. "Never mind. You don't need to answer that. You've answered enough of my questions. Bring your regiment—the Unauthorized Regiment"—amusement glinted in his eyes—"up here, and I'll swear 'em in. If they're half as good as they sound, Colonel Roosevelt, Uncle Sam's getting himself a bargain."

"Yes, sir!" Theodore Roosevelt sprang to his feet and saluted as crisply as he knew how. As soon as he did it, he realized he shouldn't have, not while he was wearing civilian clothes. He felt ready to burst with pride when the Regular Army officer returned the salute: even if it wasn't proper, Welton accepted it in the spirit with which it was offered. Roosevelt hardly remembered the polite words they exchanged in parting. He was amazed the soles of his boots kicked up dust as he left Fort Benton: he thought he was walking on air.

No one had absquatulated with the wagon while he was in the fort talking with Lieutenant Colonel Welton. He didn't see Philander Snow's body stretched out on the planks of the sidewalk, either bloodied or just stupefied from too much whiskey downed too fast. It was, in fact, in his judgment, as near a perfect day as the Lord had ever created.

A woman in a basque so tight-fitting it might have been painted on her torso and a cotton skirt thin almost to translucence came strolling up the street twirling a parasol for dramatic effect. She paused in front of Roosevelt. "Stranger in town," she remarked, and set the hand that wasn't holding the parasol on her hip. "Lonely, stranger?"

He studied the soiled dove. She had to be ten years older than he was, maybe fifteen. The curls under her battered bonnet surely got their color from a henna bottle. Despite inviting words, her face was cold and hard as the snow-covered granite of the Rockies. Roosevelt had broken an understanding of sorts with Alice Lee when he came out West, and was far from immune to animal urges. He sometimes slaked them down in Helena, but tried to pick friendlier partners than this walking cashbox who smelled of sweat and cheap scent.

Besides, the exultation filling him now was in its way nearly as satisfying as a thrashing tussle between the sheets. As politely as he could, he shook his head. "Maybe another time."

"Tightwad," the harlot sneered, and strutted off.

Roosevelt almost called after her to let her know a new cavalry regiment was coming to town. That would put fresh fire under her business. But no; Philander Snow deserved to know first. Roosevelt strolled through the swinging doors of the saloon. There sat Phil, still upright but showing a list. "We're Authorized!" Roosevelt shouted in a great voice.

"Hot damn!" Snow said when the news penetrated, which took a bit.

"Drinks are on me!" Roosevelt said. Such open-handed generosity had won him friends in Helena, and it did the same in Fort Benton. *Good,* he thought. *I'll be coming back here soon.*

Colonel Alfred von Schlieffen had hoped that, by traveling to Jeffersonville, Indiana, to observe the U.S. attack on Louisville, he would escape the ghastly summer weather of Washington and Philadelphia. In that hope, he rapidly discovered, he was doomed to disappointment. Along the eastern seaboard, the Atlantic exerted at least some small moderating effect on the climate.

Deep in the interior of the continent, as Schlieffen was now, nothing exerted any moderating effect whatever. The air simply hung and clung, so hot and moist and still that pushing through it required a distinct physical effort. His uniform stuck greasily to his body, as if someone had taken a bucketful of water from the Ohio and splashed it over him. Almost every house in Jeffersonville, even the poorest shanty, had a porch draped with mosquito netting or metal-mesh screen on which people slept in summer to escape the furnacelike heat inside the buildings. Even the porches, though, offered but small relief.

All the Americans insisted the climate in the Confederate

States was even hotter and muggier. Schlieffen wondered if they were pulling his leg, as their slang expression put it. This side of the Amazon or equatorial Africa, a worse climate seemed unimaginable.

Under canvas in among General Willcox's headquarters staff (not that, to his mind, it was a proper staff for a general: the men around Willcox were more messengers than the specialists and experts who could have offered him advice worth having), Schlieffen was as comfortable as he could be. He also found himself happy, which puzzled him till, with characteristic thoroughness, he dug out the reason. The last time he'd been under canvas, during the Franco-Prussian War, had been the most active, most useful stretch in his entire career, the time when he'd felt most alive. He could hardly hope to equal that feeling now, but the back of his mind had recalled it before his intellect could.

Accompanied sometimes by Captain Richardson (who, like General Rosecrans' adjutant, had a smattering of German he wanted to improve), sometimes by another of General Willcox's staff officers, Schlieffen explored the dispositions of the building U.S. army. "You have indeed assembled a formidable force," he said to Richardson as they headed back toward headquarters from another tour. "I would not have thought it possible, not when a large part of your numbers is made up—are made up?— of volunteers."

"Is made up." Richardson helped his English as he helped the American's German. *"Danke schön, Herr Oberst."* He fell back into his own language: "We fought the War of Secession the same way."

"Yes." Schlieffen let it go at that. The results of the war did not seem to him to recommend the method, but his guide would have found such a comment in poor taste.

Nevertheless, the U.S. achievement here was not to be despised. Kurd von Schlözer was right: Americans had a gift for improvisation. He did not think Germany could have come so far so fast from nearly a standing start (whether the USA should have begun from nearly a standing start was a different question). Fifty thousand men, more or less, had been gathered in and around Jeffersonville and the towns nearby, with the supplies they needed and with a truly impressive concentration of artillery.

"How is the health of the men?" Schlieffen asked. The hellish climate hereabouts only added to the problems involved in keeping large armies from dissolving due to disease before they could fight.

"Ganz gut." Richardson waggled a hand back and forth to echo that. "About what you'd expect. We've had some typhoid. No cholera, thank God, or we'd be in trouble. And a lot of the volunteers are country boys. They won't have had measles when they were little, not living out on farms in the middle of nowhere. You come down with measles when you're a man grown, you're liable to die of 'em. Same goes for smallpox, only more so."

"Yes," Schlieffen said, this time without any intention of evading the issue. The German Army faced similar problems. He wondered whether relatively more German or American soldiers had been vaccinated against smallpox. Then he wondered if anyone knew, or could know. So many things he might have liked to learn were things about which no one else bothered to worry.

"One thing," Oliver Richardson said: "I know the Rebs won't be in any better shape than we are."

Schlieffen nodded. That was, from everything he'd been able to gather, a truth of wider application than Richardson suspected or would have cared to admit. The two American nations, rival sections even before the Confederacy broke away from the United States, thought of themselves as opposites in every way, as enemies and rivals were wont to do. They might indeed have been head and tail, but they were head and tail of the same coin.

"Oh, Christ," Captain Richardson muttered under his breath. "Here comes that damn nigger again."

The Negro walking toward them was an impressive man, tall and well made, with sternly handsome features accentuated by his graying, nearly white beard and head of hair. His eyes glittered with intelligence; he dressed like a gentleman. Schlieffen had thought *nigger* a term of disapproval, but perhaps his mediocre English had let him down. "This is Mr. Douglass, yes?" he asked, and Richardson nodded. "You will please introduce me to him?"

"Certainly," Richardson replied. Now that the black man had come within earshot, the adjutant was cordial enough. "Mr. Douglass," he said, "I should like to introduce you to Colonel von Schlieffen, the German military attaché to the United States. Colonel, this is Mr. Frederick Douglass, the famous speaker and journalist."

"I am pleased to make your acquaintance, Colonel." Douglass' deep, rich voice left no doubt why he was a famous speaker. He held out his hand.

Schlieffen shook it without hesitation. "And I am also pleased to meet you," he said. He'd asked Captain Richardson to introduce him to Douglass, not the other way round. Had the captain assumed Schlieffen was of higher rank because he was a soldier or because he was a white man? On the other side of the Ohio, in the CSA, the answer would have been obvious. Maybe it was obvious on this side of the river, too.

Douglass said, "It is good to see, Colonel, that Germany maintains a friendly neutrality with my country despite the affiliation of the other leading European powers with our foes who set freedom at nought and whose very land groans with the clanking chains of oppression."

Germany also remained neutral toward the Confederate States, a fact Schlieffen thought it wiser to pass over in silence. Instead, he asked, "And when you speak and write of this campaign, what will you tell your . . . your"—he paused for a brief colloquy in German with Captain Richardson—"your readers, that is the word?"

"What shall I tell them about this campaign?" Douglass repeated the question and so gained time to think, a trick Schlieffen had seen other practiced orators use. His answer, when it came, surprised the German officer: "I shall tell them it should have started sooner."

Oliver Richardson scowled angrily. "General Willcox will have overwhelming force in place when he strikes the Rebels," he said.

"And what force will the Rebels have—when he finally strikes them?" Douglass asked, which did nothing to improve Richardson's temper.

"Knowing when to strike is an important part of the art of war," Schlieffen said, in lieu of agreeing out loud with Douglass. A few sentences from the man had convinced him that Negroes, of whom he knew little, were not necessarily fools.

"As I happen to know, the general commanding the Army of the Ohio has informed Mr. Douglass that he has conceived his own understanding of when that time is," Captain Richardson said, "and I am willing to presume that a career soldier knows more of such things than one who has never gone to war."

"The United States have refused to let men of my color go to war, though we would be their staunchest supporters," Douglass rumbled, his temper rising to match that of Willcox's adjutant. Then he shook his massive head. "No, I am mistaken. The United States permits Negroes to serve in the Navy, but not in the Army." He held out his hands, pale palms up, toward Schlieffen in appeal. "Colonel, can you see the slightest shred of reason or logic in such a policy?"

Schlieffen said, "I have not come to the United States to pass judgment on my hosts." *Certainly not in front of my colleagues in U.S. uniform,* he added to himself. *What goes back to Berlin is another matter.*

"When the attack goes in, we shall see who had the right of it," Richardson said. "After the attack succeeds, I trust Mr. Douglass will be generous enough to acknowledge his mistake."

"I have acknowledged my errors many times," Douglass said, "which is a good deal more than many of our career soldiers have done, judging by the memoirs that have seen print since the War of Secession. As for career soldiers' knowing when to strike, was it not President Lincoln who said that, if General McClellan was not using the Army of the Potomac at the moment, he would like to borrow it for a while?"

Richardson rolled his eyes. "If you're going to hold up Lincoln as a paragon of military brilliance—" His expression said what he thought of that.

But he'd misjudged—and underestimated—Douglass. "By no means, Captain." The Negro took obvious pleasure in demolishing his foe's argument: "But he seemed to have a better notion of when to fight than the career soldier in charge of that army, wouldn't you say?"

Oliver Richardson stared. He turned even redder than heat and humidity could have accounted for. But when he found his tongue, he spoke in chilly tones: "*If* you will excuse me, *Mister* Douglass, I am going to take Colonel Schlieffen back to his accommodations."

"I'm so sorry, Captain. I didn't mean to keep you." Douglass tipped his bowler, as if to apologize. His courtesy was more wounding than spite would have been. He tipped the hat to Schlieffen, too, this time, the German officer thought, with genuine goodwill. "Colonel, a pleasure to meet you."

"Very interesting also to meet you," Schlieffen replied. They shook hands again.

Douglass went on his way, his step jaunty despite age and imposing bulk. He knew he'd won the exchange. So did Captain Richardson. "Come on, Colonel," he said sharply. A moment later, he muttered something to himself. Schlieffen thought it was *God* damn *that nigger,* but couldn't be sure.

After a few steps, the military attaché asked, "If the United States let blacks into the Navy, why do they not let them into the Army as well?"

"In the Navy, they're cooks and fuel-heavers in the engine room," Richardson answered patiently. "Mr. Douglass is glib as all get-out, I grant you that, Colonel, but you can't expect a Negro to have the courage to advance into the fire of the foe with a rifle in his hands."

If *glib* meant what Schlieffen thought it did, it was about the last word he would have applied to Frederick Douglass. Richardson's other point perplexed him, too. "Why can you not expect this?" he asked.

Patient still, Richardson explained, "Because most Negroes haven't got the necessities—the spirit, the courage—to lay their lives on the line like that."

"I think perhaps the Englishmen fighting the—Zulus, I believe to be the name of the tribe—in the south of Africa would about this something different say," Schlieffen observed.

Richardson gave him the same stony stare he'd sent toward Douglass. General Willcox's adjutant walked along without another word till they came to Schlieffen's tent. "Here are your quarters, Colonel," he said then, and stalked off without a backwards glance. As Schlieffen ducked his way into the tent, he realized he might as well have challenged Captain Richardson's faith in God as his faith in the inferiority of the Negro.

Though coarse canvas hid the land on the other side of the river, the German military attaché glanced south, toward it. The men of the Confederate States held similar opinions. Did that make them right, or merely similar? With his limited experience, Schlieffen could not say.

He wanted to get another chance to talk with Douglass at supper that evening, but the Negro must have chosen a different time to eat or eaten away from the headquarters staff. If Captain

Richardson's attitude toward him was typical, Schleiffen didn't blame him for that. After supper, he decided not seeing Douglass might have been just as well. He himself still had to remain in the good graces of the staff, or he would not learn everything he wanted to know about the U.S. plan to cross the Ohio and invade the CSA.

He wondered if General Willcox was coming to regret having chosen to concentrate against Louisville rather than, say, Covington farther east. Bringing invasion barges down to Cincinnati would have been easy, since the Little Miami River ran by the town. The streams that flowed into the Ohio opposite Louisville—the Middle, the Falling Run, the Silver, the Mill— were small and feeble. Most of the barges came to them by rail. That that could be done impressed Schleiffen; that it had to be done impressed him in a different way.

The next morning, the Confederates started shelling the barges and boats that were being gathered. U.S. artillery promptly opened up on the Confederate guns. Schleiffen had already noted how many cannon the United States had brought to support their attack. Now the USA used the guns to keep the Confederates from disrupting it.

A considerable artillery duel developed. The C.S. gunners had to take on the U.S. cannon bombarding them, lest they be put out of action without means to reply. That meant they had to stop hammering away at the barges, so the U.S. shelling served its purpose. Schleiffen judged the United States had more guns here than did their foes. They did not put the Rebels out of action, though.

Schleiffen shook his head. The Confederate States were bringing men and matériel to Louisville, as the United States were on this side of the river. He didn't think the CSA had as much, but defenders didn't need as much, either. Had Willcox struck fast and hard two weeks before, even a week before, he might have had a better chance of carrying the town by main force. That wouldn't be so easy now.

Men and guns and barges kept pouring into Jeffersonville and Clarksville and New Albany, though. When all else failed, numbers worked wonders. Orlando Willcox had numbers on his side. If only, Schleiffen thought, he would get around to using them.

* * *

Abraham Lincoln watched in fascinated wonder as U.S. troops marched into Salt Lake City from the north. The soldiers, some mounted, others afoot, tipped their hats and grinned widely at the flag-waving crowds who cheered their arrival. Down State Street they came, under the Eagle Gate at the corner of State and Temple. The wooden eagle, its wingspan more than twice as broad as a man was tall, perched on a beehive supported by curved iron supports mounted on pale stone posts. Though the Latter-Day Saints had erected it, and though the beehive was their symbol, its fierce beak and talons now seemed to symbolize the power of the United States.

Leaning over toward Gabe Hamilton, who was cheering as loudly as anybody else, Lincoln asked, "In all these people on the street, do you see a single, solitary Mormon?"

"Not a one," Hamilton answered at once. "Not many Gentiles who're missing, though, I'll tell you that."

Surveying the soldiers in their natty blue jackets, the metal-work of their rifles bright and shiny, the sun glaring off the steel barrels of the field guns that rolled along after a troop of cavalry, Lincoln was moved to quote Byron:

> *"The Assyrian came down like a wolf on the fold,*
> *And his cohorts were gleaming in purple and gold;*
> *And the sheen of their spears was like stars on the sea,*
> *When the blue wave rolls nightly on deep Galilee."*

Gabe Hamilton clapped his hands together. "That's first-rate stuff. And remember how it ends?

> *"And the might of the Gentile, unsmote by the sword,*
> *Hath melted like snow in the glance of the Lord!*

I think that's how it goes. I know damn well that's how the Mormons hope it goes."

"True enough," Lincoln said, "I am of the opinion that they are doomed to disappointment in those hopes, however. President Blaine, whatever else may be said of him, is not a man to take half measures, as we have seen in his recent conduct of foreign affairs. Having decided not to suffer the semisecession of Utah, he will aim to make certain such a mischance cannot occur again."

A tall, handsome man with a fine gray beard came riding down the street on a gray gelding that was a splendid piece of horse-flesh. The fellow's coat was endowed with a superabundance of brass buttons; as he got closer, Lincoln saw that each of his shoulder straps bore a single silver star.

Though they had not set eyes on each other for almost twenty years, Lincoln and Brigadier General John Pope recognized each other at about the same time. Pope broke out of the parade and rode over toward Lincoln, the horse's hooves kicking up dust at every step. "I heard you were in Salt Lake City, sir," the general said, nodding. "Are you well?"

"Very well, thank you," Lincoln replied. "I am glad to see the power of the United States return to Utah. It has been sorely missed."

"Glad to see it even under my command, eh?" Pope might not have seen Lincoln since the War of Secession, but his glare made it plain he had forgotten nothing in all that time.

"Yes, very glad," Lincoln said simply.

"You shipped me away from the real war," Pope said. "You sent me off to fight redskins and gave my men back to the Young Napoleon, that lazy, pompous fraud—and look how much better than I he did with them." No, Pope hadn't forgotten a thing. His sarcasm was meant to wound, and it did. "But my duty is to serve my country in whatever place I am given, Mr. Lincoln, and I have done that duty. And so now I find myself able to liberate you along with the rest of this rebellious Territory. Strange how things come full circle, is it not?"

"General, you made errors during the War of Secession. I like-wise made errors, and those far worse than yours, else the war should have been won," Lincoln said. "If you believe a day has passed from that time to this when those errors were not upper-most in my mind, I must tell you, sir, that you are mistaken."

Pope grunted. The soft answer, giving him nothing against which to strike, seemed to discomfit him. "Well," he said at last, roughly, "I aim to make no mistakes here. I intend putting the fear of God—the proper Christian God, mind you, the God of wrath and vengeance—in these Mormons. They shall obey me or suffer the consequences. No—they shall obey me *and* suffer the conse-quences." He gave a stiff nod, then kicked his horse up into a canter so he could resume his place in the military procession.

"Well!" Juliette Hamilton said, in a tone altogether different from General Pope's. "Did I hear that man call General Mc-Clellan pompous? Has he looked in a mirror any time lately?"

Lincoln smiled at that. He thought she spoke to vent her own feelings, not to make him feel better. Paradoxically, that did make him feel better. His relief, however, was short-lived. A cavalry colonel with long golden locks and a fierce mustache gave him a look that made Pope's seem mild and benevolent. The horseman kept scowling back over his shoulder at Lincoln till he was out of sight.

"Fellow doesn't seem fond of you," Gabe Hamilton remarked.

"No," Lincoln said. Resignedly, he went on, "Not many who served during the War of Secession are, for which who can blame them? I can't remember that man's name, but he was one of McClellan's staff officers. I wonder how he likes serving under McClellan's rival now."

"What are his choices? He can like it or lump it." Hamilton leaned forward like a hunting dog going on point. "What the devil are those funny-looking things on the gun carriages? Haven't seen anything like them before."

"Neither have I. They don't look like cannon, do they?" Lincoln's curiosity was piqued. During the War of Secession, he'd taken a keen interest in military inventions of all sort. He was something of an inventor himself, and held a riverboat patent, though nothing had ever come of it. "Rifle barrels sticking out of a brass case . . ." He shrugged. "My chief hope is that we need not see what destruction they can reap."

A last company of infantry marched past. Following them came a mounted sergeant who called out in a great voice: "Brigadier General Pope, the military governor of Utah Territory, will speak in Temple Square at three this afternoon. Everyone should hear him, Mormons and Gentiles alike." He rode on a few yards, then repeated the announcement.

"Military governor, is it?" Lincoln thoughtfully clicked his tongue between his teeth. "No, President Blaine isn't doing things by half. With that title, General Pope will have the power to bind and to loose, sure enough." Pope was not the first man to whom he would have entrusted such power, but President Blaine could not have asked his opinion, and would not have if he could.

Juliette Hamilton said, "Someone needs to bring the Mormons into line." Since that was also true, Lincoln held his peace.

He would have gone to Temple Square alone, but Gabe Hamilton also wanted to hear what Pope had to say. Lincoln hadn't thought the square could be any more crowded than it had been on the Sunday when he'd gone to the Tabernacle, but discovered he was wrong. Both Mormons and Gentiles were thronging to it to hear John Pope lay down the law.

Pope was ready for any trouble the Mormons might cause, which was likely the best way to keep them from causing trouble. He himself stood on one of the granite blocks that would eventually be raised to the Mormon Temple. The men on the Temple now were not Mormon masons, however; they were bluecoats with Springfields. More riflemen were atop the Tabernacle. Behind Pope, a couple of field guns, probably loaded with case shot, bore on the crowd. In front of him stood one of the unfamiliar brass-cased contraptions.

Hamilton took his watch out of his vest pocket and looked at it. Either it was a little slow or the one Pope was using ran fast, for it showed a couple of minutes before the hour when the military governor of Utah Territory held up his hands for silence. He got it, faster and more completely than he would have anywhere else in the USA: except in matters bearing on their faith (*a large exception*, Lincoln thought), the Mormons obeyed authority.

"Fellow citizens," Pope boomed, the dusty breeze carrying his words out across Temple Square, "with my arrival here, the government of the United States resumes control over this Territory after the illegal and outrageous attempt on the part of the authorities of the Church of Jesus Christ of the Latter-Day Saints to extort acquiescence to its immoral creed by impeding the flow of men and goods and messages across the continent. No government sensitive to its right could possibly yield in the face of the threats and intimidation proffered by these so-called authorities."

Telling Mormons and Gentiles apart by looks or dress was usually impossible. Lincoln had no trouble seeing who was who now. Gentiles cheered and waved their hats. Some of them waved the flags with which they'd greeted the soldiers, too. Mormons stood silent, listening, hardly moving, almost as if they'd been turned to stone.

Pope went on, "Fellow citizens, we are at war: against the Confederate States, against England and lickspittle Canada, against France. In time of war, the leaders of the Mormon Church, through their deliberate actions, offered aid and comfort to the enemies of the United States by blocking the rail lines and by cutting the telegraph wires. Offering aid and comfort to the enemy in time of war is treason, nothing less."

"Oh, my," Gabe Hamilton whispered. "He's going to hit them hard."

"He surely is," Lincoln whispered back.

"By order of President Blaine," Pope continued, "the former civilian government of Utah Territory is dissolved, it having proved unable to maintain the authority of the U.S. Constitution in this area. Utah being a territory in rebellion against the United States and now returned to the authority thereof by military might"—he gestured up at the riflemen and back toward the cannon—"it is considered to be under military occupation. As military governor, I—"

"Am the new dictator," Hamilton murmured. Lincoln nodded.

Pope proceeded to prove them both right: "—hereby declare the suspension of the right to obtain a writ of *habeas corpus*. I declare the suspension of the right to trial by jury, Mormons having corrupted the process by repeated false and outrageous verdicts. Justice henceforward shall be by military tribunal."

"Can he do that?" Hamilton asked.

"Legally, do you mean? Maybe the Supreme Court will say he can't—years from now," Lincoln answered. "If this Territory is defined as hostile soil under occupation, though, he may well be able to do as he pleases."

"Every male citizen of Utah Territory shall be required within the next sixty days to take an oath of loyalty to the government of the United States," Pope declared. "The oath shall also include a denial that the said male citizen is or shall henceforth be wed to more than one woman at any one time. Perjury pertaining to this section shall be punished with the utmost severity by the aforesaid military tribunals. Polygamy within the boundaries of Utah Territory is from this time forward abolished and prohibited."

Again, the Gentiles applauded. Again, the Mormons revealed themselves by stonelike silence. Being taller than almost everyone around him, Lincoln could see a considerable part of the crowd. Here and there, two or three or four women, sometimes with children in their arms, stood grouped around one man. What was going through their minds?

Pope said, "Because of its role in instigating and carrying out the rebellion of Utah Territory against the United States, the Church of Jesus Christ of the Latter-Day Saints is declared not to be a religion liable to protection under the First Amendment, but a political organization subject to sanctions for its acts. Until further notice, construction of the so-called Mormon Temple is suspended. Public worship at the Mormon Tabernacle and other so-called Mormon churches is also suspended, as are all other public meetings of more than ten persons.

"One last point: any resistance to military authority will be crushed without mercy. Shooting at soldiers and destroying trains, tracks, telegraph lines, or other public necessities of any sort will result in hostages' being taken. If the guilty parties be not promptly surrendered, the hostages shall be hanged by the neck until dead. Anyone doubting my ability or will to fulfill that promise mistakes me." General Pope looked out over Temple Square. "Return peaceably to your homes, people of Utah. Obey the legally constituted authority of the military government and all will be well. Disobey only at your peril."

As Lincoln and Hamilton walked back to the carriage in which they'd come to Temple Square, the Salt Lake City man asked, "Does he mean what he says?"

"I should not care to try to find out the contrary by experiment," Lincoln answered. "John Pope had a name as a hard man during the War of Secession, and I've heard nothing of how he has conducted himself here in the West in the years since to make me believe he's changed."

That evening, Lincoln was about to sit down to supper at the Hamilton's table when someone knocked on the door. Gabe Hamilton went to open it. He called, "An officer to see you, Mr. Lincoln."

"I'm coming." Lincoln walked to the door, to find himself facing the short, energetic blond cavalry officer he'd noted in the parade. "What can I do for you, Colonel?"

"George Custer, Fifth Cavalry," the man said briskly. "I am told, Mr. Lincoln, that you had conversations with Mr. John Taylor, the Mormons' president." When Lincoln didn't deny it, Custer went on, "Do you know his present whereabouts?"

"No," Lincoln said. "If he's not at home, or perhaps at the Tabernacle, I have no idea where he might be. Why, if you don't mind my asking?"

"He is to be arrested for treason, along with the rest of the Mormon leaders," Custer answered. "We can't lay hands on him, though. He's run off, God knows where—I was hoping you might, too. When we catch him, General Pope aims to hang him higher than Haman."

Harry Turtledove

He wasn't interested for a moment, or even moved in the direction toward ... his mouth. "... ..., he ..." seemed truthful enough. He cried out, God knows what. I was home for supper too. When we came here, General, we weren't long gone from a different ...

☆ VIII ☆

General Thomas Jackson peered north across the Ohio River through a telescope. "The onslaught cannot now be long delayed," he said to Brigadier General Peter Turney, who stood by his side. "I thank our heavenly Father for having given us this much time in which to ready Louisville for the storm."

"The Yankees were slowcoaches in the last war," Turney answered, his Tennessee twang contrasting with Jackson's softer Virginia accent. "Doesn't look like they've learned a whole hell of a lot since."

"For which we should also give thanks to God," Jackson said, and Turney nodded.

Negro labor gangs in tunics and trousers of coarse, undyed cotton—almost the same color as old-style Confederate uniforms— were still busily digging firing pits and building earthworks and abatis throughout Louisville, but especially down by the waterfront. Without the slaves, the defenses of the city would have been far weaker than they were.

Brigadier General Turney asked, "Sir, is it true what I hear, that President Longstreet's going to try and manumit the niggers after the war?" Under bushy gray eyebrows, his broad, earnest face was worried.

"It is true, General," Jackson said, and Turney grimaced. "He feels the effort to be necessary for reasons of state."

"Reasons of state be damned." Turney pointed toward a gang marching along with picks and shovels shouldered like rifles. "Without slaves like that bunch there, what in blazes are we supposed to do the next time the Yankees pick a fight with us?"

"I can hope that, even if free, the Negro shall not be equal to the white man, and shall be subject to some form of conscription in time of need."

"Turn 'em loose and they'll get uppity—you mark my words,"
Turney said. Then (rather to Jackson's relief, for he agreed with
the views the Tennessean expressed) he changed the subject: "Do
you think we knocked out enough of their invasion boats to have
held them up?"

"I wish I did, but I very much doubt it," Jackson answered.
"Artillery is ideally suited for breaking up an attack once
launched, but I fear the science has not advanced to the point
where it can preempt one. That day may be coming, but has not
yet arrived."

"We'll hurt 'em when they do come—whenever that is,"
Brigadier General Turney said.

"We shall do more than hurt them, General," Jackson said.
"We shall smash them and wreck any further hopes for the invasion of our country they may have—we shall do that, or I will
know the reason why and the men responsible."

He did not raise his voice or make any histrionic gesture.
Nevertheless, before Turney quite realized what he was doing, he
gave back a pace from Jackson. The brigadier general laughed
nervously. "The men won't dare lose," he said. "They're more
afraid of what you'd do to 'em than they are of the damnyankees."

Jackson considered. "That is as it should be," he said at last,
and swung up onto his horse. Leaving Turney to stare after him,
he rode back through Louisville to the headquarters he'd established south of the city, beyond U.S. artillery range.

Even in its present state, with most of the civilian population
fled, Louisville struck him as the least distinctively Southern city
in the Confederate States. That didn't spring only from its having
been the last town to fall into Confederate hands. Many of the
people hereabouts were Yankees by origin or descent, from New
York and New England.

And Louisville, like Covington farther east, still looked across
the border to the United States, in the same way that Cincinnati,
on the other side of the Ohio, looked south to the Confederacy.
All three were towns that had grown up trading what the North
made for that the South did. That North and South were now two
different countries made trade more complicated, but had neither
stopped it nor even slowed it much.

Coins jingled in Jackson's pocket. Some had been minted in
the USA, some in the CSA. Both nations coined to the same
standard; along the border, that was all that mattered. Yankee

greenbacks circulated as readily as the brown banknotes issued in the Confederate States. A lot of people hereabouts not only didn't much care whether the Stars and Bars or the Stars and Stripes flew over them, they hardly noticed which flag did fly.

"They will, I expect, learn the difference in short order," Jackson said to himself.

A company of infantry, the soldiers in gray, the officers in the new butternut uniforms, was marching north as he rode south past them. The men grinned and whooped and tossed their hats. "Stonewall!" they shouted. Abstracted, Jackson was by them before he raised his own hat to acknowledge the cheers.

He rode past the University of Louisville, past the downs where, locals told him, people were talking about building a race-track, and into a grove of oaks where he'd pitched his tent so he could rest under the shade of the trees. After giving his horse to an orderly, he hunted up his own chief artillerist, Major General E. Porter Alexander. "It won't be long," he said bluntly.

"Good," Alexander answered. "High time." He was more than ten years younger than Jackson, with a perpetually amused look on his long, handsome face and a pointed brown beard flecked with gray.

"Much will depend on your guns, General," Jackson said. "I shall want as much damage as possible done to the Yankees' boats while they are in the water, and to their installations on the northern bank of the river."

"I understand, sir," Alexander said. "We've been trying to hurt them before they launch, but we unmask ourselves when we bombard them, and they have a lot of guns over there trying to knock us out. Say what you will about the rest of the U.S. Army, their artillery has always been good."

He and Jackson smiled at each other. Jackson had begun his military service in the U.S. Artillery. Alexander himself had started out as an engineer, switching to big guns not long after choosing the Confederate side in the War of Secession.

"It is of the most crucial importance that they not gain such a lodgment on the southern shore of the Ohio that they drive us beyond rifle range of the river," Jackson said. "That would enable them more easily to erect bridges to facilitate the flow of men and equipage into our country, and their engineers are not to be despised, either." He didn't often think to return compliments, and was always pleased with himself when he did remember such niceties.

"As long as they don't drive us out of cannon range, we can still give them a rough time," Alexander said. "And our guns range a deal farther than they did in the last war."

Jackson noted the artillerist did not promise he could put the bridges out of action with his guns. One reason he appreciated Alexander was that the younger officer never made promises impossible to keep.

"I shall rely on your men quite as much as on the infantry," Jackson said.

"Coming from you, sir, I'll take that," Alexander replied. "In fact, I'll let the men know you said it. If anything will make them fight harder, that'll do it."

They conferred a while longer. Jackson went back to his own tent, where he spent an hour in prayer. He had heard that General Willcox, the U.S. commander, was also a man of thoroughgoing piety. That worried him not in the least. "Lord, Thou shalt surely judge the right," he said.

After a frugal supper of stale bread and roasted beef with salt but no other seasoning, a regimen he had followed for many years, he checked with the telegraphers to see if President Longstreet had sent him any further instructions. Longstreet hadn't. Having ordered him to make a defensive fight, Longstreet seemed content to let his general-in-chief handle the details. Robert E. Lee, God rest his soul, had known how to write a discretionary order. Seeing that Longstreet had learned something from the man who had commanded them both was good.

On returning to his tent, Jackson reviewed his dispositions. He was, he decided, as ready as he could be. He doubted the same held true on the other side of the river. Taking that as a sign God favored the Confederate cause, he pulled off his boots, knelt beside his iron-framed cot for the day's last petition to the Lord, then lay down and fell asleep almost at once.

Whenever he was in the field, he had himself roused with the first twilight at latest. He'd just sat up in bed after the orderly woke him when a great thundering rose from the north. None of the artillery duels his forces and General Willcox's had fought were anything close to this. "It begins!" he exclaimed. As usual, all he needed to put on were his boots and his hat. That done, he rushed out of the tent.

He almost collided with E. Porter Alexander, who emerged from under canvas as fast as he did. Alexander had shed his tunic for the night and was wearing only shirt and trousers, which made him look more like a Yankee laborer on a hot afternoon than a Confederate general before sunup.

"Now we shall see what we shall see," Alexander said, for all the world like a chemistry professor about to drop a bit of sodium into water for the sake of the flame and smoke. "Artillery can do so much more than it could during the last war, but we knew much more about sheltering from it, too."

"A lesson learned from painful experience," Jackson said. Now, all at once, he wished he'd encamped in the open. The leafy canopy overhead kept him from having any better notion of what was going on than his ears could bring him, and all he could learn from them was that both U.S. and Confederate guns were in action, every one of them sounding as if it was pounding away as hard as it could.

An orderly led up Jackson's horse. At the same time, another man dashed up to the general-in-chief with a telegram clutched in his fist. "This just in from General Turney, sir," he said. "It cuts off halfway—don't know if a shell broke the wire or his operator got hit."

"Give it to me." Jackson put on his glasses, then took the wire. It was hard to read in the still-dim light. A soldier brought over a candle. By the flickering light, Jackson read, U.S. FORCES ON THE RIVER IN LARGE NUMBERS. RESISTING WITH ARTILLERY AND RIFLE FIRE. NEED . . . As the private from the signals office had said, it ended there.

Deducing what General Turney required, though, required no great generalship: a schoolchild could have done it. Jackson shouted for a messenger. When one appeared, he said, "The two brigades quartered near the Galt House are ordered to the waterfront to resist the invaders if their commanders have not sent them forward on their own initiative." The messenger saluted and dashed off, shouting for a horse. Jackson gave the identical order to the soldier who'd passed him the telegram. "With the U.S. bombardment, I do not know if a wire can get through, but make the effort."

Not far away, E. Porter Alexander was also giving orders, in a calm, unhurried voice: "Until we know different, we'll go on the notion that the Yankees are doing what we expect. That means

Fire Plan One, with guns ranged in on the river and on the Indiana docks to stick to their assigned targets. Any changes from the plan are to be reported to me at once."

When he was done, he turned to Jackson with a smile on his face. "A pity, isn't it, General, that battles have grown too large to be commanded from the front? If messengers and telegrams don't constantly tell us what's happening across the field, how can we direct the fighting?"

"In a fight this size, we can't, and I hate that," Jackson said. "Leading a brigade against Winchester made me feel a young man again. I tell you this, though, General: I am going to see the fighting for myself, even if only from a distance." He mounted the horse the orderly had brought, and rode out from under the spreading branches of the oaks toward a nearby hilltop.

Sunrise was near. The eastern horizon glowed with pink and gold light, the spark that was Venus gleaming through it. Only the brightest stars still shone in the darker sky farther west. But the northern quadrant was ablaze with bursting shells; Jackson might have been watching a Fourth of July fireworks display from some distant house.

By where the smoke was thickest, he could tell that the U.S. gunners were giving the wharves of the waterfront a fearful pounding. Had he led the Yankees, he would have ordered the same, to make the Confederate infantrymen keep their heads down and prevent them from bringing too heavy a fire to bear against the invasion boats. The smoke kept him from discerning much more than that. And, with every passing minute, though the light got stronger, the smoke got worse: smoke from the Yankees' guns on the other side of the Ohio, smoke from bursting shells, and smoke from the C.S. cannon responding to the enemy's fire.

Jackson's frown was venomous. He wanted nothing so much as to grab a Tredegar and go where the fighting was hottest. But Major General Alexander had the right of it: if he did that, he could not at the same time command. More men were capable of fighting the damnyankees than of leading the entire army against them. And, had he snatched up a rifle and run off to pretend he was a private soldier, he would have been able to see even less of the battlefield than he could from his present vantage point.

He'd already been too long away from his electric eyes and ears. And messengers would be getting back to headquarters from

the fighting by now, too. Regretfully, he used feet and reins to
start his horse back toward the tent among the trees.

No sooner had he dismounted than the first messenger arrived,
dirty-faced, with a torn and filthy uniform, eyes wide and staring
from what was surely his first taste of combat. He stared at
Jackson, too. Was that because he was meeting a man legendary
in the CSA or simply because he was too battered to recall the
message he was supposed to deliver?

Then, very visibly, his wits began to turn, as if they were a
steamboat's paddlewheel. "General Jackson, sir!" he exclaimed.
"The damnyankees have men ashore on our side of the river." He
gulped. "Lots of 'em, sir."

Even in the predawn stillness, southern Indiana remained sul-
try, sticky. Frederick Douglass stood in a field just outside the city
limits of New Albany. Every couple of minutes, he would slap at
himself as a mosquito bit him. "I'm an old man," he said sadly. "I
remember being able to hear the mosquitoes buzzing around, so
that sometimes I could get them before they got me. No more, not
for years. Now they take me by surprise."

That amused the U.S. artillerymen standing by their pieces
awaiting the word to commence. "It ain't no big loss, Pop," one
of them said. "That goddamn buzzing drives me crazy, nothin'
else but." A couple of his comrades spoke up in agreement.

"Better to know the enemy than to let him take you by surprise," Douglass insisted, which drew another chuckle from the
Massachusetts volunteers. In the couple of days he'd been with
them, they'd treated him well: General Willcox had made a good
choice in assigning him to their battery when he'd asked to watch
the bombardment of Louisville from among the guns.

A rider came trotting down the road. He halted when he saw
the guns: big, dark shapes in what was otherwise an empty field.
"Open fire at four A.M. sharp," he called, and rode on to give
the next battery the word.

Someone struck a match, first stepping well away from the
guns and limbers to do so. The brief flare of light showed the
boyish features of Captain Joseph Little, the battery commander.
"Fifteen minutes," he said after checking his pocket watch. "Men,
we'll load our pieces now, so as to get the first shots off precisely
on the mark."

In darkness just this side of perfect, the gun crews handled unscrewing the breech blocks, loading in shells and bags of powder after them, and sealing the guns once more as smoothly as they might have done at high noon. Douglass had already seen that the artillery volunteers, most of whom were militiamen of long standing, were trained to a standard close to that of their Regular Army counterparts, which could not have been said about the volunteer infantry.

Captain Little spoke up again: "Mr. Douglass, you'll want to make certain"—his Bay State accent made the word come out as *suht'n*, almost as if he were a Rebel—"you're not standing right behind a gun. When they go off, the recoil *will* send them rolling backwards at a pretty clip."

Douglass made sure he would be out of harm's way. The quarter of an hour seemed to take forever. Douglass was beginning to think it would never end when, off to the east toward Jeffersonville, several cannon roared all at once.

"Well! I like that," Captain Little said indignantly. "Still lacks two minutes of the hour by my watch." He must have been staring at it in the faintest early twilight. "Some people think they have to come to the party early. If we can't be the first, we shan't be the last, either." More guns were going off, some of them much closer than the earliest ones had been. Little raised his voice: "Battery B . . . Fire!"

All six guns bellowed at essentially the same instant. The noise was a cataclysmic blow against Douglass' ears. Great long tongues of yellow flame burst from the muzzles of the cannon, illuminating for half a heartbeat the men who served them. Dense smoke shot from the muzzles, too.

Douglass paid that scant heed for the moment. As Captain Little had warned, the cannon recoiled sharply. A couple of artillerymen had to step lively to keep from being run down by the creaking gun carriages.

"Come on, lads!" Little yelled. "Get 'em back in place and give the damn Rebs another dose of the same." Grunting and cursing, the crews manhandled the cannon up to the positions from which they'd first fired. The breeches were opened, swabbed out to make sure no burning fragments of powder bag remained. Then in went another shell, another charge, and the loaders screwed the breeches shut. The guns bellowed once more, not in a single salvo this time but one after another, each crew struggling to be faster than those to either side of it.

The smoke quickly filled the field. Coughing, Douglass moved to one side, seeking not only cleaner air to breathe but also an unimpeded view of the battlefield. As twilight brightened toward day, it was as if the curtain lifted on an enormous stage set out before him.

Seeing that panorama, he understood for the first time why men spoke of the terrible grandeur of war. Barges and boats packed with soldiers raced across the Ohio so the men they carried could close with the foe. Shells from the U.S. guns poured down like rain on the waterfront of Louisville. Each one burst with a flash of sullen red fire and a great uplifting cloud of black smoke. Douglass could not imagine how any Confederate soldiers compelled to endure such a cannonading could hope to survive.

But the enemy not only survived, he fought. Not only did shells burst along the waterfront. They also burst in the Ohio. Looking across the river, Douglass could see flashes from the muzzles of Confederate guns, cannon similar to those the Massachusetts volunteers served. Their thunder reached his ears, too, attenuated by distance but still very real.

Tall plumes of water flew up from the shells that splashed into the Ohio. When Douglass noticed those, the spectacle before him suddenly seemed less grand. His breathing came short. His palms got sweaty. Remembered terror was almost as vivid as the original. He did not need to wonder what the blue-clad men in the invasion boats were feeling. He'd felt it himself, when the Rebel battery shelled the *Queen of the Ohio*.

Those Confederates had been but a handful, with only a single battery of old-fashioned guns to bring to bear on their target. The Rebels here had modern cannon by the score and targets to match. Many of them, too, would be their Regular Army men, the best they had.

Not all their shells, then, burst in the river. Some struck the hurrying boats full of U.S. troops. Douglass groaned when one of those simply broke up and sank, throwing its heavily laden soldiers into the water. Another stricken vessel must have had either its helmsman hit or its rudder jammed, for it slewed sharply to one side and collided with its neighbor. Both boats capsized.

And, as the barges and boats neared the bank the Confederates held, tiny yellow flashes, like far-off fireflies, began appearing in the midst of the shell-bursts from the U.S. guns: Confederate riflemen got to work. Incredible as it seemed to Frederick Douglass, they had not only lived through the bombardment that still continued, but also retained enough spirit to fight back strongly. Loathe their cause though he most sincerely did, Douglass could not help respecting their courage.

The first boats began to reach the far bank of the river. Tiny as blue ants in the distance, U.S. soldiers swarmed off them, rushing forward to find cover from the galling fire of their foes—and also from the fire of their friends, which had not shifted its targets despite the landings. Artillery put Douglass in mind of some great ponderous stupid beast, liable to step on and crush anyone who came too near it.

He scrawled his impressions of the fight down in a notebook, intending to weave them into a coherent whole back at his tent when he had the leisure. He had, as yet, no idea whether the battle would be won or lost. All he could discern at the moment was that both sides were fighting not only with desperate courage but also with all the resources science and industry could give them.

And then, in the twinkling of an eye, the battle lost its abstract, panoramic quality and the face of war changed for him forever. The C.S. artillery had concentrated on the invasion boats on the Ohio and, to a lesser degree, on the quays where the barges and boats took on their cargo of soldiers. Every so often, though, the Rebs would lob a few shells at the U.S. guns bombarding them, no doubt aiming more to harass than to stop the cannonading.

By the time the sun came up, Frederick Douglass had grown intimately familiar with the astonishing cacophony emanating from an artillery battery working at full throttle. He did not, however, understand what shrill, rising screams in the air meant until three shells burst in swift succession among the Massachusetts volunteers whose deeds he'd intended chronicling.

The ground shook under his feet. Something hissed past his head. Had it flown a few inches to one side of its actual path, any hopes of his chronicling the artillerymen's adventures would have died in that instant.

More screams, these from the ground, not the air: the sounds of agony. Douglass forgot he was a reporter and remembered he was a man. Stuffing the notebook into a pocket, he ran across the field—even now, under the stink of gunpowder, the grass smelled sweet—to give what aid he could.

"Oh, dear God!" He stopped short with an involuntary exclamation of horror. There lay brave, clever Captain Joseph Little, who had never by word or deed shown he thought Douglass less than himself on account of the color of his skin. Captain Little would never think good or ill of Douglass again, not in this world. One of the Confederate shells had burst quite near him. Now he lay like a broken doll. Broken quite literally: his head had been torn from his body, and lay several feet away from the still-twitching corpse. Half the top of it had been blown off, too; red blood pooled on gray brains. More red soaked the green grass under him. The first flies were already landing.

Captain Little, of course, did not scream. The one virtue of his death was that he could have had no notion of what hit him. One second, he was directing his guns, the next . . . gone. The fellow down on the ground beside him—no, by some miracle or insanity, sitting up now—wasn't screaming, either. When the artilleryman sat, his intestines spilled out into his lap. A shell fragment had laid open his belly as neatly as the slave butcher gutted hogs back in Douglass' plantation days.

The Massachusetts volunteer looked down at himself. "Isn't that something?" he said, his voice eerily calm. Douglass had heard of men with dreadful injuries who seemed unaware of pain, in stories from railroad accidents and such. He hadn't believed them, but now he saw they were—or could be—true. The artilleryman's eyes rolled up in his head. He slumped back to the ground, dead or unconscious. If he was unconscious, Douglass hoped he'd never wake, for he had no hope of surviving, not with that dreadful wound.

By one of the hellish freaks of war, another soldier had had his guts torn out in almost identical fashion. He was not quiet. He was not calm. He rolled and thrashed and shrieked and wailed, spraying blood and fragmented bits of himself in every direction. Douglass heard one of his teeth break as he clenched his jaws against yet another scream. He was perfectly conscious, perfectly rational, and looked likely to stay that way for hours to come.

His eyes, wide and wild and staring, fixed on Douglass and held the Negro's in an unbreakable grip. "Kill me," the artilleryman growled, his voice rough and ragged and ready to dissolve into yet another howl of anguish. "For God's sake, kill me. Don't make me go through any more of this."

He wore a revolver on his belt. With what looked like a

supreme effort of will, he jerked one dripping hand away from his belly long enough to get the pistol out and shove it along the ground toward Douglass.

Before Douglass knew what he'd done, he picked up the revolver. It was heavy in his hand. He knew how to use one. He'd carried one in the grim days just after the War of Secession, when whites were liable to blame any Negro they saw for the war and, perhaps, to go from blaming him to hanging him from the nearest lamppost.

He looked around. None of the other artillerymen was paying him the least attention. Some were tending to less dreadfully wounded comrades. Others, farther away, kept on serving their own guns, so as to make sure the Confederates on the other side of the river got their fair share of death and mutilation and horror and torment.

"Shoot me," the eviscerated soldier groaned. "Don't stand there with your thumb up your ass, damn you to fucking hell."

For the first twenty years of his life and more, Douglass had been caught up in the nightmare of slavery. Now he found another nightmare, one that turned men into beasts—into beasts straight from the abattoir—in different, more abrupt fashion. Caught in the toils of this new nightmare, he pointed the revolver at the artilleryman's forehead and, with a convulsive motion, squeezed the trigger.

The pistol bucked in his hand. A neat, blue-black hole appeared above the wounded soldier's left eye. The back of his head blew out, splashing hair and shattered bits of skull and brains and blood over the grass. With a cry of disgust and dismay, Douglass set down the pistol and rubbed his blood-smeared palm against a trouser leg again and again, as if by that means he could wipe off the mark of Cain.

Several artillerymen spun toward him at the sound of the shot. Most of them, seeing what he had done, simply went back to what they were doing. One, though, with a sergeant's three red stripes on his sleeve, walked over toward the distraught Negro. After looking at the dead gunner's ghastly wound for a few seconds, he put an arm around Douglass' shoulder. "I want to thank you for what you did, sir," he said. "Noah was my cousin, and you put him out of his pain. If you hadn't been there, I believe I'd have had to do the job myself, and that would have been mighty hard, mighty hard indeed."

"It was—the only thing I could do," Douglass said slowly. So often, words like that revealed themselves for the shallow self-justification they were. This once, he heard truth in them.

So did the sergeant, Noah's cousin. "That's right," he said. "That's just exactly right, and don't you let it trouble your mind again." He went back to his cannon, leaving Douglass, who was not a Roman Catholic, fully understanding for the first time in his life the power of absolution.

Alfred von Schlieffen paced along the northern bank of the Ohio, growing more frustrated by the moment. A great battle raged a mile away, and he could not get to it. He could not even do a proper job of observing, not from where he was. Too much smoke hung in the air to let him have more than the vaguest notion of how the fight was going. And the U.S. authorities flatly refused to let him board a boat and cross over to the Kentucky side of the river.

"I'm sorry, sir," said Second Lieutenant Archibald Creel, who accompanied him today because General Willcox had more urgent things for Oliver Richardson to do. "The general doesn't want us to have to explain to Berlin how we let their military attaché go and get himself killed."

A couple of Confederate shells smashed to earth within a hundred yards of Schlieffen. "I am on this side of the river to do that," he remarked with some asperity. As if to underscore his words, more shells screamed in.

Lieutenant Creel did not look as if he had been out of West Point more than a week. He stood firm, both against the shelling and against the foreign officer he was required to shepherd. "I have my orders, sir," he said. He might have been quoting Holy Writ. In a soldierly way, he was.

"To the devil with your orders," Schlieffen muttered, but in German, which the youngster did not speak. He tried again: "I am a military man. I am obliged to take risks for my fatherland."

"No, sir," Creel said, and stuck out his chin.

"*Donnerwetter,*" Schlieffen said. No doubt about it: he was stuck.

Since he was stuck, he decided to make the most of it. He set off at a brisk walk toward the Jeffersonville wharves, which, as an accomplished map reader, he knew to be closer than those of

Clarksville. Like a dog on a leash—and so he was, a watchdog—Second Lieutenant Creel tagged along.

Men in blue—some in the faded uniforms of the regulars, more wearing the dark and almost spotless clothes the volunteers had recently donned—waited in long, stolid lines to board the barges and steamboats that would ferry them over the river so they could fight. Schlieffen had watched boats get hit in midstream. No doubt the soldiers had, too. They kept moving toward the boats anyhow, exactly as Germans would have done. That took discipline and courage both, the combination being especially remarkable for volunteer troops.

Long trenches paralleled the lines that led down to the waterfront. When the Confederates started sending shells at the men near Schlieffen, they lost their stolidity in a hurry, diving into the trenches to shelter from blast and flying splinters.

Schlieffen stayed upright. So did Lieutenant Creel. It was surely the first time he'd been under fire. He handled himself well. As soon as the shells stopped falling, the U.S. soldiers scrambled out of the trenches and resumed their places in line as if nothing had happened. Stretcher-bearers carried away a couple of groaning wounded men, but only a couple.

"These ditches are a good idea," Schlieffen said. "They save casualties."

"That they do." Archibald Creel sounded as proud as if he'd thought of them himself.

So, Schlieffen thought, *I have here one small worthwhile thing. Is this enough for sending me so far? Is this enough to have gathered from the greatest battle of the war?* The answer, in both cases, was painfully obvious. With more temper than he usually showed, Schlieffen rounded on Second Lieutenant Creel: "You can tell me for a fact that U.S. troops are at this time fighting in Louisville?"

"Yes, sir, I can tell you that," Lieutenant Creel said.

"*Sehr gut.* You cannot, however, tell me where in Louisville or how in Louisville or how well in Louisville they are fighting, *nicht wahr?*"

"I don't know those things for certain, no, sir," Creel said. "I wish I did." He laughed nervously. "The fog of war." His wave encompassed the very real layer of thick gray smoke that blanketed Louisville, that hung low and close to the Ohio, and that drifted and swirled in eddies on the U.S. side of the river.

"Where will they know—where will they have some idea— how goes the fighting in Louisville?" Schlieffen demanded.

"One place is over across the river, sir," Creel said.

"Where I cannot go."

"Where you can't go," the young lieutenant agreed. "The other place would be General Willcox's headquarters." He laughed again. "Well, Confederate headquarters, too, I suppose, but you can't go there, either."

"No," Schlieffen wondered if the German military attaché to the Confederate States was over there. He hoped so. Having reports from both sides of the line would be useful back in Berlin—provided he learned enough here to give his report any value. "Be so good, then, as to conduct me back to General Willcox's tent. To go to the front is for me forbidden, and here in the middle I might as well be in the middle of the sea. Take me back."

"Yes, sir," Lieutenant Creel said. "I don't know how much the general will let you see with the battle still going hot and heavy, but we'll find out. You come along with me, sir, and I'll take you there."

Schlieffen would have got there faster by himself, but not much. The young U.S. officer had some notion of where he was and a pretty good idea of how to reach headquarters. Schlieffen, who laid a map in his head over the territory it represented as automatically as he breathed, had to do some unobtrusive guiding only once or twice to keep Creel headed in the right direction.

Creel's presence was enough to get Schlieffen past the sentries outside General Willcox's tent. Given the stream of messengers rushing in and out, Schlieffen suspected he could have got past them without the young lieutenant. Some of those messengers clutched telegrams in their fists. Schlieffen noted that, though he didn't remark on it for fear the Americans would notice him noticing. So they'd managed to get an insulated wire across the Ohio, had they? That would help them. General Willcox would have far more intimate knowledge of what his troops were doing and would be able to send them orders far quicker than if he'd had to rely on boat traffic alone.

Getting to see him actually directing the battle, though, took a bit of doing. A staff officer senior to Second Lieutenant Creel halted Schlieffen, saying, "This isn't anything we want any foreigners watching."

"I am not an enemy," Schlieffen said indignantly. "I am a neutral. When General Rosecrans let me come here, he gave me leave to observe the actions of the Army of the Ohio. You are preventing me from doing my duty to my country when you keep me from observing."

"I'm doing my duty to my own country," the staff officer retorted.

"I protest," Schlieffen said loudly. He was half the size and twice the age of the soldier barring his path. If the idiot in blue didn't get out of his way, though, he was going to do his best to break him in half.

Lieutenant Creel saw as much, and put a restraining hand on his arm. "Wait a second, Colonel," he said. "Let me get Captain Richardson. He'll straighten this out." He hurried past the other staff officer, who suffered him to enter General Willcox's *sanctum sanctorum.*

"What's all this about?" Richardson said when he came out. "I haven't got time for any nonsense right now." Schlieffen and the other U.S. staff officer both started talking at once, glaring at each other while they did. Richardson listened for a little while, then threw up his hands. "Yes, Colonel Schlieffen, you may observe. Hickenlooper, keep out the Rebs and the Englishmen. Germany's friendly, and she's likelier to stay that way if you let the attaché here do his job."

"*Danke,* Captain Richardson," Schlieffen said. He gave the dejected Hickenlooper a severe look as he strode past him.

As he might have expected, the command center of the Army of the Ohio was more chaotic than that which he'd known while serving in the Franco-Prussian War. Messengers and officers rushed in and out and stood around arguing with one another in a fashion no German general would have tolerated for an instant.

Orlando Willcox looked up from the enormous map held flat on a table by a couple of stones, a government-issue tin cup, and one bayonet stabbed through the paper and into the wood. "Ah, Colonel Schlieffen," he said. "Glad to see you. We have our landings on the other side of the river, you see."

Schlieffen bent over the map. Sure enough, pins with blue glass heads showed U.S. forces scattered along the Kentucky shore of the Ohio and controlling the sandy islands in the middle of the river. Even as the attaché watched, an aide stuck in another blue-headed pin, this one a little farther from the riverbank.

"We have to push them back," Willcox said. "We can't bridge the river with snipers picking off our engineers as fast as they get into range. Artillery is bad enough, but Confederates, say what you will about them, produce first-rate sharpshooters. And they'll have every stretch of the Ohio ranged to the inch, too, so they'll know precisely how to sight their rifles."

"The need for accurate sighting is the major drawback of the modern military rifle," Schlieffen agreed. To reach longer ranges, rifle bullets needed considerable elevation, which meant the angle at which they descended was far from insignificant. It also meant a minor error in estimating range was almost sure to result in a miss out past a couple of hundred yards.

Willcox pointed to the red pins measling the map of Louisville. "It would appear that the C.S. commander, rather than withdrawing from the city here to engage us on open ground, intends to make his fight within Louisville itself, thereby subjecting it to all the rigors of war. Such callousness as to its fate and the fate of those civilians remaining there cannot win him favor either with his own people or in the eyes of the Lord."

"This may well be so," Schlieffen said, "but fighting in a built-up area is a good way to cause the foe many casualties. Remember the battle the French had to wage to put down the Paris Commune." He granted the Communards a good deal of thoughtful respect. Their ferocity, along with some of the fighting Napoleon III's army had waged even after its cause was lost, in his view gave the lie to those Germans who reckoned France too weak and decadent ever to be a menace again.

"Fighting like that is uncivilized," Willcox declared.

There, he had a point. European practice had long been for armies to engage away from centers of population, both to avoid endangering civilians and to give both sides the greatest possible opportunity to maneuver. The Americans had generally followed the same rules during the War of Secession. If the Confederates were changing those rules now . . . "Have you learned for certain who the C.S. commander is?"

Willcox looked unhappy. "Rebel prisoners are confirming the rumors we had heard. We do face General Jackson."

"Ach, so? Sehr interessant," Schlieffen murmured. In the War of Secession, Jackson's reputation had come from maneuvers so relentless, his infantry got the name of "foot cavalry." A man who

could change his entire strategic concept was one who demanded to be taken seriously.

A messenger burst in and said, "General Willcox, sir, Colonel Sully says the First Minnesota is melting like St. Paul ice in May. They're pinned down on the waterfront, down to a couple of hundred men now. The Rebs in front of 'em are too strong for 'em to go forward, and if they retreat they swim."

"What in heaven's name does Sully want me to do?" Willcox demanded.

"Sir, he asks if you could put some artillery on the Rebs in his front," the messenger answered. "They're either behind barricades or fighting from houses and shops and all. Makes the goddamn sons of bitches twice as hard to kill, sir, hopin' you'll pardon my French."

"Thou shalt not take the name of the Lord in vain," Willcox said, which gave Alfred von Schlieffen at least a partial understanding of what the idiom meant. Schlieffen knew French, and knew the man had not been speaking it. Willcox consulted the map, then went on, "The First Minnesota is close by Second Street?"

"No, sir—more like Sixth Street," the messenger told him. "Somebody's boats next to ours took a—a goldanged pounding, sir, and we had to slide downstream a ways to keep from gettin' rammed."

"*Sixth* Street," Willcox snarled, as if it were an obscenity. "I'll do what I can, soldier. I make no promises. Has Colonel Sully no other way to escape his predicament?"

"Sir, yes, sir," the messenger said. "He told me to tell you if he didn't get some kind of help some kind of way pretty . . . danged quick, he was going to have to surrender."

Willcox jerked as if wounded. "I'll do what I can," he repeated. The messenger saluted and hurried away. When the fellow was gone, Willcox turned to a runner from the signals office. "A wire across the river: Colonel Sully is to attempt to regain his position as indicated in the plan for the attack. That failing, he is at minimum to hold his present position at all hazards. He is to be informed that I am endeavoring to obtain artillery support for him."

The runner departed with a scrawled order. Schlieffen noted that Willcox made no effort to give the First Minnesota the artillery support he'd said he was trying to arrange. Sometimes, when all resources were committed elsewhere, that kind of deception was necessary to keep a unit fighting a while longer. Sometimes it meant only that the commanding officer wasn't doing as much as he should to solve a problem.

Which was it here? Schlieffen didn't know enough to be certain. The Army of the Ohio had a foothold on the far side of its eponymous river. Schlieffen would not have given good odds on that before the battle began. The next question was what Willcox would do with his bridgehead—and what Stonewall Jackson would do to it.

Edgar Leary dumped three telegrams on Sam Clemens' desk. "Here you go," the young reporter said: "More wires on the Louisville fighting."

"These are—what? The sixth, seventh, and eighth today?" Clemens asked. Leary nodded. The editor of the *San Francisco Morning Call* puffed out smoke like a steamboat. "Almost makes me wish the lines in Utah were still down."

He skimmed through the wires. Except for some new casualty figures, higher than the ones he'd seen a couple of days before, he didn't see anything he hadn't known already. He threw two of the telegrams into the trash, keeping the one with the numbers. He'd been about to start a new editorial; they would come in handy.

War, he wrote, *is a good deal like a meat grinder, in that you feed in fresh chunks of whole meat at one end, and what comes out the other is fit only for stuffing into frankfurters. By all reports, General Willcox is working the crank for all he is worth in the Louisville campaign. Military meat is different from the ordinary kind, because some of the fragments that come out the business end of the grinder are still able to tell you what they were like before they went into the hopper.*

If the figures we have are accurate—and God save the soul of the poor devil charged with aggregating the total—the United States have in the past several days gained anywhere from a quarter of a mile to a mile of land formerly having suffered the great misfortune of flying the Confederate flag, and have purchased this real estate at a cost of, to date, 17,409 young soldiers mutilated and killed. That we have here a great bargain can hardly be denied, for—

"Excuse me, Mr. Clemens," Edgar Leary said. "A couple of gentlemen are here to see you."

"If they're gentlemen," Clemens replied without looking up, "they'll wait till I'm ready to see them. Christ, Edgar, you know better than to jog my elbow when I'm trying to get words down on paper."

"It's not a social call, Clemens," a rough, unfamiliar voice said.

Angrily, Sam spun his chair around. He discovered he was looking down the barrels of two Colt revolvers, each held by a burly individual who did not look as if he would have much compunction about pulling the trigger. Ignoring the guns, he said, "People who use my surname commonly have the courtesy to put *Mister* in front of it, as my friend there did."

The larger of the two men—the one who had spoken before—said, "Next Rebel spy I hear tell of who deserves to get called *Mister*'ll be the first."

"Rebel spy?" That sent Clemens bouncing to his feet in fury. "Who the devil says I am, and how in hell has he got the nerve to say it?"

Quick as a striking rattler, the smaller ruffian snatched from his desk the editorial on which Sam had been working. After reading the couple of paragraphs there, he said, "Sure as hell sounds like treason to me."

"God damn you!" Clemens shouted. "Give me that back before I punch you in your stupid nose." He kept on ignoring the Colts leveled at him. So did the men holding them. "If Adolph Imbecile Sutro tries to throw a newspaperman in jail for what he writes, he'll have every newspaperman in San Francisco by this time tomorrow, and that includes the heathen Chinese. There still is such a thing as the First Amendment to the Constitution, which has a thing or two to say on the subject of a free press. Has either of you blockheads ever heard of it?"

Reporters, typesetters, and printers had been edging through the *Morning Call* offices toward the altercation. A savage grin stretched across Sam's face. If these hooligans tried hauling him away by force, they'd have a battle on their hands. Newspapermen looked after their own.

But then the bigger intruder said, "We ain't here on account of what you write, *Mister* Clemens." Unexpectedly, he had the wit to load that with irony, and to add, "Hell, nobody reads it, anyways. We're here on account of it's done been reported that you are a veteran of the Confederate States of America. Is it so or ain't it that you were in the Confederate Army during the War of Secession?"

Clemens started to laugh. Then he got a look at the faces of the men who worked with him at the *Morning Call*. None of them had ever heard the story of his brief, absurd stint as a Rebel private in Missouri. None of them looked interested in hearing it, either. Even before he could answer, they started slipping back toward the places where they worked.

"Is it or ain't it?" the ruffian repeated.

"Not to speak of," Sam said at last. "The company I was in never did more than mooch around a bit to impress the girls."

"But you were in, were you?" the big man with the revolver said. "You come along with us, then, pal. You can do your explaining to the soldiers. If they reckon you're on the up and up, then they do, is all. But if they don't, they'll put you away where you can't get into any mischief."

"This is an outrage!" Clemens thundered. Nobody else in the offices said anything at all. The smaller ruffian seemed to remember he had a gun. He jerked the muzzle in the direction of the doorway. With a sigh, Clemens walked to the door. He grabbed his hat off the tree as he went by. "Let's get this over with. The sooner we do, the sooner I can come back here and let the world know what a pack of damned fools we've got running around loose these days."

The men with revolvers didn't seem inclined to argue with him. As long as he did what they said, they didn't care what else he did: stacked against a Colt, what did an insult or two matter? They had a buggy tied up outside the building. The silence behind Sam as he shut the door hurt him worse than his sallies hurt the spy-hunters.

"The both of you are plumb loco," Clemens said as the smaller fellow took up the reins and began to drive. "If I've been such a grand and dreadful terror to the United States lo these many years, what in sweet Jesus' name was I doing as assistant to the governor's secretary in Nevada Territory even before the blamed war was over?" That the secretary had been his brother Orion, after whom his son was named, he did not bother mentioning.

"Don't know," replied the bigger gunman, the one with some trace of wit. "What *were* you doing there?" By his tone, Sam might have been sending a daily telegram to Richmond from Carson City.

Clemens replied only with dignified silence. He also did not ask where they were going, as he had intended. He judged that would become obvious in short order, a judgment vindicated when the little ruffian headed north and west, away from the heart of the city. The only thing of any consequence in that direction was the Presidio, the Army base charged with defending San Francisco.

No matter how long Sam had lived in these parts, he never ceased to marvel at the beauty of the view across the Golden Gate, looking north toward Sausalito: blue sky, green-blue sea, the wooded headland rising swiftly above it. A ferry boat, thin black plume of smoke rising from its stack, gave a touch of human scale to nature's grandeur.

So did the stone walls of Fort Point. When a sentry came forward to demand the business of the new arrivals, the bigger of Sam's captors said, "We got a feller here might be a spy."

"Like hell I am!" Sam shouted. As far as the sentry was concerned, he was invisible and inaudible. The bluecoat waved the wagon into the fort.

Having reached the garrison commander's waiting room in jig time, Clemens proceeded to put it to the purpose for which it was named: he waited, and waited, and waited. The bravos who'd shanghaied him didn't wait with him: they had better things to do. When he poked his head out of the door to the parade ground through which he'd come in, a soldier pointed a bayoneted Springfield at him and growled, "You get back in there. The colonel'll see you in his time, not yours." Fuming, Sam retreated.

At last, after what had to be closer to two hours than one, the door to Colonel William T. Sherman's office opened. "Come in, Mr. Clemens," Sherman said. Lean and erect, he wore a close-trimmed beard that had once been red and was now mostly white. His mouth was a thin slash; his pale eyes did their best to stare through Sam. Harsh lines ran down his pinched cheeks, losing themselves in his beard near the corners of that narrow mouth. The word that sprang to Clemens' mind for him was *bitter*.

His office presented a stark contrast to the genial clutter that made finding things on Sam's desk an adventure. Everything here was obviously just where it belonged. Sam was sure anything that had the gall to go where it didn't belong, even to sidle an inch out of place, would end up in the guardhouse to teach it never to get gay again.

Sherman sat; he did not invite Clemens to sit. Glancing down at the beginning of the editorial the smaller gunman had purloined, and also at a large, neatly written sheet of paper on which Sam could make out his name, he said, "Why don't you tell me why you're here, sir?"

Clemens normally wisecracked without thinking, much as he breathed. Facing this man, he restrained himself. "I am here, Colonel, because I served something less than a month in the Marion Rangers, a Confederate unit of sorts in Missouri, during the War of Secession. Because of that, someone has decided I must be a spy."

Sherman said, "When Louisiana seceded, I was teaching at a military academy there. I resigned at once, and came north to serve my country as best I could. How is it that you fought under the Stars and Bars?"

"I never fought under them," Sam replied. "I marched a bit and rode a horse a bit, but I never once fought. Governor Jackson called for soldiers to repel the U.S. invaders—so he named them—which is how the Marion Rangers came to be. It was a grand and glorious unit, Colonel—there were fifteen of us, all told. The one time we got near a farmhouse that some U.S. troops were guarding, our captain—Tom Lyman, his name was—told us to attack it. We told him no; to a man, we said no. The rest of my so-called military career was cut from the same stuff. I never fired a shot at a soldier of the United States. None of us did, before the Marion Rangers became as one with Nineveh and Tyre."

Sherman's jaw worked. "You put this down to youthful indiscretion, then?—for you would have been a young man in 1861."

"That's just what I put it down to, Colonel," Sam said with an emphatic nod.

"And you did serve the U.S. government in Nevada," Sherman said, checking that paper again. Sam wondered how much of his life's story was contained thereon. In musing tones, Sherman continued, "Yet these days, you speak out strongly in the papers against the war, as you have here." He let a finger rest on the editorial fragment for a moment. "What connection, if any, has the one to the other?"

"Colonel, you've seen real war at first hand, which is far more than I ever did," Clemens said. "What is your opinion of it?"

"My opinion?" He'd startled Sherman. But the officer did not hesitate long; Sam got the idea he seldom hesitated long about anything. "War is cruelty, and you cannot refine it. Its glory is all moonshine. Only those who have neither fired a shot nor heard the shrieks and groans of the wounded cry aloud for blood, vengeance, and desolation. War is as close to hell as a merciful God allows upon this earth."

That was more than Sam had bargained for. "If you can speak so strongly and still defend our country, how does questioning the wisdom and conduct of this war make me a Confederate agent?"

Sherman stroked his chin. "You might be an agent, using such a pretext as concealment." His mouth thinned further; Clemens had not thought it could. "But I have no evidence to say you are, not a particle. What you say of the Marion Rangers squares with what I have on this sheet here—the men who brought you in were overzealous. We were all quite mad twenty years ago. It should never have happened." That thin mouth twisted. "I shall write you a good character, Mr. Clemens, which you must show to be released from this fortress, and may show to anyone seeking to trouble you hereafter." He inked a pen and began to write.

"Thank you, Colonel," Clemens said fervently. "One thing more?" Sherman looked up from his work. Sam went on, "May I beg the use of a horse or buggy? The gentlemen who brought me here did not wait upon the outcome of your hearing." He said not a word about how long he'd waited himself.

"I'll see to it," Sherman said. The pen scratched over the paper. Sam did not mind waiting now, not a bit.

Bountiful, Utah lay about ten miles north of Salt Lake City, on the railroad line. George Custer had come south past it on the army's triumphal march toward and then into the capital of Utah Territory. He'd paid it no special mind then: just one more no-account town among so many. Now, though, he wasn't going to pass it by; along with the two troops of cavalry at his back, he was going to go through it like a man searching his pockets for a five-cent piece with which to buy his sweetheart a sarsaparilla. His own sweetheart, worse luck, was back at Fort Dodge.

"Blast John Taylor anyhow," he grumbled. "Dash and double-dash him. Why couldn't the old fraud have stayed in Salt Lake City, so we could snatch him up and stretch his neck and have done?"

"Don't be such a sourpuss, Autie," his brother Tom said. "If it weren't for Taylor and the rest of the scoops who ran away, we'd be stuck with garrison duty instead of doing something halfway useful out here."

"Halfway useful is right. We ought to be fighting the Rebs, not sitting on these confounded Mormons." Custer paused and sent Tom a quizzical look. " 'Scoops'? What's a scoop?"

"A Mormon. Heard it the other day," his brother answered. After removing his hat, Tom mimed removing the top of his skull in the same way and scooping out a large portion of its contents. "Have to have most of your brain missing to buy what they're selling, don't you think?"

"Mm, you're likely right." Custer weighed the word. "Scoops. I like that." He laughed, then pointed ahead. "We've got a whole scoopful of scoops coming up."

Much the biggest building in Bountiful was the Mormon chapel, a wood-and-adobe structure with five spires that looked as if it might have grown from the ground instead of being built. The lands around the chapel were bountiful enough; no matter how foolish the Mormons' religion was in Custer's eyes, he couldn't deny they made skillful, diligent farmers.

People came out into the street from the chapel, from the houses, and from the barbershop and dry-goods store to stare at the soldiers. Their dogs came out with them. The troopers had shot several dogs on the way up from Salt Lake City. They'd probably shoot more here. Mormons' dogs ran from mean to meaner.

Nobody said anything as the troopers rode up. Custer knew he wasn't loved here. He didn't care. Whatever the Mormons loved, as far as he was concerned, had to have something wrong with it.

He held up his hand. Behind him, the cavalrymen reined in. Every one of them carried a loaded carbine across his knees. That wasn't just for dogs. So far, the Mormons hadn't given any trouble. The best way to make sure they didn't give any trouble was to be ready to smash it down ruthlessly if it arose.

Tom Custer said, "I hate all these staring faces. Back in Salt Lake, at least the Gentiles were on our side. Out here, there aren't any Gentiles to speak of, and nobody's on our side."

"We are in the right. We must never forget it," Custer declared. He raised his voice and called out to the people of Bountiful: "We are searching for John Taylor. Anyone who knows where this fugitive from justice is lurking will be handsomely rewarded." He waited. No one said a word. The wind, full of the salty tang of the Great Salt Lake, blew up little dust devils in front of his horse.

He'd expected nothing different, but the effort had to be made. His orders said so. The silence from the Mormons persisting, he moved on to the next step in the program: "We are going to search the houses and buildings of this town for the person of John Taylor, and for the persons of other fugitives from justice in this Territory. You are required to assist and cooperate with the brave soldiers of the United States engaged in this task. Any resistance will leave the guilty party subject to summary trial and the full rigors of military justice."

That drew a response from the crowd: somebody called, "Where's your search warrants at?"

Custer's smile was anything but pleasant. "We have none. We need none. Utah Territory, having been declared a region in rebellion against the lawful authority of the government of the United States of America, has forfeited the protections enshrined in the Constitution. You people should have thought more about what would follow from your actions before you attempted to coerce the national government into approving of your hideous practices. Having willfully flouted the government, you will have to earn its good graces once more by showing you are deserving of them."

He waved to his men, who swung down off their horses. Custer told a squad to follow him to the Mormon chapel. They searched the grounds, finding nothing out of the ordinary, and then went inside. Other than being ornamented with a large portrait in oils of Joseph Smith, the founder of Mormonism, the interior might have belonged to any church.

One of the men of Bountiful came inside. "Gentlemen, Mr. Taylor is not here," he said. "He has not been here."

"Who are you, and how do you know?" Custer growled.

"I'm O. Clifton Haight, and I have for many years been a lay preacher at this chapel," the man replied, "and I know Mr. Taylor has not been in Bountiful because I should have heard of it if he were."

"Not if he's lying low—and not if you're just plain lying, either," Custer said. Haight assumed an indignant expression. Custer, feeling briefly charitable, ignored it. He waved. "This church looks nice and fresh and clean, as if people had been in it just the other day, say, or last Sunday. Public worship in Mormon churches is forbidden by order of General Pope, you will recall."

"Oh, yes, of course," O. Clifton Haight said.

"You haven't by any chance forgotten that order?" Custer said.

"Why, no, of course not." Haight's eyes were wide and candid. He was lying. Custer knew he was lying. He undoubtedly knew Custer knew he was lying. But he also knew Custer couldn't do anything about it. Until Pope had enough men to put a permanent garrison into every one of these miserable little towns, the Mormons would ignore every order they could. No one was likely to betray them, not when they all conspired together to set at nought the commands of the military governor.

Shaking his head in angry frustration, Custer stalked out of the chapel. His soldiers followed. His eyes lighted on a house across the square. It was built in a pattern with which he'd become all too intimately acquainted in Salt Lake City: a central structure that had undoubtedly been erected first, with several white-washed wings spreading out from it. Pointing toward the house, he asked, "Who lives there?"

"That's the Sessions place," Clifton Haight answered. "Peregrine Sessions was the first settler here, better than thirty years ago now. That house there, that belongs to his brother, Zedekiah."

"General Pope forbade more than public worship to you Mormons," Custer said, a certain hard anticipation gleaming in his eyes. "He also forbade the practice of polygamy, which has made you people a stench in the nostrils of decent Americans everywhere. Looking at that house, Mr. Haight, how many wives would you say, uh, Zedekiah Sessions is likely to have?"

"I only know of one," Haight said. "Irma Sessions is a pillar of our little community here."

"I'll bet she is," Custer sneered. "And how many other community pillars carry the name of Sessions?"

"I know of no others," Haight said. Custer had heard that in Salt Lake City, too. The Mormons habitually dissembled about their plural marriages.

He gathered up his troopers by eye. "We are going to search that house for John Taylor. We are also going to search it for any evidence the abhorrent vice of polygamy is being practiced within. If by some chances we find such evidence, despite the statements of Mr. Haight here, we shall take whatever action I deem at the time to be appropriate. Come along."

Grinning, the soldiers followed him. As they tramped toward the large, rambling house, they told lewd jokes. Custer pretended not to hear them, except when a good one made him laugh out loud.

He walked up to the front door and rapped smartly upon it. When it opened, standing before him was one of the formidable middle-aged women of the sort Brigham Young had apparently married in battalions: broad through the shoulders, broader through the hips, graying hair pulled straight back from a face that had not approved of anything since the War of Secession. Custer thought how good her head would look stuffed and mounted on the wall back at Fort Dodge next to a pronghorn or a coyote. "You are Mrs. Irma Sessions?" he asked.

"I am. And you are a United States soldier." By her tone, that put Custer somewhere between a Comanche and a polecat.

"My men and I are going to search these premises for the possible presence of the fugitive John Taylor," Custer announced. "All persons inhabiting this residence must first come forth."

"And if we do not?" Irma Sessions inquired.

Custer folded his arms across his broad chest. "Then we shall remove you with whatever force proves needful and bind you over for trial for defying the authority of the United States Army." He pulled out his pocket watch. "You have five minutes."

He watched Mrs. Sessions contemplate calling his bluff. He watched her decide, with obvious reluctance, that he wasn't bluffing. He watched her start to slam the door in his face and then, with even more obvious reluctance, think better of it.

Within the appointed deadline, half a dozen women emerged, the other five as like Irma Sessions as peas in a pod. Along with them came something like two dozen children, ranging from babes in arms up to youths old enough to carry a gun and girls well on their way to becoming stolid copies of their mothers. "Where is Mr. Sessions?" Custer asked when the patriarch of the family proved not to be in evidence.

"In Salt Lake City, on business," Irma Sessions replied. Maybe it was true, maybe it wasn't.

"And all six of you are his wives?" Custer persisted.

"Oh, no," one of the other women said. "I am his widowed cousin." Another claimed to be his sister, still another said she was Irma's sister, and the last two didn't explain how or why they were living there, save to assert that they were not affiliated with Zedekiah Sessions in any illegal or immoral manner. They were so shrill, so insistent, Custer would not have believed them even had he previously been inclined to do so, which he was not.

In the midst of the women's denials, a leering trooper brought Custer a photograph in a fancy gilt frame. It was a family group: a stout, bearded man, presumably Mr. Sessions, surrounded by the six women and their multifarious offspring. He displayed it to them. They went quiet. Rudely, he wondered if Sessions could get the same effect with it. For the sake of the man's peace of mind, he hoped so.

"I say that this photograph shows me you have been imperfectly truthful here," he told them, having been too well brought up to call a woman a liar to her face. "As you must know, General Pope has commanded that polygamy shall be suppressed in this Territory by all available means." He turned to the cavalryman. "Any sign of Taylor, Corporal?"

"No, sir," the soldier answered. "Nobody in there now."

"Very well. Put this place to the torch, that sin may have no dwelling place to call its own. If we needs must cleanse Utah with fire and sword, that is what we shall do."

The six wives of Zedekiah Sessions screamed and wailed, as did their female children. The boys, the older ones, cursed Custer and his men as vilely as they knew how. He'd heard worse. Despite screams and wails and curses, the house burned. Going through the town, he and his men found three more homes obviously belonging to polygamists. Those went up in flames, too. He wondered if the Mormons would shoot at his men for that. He almost hoped they would. They didn't.

"It's not so Bountiful any more," he said to his brother as they led the two cavalry troops north to the next little town. Both Custers laughed.

☆ IX ☆

Tubac drowsed under the relentless sun of the western part of New Mexico Territory. It had been a Mexican village, adobe houses clustered around a Catholic church that was also adobe but whitewashed. Then it had been a Mormon settlement, one of the many sprouts from the main tree in Utah. Since the War of Secession, unending raids by Apaches and by Mexican and white bandits had left it a sad shadow of its former self.

That left Jeb Stuart, whose army was camped nearby, something short of brokenhearted. "Mormons," he said to his aide-de-camp. "You ask me, the damnyankees are welcome to them."

Major Horatio Sellers nodded and said, "Yes, sir." His principal bugbear, though, was not the Mormons, of whom only a handful were left hereabouts, but the Apaches—not those who'd raided Tubac halfway back to savagery, but those now accompanying the Confederate forces (assuming a distinction could be drawn between those two groups, which was by no means obvious). After coughing once or twice, he said, "The more time we spend with these Indians, sir, the more I think one of the reasons the Empire of Mexico sold us Sonora and Chihuahua was to give us the joy of putting them down."

"It could be so, Major," Stuart allowed. "If there were more of them, they would be even worse trouble than they are."

"Too damned many of 'em as is," Sellers said, stubbornly sticking out his chin. "If there were more—" He shuddered. "Sir, we have good men, tough men. But these Apaches, there isn't a one of 'em can't go through this country on foot faster than a trooper can on horseback, come up behind you in the middle of a crowded church, cut your throat, and be out the window before anybody notices you're dead."

He was exaggerating only slightly, and not at all about the

Apaches' ability to outperform cavalry. "But they don't want to cut *our* throats," Stuart said. "They want to cut the Yankees' throats, and especially the Mexicans'."

"*Now* they do," Sellers said. "When is it our turn?" He looked around and lowered his voice almost to a whisper: "I still say we ought to fill 'em full of whiskey and get rid of them when they're too polluted to fight back."

"That will be enough, Major," Stuart said sharply. "That will be more than enough. One of the reasons the Apaches hate the Mexicans so much is that the Mexicans would pull that on them again and again. It would work—they like popskull, no two ways about it—but it made enemies forever out of the braves the Mexicans didn't get. I want to use these Indians against the United States; I don't want to give the damnyankees any chance to use them against us."

"Yes, sir," Sellers said.

Stuart hid a smile. He recognized that tone: it was the one a soldier used when he thought a superior was out of his mind. He said, "In the end, my guess is that we civilize them, Major. Geronimo's son, Chappo, now—he's a sharp young fellow. And his cousin, that Batsinas: I've had two different blacksmiths tell me he's been after them to teach him their trade. He's got only a few words of English, and a few more of Spanish, but one of the men who was showing him things said he picked them up as fast as you'd want with a white man."

Major Sellers said nothing at all. He tried to make his face say nothing at all, too. He wasn't as good at it as the Apaches. Clear as if he were shouting, Stuart read his thoughts: *learning things from white men doesn't civilize Indians, it only makes them more dangerous.*

"Cherokees," Stuart said quietly. "Choctaws. They might as well be white themselves—well, some of them."

"That's different," his aide-de-camp answered, but, when Stuart pressed him, he couldn't say how.

"It doesn't matter, anyway," Stuart said after looking at his watch. "We've got to meet with Geronimo anyhow, get everything in a straight line for his run up to Tucson and where we'll bushwhack the Yankees when they come after him."

Actually, the meeting hadn't been set for a specific time; the Indians, though they used telescopes most often taken from dead soldiers, didn't care about watches. But nine-thirty was a close enough equivalent to midway through the morning, which was how Geronimo had put it.

The Apaches approved of the Confederate-issue tents Stuart had given them: they were roomier and faster to put up than the hide-covered brush wickiups the Indians made for themselves. Geronimo was sitting cross-legged in front of a little cookfire, drinking coffee from a tin cup stamped *CSA*. Next to him sat Chappo, whose bronze, broad-cheekboned face showed what his father had looked like as a young man.

As Stuart came up to Geronimo, so did the Apaches' war leaders: Cochise's handsome son Naiche (whom half the Confederates called Natchez, that having a more familiar sound to their ears); a clever old man named Nana; and Hoo, a tough veteran. Only gradually had Stuart realized that Geronimo's influence, despite lurid tales to the contrary, came more from religion than generalship.

Polite greetings used up some time; both the Apaches and the Confederates were ceremonious folk. Then, through Chappo, Geronimo said, "Our scouts have found the perfect canyon for us. We can lead the bluecoats into it, and you can be waiting for them with your rifles and your wagons."

"Wagons?" That puzzled Stuart. He and Chappo went back and forth for a couple of minutes before he figured out the Indian was talking about artillery. The cannon traveled on wheels; as far as the Apaches were concerned, that made them wagons. When the misunderstanding was cleared up, Stuart nodded. "It is good. Where is this place?"

"Let me see the paper with places on it, and I will show you," Geronimo said. Stuart drew from his pocket a map of New Mexico Territory and unfolded it. He'd watched Geronimo take in the concept of maps at one big bound. The Apache had gone from complete incomprehension to rapt admiration when he realized what the line of the Southern Pacific (printed complete with little cross ties) represented. From that beginning, he'd made sense of the rest of the symbols in a hurry. Naiche, who could sketch very well himself, also understood maps now. The Apaches weren't stupid. The more Stuart dealt with them, the clearer that became.

He wished they were, almost as much as Major Sellers did. It would have made his life easier.

Geronimo drew a knife from his belt, to use the tip as a pointer.

"We are here." He touched it to Tubac with complete confidence. He could not read, but he knew how to make the map in his head, the one a lifetime in these parts had given him, match the map on the paper. "The canyon is here, a little more than halfway to Tucson." He moved the knifepoint.

"If we are to ambush the bluecoats, we will have to wait there till you have lured them," Stuart said. "Is there water?" In so much of the Southwest, that was the overriding concern.

"Yes." Geronimo smiled for a moment: he'd asked the right question. "Two springs close by. Good water, even in summer: not much water, but enough." He waved around at the Indian encampment. "Some of us will be with you. If it is not as I say, they are men you may kill."

"Hostages," Stuart said. Chappo's lips moved as he repeated the word to himself so he could learn it. Stuart plucked at his beard, considering. The Apaches were short on manpower. They thought a raid where they lost a couple of warriors a misfortune, because the fighters could not easily be replaced. Stuart didn't think Geronimo would offer hostages unless he was sincere. "We'll try it," he said. "My men can ride this afternoon."

"It is good," Geronimo said through Chappo. "We, most of us, will ride north now. When you are at the canyon, you will see what sort of place it is. You will see where to place your men where they can kill the bluecoats without being seen. You will see where to place your big rifles on wagons so the bluecoats do not know they are there till too late."

Even though Stuart could not understand a word of the Apache lingo, he paid close attention to Geronimo's tone. The Indian sounded as if he was trying to reassure himself that Stuart, though only an ignorant white man, would indeed be able to see these things and do what was required of him. The Confederate general, civilizedly certain of his own expertise, smiled at the savage's conceit.

"I will see these things," he answered gently, trying to ease Geronimo's mind. "You will bring me the U.S. soldiers, and I will kill them."

That seemed to satisfy the Apache. Geronimo and the war leaders exchanged a few words, which Chappo did not translate. Stuart resolved to scare up some interpreters who would be on his side, not the Indians'. Half-breeds, Mexicans ... one way or another, he'd manage. If his allies let something slip, he wanted a chance to know about it.

Geronimo was as good as his word. Most of the Apaches rode out inside the hour. About thirty stayed behind under Naiche. Chappo stayed, too, to translate, though Naiche and some of the others spoke Spanish. Batsinas also stayed, for no better reason Stuart could find than that he was fascinated by everything the white men did, and wanted to learn from them.

A lot of the Indians, though, found the Confederates more amusing than instructive. While the army broke camp, Horatio Sellers came up to Stuart shaking his head. "One of those red devils used a farmer to ask me what I'd do if I heard a gunshot," he said indignantly. "I told him I'd go over and see what in blazes had happened, of course. He thought that was the funniest thing he'd heard in all his born days. So I asked him what he'd do, if he was so blasted smart. He said he'd scout around and find out what was going on without letting anybody ever know he was there. Looked at me like I was a chuckleheaded nigger; and him with a line of yellow paint across his face to show he was on the warpath, the damn savage." Sellers sounded like a man on the warpath himself.

"Don't worry about it, Major," Stuart said soothingly, using much the same tone of voice he had with Geronimo. "We'll position ourselves in this canyon and lick the stuffing out of the damnyankees. That will make the redskins respect us, and I don't think anything else will."

Riding to battle, Stuart felt the same exhilaration he'd known during the War of Secession. Somewhere back in Kentucky, his young son and namesake was going up against the Yankees, too. He hoped Jeb, Jr., would be all right. The boy—no, not a boy, not if he was fighting—had all of his own impetuous spirit, and hardly any years to temper it.

Stuart would have navigated by map and compass. The Apaches knew the country as well as—better than—he knew northern Virginia. He got the feeling they could have ridden along with their eyes closed and found their way across three hundred or three thousand miles of desert by the way the dust smelled and how the echoes from their horses' hoofbeats came back to their ears. They'd been here a long time; the roadrunners probably talked with them.

As far as he was concerned, they and the damnyankees were

welcome to the country, if you took it strictly as country. Rocks and sand and dust and cactus and brush and lizards and rattlesnakes and endless sun pounding down out of the sky so that, nearly as reliable as clockwork, every hour a Confederate would slide from the saddle and plop to the ground. Most of them recovered after they'd been splashed with precious water and ridden in the wagons for a while, but a couple had died, running unquenchable fevers that cooked them from the inside out.

It was, in fact, country for camels. The Fifth Confederate Cavalry's humped livestock flourished here. The camels ate cactus, thorns and all, with every sign of relish. They didn't need much water, and the succulent pulp gave them a lot of what they did need. They were gloriously bad-tempered, reveling in the heat where the horses labored under it.

The Apaches found them endlessly fascinating. The Indians admired the animals' ability to handle the rugged terrain, but thought them the ugliest things they'd ever seen. Chappo rode up alongside Stuart after traveling with the Fifth Camelry for a while and said, quite seriously, "The god who made those beasts was trying to shape horses, but did not know how."

Stuart started to laugh, then checked himself. He didn't want to offend Geronimo's son. And it was a better explanation of how camels had got to be the way they were than anything else he'd heard.

They crossed the Santa Cruz River, such as it was, not long before nightfall, and camped close by. The next morning, Naiche and the rest of the Apaches led the Confederates into the desert east of the little town that had grown up around the stagecoach station at Sahuarita, about twenty miles south of Tucson.

About nine o'clock the next morning, Naiche trotted his horse back to Stuart with a broad smile on his wide, Roman-nosed face. *"Aquí está,"* he said, and then, to his own obvious delight, came up with a word of English: "Here."

Stuart rode ahead with him. The farther ahead he went, the better the place looked. It wasn't one of the narrow valleys down which no pursuers in their right minds would follow fleeing redskins for fear of being bushwhacked. But it wasn't so wide as to make an ambush impossible, either. As Geronimo had said he would, he spotted just the place to site his horse artillery, too: a low rise off to one side with a good view of the track down which the enemy would likely come, but not a feature of the landscape that would draw the Yankees' notice too soon.

"Water?" he asked, and made his canteen slosh.

"Ah. *Agua. Sí,*" Naiche said. And *agua* there was: two springs, as Geronimo had promised. Stuart's force would have no trouble waiting a couple of days, until the Apaches who had gone on to raid Tucson could bring the damnyankees back here in hot pursuit. "*¿Está bien?*" Naiche asked. He grinned, finding another English word: "Good?"

"Yes. *Sí.*" Stuart didn't have a dozen words of Spanish himself, but that was one of them. "Good. Very good."

"There it is!" Theodore Roosevelt swept out his right hand in the sort of dramatic gesture that came so naturally to him. "There it is, straight ahead: the Promised Land!"

Probably never before had anyone called Fort Benton the Promised Land. But it was as dear to Roosevelt as the land of Israel could ever have been to the Hebrews. And Roosevelt's Unauthorized Regiment had wandered in the bureaucratic wilderness: not for the forty years Moses' followers had endured, true, but everything moved faster in the bustling, mechanized, modern world of the nineteenth century. The weeks that had passed before the volunteers were accepted were far too long.

Behind Roosevelt, the men of the Unauthorized Regiment raised a cheer. Many of them, like their colonel, were delighted at finally becoming U.S. Volunteers. And others (and some of the same men, too, perhaps) were also delighted at the prospect of mustering close by a town, with all the pleasures attendant thereto. Out on Roosevelt's ranch, they'd been living a life not far removed from the monastic.

"The Promised Land!" Roosevelt shouted once more, and his troopers cheered louder than ever. He nodded in enormous satisfaction and spoke again, this time more quietly: "If you want something done, by jingo, you have to pitch right in and do it yourself."

Soldiers up on the mud-brick wall of Fort Benton were staring at the oncoming cavalry regiment. Roosevelt could see their arms outstretched as they pointed to the cloud of dust in which the horsemen traveled. He was still too far away to make out the amazement on their faces or to hear their exclamations, but his active imagination had no trouble supplying the lack.

Not far from the fort was a stretch of level ground where the Seventh Infantry was in the habit of practicing its maneuvers. Roosevelt led the Unauthorized Regiment toward it. "Assemble by troops!" he shouted, and the trumpeters amplified the command.

He'd made sure the troopers practiced that evolution every day of the journey along the Missouri from the ranch outside of Helena to Fort Benton. They performed it flawlessly now. He grinned from ear to ear. Maybe the only uniform they had at the moment was a red bandanna on the sleeve, but he'd turned them into soldiers, not an armed mob.

"If at the age of twenty-two I can bring order to a cavalry regiment," he murmured, suddenly thoughtful, "what will I be able to do when I have Lieutenant Colonel Welton's years behind me?"

But those years, as yet, lay ahead of him. He rode toward Fort Benton, to bring the commander of the Regular Army garrison out to inspect the Unauthorized Regiment.

Henry Welton did him the courtesy of meeting him halfway. Now Roosevelt was wearing his colonel's uniform. Nevertheless, he saluted Welton first—and, as he did so, noticed the Regular officer had eagles on his shoulder straps, too, not the silver oak leaves he'd worn when they met before. "Congratulations, Colonel Welton!" Roosevelt exclaimed.

"It's your fault, Colonel Roosevelt," Welton answered with a smile, returning the salute. "The War Department had to accept you as a colonel in the U.S. Volunteers, so they gave me the same brevet rank, and made me five minutes senior to you while they were about it."

"As I told you when we first met, sir, that is as it should be," Roosevelt said.

"I'd be lying if I told you I thought you were wrong," Welton said. Roosevelt nodded; he had nothing but approval for a man who knew his own worth. Welton went on, "Now, by thunder, let's have a look at the men who stirred up all this fuss."

"With great pleasure, sir." Side by side, the two colonels rode out toward the regiment Roosevelt had raised. They were drawing near when Roosevelt, unwontedly hesitant, said, "Even after our formal incorporation into the U.S. Army, sir, might we continue to style ourselves the Unauthorized Regiment? I believe it would have a salutary effect on the men's morale."

"I don't see why not," Welton said. "If you look at things from England's point of view, we're an unauthorized country, wouldn't you say? Formally, what we have here is the First Montana Volunteer Cavalry. I can't do anything about that. Informally—well, since it is informal, no one will fuss at what you call yourselves. Plenty of regiments—even companies—in the War of Secession had nicknames by which they were better known than by their official titles."

Roosevelt started to say something more, but checked himself, for Welton and he had come up to the troops, who, as one man, saluted them. Henry Welton rode gravely from troop to troop. He was not a cavalry officer, but his examination struck Roosevelt as being as thorough as the grilling to which he himself had been subjected. Welton had been assessing soldiers for as long as Roosevelt had been alive, and knew what he was doing.

He puzzled the commander of the Unauthorized Regiment for a moment when, instead of keeping on the open path between troops, he rode through one, pausing every now and then to examine one man's Winchester, another's saddle, the cartridge belt of a third. And then enlightenment struck Roosevelt almost as abruptly as it had struck Paul on the road to Damascus. "Colonel Welton, had you asked, I would have told you that I did not place the best men on the outer edges of the troops, as a dishonest grocer will place a few pieces of good fruit on top of a great many bad ones."

"Had I asked, Colonel Roosevelt, I'm sure you would have told me that, whether it was so or not." Welton softened the words with a disarming grin. "I'd sooner see for myself. If you possibly can, you should always see for yourself. If you don't make a habit of that, you *will* be disappointed, generally when you can least afford it."

"Thank you, sir. I'll remember that." Doing as much as he could by and for himself was always one of Roosevelt's guiding principles. Having the veteran espouse it only strengthened it in his mind.

Not satisfied with riding through one troop, Henry Welton rode through another. That done, he gave his verdict: "These men are not up to the standards of the Regular Army, Colonel, but they are some of the finest volunteer troops I have ever set eyes on, especially for volunteers who have yet to see the elephant. If and when they do, I believe they'll manage as well as anyone could hope."

"Thank you again, sir," Roosevelt said. "You make me feel my efforts on our beloved country's behalf have proved worthwhile."

"And so they have." Welton rode out before the assembled troopers. "Men of Roosevelt's Unauthorized Regiment," he began, and then had to stop while the cavalrymen yelled themselves hoarse and several of the officers made their mounts caracole. "Men of the Unauthorized Regiment, will you take the oath that makes you into U.S. Volunteers?"

"Yes!" the men cried: one great roar of sound. Roosevelt shouted as loud as he could, but even in his own ears his voice was small and lost amid the others.

Colonel Welton administered the oath to them, one ringing phrase at a time. Behind his spectacles, Roosevelt felt his eyes fill with tears as he spoke the words that took him into the service of the United States. Reaching this point had proved a greater struggle than it ever should have, but, unlike Moses, he, having overcome every obstacle, was allowed to enter the land of milk and honey—or, the U.S. Army being what it was, at least the land of hardtack, salt pork, and beans.

The oath completed, he gave Henry Welton another crisp salute. "What are your orders, sir?"

"For now, Colonel, my orders are going to be very simple, very unexciting, and, I fear, very unwelcome," Welton answered. "Your men are to bivouac by troops here on this plain until such time as my regimental clerks have completed the boring but necessary business of taking down their names and other particulars. This will, among other things, put them on the government's payroll and get them off of yours, and will assure pension benefits to their next of kin in the event of their becoming casualties of war."

Roosevelt sighed. "I do see the necessity, sir, but must it be done on the instant? You have no conception of how I long to strike the British a smart blow, nor of how hard it has been to sit by Helena knowing I had the men at hand for the task but also knowing I was not legally entitled to use them."

"Patience, Colonel." Welton chuckled. "I *do* feel like I'm talking to my son. I say again, patience. The British have made no moves against us as yet in this quarter, nor, even if they do in the next two days—which is not likely—can they sweep down on Fort Benton and catch us unawares in that space of time. You shall have your chance, I assure you. Not quite yet, though."

"Yes, sir." Suddenly and painfully, Roosevelt realized that

coming under the authority of the United States not only meant he could lead his troops against the English and the Canucks, it also meant he was required to obey orders he did not like. Then he brightened. "Sir, I shall place at your disposal all my regimental records, which should help your clerks do their jobs more quickly."

"Thank you. I'm sure that will help a great deal." Colonel Welton cocked his head to one side. "I shouldn't be a bit surprised if what you've got is a good deal more complete than anything I'm required to keep. There are some forms, though, on which we'll have to get your men's signatures or witnessed marks. Everyone talks about the exploits of the Army in the field. No one mentions the paperwork that makes those exploits—and the survival of the Army between them—possible, but it's part of the life, too."

"I discovered something of this myself, on commencing to recruit the Unauthorized Regiment." Roosevelt bared his teeth in what was not quite a smile. "I should be lying if I said it was the most welcome discovery I ever made."

"Yes, I believe that," Welton said. "This being wartime, you'll have your chance for action, and soon enough, even if not so soon as you might wish. Had you spent as much time in the Regular Army as I have done, you might by now have concluded that for a commanding officer the duty entails paperwork to the exclusion of nearly everything else."

Roosevelt tried to imagine himself on garrison duty at some dusty fort out here in the heart of the West, a fort without any hostile Indians nearby to give an excuse for action. He tried to imagine passing year after year at such duty. His conclusion was that, were the fort anywhere close to a high cliff, he would have been likely to throw himself off it.

That must have shown on his face. Colonel Welton said, "Well, it's not a fate you have to worry about. Now, would you like to order your regiment to pitch their tents here, or shall I?"

"Sir, why don't you?" Roosevelt answered. "The sooner the men fully understand they are obliged to take orders from any man of rank superior to theirs, the sooner they will become soldiers in every sense of the word."

"Very well." Welton nodded. "And well reasoned, too." Effortlessly, he raised his voice so the entire Unauthorized Regiment could hear him. He did not seem to be shouting, either—Roosevelt wondered if he could learn the trick.

Having given the orders, Welton watched with interest to see how they were obeyed. He chuckled as the troopers pitched their tents. "A bit of variety in the canvas they're living under, eh, Colonel?" A moment later, he stopped chuckling and stared. "Good heavens, is that a teepee?"

"Yes, sir. We have several of them in the regiment. They seem to work about as well as anything we white men make."

"That they do, Colonel. I've served enough time on the plains to be convinced of it. They caught me by surprise, is all." Henry Welton wasn't only watching the soldiers of the Unauthorized Regiment set up their camp. Every so often, he pulled out his pocket watch to see how fast they were doing it.

Roosevelt wanted to get in there among them, to yell and wave his arms and urge them to greater speed. He made himself quietly sit on his horse and let them do it on their own. If they hadn't learned what he'd worked so hard to drill into them, his harangues wouldn't help now.

His gaze flicked from the troopers to Colonel Welton and back again. The men seemed to take forever. But, when the last tent was up, Welton put the watch back in his pocket and nodded pleasantly to him. "Not bad, Colonel. Once again, not bad at all."

"Thank you very much, sir." Colonel Theodore Roosevelt beamed.

Colonel Alfred von Schlieffen and Second Lieutenant Archibald Creel strode along what had been the waterfront of Louisville, Kentucky. Instead of his own uniform, Schlieffen wore the light blue trousers, dark blue blouse, and cap of a U.S. infantry private. The waterfront was in U.S. hands, but the Confederates had a way of sneaking snipers forward that made being in any way conspicuous a conspicuously bad idea.

In his trouser pocket, Schlieffen had one telegram from General Rosecrans authorizing General Willcox to allow him to cross the Ohio to observe the battle at close quarters and another telegram from Minister Schlözer assuring Willcox the Fatherland would not hold him responsible if, while Schlieffen was performing his military duty, he was wounded or killed. The military attaché had needed both wires to get Willcox to let him cross.

Lieutenant Creel kept staring around in disbelief. "I've never seen anything like this in my life," he would say. A few minutes later, he would say it again, apparently forgetting his earlier words. After a bit, he rounded on Schlieffen. "Have you ever seen anything like this, Colonel?"

And Schlieffen had to shake his head. "No, I do not think I have."

Wherever war went, it left a trail of devastation. That Schlieffen knew. That he had seen for himself. But he had never seen war visit a good-sized city, decide it liked the place, and settle in for a long stay, as if it were a good-for-nothing brother-in-law. Never till now.

Stonewall Jackson had chosen to make his stand inside Louisville, to make the United States, if they wanted the city so badly, pay the greatest possible price for it, and to make sure that, if they ended up taking it, what they took would amount to nothing. The Confederates had fought in every building. They had forced the U.S. to shell whole blocks into rubble, and then fought in the rubble until cleared out by rifle and bayonet. They had taken horrible casualties, but those they'd inflicted were worse.

Schlieffen shook his head as he looked south toward the fighting front, which was still only a few hundred yards away. He could not see a single untouched building, not anywhere. Every single structure had big chunks bitten out of it from artillery, whether U.S. or C.S. Fire had licked through every building, too, leaving streaks of soot along what battered brickwork remained standing.

Off to Schlieffen's left, a battery of U.S. field guns started barking. When the battle for Louisville began, General Willcox hadn't worried overmuch about getting cannon onto the southern bank of the Ohio. He'd realized soon enough, though—probably as fast as any German general would have—that infantry couldn't do this job by itself. The shells would blast some new part of Louisville into ruins. If they went where they were supposed to go, they might help the infantrymen advance a few more yards.

The air stank of smoke and death. How many men lay entombed in the wreckage both sides had created? Whatever the number, it was not small. Schlieffen had never smelled the battlefield stench so thick. Some of that was due to the intolerable weather, which hastened corruption. More sprang from the battle's having gone on so long without moving to speak of.

Several pairs of litter-bearers came by, carrying wounded U.S. soldiers out of the fight. A couple of the hurt men lay limp; scarlet soaked through bandages on heads and torsos. Others screamed and thrashed. Those were the ones who felt worse torment now, but they were also liable to be the ones with the better chance of recovering.

Confederate shells screamed in. Lieutenant Creel threw himself to the ground before they burst, huddling behind a heap of bricks that had once been part of some fine riverfront office or shop or hotel. So did Schlieffen. No hint of cowardice accrued to sheltering from splinters that killed without the courage of a proper human foe. This wasn't his war, either.

He thought the C.S. gunners were aiming for their U.S. counterparts. As happened in war, their aim went awry. The shells fell closer to the litter-bearers. Fresh screams rose from them, some from already injured men crying out as they were dropped, others from bearers crying out as they were wounded.

"Bastards," Lieutenant Creel said. Mud streaked his uniform. More streaked his face.

"I do not believe this was their purpose, to hurt these men," Schlieffen said.

"Bastards anyhow," Creel answered. He did not seem so young now as he had when Schlieffen first made his acquaintance not long before. He went on, "I'd like to see every one of those Rebel sons of bitches dead."

His fury gave Schlieffen an opportunity he had not been sure he would have. The German military attaché, a General Staff officer to the core, had long since planned what to do if that opportunity arose. He did not hesitate to put the plan into effect, saying, "Let us forward go, then, to the very front, so we have the best chance of seeing the enemy fall."

Creel had courage. Schlieffen had already seen that. Now his blood was up, too. He nodded. "All right, Colonel, we'll do that. I wish I were carrying a Springfield, not this blamed revolver on my hip. I'd have a better chance of potting some of them myself."

Being a neutral, Schlieffen bore no weapon of any sort. He did not acutely feel the lack. He knew a certain sympathy for the USA over the CSA because he was attached to the U.S. forces, and another certain sympathy for the United States because the Confederate States were allied with France. None of that, however, was enough to make him anxious to go potting Confederates himself.

Together, he and Second Lieutenant Creel picked their way forward through the cratered, rubble-strewn streets. Shirtsleeved soldiers with picks and shovels labored to clear the paths so fresh troops and munitions could go forward and wounded men come back.

Craack! Before Schlieffen could react, a bullet slapped past his head and buried itself with a slap in some charred timbers. Archibald Creel turned back to him with a wry grin. "You were the one who wanted to do this, remember."

"I remember, yes," Schlieffen said calmly, and kept on.

Trenches started well before the front line. Schlieffen and Creel had been passing trench lines ever since they entered Louisville, in fact, but the ones close by the Ohio were hard to recognize because shellfire had all but obliterated them. Shells were falling on these trenches, too, but they still retained their shape.

"You fellers want to watch yourselves," a grimy, unshaven soldier said as Creel and Schlieffen went by. "The Rebs got a sniper in one o' them buildings up ahead who's a hell of a shot. Ain't nobody been able to cipher out just where he's at, but he done blew the heads off three of our boys already today."

The closer to the front Schlieffen got, the deeper the trenches grew. That hadn't helped the luckless three the soldier had mentioned, but it did offer their comrades some protection. The German military attaché pondered as he lifted his feet over broken bricks. The French could fight for a town tooth and nail in the same way the Confederates were doing here. If they fought in several towns in a row with this bulldog tenacity, how could an army hope to defeat them without tearing itself to ribbons in the process?

Posing the question, unfortunately, looked easier than answering it.

"I think we're here," Lieutenant Creel remarked. The only way Schlieffen could judge whether the U.S. officer was right was by how alert the riflemen here looked, and by the fact that no trenches ran forward from this transverse one.

"Where are the Confederates?" Schlieffen asked.

"If you stick your head up, you can see their line plain as day, maybe fifty yards thataway," answered another soldier who looked as if he'd been here for months, not days. " 'Course, if you stick your head up, they can see you, too, and a couple of our fellows here'll have to lug you back to the Ohio feet first." He studied Schlieffen. "You're the oldest damn private I ever did see."

"I am the German military attaché, here to learn what I can of how you are fighting this war," Schlieffen explained.

"Ah. I got you." The soldier nodded knowingly. "That's why this here baby lieutenant is taking care of you 'stead of the other way round."

No German officer would for an instant have tolerated such insolence, even if offered only indirectly. All Creel did was grin and shrug and look sheepish. Schlieffen had already seen that standards of discipline were lax in America. He had heard that was even more true in the CSA than in the USA. If that was so, he wondered how the Confederates could have any standards of discipline whatever.

He shrugged. Except as data, standards of discipline in American troops, U.S. or C.S., were not his problem—unless, of course, they made the men fight less well. For reasons he did not fully grasp, that was not the case. Had it been so, the soldiers here would not have performed so steadily and so bravely in a battle waged under conditions more appalling than any he had known in Europe.

And now that he was here at the front to see them fight, he discovered that, like a man who had wandered down to sit in the first row of seats at a theater, he was too close to the action to get a good view of it. Off to his right, the rifle fire, which had been intermittent, suddenly picked up. He couldn't look to see what was going on there, not unless he wanted to get killed. All he could do was listen.

"I think they drove us back a bit," said the soldier who'd spoken before. "Hope they paid high for it."

"I think perhaps you are right," Schlieffen said: his ears had given him the same impression. But, had he wanted to follow the battle with his ears alone, he could as well have stayed on the Indiana side of the Ohio River. He turned to Lieutenant Creel. "Have you any idea how many killed and wounded the Confederates have suffered, compared to your own?"

"No, Colonel," Creel answered. "Only person who'd know that for certain is Stonewall Jackson." He checked himself. "No, probably not him, either, for he'd know their losses, but not ours."

"Yes." Schlieffen hid his amusement. Second Lieutenant Creel was naïve. U.S. papers reported the casualty figures in Willcox's army. Schlieffen would have bet papers in the CSA did the same for those of Jackson's army. Hard-headed officers in Philadelphia and Richmond—and, no doubt, in London, Paris, Berlin, Vienna, St. Petersburg—would know both sides of the story. So would Willcox and Jackson themselves. If the Army of the Ohio was holding the numbers tight, that suggested they were not in its favor.

The grimy soldier echoed his thoughts, saying, "Whoever goes forward in a fight like this gets hurt worse, seems like. That's why I'm hoping the Rebs took a licking there over yonder."

Schlieffen nodded. He had seen in Europe that soldiers at the front often developed a keen instinct for how things were going and for which tactics worked and which didn't. That looked to be the same on both sides of the Atlantic.

"Let us go back," he said to Lieutenant Creel. "I have seen what is here worth seeing."

"Stay low and watch out for Rebel sharpshooters," said the soldier who'd been talking with them. "Them bastards know their business."

Heading north toward the river, Creel dove for cover whenever artillery came near. Bullets, however, he ignored, striding along with his head held high. Schlieffen wondered whether to call that courage or bravado. He recognized the difference between facing danger and courting it. A lot of officers, especially young officers, didn't.

For his part, Schlieffen was not in the least ashamed to duck and hide behind rubble when the Rebels started taking potshots at him. With the indulgent tolerance of youth, Creel smiled. "You don't really need to worry, Colonel, not now," he said. "We're almost back to the Ohio. They couldn't hit an elephant at this distance."

Less than a minute later, a wet, smacking sound announced that a bullet had struck home. Second Lieutenant Archibald Creel crumpled to the ground, blood gushing from a head wound. Schlieffen knelt beside him. He saw at once he could do nothing. Creel gave three or four hitching breaths, made a noise halfway between a cough and a groan, and simply . . . stopped.

"God, judge his courage, not his sense," Schlieffen murmured. He stayed by the fallen lieutenant until a couple of litter bearers carried the body away.

Abraham Lincoln came out of the general store with a cake of shaving soap wrapped in brown paper and string. Having stayed in Salt Lake City so much longer than he'd planned, he kept needing to replenish such small day-to-day items. With the telegraph back in service, he'd been able to wire for money, and had started staying with the Hamiltons as a paying boarder.

As Lincoln started down the sidewalk, a closed carriage stopped in the street alongside him. The curtains were drawn; he could see nothing within. The driver spoke to him in a low, urgent voice: "Please get in, Mr. Lincoln."

"Who . . . ?" Lincoln paused, then stiffened as he recognized the bright young man who'd escorted him to John Taylor's home. That home stood no more; soldiers had wrecked it, giving as their reason the suppression of polygamy.

"Where do you propose to take me?" Lincoln asked. He supposed he might be worth something as a hostage for radical Mormons. Given his own economic radicalism, and the embarrassment he'd become to the Republican Party, he had the idea he'd be worth less than the Mormons thought. That might lead to unpleasant personal consequences for him.

"I can't tell you that," the driver answered. "No harm will come to you, though: by God I swear it." He bit his lip. "If you aim to come, sir, come now. I cannot let soldiers spy me loitering here."

Lincoln got aboard the carriage. Not since his ignominious passage through Baltimore on his way to his inauguration in Washington had he let concern for his safety change how he behaved. Maybe he could do some good here, if the Mormons hadn't simply snatched him.

"Thank you, sir," the bright young man said as the carriage started to roll. Lincoln did not think he was the sort who made a habit of wearing false oaths. He realized he was betting his life on that.

The carriage made several turns, now right, now left. The Mormon driver had the two-horse team up into a trot; their hoofbeats and the jolts and rattles Lincoln felt said they were going at a fine clip. Nothing at all prevented him from opening the curtains and seeing where they were going. He sat quiet. Sooner or later, General Pope or one of his inquisitors would be interrogating him about this ride. He was as sure of that as of his own name. Truthfully being able to claim ignorance looked useful.

After about three-quarters of an hour, the carriage pulled into a building of some sort and stopped. Lincoln thought he was outside Salt Lake City; it had been quiet outside the carriage for some time, and the driver had stopped making turns to throw off pursuit or to confuse his passenger. In the latter, at least, he had succeeded; Lincoln did not know whether he was north or south or east or west of the Mormon metropolis.

"You may get out now, Mr. Lincoln," the driver said, climbing down from his own high seat. Outside, someone was closing a door. A bar thudded down.

Barn, was Lincoln's first thought on emerging from the carriage. He revised it a moment later: *no, livery stable.* His nose filled with the good odors of horse and hay and leather. But for the carriage, the stable was deserted. With the door closed, it was also twilight-gloomy.

The man who had shut the door was coming toward Lincoln. Though he had expected to meet John Taylor, he needed a moment to recognize him. The fugitive Mormon president was dressed like a stablehand, in canvas trousers, collarless four-button work shirt, and straw hat. He had shaved his beard and was growing a mustache on his formerly bare upper lip.

"Thank you for agreeing to see me," he said after shaking hands. "To come with Orem here took considerable moral and physical courage."

"I will do what I can for you, Mr. Taylor," Lincoln said, "for that strikes me as a likely way to bring peace to this Territory. But I must warn you, I do not think I can do much. Bearing a grudge against me as he does, General Pope will not be inclined to act favorably upon any request I make."

"You are the former president of the United States!" Taylor exclaimed.

"I told you at our last meeting, you exaggerate the influence that gives me. I told you also, you exaggerated your ability to coerce the government of the United States into doing as you desired. Events have proved me right in the second instance. Will you not credit me for knowing whereof I speak in the first, also? In both, you would have done better to leave well enough alone."

Taylor slowly shook his head. It was not so much disagreement as disbelief. "All we wish—all we ever wished—is to live our own lives as our conscience dictates. We harm no one, and what has been our reward? Treatment that would not be meted out to redskins or Negroes. Do the people condemn the outrages we have suffered? No. They applaud, and pile on more."

"Mr. Taylor, from all I have seen in my extended stay in Salt Lake City, the only way you Mormons differ in the general run of your behavior from the mass of the American people is that you excel over them," Lincoln said. "But—"

"Of course we do," Taylor said, while the driver—Orem—nodded vigorously.

Lincoln held up a hand. "I had not finished. However fine you may be in the general run of your behavior, you have not the slightest chance, so long as you condone and practice polygamy, of ever gaining the acceptance of the vast majority of your fellow citizens."

"This is most unjust," Taylor said. "We cast no aspersions on anyone else's usages; in principle, none should be cast on ours."

Lincoln sighed. "If you wish to speak of principle, maybe you are right. Do you not see, however, that by insisting on principle in this regard, you have caused the overthrow of the principle of representative government and the principle of rule under the Constitution throughout Utah Territory? Is that what you intended when you led your people into rebellion?"

"Of course not," Taylor snapped.

"Well, then—" Lincoln spread his hands. "The simplest way for your church to make its peace with the rest of the United States would be for it to renounce the doctrines unacceptable to the nation as a whole, and to do so in all sincerity."

"That would require a divine revelation," the Mormon president replied. "None has been forthcoming, nor do I reckon one likely."

"Pity." Lincoln raised one eyebrow. "A convenient revelation now would save your people enormous heartache, enormous grief, later on."

"Revelations are not born of convenience," John Taylor said. "They spring from the will of God."

He thrust his head forward like a stubborn snapping turtle. Lincoln realized he meant what he said from the bottom of his heart. Lawyer and politician, Lincoln reckoned almost everything negotiable. When he had stood foursquare for the principle of the indissolubility of the Union, rifle musket and cannon had refuted him.

"If you will not change your views in any particular," he said, "what point to asking me to meet with you? You give me nothing to take to General Pope, even assuming the military governor were inclined to accept anything I might take him."

"We have yielded peacefully to the military power of the United States," Taylor said. "We might have done otherwise. If we continue to be oppressed, to be treated as a conquered province, we are liable to do otherwise. We are men. We can act as men. General Pope and his Cossacks should remember as much."

"Mr. Taylor, if you value your faith, if you value the lives of your followers, I implore you, sir, do not take this course." Lincoln had never spoken more earnestly. "If you rise in arms against the United States, they will slaughter you and sow your cities with salt, as the Romans did to Carthage long ago. Do you not understand that many in the Army, many in the government, and many among the citizenry at large would be delighted to have an excuse to do exactly that?"

"We fled here to Utah to escape persecution," Taylor said. "Persecution pursued us. Should we welcome it with open arms? Should we bow to it, as the Israelites bowed to the Golden Calf?"

"You will have to judge the right for yourself, as every man must," Lincoln answered. "But I tell you that open resistance will bathe Utah in blood in a way never before seen upon this continent. We left religious war behind in Europe. We should be well advised not to let it emigrate from that place to our shores."

"What would you do, Mr. Lincoln, were your faith under attack instead of mine?" John Taylor did not try to hide his bitterness.

He framed sharp questions. He would have been dangerous in a court of law. But none of that mattered. Taylor's failing was his inability to see that it did not matter. Lincoln said, "I believe I should have only two choices. One would be to pay the martyr's price, the other to accommodate myself to my neighbors' usages to the degree I could do so without tearing the living heart from what I believed in."

"No accommodation we can make and still keep to our principles would satisfy our foes," Taylor said.

"That is why I hoped God in His wisdom might reveal to you a course that would let you do so," Lincoln said delicately. He remained of the opinion that John Taylor and the other leaders of the Mormon Church could produce a revelation if they put their minds to it. "The promise of peace and reconciliation might—and I can say no more than *might*, hardly being in the confidence of General Pope or President Blaine—might, I say, persuade the authorities to rescind the harsh sentences passed against you and your colleagues."

"If I must die on the gallows or in hunted exile, I am prepared," Taylor said.

Lincoln believed him, having seen the same implacable purpose on the faces of abolitionists and Confederate leaders alike. With another sigh, he said, "Then I fear this meeting had little point. I shall take your warning back to General Pope, but I warn you in the strongest terms not to act upon it. Do with your own life what you will, but spare your people the horrors of a war of extermination harsher than any we ever waged against the Sioux." He turned to Orem. "You may as well take me back to town. My friends will be wondering why I needed so long to buy a cake of shaving soap."

The bright young Mormon held the carriage door open so Lincoln could get in, then closed it after him. He did not ask Lincoln not to open the curtains, but the former president again left them alone. From inside the dark, cramped box of the carriage, he heard John Taylor undo the bar and push the livery-stable door open. Orem clucked to the horses. They leaned into their work.

After the trip back into Salt Lake City, the driver halted the carriage and said, "If you get out here, sir, you'll have no trouble finding your way to the home where you are staying."

Sure enough, Lincoln saw he was only a couple of blocks from the Hamiltons'. "Obliged," he said to Orem, and tipped his tall hat. The bright young man returned the courtesy and drove away. Lincoln supposed he had some secure place where he could go to earth. He needed one.

Juliette Hamilton looked up from the chicken she was plucking when Lincoln came into the kitchen. "Well, I never," she said in arch mock annoyance. "I was beginning to think you'd come down with a case of Valley Tan." Her eyes twinkled.

"My dear lady, although I have passed my Biblical threescore and ten, I am not suddenly taken with the urge to shuffle off this mortal coil," Lincoln said. He and Mrs. Hamilton both laughed, and he went on, "In my view, Valley Tan bears the same relation to proper whiskey as a slap in the face does to a kiss on the cheek. Both will get your attention, but I know which I prefer."

"If you're trying to sweet-talk me out of a kiss on the cheek—" Juliette walked over and gave him one. Then she wagged a finger at him. "But Valley Tan is cooked up complete with added sanctity, or so the Mormons say."

"I have never tasted a better reason for declaring sanctity unconstitutional," Lincoln answered.

"You are the funniest man," Juliette Hamilton exclaimed. "Why is it that everyone makes you out to be so somber and serious?"

"Part of it is that no one has ever told my face it has the right to be amused," Lincoln said, "and the other part is that I commonly speak of serious things, even if not always in a serious manner."

"If you mix some honey with the physic, the dose goes down easier," Juliette said.

"That's so," Lincoln said, "and with your kind permission I'll borrow the notion in a speech one day." Seeing how astonished Mrs. Hamilton looked, he added, "I am glad to employ any figure that strikes me as both true and well said, and in all my days I have never yet heard a better answer to give to the occasional person who complains of what he calls my unsuitable levity."

Gabe Hamilton had just come into the house when someone pounded on the front door. "Who the devil's that?" he said. The pounding went on. His scowl got darker. "Whoever it is, maybe I ought to have a revolver in my hand when I open the door."

"I think that would be most unwise," Lincoln said hastily.

He followed Hamilton up the entranceway to the door. When his host angrily threw it open, he was not surprised to find a squad of blue-coated U.S. soldiers outside. A young lieutenant began, "Is Abraham Lincoln—?" and then caught sight of him. "Mr. Lincoln, you are to come with me at once."

"Why should he?" Gabe Hamilton demanded, before Lincoln could speak.

"By order of the military governor, General Pope, he is under arrest," the lieutenant answered. The soldiers behind him aimed their rifles at Lincoln.

"I'll come quietly," he said. "You may lower those, lest someone be injured by mischance." He walked out of the house, leaving Hamilton staring after him.

* * *

The portly, gray-bearded man in the tweed sack suit, four-in-hand tie, and derby did not at first glance seem to belong in an army headquarters full of bustling young men in uniform. General Thomas Jackson would have been just as well pleased—far better pleased—had his visitor chosen to remain in Richmond.

"I am glad to welcome you to Louisville, Mr. President," he said, and prayed his stern God would forgive the lie.

"Thank you, General," James Longstreet said. "One of the things I found during the War of Secession was that military reports, however detailed, often conveyed a distorted view of an action. I also learned that newspaper reports seldom conveyed anything but a distorted view."

"There, Your Excellency, we agree completely," Jackson said. "If you believe what the reporters write, we have by now slain the entire population of the United States in this engagement, men, women, and children alike. It is a sanguinary fight, sir, but not so sanguinary as that."

"I had not thought it would be." Longstreet's voice held a rumble of amusement. "I came here to see what sort of fight it *is*, having acquired a fairly good notion of the sorts of fight it is *not*."

"It is, as you requested and required, a defensive fight, Mr. President." Jackson's voice had a rumble in it, too: a rumble of discontent. "Being thus constrained, I have endeavored to cause the United States the maximum of harm while yielding to them the minimum of ground."

"That is precisely why I set you in charge here, General," Longstreet said with a courtly dip of his head. "Precisely. And you have most handsomely done as I hoped you would. Papers in the United States are no less given to distortion and exaggeration than our own. Many of them quite vehemently assert you are indeed intent on slaughtering every damnyankee in creation."

"If General Willcox will continue funneling the Yankees into Louisville, I may in fact accomplish that," Jackson replied. "It will, however, take me some little while."

Longstreet laughed and slapped him on the back. From under his eyebrows, Jackson shot the president of the Confederate States a suspicious look. Longstreet restraining him, Longstreet arguing with him, Longstreet undercutting him—he'd grown used to those since his former fellow corps commander was inaugurated. Longstreet enthusiastic about what he did—that was so unusual, he didn't know how to react to it.

Military formality gave him a framework in which to respond, just as it gave him a framework for his entire life. He said, "Will you come with me, Your Excellency? You can examine the map, which will give you a good notion of where we are now and what I hope to do in the near future."

"Thank you. I shall take you up on that—it will do for the time being. Later, I intend to go up to the front, to see for myself this new sort of warfare you are inventing here."

Jackson stared. No one had ever questioned James Longstreet's courage. Jackson had found plenty of fault with Longstreet's common sense over the years, but never for a reason like this. "Mr. President, I beg you to reconsider," he said. "One lucky sharpshooter, one shell landing at the wrong spot—"

"Would you not be just as well pleased, General?" Longstreet said. "Were I to fall, I have no doubt my plan for manumission, which you have made it unmistakably clear you oppose, would fall with me."

Jackson looked down at his scuffed, oversized boots. Usually, he was the one who spoke with relentless frankness. After coughing a couple of times, he said, "Of one thing you have convinced me, Your Excellency: that no one in the Confederate States but yourself can hope to guide us through the intricacies of our relations with our allies in this time of crisis."

"I think you do Vice President Lamar a disservice, for he has more experience dealing with the Europeans than I do myself."

"He has not your deviousness," Jackson declared.

Longstreet smiled at that. "Flattery will get you nowhere," he said roguishly. "To the maps, and then on to the front." His smile got wider as he took in Jackson's expression. "I assure you, General, I am not indispensable to the cause. So long as you continue to make Louisville and the Ohio run red with Yankee blood, our success is assured."

"We bleed, too," Jackson said as he led the president toward the tent where he devised his strategy and whence he sent orders to his commanders at the battle line.

Longstreet pointed to the telegraphic operators who sat ready to tap out any commands the general-in-chief might give them. "A good notion," he said. "It saves you the time involved in sending a messenger to the signals tent, and minutes in such matters can be critical."

"Exactly so," Jackson said. He pointed to the big map of

Louisville. "As you see, Mr. President, forces of the United States unfortunately have, despite our best efforts to repel them, gained a stretch of ground several miles long and varying in depth from a few hundred yards to nearly a mile. I console myself by noting the price they have paid for the acquisition."

"How well have they fought?" Longstreet asked.

"As we saw in the last war, they have courage to match our own," Jackson replied. "They also have numbers on their side, and their artillery is both strong and well handled. Having said so much, I have exhausted the military virtues they display. General Willcox's notion of strategy seems to be to send men forward and ram them headlong into the——"

"Into the stone wall of your defense?" Longstreet interrupted, his voice sly.

Jackson went on as if the president had not spoken: "——into the positions we have prepared to repel them. One thing this battle has proved once and for all, Your Excellency, is the primacy of the defensive when soldiers in field works are provided with repeating rifles."

"So we had surmised, based on our own maneuvers and the recent Franco-Prussian and Russo-Turkish Wars," Longstreet said. "Encouraging to know our pundits were in this instance correct."

"Encouraging? I would not say so, Mr. President," Jackson answered. "The advantages accruing to the defensive make a war of maneuver far more difficult than it was in our previous conflict with the United States."

"But, General, we do not seek to invade and conquer the United States. They seek to invade and conquer us," the president of the Confederate States said gently. "I profess myself to be in favor of that which makes their work harder and ours easier."

"Hmm," Jackson said. "There is some truth in what you say." Longstreet showed a perspective broader than his own. From the viewpoint of the Confederacy as a whole, the ability to conduct a strong, punishing defense was vital. From the viewpoint of a general with the inclination to attack, the ability of the enemy to conduct a strong, punishing defense was constipating.

"Of course there is." In his own way, Longstreet had a certainty to match Jackson's. Jackson's sprang from faith in the Lord, Longstreet's, the general judged, from faith in himself. The Confederate president went on, "Now that I have seen the outline of our position in Louisville, I will see the position itself."

He looked as if he expected Jackson to argue with him. He looked as if he expected to enjoy overruling his general-in-chief. Saluting, Jackson replied, "Yes, sir. I look forward to accompanying you."

"What?" Longstreet emphatically shook his head. "I cannot permit that, General. You are—"

"Indispensable, Your Excellency?" Jackson presumed to break in on his commander-in-chief. "I think not. The arguments applying to you and Mr. Lamar apply with equal force to me and General Alexander."

"You are insubordinate, General," Longstreet snapped. Jackson inclined his head, as at a compliment. Longstreet glowered at him, then started to laugh. "Very well—let it be as you say."

Jackson put E. Porter Alexander in overall command until he should return, then, Longstreet at his side, rode down into Louisville, toward the sound of the guns. He went toward that sound as toward a lover. His wife knew of and forgave him his infidelity, one of the many reasons he loved her.

Even well behind the fighting line, shellfire and flames had taken their toll on Louisville's houses and offices and warehouses and manufactories. Some were burnt-out skeletons of their former selves, while others had had pieces bitten out of them, as if caught in the grip of monstrous jaws. The air smelled of stale smoke and gunpowder, with the sick-sweet fetor of death under them.

Longstreet drew in a long breath. His mouth tightened. "I have not smelled that smell since the War of Secession, but it never escapes the mind, does it?"

"No, sir." Jackson had his head cocked to one side, savoring the sounds of battle at close range. For the moment, the artillery was fairly quiet. After some consideration, though, he said, "I do not believe I ever heard such a terrific volume of musketry on any field during the War of Secession. Put that together with the increased power of the guns, and no wonder an attack crumples before it is well begun."

"Yes," Longstreet said abstractedly. A couple of ambulances rattled past them toward the rear. "I have not heard the cries and groans of wounded men since the War of Secession, either, but those likewise remain in memory yet green."

Soldiers coming back from the front, even the unwounded, looked like casualties of war: tattered uniforms, filthy faces, their eyes more full of the horror they had seen than of the debris-strewn paths down which they walked. Soldiers going forward, especially those who had been in the line before, advanced steadily, but without the slightest trace of eagerness. They knew what awaited them.

With every block now, the wreckage of what had been a splendid city grew worse. After a while, a corporal held up a hand. "Nobody on horseback past here," he declared, and then looked foolishly astonished at whom he had presumed to halt.

"Corporal, you are doing your duty," Jackson said. He and Longstreet dismounted and went forward on foot, soon moving from one trench to another along zigzags dug into the ground to minimize the damage from any one shellburst and to keep any advancing Yankees who gained one end of a trench from laying down a deadly fire along its entire length. Some of the trench wall was shored up with bricks and timbers from shattered buildings.

Slaves in coarse cotton labored to strengthen the defenses further. Jackson made a point of looking at them, of speaking with them, of urging them on. Longstreet made a point of taking no notice of Jackson.

Up above the trench, on bare ground, a sharpshooter with a long brass telescope mounted on his Tredegar crouched in the military equivalent of a hunter's blind: rubbish cunningly arranged to conceal him from view from the front and sides while he searched for targets behind the U.S. line. Jackson wondered how many snipers he'd passed without noticing them. He also wondered how many similar sharpshooters in Yankee blue were peering south, looking for unwary Confederates.

In the front-line trenches, the soldiers started to raise a cheer for their general-in-chief and president. Officers in butternut frantically shushed them, lest the damnyankees, getting wind of the arrivals, send a torrent of shells down on Jackson and Longstreet.

The president walked along, examining the trench and pausing now and then to chat with the soldiers defending it. Jackson followed. After a couple of hundred yards, Longstreet turned to him and asked, "Is it possible that the U.S. Army of the Ohio may bring in enough in the way of guns and men to drive us out of Louisville?"

"Yes, Mr. President, much as it pains me to say so, that is possible," Jackson answered. "They would pay a fearsome price, but it is possible."

"Having taken Louisville at such a price, could they then rapidly overrun the rest of Kentucky?" Longstreet inquired. Jackson laughed out loud, which made the president smile. But he had another question: "Are the Yankees as aware of these facts as we are ourselves?"

"I hardly see how it could be otherwise," Jackson said. "Why do you ask?"

"To see if your conclusions march with mine," Longstreet said, which, to the general's annoyance, was not an answer at all.

☆ X ☆

Colonel George Custer rode back toward Salt Lake City in high good humor. He had not succeeded in running the elusive John Taylor to earth, but he was bringing back to U.S. justice George Q. Cannon, another eminent leader of the Church of Jesus Christ of Latter-Day Saints. Cannon, his hands manacled and his feet tied together under his horse, glumly rode along behind Custer and his brother.

In splendid spirits himself, Custer said to Tom, "Did you hear about the Mormon bishop who passed away leaving behind nine widows?"

"Why, no, Autie, I can't say as I did," Tom Custer answered. "Why don't you tell me about the poor fellow?" By his expression, he suspected a joke of lurking in there somewhere. Since he couldn't see where, he willingly played straight man.

"It was very sad," Custer said with a sigh. "As the preacher put it by the graveside, 'In the midst of wives we are in death.'"

Both Custer brothers laughed. So did the other soldiers in earshot. Tom Custer looked over his shoulder at their prisoner and asked, "How many wives are you in the midst of, Cannon?"

"One," the Mormon answered tightly. He was a round-faced little man, his hair cut close to his head, cheeks and upper lip clean-shaven, with a short, curly tangle of graying beard under his chin.

"Why lie?" Custer said with something approaching real curiosity. "We know better. You must know we know better."

"First, I am not lying." Cannon had a precise, fussy way of speaking, more like a lawyer than a revolutionary. "Second, and now speaking purely in a hypothetical sense, if the penalty for polygamy be harsher than the penalty for perjury, would it not profit one in such a predicament to lie?"

274

"It might, if those were the only charges you were up against," Custer answered. "Next to treason, though, they're both small potatoes."

"I am not a traitor," George Cannon said, as he'd been saying since Custer's troopers caught him in a hayloft near Farmington. "I want nothing more for my people than the rights guaranteed them under the Constitution of the United States."

"Life, liberty, and the pursuit of wives?" Custer suggested, which drew another guffaw from his brother and made the captured Mormon fugitive set his jaw and say no more.

John Pope had established his headquarters at Fort Douglas, north and east of the center of Salt Lake City. The fort sat on a bench of land higher than the town. From it, the artillery Pope had brought with him—and the guns that had come in since government forces reoccupied Utah Territory—could direct a devastating fire on any insurrection that broke out.

Custer rode into the fort like a conquering hero. "Another Mormon villain captured!" he cried in a great voice. The soldiers manning the gates and up on the stockade raised a cheer. Custer took off his hat and waved it about. That drew another cheer.

Hearing the commotion, Brigadier General John Pope came out of his office to see what was going on. "Ah, Colonel Custer!" he said, and then looked past Custer to the prisoner. "So this is the famous George Cannon of whom you telegraphed me, is it? He doesn't look so much like a wild-eyed fanatic as some of the ones we snared before."

"No, sir," Custer agreed: close enough for his superiors to hear him, he made a point of agreeing with them. "But without their coldhearted, coolheaded comrades egging them on, the wild-eyed fanatics could not do so much damage."

"That, as we have seen here, is nothing less than the truth," Pope said heavily. "Well done, Colonel. Get him down from his high horse"—the military governor laughed at his own wit, and so, of course, did Custer—"and take him to the stockade. In due course, we shall try him, and, in due course, I have no doubt we shall hang him by the neck until he is dead."

Politely, Cannon said, "I presume you shall be the judge at these proceedings? Good to know you come into them unbiased."

"You Mormons have corrupted courts in Utah Territory too long," Pope replied. "You shall not have the opportunity to do so any more."

Dismounting, Custer walked over to George Cannon's horse and cut the ropes that bound his feet. He helped the manacled prisoner get down from the animal, then started to lead him to the row of cells that had been intended for drunk soldiers who got into brawls but now held as many Mormon leaders as the U.S. Army had been able to track down.

After a couple of steps across the parade ground, Custer stopped dead. Since he had his arm hooked to Cannon's, the Mormon bigwig perforce stopped, too. Custer, for the moment, entirely forgot the prisoner he'd been so proud of capturing. Pointing across the grounds, he growled, "What in blazes is *he* doing here?"

John Pope's gaze swung toward the tall figure walking along at a loose-jointed amble. In something approaching a purr, the military governor answered, "Honest Abe? He's under arrest for consorting with John Taylor, and for refusing to tell us the miserable rebel's whereabouts."

"Is that a fact, sir?" Custer's eyes glowed. "Can you hang him, too? Heaven knows he's deserved it, these past twenty years. If it hadn't been for him, we wouldn't have had to fight the War of Secession—and, if it hadn't been for him, I think we should have won it." By putting it that way, he managed to blame Lincoln for his treatment of both McClellan and Pope.

"I am forbidden to hang him," Pope said unhappily. "I am even forbidden formally to keep him under lock and key, though President Blaine in his generosity does permit me to retain him in custody here at the fort." He muttered something into his beard. Aloud, he added, "Blaine is a Republican, too."

"Republicans," Custer made the word a venomous oath. "They get us into wars, and then they fight them every wrong way they can find. If half—if a quarter—of what the wires are saying about the fighting in Louisville is true—" He kicked up a small cloud of dust, then rubbed his boot clean on the back of his other trouser leg.

"Orlando Willcox always was better at praying than he was at fighting," Pope said. "That impressed the redskins when he was out here in the West. He's not fighting the redskins any more. He's fighting Stonewall Jackson."

"We both know about that," Custer said with a grimace. He abruptly seemed to remember he still had hold of George Q.

Cannon. "Come along, you." He jerked the Mormon prisoner forward.

Once he had raced through the formalities of turning Cannon over to the warder, he hurried out to the parade ground once more. He needed only a moment to spot Lincoln, who was strolling along with as little apparent concern as if in a hotel garden. Custer trotted over to him. "How dare you?" he demanded.

Lincoln looked down at him: a long way down because, even though beginning to be shrunken by age, the former president was still the taller of them by half a foot or more. "How dare I what?" he asked now, his voice mild. "Take a walk here? I didn't know it was private property, and I'm not stepping on the grass to any great degree."

The parade ground being bare dirt, there was no grass on which to step. Custer scowled at Lincoln, who bore the glower with the air of a man who had borne a lot of glowers. "How dare you treat with the Mormons without leave?" he snapped.

"I hoped I might persuade Mr. Taylor to yield in such a way as to make this occupation do as little damage to the Constitution as possible," Lincoln answered. "In this, I fear, I was unsuccessful, Mormons possessing the same aversion to having their necks stretched as any other segment of the populace."

"Force is the only lesson the Mormons understand," Custer said.

"He who sows the wind will one day reap the whirlwind," Lincoln returned. "The store of hatred the U.S. Army builds for itself will come back to haunt it."

"As the Confederate States ought now to be reaping the whirlwind whose wind you sowed," Custer said. That got through to Lincoln; Custer smiled to watch him grimace. He went on, "How dare you presume to hide from us John Taylor's whereabouts?"

To his surprise, Lincoln laughed at that. "My dear Colonel, do you mean to tell me you believe Taylor will still be where he was?"

Custer felt foolish. He covered that with bluster. "No, of course not. Had you come to the U.S. military authorities directly you returned from this illicit meeting, we might have been able to capture the traitor, as he would have had only a short head start on our men."

"There you may possibly be correct, Colonel Custer," Lincoln answered. "But, in his seeking to use me as an intermediary, I judged—and judge still—that Mr. Taylor in effect made me his client, and I would be violating my responsibility to him in revealing where we met."

"If you are going to hide behind every jot and tittle of the law to save a criminal and a traitor from his just deserts, then in my view you deserve to go up on the gallows with him when we do seize him," Custer said. "I have no patience with legalistic folderol and humbug."

"If we do not live by law, what shall we live by?" Lincoln asked.

"When the law fails us, as it has plainly done in Utah Territory, shall we live by it no matter how dear that may cost us?" Custer returned.

Lincoln sighed. "There, Colonel, you pose a serious question, whether that be your intention or not. Much of the history of the law in the United States—and, indeed, in the world, or what I know of it—springs from the dialectical struggle between your observation and mine."

"The what kind of struggle?" Custer asked.

"Never mind," Lincoln said. "I would not expect you to be a student of either Hegel or Marx. Their works have come late to this side of the Atlantic, and are not yet appreciated as they should be."

Custer had not heard of either of them. That made him feel smugly superior, not ignorant. "We've got no need for a pack of damned foreign liars. We've got enough homegrown liars, seems to me." He glared fiercely up at the former president. "And if you didn't have a president of your own miserable party to protect you from the consequences of your treason, we would see if we could build a gallows tall enough to stretch you on it."

"My legs have always been long enough to reach the ground," Lincoln said. "I should prefer that they continue to do so."

"I shouldn't," Custer said, and turned his back on the man he blamed for so many of the country's misfortunes of the previous generation. He strode off. Although he thought he heard Lincoln sigh again behind him, he didn't turn around to make certain.

Instead, he sought out General Pope, who was glad enough to see him after his capture of George Cannon. "One by one, Colonel, they fall into our hands," Pope said, "and one by one we shall dispose of them."

"Yes, sir," Custer replied. "It is truly a pity we can't dispose of

Lincoln in the same way, or perhaps have him meet with an accident while attempting escape."

"I have been specifically cautioned against letting any such accident befall him, though he does not know that," Pope said. "It *is* too bad, isn't it?"

"Hiding behind the law to break the law," Custer muttered. Lincoln could put whatever fancy name on it he wanted. In Custer's eyes, that was what it was.

"Just so. Well, we've both known lo these many years the man is a scoundrel, so why should one more proof of it surprise us?" Pope started to say something else, then caught himself. "I remember what I wanted to tell you, Colonel. The War Department is letting us have another half-dozen Gatling guns. As you've had experience with the weapons, I'm assigning them to your regiment."

"Yes, sir," Custer said. "Lord only knows what I'll do with eight of the contraptions, but I will say I can't think of anything handier than one of them for making a pack of rioters wish they'd never been born."

"Just so," Pope repeated. "Once we start hanging Mormon big shots, we may have those rioters. I hope not. If we should, however, I'll expect you and these fancy coffee mills to play a major part in putting them down."

"Sir, it will be a pleasure," Custer said.

Chappo came up to General Stuart. Geronimo's young son politely waited to be noticed, then said, "Our first men come in. The bluecoats are not far behind them. They push hard; they think they have only us to fight. In another hour, maybe two, you will show them they are wrong."

"Yes." Stuart rubbed his hands together. He waited for the action to begin as eagerly as a bridegroom for the night of his wedding day. "You're sure about the time?"

"How can a man be sure?" Chappo asked reasonably. "If the bluecoats do not scent a trap, though, that is when they will be here."

"Good enough." Stuart turned to his trumpeter. "Blow Prepare for Battle."

As the martial notes rang out, Chappo said, "For white men, you hide yourselves well. You should fool other white men."

With the precision of youth, he revised that: "You should fool them long enough."

Jeb Stuart reminded himself the redskin meant it as praise, not as a slight. This desert was the Apaches' country, not his own. He and his men would never know it as they did. That was why they made such useful allies against the damnyankees.

That was also why, while he wouldn't turn on them himself as Major Sellers kept urging, he wouldn't mind seeing a good many Apaches killed and wounded in the fight that lay ahead. They wouldn't be able to blame that on him if it happened. They'd been as ready for this fight with the U.S. soldiers as he was: more ready, since the fight had been their idea. He'd sound as sympathetic as an old mammy when they counted up their losses.

Meanwhile, he sent messengers to the men who'd been sweating in the hot, hot sun the past few days. All the runners bore the same order: "Don't open fire too soon," Stuart instructed them. "Wait for the signal. Wait till the Yankees are well into the canyon. We don't want to just frighten them. We want to ruin them."

Chappo listened to that with approval. "The only reason to fight is to win," he said. "You see this clear."

"You bet I do," Stuart answered. Even with a general's wreathed stars on his collar, he carried a Tredegar carbine like any other cavalryman. Some officers felt their duty in battle was to lead and inspire the enlisted men, without actually doing any fighting past self-defense. Stuart had never seen the sense in that. He wanted to hurt the enemy any which way he could.

Waiting came hard, as waiting always did. When, off in the distance to the north, he heard rifle fire, his head swung that way like a hunting dog's on taking a scent. He looked around for Chappo. The Apache had vanished, Stuart could not have said exactly when. One second he was there, the next gone. No white man was able to move like that.

Here came the Apaches, some mounted, others afoot. They retreated steadily through the canyon. Watching them, Stuart knew nothing but admiration. By the way they were carrying out their fighting retreat, they gave the U.S. forces not the slightest clue they had allies lying in wait. When they formed a line of sorts near the southern end of the canyon, it looked like nothing more than a delaying action on the part of a few to let the rest put more distance between themselves and their pursuers.

And here came the Yankees, riding in loose order, a puff of gray smoke rising every now and then as one of them or another fired at the retreating Indians. Some, a couple of troops' worth, weren't properly bluecoats at all, but men in civilian-style clothes: volunteers, Stuart supposed. Now that the Indians weren't retreating but had formed a line, the U.S. soldiers began to bunch, those in front slowing while those in back came on.

It was the sort of target of which artillerymen dreamt. Stuart waited for the gunners, off on their rise, to decide they had enough damnyankees in their sights. If they waited much longer, some trigger-happy idiot was going to start shooting before they did, and warn the enemy of the trap.

Crash! All the field guns fired as one. All the shells burst close together among the Yankees. The result, seen through smoke and kicked-up dust, was gruesome: men and horses down and thrashing on the burning desert floor, other men and horses, and pieces of men and horses, down and not moving at all.

As to sweet music, Stuart listened to the confused and dismayed cries rising from the U.S. forces. As he'd hoped, they hadn't yet spotted his guns, and thought the Apaches had waylaid them with torpedoes. "Go wide!" someone yelled, which sent bluecoats riding toward the gentle slopes of the canyon walls— and straight into the withering rifle fire the Confederates, now waiting no longer, poured down on them.

Stuart's Tredegar bucked against his shoulder. The Yankee at whom he'd aimed slid off his horse into the dirt. The Confederate general whooped with glee as he slipped a fresh round into the rifle's breech, though he wasn't absolutely sure his was the bullet that had brought down the U.S. cavalryman. Other soldiers might also have aimed at the fellow.

Now the U.S. soldiers realized they'd run headlong into a box. They still hadn't figured out what kind of box, though. "Straight at 'em!" shouted an officer leading a squadron of volunteers. "You charge 'em, the damn redskins'll run every time." He swung his hat. "Come on, boys!"

He rode forward at the gallop, brave but stupid. A moment later, he was brave and stupid and dead. The bullet that caught him in the face blew off the back of his head. Another bullet took his horse in the chest. The beast went down, and in falling tripped up the horse behind it, which fell on its rider.

More shells crashed down on the U.S. troops, not in a single neat salvo but one by one as the guns reloaded and fired. "Christ almighty, it's the Rebs!" That cry and others like it announced that, too late, the Yankees had figured out what was going on.

They fought back as best they could. The volunteers seemed to be armed with Winchesters rather than government-issue Springfields. The hunting rifles' magazine feed and lever action meant those volunteers could fire faster than the regulars on both sides with their single-shot breechloaders. At close range, they did a fair amount of damage.

But not many of them got to close range. The U.S. forces were at the center of three fires: the Apaches and artillery from ahead, and dismounted Confederate cavalry to either side. Had Stuart been their commander, he didn't know what he would have done. Died gallantly, he hoped, so nobody afterwards would have the chance to blame him for sticking his head in the noose in the first place.

After dying gallantly, the next best thing the officer in charge of the U.S. force could have done was pull back and escape with as many men as he could, perhaps sacrificing a rear guard to hold back pursuit. The enemy commander didn't try that, either. Instead, though he could not have helped knowing what he was up against, he tried to punch his way through the Confederates dug in on the sides of the canyon.

A young lieutenant close by Stuart screamed as he was wounded. Then he examined the wound and screamed again: "My God! I am unmanned!" Stuart bit his lip. He knew the horrid chances war could take, but no man ever thought of that particular injury without a shudder of dread. Then a bullet cracked past his own head, so close he thought he felt the breeze of its passage. That refocused his mind on his own survival.

He had never seen a battle that came so close to running itself. That was as well, for, with the Yankees in the trap, his messengers had to travel a long, roundabout route to reach the Confederates on the other side of the canyon. But the other half of the army knew perfectly well what it had to do: hold its place and keep shooting at the damnyankees either till none was left or till the ones who were left had enough and ran away.

The same applied to the men on the west side of the canyon with him. The U.S. soldiers, regulars and volunteers alike, pushed their attacks with the greatest courage. Many of them advanced on foot, to present smaller targets to their foes. Some got in among the Confederates. The fighting then was with clubbed rifles and bayonets and knives as well as with bullets. But, though the Yankees got in among the C.S. troopers, they did not get through. Those few who survived soon ran back toward the center of the canyon, bullets kicking up dirt near their heels and stretching them lifeless under the sun.

Stuart looked up to the sky. Buzzards were already doing lazy spirals. How did they know?

"Forward!" Stuart called. "If they're going to stand there and take it, let's make sure they have a lot to take."

Cheering, his men advanced. Neither butternut nor gray perfectly matched this country, but both came closer than the dark blue the U.S. soldiers wore—and both were covered with a good coat of dust and dirt, too. The damnyankees found few good targets among their oncoming foes.

The officer in charge of the U.S. forces—whether he was the original commander, Stuart had no way of knowing—finally decided, far too late, to pull out with whatever he would save. By then, rifle fire from both sides of the canyon was far closer than it had been. The Confederate field guns kept sending shells wherever the Yankees were thickest. Only a battered remnant of the force that had pursued the Apaches south from Tucson rode back toward it.

"Splendid, General, splendid!" Major Horatio Sellers shouted.

"Thank you, Major," Stuart told his aide-de-camp, and then went on, in a musing voice, "Do you know you have a bullet hole in your hat?"

Sellers doffed the headgear and examined it. "I know now, yes, sir," he said, and then, with studied nonchalance, set the hat back on his head. "How vigorous a pursuit were you planning to order?"

"Not very," Stuart answered. "President Longstreet has made it all too plain that our mission is to protect Chihuahua and Sonora, not to try to annex any of New Mexico Territory. A pity, but there you are. After this licking, I don't think the Yankees will be panting to invade our new provinces any time soon."

"I think you're right about that," Sellers said. "And I also have to say that you were right about the Apaches. They served us very handsomely here." He looked around and lowered his voice. "And I hope a lot of them bit the dust, too. What they helped us do to the Yankees, they could do to us one fine day."

"They could," Stuart agreed. "We have to persuade them that it's not in their interest. As I've said, being neither Yankees nor Mexicans, we have a leg up on that game." He pointed toward the mouth of the canyon, where the artillery, lengthening its range, was paying the retreating U.S. soldiers a final farewell. "And we have a leg up on this game, too."

On what had been the main battlefield, gunfire ebbed toward silence. More and more Confederates broke cover to round up prisoners, do what they could for the U.S. wounded, and plunder the dead. The Apaches emerged from their places of conceal-ment, too. Some of those seemed incapable of concealing a man until an Indian, or sometimes two or three, came forth from them.

A fair number of the Confederates—especially members of the Fifth Cavalry, who had done a lot of Comanche fighting—took U.S. scalps as souvenirs of victory. To Stuart's surprise, the Apaches didn't.

"No, that is not our way," Chappo said when the general asked him about it. He frowned in thought, then qualified that: "Some of the wildest of us will sometimes take one scalp"—he held up his forefinger—"only one, for a special . . ." He and Stuart hunted for a word. ". . . a special ceremony, yes. The one who does this spends four days making clean. Not like—" He pointed to the cavalry troopers, who were busy with their knives.

Stuart suffered a timely coughing fit. He was used to whites' being disgusted at Indians' brutality. Here he had an Indian unhappy with the brutality of his own men. When worn on the other foot, the shoe pinched.

To keep himself from dwelling on that, he walked over to have a look at the prisoners. He found that the U.S. Regular Army troopers his men had captured wanted nothing to do with the vol-unteers who had ridden into battle with them. "You better keep us separate from those sons of bitches," said one blue-coated cavalryman, a dirty bandage wrapped around a bloody crease to his scalp. "God damn the Tombstone Rangers to hell, and then stoke the fire afterwards. 'Got to get them Injuns,' they said. 'Them Injuns is runnin' on account of they's a pack of cowards,' they said. And God damn Colonel Hains for listening to 'em, the stupid fool."

Colonel Hains was not in evidence among either the dead or the captured. The commander of the Tombstone Rangers, how-ever, had had his horse shot under him; the beast had pinned him when it crashed to earth. When Stuart came up to him, he was cursing a blue streak as a Confederate medical steward put splints on his ankle. "If I knew who the shitepoke was that killed my horse, I'd cut the balls off the asshole," he greeted Stuart. "I'm going to hobble around on a stick the rest of my born days, god-damn it."

"Sorry to hear it," Stuart said, a polite fiction. "Your men fought courageously, Colonel . . . ?" They'd charged into a trap—by what the Regular had said, they'd ignored the possibility that it might be a trap, too—so they hadn't fought very cleverly, but they had indeed been brave.

"Earp," the colonel of Volunteers said. Stuart thought it was a nauseated noise, perhaps from the pain of his injury, till he ampli-fied it: "Virgil Earp." He was about thirty, with a dark mustache and a complexion, at the moment, on the grayish side. "You damn Rebs went and slickered us."

"There's nothing in the rules that says we can't," Stuart answered.

"Wish my brother'd come out West with me," the captured Colonel Earp said. "He's the best poker player I ever knew. You wouldn't have fooled him. *Careful* there, you son of a whore!" That last was directed at the man tending to his ankle. He gave his attention back to Stuart. "We wanted to wipe out the dirty red-skins, but it didn't quite come off."

"No, it didn't." Stuart knew he sounded smug. He didn't care. He'd earned the right.

Virgil Earp surprised him by starting to laugh. "That's all right, Reb. You go ahead and gloat. Those bastards are your trouble now."

Abruptly, Stuart turned away. The Volunteer might not have been much of a soldier, but he'd put his finger right on the Con-federate commander's biggest worry. If the need to worry was so obvious even an arrogant fool could see it at a glance . . . Stuart didn't care for anything that implied.

Across the Ohio, the guns had fallen silent. Frederick Douglass peered suspiciously over the river toward the wreckage of what had been Louisville. The Confederates had asked for an eight-hour truce so they could send a representative to General Willcox's headquarters, and Willcox, after consulting by telegraph with President Blaine, had granted the cease-fire.

Here came the Confederate now: a major carrying a square of white cloth on a stick as his *laissez-passer*. Seeing Douglass standing close to Willcox's tent, he snapped, "You, boy! What business do you have hanging around here? Speak up, and be quick about it."

He might have been speaking to a slave on a plantation. To Douglass' hidden fury, a couple of the U.S. soldiers escorting the messenger chuckled. With ice in his own voice, Douglass replied, "What business have I? The business of a citizen of the United States, sir." He spoke with as much pride as St. Paul had when declaring himself a Roman citizen.

"Any country that'd make citizens out of niggers—" The Confederate emissary shook his head and walked into General Willcox's tent.

Douglass was shaking all over, shaking with rage. He turned to one of the U.S. soldiers who had not joined in the amusement at his expense and asked, "Why is that—that individual here, do you know?"

"I'm not supposed to say anything," the bluecoat answered. Douglass stood as quietly as he could and waited. In his years as a newspaper reporter, he'd seen how proud most people were of knowing things their friends and neighbors didn't, and how important that made them feel. He'd also seen how bad most of them were at keeping their secrets. And, sure enough, after half a minute or so, the soldier resumed: "What I hear, though, is that there Reb is going to put terms to us for ending the war."

"Terms?" Douglass' ears stood to attention. "What kind of terms?"

"Don't know," the soldier said. His obvious disappointment convinced Douglass he was telling the truth. "Tell you this much, Uncle: after what I've been through over on the other side of the river, any terms at all'd look pretty damn good to me, and you can take that to the bank."

His companions nodded, every one of them. Douglass made as if to write something in his notebook, to keep the white men from seeing how they had wounded him. Where he'd envisioned a crusade—literally a holy war—to sweep the curse of slavery from the face of the earth forever, they, having fought a bit and seen that the enemy would not fall over at the first blow, were ready to give up and go home.

No feeling among the soldiery for the plight of the Negro in

Confederate bondage, Douglass scrawled. The plight of the Negro, in fact, was not what had engendered the war. He reminded himself of that, grimly. Not even Lincoln had sent men off to battle for the express purpose of freeing the bondsman. Blaine hated the Confederate States because they were a rival, not because they were tyrants. Had they been exemplars of purest democracy, rivals they would have remained, and he would have hated them no less.

Presently, Captain Oliver Richardson came out of the tent. He was puffing on a cigar and looked mightily contented with the world. When he saw Douglass, he stared right through him. Douglass would have bet he knew the terms the major in butternut had brought. The Negro did not waste his time asking Richardson about them. General Willcox's adjutant cared for him no more than did the Confederate emissary.

A couple of minutes later, a corporal with the crossed semaphore flags of the Signal Corps on his sleeve hurried from Willcox's tent to that of the telegraphers nearby. Slowly, as if without the slightest need to hurry, Frederick Douglass strolled in the same direction. He positioned himself not far from the entrance, looked busy (in fact, he was jotting down unflattering observations about Captain Richardson, of which he had a never-failing supply), and waited.

In due course, the corporal came out once more. Douglass intercepted him in a way that, like any great art, looked effortless even when it wasn't. In confidential tones, he asked, "What sort of impossible terms are the Rebs proposing?"

"They don't sound so impossible to me," the soldier answered. When he said no more than that, Douglass was tempted to grab him by the front of his blouse and shake the news out of him. Restraining himself with an effort, he said, "What are they, then?" The soldier hesitated, visibly considering whether to reply. "It doesn't matter if you tell me," Douglass assured him. "Whatever the terms may be, I can neither accept nor refuse them."

"That's true enough," the Signal Corps corporal said, half to himself. "All right, I'll tell you: the offer is to end the war and pretend it never happened, near enough. Both sides to pull back over the border. No reparations, nothing of the sort. We just go on about our business."

Douglass sucked in a long breath of air. Those were generous terms, far more generous than he'd expected the Confederate

States to offer. Some—maybe many—in the United States would want to accept them, especially as word of the horrors of the battle of Louisville spread through the land. Douglass had done some spreading of that word himself, and now all at once bitterly regretted it.

"What of Chihuahua and Sonora?" he asked.

"Huh? Oh, them. Right." The corporal needed to be reminded of the immediate cause of the war. "The Rebs'd keep 'em."

"I see," Douglass said slowly.

"General Willcox said that, far as he was concerned, the Confederates were welcome to 'em, that they weren't worth owning in the first place, and that the only things in 'em was cactuses and redskins and greasers."

Rather than keeping too quiet, the soldier was suddenly talking more than Douglass had expected. "Did he?" the Negro journalist murmured. If an important U.S. commander didn't think the Mexican provinces were worth the cost the country was paying to try to make the Confederate States disgorge them, how would President Blaine feel?

"He did, sure as I'm standing here next to you," the Signal Corps corporal answered. "And I'm not going to stand next to you any more, though, on account of somebody's gonna spot me and figure I've been bangin' my gums too much." He sidled off, doing his best to look as if he'd never been there at all.

Frederick Douglass wrote down the details the soldier had given him while they were still fresh in his mind. Then he shoved the notebook back into his pocket and walked over to his tent. He'd been under canvas long enough to have grown used to the stark simplicity of a stool, a kerosene lamp, and an iron-framed military cot. They made his home in Rochester, which before leaving it he'd thought of as having all the modern conveniences, instead seem overcrowded and overstuffed.

He sat down on the stool and covered his face with his hands. He was not quite so appalled as he had been after shooting the disemboweled Massachusetts artilleryman. The physical shock of that deed would stay with him till his dying day. The grief flowing through him now, though, ran deeper and stronger than that which had followed the mercy killing.

"I was right then," he said. "Now . . ."

Now, instead of watching a man die before his eyes, he was seeing a lifetime's effort and hope take their last breaths.

James G. Blaine had started this war, basically, to punish the Confederate States for winning the War of Secession. Now that he had discovered he was punishing the United States even more severely, how could he continue after getting an honorable—no, an honorable-sounding—peace proposal from the CSA?

In Blaine's place, Douglass would have been hard pressed to keep from accepting such a peace. But if it was made, the USA and CSA would live side by side for another generation, maybe two or even three, and the vast white majority in the United States would go right on despising the handful of Negroes in their midst and doing their best to forget the millions of Negroes in the Confederate States even existed.

Douglass looked up and scowled at the canvas wall of the tent as if it were Oliver Richardson's smoothly handsome face. "I shall oppose this peace with every fiber of my being," he said aloud, as if someone had doubted him. "No matter what the cost, I shall urge that the war go forward, for the sake of my people."

The guns did not resume their deadly work immediately the peace expired. Both sides held back, awaiting President Blaine's decision. Douglass did not realize how constant a companion the roar of battle had been until he discovered the long stretch of silence was making him jumpy.

When he messed with the staff officers in the seemingly unnatural quiet that evening, he found he did not have to pretend ignorance of the proposed peace terms. Everyone was talking about them, and everyone assumed someone else had let Douglass know what they were. Almost to a man, the officers thought President Blaine would accept President Longstreet's offer.

"We'll be going home soon," Captain Richardson predicted. "I'd have liked to lick the damn Rebs, I'll say that, but it doesn't look like it's in the cards here."

Alfred von Schlieffen spoke up: "Did I not hear from the far-writer—no, the telegraph, you say; I am sorry—did I not hear that the Confederate States have in New Mexico a victory won?"

"I heard that," several people said around mouthfuls of fried chicken. Douglass had not heard it, but he'd been moping in his tent since getting word of the Confederate peace proposal. Somebody said, "The Rebs used the goddamn Apaches to lure our boys into a trap, that's what happened."

"We should have given the Apaches what we gave the Sioux," Richardson said. He slammed his fist down on the table, making silverware and tin plates jump. "We would have done it, too, I reckon, if they hadn't run down into Mexico every time we got on their tail."

"Yes, and now, instead of running into the Empire of Mexico, which was weak enough to allow our pursuit, they shall, if President Blaine accepts this peace, run down into Confederate territory, where we can no more pursue them than we can the Kiowas of the Indian Territory," Douglass said.

As always, the power of his voice let him command attention. Somebody a long way down the table—he didn't see who—said, "Damned if the nigger isn't right." For once in his life, he felt happier about the agreement than angry at the insulting title.

Thoughtfully, someone else said, "Maybe we've been looking too hard at all the blood we've spilled here in Louisville and not enough at the whole war."

"I don't know what's to look at," Oliver Richardson said. "We aren't doing any better anywhere else."

"But you are not invaded," Colonel Schlieffen said, "but only in this one far-off Territory. Your armed forces are not beaten. If the United States have the will, you can go on with this war."

"You're right, sir," Frederick Douglass exclaimed. "We *can* beat the Confederate States. We are larger and stronger than they. Do you soldiers want them laughing at us for another twenty years, as they've done ever since the War of Secession? If we give up the fight without being defeated, we shall make ourselves a laughingstock before the eyes of the whole world."

"If we go on and keep getting our ass kicked, the rest of the world is going to think that's pretty damn funny, too," Richardson said.

"But if we win," Douglass replied, "if we win, what glory! And what a triumph for the holy cause of freedom."

"Oh, Christ," Richardson muttered to the officer next to him, "now he's going to start going on about the slaves again." The other soldier nodded. Douglass almost threw a bowl full of boiled beets at them. With so many in the USA feeling as Oliver Richardson did, would even victory over the Confederate States bring liberation? And if it did not, what in God's name would?

Colonel Theodore Roosevelt raised the Winchester to his shoulder, squinted down the sights, and pulled the trigger. The rifle bucked against his shoulder. "Take that, you damned Englishman!" he shouted, working the lever. A brass cartridge case leaped into the air, then fell to the ground with a small clink. He aimed the rifle again, ready for another shot.

He didn't fire. A couple of hundred yards away, the pronghorn, after its first frantic bound, was already staggering. As its herd-mates raced off over the plains of northern Montana Territory, it took three or four more wobbly steps, then fell. Roosevelt shouted again, this time in triumph. He ran toward the mortally wounded antelope. His boots kicked up dust at every stride.

"Good shot, Colonel!" First Lieutenant Karl Jobst exclaimed. Jobst, only a few years older than his superior, was a Regular Army officer, not an original member of Roosevelt's Unautho-rized Regiment. Colonel Henry Welton had detailed him to the Volunteers as Roosevelt's adjutant and, Roosevelt suspected, as his watchdog, too. He'd stopped resenting it. Jobst had already made himself very useful.

"Right in the lung, by jingo! That's bully," Roosevelt said, seeing the bloody froth on the antelope's nose and mouth. The animal tried to rise when he came up to it, but could not. Its large, dark eyes reproached him. He stooped, pulled out a knife, and cut its throat to put it out of its misery. After watching its blood spill over the dirt, he rose, a broad grin on his face. "Good eating tonight!"

"Yes, sir," Jobst said with a grin of his own. "If there's any-thing better than antelope liver fried up with salt pork, I'm switched if I know what it is." He drew his knife, too. "Let's butcher it and take it back to camp."

They opened the body cavity and dumped the guts out onto the ground. Flies buzzed around them. Roosevelt plunged his knife into the soil again and again to clean it. "I wish this had been an Englishman, by Godfrey," he said. "I chafe at the defensive."

"Sir, our orders are to patrol the border but not to cross it," Lieutenant Jobst said. "If the enemy should invade us, we are expected to resist him. But we are not to provoke him, not when the United States have enough on their plate fighting the Confederates."

He spoke politely, deferentially: Roosevelt outranked him. He also spoke firmly: he was there not only to give the colonel of Volunteers a hand but to make sure he didn't go haring off on his own. Roosevelt knew how tempted he was to do just that, and gave Colonel Welton a certain amount of grudging respect for having anticipated his impulses.

He grabbed the carcass' hind legs, Jobst the forelegs. They carried the dead antelope back to the horses. The pack animal to whose back they tied the antelope snorted and rolled its eyes, not liking the smell of blood. Jobst, who was very good with horses, gave the beast a lump of sugar and calmed it down.

Camp lay close by the bank of the Willow River, which at this season of the year was little more than a creek. Roosevelt had patrols scattered from the Cut Bank River in the west all the way to the Lodge in the east, covering better than a hundred miles of border country with his regiment. Placing his headquarters roughly in the middle of that broad stretch of rolling prairie did not leave him reassured. "How are we supposed to fight the British if they do cross the border?" he demanded of Lieutenant Jobst, not for the first time. "They'll brush aside the handful who discover them the way I brushed off those deerflies back where we made the kill."

"Sir, we aren't supposed to fight them singlehanded," his adjutant replied. "We'll fall back, we'll harass them, we'll concentrate, we'll send word of their whereabouts down to Fort Benton so Colonel Welton can bring up the infantry, and then we'll lick 'em."

"I suppose so," Roosevelt said, not quite graciously. He admitted to himself—but to no one else—that he had trouble with the idea of not fighting the foe singlehanded. In all his visions of battle with the British, he saw himself. Sometimes he alone was enough to defeat the foe, sometimes he had help from the Unauthorized Regiment. In none of them did the rest of the U.S. Army play any role. He knew what he imagined and what was real were not one and the same. Knowing it and coming to terms with it were not one and the same, either.

The rest of the small regimental staff greeted him with enthusiasm and the antelope with even more. The cook, an enormous Irishman named Rafferty, had an equally enormous pot of beans going, but he was among the loudest of the men cheering the kill. "Beans'll keep you from starving, that they will," he said, "but after a while you don't care. This here, now—" He ran his tongue over his lips in anticipation.

Roosevelt was gnawing on an antelope rib and getting grease in his mustache when a rider came trotting up from the south. "What's the news?" Roosevelt called to him. "Have some meat, have some coffee, and tell us what you know."

"Thank you, sir," the soldier from Fort Benton said. He loaded a tin plate with food—not only a chunk of roast antelope haunch but also a big dollop of Rafferty's beans—and then sat down by the fire. "News could be better."

"Well, what is it?" Roosevelt said. North of Fort Benton lived only a few scattered farmers and sheepherders. No telegraph lines ran north from there, which made Roosevelt feel cut off from the world beyond the circle of prairie he could see.

"Rebs and Indians done licked us south of Tucson, down in New Mexico Territory," the courier answered, which produced a chorus of groans from everyone who heard it. "And there's no good news to speak of out of Louisville, neither. We throw in some men, they get themselves shot, we throw in some more. Don't know what the devil we got to show for it."

Louisville, Roosevelt thought, was the very opposite of the fight he would have to make against the British if they did invade Montana Territory. Down in Kentucky, too many men were jammed into too little space, and all of it built up. That was a recipe for slaughter, not war.

Thinking along with him, Lieutenant Jobst said, "Louisville's a bad place to pick for a battle. If the Rebels had gone into Washington or Cincinnati, it's the sort of battle we'd have given them. As things are, we get that end of the stick."

"What happened down in New Mexico?" Roosevelt asked the man from Fort Benton.

"Sir, I don't rightly know," the soldier said. He took a note from the pocket of his blouse. "This here is what Colonel Welton gave me to give you. He said I should read it before I set out so I could tell you what it said in case it got soaked or somethin'."

Roosevelt read the note. It told him no more than the courier had: the bare facts of defeat in New Mexico and bloody stalemate in Kentucky. He crumpled it and threw it into the fire, then rounded on Lieutenant Jobst. "If you ask me, Lieutenant, an invasion of Canada is likely to be the best thing we could do right now. Heaven knows we're going nowhere on any other front."

"That's not for me to say, sir," Jobst replied, "nor, if you'll forgive me for reminding you, for you, either."

"I know it's not." Roosevelt paused to light a cigar. He blew out a cloud of fragrant smoke, then sighed. "The tobacco in this one's from Confederate Cuba. We don't grow such good leaf here in the USA, more's the pity."

Taking his change of subject as acquiescence, Karl Jobst said, "I'm sure the War Department will notify Fort Benton if they want us to undertake any offensive action."

"And why are you so sure of that?" Roosevelt inquired, as sardonically as he could. "Look how long the powers that be took to decide that the Unauthorized Regiment should go into service, and at everything I had to do to convince them."

Lieutenant Jobst hesitated. Roosevelt was, for the moment, his superior, yes. But, when the war ended, Roosevelt would go back to being a civilian while Jobst stayed in the Army. And, despite being a young man, Jobst was older than his regimental commander. Both those factors warred with his sense of subordination. He picked his words with obvious care: "The powers that be did not know how fine a regiment you'd recruited, sir. I assure you, they are aware of the threat the British and Canadians pose to our northern frontier."

Roosevelt wanted to argue with that. He wanted to argue with everything keeping him from doing what he most wanted to do: punish the enemies of the United States. Try as he would, he found no way; Jobst was too sensible to be doubted here. "I suppose you have a point," Roosevelt said with such good grace as he could.

"Sir," the courier asked, "what word should I bring back to Colonel Welton at the fort?"

"All's quiet," Roosevelt answered. That didn't make him happy, either, for it gave him no excuse to strike back at the British Empire. But, he felt, having become a U.S. Volunteer obligated him to give his own superior nothing but the truth. "I have riders constantly going back and forth from each of my troops to this place. Should the foe make so bold as to pull the tail feathers of our great American eagle, I would know it before a day had passed, and would send a messenger to Colonel Welton with orders to kill his horse getting the news down to Fort Benton."

"Pull the tail feathers of the American eagle," the soldier repeated. Then he said it again, quietly, as if memorizing it. "That's pretty fine, sir. You come up with things like that, you ought to write 'em down."

"You're not the first person who's said so," Roosevelt purred; he was anything but immune to having his vanity watered. "One day, perhaps I shall. Meanwhile, though"—he struck a theatrical pose, not altogether aware he was doing it—"we have a war to win."

"Yes, sir!" the courier said.

Lieutenant Jobst studied Roosevelt. "Sir, I hope we do get the chance to fight the British," he said. "I think your men would follow you straight to hell, and that's something no one but God can give an officer."

"I don't aim to lead them to hell," Roosevelt said. "I may lead them *through* hell, but I intend to take them *to* victory."

Jobst didn't say anything to that. The courier from Fort Benton softly clapped his hands together once, before he'd quite realized he'd done it. In the firelight, his eyes were wide and bright and staring.

Roosevelt chose not to sleep inside his tent, not when the weather was dry. Curled in his bedroll later that night, he stared up and up and up at the sky. Stars were dusted across that great blue-black bowl like diamonds over velvet, the Milky Way a ghostly road of light. As he watched, two shooting stars glowed for a heartbeat, then silently vanished.

He sighed. You never saw skies like this in New York: too much stinking smoke in the air, too many city lights swallowing the fainter stars. This perfection struck him as reason enough by itself to have come to Montana Territory. So thinking, he took off his spectacles, slid them into their leather case, and drifted off in bare moments.

He woke, refreshed, at sunrise, breathing cool air like wine. Even in August, even when the day would be hot and muggy by noon, early morning was to be cherished. He pulled on boots, put on spectacles, and began mixing calisthenics with rounds of shadow boxing.

"Colonel, you make me tired just watching you," Lieutenant Jobst said when he woke up a few minutes later.

"You should try it yourself," Roosevelt panted. "Nothing like exercise for improving the circulation of the blood."

"If I felt any healthier now, I do believe I'd fall over," Jobst replied. Roosevelt snorted and ripped off a couple of sharp right-left combinations that would have stretched any invading Englishman—at any rate, any invading Englishman without a rifle—senseless in the dust.

After antelope meat, hardtack, and coffee, Roosevelt mounted and rode off across the plains on patrol. Along with commanding his soldiers, he wanted to do everything they did. And, if the British did presume to invade the United States, he wanted at least a chance of being the first to discover them.

Duty and the siren song of paperwork brought him back to camp in a couple of hours. He was busy writing up a requisition for beans and salt pork for A Troop, far off to the west by the Cut Bank River, when someone rode in from the south. Curiosity and a distaste for requisitions, no matter how necessary, made him stick his head out of the tent to see what was going on.

He'd expected the newcomer to belong to one troop or another of the Unauthorized Regiment. But the soldier wore no red bandanna tied to his left sleeve. That meant he was from Fort Benton. Roosevelt's eyebrows pulled down and together. Colonel Welton wasn't in the habit of sending couriers up to him two days running.

"What's the news?" he called.

The soldier, who had been talking with Lieutenant Jobst, saluted and said, "Sir, I have an urgent message for you."

"I didn't think you'd ridden fifty miles or so for your amusement," Roosevelt returned. "Go ahead and give it to me."

"Sir, it's only in writing," the courier said. Roosevelt blinked. That wasn't what Welton usually did, either. He saw Lieutenant Jobst also looking surprised. The rider took from his saddlebag an oilskin pouch that would have protected its contents regardless of the streams through which he might have splashed. He handed it to Roosevelt. "Here you are, sir."

"Thank you." Roosevelt drew away. Had Welton wanted the courier to know what the message said, he would have told him. Lieutenant Jobst followed Roosevelt, who frowned a little but said nothing.

He opened the pouch. Inside lay a sealed envelope. He opened that, too, and drew out the folded sheet of paper it contained. Together, he and Jobst read the note on that sheet of paper. Both of them let out low whistles, neither noticing the other.

"Longstreet offers peace on the *status quo ante bellum*, except the Rebs get to keep their Mexican provinces?" Jobst murmured. "That could be damned hard for President Blaine to turn down."

"Yes." Roosevelt faced southeast, all thoughts of keeping secrets from Colonel Welton's courier flown from his head. He shook his fist in the general direction of Richmond. "You son of a bitch!" he shouted. "You filthy, stinking son of a bitch! God damn you to hell and fry you black, I went to all the trouble of putting a regiment together, and now I don't even get the chance to fight with it? You *son* of a bitch!" To his own mortification, he burst into tears of rage.

"Morning, boys," Samuel Clemens called as he took off his straw boater and hung it on a hat tree just inside the entrance to the *Morning Call* offices.

"Mornin', boss." "Good morning, Sam." "How are you?" The answers came back in quick succession, as they had for as long as he'd been working on the newspaper. No outside observer would have noticed anything different from the way it had been, say, a month before. As he walked to his desk, Clemens told himself that was because there was nothing to notice.

He paused to light a cigar at a gas lamp, then sat down and took a couple of puffs. On the desk in a fancy gilt frame sat a tintype of himself, Alexandra, and the children. He could see his reflection in the glass in front of the photograph. He was unsmiling on the tintype because smiles were hard to hold while waiting for the exposure to be completed. His reflection was unsmiling because . . .

"Because there's nothing to smile about," he muttered. Try as he would, he couldn't convince himself things were as they had been before those two ruffians hauled him off to the Presidio. He still carried in a vest pocket the good character Colonel Sherman had given him. No one had accused him of disloyalty since, not out loud.

But when he greeted people, didn't their responses come a quarter of a second slow? Didn't they sound ever so slightly off, like those of a good actor who would die prosperous but whom no one would remember three days after they shoveled dirt over him? And these were his colleagues, here at a newspaper that opposed the present war. If this was what his brief brush with Confederate service got him here, he shuddered to think what the rest of San Francisco thought. None of the other papers had made him out to be a traitor, but that was probably only a matter of time.

He was scowling as he sorted through the telegrams that had come in during the night. For one thing, none of them had the news he really needed. For another, he wasn't sure it even mattered. If people thought he was tarred by the brush of the CSA, if they didn't take seriously what he wrote because he was the one who wrote it, what good was he in the spot he was holding?

Sharp, quick, abrupt footsteps behind him. He recognized them before Clay Herndon said, "Good morning to you, Sam."

"Morning, Clay." Sam spun around in his chair. It squeaked. "I've got to oil that, or else set a cat to catch the mouse in there." He felt a little less morose as he blew smoke at Herndon. The reporter didn't treat him as if he suffered from a wasting sickness. Clemens ruffled the telegrams on his desk. "Still nothing out of Philadelphia, I see."

"Not a word," Herndon agreed.

"How long can President Blaine sit there like a broody hen before he hatches a yes or a no?" Clemens demanded.

"Been a day and a half so far," Herndon said. "He doesn't seem to be in much of a hurry, does he?"

"He was in a hurry to start the damned war," Sam said. "Now that he's got a chance to get out of it easier and cheaper than anybody thought he would, I don't know what in creation he's waiting for."

"Chihuahua and Sonora," Clay Herndon said.

Clemens rolled his eyes. "If he thinks a slab of Mexican desert is worth the Children's Crusade he's thrown against Louisville, he's . . . he's . . . he's the fellow who was in a hurry to start the damned war." He sighed. "Since he is that fellow, he's liable to keep right on at it, I suppose. But if he can't live with this peace, I don't know where he'll find a better one."

"But if he says yes to it, then he has to go and tell the voters why he went and started a war and then quit before he got anything out of it," Herndon said.

"That's true," Clemens admitted. "But if he says no, he's liable to have to go and tell the voters why he went and started a war and then lost it. That made Abe Lincoln what he is today."

"A rabble-rousing blowhard, do you mean?" Herndon said, and Sam laughed. The reporter went on, "What I think is that Blaine's like a jackass between two bales of hay, and he can't figure out which one to take a bite out of."

"Blaine's like a jackass more ways than that." Sam threw back his head and did an alarmingly realistic impression of a donkey.

That made Herndon laugh in turn. "Time to get to work," he said, and headed off to his own desk.

"Time to get to work," Clemens repeated. He looked upon the notion with all the enthusiasm he would have given a trip to the dentist. What he wanted to do was write an editorial. He couldn't do that till Blaine figured out which bale of hay made him hungrier.

Edgar Leary came up with a couple of sheets of paper in his hand. "Here's that story about the people who were stranded in Colorado when the Mormons closed down the railroad, boss," he said. "You should hear the way they go on. If it were up to them, there wouldn't be enough lampposts to hang all the Mormons from."

"Give it here. I'll have a look at it." Sam took the sheets and proceeded to edit them almost as savagely as he'd dealt with Mayor Sutro's inanities over at City Hall. Leary had the *Morning Call*'s slant on the story straight: the Mormon troubles were Blaine's fault, for the settlers in Utah would never have dared defy the power of the United States were that power not otherwise occupied. But the young reporter was wordy, he had trouble figuring out what was important and what wasn't, and once, perhaps absently—Sam hoped absently—he'd written *it's* when he meant *its*.

By the time Sam finished butchering the story, he felt better. He took it over to Leary. "See if I've done anything to it that you can't stand. If I have, tell me about it. If I haven't, clean it up and take it to the typesetters."

"All right, boss," Leary said. Clemens' tone warned him he would not be wise to defend his original version too strenuously. He looked down at the paper, then up at his editor. His unlined face turned red. "Did I write that?"

"The apostrophe, you mean? It's not in *my* handwriting." Sam strode off.

He spent the rest of the morning arguing with people who didn't want their stories shortened; with people who hadn't finished stories that would eventually need shortening; with typesetters who, by all appearances, couldn't spell *cat* if he spotted them the *c* and the *a*; and with printers who hadn't tightened the nine wood blocks of an engraving of the ruins of Louisville enough to keep the spaces between them from showing on the page as thin white lines.

"No, of course it wasn't you fellows," he said when the printers tried to deny responsibility. "A British spy sneaked in and did it while you weren't looking. If he's hiding under one of your presses and jumps out and does it again, though, I'm going to be very unhappy—and so will you."

Quarreling till noon helped him work up an appetite—or maybe his stomach was growling from nerves because he still didn't know which way President Blaine would jump. However that was, he'd grown ravenous by the time twelve o'clock rolled around. He collared Clay Herndon and said, "Let's go over to the Palace for lunch."

"Bully!" Herndon lifted a gingery eyebrow. "Are you counterfeiting double eagles down in your cellar, or is Mayor Sutro paying you not to run that picture of him and Limber Hannah?"

Clemens' ears burned. He rallied quickly, saying, "If I had that picture, I'd run it on the front page, and I'd make damned sure the printers screwed the engraving blocks together good and tight. In a manner of speaking. Come on. If we're going to live, let's live a little."

"Sold!" Herndon sprang from his seat.

Being on Market Street, the Palace Hotel was only a few minutes' walk from the *Morning Call* offices. Going into the restaurant, though, was entering another world. Sam felt released from prison: no more dingy cubbyholes crammed with wisecracking newspapermen and smelling of printer's ink. The restaurant was bright and airy, full of starched white linen and gleaming cutlery, and as full of the odors of good food and even better tobacco. In such surroundings, Sam was almost ashamed to light up one of the cheap cheroots he enjoyed more than any other cigars—almost, but not quite.

He ordered toasted angels—oysters wrapped in bacon, flavored with red peppers and lime juice, and grilled on skewers—and deviled pork chops. Herndon chose oysters, too, in an omelet with flour and heavy cream. The waiter started to suggest that might make a better breakfast than a luncheon. Herndon fixed him with a steely glare. "If I wanted advice, pal, I'd have ordered some," he said. The waiter bowed and retreated. The reporter got his omelet.

"That's telling him," Clemens said, lifting a sparkling tumbler of whiskey in salute. "Put a fancy suit on some people and they

think they own the world—and they make you believe it, too."
He sipped from his drink, looked thoughtful, and went on,
"That's probably why generals look like gold-plated peacocks."

"You're likely right," Herndon answered. Struck by the aptness of his own thought, Sam looked around the restaurant for
officers. There wouldn't be any generals here, not with Colonel
Sherman commanding the garrison, but the principle applied, in
diminishing degree, to other ranks as well. He spotted a major, a
couple of captains, and a lieutenant commander from the small
Pacific Squadron of the U.S. Navy: all in all, enough in the way
of epaulets and gold buttons and plumed hats to convince him
he'd stumbled across a new law of nature.

Then the food arrived, and he stopped worrying about the U.S.
Army, or even the Navy. The toasted angels were perfect, or
maybe a little bit better: the bacon brought out the delicate,
oceanic flavor of the oysters, with the pepper and lime juice adding a piquant counterpoint. And the pork chops, served in a sauce
of mustard, horseradish, and chutney, had a solid, fatty taste that
made him demolish them one after another.

Across the table from him, Herndon was methodically laying
waste to the omelet. "God damn, Sam," he said, features working
in the throes of some deep emotion, "why don't we do this more
often?"

"Only reason I can think of is that I'm not stamping out double
eagles downstairs," Clemens answered, real regret in his voice. "I
felt like it today, that's all. I'll feel like it tomorrow, too, but my
wallet won't."

After more whiskey, Turkish coffee, and zabaglione, the two
newspapermen sorrowfully paid the bill and even more sorrowfully walked back to the *Morning Call*. As soon as they came
through the door, Edgar Leary all but leaped on them. He was
waving a telegram in his hand and dancing around as if about to
hit the warpath.

"Easy, there," Sam said. "Get the rattlesnake out of your unmentionables and tell us what the devil's going on."

"We've got Blaine's answer," Leary said, waving it in Clemens'
face. "Came over the wire not five minutes ago." Before Sam
could snatch it out of his hand, he went on, "Blaine says no—a
big, loud, no. We aren't licked anywhere, he says—"

"Anywhere but New Mexico Territory," Sam broke in. He

checked himself. "Never mind. I'll shut up. What else does he say?"

"Says we were right to fight at the beginning, and says we're still right now. Says we're going to make the Confederate States cough up what they had no business taking in the first place. Says—"

Clemens could restrain himself no longer: "He says we'll make the Empire of Mexico keep those two worthless provinces if we have to kill every man in the United States to do it."

"That's not quite how he put it," Leary said.

"No, but that's what it means." Now Clemens did take the telegram from him. He rapidly read through it, then nodded. "Yes, that's what it means, all right. If we'd spent five millions a few months ago, we could have made Maximilian happy and taken all the steam out of Longstreet's boiler. Now we'll spend ten or twenty or fifty times that much, and for what? What do we get? A war that isn't going anyplace, soldiers maimed and murdered by the thousands, and tomorrow's editorial for me. Isn't that grand?"

Without waiting for an answer, he carried the telegram back to his desk, read it again, and began to write:

"Throw some good money after the bad," you will hear them say, after you have thrown away half your life's savings on a railroad that goes up a mountain but does not come down the other side; or on a street-paving company whose president has lacked the forethought to cross your mayor's palm with silver; or on your brother-in-law, whom you reckon must surely be right this once, having been wrong so often, "throw some good after the bad, and you will earn it all back, and more besides."

This is what they tell you, and once in a blue moon they tell you the truth. The rest of the time, they buy themselves railroad cars—heavens! railroads!—and yachts and shooting boxes in Scotland and Congressmen to shoot from the shooting boxes, and they do it with your bad money and your good impartially.

Yet this appears to be the theory upon which James G. Blaine has chosen to go on with this war, no other theory looking to hold. Not only has he chosen to throw good money after bad, but to throw good men after good. The dead mount up, and the peg-legged, and the hook-handed, and the blind, but never you fear, for we have gained a mile of ground in Kentucky, near enough, and have not lost above forty or fifty miles of New Mexico to make up for it, and have had Washington, D.C., knocked flat besides, and so victory must be right around the corner.

He rubbed his chin, studying what he'd done. "Will this cause them to make me out to be a Confederate spy again?" he murmured. He read the words once more. "To hell with that. It's the truth." He inked his pen and kept on with the editorial.

☆ **XI** ☆

Abraham Lincoln watched the soldiers building the gallows outside Fort Douglas. It was a touch of General Pope's, either extraordinarily good or extraordinarily bad, depending on how things worked out, for Lincoln was not the only one watching that exercise in practical carpentry. Far from it: the work had to be visible from a goodly part of Salt Lake City, and those of the Latter-Day Saints who could not see it would have heard of it.

As Lincoln watched the men labor, stripped to their shirts, a guard in a blue blouse watched him. He suspected the guard had stretched the truth about his age to get into the Army. The fellow was trying to raise a mustache, but had only a little pale fuzz on his upper lip. His eyes never left Lincoln. It was as if he were tracking a nine-point buck, a resemblance only strengthened by the loaded Springfield he carried. The index finger of his right hand never got far from the trigger.

"You want to be careful with that," Lincoln said mildly, "lest something happen we would both regret afterwards."

"Oh, no, Mr. Lincoln." The guard shook his head. "I wouldn't regret it one bit." His smile was wide and bright and pitiless and about half crazy. "So you're the one who wants to be careful."

"Believe me, I shall," Lincoln said. *Shot while trying to escape.* How many murders hid behind that stern mask of rectitude? He did not care to add another to the number.

Half a dozen traps on the gallows. Half a dozen nooses, though the ropes were not yet in place. Half a dozen Mormon leaders to dance on air at a time, though they were not yet in place, either. Lincoln knew John Pope wanted to hang him, too. Had Pope had his way, he would soon climb those steps with Orson Pratt and George Cannon and the rest of the high-ranking Mormons the

U.S. Army had managed to run down. A Democrat in the White House might have let Pope hang him.

Of course, with a Democrat in the White House, the United States would no doubt have passively acquiesced to the Confederacy's acquisition of Chihuahua and Sonora. The Mormons would not have gained an excuse for showing their disloyalty to the government that loved them so little. Would that have been better? Lincoln shook his head. The United States should have resisted the expansion of the slave power, and should have started resisting long since. His smile reached only one corner of his mouth. The United States should have done a better job of resisting, too.

One of the soldiers up on the multiple gallows tried a trapdoor. It didn't drop. "God damn it," he said, as any workman would have when what he was making didn't perform the way it should. He called to another soldier: "Hey, Jack, bring me over that plane, will you? Got to smooth this old whore down." Yes, it was just work to him. If he thought about what the work would do, he didn't show it.

Lincoln turned away from the gallows and slowly walked back into the fort. The guard followed, finger still near the trigger of his rifle. "Son, I am not going to run away," Lincoln told him. "I am seventy-two years old. The only way I could move faster than you would be for someone to throw me off a cliff yonder." He pointed north and east, toward the brown, sun-baked Wasatch Mountains.

"That'd be good," the guard said, showing his teeth. Lincoln kept quiet.

Inside Fort Douglas, Colonel George Custer was strutting across the parade ground. When he saw Lincoln, he scowled and trotted toward him. For a moment, Lincoln thought the cavalry officer would collide with him. But by what he'd seen, Custer lived his entire life going straight ahead at full throttle. That struck Lincoln as needlessly wearing, but the cavalryman wasn't going to ask his advice.

Custer wanted to go chest-to-chest with him, but wasn't tall enough. He had to content himself with going chest-to-belly and fiercely scowling up into Lincoln's face, as he'd done several times before. "If it were up to me," he growled, "you'd swing."

"I thank you kindly for the vote of confidence, Colonel," Lincoln said.

Irony to Custer was like a mouse on the tracks to a locomotive: not big enough to notice. He rolled right over it, saying, "You dashed Black Republican, they should have hanged you after we lost the last war, they should have hanged you again for a Communard, and now they should hang you for a traitor. You're luckier than you deserve, do you know that?"

"I'm lucky in all the people who love and admire me, that's plain," Lincoln answered.

Again, it sailed past the cavalry colonel. He paused to kick dust on Lincoln's shoes, another of his less endearing habits, then jerked a thumb back in the direction of General Pope's office. "The military governor is going to want to see you. You may as well go on over there now."

"I'll do that," Lincoln said, amiably enough. When Custer did not move, he added, "Just as soon as you get out of my way, I mean." With another growl, the commander of the Fifth Cavalry stepped aside.

As Lincoln ambled along in the direction of Pope's office, the young lieutenant who'd arrested him at Gabe Hamilton's house came out of the stockade, spotted him, and came over at a run. "Mr. Lincoln! I was looking for you. General Pope—"

"Wants to invite me to take some tea with him," Lincoln said as the lieutenant gaped. "Yes, so I've been informed." Resisting the urge to pat the youngster on the head, Lincoln walked past him toward the beckoning shade.

General John Pope looked up from the sheet of paper he was reading. "Ah, Mr. Lincoln," he said, taking off his spectacles and setting them on the desk. "I wanted to speak with you."

"So I've been told," Lincoln said. A moment later, he repeated, "So I've been told." It meant nothing to Pope. It probably would have meant nothing to him had he seen both Custer and the young lieutenant come up to Lincoln. The former president started to sit, waited for Pope's brusque nod, and finished setting his backside on a chair.

The military governor of Utah Territory glowered at him. It was probably a glower that put his subordinates in fear. Since Lincoln already knew Pope's opinion of him and was already in his power, it had little effect here. Perhaps sensing that, Pope made his voice heavy with menace: "You know what would happen to you if your fate were in my hands."

"I have had a hint or two along those lines, yes, General," Lincoln answered.

"President Blaine forbids it. You know that, too. It's too damned bad, in my opinion, but I am not a traitor. I obey the lawful orders of my superiors." Pope tried the glare again, not quite for so long this time. "Next best choice, in my view, would be putting convict's stripes on you and letting you spend the rest of your days splitting rocks instead of rails."

"In my present state, I doubt the gravel business would get as great a boost from my labors as you might hope," Lincoln said.

Pope went on as if he had not spoken: "The president forbids that as well. His view is that no one who has held his office deserves such ignominy—no matter how much he deserves such ignominy, if you take my meaning."

"Oh yes, General. You make yourself very plain, I assure you."

"For which I thank you. I am but a poor bluff soldier, unaccustomed to fancy flights of language." Pope was a grandiloquent twit, given to flights of bombast. He didn't know it, either; he was as blind about himself as he had been about Stonewall Jackson's intentions during the War of Secession.

"If you can't hang me and you can't put me at hard labor for the rest of my days, what do you propose to do with me?" Lincoln asked.

Pope looked even less happy than he had before. "I have been given an order, Mr. Lincoln, for which, to make myself plain once more, I do not care to the extent of one pinch of owl dung. But I am a soldier, and I shall obey regardless of my personal feelings on the matter."

"Commendable, I'm sure," Lincoln said. "What is the order?"

"To get you out of Utah Territory." Pope truly did sound disgusted. "To put you on a train and see your back and never see your face again. To make sure you interfere no further in the settling of affairs here."

That was better than Lincoln had dared hope. He did his best to conceal how happy he was. "If you must, General. I was bound for San Francisco when matters here became unfortunate. I shall have to set up some new engagements there, having been detained so long, but—"

"No," Pope interrupted. "You are not going to San Francisco. Neither are you going to Denver, nor Chicago, nor St. Louis, nor

Boston, nor New York. President Blaine has shown so much sense, if no more."

"Whither am I bound, then?" Lincoln inquired.

"You have a choice. You may go south to Flagstaff, in New Mexico Territory, or north to Pocatello, in Idaho Territory, and points beyond. For the duration of the war, you are to be restricted to the Territories north or south of Utah Territory. I am to advise you that any attempt to evade the said restriction will, upon your recapture, result in punishment far more severe than this internal exile."

"Ah, I see." Lincoln nodded sagely. "I may go wherever I like, provided I go to a place with, for all practical purposes, no people in it."

"Precisely." Pope was almost as deaf to irony as Custer.

"If you wish to muzzle me, why not simply leave me in confinement here in Utah?" Lincoln asked.

"Confining you embarrasses the present administration, you being the only other Republican president besides the incumbent," General Pope replied. "Leaving you to your own devices here in Utah, on the other hand, embarrasses *me*. You have already proved beyond the slightest fragment of a doubt that you are not to be trusted here, but delight in meddling in affairs properly none of your concern."

"General, nothing that has happened in Utah since the outbreak of the war has delighted me," Lincoln said: "neither the deeds of the Mormon leaders nor those undertaken since U.S. soldiers reoccupied this Territory."

"If you equate the Mormons and the United States Army, we are well shut of you," Pope declared. "Had John Taylor and his henchmen simply remained good citizens, none of what we have had to do would have been necessary."

When phrased thus, that was true. But Lincoln had listened to Taylor and the other Mormons enough to know they thought every effort to abolish polygamy a persecution of beliefs they held dear. From what he had seen, they had a point. But did that matter? To anyone who took the view on polygamy of the vast majority of the American people, it mattered not at all.

Pope went on, "The time for coddling the rebels here is past. We have tried to persuade them to obedience, and failed. Persuasion having failed, we shall force them to obedience. One way or another, however, obedience we shall have."

"What you shall have is hatred," Lincoln said.

"I don't care this much"—Pope snapped his fingers—"if every Mormon wakes up in the morning and goes to bed at night and spends all the time between praying that I roast in hell forever, so long as he obeys me while so praying. When you treat with Taylor, when you hold silence after treating with Taylor, you suggest to these poor ignorant folk that they too have some hope of successfully defying me. That I cannot tolerate, and that is why I am sending you out of this Territory."

Lincoln sighed. If singleminded ruthlessness could bring the Mormons to heel, Pope was the right man for the job, and Custer a good right hand for him. The question, of course, was whether such ruthlessness could do the job. Lincoln had his doubts. If John Pope had ever had doubts about anything, he'd had them surgically removed at an early age.

"I would sooner send you out of this Territory to your eternal reward," Pope said, "but, as I have noted, that is not among the choices President Blaine has left me. In fact, he has left the choice to you, and a better one than you deserve, too: north, Mr. Lincoln, or south?"

Lincoln wondered if promising to arrange the peaceable surrender of John Taylor would let him stay here and work to avert the tragedy he so plainly saw coming. Had he seen the slightest hope of success in keeping such a promise, he would have made it. But he did not think the Mormon president would surrender. Even had he reckoned Taylor willing, he did not think General Pope would let him make the arrangements. And he did not think that, if Taylor should surrender, Pope would do anything but hang him.

"North or south?" the military governor repeated. "That is the sole choice left you."

He was right. Knowing he was right saddened Lincoln as he had not been saddened since having to recognize the independence of the Confederate States. "North," he said.

Pope clapped his hands together. "And I win an eagle from Colonel Custer. He was ten dollars sure you'd say south. But for that, though, it matters little. During the War of Secession, you exiled me to Minnesota to fight redskins, and then lost the war anyhow. Now I get to return the favor, and, if you think it isn't sweet, you're wrong."

"I hope you don't lose the war here," Lincoln said.

Being in Pope's power, he was not suffered to have the last word. "There is no war here," the military governor said harshly. "There shall be no war here. Your going makes that the more likely. You leave tomorrow."

General Orlando Willcox studied the map of Louisville. "Give me your frank opinion, Colonel Schlieffen," he said. "Might I have been wiser to attempt a flanking movement than a frontal assault?"

Alfred von Schlieffen's frank opinion was that General Willcox would have made an excellent country butcher, but was less than ideally suited to command an important army—or even an unimportant one. He did not think Willcox would appreciate his being so frank as that. Instead, he said, "Perhaps you might have made a small attack here to hold the foe, and a larger one on the flank to beat him."

"That's what I have in mind doing now," the commander of the Army of the Ohio said. "I have reinforcements coming; President Blaine is committing the resources of the entire nation to this fight. Instead of sending them straight into Louisville, I purpose invading Kentucky at another point farther east, whence I can take the Confederates' defenses of the city in the flank. What is your view of the matter?"

Again, Schlieffen could not make himself be so forthright as he might have liked. "What could have at the campaign's beginning been done and what can now be done are different, one from the other," he said.

"Oh, no doubt, no doubt," Willcox said. "But we have the Rebs well and truly pinned down inside of Louisville now, thanks be to God. They won't be able to shift quickly to respond to such a move now."

Some truth lurked at the bottom of that. How much? Schlieffen admitted to himself he did not know. He did not think the world had ever known a battle like this one. Sieges had been fought around cities, yes, but in all history before now had a siege ever been fought in the heart of a city? That, in essence, was what the fight for Louisville had become.

When he said so aloud, Willcox nodded. "That's just what it's turned into," he agreed. "The question is, are we the besiegers or the besieged?"

"Both at the same time," Schlieffen answered. "Each of you

thinks you can the other force back, and so you both push forward—and you collide, and neither of you can go ahead or to fall back is willing. Have you ever seen rams bang heads together?"

"Oh, yes," Willcox said. "That's why I aim to try out this flanking maneuver. A ram that butted another in the ribs before it was ready to fight would tup a lot of ewes."

"Before it was ready to fight? Yes, in this you have right—*are* right." Schlieffen corrected himself with a grimace of annoyance at his imperfect English. Anything imperfect annoyed him. "But if the second ram were already fighting, it would be harder to surprise."

"I don't even know whether this flank move will surprise the Confederates," Willcox said. "My bet is, surprised or not, they'll be too badly beaten up to do anything save ingloriously flee."

"You place on this bet a large stake," Schlieffen said, in lieu of asking Willcox where he was hiding his wits these days.

"Our cause being just, God will provide," the general said. "I have prayed over this decision, and I am confident it is the best thing we can do."

"Prayer is good," Schlieffen agreed from the bottom of his heart. "To prepare is also good. If you do not prepare, prayer asks of God a miracle. God will work a miracle when it suits Him, but suit Him it does not often."

"No, indeed," Willcox said. "If miracles were common, they would not be miracles." Schlieffen waited from him to draw the proper lesson from that. He drew . . . some of it. "We shall get these men into Kentucky and hurl them against the foe as expeditiously as possible."

Schlieffen took *expeditiously* to mean something like *expedition*, and had to have that straightened out, which Willcox did with patience and tact. The German military attaché admired Orlando Willcox the man, who from all he could see lived an exemplary Christian life. He wished his opinion of Orlando Willcox the commander were higher. The man did not lack courage. He had the ability to inspire his subordinates. Both of those were important parts of the general's art. These days, though, the art entailed more.

"In Germany," Schlieffen said, "we would have done more planning before this battle began. We would have looked at the choices we might make. If so-and-so happened in the fighting in

Louisville, we would have known we then needed to do this thing or that. We would have done the thing. We would not have had to think out on the spot what the thing would be to do."

Willcox looked at him with wide eyes. "We haven't got anything like that in the United States."

"I know you have not this thing in your country," Schlieffen said in the pitying tones he would have used to agree with a Turk that railroads were sadly lacking in the Ottoman Empire. "You have not in your country the understanding of a general staff."

"General Rosecrans heads up a staff in the War Department," Willcox said, shaking his head. "I have a staff here, and a sizable one, too."

"Yes, I have seen this," Schlieffen said. "It is not the sort of staff I mean. Your staff, when you decide the army will do thus-and-so, take your orders to the commanders of corps and divisions. They to you bring back any troubles these men may have with the orders."

"Yes," Willcox echoed. "What else are they supposed to do, for heaven's sake? Aside from the quartermaster and such, I mean."

"The staff of the War Department should have in peacetime been busy at making plans for how you would fight when you had to fight." Schlieffen remembered the incomprehension with which Rosecrans had greeted the idea of having ready-made plans to roll out in case of war, and his own dismayed astonishment at the U.S. general-in-chief's lack of preparation. "Your staff here should on a smaller scale the same thing do."

What he was trying to say was that Willcox shouldn't have decided on the spur of the moment to try a flanking maneuver against Louisville, and only then begun to make plans for such a maneuver. It should have been one of the possibilities all along, as thoroughly studied as any of the others. (So it was, zero equaling zero, but that was not what Schlieffen had in mind.) If and when the time came to use it, everything would be in place beforehand: railroad transport, manpower, artillery, supplies, so much of each, to be delivered to the right place at the right time. What the Army of the Ohio had instead was frantic improvisation. Some of it was inspired improvisation, as seemed to be the American way, but not all, not all.

Those thoughts ran through his mind far faster than he could hope to turn them into English. "No, we haven't got anything like that here," General Willcox said in wondering tones, impressed enough by what Schlieffen had managed to bring out. "You Germans really do that? Plan everything out ahead of time, I mean?"

"Aber natürlich," Schlieffen said, and then went back to English: "Of course."

"Maybe we ought to take some lessons from you, then," Willcox said, after a moment adding, "The Confederates haven't got anything like that, either."

"This I believe, yes," Schlieffen said. "They also—is it that you say in English, they make it up as they go along."

"We say that, all right," Willcox answered. "I say something else, too: I say I'm going to send a couple of telegrams to Philadelphia, one to General Rosecrans and the other to President Blaine. Sounds like the USA ought to know more of what you're talking about."

"The French have adopted this method," Schlieffen said with something less than delight. "They are our neighbors. They have seen what this lets us do. You are not our neighbors, but you have neighbors to north and south who are strong and with whom you fight, as we do to east and west and south. It may help you better help yourselves."

"If it can make us win wars the way you Germans have won wars, I don't see how it could be better than that," Willcox said. He suddenly looked like what he was: a tired man, not so young as he had been, saddled with an assignment even he might have sensed was too big for him. In a wistful voice, he went on, "Been a long time since we won a real war. Indians don't count; sooner or later, they get worn down. But we haven't trounced anybody since the Mexicans, and losing the War of Secession threw us down in the dumps for years."

"This I believe. We in Prussia were downcast when we lost to Napoleon, but we rose up and were soon again strong." Generously, Schlieffen added, "The United States can also do this."

"I ask the Lord on bended knee every night to make it so," Willcox said. "I am nothing. My country is everything to me."

"You are a good man, General. This is how a soldier must think." Schlieffen turned to go. "I thank you for giving of your time to me. I know you have much to do." Willcox nodded abstractedly. His eyes were back on the map. Of itself, one of his fingers traced the flanking move he was planning. He sighed and plucked at his beard.

As Schlieffen left the army commander's tent, Confederate

artillery began tearing at the pontoon bridges U.S. Army engineers had thrown over the Ohio. Every so often, the guns of the South managed to put one span or another out of action for a while, but the U.S. engineers were adept at making repairs. *Improvisation again,* Schlieffen thought.

Smoke mantled Louisville, as it always did these days. Smoke also rose from the docks on the Indiana side of the river; Confederate gunners did not neglect them, either. In one regard, Orlando Willcox was assuredly correct: a fight on this line would take all summer, and would gain little ground if he kept fighting it the same way.

Schlieffen turned and looked to the north and east. He saw smoke plumes there, too, smoke plumes from the trains bringing in endless streams of reinforcements to be thrown into the fire as children in ancient days had gone into the fire of Moloch.

Maybe Willcox had the right of it after all. What he was doing did not work. That argued some other approach might work better. In the German Army, he would have had a list of such approaches at his fingertips, with similar lists of everything he needed to do to use any one of them. Here, he had to think of them for himself and then figure out their requirements. *Poor devil,* Schlieffen thought.

If the United States did try a flanking attack, could they conceal it till the time came to loose it? Schlieffen had his doubts, for a couple of reasons. One was that he doubted the ability of the United States to keep secrets as a general principle. Courage, yes. Growing industrial capacity, yes. Discipline? No.

But even with discipline, it wouldn't have been easy. When Prussia had fought the Austrians fifteen years before, each side easily spied on the other. Why not? They both spoke the same language, with only minor differences of dialect. The same applied here. The Confederates could easily sneak men into Indiana to observe their foes' preparations.

Of course, General Willcox and his henchmen could as easily send spies into Kentucky to keep an eye on Confederate troop movements and such. If Willcox was doing that, Schlieffen had seen no evidence of it. Did the commander of the Army of the Ohio know whether his opponents were readying field fortifications to help their men withstand the blow he had in mind?

Schlieffen was tempted to go back and ask General Willcox whether he knew that. The map over which Willcox had been poring had not shown any Confederate field fortifications east of Louisville. Did that mean none were there, or did it mean he didn't know whether any were there?

After taking a step in the direction of Willcox's tent, Schlieffen turned away once more. He was a neutral here. His duty was to observe and report and analyze the war between the USA and the CSA, not to involve himself in the result of the struggle.

With a shrug, he headed off toward his own tent to write up what Willcox had told him. Even if he did make suggestions to the U.S. commander, he doubted Willcox would comprehend them anyhow.

Colonel George Custer strode slowly down the row of men drawn up outside Fort Douglas. He had on his stern face, the one he always used at inspections. *Nothing will escape my eye,* that scowl said. *You had better be perfect—anything less and you will pay.*

It was, to a certain degree, humbug. Custer knew it. Enlisted men had been inventing ways to hoax inspectors since Julius Caesar's day, if not since King David's. Sometimes, though, they got nervous when the commanding officer's glare fell on them. Then they gave away things he might otherwise have missed.

Privately, he doubted that on this inspection. For one thing, he wasn't so sure about what to look for as usual. For another, he had trouble keeping up that stern façade.

About three-quarters of the way down the line, he gave up and let himself grin. "Well, boys," he said, "I expect you'll be able to give the Mormons holy Hades if they step out of line. What do you say to that?"

"Yes, sir!" chorused the soldiers with the red facings on their uniforms.

"And if you do have to open up on them, I expect they'll die laughing," Custer went on. "I declare, you've got the funniest-looking contraptions there in the complete and entire history of war. I've seen them in action, and they're still funny-looking. What do you say to *that*?"

"Yes, sir!" the Gatling-gun crews chorused once more.

Eight Gatlings now, each one with the brass casing polished till it gleamed like gold. "Do you know what General Pope calls your toys?" he asked the men who served them.

"No, sir," they answered, still in unison.

"Coffee mills," Custer told them, and grins came out on their faces, too. With the big magazines set above those polished casings, with the cranks at the rear of the weapons, they did look as if they'd be suited to turning coffee beans into ground coffee. They could take care of more grinding than that, though. Custer said, "If the Mormons *do* give us trouble, we'll have them ready for boiling up in the pot in nothing flat, won't we?"

"Yes, sir!" the soldiers in artillerymen's uniforms responded.

Some of them glanced toward the gallows not far away. Custer's eyes traveled in that direction, too. The exercise in carpentry was finished now. Each trap had a noose above it. The ropes twisted in the breeze off the Great Salt Lake. Before long, blindfolded men would twist at the ends of those ropes.

"Traitors," Custer muttered. "Just what they deserve. Pity we couldn't give it to Honest Abe, too." He raised his voice: "If the Mormons riot when we hang the devils who held the United States to ransom, will we do our duty, no matter how harsh it may prove?"

"Yes, sir," the Gatling gunners said.

Custer's grin got wider. The next enlisted man he found with any sympathy for the Mormons would be the first. "Remember, boys," he said, "if we do have to shoot them down, we'll be making an uncommon number of widows." The gun crews laughed out loud. A couple of soldiers clapped their hands with glee.

As far as Custer was concerned, the Mormons were a dirty joke on America. Whatever happened to them, he thought they had it coming. He peered down the row of Gatling guns. As far as he was concerned, they were a joke of a different sort. A couple of them had proved useful against the Kiowas and the Confederates. Eight, now, eight struck him as excessive.

Major Tom Custer came strolling out from Fort Douglas to join his brother. The two of them had matching opinions on the new weapons. In a low voice, Tom asked, "Suppose we really have to go and fight the Rebs, Autie. What in blazes will we do with these ungainly critters?"

"Don't rightly know," Custer admitted, also out of the side of his mouth. He walked a little farther away from the Gatlings so he and Tom could talk more freely. "Best thing I can think of is to do what we did to the Kiowas—put 'em on good ground and let the enemy bang his head against them."

"I suppose so," Tom said. Like his brother, he would have led his men at full tilt against any foe he found. Also like his brother, he assumed any other officer would do the same.

"I just hope we get the chance to try it, or to move against the Rebs without the Gatlings," Custer said. "Frankly, I'd prefer that. What good will eight of the things do us? None I can see, and they'll slow us down as soon as we get away from the railroad line."

"Two didn't, not too much," Tom observed.

"That's so, but with eight there are four times as many things to go wrong," Custer replied, to which his brother had to nod. He went on, "Right now, though, everybody thinks they're a big thing, so we're stuck with them come what may. Sooner or later, my guess is that the War Department will decide they're nothing but a flash in the pan."

"You're likely right," his brother said.

"Of course I am." Custer spoke with his usual sublime confidence. He pulled out his pocket watch, looked at it, and let out a low whistle. "Tom, I'm late in town." He pointed down toward Salt Lake City. "Will you dismiss these fellows and tell them what good boys they are? If I'm not where I'm supposed to be on time or dashed close to it, I'm going to get skinned."

"Sure, I'll take care of it for you," Tom answered, "but what's so all-fired important down there?"

Custer set a finger in front of his lips for a moment. "I've got a lead that needs following up," he whispered melodramatically. "If it turns out the way I hope it will—well, I don't want to say too much."

Tom's eyes widened. "Don't tell me you've got a line on John Taylor."

"I won't tell you anything," Custer said. "I can't tell you anything. But believe me, I've got to go."

"All right, Autie. If you do bring that scoop back, I'll bet you'll have a brigadier general's stars on your shoulder straps this time tomorrow."

"That would be fine, wouldn't it?" Custer slapped his brother on the shoulder, then hurried off to the stables. The hands in there were supposed to have his horse ready. He was glad they did. He sprang up into the saddle, let the horse walk out of Fort Douglas, and then urged it up into a trot. Tom had the Gatling-gun crews well in hand. Custer had been sure he would. Tom was ready for a regiment of his own. He didn't much want one, fearing higher rank would keep him out of the field more than he fancied.

The road into Salt Lake City ran south and west. The Mormons Custer passed on it either gave him hate-filled snarls and glares or pretended he didn't exist. He preferred the former: it was honest. Every so often, a man would clap his hands or wave his hat to the commander of the Fifth Cavalry. Custer always waved back, knowing the Army needed backing from Utah's Gentiles, as it would surely get none from the Latter-Day Saints.

He did admire the way the Mormons had lined their boulevards with trees. That helped make the heat more bearable. Under the Eagle Gate he rode, as he had when first entering Salt Lake City. He kept looking around in all directions while doing his best not to let that be noticed. He wanted nobody, soldier or Mormon, on his trail. The fewer who knew of the business he was on, the better for everyone.

No one was following him when he turned onto a narrow street, really more of an alley, a few blocks southeast of Temple Square—though when the Temple would be completed was anyone's guess now. *Probably about the time the Jews rebuild theirs in Jerusalem,* Custer thought derisively.

He hitched his horse in front of a battered adobe building with CAFE painted in faded letters on the whitewash above the door. Before he went in, he looked around again. Nobody but he was on the street. The nearby shops and houses drowsed in the afternoon sunshine. Satisfied, he went through the door.

Inside, the place was full of the good odors of roasting pork and fresh-baked bread. It was, however, empty of customers. In a way, that was too bad: it deserved better. In another way, though, it was perfect for the meeting Custer had in mind.

Hearing the door open and close, the proprietress came out from the back room: a redheaded woman in her late twenties, the map of Ireland on her saucy face. She walked up to Custer and asked, "And what can I do for you today, sir?"

"Ah, Katie, my very dear, it's what we can do for each other," he replied, and took her in his arms.

The first time he'd tried the café, he'd been after nothing more than dinner. He'd got that—and a fine one it was, too—and a deal of friendly banter from Katie Fitzgerald besides. That and the food had brought him back. On his second visit, he'd learned she was a widow, doing her best to make ends meet. On his fourth visit . . .

Now, their lips clung, their hands clasped, their bodies molded to each other. Custer, exulting in his strength, picked her up and carried her back to the bedroom. She laughed. She'd squealed, the first time he did it.

"Hurry," she said when he set her down. He needed no urging along those lines. Fast as he could, he divested himself of blouse and shirt, of boots and socks, of trousers and drawers. He was fast enough to be ready to help her loosen the stays of her corset and slide it down over her hips before they embraced again, naked this time, and tumbled down onto the bed.

Custer had strayed off the path of perfect rectitude before, sometimes with Indian women, sometimes with whites. When Libbie was close by, he made himself a model of circumspection. When she wasn't, he did what he did, as discreetly as he could, and worried about it very little afterwards.

"I love you," Katie Fitzgerald breathed into his ear. He had never said that to her. He was, in his own fashion, honest. But the way his fingers stroked the softness not quite hidden in the fiery tuft of hair between her legs might almost have been an equivalent. Her soft moan said she took it for one.

She moaned again when he went into her, and shut her eyes tight, lost in her own world of sensation. Custer laughed, deep in his throat. Libbie did the same thing. Then he stopped thinking about Libbie, or about much of anything at all. His hips pistoned, faster and faster. Beneath him, Katie yowled like a catamount. Her nails scored his back.

At the last possible moment, he pulled out of her and spurted his seed over her soft, white belly. He prided himself on his control there as much as he did on his skill with a gun or on horseback.

"It's a sin," Katie whimpered halfheartedly. She was a good Catholic, but she did not want to find herself in a family way. One side of her mouth quirked upward. "It's messy, too. Get off me, so I can clean myself." She did just that, with a rag and some water from the pitcher on the bedside nightstand.

As fast as he'd got out of his uniform, Custer got into it again. As he'd helped Katie undress, he helped her dress, too. When they were both fully clothed once more, he said, "My brother thinks I'm out hunting John Taylor." He found that deliciously funny; a reputation for singleminded devotion to the task at hand was a disguise as effective as false beard and wig. There were tasks, and then there were tasks.

"Well, when you're not here, that's a good thing for you to do," she answered seriously. "The sooner he's on the end of a rope, the better off this place will be." Custer had never yet heard any Gentile with a good word to say about the Mormon president.

"Now I've got to go," he told her. He kissed her and caressed her and pretended he didn't see the tear slide down her cheek. He'd never told her he was married, not in so many words, but he hadn't pretended to be a bachelor, either. He said, "I'll see you again as soon as I can."

"What if I have a customer?" she asked with a sly little smile.

"I'll be disappointed," he answered, which changed the smile to a different sort. She hugged him one more time, fiercely, then let him go.

No one paid any more than the usual attention to him as he rode back up to Fort Douglas. He whistled "Garry Owen," as he might have done going into battle. But he'd fought his battle here, fought it and won it.

When he got back to the fort, his younger brother collared him at once, as he'd known Tom would. "Any luck?"

Yes, but not the sort you're thinking of. "Not so much as I should have liked," Custer said, and made himself look unhappy with the world.

"They're wily devils, the Mormons," Tom said sympathetically. "But you have more luck than you know, as a matter of fact."

"Do I?" Custer looked up his sleeve, as if hoping to find it lurking there. As his brother laughed, he asked, "Whereabouts?"

To his surprise, Tom turned and pointed across the parade ground. "Here it comes now," he said.

"Hello, Autie, darling!" Libbie Custer waved to her husband. "They finally let me escape from Fort Dodge, so here I am, with all the animals in tow. I expect they're unpacking the trophies even now." She hurried forward to give Custer a hug.

He had faced death more times than he could count, against Confederates and Indians both. What he did now, he thought, took more courage than any of those desperate fights. He threw his arms wide. "Ah, Libbie, my very dear!" he said enthusiastically, and smiled a big, broad smile.

* * *

"Tombstone is still ours," Theodore Roosevelt said, the name tolling like a mournful bell in his mouth. "Let's hope plenty of Rebel tombstones will go up there if General Stuart does choose to attack it."

"Hasn't happened yet, like I told you," the courier from Fort Benton said.

"I pray to the Lord it does not happen," Roosevelt declared. "I pray to the Lord that we instead attack the Confederate forces in New Mexico Territory and drive them from our soil."

Lieutenant Karl Jobst had been taking a swig of coffee. When he lowered the tin cup from his lips, he said, "We already tried that, sir, and got licked. That's why Tombstone is in so much trouble now."

"A shame and a disgrace," Roosevelt growled. "Wherever the fighting truly matters—wherever it's bigger than I'll raid your farms and you raid mine—the damned Rebels have the bulge on us."

"There's a reason for that, sir," Jobst said. Roosevelt raised an eyebrow. His adjutant went on, "Wherever the fighting matters, it's fighting between enough men on each side to have a general commanding them. Our generals fought in the War of Secession and lost. Theirs won. Need I say more?"

"That's pretty damned cynical for so early in the morning," Roosevelt said. Lieutenant Jobst grinned at him. His own smile was on the strained side. "It also has the unpleasant ring of truth."

The courier spoke up: "Sir, have your men seen any sign that the British are likely to move soon? Colonel Welton asked me to ask you special."

"Nary a one." Roosevelt sprang to his feet and paced around the cookfire. When he'd recruited the Unauthorized Regiment, his head had been full of the rasping roar of the rifles and the fireworks smell of burnt gunpowder. He'd wanted battle. What he'd got was boredom, and he was beginning to chafe under it. "If he hadn't told me they were in Lethbridge, I'd have guessed they hadn't come any closer than Labrador, or maybe London."

"Yes, sir. That's right good, sir." The soldier chuckled. "Sir, if it's like you say and them bastards are being quiet, Colonel Welton asks if you reckon you can leave your command for a couple-three days, come down to the fort and talk things over:

how it's all working out up here and what you'll do if the limeys ever should decide to get off their asses and try something."

"Yes!" Roosevelt sprang into the air. This was action. If not the action against the British his heart wanted as much as his body craved a woman—which was no small yearning—it was something different from what he was doing now. After sameness that seemed unending, that drew him like a magnet. "Let's be off. I can leave as soon as I saddle my horse. We'll get you a fresh animal, so you won't slow the journey with your worn one. Aren't you done with that coffee yet? Good heavens, man, hurry!"

That was pushing things somewhat, but when any idea bit Roosevelt, it bit him hard. Inside half an hour, he and the courier, him with a Winchester on his back, the other man with a Springfield, were riding south toward Fort Benton. Roosevelt pounded a fist down onto his thigh in anticipation of his first return to the civilized world since taking the field. Then he laughed at himself. If Fort Benton counted for civilization, he'd been out in the wilderness too long.

Walk, trot, canter, walk, trot, canter. The two men kept their horses as fresh as they could by varying their gaits. Roosevelt held his mount to a canter longer than usual: as long as his kidneys could stand the jarring. No matter how rough it was, it ate up the miles.

He got into Fort Benton a little past sundown, riding along the Missouri the last few miles. When he dismounted, he discovered his own gait resembled nothing so much as that of a bear with the rheumatism. As a couple of enlisted men took the horse away to be seen to, he stumped across the parade ground to Colonel Welton's office.

"My dear fellow!" Welton exclaimed. "You look as if you could use a good brush-down and a blanket across your back, and to the devil with your horse." He reached into a desk drawer. The kerosene lamps that lighted the chamber sent shadows swooping in every direction. Welton pulled out a corked bottle full of tawny liquid. "Can't give you that, I'm afraid, but what do you say to a small restorative?"

"I say, 'Yes, sir!' I say, 'Thank you, sir!' " Roosevelt sank into a chair. Sitting hurt as much as moving did. "Oof! I say, 'Good God, sir!' "

"Don't blame you a bit." Welton poured him a restorative that might have been small for a rhinoceros. "I didn't expect you till tomorrow morning some time. That's a long ride for one day, but you are a chap who takes the bull by the horns. Wouldn't have eagles on your shoulder straps if you didn't, eh?"

"That's about the way I see it, sir." Roosevelt drank. Fire ran down his throat and exploded into contentment in his belly. "Ahh. I say, 'God bless you, sir!' You're right. A man without pluck goes nowhere."

Henry Welton sipped at his own glass of whiskey. "If that's the measure of success, you'll go far—and heaven help anyone who stands in your way." He took another sip. He was still behind Roosevelt, but he didn't need the drink so badly and was wise enough to remember he carried twice his guest's years. "So the British are quiet, are they?"

"Yes, sir—quiet as the tomb." Roosevelt did not even try to keep the regret from his own voice.

"I know how tempted you've been to go over the border and take a whack at 'em, the way a boy whacks a hornets' nest with a stick." Welton chuckled. "Be glad you've restrained yourself. Were you foolish enough to try anything of the sort, you'd get what the hornets would give the boy—if not from the British, then from your own side for disobeying orders."

"I understand that, sir. I'm switched if I like it, but I understand it." Roosevelt stared at his glass. Where had the whiskey gone? "When President Blaine told Longstreet we weren't whipped yet, I thought the Englishmen would come down over the border, to try and make us change our minds. Er—I say, 'Thank you again, sir!'" Welton had restored the restorative.

Setting the bottle back on the desk, the commander of the Seventh Infantry studied Roosevelt with considerable respect. "I looked for the very same thing, as a matter of fact," he said slowly. "You may be an amateur strategist, Colonel, but you're a long way from the worst one I've ever seen. If you can lead your men in action, too—well, in that case, you'll make a first-rate soldier."

"And I thank you yet one more time for that, sir." Roosevelt made himself be deliberate with his second glass of whiskey. After getting such a compliment, the last thing he wanted was to act the drunken fool—the young drunken fool—before his superior. "You called me down—that is, you said I might come down—so we could confer on how best to resist the British should they happen to recall they are men."

"Your men delay them and concentrate against them, mine join you, we pick the best ground we can, and we fight them," Henry Welton said, ticking the points off on his fingers. "How does that sound to you?"

"It sounds bully," Roosevelt said, "but, begging the colonel's pardon, I don't see how it's any different from what we'd planned before the Unauthorized Regiment went up to watch the border."

"It's not," Welton admitted cheerfully, "but I figured a few days in town—even so small a town as Fort Benton—would do you a world of good. You're not used to going off on your lonesome for long stretches. Blowing off steam while everything's quiet won't hurt the war, and it'll help you."

As Roosevelt had seen, the fleshpots of Fort Benton were nothing to threaten New York City, or even Great Falls. But Welton was right—the little town by the fort seemed positively sybaritic when set beside a regimental headquarters out in the middle of the empty Montana prairie.

Still . . . "Sir, if you're generous enough to give me a few days of ease like this—and I do thank you for them; don't mistake me—might I give the troops in the regiment leave to come into Fort Benton one at a time, to blow off their steam? The troops adjacent to that coming in on furlough could spread themselves thinner to cover its ground. I should hate to take advantage of a privilege my men cannot enjoy."

"Well, I hadn't thought of it, but I don't see why not," Welton said. He stared across the desk at Roosevelt. "Colonel, have your troopers any conception of how fortunate they are in their commanding officer?"

"Sir, in this request I am only seeking to apply the Golden Rule."

"You *are* a young man," Henry Welton said. He raised a hand. "No, I mean nothing by that but praise. We need young men, their energy and their enthusiasm and their idealism. Without them, this part of the country will never come to its full growth."

Had Welton meant nothing by the remark but praise, he wouldn't have felt the need to amplify and justify it so. Roosevelt was not so young as to fail to understand that. But, even with whiskey burning through him, he refused to take offense. Instead, he answered, "Some few men are fortunate enough to retain their youthful energy and enthusiasm and idealism throughout the whole span of their lives. They are the ones the history books written a hundred years after they are dead call great. I cannot judge the course of my life before I run it, but that is the goal to which I aspire."

Henry Welton didn't say anything for fully five minutes after that. One of the lamps burned out, filling the room with the sharp stink of kerosene and throwing new dark shadows across his face. When at last he spoke, it was from out of those shadows and in a meditative tone suited to them: "I wonder, Colonel, what the old generals and captains who had fought so long and so well under Philip of Macedon thought when Alexander gathered them together and told them they were going to go off and conquer the world. Alexander would have been about the age you are now, I expect."

Roosevelt stared. Nothing he could say or do sitting down seemed thanks enough. Forgetting his aches and pains, he sprang to his feet and bowed from the waist. "I can't possibly live up to that." Now he felt the whiskey; it put him at risk of sounding maudlin. "God made only one Alexander the Great, and then He broke the mold. But a man might do much worse than trying to walk as far as he can in his footsteps."

"Yes. So a man might." Welton paused again, this time to light a cigar. When he had it going, he chuckled self-consciously. "*In vino veritas,* or so they say. Lord only knows what they say about whiskey from a Fort Benton saloon." He suddenly seemed to notice the lamp had gone out. "Heavens, what time has it gotten to be?"

"It's a little past ten, sir," Roosevelt said after looking at his watch.

"I didn't mean to keep you gabbing here till all hours," Colonel Welton said. "You must be about ready to fall over dead. Let me gather you up and take you off to the bachelor officers' quarters for the night."

"As a matter of fact, I'm fine," Roosevelt said, and, to his surprise, it was true. "Much better than I was when I first rode into the fort. Must be the excellent company and the equally excellent restorative."

"If you don't get some rest now, you won't be fine in the—" A knock on the office door interrupted Welton before he could finish the sentence. "Come in," he called, and a soldier did, telegram in hand. Welton raised an eyebrow. "It must be after midnight back in Philadelphia. What's so important that it won't keep till daybreak?"

"It's not from Philadelphia, sir," the soldier answered. "It's from Helena, from the Territorial governor."

"All right, what's so important in Helena that it won't keep till daybreak?" Welton took the wire, read it, growled something vile under his breath, crumpled up the paper, and flung it across the room. "God damn that lazy bastard!"

"What's wrong, sir?" Roosevelt asked.

"You may have heard they booted Abe Lincoln out of Utah Territory for interfering with the military governor? No? Well, they did. He turned up in Helena preaching the power of labor, and started a riot down there. Now he's on his way up to Great Falls, probably to preach on the same text. I'm supposed to help keep order there, and I'd have had a hell of a lot better chance of doing it if His idiotic Excellency hadn't waited till the day before Lincoln was getting into Great Falls before bothering to tell me he was on his way. He's talking there *tomorrow night*."

"Sir, whomever you send, send me, too!" Roosevelt exclaimed. "I've always wanted to hear Lincoln."

"I'm not sending anyone," Welton said. "I'm going myself. You're welcome to ride along if you like." He waited for Roosevelt's eager nod, then went on, "And now I will put you to bed, and put myself to bed, too. We have a busy day ahead of us tomorrow, and likely a busier night."

"Good!" Roosevelt said, which made Henry Welton laugh.

As far as Frederick Douglass knew, he was by at least twenty-five years the oldest correspondent crossing the Ohio with the second wave of invaders—no, of liberators—entering Kentucky. He'd wondered how much trouble he would have in getting permission to see the action at first hand.

He'd had no trouble at all. The officer in charge of granting such permissions was Captain Oliver Richardson. Instead of being difficult, General Willcox's adjutant had proved the soul of cooperation. When the process was done, Douglass had said, "Thank you very much, Captain," with a certain amount of suspicion in his voice, hardly believing Richardson wanted to be helpful.

And then the captain had smiled at him. "It's my pleasure, Mr.

Douglass, believe me," he'd said, and the smile had got wider.
That wasn't pleasure; it was gloating anticipation.

He thinks he's sending me off to be killed, Douglass had realized. *He hopes he's sending me off to be killed.* Worst of all, the
Negro journalist couldn't say a word. Richardson had only done
what he'd asked him to do.

And now, along with a raft—actually, a barge—full of nervous
young white men in blue uniforms, a nervous elderly black man
in a sack suit set out across the Ohio to go into the Confederate
States of America for the first time in his life. On his hip was the
comforting weight of a pistol. He didn't expect to do much
damage to the Rebels with it. It would, however, keep them from
ever returning him to the life of bondage he had been fortunate
enough to escape.

U.S. artillery opened up, thunderous in its might. As had happened before the direct assault on Louisville, the southern bank of
the Ohio disappeared from view, engulfed in smoke. If all went
according to plan, the bombardment would leave the Confederates too stunned to reply.

If all had gone according to plan, Louisville would have fallen
weeks before, and this second assault would have been unnecessary. Douglass did his best not to dwell on that.

At the rear of the barge, the steam engine began hissing like a
whole nestful of snakes. "Here we go, boys!" shouted Major Algernon van Nuys, who commanded that part of the Sixth New
York Volunteer Infantry crammed aboard the awkward, ugly vessel. The soldiers cheered. Douglass wondered whether they were
outstandingly brave or outstandingly naive.

No matter what sort of noises the engine made, the barge
wasn't going anywhere in a hurry. It crawled away from the
wharf and waddled south toward the Kentucky shore of the Ohio,
one of many boats and barges in the water. As soon as they started
moving, shells started falling among them. "We've been hoaxed!"
somebody near Douglass exclaimed. "They said they were gonna
knock all these Rebel guns to kingdom come. They lied to us,
lied!" He sounded comically aggrieved.

One of his friends, a youngster with a more realistic view of
the world, replied, "Likely they said that to the fellows who went
over the Ohio the first time, too. You think they were right then,
Ned?"

Ned didn't answer; a shell that came down very close to the

barge drenched everyone and set all the men cursing and trying to dry off. Douglass decided, too late, that the occasion was probably informal enough for him to have escaped criticism even if he hadn't worn a cravat and wing-collared shirt.

How slowly Kentucky drew near! He felt he'd been on the barge forever, with every cannon in the Confederate States of America taking dead aim at him and him alone. The logical faculty he so prized told him that was an impossibility: it had been bare minutes since he'd set out from the northern bank of the river. With death in the air, though, logic cowered and time stretched like saltwater taffy.

"Once we land, we'll have to step lively," Major van Nuys called, cool as if his men were going onto the parade ground for drill, not into enemy territory to fight for their lives. "We'll form columns of fours and advance southwest in column till we meet the enemy, then deploy into loose order and sweep him aside. Our shout will be 'Revenge!' "

His men raised another cheer for that. Only a handful of them were old enough to remember the War of Secession, but the scars from that defeat had twisted the national countenance ever since. Even the young soldiers knew why they wanted revenge. Douglass would have preferred *Liberty!* for a shout, or perhaps *Justice!*—but *Revenge!* would do the job.

The *Queen of the Ohio* had gone aground far harder than the invasion barge did. The steamboat had been going far faster when she grounded, too. Yelling fit to burst their throats, the soldiers of the Sixth New York swarmed off the barge. They swept Douglass along, catching him up in their resistless tide. He counted himself lucky not to be knocked down and trampled underfoot.

"Get the devil out of the way, you damned old nigger!" somebody bawled in his ear. The soldier, whoever he was, didn't sound angry at him for being a Negro so much as for being an obstruction. Whichever his reason, Douglass could do nothing to accommodate it. He had no more control over his own movement than a scrap of bark borne downstream by a flood on the Mississippi.

And then, suddenly, he spun out of the main torrent of men and realized the muddy ground on which he was standing was not just any muddy ground but the muddy ground of Kentucky, of the Confederate States of America. He had carefully planned what he would do when at last he bestrode enemy soil. Shaking his fist toward Stonewall Jackson in Louisville, he cried out, *"Sic semper tyrannis!"*

" 'Thus always to tyrants,' " Major van Nuys echoed. "Well said. But do you know what, Mr. Douglass? That is the motto of the Confederate state of Virginia."

"Oh, they are great ones for taking a high moral tone, the Confederate States," Douglass said. "Taking a high moral tone costs them nothing. Living up to it is something else again."

Van Nuys did not linger to argue the point. He waved his sword to draw the attention of the men under his command— about the only use a sword had on a battlefield dominated by breechloaders and artillery. Disembarking from the barge had mixed the soldiers promiscuously. Officers, sergeants, and corporals screamed like madmen to get them into some kind, any kind, of order and moving forward against the foe.

A few bullets cut the air. Even as the Sixth New York began its part of the U.S. flanking assault against Louisville, a man fell with a dreadful shriek, clutching at his belly and wailing for his mother and someone named Annie. Sister? Sweetheart? Wife? Whoever she was, Douglass feared she would never set eyes on her young hero again. He hoped his own Anna would see him once more.

When the soldiers began to march, the Negro journalist discovered that, with the best will in the world, a man in his sixties had a hard time keeping up with fellows a third his age. He did his best, stumping along heavily and managing to keep the tail of the column in sight.

Panting, he muttered, "The faster they go, the better I like it." If the men of the Sixth New York and all the other regiments thrown into the fight moved swiftly, they did so because the Confederate defenders had not the strength to withstand them. No one going straight into Louisville had moved swiftly.

Two shells burst up ahead. A man flew up into the air, limp and boneless as a cloth doll tossed away by a girl who didn't feel like playing with it any more. Others were simply flung aside. Still others screamed when shell fragments sawed into their tender flesh.

"Come on, lads! Keep it up. Come on!" Major van Nuys called. "We can't play these games without paying a little every now and then. Believe you me, whatever it costs us, the Rebs will pay more."

More cheers rose from the Sixth New York. Van Nuys then ordered them into open echelon, which suggested to Douglass not only that they were already in the zone of combat but that they were liable to pay more than a little. How much the Confederates were paying was anyone's guess.

One thing was plain: the CSA had not resisted this thrust as they had the one aimed straight at Louisville. That the U.S. soldiers were advancing and not entrenching to save their lives from devastating Confederate fire proved as much. Douglass hoped that meant the Rebels were at full stretch to contain the USA in Louisville itself, and had little left to resist elsewhere.

The countryside was pretty: farms with belts of oaks and elms between them. After a moment, Douglass revised his first impression. The countryside had been pretty, and might one day be pretty again. War was rapidly doing what war did—making ugly everything it touched. Shell craters scarred meadows and fields. A couple of farmhouses and barns were already burning, smoke from their pyres staining the morning air. Several small cabins near a farmhouse also burned. For a moment, Douglass simply noted that, as any reporter would. Then he realized what those smaller buildings were.

"Slave shanties," he said through clenched teeth. "Even here, so close to the Ohio and freedom, they had slave shanties. May they all burn, and all the big houses with them."

A few minutes later, a couple of U.S. soldiers with long bayonets on their Springfields led half a dozen or so Confederate prisoners back past him toward the river. A couple of the Rebs were wounded, one with his arm in a sling made from a tunic, the other wearing a bloody bandage wrapped round his head. All of them were skinny and dirty and surprisingly short: rumor made six-foot Confederate soldiers out to be runts. They did not look like invincible conquerors—petty vagrants was more like it.

"May I speak to these men?" Douglass asked their guards.

"Sure, Snowball, go right ahead," one of the men in blue replied. "Can't think of anything liable to make 'em feel worse, not off the top of my head I can't."

Douglass ignored that less than ringing endorsement. "You prisoners," he said sharply, to remind them of their status, "how many of you are slaveowners?"

Two men in gray nodded. The fellow with the bandaged head

said, "*You* wouldn't bring me fifty dollars. You're too damn old and too damn uppity."

"I can't help being old, and I'm proud to be uppity," Douglass said. "How dare you presume to own, to buy and to sell and to ravish, your fellow human beings?"

The captured Confederate laughed hoarsely. "You damn crazy nigger, I'd sooner ravish my mule than ugly old Nero who helps me farm." He spat a stream of tobacco juice. "And you got a lot of damn nerve tellin' me what I can and can't do with my property, which ain't none o' your business to begin with."

"Men and women are not property," Douglass thundered, as if to an audience of twenty thousand. "They are your brothers and sisters in the eyes of God."

"Not where I come from, they ain't," the prisoner said, and spat again. He turned to the U.S. soldiers guarding him. "You done caught us. Ain't that bad enough? We got to put up with this damn mouthy nigger, too? Take us away and put us somewheres, why don't you?"

"You're damn lucky you're breathin', Reb," one of the soldiers in blue answered. "You want to stay lucky, you'll do like you're told."

Douglass had often anticipated interviews with ordinary Confederates. This one wasn't going the way he'd anticipated. The other Rebel who admitted to being a slaveholder said, "What in blazes are the *Yew*-nited States invadin' us for, anyways? We ain't done nothin' personal to you, nigger. We ain't done nothin' to nobody in the USA. All we done is buy up a chunk o' Mexico wasn't doin' nobody no good nohow. An' you-all start shootin' at us an' blowin' us up on account of *that*? My pappy always told me they was funny up in Boston and Massachusetts and them places, and I reckon he was right."

"The existence of a nation built on bondage is a stench in the nostrils of the entire civilized world," Douglass said.

"It ain't your business." Both Confederate soldiers spoke as one.

"It is the business of every man who loves liberty," Douglass declared. He threw his hands in the air; he and the slaveholders might have been speaking two different languages. He asked them, "How were you captured?"

The uninjured one said, "Three Yankees yelled at me to throw down my rifle at the same time. Right about then, I reckoned that'd be a plumb good idea."

"What about you?" Douglass asked the other one.

"You really want to know, nigger?" the Reb with the bandaged head answered. "I was squattin' in the bushes with my pants around my ankles, doin' my business, when this motherfucker in a blue coat says he'll blow me out a new asshole to shit through if'n I don't put my hands high. So I done it." He gave Douglass a sour stare. "An' looky here—I got me the new asshole anyways."

That set not only the Confederate prisoners but also their guards braying like donkeys. Douglass stomped off. The Rebels' jeers pursued him. He paused to scribble in his notebook: *They are now, as they have long been, ignorant, uncouth, and stubbornly indifferent to the sentiments of their fellow men and to the appeals of simple human justice. Only a brute-like hardiness—ironically, the very trait they impute to their enslaved Negroes—enables them to persist in their infamous course.*

A second look told him that was hardly objective. He grunted. "So what?" he said aloud. He put the notebook in his pocket and tramped off toward the southwest.

☆ **XII** ☆

General Thomas Jackson looked up from the map. "They are throwing everything they have into this," he observed. "Can we reduce our forces within the city of Louisville to add a core of battle-hardened men to the forces we are deploying against their flanking maneuver?"

"I believe so, sir," Major General E. Porter Alexander answered. "They have stepped up their attacks within the city, but their troops there have not the dash and spirit they did when the fighting was new. They know they are likely to gain little and to pay dearly for what they do get. Few men give their best under such circumstances."

"Any men who fail to give their best under any circumstances deserve the sternest treatment from their own superiors," Jackson said. "The old Roman custom of decimation has much to recommend it."

"I wouldn't go so far as *that*, sir," Alexander said, trying to turn it into a joke.

"*I* would," replied Jackson, who saw nothing funny in it. Raising one arm above his head, he went on, "But back to the nub of things. What can you do, General, about the Yankees' artillery? Their guns seriously hamper our efforts to move troops to face the attack from the east."

"They have more guns than we do," E. Porter Alexander said unhappily. "They've taken some off the Louisville front to do just as you say: to make shifting soldiers harder for us. It's a good thing you had the forethought to build so many trench lines around the city before the Yankees started moving against our flank. If we had to dig while we were fighting, we'd be in worse trouble than we are already."

"This demonstrates a point I have repeatedly stressed to President Longstreet," Jackson said: "namely, that having a servile population upon which we can draw in time of need confers great military advantage on us." He sighed. "The president is of the opinion that other factors militate against our retaining this advantage. Perhaps he is even right. For the sake of the country, I pray he is right."

"Yes, sir." General Alexander hesitated, then said, "Sir, do you mind if I ask you a question?"

"By no means, General. Ask what you will."

Despite that generous permission, Alexander hemmed and hawed before he did put the question: "Sir, why do you stick your arm up in the air like that? I've seen you do it many times, and it's always puzzled me."

"Oh. That." Jackson lowered the arm; he'd all but forgotten he'd elevated it in the first place. "One of my legs, it seems to me, is bigger than the other, and one of my arms is likewise unduly heavy. By raising the arm, I let the blood run back into my body and so lighten the limb. It is a habit I have had for many years, and one, I believe, with nothing but beneficial results."

"All right, sir." Alexander grinned at him. "I expect I ought to be glad I'm the same size on both sides, then."

"Is that levity?" The general-in-chief of the C.S. Army knew he had trouble recognizing it. "Well, never mind. The key to this fight will lie in halting the new Yankee thrust before it can crash into the flank of the position we were previously maintaining. The foe has been generous enough to give us considerable room in which to maneuver."

"He's given himself considerable room to maneuver, too," Alexander pointed out.

"You have set your finger on an unfortunate truth." Jackson studied the map again. "We have to maneuver more effectually, then. We have no other choice. As best I can judge from the reports reaching this headquarters, the intended direction of the Yankee column is—"

"Straight at us, near enough," Porter Alexander broke in.

"I believe you are correct, yes." Jackson took another long look at the indicated U.S. line of attack. "Absent interference, they would be here in a couple of hours. I intend to see that such interference is not absent."

"Sir!" A telegrapher waved for Jackson's attention. "I have an urgent wire here from Second Lieutenant Stuart, commanding the Third Virginia south and west of St. Matthews. His line to divisional headquarters is down, so he calls on you. He says the Yankees are there in great numbers. He's thrown an attack at them to delay and confuse them, but requests reinforcements. 'Whatever you have,' he says."

"He shall be reinforced." Jackson's head came up. "A lieutenant, commanding a regiment?"

"I don't know anything about that, sir, past what the wire says," the telegrapher answered. "Shall I order him to report the circumstances?"

"Never mind," Jackson said. "If he has the command, he has it, and does not need his elbow jogged for explanations. Afterwards will be time enough to sort through the whys and wherefores."

E. Porter Alexander said, "One way or another, he won't be a second lieutenant by this time tomorrow. Either he'll be a captain or maybe a major, or else he'll wind up a private with no hope of seeing officer's rank ever again." He paused. "Or, of course, he may well end up more concerned about his heavenly reward than any he might gain upon this earth. A lot of good men must have fallen for a lieutenant to assume regimental command. If afterwards he ordered an attack, he would hardly be removing himself from danger."

"That's true, General." Jackson studied the telegram, trying to divine more from it than the operator's bald statement had given him. Then, suddenly, his tangled eyebrows rose. "Second Lieutenant Stuart—that's S-T-U-A-R-T, General Alexander. Is our colleague's son not of that rank, and in this army?"

"Jeb, Jr.?" Alexander's eyebrows went up, too. "I believe he is, sir. Of course, even with that spelling, it's far from the least common of names. Would you answer his request any differently if you knew he was, or, for that matter, if you knew he wasn't?"

"In the midst of battle? Don't be absurd." Jackson tossed his head. As he did so, he remembered Robert E. Lee's habitual gesture of annoyance—Lee would jerk his head up and to one side, as if trying to take a bite out of his own earlobe. It was, in Jackson's view, ridiculous. Raising his arm over his head again, he concentrated on the map. "The Fourth Virginia, the Third Tennessee, and the Second Confederate States are ordered to support the attack of the Third Virginia, if their commanders shall not have already moved to do so of their own initiative."

"Yes, sir." The telegrapher's key clicked and clicked, almost as fast as the castanets of the Mexican *señoritas* whose sinuous grace and flashing eyes Jackson had admired during his long-ago service in the U.S. Artillery.

No sooner had he thought of artillery in one way than General Alexander did in another, saying, "We have three batteries by the village of West Buechel, sir, that could lend the infantry useful assistance."

"Let it be so," Jackson agreed, and the telegrapher's key clicked anew.

More and more wires began coming in to headquarters from that part of the field. Second Lieutenant Stuart, from whom nothing further was heard, had been right in reporting that U.S. troops were there in great force. They had been driving forward, too. They no longer seemed to be doing so; Stuart's attack had done what he'd hoped, rocking them back on their heels. They must have thought that, if the Confederates were numerous enough to assault them, they were also numerous enough to beat back an assault.

Jackson knew perfectly well that they had not been so at the time when Second Lieutenant Stuart ordered the attack. (Was it Jeb, Jr.? Hadn't Jeb, Jr., been born day before yesterday, or last week at the outside? Hadn't he just the other day graduated from a little boy's flowing dress into trousers? Intellectually, Jackson knew better. Every so often, though, the passing years up and ambushed him. They had more skill at it than any Yankees. One day, they would shoot him down from ambush, too.)

Even had it not been so then, it was rapidly becoming so now. *He who hesitates is lost* was nowhere more true than on the battlefield. The brief halt Stuart had imposed on the enemy let Jackson bring forces up to yet another of the lines he had had the conscripted Negro slaves of the vicinity build. (He had every intention of sending President Longstreet an exquisitely detailed memorandum relating everything the slaves' labors meant to his forces. Longstreet, no doubt, would consign it to oblivion. That was his affair. Jackson would not keep silent to appease him.)

By midafternoon, the line had stabilized. Jackson called off the counterattack, which, he knew, must have cost him dear in terms of men. Though his instinct was always to strike at the enemy, he had come to see a certain virtue in the defensive, in making U.S. forces rise from concealment to attack his men while the soldiers in butternut and gray waited in trenches and behind breastworks. (Unlike his thoughts on slave labor, he did not plan on confiding that one to James Longstreet.)

When the crisis was past, he told the telegrapher, "Order Second Lieutenant Stuart to report to his headquarters immediately." As the soldier tapped out the message, Jackson sent a silent prayer heavenward that the lieutenant would be able to obey the command.

He caught E. Porter Alexander looking at him. His chief artillerist crossed his fingers. Jackson nodded. Alexander had been thinking along with him in more than matters strictly military, then.

When Lieutenant Stuart did not report as soon as Jackson thought he should, the Confederate general-in-chief began to fear the officer was now obeying the orders of a higher commander. But then, to his glad surprise, a sentry poked his head into the headquarters tent to announce that Stuart had arrived after all. "Let him come in; by all means let him come in," Jackson exclaimed.

He and E. Porter Alexander both exclaimed then, for it was Jeb Stuart's son. "*How* the devil old are you?" Alexander demanded.

"Sir, I'm seventeen," Jeb Stuart, Jr., answered. He looked like his father, though instead of that famous shaggy beard he had only a peach-fuzz mustache. But for that, though, he looked older than his years, as any man will coming straight out of battle. With his face dark from black-powder smoke, he had the aspect of a minstrel-show performer freshly escaped from hell.

"How did you become senior officer in your regiment, Lieutenant?" Jackson inquired. How young Stuart had become a lieutenant at his age was another question, but one with an obvious answer—his father must have pulled wires for him.

"Sir, I wasn't," Stuart answered. "Captain Sheckard sent me back to Colonel Tinker with word that the Yankees were pressing my company hard."

"I see." Jackson wasn't sure he did, not altogether, but he didn't press it. Had Sheckard decided to get his important subordinate out of harm's way, or had he chosen him because he was worth less on the fighting line than an ordinary private? No way to tell, not from here. "Go on."

"There I was, sir, and a Yankee shell came down, and, next thing I knew, Colonel Tinker was dead and Lieutenant-Colonel

Steinfeldt had his head blown off and Major Overall"—Stuart gulped—"the surgeons took that leg off him, I heard later. And the Yankees were coming at us every which way, and everybody was yelling, 'What do we do? What do we do?' " He looked a little green around the gills, remembering. "Nobody else said anything, so I started giving orders. I don't know whether the captains knew they were coming from me, but they took 'em, and we threw the Yankees back."

Jackson glanced at Alexander. Alexander was already looking at him. They both nodded and turned back to Jeb Stuart, Jr. Alexander spoke first: "Congratulations, son. Like it or not, you're a hero."

That summed it up better than Jackson could have done. He did find one thing to add: "Your father will be very proud of you."

"Thank you, sir." Stuart was less in awe of Jackson than most young officers would have been, having known him all his life. But the wobble in his voice had only a little to do with his youth. More came from the question he asked: "Sir, what would have happened if it hadn't worked out?"

Jackson was not good at diplomatic responses. He managed to come up with one now: "You probably would not be here to wonder about that."

The young officer needed a moment to see what he meant. Jackson was unsurprised; at that age, he'd thought he was immortal, too. Stuart licked his lips. He understood what might have happened, once Jackson pointed it out. He said, "I meant, sir, if I'd failed but lived."

"Best to draw a merciful veil of silence over that," E. Porter Alexander said.

Beneath his coating of smoke and soot, Jeb Stuart, Jr., turned red. "Er, yes, sir," he said, and turned back to Jackson. "Sir, *will* we hold the Yankees from our flank?"

"That still hangs in the balance," Jackson replied. "I will say, however, that we have a better chance of doing so thanks to your action, Lieutenant Stuart." He inclined his head to his old comrade's son. "You will be changing the ornaments on your collar in short order."

Jeb Stuart, Jr., understood that right away. He raised a hand to brush one of the single collar bars marking him as a second lieutenant. His grin lit up the inside of the headquarters tent, brighter than all the kerosene lamps hung there.

* * *

Orion Clemens rolled a hard rubber ball through a couple of squads of gray-painted lead soldiers. "Take that, you dirty Rebs!" he shouted as several of them toppled. Sutro ran barking after the ball and through the soldiers, completing the Confederates' overthrow. With a cry of fierce glee, Orion sent blue-painted lead figures swarming forward. "They're on the run now!"

His father looked up from *Les Misérables*. "If only it were that easy, for our side or theirs," Sam Clemens remarked to his wife. "The war would be over in a fortnight, one way or the other, and we could slide back to our comfortable daily business of killing one another by ones and twos—retail, you might say—instead of in great wholesale lots."

Alexandra set Louisa May Alcott's *After the War Was Lost* on her lap. "I think too many telegrams from the front have curdled your understanding of human nature."

"No." He shook his head in vigorous denial. "It's not the wires from the front that make your belly think you've swallowed melted lead. It's the ones from the politicians, who keep on claiming the boys die to some better purpose than their own stubborn greed and the generals' stupidity."

Even Orion's triumphal advance was interrupted. Ophelia got the ball away from Sutro and threw it at the toy soldiers who wore blue paint. The missile struck with deadly effect. One of the many casualties flew into the air and bounced off Sam's shin.

"Artillery!" Ophelia cried. "Knock 'em all down!"

Sam studied his daughter with the mixture of admiration and something close to fear she often raised in his mind. She couldn't possibly have read the latest despatches out of Louisville ... could she? He shook his head. She was, after all, only four years old. She knew her ABCs, she could print her name in a sprawling scrawl, and that was about it. How, then, had she been so uncannily accurate about what the Confederate guns were doing to U.S. attackers?

She was Ophelia. That was how.

"Pa!" Orion shouted angrily. "Look, Pa! See what she did? She broke two of 'em, Pa! This one got his head knocked off, and this other one here, this sergeant, his arm is broke."

"Casualties of war," Clemens said. "See? You can't even fight with toy soldiers without having them get hurt. I wish President

Blaine were here, I do. It would learn him a good one, if you don't mind my speaking Missouri."

"Sam." Alexandra Clemens somehow stuffed a world of warning into one syllable, three letters' worth of sound.

"Well, maybe I could find a better time to talk about politics," her husband admitted. With a sigh, Sam raised his voice. "Ophelia!"

"Yes, Pa?" Suddenly, she sounded like an ordinary four-year-old again.

"Come here, young lady."

"Yes, Pa." No, not an ordinary four-year-old after all: as she walked toward him, a halo of rectitude sprang into glowing life above her head. Sam blinked, and it was gone. A trick of the gaslights, or perhaps of the imagination, though what a newspaperman needed with such useless stuff as an imagination was beyond him.

"You broke two of your brother's lead soldiers," he said, doing his best to sound stern and not break out laughing at the sight of the oh so precious, oh so innocent countenance before him. "What have you got to say for yourself?"

"I'm sorry, Pa." The voice was small and sweet and pure, like the chiming of a silver bell.

Probably sorry you didn't wipe out the whole blasted regiment, Clemens thought. He turned her over his knee and gave her a swat on the bottom that was as much ritual as punishment. That opened the floodgates for a storm of tears. Ophelia always howled like a banshee when she got smacked. Part of that, Sam judged, was anger that she should be subjected to such indignities. And part of it probably stemmed from a calculation that, if she made every spanking as unpleasant as possible, she wouldn't get so many of them.

Orion seemed properly gratified at the racket his sister made. When she stalked off to sulk in her tent, he held out the broken lead soldiers and asked, "Can you fix 'em, Pa?"

"I'll take 'em to the paper tomorrow," Clemens answered. "The printers can melt 'em down for type metal."

"Sam!" Three letters and an exclamation point from Alexandra this time. Too late. Orion started crying louder than Ophelia had.

Over those theatrical groans, Sam said, "I was only joking. They'll be able to solder the soldiers back together." He had to say it twice more, once to get his son to hear him through the caterwauling he was putting out and again to get the boy to believe him.

"Can't you remember to save all that for the editorial page and not to bring it home to your family?" Alexandra asked after relative calm—and calm among the relatives—returned.

"I'm all of a piece, my dear," Clemens answered. "You can't very well expect me to flow like a Pennsylvania gusher at the *Morning Call* and then put out pap for no better reason than that I've come home at night."

"Can I expect you to keep in mind that your son *will* believe you no matter what you say, while the politicos who read your editorials *won't* believe you no matter what you say?" Alexandra was never more dangerous than when she worked hardest to hold on to her patience.

Sam wagged a finger at her. "You had better be careful. You will make me remember that once upon a time I was fitted out with a sense of shame, and that's dangerous excess baggage for a man in my line of work."

"Hmm," was all Alexandra said. "Joke as much as you like, but—"

Orion broke in: "Pa, will you really and truly fix my soldiers?"

"They will rise from the dead—or at least the maimed—like Lazarus coming forth from his tomb," Clemens promised. Orion looked blank. His father explained: "In other words, yes, I will do that. If only General Willcox could make a similar—"

Alexandra suffered a coughing fit of remarkable timeliness. Sam shot her a look half annoyed, half grateful. Orion said, "As long as they really and truly get fixed, it's all right." He paused, then asked, "When you get 'em soldered, will it leave scars on 'em, like?"

"I expect it may," Sam said solemnly. "I'm sorry, but—"

"Bully!" Orion exclaimed, which made his father shut up with a snap.

The next morning, Sam walked over to the *Morning Call* carrying the mortal remains of the lead soldiers in a jacket pocket. One of the printers, a wizened little Welshman named Charlie Vaughan, took a look at the casualties of war and said, "Yeah, we can set 'em right again." His cigar, made from a weed even nastier than those Clemens favored, bobbed up and down as he spoke. "Damn shame we can't fix the real soldiers this easy, ain't it?"

"You, sir, have been listening at my window," Sam said. Vaughan shook his head before realizing the editor was joking. He gave Sam a sour look. "Never mind," Clemens told him. "You'll make my son very happy and help my daughter out of trouble." He rolled his eyes. "And God forbid I should use that particular phrase fifteen years from now."

Jerk, jerk, jerk went the printer's cigar as he chuckled. "Know what you mean," he said. "I have three of 'em. Married the last one off a couple years ago, so I don't have to worry about that any more."

"All your children out of the house, then?" Clemens asked. When Charlie Vaughan nodded, he aimed another question at him: "How the devil do you stand so much quiet?"

"You think you're making fun of me again, only you ain't," Vaughan said. "Gets almost spooky-like, sometimes." The cigar twitched. "Would be worse, I suppose, if my missus'd ever learned to shut her trap."

"I'll be sure to tell her you said that, next time I see her," Sam said, and beat a hasty retreat in the direction of his desk before the printer could choose one of the numerous small, heavy objects within arm's length and throw it at him.

"Morning, Sam," Clay Herndon said when he walked in a few minutes later. "What have you got there?"

"This? Police-court story Edgar turned in last night," Clemens answered, excising an adverb. "Man bites dog, you might say: three Chinamen charged with setting on an Irish railroad worker, whaling the stuffing out of him, and departing with his wallet. Since the Celestials decided the wallet was worth keeping, they must have caught the mick before he started his round of the saloons."

"Ha," Herndon said, and then, "You're right—that's not the way it usually goes. The Irish get liquored up, they cave in John Chinaman's skull, and the judge slaps 'em on the wrist. We've seen that story so many times, it's hardly news enough to put in the paper."

"Back when I first started working for this sheet, in the days when the office was over on Montgomery, you couldn't have put that story in the paper," Sam said. "Publisher wouldn't let you get by with it. He thought it would offend the Irish, though I always reckoned not more than a double handful of 'em could have read it."

"Those must have been the days," Herndon said. "This would have been a rip-snorting town back then."

"It was, when I first got here," Clemens agreed. "Then the United States went and lost the war, and San Francisco got a lot of the snorts ripped clean out of it. The panic was a hell of a lot worse than it ever got back in the States." For the first time in a long while, he hauled out the old California expression for the rest of the USA. "The railroad hadn't gone through yet, remember, and we were about as near cut off from the rest of the world as made no difference—and the rest of the world seemed to like it just fine that way, too."

"I've heard it was pretty grim, all right," Clay Herndon allowed.

"Grim?" Clemens said. "Why, it made dying look like a circus with lemonade and elephants, because once you were dead you didn't have to try and pay your bills with greenbacks worth a hot four cents on the gold dollar—oh, they dropped down to three cents on the dollar for a week or two, but by then everybody who could be scared to death was already clutching a lily in his fist."

"Hard times," Herndon said. "Every time somebody who went through it here starts talking about it, you wonder how people got by."

"You hunker down and you hang on tight to what you've got, if it isn't that damn lily," Sam answered. "The great earthquake of '65 didn't do us any good, either. You'll have felt 'em here now and again, but there's never been anything like that since, thank heavens, not even the quake of '72, which wasn't a piker. I don't reckon we'll see the like again for another couple of hundred years, and, if God pays any attention to what *I* think, that'd be too soon, too."

"Even the common, garden-variety earthquakes are bad enough," Herndon said with a shudder. "Makes me queasy just thinking about 'em." He deliberately and obviously changed the subject: "What's the war news?"

"They're killing people," Sam said, and let it go at that. When his friend coughed in annoyance, he blinked, as if surprised. "Oh, you want the *details*." He pawed through the blizzard of telegrams on his desk. "General Willcox has proved he can get stuck in two different places at the same time—a lesser man would have been incapable of it, don't you think? The British gunboats on the Great Lakes have bombarded Cleveland again, though

Lord knows why, having visited the place once, they felt inclined to come back. The Indians are on the warpath in Kansas, the Confederates are on the warpath in New Mexico Territory, and Abe Lincoln's on the warpath in Montana Territory. And, with ruffles and flourishes, the War Department announced the capture of Pocahontas, Arkansas."

"Pocahontas, Arkansas?" Clay Herndon asked in tones that suggested he hoped Sam was kidding but didn't really believe it.

And Sam wasn't. He waved the telegram to prove it. "In case you're wondering, Pocahontas is almost halfway from the border down toward the vital metropolis of Jonesboro," he said solemnly. "I looked it up. At first I thought it was only a flyspeck on the map, but I have to admit that further inspection proved me wrong. Hallelujah, I must say; no doubt the shock waves of the seizure are reverberating through Richmond even as I speak."

"Pocahontas, Arkansas?" Herndon repeated. Sam nodded. "Ruffles and flourishes?" the reporter asked. Clemens handed him the wire. He read it, grimaced, and handed it back. "Ruffles and flourishes, sure enough. Good God Almighty, we shouldn't cackle that loud if we ever do take Louisville."

"You can't cackle over the egg you didn't lay," Clemens pointed out. "We haven't got Louisville, but Pocahontas, Arkansas, by thunder, is *ours*." He clapped his hands together, once, twice, three times.

"Sam . . ." Herndon's voice was plaintive. "Why do we have such a pack of confounded dunderheads running this country?"

"My theory used to be that we get the government we deserve," Sam said. "Bad as we are, though, I don't think we're *that* bad. Right now, I'm taking a long look at the notion that God hates us." He glanced up at his friend. "I know somebody who's going to hate you if you don't set your posteriors in a chair and get some work done." To soften that, he added, "And I'd better do the same." Returning his attention to Edgar Leary's story, he killed seven adjectives at one blow.

A brisk crackle of gunfire came from the northern outskirts of Tombstone, New Mexico. Major Horatio Sellers turned to Jeb Stuart and said, "You were right, sir. They are going to try and hold the place. I didn't reckon they'd be such fools."

"I think we rolled most of the real Yankee soldiers back toward Tucson—the ones we didn't capture at Contention City, I mean,"

Stuart answered. "What we've got left in these parts is mostly Tombstone Rangers and the like, unless I miss my guess. They'll be fighting for their homes here."

"And they haven't got the brains God gave a camel," Sellers said, with which Stuart could not disagree, either. His aide-de-camp rubbed his hands together in high good cheer. "They'll pay for it."

Boom! A roar louder than a dozen ordinary rifle shots and a large cloud of smoke rising from the graveyard north of Tombstone declared that the U.S. defenders had found a cannon somewhere. Stuart stayed unperturbed. "I hope to heaven we know better by now than to pack ourselves together nice and tight for a field gun to mow us down." His smile was almost found. "Those smoothbore Napoleons did a good business during the last war, but we've come a long way since."

His own field artillery, posted on the hills that led up to the Dragoon Mountains north and east of town, consisted of modern rifled guns that not only outranged the Tombstone Yankees' obsolete piece but were more accurate as well. No sooner than the Napoleon revealed its position, shells started falling around it. It fired a couple of more times, its cannonballs kicking up dust as they skipped along, then fell silent.

"So much for that," Horatio Sellers said with a chuckle.

A couple of minutes later, though, the old-fashioned muzzle-loader came back to life. "We must have knocked out their number-one crew," Stuart guessed, "and sent them scrambling around for replacements. They've got some brave men serving that gun."

"Much good may it do them." Sellers grunted. "They likely never did have a whole lot of men with much notion of what to do with a cannon. If you're right, sir, and their best gun crew's down, they won't be able to hit a blamed thing now, not without fool luck they won't."

"That makes sense to me," Jeb Stuart agreed. "We don't want 'em to get lucky, though." He turned to Chappo, who, along with Geronimo, was watching the fight for Tombstone alongside the Confederate commander. "Will you ask your father if he can slide some Apaches forward and pick off the Yankees who are tending to their gun?"

"Yes, I will do that." Chappo spoke to Geronimo in their own language. Young man and old gestured as they spoke back and forth. The Apaches used their hands as expressively as Frenchmen when they talked. Chappo returned to English. "My father says he will gladly do this. He wants to punish the white men of Tombstone, to hurt them for all the times they have hurt us. If we take this place together, he will burn it."

Stuart looked down at Tombstone's wooden buildings, baking under the desert sun and no doubt tinder-dry. "If we take this place, it's going to burn whether he burns it or not, I reckon."

Even though he watched with a telescope, he could not spy any of the Apaches moving up toward the Napoleon the Tombstone volunteers were still firing. He wondered whether Geronimo had ordered them forward. The ground beyond the graveyard offered more cover than a billiard table, but not much. He wouldn't have cared to send his own men up to try to knock the gunners out of action.

That's why we're allied with the Apaches, the cold, calculating part of his mind said. *Let them get hurt doing the nasty little jobs like that.*

He glanced over at Geronimo. The Indian—medicine man, was the closest term Stuart could find for his position—was watching litter-bearers carrying wounded Confederate soldiers back toward the tents where the surgeons plied their grisly trade. When Geronimo felt Stuart's eye on him, the old Indian quickly moved his head and looked in a different direction.

He didn't do it quite quickly enough. *I will be damned,* Stuart thought. *I know just what that dried-up devil of a redskin is thinking, and nobody will ever make me believe I don't. He's thinking, sure as hell he's thinking,* That's why we're allied with the Confederates. Let them get hurt doing the nasty big jobs like that. *To hell with me if he's not.*

Stuart whistled "Dixie" between his teeth. Weeks of travel with Geronimo and the other Apache leaders had taught him they were more than the unsophisticated savages the dime novels made them out to be. They were, in fact, very sophisticated savages indeed. Not till that moment, though, had Stuart paused to wonder who was using whom to the greater degree.

Now Geronimo looked over toward him. The Apache seemed to realize Stuart had peered into his thoughts. He nodded to the white man, a small, tightly controlled movement of his head. Stuart nodded back. The two of them might have been the two sides of a mirror, each reflecting the other's concerns and each surprising the other when he realized it.

All at once, Stuart noticed the Napoleon had fallen silent again. Now Geronimo looked his way without trying to be furtive about it. The Apache raised his Tredegar to his shoulder and mimed taking aim. Stuart nodded to show he understood and doffed his hat for a moment in salute to the Apache warriors' skill. Geronimo's answering smile showed only a couple of teeth.

Losing their cannoneers once more dismayed Tombstone's defenders. They fell back from the graveyard into the town. Had Stuart commanded them, he would have had them hold out among Tombstone's tombstones as long as they could; when they retreated, the Confederates and Apaches promptly seized the high ground.

The Confederate field guns started hammering away at Tombstone itself. When shells struck bare ground, smoke and dirt leapt skyward. When a shell hit a building, it was as if a spoiled child kicked a dollhouse. Timbers flew every which way. No doubt glass did, too, though Stuart could not see that even with his telescope. But he knew what flying bits of glass could do to a man's body, having been educated in the War of Secession.

"Do we wait for fire to do our work for us?" Major Sellers asked. A couple of thin threads of smoke were already rising into the sky.

"No, we'll press it a bit," Stuart replied. "Even in fire, the damnyankees can hold out for a long time down there, and it wouldn't burn them all out. Besides, if we take the town instead of burning it, we also get to forage to our hearts' content."

"Yes, sir," his aide-de-camp said enthusiastically. The Confederate army in New Mexico Territory operated on the end of an enormously long supply line. Thanks to their victories, Stuart's troopers had plenty of food for themselves and fodder for their animals. They had enough powder and munitions for this fight, too. Looking ahead to the next one, Stuart didn't like the picture he saw.

Down from the hills toward Tombstone came the dismounted Confederate cavalrymen, four going forward for every one who stayed behind to hold horses. Down from the hills, too, came the Apaches. Stuart was sure that was so although, again, he could see next to no sign of the Indians.

After a bit, he watched Geronimo instead of trying to spot red-skinned wills-o'-the-wisp. The Indian could plainly tell where his braves were and what they were up to, even if Stuart's eyes could not find them. The Apaches were convinced Geronimo had occult powers. Watching him watch men he could not possibly have seen halfway convinced Stuart they were right.

The volunteers in Tombstone kept on putting up a brave fight. As they had been in the valley south of Tucson, the U.S. forces were caught in a box with opponents coming at them from three sides at once. Here, though, they had good cover. They also had no good line of retreat from Tombstone, which made them like-lier to stand where they were. Whenever Confederates or Indians pushed them, they drove off their foes with an impressive volume of fire from their Winchesters.

But then more and more of the saloons and gambling halls and sporting houses—which seemed to make up a large portion of Tombstone's buildings—on the northern edge of town caught fire. The flames forced the defenders out of those buildings and farther back into Tombstone. The smoke from them also kept the Tombstone Rangers from shooting as accurately as they had been doing. Confederates and Apaches began dashing between flam-ing false fronts and into Tombstone. As Stuart rode closer to the mining town, the cheers of his men and the Indians' war cries drowned the shouts of dismay from the U.S. Volunteers.

Major Horatio Sellers rode alongside him. "Sir, will you send in a man under flag of truce to give the Yankees a chance to surrender?"

Geronimo and Chappo were also riding forward with the Con-federate commander. Before Stuart could answer, Chappo spoke urgently to his father in the Apache language. Geronimo an-swered with similar urgency and greater excitement. Chappo returned to English: "Do not give them a chance to give up. They have done us too many harms to have a chance to give up."

Sure as the devil, the Apaches were using the Confederates to pay back their own enemies. But then Major Sellers said, "It's not as if they were Regular Army men, sir, true enough. Probably better than half of them are gamblers or road agents or riffraff of some kind or another."

The spectacle of his aide-de-camp agreeing with Geronimo instead of trying to find a persuasive excuse to massacre him bemused Stuart. It also helped him make up his mind. "If the

Tombstone Rangers want to surrender, they can send a man to us. I won't make it easy for them."

Chappo translated that for Geronimo. His father grunted, spoke, gestured, spoke again. Chappo didn't turn his response back into English. From the old Indian's tone and expression, though, Jeb Stuart thought he could make a good guess about what it meant: something to the effect of, *Oh, all right. I'd sooner every one of them bit the dust, but if they give up, what can you do?*

A dirty-faced Confederate came running back to Stuart. "Sir, the damnyankees put a couple of sharpshooters up in that church steeple"—he pointed back through drifted smoke toward what was plainly the tallest structure in Tombstone—"and they've done hit a bunch of our boys."

"I can't knock 'em out by myself, Corporal," Stuart answered. He looked back to see where the field guns were. A couple of them had already taken up positions in the graveyard, not far from where the Napoleon had stood. "Go tell them. They'll take care of it."

The range was short; the gunners were barely out of effective Winchester range from the outskirts of Tombstone, and might have come under severe fire from U.S. Army Springfields. Stuart watched shells fall around the church. Then one gun crew made a pretty good shot and exploded their shell against the topmost part of the steeple. No further reports of Yankee sharpshooters there came to Stuart's ears.

That church, he found when he rode into town, was at the corner of Third and Safford. The Tombstone Rangers made a final stand a block south of it, at the adobe Wells Fargo office at Third and Fremont and the corral across the street from it, whose fences they'd reinforced with planks and stones and bricks and whatever else they could find. The OK Corral was a target artillerists dreamt of. After a couple of salvos turned the place into a slaughterhouse, the defenders raised a white flag and threw down their guns, and the fighting stopped.

Geronimo, seeing the men who had so tormented the Apaches now in his allies' hands, wanted to change his mind and dispose of them on the spot. "No," Stuart told him through Chappo. "We don't massacre men in cold blood."

"What will you do with them?" the medicine man asked.

"Send them down to Hermosillo, along with the rest of the U.S. soldiers we've captured," Stuart answered.

Geronimo sighed. "It is not enough."

"It will have to do," Stuart told him. "We haven't done too badly here, when you think about it. We've cleared U.S. forces from a big stretch of southwestern New Mexico Territory, and we did it without getting badly hurt at all."

"Much of what you did, you did because we helped you," Geronimo replied through Chappo. "We should have some reward."

He could not force the issue; he had not the men for that. Stuart said, "You do have a reward. Here is all this land with no Yankee soldiers on it. Here are your braves with the fine rifles they have from us. How can you complain?"

"It is not enough," Geronimo repeated. He said nothing more after that. Stuart resolved to keep a close eye on him and his followers.

As soon as Abraham Lincoln saw the crowd that had come to hear him in Great Falls, he knew he would not have such an appreciative audience as he had enjoyed in Helena. By the standards of Montana Territory, Helena was an old town, having been founded just after the end of the War of Secession. Great Falls, by contrast, was so new the unpainted lumber of the storefronts and houses hardly looked weathered.

More to the point, though, Helena was a mining town, a town built up from nothing by the laborers who worked their claims—and who, most of them, worked luckier men's claims these days—in the surrounding hills. Great Falls, by contrast, was a foundation of capital, a town that had sprung to life when the railroad out to the Pacific went through. If it hadn't been for fear of the British up in Canada, the railroad would probably still remain unbuilt. But it was here, and so were the people it had brought. Storekeepers and merchants and brokers predominated: the bourgeoisie, not the proletariat.

Lincoln sighed. In Helena, he'd got exactly the response he'd wanted. He'd told the miners some home truths about the way the country treated them. Without more than a handful of Negroes to exploit, it battened off the sweat of the poor and the ignorant and the newly arrived and the unlucky. Capitalists didn't want their victims to know that.

Capitalists had reasons for not wanting their victims to know that, too. After he'd told the miners some things of which their bosses would have preferred them to remain ignorant, they'd torn up Helena pretty well. He smiled at the thought of it. He hadn't touched off that kind of donnybrook in years.

He'd won the supreme accolade from one of the local capitalists, a tough, white-bearded fellow named Thomas Cruse: "If I ever set eyes on you again, you son of a bitch," Cruse had growled, "I'll blow your stinking brains out."

"Thank you, sir," Lincoln had answered, which only served to make Cruse madder. Lincoln wasn't about to lose sleep over that. From what he'd heard, Cruse had once been a miner, one of the handful lucky enough to strike it rich. Having made his pile, he'd promptly forgotten his class origins, in much the same way as an Irish washerwoman who'd married well would come back from a European tour spelling her name Brigitte, not Brigid.

Another sigh came from his lips. No, no sparks tonight, not from these comfortable, well-dressed people. A couple of Army officers sat in the second row, no doubt to listen for any seditious utterances he might make. One of them looked preposterously young to be wearing a cavalry colonel's uniform. Lincoln wondered what sort of strings the fellow had pulled to get his command, and why he'd tied a red bandanna around his left upper arm.

Rather nervously, a local labor organizer (not that there was much local labor to organize) named Lancaster Stubbins introduced Lincoln to the crowd: "Friends, let's give a warm Montana welcome to the man who makes it hot for capital, the fiery champion of the working man, the former president of the United States, Mr. Abraham Lincoln!"

Despite Stubbins' images of heat, the most enthusiastic word Lincoln could in justice apply to the round of applause he got was *tepid*. That did not surprise him. Here in Great Falls, he would have been surprised had it proved otherwise. When he took his place behind the podium, he stood exposed to the crowd from the middle of his belly up. That didn't surprise him, either; almost every podium behind which he'd ever stood—and he'd stood behind a great forest of them—had been made for a smaller race of men.

He sipped at the glass of water thoughtfully placed there, then began: "My friends, they ran me out of Helena because they said

I made a riot there. As God is my witness, I tell you I made no riot there."

No applause came from the crowd. Shouts of "Liar!" rang out. So did other shouts: "We have the telegraph!" and "We know what happened!"

Lincoln held up a hand. "I made no riot there," he repeated. "That riot made itself." More outcry rose from the audience. The young colonel in the second row wearing a red bandanna seemed ready to bounce out of his chair, if not out of his uniform. Lincoln waited for quiet. When he finally got something close to it, he went on, "Do you think, my friends, the honest laborers who heard me in Helena would have turned the town on its ear had they been happy with their lot? I did not make them unhappy with it. How could I have done so, having only just arrived? All I did was remind them of what they *had*, and what in law and justice they were *entitled to*, and invite them to compare the one to the other. If that should be inciting to riot, then Adams and Franklin and Washington and Jefferson deserved the hangings they did not get."

Sudden silence slammed down. He had hoped for as much. The people still remembered freedom, no matter how the plutocrats tried to make them forget. Heartened, Lincoln continued, "So many in Helena, like so many elsewhere in the United States—so many even here, in Great Falls—labor so that a few who are *rich* can become *richer*. Ignorant old man that I am, I have a moderately hard time seeing the fairness there.

"A capitalist will tell you that *his* wealth benefits everyone. Maybe he is even telling you the truth, although my experience is that these capitalists generally act harmoniously and in concert, to fleece the people. Or do you not think his wealth would benefit *you* more, were some part of it in *your* pocket rather than his?"

That got a laugh—not a large one, but a laugh. "Tell 'em, Abe!" somebody called. Somebody else hissed.

Lincoln held up his hand again. Quiet, this time, came quicker. He said, "Even before the War of Secession, I made my views on the matter clear. As I would not be a slave, so I would not be a master. Democracy has no place for slaves *or* masters. To whatever extent it makes such a place, it is no longer democracy. A man with silk drawers, a gold stickpin, and a diamond on his pinky may disagree. What of the miner in his tattered overalls or the shopkeeper in his apron? Does not the capitalist trample them down, by his own rising up?

"And does he not sow the seeds of his own destruction in the trampling? For when, through this means, he has succeeded in dehumanizing the laboring proletariat by whose sweat he eats soft bread, when he has again and again put the working man down and made him as nearly one with the beasts of the field as he can, when he has placed him where any ray of hope is extinguished and his soul sits in darkness like the souls of the damned . . . When the capitalist has done all this, does he not fear, while he sips his champagne, that the demon he has made *will one day turn and rend him*?"

That was the sentence upon which his speech in Helena had ended. He had not intended it to end there. He had planned to go on for some time. But the ragged miners there construed his words literally, and acted on what he had taken for (or part of him had taken for) a mere figure of speech.

Here in Great Falls, he got no riot. He did get an audience perhaps more attentive than it had planned on being. When he saw men leaning forward to hear him better, he knew he'd succeeded. "My friends, the defense of our nation lies not in our strength of arms, though I wish our arms every success in this war upon which we are engaged. Our reliance is in the *love of liberty* which God has planted in us. If we let it perish, we grow the seeds of tyranny on our own soil. If we suffer our laborers to wear the chains of wage slavery, we look forward to the day when the nation is enchained.

"To our north, in Canada, we find a people with a different government from ours, being ruled by a Queen. Turning south to the Confederate States, we see a people who, while they boast of being free, continue to hold their fellow men in bondage. At present, we are at war with both these peoples, not least because we do not wish to permit their unfree power to be extended. It is altogether fitting and proper that we should struggle, if struggle we must, for such a cause.

"Yet will we fight for the cause of freedom *abroad*, while allowing the same cause to perish *at home*? We all declare for liberty; but in using the same *word* we do not all mean the same *thing*. With some, the word means for each man to do as he pleases with himself, and with the product of his labor. With others, the same word means for some men to do as they please with other men, and the product of other men's labor. The fullness of time, I am convinced, will prove to the world which is the true definition of the word, and my earnest hope remains that the United States of America shall yet lead the way in the proving."

In Great Falls, he got applause, warmer than when he was introduced. In Helena, that passage might have touched off the riot had the previous one not done it. In a way, he appreciated the polite hearing. In another way, he would sooner have been booed off the platform. People who listened politely and forgot an hour later what they'd heard were no great asset to the cause of liberty.

"We *shall* have change in this country, my friends," he said. "I leave you tonight with this thought to take to your homes: if we cannot find a *peaceable* way to bring about this change, we shall find *another* way, as our forefathers did in 1776. We have now, as we had then, the revolutionary right to overthrow a government become a tyranny to benefit only to the rich. I pray we shall have no need to exercise this right. But it is there, and, if the need be there as well, we *shall* take it up, and the foundations of the nation *shall* tremble. Good night."

As he stepped down, he got about what he'd expected: cheers and catcalls mixed together. One fight started in the back of the hall. Instead of joining in, the men around the fighters pulled them apart and hustled them outside. Lincoln smiled, ever so slightly: no, it hadn't been like that in Helena.

Lancaster Stubbins came up to Lincoln and shook his hand. "That was very fine, sir, very fine indeed," he said. "You'll stay the night with my family and me?"

"I should be honored," Lincoln said. Stubbins was earnest and sincere, and, when and if the new revolution came, would undoubtedly be swept away. Still— "It will prove a better bed, I am sure, than the one I enjoyed—though that is scarcely the proper word—in Fort Douglas."

Getting to the promised bed would take a while. Some people came forward to congratulate him. Some people came forward to argue with him. Half an hour after the speech was done, he was still alternately shaking hands and arguing. That brash young cavalry colonel stuck a finger in his chest and growled, "You, sir, are a Marxian Socialist."

His tone was anything but approving. Lincoln found himself surprised; men who so emphatically disagreed with his positions seldom came so close to identifying their true nature. "That is near the mark—near, but not quite on it, Colonel . . . ?" he said.

"Roosevelt," the cavalry officer answered impatiently. "Theodore Roosevelt." He scowled up at Lincoln through his gold-framed spectacles. "How do you mean, sir, not quite on the mark? In what way am I in error?" The challenge in his voice declared that, like George Custer, he saw disagreement as affront.

Still, Lincoln judged the question seriously meant, and so answered seriously: "A Marxian Socialist, Colonel Roosevelt, believes the revolution *will* come, no matter what measures be taken to prevent it. My view is, the revolution will come *unless* strong measures be taken to prevent it."

"Ah." Roosevelt gave a slow, thoughtful nod. "That is a distinction." Unlike Custer, he evidently could feel the intellectual force of a counterargument. That index finger stabbed out again. "But you do believe the pernicious Marxian doctrine of the class struggle."

"I do believe it, yes," Lincoln said. "I do not believe it pernicious, not after spending my time since the War of Secession observing what has been afoot in the United States, in the Confederate States, and, as best I can at a distance, in Britain and Europe as well."

"Class struggle is balderdash! Poppycock!" Roosevelt declared. "We can attain a harmonious society by adjusting our laws and their interpretation so as to secure to all members of the community social and industrial justice."

"We *can*, surely. I said as much," Lincoln replied. "But *shall* we? Or will those in whose hands most capital now rests seek only to gain more? That looks to be the way the wind is blowing, and it blows a fire ahead of it."

Roosevelt surprised him again, this time by nodding. "The worst revolutionaries today are those reactionaries who do not see and will not admit that there is any need for change."

"You had best be careful, Colonel Roosevelt, or people will be calling *you* a Marxian Socialist," Lincoln said.

"By no means, sir. By no means," the brash young officer said. "You believe the damage to our body politic is . . . I shall give you the benefit of the doubt and say, *all but irreparable*. My view, on the contrary, is that the political system of the United States remains perfectible, and that resolute action on the part of the citizens as voters and the government as their agent can secure the blessings of both liberty and prosperity for capital and labor alike."

"I have heard many men with your views, but few who express them so forcefully," Lincoln said. "Most, if you will forgive me, have their heads in the clouds."

"Not I, by jingo!" Theodore Roosevelt said.

"I wish I could believe you likely to be correct," Lincoln carried out. "For reform to be carried out in the manner you describe, though, a man of truly titanic energy would have to lead the way, and I see none such on the horizon. I do see workers by the millions growing hungrier and more desperate day by day. Now if you will excuse me, Colonel, this other gentleman wished to speak with me."

Roosevelt turned away. Lincoln heard him mutter "Poppycock!" under his breath once more. Then the former president, being greeted by a supporter, forgot about the young cavalry colonel.

Frederick Douglass wished he could go home to Rochester. In fact, nothing save his own pride and stubbornness kept him from going home to Rochester. If he went home, he would be admitting defeat: not only to those who read his despatches from the Louisville front in their newspapers, but also, and more important, to himself.

As he got out of a carriage Captain Richardson had furnished him and headed for the newly built wharves several miles east of Louisville, he knew defeat was there whether he admitted it or not. Captain Richardson kept right on being obliging, still, Douglass was convinced, in the hope that he could get him killed. With each new time Douglass crossed the Ohio into Kentucky, the total chance of his getting killed grew more likely, and he knew it. He kept crossing anyhow, every time he could.

The United States now held two tracts on the southern side of the river, one inside battered Louisville itself, the other projecting toward it from the east. The shape of that second salient, sadly, was deceiving; the front had not advanced more than a couple of furlongs in the past several days. Hope that the flanking maneuver would drive the Confederates from Louisville had all but died. With it had also died a great many young men in U.S. blue.

Confederate artillery pounded away at the U.S. positions east of Louisville. This salient was bigger than the one in the city, and had pushed the Rebels out of range of the Indiana side of the Ohio. The amount of ground gained, however, was not the be-all and end-all of the campaign. The *be-all* had not come to be, and the *end-all* was not in sight.

Another barge was loading. Barges were always loading, sending in more soldiers to do what they could against the Rebels' entrenchments and rifles and cannon. Some soldiers came back on barges, too, shrieking in anguish. Some stayed in Kentucky and fought and did not go forward. Some stayed in Kentucky and died and were hastily buried. Some stayed in Kentucky and died and were not buried at all.

Sometimes Douglass had trouble persuading the soldiers he had the right to cross. This time, though, he met no difficulties. Even before he drew from a pocket Captain Richardson's letter authorizing him to go into Kentucky, one of the men tending to the barge's engine waved and said, "Got a letter from my cousin, sayin' she really likes the way you're writin' about the war."

"That's very kind of her," the Negro journalist said as he stepped aboard the barge. Had he been white, he thought the soldier would have called him *Mr. Douglass.* Few white men could bring themselves to call a Negro *Mister.* Making an issue of an act of omission, though, was much harder than doing so about an act of commission. Douglass kept quiet, consoling himself with the thought that he might have been wrong.

Once the one white man had accepted him as an equal, or something close to an equal, the rest did the same. He'd seen that before, too. People all too often put him in mind of sheep. Had that fellow mocked him and called him a nigger, the others packing the barge likely would have followed that lead as readily as the other.

U.S. guns on the Kentucky shore not far from the riverbank belched smoke and flames as they tried to put their Confederate counterparts out of action. Near the guns lay wounded soldiers who would go back to Indiana aboard the barge once it had unloaded the men it carried. Some cried out, some groaned, and some lay limp, too far gone in suffering to complain. Along with the soldiers headed toward the battle line, he averted his eyes from the bloodstained evidence of what war could do.

He did not accompany the fresh troops to whatever position they had been assigned. Instead, he made his way toward the men of the Sixth New York. They had come closer than any other U.S. troops to breaking the Confederate line and smashing into Louisville as General Willcox had envisioned. Only a desperate countercharge by a Rebel regiment—led by a lieutenant, some said, though Douglass didn't believe it—had knocked them back on their heels and let C.S. forces bring in more troops and solidify their position.

Several Confederate shells came screaming down within a couple of hundred yards of him. He took no notice. Back before the battle began, they would have sent him diving, panicked, for the closest hole he could find. He was astonished at how blasé he'd grown about shellfire.

On toward the line of battle he tramped, not at any great speed but as steadily as if powered by steam. That comparison made him smile. He puffed less now on such hikes than he had when he'd first made them; his wind was better than it had been for years. He'd always been blessed with a robust constitution, which served him in good stead today.

He'd gone up to the Sixth New York's position so often by now, some of the troops behind the line had grown used to his presence. One made as if to set his watch by Douglass. "How are you this morning, Uncle?" another called. The Negro answered that with a nod and nothing more; as usual, *Uncle* straddled the line between polite and insulting.

Another U.S. soldier whistled and waved and said, "Good morning to you, Fred."

"And to you, Corporal," Douglass answered, this time feeling his face stretch into a broad, almost involuntary grin. A white man who called him *Fred* might be short on formality, but was also short on prejudice. Douglass reckoned that a fair exchange.

He was drawing near the front line, up into the area where entrenchments seamed Kentucky's smooth fields as scars from the lash seamed his own back, when an officious provost marshal whom he hadn't seen before challenged him: "Who the devil are you, and what business have you got here?"

"Don't you recognize Jefferson Davis when you see him?" Douglass demanded. The joke fell flat; like most provost marshals, this one had no sense of humor. Douglass produced the letter from Captain Oliver Richardson. The soldier read it, moving his lips. At last, reluctantly, he returned it to the journalist and stood aside.

Up in the trenches, the men of the Sixth New York hailed him as an old friend. "You're a crazy old coot, you know that?" one of them said by way of greeting. "We've got to be here, and you don't, but you keep comin' anyhow."

"He reckons we'll keep him safe, Aaron, that's what it is," another soldier said. "Looky! He ain't even carrying his six-shooter no more."

"As you say, I am among heroes." Douglass smiled at the blue-coat, who, along with his companions, hooted and jeered. Many of them *were* heroes, but they bore that heroism lightly, as if mentioning it embarrassed them. Douglass had stopped wearing a revolver once the line stabilized, no longer seeing much likelihood he would need it for self-defense. Instead of a Colt, he pulled out a notebook. "And what has gone on here since my latest visit?"

"Snaked a raid over into the Rebs' trenches yesterday afternoon, we did," Aaron said proudly. "Killed two or three, brought back a couple dozen prisoners, only had one feller hurt our ownselves."

"Well done!" Douglass said, and scribbled notes. Inside, though, he winced. This was what the bold if tardy flank assault had come down to: little raids and counterraids that might move the front a few yards one way or the other but meant nothing about when or if the Army of the Ohio would ever drive the Confederates out of Louisville.

Douglass listened to the volunteers as they talked excitedly about the raid. They were caught up by it; because they'd done well in a tiny piece of the war, they thought the whole of it was going well. Douglass had not the heart to disillusion them, even had they chosen to listen to him in turn. He pressed on up to the foremost trench, knowing he would find Major Algernon van Nuys there.

Sure enough, van Nuys squatted by a tiny fire, eating hardtack and waiting for his coffee to boil. "Ah, Mr. Douglass, you come back again," the regimental commander said. His knees clicked as he straightened up. "You must be a glutton for punishment. Here, you can prove it: have a hardtack with me." He offered Douglass one of the thick, pale crackers.

"Why do you hate me so?" Douglass asked, which made Major van Nuys laugh. Accepting the hardtack, Douglass took a cautious bite. When fresh, the crackers weren't bad. By the way this one resisted his teeth, it might have been in a warehouse since the War of Secession. After he'd managed to swallow, he said, "Do I rightly hear that you poked the Rebels yesterday?"

"A poke is about what it was, a little poke," van Nuys said with a sour smile: he knew too well this wasn't what Orlando Willcox had intended for the flanking move. "Today, tomorrow, the next day, the Rebs'll try to poke us back, I expect. We might as well be playing tag with 'em."

"No, thank you," Douglass said, and the colonel chuckled again. Van Nuys stooped to see how the coffee was doing, and, as if to confirm his words, Confederate artillery opened up on the Sixth New York. Now Douglass did throw himself flat; these shells came crashing down far closer than a couple of hundred yards away. Fragments scythed through the air above his head, hissing like serpents.

Through the din of the shelling, the roar of rifle fire also picked up. "To the firing steps!" Major van Nuys shouted. "Here they come! Let's give it to 'em, the sons of bitches."

A moment later, he cried out wordlessly and reeled back into the trench. The cry was necessarily wordless, for a bullet had shattered his lower jaw, tearing away his chin and leaving the rest a red ruin. He gobbled something unintelligible at Douglass. Maybe it was *I told you so*, but it could have been *Tell my wife I love her* or anything else. Then his eyes rolled up in his head and, mercifully, he swooned, his blood pouring out onto the floor of the trench. Douglass wondered if he would ever wake again. With that wound, eternal sleep might be a mercy.

High and shrill, Rebel yells rang out from the stretch of ground between C.S. and U.S. trench lines. "Reinforcements!" Douglass shouted. "We need reinforcements here!" But no reinforcements came. Cleverly, the Confederates were using the artillery bombardment to form a box around the sides and rear of the length of entrenchments they had chosen to attack. Anyone who tried to get through that bombardment was far likelier to get hit.

A U.S. soldier a few feet away from Douglass fired his Springfield. One of the Rebel yells turned into a scream of a different sort. But as the bluecoat was slipping another cartridge into the breech, a Confederate bullet caught him in the side of the head. Unlike Algernon van Nuys, he never knew what hit him. He slumped to the ground, dead before he touched it. The rifle fell from his hands, almost in front of Frederick Douglass.

He grabbed for it, wishing it were a carbine, whose shorter barrel would have made it easier for him to reverse it and blow out his own brains. But all his resolve about not being taken alive came to nothing, for a Confederate in dirty butternut leaping down into the trench landed on his back. Pain stabbed through him—a broken rib? He didn't know.

He didn't have time to think, either. "Come on, nigger!" the Reb screamed. "Up! Out! Move! You're caught or you're a dead man!" No matter what his head thought, Douglass' body wanted to live. However much it hurt, he scrambled out of the trench and, after getting jabbed in a ham by the Confederate's bayonet, stumbled toward the C.S. lines.

A Rebel captain was shouting, "Come on, you prisoners! Move! Move fast!" When he saw the journalist captured with eight or ten U.S. soldiers, his eyes widened. "Good God," he said. "It can't be, but it is. Frederick Douglass, as I live and breathe."

"The nigger rabble-rouser?" Three Confederates asked it at once. "Him?"

"Him—the same." The captain had no doubt whatever.

The soldier who'd captured Douglass jabbed him again, harder. "Let's string the bastard up!" His friends bayed approval.

☆ XIII ☆

As the Louisville campaign ground on, Colonel Alfred von Schlieffen found himself with ever freer access to Orlando Willcox and to the map-filled tent where the commander of the Army of the Ohio planned his operations. He found himself less and less happy each time he visited the U.S. general. It was too much like having ever freer access to a sickroom where the patient grew visibly more infirm as day followed day.

Brigadier General Willcox seemed uneasily aware of the wasting sickness afflicting his campaign, aware but doing his best to pretend he wasn't. "Good afternoon, Colonel," he said when he spied Schlieffen through the partly open tent fly. "Come in, come in. Ah, I see you have coffee. Very good."

"Yes, General, I have coffee. Thank you." Carrying the tin cup stamped *USA*, Schlieffen ducked his way into the tent and came over to stand beside Willcox. "The guns in the night were not noisier than usual. Have I right—no, *am* I right; this mistake I make too often—nothing new happened?"

"Nothing new," Willcox agreed with a small sigh. He stared down at the maps, at the blue lines and the red that had moved so much less than he'd hoped. "It's always good to see you here, Colonel. I want you to know that."

"You are too kind to a man who is not of your country," Schlieffen said.

Without looking over at the German military attaché, General Willcox went on, "You always keep your temper. You never judge me. My corps commanders, my division commanders— sometimes this tent gets like a kettle full of live lobsters over the fire. But I never hear recriminations from you, Colonel, and, if you send telegrams to Philadelphia, you don't send them to General Rosecrans."

Schlieffen hadn't heard the word *recriminations* before, but he didn't bother asking Willcox to explain it; context made the meaning plain. An army that was winning had little backbiting. When things went wrong, everyone was at pains to prove the misfortune could not possibly have been his fault.

Willcox said, "Tell me what you think of our position at the present time."

"Let me examine the map before I answer." Schlieffen seized without hesitation the chance to think before he spoke. He wished he had Kurd von Schlözer's diplomatic talents, so he might come somewhere near the truth without destroying the U.S. commander's good opinion of him. At last, he said, "I think it now unlikely that you will from the east into Louisville break."

Willcox sighed again. "I'm afraid I think the same thing, although, if I admit it to anyone but you, I'll see my head go on a platter faster than John the Baptist's after Herodias' daughter danced before King Herod. We came close; I'll wager we scared old Stonewall out of a year's growth. But in war, the only thing that does any good if it's close to where it ought to be but not quite there is an artillery shell."

That was an effective image; Schlieffen filed it away to use if and when he had the luck to return to General Staff duty in Berlin. He said, "In the salient you made with the flanking move, you still have most of your men on the line facing Louisville, and in other places not so many."

"Well, yes, of course I do," General Willcox replied. "I have orders that I am still to do everything I can to capture the city, and I must obey them."

"If you think you can do this, then naturally you . . . are right," Schlieffen said, pleased he'd remembered the English idiom this time. "If you think you cannot do this, and you leave your flank as weak as it is—"

"The Rebs looked to have a weak flank," Willcox said. "It got strong a lot faster than we wished it would have, and that's the Lord's truth. If the Confederates could stop us, I reckon we'll be able to stop them."

"This may well be so, but your situation here seems to me not to be the same as that of the Confederate States," Schlieffen said.

"And why not?" Willcox bristled at what was to Schlieffen a gentle suggestion of something so obvious a schoolchild should see it.

Patiently, the attaché spelled it out in words almost literally of one syllable: "The Confederate States had more depth to use than you have now. They could halt you for a little while, fall back, halt you again, and so on. This is not something you enjoy. If they break through your trenches from the south, they will go into the rear of the main body of your forces there."

"Ah, I see what you're saying." General Willcox was mollified. Nonetheless, he brushed aside Schlieffen's concern. "We do have men enough and guns enough to make them pay a high price if they try that. Myself, I don't think they'll do it. All their attacks up till now have been aimed at the line closest to Louisville." Someone came into the tent. Willcox nodded a greeting. "What is it, Captain Richardson?"

After saluting Willcox and politely inclining his head to Schlieffen, the adjutant answered, "Sir, we just got a report that the Rebels have raided the stretch of trench the Sixth New York was holding."

After a glance at the map, Willcox turned triumphantly to Schlieffen. "There? Do you see? They persist in striking us where we are strongest." He spun back toward Oliver Richardson. "A raid, you say? They didn't break through, did they?"

"Oh, no, sir," Richardson assured him. "I'm sorry to say Major van Nuys was killed in the attack, but they seemed to be trolling for prisoners more than anything else—and, I daresay, paying back the Sixth for a raid yesterday. They captured a few men, then withdrew to their own entrenchments."

"Why even bring this to my notice, then?" Willcox asked. He took a longer look at the young captain. "And why, after a raid in which a colonel was killed, have you that smirk on your face?"

Schlieffen wondered if Richardson had an enemy in the Sixth New York, of whose demise in the raid he had heard. The adjutant had sounded properly regretful when reporting Major van Nuys' death, so Schlieffen doubted he was the man, if any man there were. He would not have wanted an officer who gloated at a comrade's death on his staff. By the building anger on Willcox's round face, the commander of the Army of the Ohio felt the same way.

And then Captain Richardson said, "Sir, you must know that Frederick Douglass has made the Sixth New York his pet regiment, and also the horse on which he mounts all his complaints about the manner in which you have conducted this campaign.

He was with them today; I gave him a letter authorizing a river crossing this morning. And I have reports, sir, that he was among those whom the Confederates captured in this raid."

"Ah," Schlieffen said: a short, involuntary exclamation. His opinion of Captain Richardson recovered to some small degree. Disliking a reporter to the point of enjoying his misfortune was a lesser matter than similarly disliking a fellow officer. And Richardson had made no secret of his distaste for Douglass, though Schlieffen could not understand what, aside from being a Negro, Douglass had done to deserve it.

"Good God!" Willcox exclaimed, taking a point that had eluded the German. "Douglass has been a thorn in the slave-holders' side since long before the War of Secession. What will the Confederates do to the poor man, if he has been so unfortunate as to fall into their hands?"

"I don't know, sir, but my bet would be that they don't do anything good." Yes, Richardson sounded delighted at Douglass' discomfiture. English lacked the word *Schadenfreude*, but not the idea behind it. Men being the sinful creatures they were, no nation, Schlieffen was sure, lacked that idea.

He said, "But is he not protected from mistreatment as a civilian citizen of the United States?"

"The Confederate States seldom feel obliged to recognize any black man's rights of any sort," Willcox said.

"You ask me, sir, they've got the right idea, too," Richardson said. "If it hadn't been for the niggers, Abe Lincoln never would have been elected president, and we never would have fought the War of Secession in the first place. Never would have lost it, either."

"How does the second statement follow from the first?" Schlieffen asked. The only answer Richardson gave him was a dirty look. That made him realize he'd been less than diplomatic. He wasn't so upset as he might have been. Failures in logic distressed him; he rejected unclear thinking as automatically as he breathed.

"Most disturbing," Orlando Willcox said. "Most disturbing indeed. I shall pray for Douglass' safety and eventual liberation, however unlikely I fear that may prove."

"I'll pray, too," Richardson said. "I'll pray, *May God have mercy on his soul*." He laughed a nasty laugh.

"That will be quite enough of that, Captain," Willcox said, as sharply as Alfred von Schlieffen had ever heard him speak. The German military attaché frowned, not understanding why Richardson's prayer was offensive. Seeing as much, General Willcox explained: "Colonel, that's what the judge in an American court says after he sentences a prisoner to death."

"*Ach, so,*" Schlieffen murmured. Truly praying for God to have mercy was one thing, a prayer any Christian ought to be glad to make or to have made for him. Praying for a man to be condemned to death was something else again; Willcox had been right to rebuke his adjutant.

Richardson came to attention, saluted, did a smart about-turn, and left the tent with precisely machined steps. That was exactly what a German officer, similarly rebuked yet still feeling himself to be correct, would have done. The only difference Schlieffen could see was that the Americans did not include a heel-click as part of coming to attention.

Willcox drew in a deep breath, held it, and let it out in a long sigh. "He's an able young man, Colonel," he said, as if Schlieffen had denied it. "He's just—unreasonable on the whole Negro question."

"Many in the United States are, is this not so?" Schlieffen said. "It is true almost as much in the United States as in the Confederate States, yes?"

"Mm, not so bad as that, I'd say," Willcox replied. "On the other hand, one man in three in the CSA is a Negro, near enough, and we have only a relative handful of colored people in the USA, so white men here have less to get exercised about. A lot of folks do wish, though, we had no Negroes among us: I can't deny that."

"This is foolishness," Schlieffen said, never for a moment thinking of the Polish peasants his ancestors had subjugated to help make Prussia the power that would reshape the German *Reich.*

"I think so myself." Willcox spread his hands, palms up. "Not everyone agrees with me, though. And you'd be hard pressed to say my adjutant is wrong in one regard: absent the Negro, I believe the United States would still remain one nation today."

"I understand this reason for resenting Negroes," Schlieffen said. "But if Negroes were not resented before your War of Secession for other reasons, there would have been no war, is this not true? And these other reasons I must say I do not understand."

"It's a hard business, that it is," General Willcox said, which most likely meant he didn't understand it, either. As if to confirm that, he changed the subject: "I fear Captain Richardson is right in thinking it will be a hard business for Frederick Douglass, too."

"If he is mistreated, will the United States avenge themselves by mistreating Confederate prisoners in their hands?" Schlieffen asked. "This is, excuse me for saying it, an ugly way to make war."

"So it is—or so it would be, at any rate," Willcox answered. "As for what will happen, Colonel Schlieffen, I just don't know, and have no way to guess. Right now, I'd say it lies in the hands of God—and of the Confederate States."

General Thomas Jackson looked as dour as usual while studying the situation map of his two-front battle in and east of Louisville, but his heart sang within him. "I truly do believe we have nothing more to fear from the Army of the Ohio," he said.

"I think you're right, sir," E. Porter Alexander agreed with a boyish grin. "Been a hard fight—they *are* brave, even if their officers could be better—but I don't really see how they can surprise us now."

"That's why they fight wars, General Alexander: to discover how the other fellow can surprise you." When Jackson essayed a joke, he was in good humor indeed. More seriously, he went on, "In my view, however, you are correct. I do not think they can break free of their present lines, and the cost of containing them within those lines appears acceptable. That being said, will you take some supper with me?"

"I'd be delighted, sir, so long as you let me put mustard on my meat," Alexander said, grinning still.

"Such sauces are unhealthy," Jackson insisted. His artillery chef looked eloquently unconvinced. Jackson yielded, as he would not have on the battlefield. "Have it your way, General. You see, I refuse you nothing." Laughing, the two men started out of the tent.

Had Alexander not teased Jackson, they would have been gone when the messenger came rushing in. Instead, he almost ran into them—he almost ran over them, as a matter of fact. "General Jackson, sir!" he gasped. "They've captured—you'll never guess who they've captured, sir! He's on his way here now, not that far behind me."

He was so excited, he didn't notice he'd failed to give Jackson the name. "*Who* is on his way here now?" the Confederate general-in-chief inquired. "By the way you sound, young man, it might be General Willcox himself."

"Even better'n that, sir," the messenger answered, chortling with glee. "They just captured Frederick Douglass his own self."

"You don't mean it!" E. Porter Alexander exclaimed. That was foolishness: the messenger obviously did mean it. Alexander turned to look at Jackson. Jackson was already looking at Alexander. The same thought had to be uppermost in both their minds. Alexander spat it out first: "We couldn't get a hotter potato right out of the fire, sir. What in blazes do we do with him?"

"I don't know." Jackson briefly felt all at sea. This was not the sort of decision he was supposed to have to make. As soon as that thought crossed his mind, he knew what needed doing. Stepping back into the tent, he walked over to the telegraphers' table. "I am going to wire President Longstreet, requesting instructions. This is more a political than a military matter, and beyond my sphere of competence." He dictated a brief telegram, then turned back to the messenger. "You said Douglass is being brought here?"

"Yes, sir," the man answered.

"I had better stay and await him, then. General Alexander, you may go and eat your mustard without me."

"Sir, by your leave, I wouldn't miss this for the world," Alexander said. "It's almost like having the Antichrist walk into the tent, isn't it?"

"I had not thought of it in those terms, but you are not far wrong," Jackson agreed. He nodded to an orderly. "Bring back supper for two, Corporal—no, for three: Douglass will be hungry, too, no doubt. And bring back as well a pot of mustard for General Alexander, since he will have it."

After that, there was nothing to do but wait. The orderly returned with three full plates, a mustard pot, and three cups of coffee. Jackson and Alexander were still wondering whether to begin on their own meals when the tent flap opened and Frederick Douglass walked in ahead of a couple of grinning young soldiers with bayoneted Tredegars. "I thank you for delivering your present, lads," Jackson told them. "I believe we shall be able to protect ourselves from him henceforward. Go on back to your regiment now." Saluting, they obeyed.

Frederick Douglass was staring at him. The Negro—mulatto,

actually, by his looks—was a fine figure of a man, despite dishevelment and obvious dismay. "You are Stonewall Jackson," he said, his voice deep and rich, his accent that of an educated man of the United States, with only the slightest hint of something else, something softer, underneath.

"I am," Jackson admitted. He pointed to the food the orderly had just brought. "Will you join General Alexander here and me for supper?"

To his surprise, Douglass burst out laughing. "I beg your pardon, General," he said, checking himself after a moment, "but, seeing you, I feel rather as if I have been ushered into the presence of the Antichrist. In that presence, the last thing I expected was a supper invitation."

Jackson said, "You may be interested to know that, not fifteen minutes before your arrival, General Alexander compared your coming to that of the Antichrist."

"To the unrighteous, the righteous no doubt seem wicked," Douglass replied.

"You are not the least bold of men, to say such a thing here," Jackson observed, more approvingly than otherwise.

E. Porter Alexander caught something he had missed: "Who here is righteous, who the reverse, and how do you go about proving it?" He held up a hand. "Since we could argue about that through the night, what say we don't, but eat supper instead?"

"I find myself unable to oppose such logic, especially when I but recently thought a noose my certain fate," Douglass said. Jackson contented himself with a single short, sharp nod.

A couple of minutes later, General Alexander said, "Do you see, sir? Douglass is among the righteous after all—for he eats mustard."

"His digestion would be better if he abstained," said Jackson, who, as usual, used only salt on his meat. Frederick Douglass looked from one of them to the other, unsure how serious they were. Jackson willed his face to reveal nothing. Only when his artillery chief smiled did the captured Negro agitator relax.

After all three men had finished, Douglass asked the question no doubt uppermost in his mind since he'd entered the tent—no doubt uppermost in his mind since he was taken prisoner: "What do you intend to do with me, General?"

"Hold you here until I have received instructions from President Longstreet," Jackson answered, "then follow them, whatever they may be." He cocked his head to one side, raised his arm in the air, and asked in turn, "What would you have us do with you?"

"What would *I* have you do?" Douglass said. "Why, release me, of course. I am a U.S. citizen, and a civilian member of the Fourth Estate."

"You are, I have heard, an escaped slave," Jackson remarked.

Douglass scowled. "I *am* an escaped slave," he said proudly, "but I escaped from Maryland, which is and has always been one of the United States, not a Confederate state, so your cruel laws pertaining to such conduct are without application to my case. Further, on payment of the sum of one hundred dollars, my former master formally manumitted me in December of the year 1846, proof of which I can readily provide if allowed to communicate in any way with my friends. I am, sir, a free man, both in my heart and in point of law."

"You are the cause of more runaways and the wellspring of more plots against the white men of the Confederate States than any other half dozen people I could name," E. Porter Alexander said.

"Thank you," Douglass replied, which nonplussed the artillerist. Douglass added, "You are telling me I have not lived my life as a free man in vain."

"Why should we not condemn you for attempting to create a servile insurrection of the sort John Brown tried raising?" Jackson asked.

"I advised Brown against that, brave patriot though I thought him—and still think him," Douglass said with a defiant toss of his head. "As for why you should not, I told you: I do not fall, and have never fallen, under your jurisdiction. I have broken none of *my* nation's laws. If you declare me *persona non grata* and deport me, you would be within your rights. Condemn me? No, not if you wish to adhere to the law of nations."

Jackson leaned forward, relishing the argument. "But uprisen slaves have committed many outrages in the Confederate States, some of them citing you as the author of their discontent. In war, shall I shoot the simple-minded soldier who goes over the hill as a deserter, while taking no notice of the wily civilian who induces him to desert? Your case strikes me as similar."

"How can it?" Douglass raised his impressive eyebrows. "Do you not aim to keep your Negroes in such abysmal ignorance that they are not allowed to learn to read and write, lest the written word lead them to the desire for freedom? How then could your servile populace come to know my words, since assuredly I have never given an address within Confederate territory?"

"We instruct them in the things that matter," Jackson said. "Why, I myself began and taught a Sunday school for the Negroes in and around Lexington, Virginia, before the War of Secession. They are, in my view, perhaps not the Regulars of the church, but they assuredly make up the militia."

Douglass started to say something, then stopped. He resumed after an evident pause for thought: "I have come to see, over the years, that few men are entirely of a piece. I did not know you had done such a thing, General; it shall redound to your credit on the day when our Father judges you. How can you, though, justify the manifold evils of slavery while preaching the Gospel that sets all men free?"

"As you must know, the Good Book sanctions slavery," Jackson replied. "If Providence sanctions it, who am I to speak in opposition? I do believe Negro slaves to be children of God no less than myself, and deserving of good treatment."

"You might be wiser, from a master's point of view, if you did not," Douglass observed. "A slave who has a bad master wants a good master. A slave who has a good master wants to be free."

"Are you not betraying slaves' secrets to tell us this?" Porter Alexander asked.

Douglass shook his leonine head. "A bad master does not become a good one at the pull of a lever. Nor does a good one easily go bad; that can and does happen, as I know to my pain, but slowly, over years."

One of the telegraph keys in the tent began to chatter. Everyone whirled to stare at it. When it fell silent, the telegrapher carried the transcription of the wire over to Jackson. Douglass' eyes followed the man's every step. Jackson read the telegram, then smiled a crooked smile. "Anticlimax, I fear," he said. "General Alexander, some of the new shipment of horses that will haul your guns has arrived."

"I'm relieved to hear it." The artillery commander glanced over at Frederick Douglass. "Rather more so than our . . . guest, I daresay."

"I am not your guest, unless I misunderstand and am in fact

free to come and go as I please," Douglass snapped. "I am your prisoner."

"Yes, you are a prisoner." Jackson minced few words, and appreciated candor in others. "Whether you will remain a prisoner, and upon what terms—these matters await President Longstreet's decision."

Porter Alexander raised an eyebrow. "I stand corrected. *Our distinguished prisoner,* I should have said, or perhaps *our notorious prisoner.* No, *distinguished* will do, for were you not distinguished, Douglass, were you, say, an ordinary white Yankee, it is moderately unlikely that you should have taken supper with the general-in-chief of the Confederate States."

A beat slower than he might have, Jackson caught the irony there. It won a smile from Frederick Douglass, too, a sour smile. "I note, General Alexander, that however distinguished I may be in your eyes and those of General Jackson, I am not distinguished enough for either of you to preface my name with *Mister.*"

Jackson blinked. "It never occurred to me to do so," he said. "To the best of my recollection, I have never called a Negro *Mister* in my entire life."

"That in itself speaks unhappy volumes on the history of my race in what are now the Confederate States," Douglass said bitterly, "and, I note, in the United States as well."

Another telegraph apparatus began to click. "This is the reply from the president, sir," said the soldier at the chair in front of it. Like every telegrapher, he enjoyed the privilege of learning the content of the message before it reached the man to whom it was addressed.

When the clicking stopped, he brought the wire to Jackson, who donned his reading glasses and skimmed through it. Longstreet made his instructions unmistakably clear. Jackson turned to Douglass. "By order of the president of the Confederate States, you are to be turned over to U.S. military authorities under flag of truce as soon as that may be arranged. You are to be freely given to those U.S. authorities; no exchange of any Confederate prisoner now in U.S. hands is to be required or requested. Until such time as you are turned over to the U.S. authorities, you are to be treated with every consideration. Is that satisfactory . . ." He hesitated, but the president had said *every consideration,* and he was not a man to disobey orders. He began again: "Is that satisfactory, Mr. Douglass?"

The Negro's eyes widened; he recognized what Jackson had done. Ever so slightly, he inclined his head to the Confederate general-in-chief. "It is more generous than I had dared hope. As soon as my identity was known to my captors, I thought a rope hoisted over a tree branch my likeliest fate, an apprehension of which they did little to disabuse me. I know your opinion of me here."

"Not far removed from your opinion of us," General Alexander remarked.

"Perhaps." Douglass shoved that aside with one word. His features took on a look of intense concentration. "President Longstreet is a clever politician. He realizes, where many in his position would not, that harming me would in the end also harm the reputation of your country even more, and refrains from taking the brief pleasure that hanging me would bring." His shoulders hunched and slumped as he sighed.

"President Longstreet *is* a clever politician," Jackson agreed. He eyed Douglass. "And you, sir"—*every consideration*— "unless I find myself badly mistaken, are at the moment somewhat dismayed that you shall not make your cause a martyr after all."

"I cannot contest the charge," Douglass said. "And yet I should also be lying were I to claim that I am not glad to go on living, and, even more so, to be restored to liberty. Having lived without it more than twenty years, I know how dear it is."

"At dawn tomorrow, I shall send an officer under flag of truce to arrange for your return to the United States," Jackson said. "I delay only because a flag of truce may not be recognized at night, and I would not willingly expose a man to danger thus."

"I understand." Douglass turned his dark, clever eyes on Jackson. "Tell me, General, what would you have done with me absent President Longstreet's instructions?"

"Since I did not know what to do with you, I asked for those instructions," Jackson answered. It was an evasion, and he knew as much. To his relief, Frederick Douglass did not press him on it.

Cananea baked in the Mexican sun. No sooner had that thought crossed Jeb Stuart's mind than he rejected it. Sonora now being part of the CSA, Cananea baked in the Confederate sun. The Stars and Bars hung limp from a flagpole in the middle of town. The tents of the Confederate army and its Apache allies vastly outnumbered the squalid adobe houses that made up the miserable little place.

Water mirages danced and shimmered on the desert. Stuart knew they weren't real. They were amazingly convincing, though. Someone thirsty who hadn't seen them before would surely have chased them till he perished or realized that, like wills-o'-the-wisp, they endlessly receded before him and were not worth pursuing.

Major Horatio Sellers walked up beside Stuart. "Good morning, sir."

"Hmm? Oh, good morning, Major," Stuart answered, a little sheepishly. "I'm sorry. I was looking at the mirages and not thinking about very much of anything. If you hadn't come along, the buzzards probably would have picked me up and carried me off in an hour or two."

"Really, sir?" Sellers looked surprised. "I would have guessed you were thinking about your son."

"Captain Stuart, do you mean?" The commander of the Department of the Trans-Mississippi smiled. "If he's not the youngest captain in the history of the Confederate Army, I'll be everlastingly surprised. What I should be is jealous. I wasn't even at West Point at his age, let alone winning battlefield promotions."

"War will give a push to things that would have happened more slowly without it," his aide-de-camp said. Sellers suddenly looked as if he'd bitten down on a lemon. Without seeing any more than that, Stuart understood what it meant.

Sure enough, Geronimo and Chappo silently came up to stand beside the two Confederate soldiers. Their soft moccasins were far better suited to quiet movement than the boots Stuart and Sellers wore. As always, Geronimo greeted Stuart as an equal. That bothered the general less than the impression he got that Geronimo was stretching a point to do so.

Through Chappo, the medicine man said, "Is it true your son is now a warrior? I have heard this from my men who have some English."

"It is true," Stuart agreed gravely. "Your son, Chappo here, fought well against the Yankees in New Mexico Territory. My son, who is Chappo's age and has the same name I do, fought well against the Yankees in a land called Kentucky, far from here."

"For boys to become men is good," Geronimo said. "Your son, I hear, did something very brave, something very fine. What is it?"

"The Yankees were attacking," Stuart answered, "and all the officers of higher rank in his regiment were killed or wounded." That was oversimplifying, but the Indian wouldn't know the difference, and explaining it struck Stuart as more trouble than it was worth. "He took charge of the regiment and fought back against the Yankees and stopped their attack."

After that was translated, Geronimo and Chappo went back and forth for a couple of minutes, as if the old man was making sure he understood correctly. Then he said, "But your son, with only Chappo's years—how did the other soldiers, the men who were soldiers for a long time, how did they obey him? They were already men, and he a boy in his first fight, not so?"

"Yes," Stuart said. "But he had higher rank"—again, oversimplifying—"and so they had to obey."

"Foolish to make men who have been in many fights obey a boy in his first. He might lead them wrongly," Geronimo said. Under normal circumstances, he would have had a point. Circumstances where Jeb Jr. was hadn't been normal. And, realizing he might have been tactless, the Indian added, "But this is your son, and he did well in the fight, you say. This is good. A father is always glad when his son grows up well." He set a hand on Chappo's shoulder, to show that he too had a son of whom he was proud.

They would have gone on, but the *alcalde* of Cananea came up and waited for Stuart to notice him. *Señor* Salazar was a round-bellied little man who wore a dirty red sash of office over a black jacket, ruffled shirt, and tight trousers that had all seen better days. "Yes, sir? What is it?" Stuart asked him, respecting the dignity of his office.

Salazar, fortunately, spoke fair English; the U.S. border lay only a few miles to the north. "Can I talk wit' you, General, by yourself?" His black eyes flicked to Geronimo and Chappo. The Apaches, Stuart had discovered, frightened the whey out of him and out of everybody in Cananea. The farmers had scarcely dared work their parched, meager fields since Maximilian's National Guards withdrew in the wake of the Confederate occupation.

Geronimo sent *Señor* Salazar the sort of look a coyote gave a pork chop, which did nothing for the *alcalde*'s composure. Stuart had mercy on the petty official. "Well, yes, *señor,* I suppose so." He stepped a few paces away from the two Indians. Salazar followed with obvious relief.

Geronimo and Chappo both frowned, though their unhappy expressions did not make Stuart start to turn to jelly, as they did with Salazar. The Confederate officer understood why the Apaches were unhappy. The *alcalde* made Major Horatio Sellers seem as if he were on the Indians' side. Salazar not only feared the Apaches, he hated them with a Latin passion beside which Sellers' feeling toward them hardly rated more than the name of mild distaste. He would have slaughtered them all if he could. He only hated them the more because he couldn't.

To forestall him, Stuart said, "I do hope you will remember, the Apaches are our allies."

"Oh, *sí*, General Stuart, I remember this." Salazar's eyes flashed. He might remember, but he didn't like it for hell. He needed a deliberate effort of will to set aside his anger. Stuart watched him make it. Like ocean waves with oil poured over them, his face smoothed. "I don't want to talk about no Apaches."

"That's good," Stuart said equably. "What do you want to talk about, then?"

"We have a ball tonight," Salazar said, "to commence when the sun go down. We have dancing and music and good food and *mescal*. You do us the honor to come? You and so many officers from your country—officers from this country now, I should say—you want to bring?"

If Cananea boasted good food, Stuart had yet to see it. The locals mostly ate *atole*, a cornmeal gruel that reminded him of library paste. Sometimes they enlivened it with chilies that would have made a man sweat at the North Pole, let alone in the middle of the Sonoran desert. As for *mescal*, it gave the vilest North Carolina moonshine a run for its money. Major Sellers swore the Mexicans distilled the stuff from kerosene, but that oath came the morning after a night of copious indulgence.

As much as anything else, curiosity impelled Stuart to say, "Thank you very much, *Señor* Salazar. My men and I will be there." Wickedly, he added, "Does your generous invitation also extend to the leaders of the Indians?"

"Maybe we do that," Salazar said, but he made no effort to hide his scorn for the Apaches. "We do it before. We get them plenty drunk, get them *loco* with *mescal*, then kill all we can. We do it three, four times, every few years. Stupid Apaches come every time. They like to drink plenty *mescal*."

"And you wonder why the ones you don't kill want to kill

you?" Stuart said. The *alcalde*'s answering shrug was as old as time. Whether Mexicans had first wronged Apaches or Apaches Mexicans no longer mattered much. Each side had been going after the other for so long, the CSA would need lots of years or lots of troops or more likely both to bring firm order here.

"You will come, and not the Indians?" *Señor* Salazar persisted.

"We will come, and not the Indians," Stuart agreed. Salazar bowed stiffly from the waist and departed.

As soon as he was gone, Geronimo and Chappo hurried up to Stuart. "What did he want?" Geronimo demanded. Stuart could hear the hard suspicion underlying the Apache words even before Chappo translated. "That man is a rattlesnake in stupid Mexican clothes. He would murder every one of us if he had the way and the courage to do it."

That being obviously true, Stuart ignored it. "What he said had nothing to do with you," he answered, which wasn't true but would keep the lid on the kettle. "He invited me and some of my officers to a ball in town tonight."

"Ah," Geronimo said when that was translated. He knew what a ball was, and what accompanied it. *"Mescal."* Longing filled his voice. He ran his tongue over his lips. Stuart hadn't altogether believed *Señor* Salazar's claim that the Apaches would frequently come into town for ardent spirits and lay themselves open to massacre. The warriors he'd seen in action had appeared too level-headed for that. Now, he decided the *alcalde* had been telling nothing but the truth.

The explanation did satisfy the old medicine man and his son. To Stuart's relief, they didn't seek to invite themselves to the ball. The commander of the Trans-Mississippi had no trouble finding enthusiastic celebrants among his officers. Those who held a high opinion of *señoritas* were eager to dance and drink with them; those who held a low opinion were even more eager.

At the appointed hour, Stuart led his contingent of officers into Cananea's central square. An orchestra of two drums, two fiddles, and an accordion greeted them with a squeaky rendition of what, about three-quarters of the way through the piece, Stuart recognized as "Dixie." It was, in its way, a compliment. So was the roast pork, basted in a red, no doubt fiery, sauce.

And so was the tumbler of *mescal Señor* Salazar pressed into Stuart's hand. The *alcalde* was armed with a similar tumbler. He raised it. "To the Confederate States of America!" he said in English and Spanish. He gulped down half his tumbler.

Stuart had to follow suit. He felt as if a shell had exploded in his stomach. His eyes crossed. His ears rang. Dimly, he realized he had to offer a return toast. He wondered if he could still talk. Duty required him to make the effort. "To Sonora and to Cananea!" he croaked, and everyone within six inches of him could hear his voice. He tried it again, and succeeded in making himself understood the second time. The Cananeans burst into applause. Stuart drank the rest of the tumbler. That he didn't fall over proved he was made of stern stuff.

"Your glass is empty," Salazar said sympathetically. He filled it from an earthenware jug. Stuart stared, glassy-eyed. The *mescal* didn't seem to bother the *alcalde*.

Food helped. The sauce on the pork was as spicy as it smelled. It started a fire of its own in Stuart's belly, and seemed to counteract the fire from the firewater. He ate bread, too, hoping it would help absorb some of the second tumbler of *mescal*.

Disappointingly few *señoritas* were in evidence. The band thumped out something that might have been a dance tune or an improvisation. Whatever it was, people started dancing to it. About seven out of eight were men. Nobody cared much. After more *mescal* flowed, nobody cared at all.

In the middle of a quadrille with the colonel of the Fifth Confederate Cavalry, Stuart said, "If a horse danced the way you do, they'd shoot it."

"If a *camel* danced the way you do, they'd shoot it," retorted Colonel Calhoun Ruggles, who, when it came to camels, knew whereof he spoke. Being considerably elevated by *mescal*, he needed a moment to remember proper military courtesy. "Sir."

After a while, Stuart decided to take a blow. While he leaned against an adobe wall and watched his officers and the Cananeans cavorting, *Señor* Salazar tapped him on the shoulder. The *alcalde* swayed where he stood; by now, whatever his capacity, he'd illuminated himself even more generously than the Confederates. But he spoke with great earnestness: "Do you know, General, those *Indios* will take your guns and take your bullets and go up into the Sierra Madre"—he pointed west, then, correcting himself, east—"and they be *bandidos* there. They go up there, they be *bandidos* forever."

"They can be *bandidos* against the United States," Stuart said. "They won't be *bandidos* against your people any more."

"Maybe you are right. *¿Quién sabe?*" The *alcalde* smiled a sweet, sad, drunk smile. "But if you are right, then the *Estados Unidos*"—his English was slipping—"will get *Indios* to be *bandidos* against us. It will be the same in the end. For us, it is *siempre* the same in the end."

How many years of disasters—and how many tumblers of *mescal*—went into that resignation? Stuart shook his head, which was beginning to throb. "It won't be the same any more. You're in the Confederate States of America now. You're going places, and you'd better believe it."

The only place the *alcalde* was going was to sleep. His eyes closed. He sagged against the wall and slumped to the ground. Jeb Stuart laughed. Five minutes later, he joined *Señor* Salazar.

"Well, Colonel," Henry Welton said, "I trust your stay in Fort Benton, and also in Great Falls, has been a pleasant one."

"Yes, sir. Thank you very much," Theodore Roosevelt answered. "Pleasant in ways I couldn't have anticipated when you ordered me down from my regimental headquarters, as a matter of fact."

Colonel Welton grinned a sly grin. "When I ordered you down, you thought you were coming for nothing but work."

"That's true, sir," Roosevelt said, "but it's not precisely what I meant. The usual pleasures of Fort Benton—and even of Great Falls—are easily named: saloons, dance halls, bathtubs with hot water." A couple of other pleasures were easily named, too, but he declined to name them.

"Hot water, yes." Henry Welton nodded. "You do miss it in the field."

But Roosevelt hadn't finished. "As I say, sir, those are the usual pleasures, the commonplace pleasures. Hearing Abe Lincoln speak, though: that I had not looked for, and I expect I'll remember it all my days."

"After he finished, you and he were going at it hammer and tongs there for a while," Henry Welton said. "You made him stop and be thoughtful once or twice, too." He chuckled. "You make everybody you meet stop and be thoughtful, seems to me. Twenty-two—you ought to be illegal."

"Twenty-three soon, sir," Roosevelt said with a grin, which

made Welton grimace and mime pathetic decrepitude. Roosevelt went on, "Plainly, Lincoln has a faction that *will* heed him in all he says. As plainly, there is a large faction that *will not* heed him in anything he says." He laughed. "He has me speaking like him, even yet—he is a demon on the stump. But both those factions I mentioned have their homes in the Republican Party. It could split on account of him."

"It could split if we lose this war, too," Welton replied, which was plain common sense. "Of course, if we lose this war, not enough men will admit to being Republicans for it to matter much whether the party splits or not."

"These things do matter, sir—they always matter," Roosevelt said seriously. "Look what happened when the Democrats, like Gaul, were divided *in partes tres* in 1860. Had that not happened, the United States might well be the only nation lying between Canada and the Empire of Mexico."

"Maybe you're right. I'm just a soldier, and soldiers are better off not meddling in politics," Welton said. "If we hadn't already learned that lesson, the War of Secession would have driven it home like a schoolmaster with a hickory switch." He slapped Roosevelt on the back. "Here come the stablehands with your horse, Colonel. Have a safe trip back to the Unauthorized Regiment, and I hope to see you again before too long."

"Likewise, whether here or in the field," Roosevelt said. "And, thanks to your generous permission, I will be sending A Troop here for rest and recreation as soon as I can draft the orders."

"That will be fine," Colonel Welton said. "I do very much approve of an officer who looks out for the well-being of his men."

Roosevelt mounted and rode out of Fort Benton, pausing in the gateway to wave back at Welton. His mount, which had done next to nothing since he'd come down to Fort Benton, felt lively, almost electric, under him. He had to hold the animal under tight rein to keep its trot from exploding into a gallop.

"Easy, old fellow, easy," he said, patting the horse on the neck. "We've got a long road ahead. If you go too fast now, you'll wear yourself down to a nub long before we get there."

The horse didn't want to listen to him. It wanted to run. Roosevelt laughed as the fort disappeared behind a swell of prairie. He was the same way. When anyone told him to slow down, he generally went faster. And not a man in the world had the right to rein him in.

He checked himself. That wasn't quite true. Military discipline did for him what reins did for the horse. Without it, he would have charged into Canada by now. But the cases weren't identical. He'd submitted to military discipline of his own free will. The horse didn't have a choice.

Jackrabbits bounded over the plains, sensibly taking no chances on whether he might try to shoot them if they stayed around to watch him ride by. He didn't need to bother with jackrabbits, not today, not with fresh-baked bread and several chunks of fried chicken in his saddlebag. If he spied a herd of pronghorns on his way north, though . . .

He saw some antelope off in the distance, but too far off for him to bother chasing them. Welton had sent a courier up to the headquarters of the Unauthorized Regiment, letting Lieutenant Jobst and the rest of the men know he would be spending some time at Fort Benton. He couldn't help feeling he'd been away too long. One thing he emphatically did not want was for his regiment to discover it could get along just as well without him.

Walk, canter, trot. Walk, canter, trot. Mile after mile of prairie unrolled behind him. More miles lay ahead. The horse was still willing, but no longer eager. Roosevelt rode north by the sun and by his compass; not nearly enough horsemen had traveled back and forth between Fort Benton and his headquarters to wear even the beginnings of a trail into the grass. Walk, canter, trot.

Every hour or so, he gave his mount a few minutes' rest and let it snatch at clumps of grass. The grass was still green. It wouldn't stay green forever, nor even much longer. Winter came early to Montana Territory, just as it left late. Blaine had rejected the Confederates' peace offer: well and good. Despite that, though, Roosevelt still hadn't been able to do any fighting. If the damned British didn't get moving, or if his own orders didn't change, he wouldn't be able to start till spring.

When he came to the Marias River, he stowed the compass in his saddlebag. He wouldn't need it any more. He rode northwest along the southern bank of the river till he came to a ford. With the water so low in summer, that didn't take long. His boots stayed dry while his horse splashed across. No steamboat had ever made it up the Marias. "And I know steamboats," he told the horse, "that can pour a barrel of beer into a dry riverbed and make fifty miles on the suds."

The horse snorted. He couldn't tell whether it was derision or appreciation.

He rode up the northern fork of the Marias, which was the Willow. "Almost there now," he told the horse as the sun sank toward the Rockies. The horse didn't answer, not this time. It had worked hard all day. He patted its neck. "Come on—not much farther."

He strayed away from the riverbank after dark, and almost rode past the camp. The night was mild—milder than the past few had been—and the men had let the fires die back to embers. He spied their red glow off to his left only a moment before a challenge came out of the night: "Halt! Who goes there?"

"Hello, Johnny," he answered, recognizing the sentry's voice. "It's Colonel Roosevelt, back from Fort Benton."

"Advance and be recognized, Colonel," Johnny Unger said, playing the game by the rules. His voice held a grin, though. As Roosevelt rode slowly forward, he whistled to the next nearest sentry and called, "Hey, Sean—the Old Man's come back from town."

"Bully!" Sean said. Neither of their voices would have disturbed the men sleeping back at regimental headquarters.

A booted foot crunched a twig. Johnny Unger materialized, one moment invisible, the next standing right beside Roosevelt. "Yes, sir, it's you, all right," he said, and chuckled. "Go on in. Did you do the trip in one day, or stretch it out over two?"

"Started this morning," Roosevelt answered. "Never waste time, Johnny. It's the one thing in the whole wide world you can't get back."

"Yes, sir," the sentry said. "If you've been riding that horse all day, I was just thinking, he'll need more seeing to than if you'd done it the easy way."

"I'll tend to him, never fear," Roosevelt said. He asked for very few of the privileges to which his rank might have entitled him. When the sentry vanished once more, Roosevelt rode the beast into camp.

He poked and fed one of the fires up to brighter life so he could see what he was doing as he brushed down the horse and checked its hooves. One of them had a pebble caught in the horseshoe. He dug it out with a curved steel pick. The beast couldn't have had it long, or it would have started favoring that leg.

Roosevelt tried to be as quiet as he could, but a couple of men sat up in their bedrolls to see what was going on. "Good to have you back, Colonel," one of them said softly. Roosevelt waved and went back to work.

After an hour or so, the horse was settled. Roosevelt patted him one last time, then got out his blanket, wrapped himself up in it like a papoose, and fell asleep even while still wriggling around to get comfortable.

He woke with the sun shining in his face, the smell of coffee in the air, and First Lieutenant Karl Jobst standing only a couple of feet away. "Good morning, sir," Jobst said while Roosevelt stretched and yawned. "By what the courier had to say, you found yourself a livelier time than you looked for when you went down to Fort Benton."

"That's nothing but the truth," Roosevelt said. "I rode down to Great Falls with Colonel Welton, as you'll have heard, to listen to Abe Lincoln. Very fine speaker—no two ways about that—but he spouts nonsense, nothing but Socialistic nonsense. Let him rave, I say. If he keeps at it, he'll split the Republican Party right down the middle, or I'm a Dutchman."

"Uh, sir . . . you are a Dutchman," Jobst pointed out. Of German blood himself, he got called a Dutchman a lot, but Roosevelt was the genuine article.

"Proves my point, doesn't it?" Roosevelt said gleefully as he got to his feet. Over coffee and hardtack and antelope, he asked, "Anything new on patrol that's worth hearing?"

"No, sir," his adjutant answered. "All routine. No, I take that back. Somebody in D Troop got bitten by a rattlesnake, but it's not a bad bite, and they're pretty sure he'll pull through."

"I'm glad to hear it—not that he got bitten, but that we won't lose him. The rattlesnakes north of the border are quiet, though?" When Jobst nodded, Roosevelt went on, "In that case . . ." He set out the scheme for leave Colonel Welton had accepted.

Karl Jobst blinked. Plainly, such an idea would never have occurred to him. Once he heard it, he liked it. "What a clever notion, sir. You're right—I'm sure it will have a tonic effect on the men's spirits."

"I'll draft the necessary orders," Roosevelt said. Jobst looked slightly miffed; a lot of regimental commanders would have let him do the job. Everything Roosevelt could do himself, he did do himself. Inside of an hour, one courier was on his way to A Troop, announcing a week's leave for its men, and another to B Troop, ordering it to stretch out to cover the ground A Troop would be clearing.

Half an hour after that, another courier rode into regimental headquarters at a pounding gallop: Roosevelt's farmhand, Esau Hunt, who was serving in B Troop. "Boss!" he shouted, and then, remembering himself, "Colonel Roosevelt, sir! The limeys are over the border, sir. Whole great big column of 'em crossed yesterday. We took a few shots at 'em, but they got a hell of a lot more men than we do."

Theodore Roosevelt stared, briefly speechless. "All leaves canceled," he murmured. Half a moment later, he was bellowing for couriers at the top of his lungs, some to concentrate his regiment and set it in motion against the British, another to ride down to Fort Benton and bring the rest of the Army the news. That done, he threw back his head and laughed out loud. "God delivered the Midianites into Gideon's hands, and He has delivered the British into mine." He raised his voice to a great shout: "For the Lord, and for Gideon!"

Colonel George Custer had a splendid view of the hanging of the Mormon traitors in front of Fort Douglas, but could not watch it so closely as he should have liked. He was too busy keeping an eye on the crowd that pressed up against the restraining rope a couple of hundred yards from the gallows.

"Be ready, men," he called to his Gatling-gun crews. "If anyone crosses that barrier, we are to open fire without warning and without mercy. The scoops know as much. They had better— we've warned them often enough."

The Mormons were splendidly law-abiding—except when their church elders led them astray. If John Taylor, who remained at large, wanted martyrs in large numbers, he would have them. The believers were likelier to heed his admonitions than those of the hated U.S. Army.

"We'll get 'em, sir," Sergeant Buckley said, and the other gunners nodded.

They were not alone out there. Riflemen stood between the Gatlings, and several cannon shotted with canister bore on the crowd. Custer wished the Gatlings weren't there at all. Their absence would have let him pay more attention to the Mormons' getting what they deserved. But General Pope had assigned him the miserable gadgets, and so he had to make the best of it.

Softly, his brother Tom said, "Here they come, Autie."

And indeed, out through the gate, guarded and led by more soldiers with Springfields, came George Q. Cannon, Orson Pratt, a Mormon apostle named Daniel Wells, Cannon's brother (whose Christian name—if Mormons' first names deserved that description—Custer had never bothered to learn) and two other leaders of the Latter-Day Saints. Their hands were bound behind them. John Pope followed in dress uniform.

None of the Mormons hesitated in mounting the thirteen steps to the multiple gallows; their steps were firm and sure. Each leader took his place at a noose, beside which stood a hangman in a black hood—Pope, sensibly, did not want the grimly silent crowd to be able to recognize the executioners.

Each hangman offered his Mormon a hood without eyeholes. Wells, Cannon's brother, and one of the men whose names Custer had not noted accepted; Pratt, George Cannon, and the other stranger refused. The hangmen set the nooses around the Mormons' necks.

In a voice just loud enough for Custer to hear, Orson Pratt asked General Pope, "May I speak to my people one last time? I give you my sacred oath the words shall be of reconciliation, not of strife."

Custer turned his head and watched Pope mull. He would have said no. But Pope answered, "Speak, then. Be brief, though, and remember that your people shall answer if you betray them into madness."

"I remember, and I thank you," Pratt said, quietly still. The salt-smelling breeze ruffled his bushy white beard. He cried out to the throng who believed as he did: "My brethren, my friends, I leave you today for a better world to come, and give you these words from the second book of Nephi as my parting gift: 'O then, if I have seen so many great things, if the Lord in his condescension unto the children of men hath visited men in so much mercy, why should my heart leap and my soul linger in the valley of sorrow, and my flesh waste away, and my strength slacken, because of mine afflictions? And why should I yield to sin, because of my flesh? Yea, why should I give way to temptations, that the evil one have placed in my heart to destroy my peace and afflict my soul? Why am I angry because of mine enemy? Awake, my soul! No longer droop in sin. Rejoice, O my heart, and give place no more for the enemy of my soul. Do not anger again because of mine enemies.'" He bowed his hoary head.

"Amen!" George Cannon cried.

"Amen!" the other Mormon leaders echoed more quietly.

"Amen!" It rippled through the crowd, along with the sound of weeping.

"He kept his word," Tom Custer murmured, his voice more serious than was his wont. "That's not the worst prayer I ever heard, either."

"It is nothing but a mockery and an imitation of the Good Book." George Custer remained unmoved.

So did Brigadier General John Pope. "These men have been convicted of treason and insurrection against the United States of America," he declared in a shout that would have been huge had it not followed Orson Pratt's. "For their crimes, I, under the authority given me by President James G. Blaine, have sentenced them to death by hanging. President Blaine having reviewed and confirmed these sentences"—he raised his right hand high in the air—"let the punishment be carried out." The hand dropped.

So did the traps beneath the six condemned Mormons as the hangmen worked their levers. So did the Mormons' bodies. Custer heard neck bones snap; the men who'd tied the hangman's nooses had known their business. The bodies kicked and spasmed briefly, then were still.

No one surged forward out of the crowd. The sound of weeping grew louder. "Shame!" someone shouted. In an instant, men and women alike took up the call: "Shame! Shame! Shame!" It washed over the soldiers and their weapons and the military governor of Utah Territory and the gallows and the bodies dangling from it. For a quarter of an hour, the Mormons repeated their one-word answer to what they had just witnessed.

John Pope had grit. He walked out in front of his men, advancing on the rope barrier till he was within easy pistol range of the crowd that hated him. He raised his hand, as he had done to order the executioners to ready themselves. "Hear me!" he shouted. "People of Utah, hear me!" And the people did grant him something close to quiet. "Go home. All is over here. Live in peace, and obey the laws and authority of the United States of America. Go home."

Some of the Mormons kept on calling, "Shame!" More, though, began the walk back down to Salt Lake City. Little by little, the crowd melted away.

Tom Custer whistled softly. "We got by with it, Autie. I was a long way from sure we would."

"So was I." Custer didn't know whether to be relieved the Mormons had not erupted at the execution of their leaders or disappointed the U.S. Army had not had the chance to teach them precisely how much rebellion could cost.

By the expression on Pope's face, the military governor was contemplating the horns of the same dilemma. "Six traitors dead," he said, walking up to Custer. Apparently choosing to look on the bright side, he added, "God grant the rest learn their lesson."

"Yes, sir." Custer looked back toward the gallows. "They died well." He shrugged to show how little that mattered to him. "Redskins die well, too. In my view, the Mormons are about as fanatical as the Sioux and the Kiowa."

"And in mine as well." Pope took off his plumed hat and mopped his forehead with a linen handkerchief. "I took a chance with that rascal Pratt, and I know it. But I reckoned he couldn't make things much worse, and might make them better. And his fanaticism, I have seen, includes a fanatical truthfulness."

"It worked out well, sir." Custer was not about to criticize a superior to his face, especially not after that superior had scored a success. What he said to Libbie come evening was liable to be something else again. He thought of Katie Fitzgerald, of her mouth, of her breasts, of her coppery bush. Ever so slightly, he shook his head. No matter how much of a tigress Katie was between the sheets, he was glad his wife had come to Fort Douglas. He could unburden himself to her as to no one else on earth.

Pope pointed to the limp bodies swaying in the breeze. "We'll have to cut that carrion down and bury it. I don't fancy giving the bodies back to the Mormons so they can riot at a funeral where they didn't at the hanging."

"That's—very clever, sir," Custer said, and meant it. Worrying about the funeral would never have entered his mind. He turned to the eight Gatling-gun crews. "Men, you have helped keep order in Utah Territory. The United States are in your debt."

"Well said, Colonel," Pope agreed. "That goes for all of us

here. We have subdued this Territory, and we are reducing it to obedience. And we have done it with a minimum of bloodshed, and with no need to summon excessive forces away from the armies in the field against the Confederate States."

"I wish I were serving in an army in the field against the Confederate States," Custer said.

"So do I," Pope replied. "We also serve here, however. I remind myself of this daily. And, were I facing the Rebels, I should not have had the opportunity, after all these years, to pay Abe Lincoln back at least in part for the bitter lot he imposed upon me and rendered far more bitter by the fact that my sacrifice was made in vain. But I am in some measure avenged for my exile to Minnesota."

"I wish he'd tried to tread the air with the Mormons here today," Custer said. "From what I hear, he continues to spread trouble wherever he goes."

"You know we are also in complete agreement on that score," Pope said. "But, being soldiers, we can only obey the orders we receive from the duly constituted civil authorities." He cocked his head to one side. "It *is* a pity, isn't it?"

"Yes, sir, it is," Custer said. "I was General McClellan's man during the War of Secession, and you, of course, were anything but, yet all soldiers who served during that unhappy time cannot possibly have any other view of Honest Abe." He freighted the title with as much contempt as it would bear.

Pope set a hand on his shoulder. "Since coming to Utah, we have proved to be in harmony on more than that view alone, Colonel. You have carried out my wishes in a fashion with which I can not only find no fault, but which pleases me very highly indeed, and I have so stated in my reports at every opportunity."

"Thank you, sir!" Custer said joyfully.

When he told Libbie about it at supper that evening, she beamed, too. "That's splendid news, Autie," she said. "Of course you deserve it, but a man does not always get what he deserves." Her lip curled. "As you said, Lincoln is the chiefest example there."

"Yes." Custer cut a piece off his beefsteak and tossed it up in the air. Stonewall caught it before it touched the ground, gulped it down, and barked for more. "Later, boy," his master told him. Custer patted the dog's head. To his wife, he went on, "I always marvel at how you manage to move everything we have, beasts and all, without missing a beat."

"Your duty is to be a soldier, Autie. My duty is to keep an eye on you, and one way or another I do it." If Libbie's mouth narrowed a little, if her voice held the slightest edge, Custer, whose gaze was ever most focused on himself, failed to notice.

The cook came out of the kitchen. "Anything else, sir, ma'am?" she asked.

"No, thank you, Esmerelda," Libbie said before Custer could reply. Esmerelda nodded and withdrew.

In a low voice, Custer said, "She cooks well—no one could deny it—but that is one of the homeliest women I have ever set eyes upon, even in Salt Lake City."

"Really? I hadn't noticed," Libbie said. Custer chuckled at women's blindness about other women. If Libbie wasn't quite so blind as he thought she was, he failed to notice that, too, as he'd failed for a good many years.

He was pouring cream into his coffee when a soldier rushed up thumping in booted feet to the door to his quarters and pounded on it, shouting, "Colonel Custer! Colonel Custer! General Pope needs to see you right away, sir!"

Custer pushed back his chair and sprang to his feet. "I wonder what it can be," he said. Whatever it was, Stonewall wanted to come along and find out, too. "Down, sir. Down!" Custer commanded. The dog stared at him with resentful eyes as he dashed off, as if to say, *Why do you get to have all the fun?*

"Hurry, sir!" the orderly said when Custer opened the door.

"Hurry I shall." To prove it, Custer dashed past the soldier and beat him to Pope's office by half a dozen strides. He wasn't quite so young as he had been, but kept himself in top shape. Not breathing hard at all, he saluted and said, "Reporting as ordered, sir."

Pope held up several telegrams. "Colonel, within the last half hour, I have learned that British forces have invaded Montana Territory."

"Good God, sir!" As if lightning had struck close by, electricity arced up Custer's spine.

"I can only presume that their goal is to plunder and ravage the mining regions of that Territory, as the Confederates have done to such unfortunate effect in New Mexico," Pope said. "Whatever their purpose, though, we must and shall beat them back, punishing them as they deserve for thus testing our mettle."

"Yes, sir!" Custer said. "We'll lick them. We *must* lick them, and so we shall." And then, hardly daring to hope, he asked, "What can we here in Utah"—by which he meant, *What can I, myself, personally*—"do to lend a hand?"

And Pope replied, "As I told you earlier today, I have spoken highly of you in my reports back to Philadelphia. That praise has apparently borne fruit." He picked through the sheaf of telegrams for one in particular. "You and the Fifth Cavalry, and, specifically, the eight Gatling guns attached to your regiment are ordered to Great Falls, Montana, there to join in defending our beloved country. And you, Colonel, are ordered to take overall command of that defense, with the brevet rank of brigadier general." He stood up and shook his hand. "Congratulations, General Custer!"

In a pink-tinged daze, Custer shook the proffered hand. "Thank you very much, sir," he whispered. He'd dreamt of stars on his shoulder straps since the day he entered West Point. Now, at last, they were his. "I shall save our country, sir," he declared, while an interior voice added, *In spite of those Gatling guns.*

☆ **XIV** ☆

Sam Clemens walked into the office of the *San Francisco Morning Call*, hung his straw hat on a branch of the hat tree, and asked, "Well, boys, what's gone wrong since I went home last night?"

A chorus of voices answered him, so loud and vigorous that he had trouble sorting out one piece of bad news from the next. The British army in Montana Territory was still moving south. British gunboats on the Great Lakes were bombarding U.S. lakeside cities again, with apparent impunity. Louisville remained a bloody stalemate.

"President Blaine didn't think he had reason enough to give over the war before," Clemens observed. "Our enemies seem to be giving him reason now, don't they?"

"And Pocahontas, Arkansas, has fallen back into Rebel hands," Clay Herndon added.

"Good God!" Sam staggered, as if taking a mortal wound. "That proves the struggle truly hopeless. How, save by the grace of a thick skull, can Blaine keep from yielding to common sense?"

Edgar Leary delivered the topper: "The wires say British ironclads have appeared off Boston and New York, and they're bombarding the harbors and the towns."

"Good God," Clemens said, this time in earnest. "They are taking the switch to us. You'd think that, if we were going to get into a war with the whole world, we might have made some sort of an effort to be ready for it ahead of time. But the Democrats reckoned saying 'Yes, Massa' to the Rebs once a day and twice on Sundays would get us by without fighting, so they didn't fret much about the Army and Navy. And Blaine didn't fret about 'em, either; he just up and used 'em, ready or not. And now we know which."

From the back of the office, somebody shouted, "Holy Jesus! Telegraph says the French Navy is shelling Los Angeles harbor."

"That does it!" Sam cried. "That absolutely does it! The Confederates wrestle us to the ground, England jumps on us as soon as we're down, and now France bites us in the ankle. Can't you see her, yapping and panting? Pretty soon, she'll piss on our leg, you mark my word."

Off in the distance, thunder rolled.

Clay Herndon frowned. "It was clear when I got here half an hour ago. Don't usually get thunderstorms this time of year, anyhow. Hell, we don't usually get any rain at all this time of year."

"Fastest thunderstorm I ever heard of," Clemens said. "It was clear when I walked in five minutes ago."

"Look out the window," Leary said. "It's still clear."

Sam couldn't see the window. He opened the door. Bright daylight streamed in. Another rumbling roar sounded, though, this one not so far away. "That isn't thunder!" he exclaimed. "It's cannon fire."

"It can't be," Clay Herndon said. "It's not coming from the direction of the forts, and we'd have heard if Colonel Sherman were moving any guns. Most of those big ones don't move, anyhow."

"I didn't say they were our guns, Clay," Clemens answered quietly. "I think somebody's navy has just brought the war to San Francisco."

"That's cra—" Herndon began. Then he shook his head. It would have been crazy yesterday. It wasn't crazy today, not with the Royal Navy shelling Boston and New York harbors, not with the French—whose ships, Sam judged, had to be sallying from some port on the west coast of their puppet Mexican empire—bombarding Los Angeles.

And, as if to confirm Clemens' words, more thunderous reports rolled out of the west. But they were not thunder. A few seconds later came another blast, close enough to rattle the front window of the *Morning Call* offices, through which Edgar Leary was still staring as if expecting rain. A rending crash followed. "That's a building falling down," Herndon whispered.

"No." Clemens shook his head. "That's a building blowing up."

Now, at last, from the northwest came the thunderous reports that had grown familiar through the summer: the cannon in San rancisco's fortifications opened up, defending the harbor against he foe. "They'll never make it through the Golden Gate!" Leary xclaimed.

"I wonder if they even care to try." Sam was thinking out loud, nd not liking any of his own thoughts. "By the sound of their ;uns, they're standing off the coast—maybe out past the Cliff House—and shooting across the peninsula, either toward the wharves or just toward us. I wonder if they know which themselves, or care."

A shell landed only a couple of blocks away. The floor jerked under Sam's feet from the explosion, as if at a small, sharp earthquake. A moment later, he heard the rumble of collapsing masonry. He'd heard that during earthquakes, too, but not during small ones. Blast and rumble were so loud, he marveled at how faint and distant the following screams seemed.

But, where the roar of the cannons had not, those screams reminded him he was a newspaperman. "Jesus Christ, boys!" he burst out. "We're sitting in the middle of the biggest story that's happened in this town since 1849. We're not going to be able to cover it standing around here or hiding under our desks. Leary! Get over to Fort Point. See what the devil the garrison's doing to drive the enemy away. See if they're doing anything to drive the enemy away. See if they know who the devil the enemy is. That'd be a good bit of news to put in a story, don't you think?"

"Right, boss!" Edgar Leary pushed past him and out the door.

"Clay!" Sam snapped. "You go to the Cliff House, fast as you can. Whatever you can see of the enemy fleet, note it down."

"I'll do it," Herndon said. Then he hesitated. "What if they've already blown the Cliff House to hell and gone?"

Clemens' exasperated exhalation puffed out his mustache. "In that case, you chowderhead, don't go inside." Herndon nodded quite seriously, as if that hadn't occurred to him. Maybe it hadn't. More explosions were rocking the city now. How could you blame anybody for having a hard time thinking straight?

Clemens sent someone to the harbor, to see if enemy shells were falling there as well as on San Francisco itself, and also to see what, if anything, the Pacific Squadron was doing about the enemy. He scattered reporters through the city. Whatever happened, he—and the *Morning Call*—would know about it.

One of the last men out the door asked, "Are you going to stay here and put everything together, boss?"

"That's what I have in mind, yes," Sam answered. "Every one of you will know more about some of this business than I do, but I'll end up knowing more about all of this business than any of you."

"Unless a shell comes down on your head," the reporter said with a nervous chuckle.

"Some people who work for this paper, that would hurt the shell more than the head in question." Clemens fixed the reporter with a glare. "Shall I name names?"

"Oh, no, boss," the fellow said hastily, and departed. Not five seconds after he was out the door, another shell made the building shake. The front window broke in a tinkling shower of glass. Somewhere not too far away, a fire-alarm bell was clanging. Sam grimaced at that. How many gas lines was the bombardment breaking? How many fires had started? How bad would they get? How was the fire department supposed to put them out, with iron-clads shelling the men as they worked?

"Those are all good questions," Clemens muttered. "I wonder if any good answers will stick to them."

He stationed himself at his desk. Every time a shell smashed down west of the newspaper office, he scowled and chewed on his cigar. What were Alexandra and Orion and Ophelia doing? This was a nasty way to make war, throwing shells around in the hope of smashing up whatever they hit and not worrying much about what that was.

Most of an hour went by. The local telegraph clicker started to chatter. No one was minding it; Clemens had sent everybody out to cover the story. He got up to see what the message was. It was from Clay Herndon: ROYAL NAVY SHELLING CITY. CLIFF HOUSE WRECKED AND BURNING. AT NEAREST TELEGRAPH OFFICE TO OCEAN. DAMAGE SEVERE ALREADY. OUR GUNS OF LITTLE EFFECT.

That gave Sam something to write. He wrote it and gave it to the typesetters. Other reports began coming in, some by wire, some by messengers the reporters had paid, some by messengers who loudly demanded to be paid. Sam suspected some of those had already been paid once, but he shelled out. They hadn't had to come here, after all.

A picture began to emerge. The enemy ships did seem to be trying to reach the harbor with their guns, or at least with some of them. Most of the shells were falling short, though. "Thanks,"

Sam muttered sourly as the *Morning Call* building rattled again. "I never would have noticed that."

The Pacific Squadron was moving out to engage the foe. He suspected the handful of antiquated gunboats would be sorry in short order, but making the effort was their job. He wished Edgar Leary would send him something, but the cub remained silent. Maybe he'd been hit on the way to Fort Point. Maybe the telegraph lines were down. And maybe Colonel Sherman wasn't inclined to let any news out of the fort and into the city. Considering how little the fort's guns were doing to drive away the British ironclads, the last explanation struck Clemens as most likely.

Men with rifles started running down Market. Other men with rifles started running up Market. "Good to see the Volunteers have everything well in hand," Sam muttered. "Chickens act this way after the hatchet comes down, but chickens aren't in the habit of carrying Springfields." Somebody fired one of those rifles. *How many of our own shall we kill?* Clemens scribbled. *How many of them shall we blame on the British?*

The telegraph clicker started up again. He hurried over to it. The message was to the point: MARINES LANDING OCEAN BEACH. HERNDON.

Sam was still carrying his notebook and pen. He looked down at the two sentences he'd just written. They were still true. They were, if anything, truer than ever. With three quick, firm strokes, he scratched them out anyhow. "Who's wearing a hogleg?" he shouted, as loud as he could. "The Goddamned Englishmen are landing troops!"

"We'll nail the sons of bitches!" a typesetter yelled. He and two of the men who served the presses dashed out the front door, pistols in their hands. Clemens wondered if the British Marines knew what they were getting into. Apart from the Volunteer companies, a lot of men in San Francisco carried guns for self-protection—not least, for protection from other men carrying guns.

He wondered whether the Regular Army garrison up at Fort Point and the Presidio knew the ironclads out in the Pacific had landed Marines. Anyone with a lick of sense would have posted lookouts—with luck, lookouts with telegraph keys—all along the ocean front opposite the built-up part of San Francisco. "Which means the Army likely hasn't done it," he said. Then he shrugged.

"If they don't know about 'em, they'll find out pretty damn quick."

He went back to his desk and started writing up some of the reports he was getting. As soon as he finished one, he carried it back to the typesetters, who set about turning it into something someone besides him and them and perhaps Alexandra could read.

By the time he'd finished a couple, a great rattle of small-arms fire had broken out to the west. It rapidly got louder and closer. People might be shooting at the British Marines, but they were shooting back, too, and evidently to better effect.

Smoke started floating in through what had been the front window. Clemens coughed a couple of times, then called, "Boys, if you want to go out in the street, I won't say a word. This is a fine paper, but it's not worth burning up for."

Most of the printers and typesetters did leave the building. As long as some of them stuck, Sam did, too, figuring the men out there would warn him before advancing flames got too close. He covered page after page of paper, wondering all the while if what he wrote would meet a hotter critic than he'd ever been.

Clay Herndon burst into the offices without his jacket, with his cravat all askew, and with blood running down the side of his face. "My God, Sam!" he cried hoarsely. "They're coming this way! Nobody can stop them. They're coming!"

Clemens pulled a bottle of whiskey out of a desk drawer. "Here," he said. "Drink some of this." Herndon did, and then wheezed and choked. Sam said, "Wipe your face and tell me what happened to you."

Herndon ran a sleeve across his cheek and seemed astonished when it came away red. "Must have been when a bullet took out a window and sprayed me with glass," he said. "It's nothing. Listen, those Royal Marines make the Regulars look sick. Nobody can shift 'em, and they're not far behind me, either."

"What in tarnation are the limeys up to?" Clemens demanded. "I thought they'd do some shooting and burning for show, but if they're on your heels"—and the ever-swelling racket of gunfire made that obviously true—"they must be after something bigger. But what?"

"Damned if I know," the reporter said. "Whatever it is, who's going to stop 'em?"

"City Hall?" Sam mused. He shook his head. "No, too much to hope for—and if they shoot Mayor Sutro, the city gets stronger."

And then, almost with the force of divine relation, he knew, or thought he did: "My God! The U.S. Mint!"

"I don't know." Herndon took another slug of whiskey. "You can't imagine what it's like out there. All fire and smoke and chaos and people shooting and people running and people screaming and horses screaming and the only ones who have any notion of what they're doing or where they're going are the Marines."

"You sound like a man talking about the devils in hell," Clemens said.

"You aren't far wrong," Herndon said. "Listen, if they are after the Mint, it's not far from here—down on Mission, by Fifth." He swayed where he stood. Shock? Whiskey? Some of both? Probably the last, Sam guessed. The reporter gathered himself. "They'll be here soon. That's not good."

"Have to get the story," Sam said, and pushed outside past Herndon. People were still dashing every which way, some with weapons, some without. And then, almost without warning, they weren't running every which way. They were all running east, with rifle fire lashing them on. Every so often, someone with a rifle or pistol would pause to send back a shot or two. After that, he'd run some more.

Except one of them didn't run any more. Instead, he fell, clutching his chest. A moment later, a skinny little man in an unfamiliar uniform not far from Confederate butternut dashed up and bayoneted him to make sure he didn't get up again. Then he yanked the long, bloody bayonet free and aimed his rifle at Sam Clemens.

Time stretched endlessly. As if in a dream, Sam raised his hands to show he was unarmed. The Royal Marine's face was sweaty and smoke-stained. His scowl showed very bad teeth. He couldn't have stood more than fifty feet from Sam: point-blank range. After a hundred years in which Sam's heart beat once, the Englishman turned the rifle aside and ran on.

All the starch went out of Clemens' knees. Even though the Marine had not shot him, he sagged to the pavement. Now, instead of once in a hundred years, his heart thudded a thousand times a second. More and more Royal Marines dashed past him. None of them gave him a second glance; no one could have imagined him a danger at that moment.

More gunfire rang out, not far to the east: the Mint, sure enough. He remained too dazed to feel proud of being right.

Some of the British fighting men must have brought dynamite, for loud explosions smote the ear. "Move against them!" shouted a fellow in a captain's uniform: surely a volunteer. No one moved against them, no matter how he bellowed and carried on.

And then, quite suddenly, or so it seemed to Sam, the Royal Marines were running west where they had been running east. He went back into the *Morning Call* offices. "You know what this is?" he said to Clay Herndon. "It's the biggest goddamn bank holdup in the history of the world."

"How much silver and gold do you think however many British Marines there are could carry away?" Herndon asked in an awed voice.

"Don't know the answer to that one, but I'll tell you this: people are going to fight over the bodies of any who got killed the way lions fought over the Christians in the Colosseum," Sam said.

As the sounds of gunfire had once advanced through San Francisco, so now they retreated toward the Pacific. Half an hour after the Royal Marines departed from whatever was left of the U.S. Mint (by the smoke billowing up from it, not much), two natty companies of Regular Army infantry marched past the *Morning Call* offices in neat formation, sun gleaming from their fixed bayonets. Sam didn't know whether to laugh or cry. He took that bottle out of his desk and got drunk instead.

Brigadier General Orlando Willcox beamed at Frederick Douglass. "How good to have you restored to my table here once more," the commander of the Army of the Ohio said, raising his coffee cup in salute as if it were a goblet of wine. "A pleasure to see you returned to freedom, and a pleasure to enjoy your company again. Your very good health." He drank the unspirituous toast.

So did all the officers at his table, even Captain Richardson. "Thank you very much, General," Douglass said. "Believe me, I feel myself delivered, as were the Israelites from Pharaoh's bondage in the land of Egypt."

"You are a pious man, Mr. Douglass," Colonel Alfred von Schlieffen said. "This is in my judgment good. It will take you through hard times in your life more surely than will anything else."

Douglass eyed the German military attaché. What did he know of hard times? In his life, Prussia had gone from triumph to triumph, and now headed a German Empire that was surely the strongest power on the European continent. He had not seen his nation split in two, nor ninety percent of his own people, his own kind, trapped in bondage—*like the Israelites indeed,* Douglass thought.

But then he recalled having heard that Schlieffen had lost his wife in childbed. That was an anguish Douglass had never had to bear. He nodded judiciously. Schlieffen could know whereof he spoke.

"They brought you before Stonewall himself, didn't they?" someone asked. "What was that like?"

What *had* that been like? Stonewall was a name with which mothers in the United States, and especially Negro mothers in the United States, had been frightening naughty children for a generation. "When the Rebel soldiers took me into his tent, I told him I thought I had come before the Antichrist."

"As well you might," General Willcox said, and then, "Oh, thank you, Grady." The cook set on a table a large tray piled high with squab.

The succulently roasted birds went from tray to plates in next to nothing flat. Douglass snagged a couple for himself. Baked potatoes followed shortly. He went on, "The very strange thing was that Jackson's artillery commander—"

"General Alexander," Oliver Richardson put in.

"General Alexander, yes," Douglass agreed. "Shortly before my arrival there, *he* had likened *me* to the Antichrist."

Richardson nodded, as if he not only believed Alexander would say such a thing but agreed with it himself. Orlando Willcox asked, "And do you and the Confederate generals still hold this view of each other?"

Cutting up a potato and grinding pepper over it, Douglass paused before answering. Then, slowly, reluctantly, he said, "I, at any rate, do not. General Jackson is a man convinced of his rightness and of his righteousness, but not the horrific figure of evil I had made of him in my mind."

Captain Richardson looked mischievous. "You'll notice, friends, Douglass says nothing of whether the Rebs changed their minds about him." He spoke lightly, so the words would be taken for a joke, but Douglass did not think he was joking. By the snide laughs that rose around the table, neither did a good many members of Willcox's staff.

"In fact, I believe they did," Douglass answered. "We shall never love one another. We may now know a certain respect previously lacking." He laughed a laugh of his own. "I cannot deny that General Jackson treated me far more respectfully than the Rebel soldiers who first took hold of me." He chuckled again. That rib didn't seem to be broken after all. He didn't know why not.

Down at the far end of the table, someone said, "They didn't worry about the Antichrist, I'll bet. They likely thought they'd nabbed Old Scratch himself." That got another laugh, this time one in which Douglass felt he could join. That major down there wasn't far wrong.

Colonel Schlieffen changed the subject, saying, "These"—he groped for the English word—"these doves are very good eating. And we have them often, so they must common be. Very good." He sucked the meat off a leg bone.

"Not doves, Colonel." Oliver Richardson enjoyed showing off how much he knew, though this was something any American schoolboy could have told the German military attaché. "They're passenger pigeons, and yes, they are very common in this part of the country."

"Not so common as they used to be," General Willcox said. "When I was a lad in Michigan, the flocks would darken the sky, as the Persians' arrows are said to have done at Thermopylae against the Greeks. Swarms of that size are no longer seen: fewer forests here in the Midwest where the birds can rear their young than in the old days, I suppose. But, as Captain Richardson says, they do remain common."

"And, as Colonel Schlieffen says, they do remain very good eating." Douglass had reduced the two he'd taken to a pile of bones. He hooked another bird off the tray and devoured it, too.

Schlieffen said, "I am glad, Mr. Douglass, you here again to see, and to know that you are safe after being captured. I will not much longer with the Army of the Ohio stay, I think. I have learned much here, and am sorry to have to go, but I think it is for the best."

"I'll miss you, Colonel," Douglass said, and meant it. Like most Europeans he'd met, Schlieffen was far more prepared to accept him simply as a man, and not as a black man, than the common run of Americans. "But, if you're still learning things here, why go?"

"I believe," Schlieffen replied after a perceptible pause for thought, "that what new things I may learn by staying will be small next to the knowledge I have already gained."

Douglass needed a moment to figure out why the German had taken such pains with his answer. Then he saw: Schlieffen was saying he didn't expect the Army of the Ohio to accomplish much more than it had already done. He didn't expect U.S. soldiers to break through the Confederate entrenchments ringing them and to rampage across Kentucky. Had he thought they could manage something like that, he might have stayed to watch them do it.

And, in saying the Army of the Ohio was unlikely to accomplish anything more, he was also saying that army had failed. It still did not hold all of Louisville; its flanking maneuver had been costly but had not dislodged the Rebels. Even if it did eventually dislodge the Rebels from Louisville, it surely could not launch any triumphal progress through Kentucky thereafter. Since triumph was what Blaine and Willcox had purposed, anything less meant defeat.

No wonder Schlieffen was so careful not to offend. His departure passed judgment on the campaign and on those who ran it.

Richardson said, "Whether he reckons you're the Antichrist or not, Mr. Douglass"—he was smooth when he wanted to be, smooth enough to use a title in public, no matter how hypocritically—"I'm surprised old Stonewall up and let you go instead of keeping you to trade for a Reb or something."

Douglass shrugged. "Had the decision been his, I do not know what he would have done with me—or to me. Had the decision been his, I gather he did not know what he would have done. He referred it to President Longstreet, however, who ordered my release. Having received the order, Jackson not only obeyed but treated me quite handsomely."

Better than you deserved, Richardson's face said.

Orlando Willcox sighed. "Longstreet was more astute than I had thought he would be. By releasing you so promptly and with such good treatment, he enabled the Confederate States to escape the odium that would have fallen on them had they sought to punish you for your views and actions over the years."

"Yes," Douglass said, and let it go at that. Martyrdom was easier to contemplate in the abstract than to embrace in the flesh.

From across the Ohio, artillery rumbled. "Confederate guns,"

Captain Richardson said, and grimaced. "We've done everything we could, but we never have been able to beat them down."

"The long range of modern guns makes this hard," Schlieffen said. "So we learned when we fought the French. When the guns you are shooting at are behind a hill or otherwise hidden out of sight, finding accurately the range is not easy."

"True, true," General Willcox said sadly. "During the War of Secession, you could see what you were shooting at, and what you could see, you could hit. Only twenty years ago, but how much has changed since."

"We do use up a lot of ammunition feeling around for where the other fellow is, and that's a fact," Richardson said. "A good thing he's doing the same with us, or we'd be in the soup."

"Who learns first how to find the range to the enemy's guns will a large advantage have in the war where this happens," Schlieffen said.

Nods went up and down the table. Oliver Richardson said, "When they're in sight, a rangefinder like the ones the Navy uses would do some good. But land isn't flat, the way water is. Guns can hide almost anywhere, and shoot from behind hills, as you say, Colonel. I'd like to see the boys in the ironclads cope with that."

The discussion grew technical. As far as Frederick Douglass was concerned, the discussion grew boring. Changing only the subject of the conversation and not its tone, the soldiers, hashing over the best ways to blow up their foes at enormous distances, might as readily have been steamboat engineers hashing over the best ways to wring a few extra horsepower out of a high-pressure engine.

Stifling a yawn, Douglass shifted in his seat. But before he could rise, General Willcox held up a forefinger. "Something I was meaning to ask you, sir," the commander of the Army of the Ohio said. "What was it, now? Oh, yes, I have it: during your captivity, did you have any occasion to speak with men of your race held in servitude in the Confederate States?"

Douglass settled himself firmly once more. "No, General, I did not. I wish I had had such an occasion, but it was denied me. My captors went to such lengths to prevent me from having any intercourse with my own people that, until I was returned to this side of the fighting line, I had all my meals from the hands of white soldiers detailed for the task. Appreciating the irony of having white servants at my beck and call perhaps more than the Confederate authorities would have done, I refrained from pointing it out to them, although I have every intention of prominently mentioning it in one of my future pieces on the experience."

"They were so afraid you'd corrupt their niggers, eh?" Richardson said. He found himself in a predicament that must have been awkward for him: Douglass had seen how he despised Negroes, but he also despised the Confederate States of America. Juggling those two loathings had to keep him on his toes.

"If, Captain, by corrupting you mean instilling the desire for freedom into the heart of any *Negro*"—Douglass stressed the proper word—"upon whom I might have chanced, then I should say you are correct. Should you desire to construe the word in any other sense, I must respectfully ask that you choose another instead."

"That is what I meant, close enough," Richardson said. Douglass sighed a small sigh. No point to taking it further. None of the officers at the table, not even General Willcox, had noticed that Richardson had called Douglass' brothers in bondage niggers—had, in effect, called him a nigger, too.

No. Colonel Schlieffen had noticed. The mournful eyes in that nondescript face held sympathy for Douglass. Schlieffen, of course, was a foreigner. None of the U.S. officers at the table had noticed anything out of the ordinary. Frederick Douglass wished that surprised him more. Had he really escaped from captivity after all, or only from the name of it and not from the thing itself?

Brakes squealed, iron grinding against iron. Sparks flew up from the rails, putting General Thomas Jackson in mind of distant muzzle flashes seen by night. The train was a special, laid on by order of President Longstreet. No conductor came down the aisle shouting, "Richmond! All out for Richmond!" Jackson's was the only Pullman behind the engine and tender.

Gaslights turned the Richmond and Danville Railroad depot bright as day. Under that yellowish light, a captain stood waiting. He sprang to attention when Jackson emerged from his car. "Sir, I have a carriage waiting for you right over yonder. You're in less than half an hour later than you were scheduled to get here; President Longstreet will be waiting up for you."

"Very well—take me to him," Jackson said. Part of him—the frivolous part he'd been fighting all his life—wished the train had been hours late, so Longstreet would have gone to bed and he would have been able to spend the night in the bosom of his family and to see the president in the morning. But duty came first. "The president would not have summoned me had he not reckoned the matter urgent. Let us go without delay."

The captain saluted. "Yes, sir. If you'll just follow me—" As he'd promised, the carriage waited just beyond the glow of the gaslights. He stood aside to let Jackson precede him up into it, then spoke to the old Negro holding the reins: "The president's residence."

"Yes, suh." The driver tipped his top hat, clucked to the horses, and flicked the leather straps. The carriage began to roll. Every so often, Jackson saw men in uniform on the streets of Richmond. But he might well have done that in peacetime, too, here in the capital of his nation. From the spectacle that met his eyes, he could not have proved the Confederate States were at war.

"Did you have a good trip, sir?" the captain escorting him asked.

"Middling," he replied. "As travel goes, it went well enough. I should be lying, however, if I said I was eager to leave Louisville with the fight unsettled." He glared at the young officer as if it were his fault. As he'd hoped, that glare suppressed further questions until the carriage had rattled up Shockoe Hill to the presidential mansion.

"Good to see you, General," G. Moxley Sorrel said, as if Jackson had come round from the War Department rather than from Louisville. "Go right in, sir. The president is waiting for you." *That* was out of the ordinary. Jackson couldn't remember the last time he hadn't had to cool his heels in the anteroom while Longstreet finished dealing with whoever was in his office ahead of the general-in-chief.

This time, Longstreet was going through papers when Jackson came in. "You made good time," he said, rising to shake Jackson's hand. "Sit down, sit down. Make yourself comfortable. Can I shout for coffee?"

"Thank you, Your Excellency. Coffee would be most welcome." As usual, Jackson sat rigidly erect, taking no notice of the chair's soft, almost teasing efforts to seduce him into a more relaxed posture. Longstreet didn't shout for coffee; he rang a bell. The steaming brew appeared with commendable promptness.

Jackson spooned sugar into his cup, sipped, nodded, and said, "And now, sir, may I inquire what was so urgent as to require removing me from the sight of my command without the battle's end in sight?"

Longstreet drank some coffee, too, before asking, "Do you expect the Yankees to break through while you're away?"

"I do not expect them to break through at all," Jackson snapped. Longstreet only smiled at him. After a moment, he had the grace to look sheepish. "Very well, Your Excellency: I take your point. Perhaps my absence will not unduly imperil the front. Nevertheless—"

"Nevertheless, I wanted you here, General." Longstreet took a president's privilege and overrode him. "Conferring by telegraph is far too cumbersome. Were the telephone improved to the point where I could remain in Richmond and you in Louisville, that might serve, but we must deal with life as it is, not with life as we wish it were or as it may be ten years or fifty years from now."

"I do take the point, Mr. President, I assure you," Jackson said. When Longstreet said *conferring*, he often meant *lecturing*. Like a lot of clever men, he enjoyed hearing himself talk. Jackson had not seen him anywhere near so happy when listening to someone else.

And the president kept right on talking. What came from his lips, though, was praise for Jackson, to which the Confederate general-in-chief was not averse to listening: "You did exactly the right thing when you wired me after Frederick Douglass fell into your hands. Next to holding the Yankees' first assault at Louisville, sending that telegram may well prove your most important action in the entire campaign."

"That's very kind of you, Your Excellency, but surely you exaggerate," Jackson said.

"I do not! In no particular do I overstate the case." Longstreet began ticking off possibilities on his fingers. "Had the soldiers who captured him shot him on realizing who and what he was, we might have claimed he was killed in the fighting. Had they lynched him after realizing who and what he was—"

"A fate he nearly suffered," Jackson broke in.

"I believe that." Longstreet shuddered. "Had they done it, I should have had to punish them and publish to the world that they had done the infamous act without authorization from anyone higher in rank. And had *you* hanged him, General"—the president of the CSA frowned most severely—"that would have been very bad. I don't know how I could have repaired it."

"Mr. President, you are starting at shadows," Jackson said. "Douglass"—he'd forgotten about saying *Mister* Douglass—"is a prominent figure in the United States, but his prominence does not translate into popularity."

"What you say is true, so far as it goes," Longstreet agreed, nodding his majestic head. "It does not go far enough. You see over the hill to the battle just ahead, but not to the larger fight three weeks later and half a state away."

"Enlighten me, then," Jackson said, more than a little testily. He knew he was no match for Longstreet as a politician, but did not enjoy having his nose rubbed in the fact.

Almost to his disappointment, Longstreet *did* enlighten him: "As you say, Douglass is not nearly so popular as he would wish in the USA. He embarrasses his countrymen by reminding them they lost the War of Secession, an unpalatable fact on which they would sooner not dwell. But Douglass is popular in France, and he is extremely popular in England, and has been for upwards of thirty years. We would have had an easier time explaining to the United States how we had killed one of their citizens than explaining to our allies how we had come to kill a man they revere."

"Ah. Now I see it plain." Jackson dipped his head to the president. "I humbly beg your pardon, Your Excellency: in such matters your mind does cast a wider net than mine."

"Each cat his own rat," Longstreet said. That was not quite the same as admitting Jackson made a better soldier than he, but it came close enough to keep the general-in-chief from being offended. Then the president of the CSA leaned forward and asked, "And how did you find Douglass, General?"

He might almost have taken that curiously avid tone had he asked Jackson about a lewd photograph or something else at the same time illicit and attractive. After meeting the Negro agitator, Jackson understood why. "He is a ... formidable man, Your Excellency," he answered after a pause spent groping for a word that fit.

"That I believe," Longstreet said.

But Jackson, once begun with his judgment, would not give over until he had completed it: "Were all men of his race endowed with gifts even approaching those he possesses, we should never have succeeded in holding them in bondage."

"I believe that, too, but they are not so endowed. I have read much of his work," Longstreet said. Jackson blinked, startled. The president saw the blink and laughed. "Do you not favor knowing the enemy, General?"

"Mm," Jackson said. "Put that way, yes, sir."

"Having done so, I will say, within the confines of these four walls and these four ears, that few white men are endowed with gifts even approaching his. In any public setting, of course, I should say nothing of the sort."

"I understand, Your Excellency," Jackson said. And he did. The Confederate Constitution mandated free speech, but no one used that mandate to proclaim the Negro's equality to the white man, let alone his superiority over him.

"As I say, you did the nation a good turn by your forbearance," Longstreet said. "I have received cables from both London and Paris thanking and congratulating us for our prompt release of Douglass. I am convinced it has made our allies more willing to play an active part in the fight against the USA."

"They certainly have done that of late," Jackson said with a smile. Now he told of the blows on his fingers: "Boston, New York, the Great Lakes, Los Angeles—nice to find the French doing something—San Francisco, that town up in Washington Territory—"

"Seattle." Longstreet supplied the name.

"Thank you, Mr. President. And this invasion of Montana Territory is one more stroke against which the Yankees will be hard pressed to find an effective response."

"Ah. I see you have not heard the latest." A smile broke through Longstreet's beard like the sun breaking through clouds. "No fault of yours, General—you've been on the train. But this morning British and Canadian troops crossed over the border from New Brunswick into Maine."

"Maine?" Jackson shivered theatrically. "Brr! Why would anyone want it? Give me Mexico any day. Or, seen from Canada, does Maine look warm?"

"There's a—chilling thought," Longstreet said with a smile. "But there are two excellent reasons for invading it. One is that the border, which was not settled until the 1840s, was not settled altogether to England's satisfaction. And the other"—the smile got wider, as if the president was inviting Jackson to share the joke—"the other is that Maine is President Blaine's home state, which makes the invasion doubly humiliating to him."

"Ah," Jackson said, appreciating the beauty of it.

With a certain savage satisfaction, Longstreet went on, "When I last offered President Blaine peace on the *status quo ante bellum*, he refused not least on the grounds that the United States were undefeated. If I make him the same offer again, he will have a harder time putting forward that claim."

"He certainly would," Jackson said with a chuckle. Then he checked himself and studied the president of the Confederate States. "Your Excellency, are you thinking of renewing that offer?"

Longstreet's big, leonine head went up and down. "I am. Along with the matter of Douglass, gaining your opinion of such a move was the other reason I asked you to come here. My view is that at this time no one in the USA or anywhere else in the world could possibly believe we would offer peace because we are weak rather than because we are strong. How say you?"

"Our Lord did say, 'Blessed are the peacemakers,' " Jackson answered, "but I must tell you that I would prefer to see the United States pay a high price for starting a war over something that was none of their proper concern in the first place."

"Having to give up the war while gaining nothing, and having to recognize our right to Chihuahua and Sonora, to prevent which acquisitions they went to war in the first place, should be price enough, don't you think?" Longstreet asked. "The United States have now twice elected Republican presidents, twice gone to war with us almost immediately thereafter, and twice failed in mortifying fashion to achieve their purpose. Based on that, General, how long do you reckon it will be before they elect a third Republican president?"

"Sooner than you think, perhaps, Mr. President, if you let them down too gently," Jackson said.

"Are you saying I should not do this?" Longstreet looked unhappy, as he did when anyone disagreed with him. "They *are* there, General." He pointed north. "They will be there. We cannot subdue and occupy them. Now they see they cannot subdue and occupy us. Is it not enough?"

Air hissed out between Jackson's teeth. "Put that way—" He

was not happy himself, nor anywhere close, but the president had a point. Grudgingly, he said, "Perhaps it could be tried."

"I knew you'd see it my way." Now Longstreet was all smiles. *Why not?* Jackson thought. *He's got what he wanted.*

Brakes squealed, iron grinding against iron. Sparks flew up from the rails. Brevet Brigadier General George Custer turned to his brother and said, "Reminds you of muzzle flashes in a night battle, doesn't it, Tom?"

Major Tom Custer shrugged. "Nobody's trying to kill us, not yet, unless it's the railroad line."

The conductor stuck his head into the car that carried the Fifth Cavalry's officers. "Great Falls!" he shouted. "All out for Great Falls!"

Custer shifted in the seat he'd occupied far too long. Something in his back gave a sharp click. He let out a sigh of relief. "That's a little better, anyhow. The railroads," he muttered. "Ah, the railroads. How I do love it when the faster way to go from hither to yon is around three sides of a square."

He stretched again. Despite that welcome click, his back remained unhappy. To get from Salt Lake City to Great Falls, his regiment had had to travel back past Denver, then up through Nebraska, into the Black Hills country of Dakota Territory, clipping a corner of Wyoming Territory before they finally entered Montana. And that had been a while ago; Montana itself was a big place.

"God's own luck it's not General Gordon and the British army meeting us here," he grumbled. "Wouldn't that be fine?—to get shelled and shot up as we were trying to leave the train, I mean."

"Happened a couple of times during the last war, didn't it, Autie?" his brother said. "But you're right—it's not what I'd want to do for fun. We're blasted lucky the Mormons didn't greet us that way when we got to Utah."

"Oh, don't I know it." Custer got to his feet as the train slowed to a stop. "Well, let's get ourselves disembarked and on the move. The sooner we set to marching, the sooner we can send the damned—the dashed—Englishmen back over the border with their tails between their legs."

He was the first one out of the car. Back in the days when he was a mere colonel, others might have tried to leave ahead of him—more likely Tom than anyone else. But those shiny stars on his shoulder straps froze the rest of the officers in their seat till he had gone by. *A general,* he thought, and walked straighter. *I'm a general.*

Down to the ground he sprang, boots scuffing on gravel. An infantry colonel stood there waiting to greet him, a blond man a few years older than he was and weathered leathery by sun and wind and snow. "Welcome to Montana, General Custer," he said, saluting.

His voice was familiar, even if his face hadn't been at first glance. Custer looked again and did a double take. "Henry Welton, you son of a gun!" he exclaimed, and clasped the other man's hand. "I'd heard you were up in these parts, but it went clean out of my head in the rush to get here from Salt Lake City. By thunder, it's grand to see you again. Been a long time, hasn't it?"

"Since we were a couple of McClellan's bright young men? Almost twenty years," Welton said. "That one didn't turn out the way we wanted it to. Here's hoping we do better this time around."

"Amen, and we'd better," Custer said. He grabbed his brother by the arm. "Henry, did you ever meet Tom here?" When Welton shook his head, Custer went on more formally: "Colonel Welton, I'd like to present to you my younger brother, Major Tom Custer. Tom, Henry Welton and I both served together at Little Mac's headquarters in our Army of the Potomac days."

"Very pleased to meet you, sir," Tom said.

"And you, Major." Welton lowered his voice as he spoke to George Custer once more: "And after all that Army of the Potomac duty, how did you find serving under Brigadier General John Pope?"

"As a matter of fact, that went better than I'd thought it would," Custer answered. "We differed, naturally, in our views of General McClellan, but discovered a common aversion to the Latter-Day Saints and another to the abilities and characters, such as they are, of Abraham Lincoln." He stiffened. "Speak of the devil! There he is on the platform. I thought I'd never set eyes on that Goddamned old undertaker again"—he forgot about *dashed* and other euphemisms—"after we sent him packing from Salt Lake City."

"He's been up here most of the time since, trying to raise trouble," Welton answered. "He managed it in Helena, but he hasn't had such good luck in Great Falls ... Christ, here he comes. What does he want with us?"

Lincoln towered over Henry Welton and both Custers. Tipping his hat to George, he said, "I know you find my good wishes superfluous, Colonel Cus—" He caught himself. He was an observant man. "Excuse me—*General* Custer. Congratulations. In any case, I do hope you enjoy all good fortune in driving the invader back from our soil."

"I aim to do exactly that, Mr. Lincoln," Custer said. "And when I have done it, and when our great nation is once more free to turn to the things of peace, I expect you, sir, will go right on setting class against class and preaching hatred and strife until they plant you in the ground."

"I preach neither of those things," Lincoln said quietly. "I preach justice and equality for all men in the United States."

"Yes, for the Mormons," Custer jeered. "We gave them justice and equality, all right—they were plenty equal at the end of a rope."

Lincoln's long, sad face grew longer and sadder. "I had already heard of that. May it not come back to haunt us."

"Pah! You care for the Mormons more than for the decent citizens of the United States." With a fine show of contempt, Custer turned his back. "I've wasted enough time. Now to get this regiment moving." Behind him, he heard Lincoln walk away. The ex-president's step was that of a much younger man, firm and regular. As long as he was leaving, Custer didn't care what he sounded like.

Cavalry troopers filed out of the cars behind the one housing the regimental officers. They hurried back to the freight cars that held their mounts. From one freight car emerged not horses but the regiment's Gatling guns and limbers, carefully guided down special, extra-wide ramps by their crews.

"Heavens!" Henry Welton's eyebrows rose in surprise. "You've got enough of those contraptions, don't you?"

"Enough and to spare," Custer answered, not altogether happily. "I had two in Kansas, and went down into Indian Territory and did good work with them. After my regiment got sent to Utah to help overawe the Mormons, the other half dozen were attached to me, for no better reason than that the first two had done good work. And when I was ordered here, I was ordered here with the Gatling guns specifically included."

Welton asked the first question that would have entered any good soldier's mind: "Can they keep up?"

"The first two did well enough in Kansas," Custer said. "I made sure the gun carriages had good horses, not screws. I've been doing the same with all of them, but now, with eight guns and eight limbers, we have four times as many things that can go wrong." He affected a tone of ruthless pragmatism: "If they cause trouble on campaign, I'll leave them behind, that's all."

"That makes good sense, sure enough," Welton said. "Well, we'll have a chance to see how well they travel from here up to join with the Seventh Infantry. From that point on, we'll be moving against the British, so if they can't keep up, they will have to fall back."

Custer's face crinkled into a frown. "I haven't been so well briefed as I would have liked," he said, which would do for an understatement till a bigger one came along. He exulted at having the command in Montana, but with command went responsibility. "You're not in contact with the enemy?" He didn't care for the sound of that.

"My infantry Regulars aren't, no, sir," Welton replied, which made Custer like it even less. Then the infantry officer went on, "But the First Montana Volunteer Cavalry are skirmishing with the limeys—that's the Unauthorized Regiment, you know."

"Volunteer cavalry?" Custer said scornfully—he didn't know, and had no way of knowing. "*Unauthorized* volunteer cavalry?"

"They're good men, sir—as good as a lot of the troopers you have," Welton said. Custer didn't believe that last for a minute, but, if the commander of the Seventh Infantry thought it was true, they might prove better than their name suggested. Welton next addressed that very point: "They started calling themselves the Unauthorized Regiment because they had a devil of a time getting into U.S. service after their colonel recruited them. They still wear the name with pride—a finger in the eye of the War Department, you might say."

"All right, Colonel—for the time being, I have to take your word about such things, not having seen them myself." Custer's tone remained dismissive.

Henry Welton held up a warning hand. "Sir, they truly are a fine-looking unit. And their colonel, the fellow who recruited them and organized them, is a lad to watch out for. One way or another, you mark my words, he *will* make the world notice him."

"Their colonel—a lad?" Custer wasn't sure he'd heard right.

"Theodore Roosevelt is twenty-two ... though he will be twenty-three soon." Welton spoke with a certain somber relish.

"By Godfrey!" Custer exploded.

"That's right, one of those." Welton nodded. "He will run rings around any three ordinary men you could name. He's run rings around me more than once, I'll tell you that. Do you know what he puts me in mind of? He puts me in mind of you, sir, the day you got yourself onto General McClellan's staff. Do you remember?"

"I'm not likely to forget," Custer said with a smile.

Welton went on as if he hadn't spoken: "There we were, on the banks of the Chickahominy, and Little Mac wondered how deep it was. And what did you do? You spurred your horse into the river, got to the other side—God knows how, because it wasn't shallow—and then came back across and said, '*That's* how deep it is, General.' Roosevelt would have done the same thing there. I can't think of anyone else I've ever seen who would."

"Hmm." Custer wasn't sure he liked that; he preferred to think of his headlong bravado as unique. "Well, we shall see. A man who goes hard at the foe will find a place for himself, sure enough."

"Yes, sir." Welton looked around. "Your regiment is shaping with remarkable speed. Won't be long before you're ready to move out, will it?"

"*We're* not Volunteers, unauthorized or otherwise," Custer said with more than a hint of smugness. "By God, it will be good to get out in the clean air on a horse's back, instead of sitting cooped up in a rolling box breathing the fumes of other men's tobacco until it was as if I were doing the smoking myself."

Welton chuckled. "Well, then, sir, I shan't offer you a cigar, as I was about to." He got one out, lighted it, and puffed up a happy cloud of smoke.

"Never took the habit," Custer said, "though I really am thinking of starting now, having made such a good beginning at it."

"Here's a habit I know you have." Henry Welton took a flask off his belt. It gurgled suggestively.

But Custer shook his head again. "I was a man who'd raise Hades, sure enough. But I haven't touched spirits and I haven't cursed—much—since I married Libbie right after the War of Secession."

"Well, well," Welton said. "Should I congratulate you or com-miserate with you?"

"One of those should do it," Custer answered. "But I'll tell you this, Henry—if we don't lick the British, we may as well get drunk, because the whole country will be up the smokestack." Henry Welton solemnly nodded.

Jeb Stuart took off his hat and fanned himself with it. "El Paso was hot," he said to Major Horatio Sellers. "Cananea's hotter. Don't know whether I'd have believed that if someone told it to me last spring, but it's so."

His aide-de-camp nodded rueful agreement. With his chunky build, the heat told harder on him. When he spoke, he spoke of a different sort of warmth: "Latest wagon train from El Paso is overdue, too. If the Yankees hit us now, they could make things hot. We still haven't caught up with all the munitions we used against them in New Mexico Territory."

"I sent a wire off yesterday, asking where the wagons were," Stuart said. "Haven't had an answer yet. Maybe the line's down again; heaven knows how it stays up, strung from cactus to fence post the way it is. Maybe a cow tripped over a wire. And maybe the Yankees are up to something farther east. If I don't hear any-thing from El Paso by this time tomorrow, I'm going to send out a troop of cavalry and see what's up."

"Railroad line might be broken east of El Paso, too," Sellers said. "It's not as if we haven't worried about that."

"No, it's not." Stuart kicked up dust as he paced along Cana-nea's main street, which would scarcely have made an alley in a proper town, a town that had some life to it. "El Paso's on the end of a long supply line from the rest of the CSA, and we're on the end of a long supply line from El Paso. I suppose I ought to get down on my knees and thank God our ammunition has come in as well as it has."

"Embarrassing to try and fight a battle without it," agreed Ma-jor Sellers, who had a sardonic cast of mind. "We almost found that out, to our cost, at Tombstone. If the Yankees had had a couple of companies of Regulars there along with the Tombstone Rangers, we might have found ourselves biting down hard on a cherry pit."

"That's so." Of itself, Stuart's tongue ran over a broken tooth on the left side of his lower jaw. He hadn't done it on a cherry pit, but on a bit of chicken bone. The comparison struck a nerve even so. He went on, "We've taught the Yankees a lesson, though. Since we licked them in that last fight, they haven't even tried moving soldiers into the stretch of their own country we overran, let alone down into Sonora."

But counting on the United States to stay quiet was a mistake, as Stuart learned that afternoon when a half-dead Confederate cavalry trooper rode a foundering horse into Cananea. A bucket of water poured over his head, another poured down him, and a tumbler of *mescal* poured after it did wonders to revive the soldier. "Drench me again," he said, whether seeking more water on him or more *mescal* in him Stuart did not know.

"What news?" the commander of the Trans-Mississippi demanded.

"Sir, the damnyankees bushwhacked our wagon train, maybe twenty miles west of this Janos place," the trooper answered. "Wasn't like they came ridin' down on us, neither. They was waitin' there, right in the road, like they got there a while ago and they was a-fixin' to stay."

"Oh, they were, were they?" Stuart's eyes lit up. "That's what they think. How many men have they?"

"Looked like a couple troops of cavalry, mebbe some infantry with 'em," the soldier answered. "I was ridin' rear guard, but I reckoned you needed to know what they was up to worse'n the folks back in El Paso, so I went wide around the ambuscade and managed to get on by them bastards without 'em spottin' me. They was too busy foragin' 'mongst the wagons to pay much heed to one rider off on his lonesome. You reckon my horse'll live, sir? That's powerful dry country I rode him over, and I didn't do much in the way of stoppin', you know what I mean?"

"Yes," Stuart said. "I don't know about your horse." He did know about foraging in a captured wagon train; he'd done plenty of that during the War of Secession. He also knew the trooper was right about how dry the land between Cananea and Janos was. If he galloped out at the head of a column of horsemen, he'd get to the Yankees a day and a half later with all the mounts at death's door, as this trooper's was now. The U.S. cavalrymen would ride rings around him.

If he galloped out at the head of a column of horsemen . . .

He hunted up Colonel Calhoun Ruggles, commander of the Fifth Cavalry, and outlined his difficulty. "Oh, yes, sir, we can do that," Colonel Ruggles said confidently. "Those Yankee sons of bitches won't reckon we can drop on 'em anywhere near so quick as we'll do it."

"That's what I hoped I'd hear you say," Stuart answered. "Get your regiment in order, Colonel; we leave as soon as may be."

Colonel Ruggles erected one of his bushy eyebrows like a signal flag. " 'We,' sir?" he asked. "Are you certain?"

"Good heavens, yes," Stuart answered. "Did you think I'd miss the chance to ride with the Fifth Camelry if it ever came up? Or do you deny that a threat to our supply line is business important enough to demand the attention of the army commander in person?"

"No, sir, and no, sir, again. It's only that—" Ruggles' eyes took on a wicked gleam. "It's only that, if you ride a camel the way you dance a quadrille, *sir,* you'll be yanking cactus spines out of your backside with pliers before we've made a mile. Meaning no disrespect, of course."

"Oh, of course. Heaven forbid you should mean disrespect," Stuart said. Both officers laughed. Stuart went on, "I have been aboard the mangy critters your regiment fancies, Colonel, but I've never seen them in this kind of action, striking across the desert from a distance horses can't hope to match."

"That's what they're for, sir," Ruggles said. "We've hit the Comanches a few licks over the years that they never expected to get, after they raided west Texas from out of New Mexico. And now we can hit the Yankees who paid 'em to do it. This'll be purely a pleasure, sir. We'll be ready to ride in an hour at the outside."

He proved as good as his word. Stuart spent most of that hour convincing Major Horatio Sellers that he wasn't just indulging himself by riding off with the Fifth Camelry. He was indulging himself, and he knew it. But a U.S. force athwart his supply line was serious business, too. "This is what we were talking about before the trooper rode in, if you'll recollect," he said. After he'd said it several times, Major Sellers, both outranked and outargued, threw his hands in the air and gave up.

Despite what Stuart had said to Colonel Ruggles, he hadn't ridden a camel in several years. He quickly discovered several things he'd forgotten: the rank smell of the beast, the strange feel of the saddle under him and the even stranger grip his legs had on the animal, and how high up he was when it reluctantly rose after reluctantly kneeling to let him mount.

Its gait was strange, too, when it set out east across the desert with the rest of the Fifth Confederate Cavalry. It had much more side-to-side sway than a good, honest horse did. Stuart began to suspect they called camels ships of the desert not only because they could travel long distances on little water but also because a man might easily get seasick atop one.

Despite that sway, in another way the camel's trot was smoother than a horse's. Along with the hard hooves on the ends of its toes, it also struck the ground with padded feet. No jolts flowed up its legs to him. Its strides were slow, but they were so much longer than a horse's that Stuart found himself astonished when he realized how quickly the barren countryside was flowing past to his left and right.

And, while the countryside might have seemed barren to him, the camels reckoned it flowing with milk and honey—or at least with cacti and thorn bushes, which they found an adequate substitute. Whenever Colonel Ruggles halted the regiment to let men and animals rest, the camels would forage. Thorns seemed to bother them not in the least. Some of the cacti they bit into dripped with juice, so they were getting something in the way of water to go along with their food.

The sun dropped toward the horizon behind the Fifth Camelry. Colonel Ruggles called out to Stuart: "I presume we go on through the night, sir?"

"I should say so." Stuart pointed ahead, where a fat, nearly full moon hung low in the southeast. "That'll light our way. We won't go so fast as we would in daylight, but we'll get some good work done—and we've done amazingly good work so far, if anyone wants to know. We should come down on the Yankees before noon tomorrow, wouldn't you say?"

"You'd best believe it, sir," Ruggles answered. "When you want to get somewhere a long way away in a hurry, camels are the best thing this side of a railroad."

They were also the noisiest things this side of a railroad. They moaned and complained when they started up, they moaned and complained when they stopped, and they moaned and complained in between times to keep from getting bored. Stuart began to see why it took a special sort of trooper to want to have anything to do with them: they were easier to hate than to love. But how their long strides ate up the ground!

On through the night the Fifth Camelry rode. Maybe some of the troopers, long used to their beasts, were able to sleep in the saddle. By the time the sun turned the eastern horizon gray and the moon sank behind Stuart in the west, he was yawning, but he and the rest of the men kept on. As dawn stretched the distance a man could see, Colonel Ruggles sent scouts out ahead of the main body of the regiment to search out the Yankee position.

They found the U.S. force a little past nine o'clock, better than an hour earlier than Stuart would have expected. "Did the damn-yankees spy you?" he asked.

"Don't reckon so, sir," one of the scouts answered, and the rest nodded.

Stuart glanced over to Ruggles. "We outnumber 'em. If we spread out and hit 'em from three sides at once, the way the whole army did with the Yanks at Tombstone, they shouldn't be able to stand against us."

"Expect you're right, sir," Ruggles said. "I wouldn't say this if we were riding horses, but I think we ought to go in mounted. The stink of camels panics horses that aren't used to them—you'll have seen that—and the sight of them ought to panic Yankees who never set eyes on the like before."

"Good," Stuart said. "We'll do it."

He swung north with three troops from the regiment. Firing had already broken out from the west when his men came into sight of the Yankee position. It was a roadblock with an encampment beyond it, fine for ambushing a supply column but not intended to hold against a serious assault.

The Fifth Camelry howled Rebel yells as their ungainly mounts bore down on the horrified U.S. forces. A few Yankees got into the saddle, but their horses wanted nothing to do with the Confederate camels. More U.S. soldiers fought as infantry, but, taken in the flank and caught by surprise, they didn't hold out long.

A couple of rounds snarled past and over Stuart. He fired his Tredegar carbine four or five times, and thought he might have wounded one running Yankee. Then white handkerchiefs and shirts began fluttering in lieu of flags of truce. The fighting couldn't have lasted more than half an hour.

"You damn Rebs don't fight like you should ought to," a disgruntled U.S. sergeant complained.

"Wouldn't have had to fight at all if it weren't for you people," Stuart said, borrowing Robert E. Lee's scornful name for the Yankees. He found himself in an expansive mood—the U.S. forces hadn't yet sent all the captured supply wagons up into New Mexico and out of his reach. That made him add, "The way we fight is to win—and I reckon we're going to do it." The sorrowful sergeant did not disagree.

☆ **XV** ☆

"Redcoats!" The scouts' cries echoed across the Montana prairie. "The redcoats are coming!"

"Come on, lads!" Theodore Roosevelt called to the men of the Unauthorized Regiment, or those troops of it that had joined him to try to impede the progress of the British column penetrating U.S. territory. "Come on!" he repeated. "The English wore red a hundred years ago, too, when we licked 'em in the Revolution. And the patriotic Continental soldiers wore blue, just as we do. They won against great odds, and so can we. Forward!"

Forward they went, with cheers on their lips. First Lieutenant Karl Jobst said, "Sir, I have to commend you. My opinion of volunteers has gone up immeasurably since we began harassing the British."

Roosevelt noted his adjutant's phrasing. Jobst didn't say, *My opinion of volunteers has gone up since I joined the regiment.* He'd waited till he saw the Unauthorized troops fight before approving of them. Maybe that made him a hard man to please. Maybe it just made him an old—or rather, a young—stick-in-the-mud.

"They do grow brave men outside the Regular Army, Lieutenant," Roosevelt said. He filled his chest with air, then let it out in a shout like the cry of a bull moose: "Close with 'em, boys, and fill 'em full of lead!"

That got another cheer. As Roosevelt rode north after the scouts, he made sure his own Winchester had a full magazine. Only the firepower his men had at their disposal let them slow down the enemy at all. Most of the British cavalry was armed with single-shot carbines much like the ones the U.S. Regulars carried. Some of the others were lancers, who but for their revolvers might have fought against Napoleon or Louis XIV or, for that matter, against Joan of Arc.

They were brave, too. He'd seen that. He hadn't seen that it helped them much.

He pointed. Bugler's horns cried out a warning. There ahead was the cavalry screen the British used to protect the infantry and baggage train advancing into Montana Territory. "Charge!" Roosevelt roared. He wanted to wave his sword about to help inspire his men, but in the end hung onto his Winchester instead. Knocking a few limeys out of the saddle would be the best inspiration possible.

Rapidly, the British horsemen swelled from little red specks visible across the prairie to an astonishing distance to scarlet-tunicked, white-helmeted men. They opened fire at several hundred yards, well beyond the reach of the Unauthorized Regiment's Winchesters. Puffs of dirty gray smoke shot from their carbines. A horse went down. A man slid out of the saddle.

But not enough horses fell, not enough saddles were emptied, to keep the U.S. soldiers from getting close enough for their Winchesters to bite. And when the magazine rifles bit, they bit hard. A man could shoot two or three times as fast with one as with a single-shot breechloader.

As had happened several times before, the British outriders recoiled back onto the rest of the cavalry in General Gordon's force. Before, the larger force had been enough to drive back the volunteers. Now Roosevelt had a couple of more troops than he'd been able to deploy at the last skirmish. "Keep at 'em, boys!" he shouted, and waved his hat.

Bullets sang past him. He'd been delighted to discover, not that he felt no fear in battle, but that he had no trouble keeping under control the fear he did feel. And the savage exultation that filled him almost canceled out even his controlled fear.

He raised the rifle to his shoulder and sent a stream of lead at the Englishmen who had stabbed the United States in the back. A redcoat dropped his carbine and clutched his right arm. Roosevelt whooped. He wasn't sure that was the limey he'd been aiming for, or that his bullet had wounded the foe, but who could prove it hadn't?

With his extra men, with his extra firepower, he drove back even the reinforced British cavalry. They in turn fell back toward the red-coated infantry. The foot soldiers shook themselves out from column into line of battle. They too fired single-shot Martini-

Henrys, but there were far more of them than troopers of the Unauthorized Regiment.

One thing coming out West had eventually taught Theodore Roosevelt: when not to raise on a pair of threes. "Back!" he yelled. A bugler always rode close by him. The order to retreat blared forth.

The British cavalry did not pursue his men when they broke off the fight and galloped off to the south. They'd learned from painful experience that they paid a high price if they got too far separated from the infantry they screened. *Lancers,* Roosevelt thought derisively. *We're nearing the end of the nineteenth century, and the British still have lancers in the line.*

"Well done, sir," Karl Jobst said, wiping sweat from his face with his sleeve. "They'll have to go back from line into column, and that will delay them. We bought our country another hour or so there."

"You have a cold-blooded way of looking at war, Lieutenant," Roosevelt said.

"It's the Regular Army way, sir," his adjutant said. "War is your hobby; it's my profession. Our job is not to drive the British back into Canada. We can't, not with one regiment against a much larger force. Our job is simply to slow them down as much as we can, so they don't get the chance to plunder anything important before reinforcements join us."

For him, it was a chess problem. He was interposing a pawn into a rook's threatening path so other pieces would have time to move forward and defend his king. As far as Roosevelt could tell, he would have been as happy deciding the result on a chessboard as on the plains of Montana, too.

Roosevelt said, "Such calculations have their place, but they are not the be-all and end-all of warfare. If strategy seemed to call for a long, continuous retreat, how would the soldiers ordered to make it have the spirit to fight once the time came for action?"

"That is an important point, no doubt about it." Jobst smiled to find his superior so acute. "Men are not steam engines, to perform at the pull of a lever." It wasn't the chessboard analogy Roosevelt had in his own mind, but it wasn't far removed. Jobst went on, "Persuading men to fight bravely under such circumstances as you describe is what makes war an art rather than a science. The Germans believe they can reduce it to a science, but I for one remain unconvinced."

"Good," Roosevelt said. "You do show signs of life after all, Lieutenant." He watched Jobst wonder whether he ought to be insulted. His adjutant finally decided it was a compliment, and smiled instead. Roosevelt smiled, too. "Stout fellow. Having delayed the British, what do we do next?"

"What we have been doing," Lieutenant Jobst answered. "We break away from them, we fall back to the next stream lying across their line of march, we post dismounted riflemen at the easiest fords to contest their crossing, we do our utmost to ensure that we are not outflanked, and, when we have no other choice, we fall back again. Colonel Welton is moving to our aid, as are the more easterly troops of our regiment, and as are reinforcements from outside the Territory."

"And, if we're lucky, we shan't be all used up by the time all those reinforcements come up," Roosevelt said.

"Yes, if we're lucky," Jobst agreed. His voice was tranquil. If you had to sacrifice a pawn to stave off the other fellow and set up moves of your own later in the game, you did it, and did it with no regrets.

Roosevelt understood that attitude, but it didn't come easy to him. The men of the Unauthorized Regiment were a force that might delay the British, yes, but they were more than that to him. They were his comrades, they were his friends, they were—in an odd sort of way, since many of them were older than he—his children. Without him, they would not have been born as a regiment. Without him, they would not be facing danger now. Like a comrade, like a friend—like a father—he felt obligated to keep them as safe as he could.

In thoughtful tones, he said, "We haven't seen much in the way of outflanking moves from this General Gordon of theirs. He seems to think only of going straight for what he wants."

Karl Jobst nodded. "So it would seem, wouldn't it, sir? I daresay it's because of his service in China and the Sudan. With properly disciplined troops, you can go through the heathen Chinese and the bush niggers like a dose of salts. He likely expects to do the same against us."

"Against Americans? Our blood is as fine as his—finer," Roosevelt declared. "When we gain the numbers to make a proper fight of it, I believe we shall give his excellency Mr. Chinese Gordon a proper surprise." He loaded with scorn the titles he had applied to the British soldier.

"Yes, sir," Jobst said. "By what I know of Brigadier General Custer, our new commander, he fights the same way. Once everything is in place, it should be like two locomotives heading down one track toward each other."

"*We* shall survive the smash," Roosevelt said. "I hold with this attitude myself, as you will have gathered. Admiral Nelson may have been a damned Englishman, but he spoke the truth when he said no captain could do very wrong if he placed his ship alongside that of the enemy."

Having made that vaunting statement, he felt the irony inherent in falling back. But he also felt the need. Having splashed through some small tributary to the Marias, he left behind a couple of dozen of his best sharpshooters. He stayed behind himself, too, to see how they did what they did. So he told himself, at any rate. He kept on telling himself so, too, and almost convinced himself that wanting to take another lick at the British out of sheer personal hatred had nothing to do with why he did not ride on.

Along with his troopers, he concealed himself among the alders and birches and cottonwoods that grew by the river. He might have been hunting canvasbacks instead of redcoats. The only difference was that Englishmen, unlike ducks, were liable to shoot back.

The oncoming British neared the river after he'd been waiting about an hour and a half. They approached with caution; the troopers of the Unauthorized Regiment had stung them at crossings even before Roosevelt came galloping in with his headquarters staff to take charge of resistance. Roosevelt drew a bead on a fellow who, by the way he was waving his comrades about, was probably an officer. The redcoat had courage. He went about his business as if without the slightest notion his foes were liable to be anywhere nearby.

Knowing when to start shooting was an art in itself. Open fire too soon and the British would gallop off and ford the stream a few miles to the east or west, without giving you the chance to hurt them. Wait too long and they'd have enough men forward to overwhelm you even if they couldn't shoot as fast.

One of his men pulled trigger a little sooner than he would have liked. An Englishman's horse screamed shrilly and fell on him. That made the Englishman cry out, too. Roosevelt fired at the officer, who was a couple of hundred yards off. To his blasphemous disgust, he missed.

He worked the Winchester's lever. A brass cartridge case flipped up into the air and fell to the damp ground at his feet. He fired again, and cried out in delight as the Englishman clutched at himself.

Along with his troopers, he emptied his magazine as fast as he could, trying to do the enemy the most damage in the shortest stretch of time. Some of the British cavalrymen fired back, though they had almost as small a chance of hurting his men as their ancestors under General Braddock had had against the skulking redskins during the French and Indian War. Most of the Englishmen, having discovered the enemy, sensibly drew out of range.

Twenty minutes passed. The Englishmen rode forward again. One of Roosevelt's troopers knocked a redcoat out of the saddle at better than two hundred yards, a fine bit of shooting with a Winchester. The rest of the British cavalrymen drew back again, to wait for reinforcements. They couldn't be sure how many men Roosevelt had waiting for them. If he'd chosen to defend the line of the river with everything he had, that could make for a large, hard fight.

He hadn't. He hooted like an owl, the signal for his troopers to withdraw to the horses a handful of their comrades were holding for them. Even in retreat, his smile was broad and triumphant. He'd given the tail of the British lion another nasty yank. "Why not?" he said aloud. "I'm a nasty Yank myself."

Sam Clemens had never liked his brother-in-law. As far as he was concerned, his wife's most prominent virtue was that she was nothing like her brother. Vernon Perkins was ideally suited to his bookkeeping job: he was bald, thin, bespectacled, fussily precise, and had as much juice in him as a brick. Save that she wasn't bald, his wife Lucy might have been stamped from the same mold. Their two daughters were insipidly well-mannered. Even their dog behaved himself.

And now Vernon Perkins was not only Sam's brother-in-law but also his landlord. Lying on the uncomfortable divan in the tatty parlor of Perkins' house, knowing he wouldn't go to sleep for a good long while yet, Clemens muttered under his breath. "What's wrong, dear?" asked Alexandra, who lay beside him.

She knew what was wrong. Bless her, she didn't mind giving him the chance to blow off steam. And he didn't mind taking it.

"Why in the name of all that's holy and a good many of the things that aren't didn't the Royal Marines pass by without setting fire to our house? And why didn't they come up here by Telegraph Hill and burn out your brother instead? Or why, at least, didn't one of their shells fall on this place? Shockingly bad gunnery, if anyone wants to know what I think."

"You don't mean that," Alexandra said.

"I don't?" In the darkness, Clemens raised an eyebrow. "Thank you for informing me of that, because I didn't know it. And why, pray tell, don't I?"

"Because if Vernon's house was wrecked and ours wasn't, he and Lucy and Mary and Jane and Rover would have moved in with us instead of the other way round," his wife answered.

"Boring names for their children. Boring name for their blasted dog, too." But Sam sighed. "All right, I don't wish your brother's house was wrecked. I wouldn't want him in my pockets, any more than I want to be in his. Heaven only knows how much I wish our house hadn't been torched, though."

Alexandra reached out and set a hand on his shoulder. "I know, Sam. I feel the same way. But we all came through safe, even Sutro, even the cat. That's what matters. How many people weren't so lucky?"

She was right, of course. She usually was. That she was right failed to lighten Sam's mood. "My soul rejoices every time I think the Royal Marines furnished you with a gentleman arsonist." He did his best, which was none too good, to put on a British accent: " 'Terribly sorry to disturb you, ma'am, but if you'd be so kind as to gather up the tykes and the pets so I can pour out the kerosene and touch a match to it?' Bah!"

From what Alexandra had told him, he wasn't exaggerating much. The British invaders had set a number of fires to cover their withdrawal to the Pacific, and Turk Street was one of the streets down which they'd pulled back. They hadn't actually set fire to his house. They'd set fire to the one next door, and the fire—what a surprise!—had spread. Lots of fires had spread through San Francisco in the wake of the British bombardment and invasion. The sour smell of stale smoke still tainted the fog.

"Try to sleep," Alexandra urged.

"I am. I do," he said. "I try every night. Sometimes, Lord knows how, I even turn the trick. A Hindu straight from his bed of nails would have trouble sleeping on this divan."

She patted his shoulder again. "It will be all right," she said. "As soon as we have a place of our own, it will be all right." And with that, and without further ado, she rolled over onto her side and did fall asleep.

Orion and Ophelia were sleeping, too, on piles of rugs and blankets. Their steady breathing mingled with Alexandra's in a rhythm that did nothing whatsoever to lull Sam to sleep. He muttered under his breath again and stared up at the ceiling. Eventually, he did doze off, and tossed and turned through the night, his head full of dreams of exploding shells and snarling rifles.

When morning came, he put on the suit he'd been wearing the day the British came. It was, at the moment, the only suit he owned. He downed a bowl of Lucy Perkins' oatmeal, which stuck to his ribs like a cheap grade of cement, declined a cup of her watery coffee, and fled the house as fast as he decently could, or perhaps a little faster.

He was farther from the *Morning Call* offices than he had been while he still had a home of his own. Trudging down to Market and then along it showed him a sample of what the British had inflicted on San Francisco.

Most of the houses along the narrow streets that led down to Market were fine. No Royal Marine incendiaries had penetrated so far north and east. Here and there, though, where a shell from an ironclad's big gun had landed, rubble took the place of what had been a home. Some gaps, where shells had started fires, were bigger still.

The northern end of Market Street was more of the same. A couple of shells had landed right in the middle of the street, and dug sizable craters. Dirt and rubble filled those craters. Work gangs—some made up of white men, including convicts in striped suits; others of pajama-wearing, pigtailed Chinese—were clearing away wreckage one ruined house or shop at a time.

And then, a little north of the *Morning Call* offices, three or four blocks were nothing but wreckage. Those were the blocks the Royal Marines had passed on their way to and from the Mint. They were also the blocks where some of the hardest, most desperate fighting had gone on. The stench of damp smoke lingered most strongly there. Another stench still lingered, too, the sickly-sweet smell of meat going bad.

A white straw boss was shouting orders to a gang of Chinese.

Clemens called out to him: "Hey, Sweeney, find any more bodies in the ruins yesterday?"

"We did that, Sam," the straw boss answered. "Only one, though; better than it has been. Heaven only knows who the poor bastard was, with him so swole up and black and all." He held his nose. "He'll go in one o' the common graves, poor sod, for not even his own mother could be naming him the now."

"Filthy business," Clemens said, and Sweeney nodded. Sam could look west and see some of the swath of devastation the invaders had cut through San Francisco. It ran straight toward the ocean; he would have been able to take in more of it had some of the city's hills not blocked his view.

"Is there any word yet on how much in the way of gold and silver the Sassenachs are after stealing?" Sweeney asked.

"If words were drops of water, Noah would be up at the top of Telegraph Hill right now, building a new Ark," Sam answered, which made the Irishman grin around the stub of his cigar. "Whether there's truth in any of them, heaven only knows. I've heard a quarter of a million dollars, but I've heard fifty million dollars, too."

He tipped his hat and went on his way. Sweeney shouted at the Chinamen. They hadn't slowed down while he was talking with Sam, as a gang of white men would have done. He shouted at them anyhow.

At the *Morning Call* offices, Sam hung his straw hat on one of the trees in the entry hall, then called out the question uppermost in his mind the past few days: "Has Blaine decided to take the carrot yet, or will they have to hit him a few more licks with the stick?"

"Still no word out of Philadelphia, boss," Edgar Leary answered. "That means the war's still on."

"Give me two synonyms for 'idiots,'" Clemens said, and then gave them himself: "'Fools' and 'Republicans.' They haven't got any notion of when to start wars but, just to make up for it, they haven't got any notion of when to quit them, either. Well, what's gone wrong since yesterday?"

"British are shelling Erie, Pennsylvania," Leary said with a certain weary relish. "Wires say there are big fires down by the waterfront. We know about that here, don't we?" He turned red and grimaced. "Uh, sorry, boss."

"Sorry I got burned out, or sorry you mentioned it?" Clemens asked. "Never mind. You don't need to answer that. You ought to live with my wife's brother; then you'd really know what sorry was all about. What's the news out of Montana Territory?"

"There is no news out of Montana Territory," Leary said. "The British are over the border, that volunteer outfit with the funny name is skirmishing with them—"

"Roosevelt's Unauthorized Regiment," Sam supplied. "I like it. Anybody who's unauthorized and proud of it is my kind of fellow. Why, I come from a long line of unauthorized—" Instead of interrupting Edgar Leary, he interrupted himself. "Montana, dammit."

"Nothing else to tell," the young reporter said. "The cavalry is skirmishing with the British soldiers, and Regulars are moving to help."

"Moving *where*?" Clemens asked irritably. "Montana's a hell of a big place. Are they all over it like measles, or sort of settled down in one spot in particular? And if they are in one spot, which one is it?"

"Whichever spot it is, it's one that's out of reach of the telegraph lines," Leary replied. "Of course, there aren't very many telegraph lines in Montana, on account of there aren't very many people in Montana."

"One of the biggest stories of the whole war, and it's happening out where nobody can take a proper look at it," Sam said. "Do you know what, Edgar? I'll bet the Army likes that just fine. After the British give us another licking, the donkeys in blue will have an extra couple of days to cipher out how to make it sound like a victory."

Grumbling about the U.S. Army, Vernon Perkins, and other calamities of nature, he went to his desk and lighted a cigar. Spotting three typographical errors in the first paragraph of a story sitting there did nothing to improve his disposition. Neither did the text of the story itself. "Whoever edited this would have done the world a favor if he'd never learned to read," he muttered. Then he remembered he'd edited it himself. He blew out as large and thick a cloud of cigar smoke as he could, to keep everyone else in the office from noticing him turning red.

Edgar Leary said, "Colonel Sherman announced that two men, Diego Reynoso and Michael Fitzpatrick, were shot at sunrise in the Presidio for looting."

"There, that's another victory," Sam exclaimed. "Can't lick

the Royal Marines—Christ, can't even find the goddamn Royal Marines—but we're death on looters, no two ways around it. Of course, if we'd done any kind of proper job fighting off the Royal Marines in the first place, the looters wouldn't have had anything to loot. Maybe, just maybe, if we give them enough hell now, this particular brand of idiocy won't happen the next time we find ourselves in a scrape."

"I hope not, I surely do," Leary said. After brief hesitation, he went on, "Boss, I do hear tell that Colonel Sherman isn't happy about what the paper's been saying since the British hit San Francisco. And if he isn't happy with the *Morning Call*, he isn't happy with you."

"Well, I have to tell you, Edgar my lad, I'm not very happy about what the Army did when the British hit San Francisco. And if I'm not happy with the Army, I'm not happy with Colonel Sherman." Sam took sardonic pleasure in turning Leary's warning on its ear.

The young reporter shuffled his feet uncertainly. "I know that. But I thought I ought to tell you anyway, because you can't throw Sherman in the stockade, but he can put you there, and throw away the key once he's done it."

"Throw a newspaperman in the stockade? He wouldn't d—" Clemens began. But he ran down, like a pocket watch that wanted winding. The trouble was, he wasn't just a newspaperman; he was a newspaperman who'd spent a few inglorious weeks as a Marion Ranger, a soldier of sorts on the Confederate side during the War of Secession. If Sherman decided he was lambasting the Army because he sympathized with the Confederate States after all rather than because he was a man who recognized damnfoolery when he saw it . . . if that happened, the commandant at the Presidio was liable to lock him up on suspicion of general frightfulness.

He threw back his head and laughed till he started to cough. "Are you all right?" Edgar Leary asked anxiously.

"I'll do, no doubt about it," Sam answered. "It just occurred to me that, considering where I'm staying now, the stockade might be a step up—so long as the estimable Colonel Sherman doesn't fling my brother-in-law into the cell next door."

Abraham Lincoln stood on the platform at the Great Falls train station, patiently waiting for disembarking passengers to get off.

Then, carrying his carpetbag, he got aboard. He looked around the car, wondering if a couple of unsmiling soldiers would come up, tap him on the shoulder, and order him off. He saw no soldiers, unsmiling or otherwise.

He smiled himself. He'd gauged things about right. When he was the principal menace to law, order, and the peace of mind of the moneyed class in Montana Territory, the Army had watched him like a hawk. As soon as the British came over the border, though, everyone forgot all about him. With the invaders heading south, nobody cared a Continental for John Pope's order limiting him to the Territories.

He would, he supposed, have been even more worried about the future of the country had the military authorities kept right on watching him closely even though the British had invaded Montana.

The conductor walked down the aisle, big gold watch in hand. "Now departing for Bismarck, Fargo, St. Paul, Milwaukee, and Chicago!" he intoned. "All aboard!"

A blast from the steam whistle also announced the train's departure. Cars jolted in their couplings as it began to roll. A vexing thought made Lincoln's long face grow longer. He wouldn't be altogether free of the Army's grip till he passed Fargo and left Dakota Territory. Maybe no one had tried to keep him from leaving Great Falls because the soldiers who would stop him were waiting in Fargo.

He shook his head. He didn't believe it. No one had tried to keep him from leaving Great Falls because no one knew, or cared, he was leaving. If no one knew he was gone or where he was going, no one could stop him.

No sooner had he settled back in his seat than the young man across the aisle, a fellow who looked like a miner in ill-fitting Sunday best, asked, "Beg your pardon, but ain't you Abe Lincoln?"

"Yes," Lincoln answered, warily and wearily. Had he had a dime for every time he'd had a conversation opened with that gambit, he would have been a plutocrat himself. The only commoner opening was, *God damn you, Lincoln, you son of a bitch!*—and that one usually came from older men, men who recalled the sorry course of the War of Secession. "Who are you, son?"

"My name's Hosea Blackford, Mr. Lincoln," the youngster said, and stuck out a hand. Lincoln relaxed a little as he shook it;

he'd had enough of curses and to spare lately. It was strong and rough-skinned and callused, the hand of a working man. Blackford went on, "Heard you talk in Helena when you was there." He nodded, half to himself. "Sure as hell did."

"Is that a fact?" Lincoln said: a little sentence polite in any context.

"Yes, sir!" Hosea Blackford's green eyes glowed. "*Hell* of a speech. Made me reckon we ought to get shut of fightin' our neighbors till we finished muckin' out our own barn first. Like you said, we had ourselves one revolution, and now we could use ourselves another one."

"Thank you, Mr. Blackford," Lincoln said. "Every now and again, when I hear a young man like you speak, my hope for the country revives."

"Ain't that somethin'!" Blackford said; after a moment, Lincoln realized it was his equivalent of *Is that a fact?*

They talked politics on and off till the miner—Lincoln had indeed pegged that one correctly—got off the train at Oriska, a tiny spot in eastern Dakota Territory, where his sister and brother-in-law had a farm. He didn't even carry a carpetbag; his suitcase was made of cardboard. When he rose to leave, he pumped Lincoln's hand again.

"You don't know what this here's meant to me," he said. "Ever since I started thinkin' about things, I could see they wasn't right, but I never seen how, or how to go about fixin' 'em. You done opened my eyes, and I reckon I can go and open some other folks' eyes my own self. You got yourself a—what's the Bible word?—a disciple, that's what it is."

"Good luck to you, Mr. Blackford," Lincoln said. "Be the truth's disciple, not mine. Follow the truth, wherever it may lead you."

The miner bobbed his head in an awkward nod, then hurried away. At a place like Oriska, the train didn't stop long. At a place like Oriska, you were lucky if the train stopped at all.

Lincoln smiled at the miner's stalwart back. He wondered how long Blackford's enthusiasm would last. Young men burned hot, but they burned out fast, too. Lincoln thought of that ridiculously young cavalry colonel back in Great Falls. He was doing something special now, too. How long before he became a lawyer or a banker or something else stuffy and boring and profitable? *Prof-*

itable. Lincoln's lip curled. The owners took the profits, and took them from the sweat of the working man.

A few hours and a few stops out of Oriska, the train halted in Fargo. No soldiers waited for Lincoln. Fargo was a fair-sized town, and the train paused there half an hour, long enough for him to get off and wire his son that he was on the way.

Boarding again, he crossed into Minnesota. Out of these flat farmlands John Pope had driven the Sioux when they rose up against white settlers in the hope that the United States would be too distracted by the War of Secession to bring any great force to bear against them. That had been a double miscalculation on the Indians' part. The USA had had soldiers enough to fight them and the Confederates both. And, after the war was lost, soldiers originally recruited for it hurled the Indians west across the plains, using numbers and firepower they could not hope to match.

Farms grew thicker and towns larger and closer together as the train carried Lincoln east. Minneapolis and St. Paul were real cities; some in the East that had been settled a hundred years longer could not compare to them.

The passengers who boarded at the two rival centers were perhaps more warmly inclined to Lincoln than people from the rest of the United States. In Minnesota, he was remembered as much for being the man who'd driven the Indians out of the state as for being the man who'd lost the War of Secession. With a sort of melancholy pride, he recalled that he'd carried Minnesota in the election of 1864. Recalling that wasn't hard; he hadn't carried many states.

The Republicans hadn't carried many states since, not till public disgust at the Democrats' unending soft line toward the CSA swept Blaine into the White House the autumn before. And now Blaine had taken a hard line, and done no better with it than Lincoln. How long would it be before the Republicans carried many states again?

Lincoln thought he had the answer, or at least an answer, to that question. He'd thought so for ten years and more now, as he'd watched factories boom and capitalists send their spaniels to Europe on holiday and workers live in squalid warrens at which those pampered spaniels would have turned up their noses. He'd been able to make only a handful of party leaders pay any attention to him till now.

Now, he thought, *now they no longer have any choice. If they don't heed me now, the party will surely go under.*

And then, as the train passed from Minnesota into Wisconsin, he closed his fat Shakespeare, took off his reading glasses and put them in their leather case, and buried his face in his hands. These past ten years, he hadn't even succeeded in persuading his own son he was right. He doubted he would persuade Robert even now. His son, having enriched himself at the practice of law, thought like a rich man these days.

Not that Robert would be anything but glad to see him. In family matters, they were close, as they always had been. Only in politics did a chasm separate them: the chasm that yawned between a man satisfied with his lot and another who could see how many in the country he loved had no reason to be satisfied with theirs.

The tracks beat south and east as they ran through Wisconsin. Lincoln knew no great joy when he left that state and came into Illinois, even though he'd lived more of his life in the latter state than anywhere else. Illinois had repudiated him in 1864, and had not looked on him kindly since, no matter how great a power in the land Robert had become.

Chicago sprawled along the shores of Lake Michigan. Everything came together there: Great Lakes commerce (however damaged that was at the moment because of the war), Mississippi River commerce (with the same caveat), and railroads from east, south, and west. Smoke from its factories darkened the skies. The great stockyards made the air pungent. The other scent in the air, the one Robert breathed day and night, was the scent of money.

Even with five train stations, Chicago seemed undersupplied. Lincoln's train waited in the yard of the Chicago and Northwestern depot for close to an hour until a platform became available. It inched its way forward, then sighed to a stop.

Robert Lincoln was waiting on the platform. As he embraced his father, he said, "By all accounts, you've had a busy time of it." His tone was no more ironic than he could help.

"Maybe a bit," Lincoln allowed, matching dry for dry. "It's good to see you, son. You look well."

"Thank you, sir." In his late thirties, Robert Lincoln was plainly his father's son; his neat beard only strengthened the resemblance. But, having his mother's blood in him as well, he was several inches shorter than Abraham, a good deal wider through the shoulders and the face, and, by all conventional standards, a good deal handsomer as well.

"So you'll put up—and put up with—your radical old father for a while, will you?" Lincoln asked, a little later, as they made their way toward Robert's carriage.

"You know I don't fancy the direction in which your politics have taken you," his son answered. "You also know that matters not at all to me when it comes to the family. If you're willing enough to put up with a son reactionary enough to believe in earning money and keeping what he earns, we'll get on splendidly, as we always have."

"Good," Lincoln said. He climbed into the carriage.

Robert tipped the porter who had carried the bags, and who now heaved them up behind the seats. The man lifted his cap, murmured thanks, and departed. To his driver, Robert Lincoln said, "Take us home, Kraus."

"Yes, sir." By his accent, Kraus had not been in the United States long. He too tipped his cap, then flicked the reins and got the carriage rolling.

"Quite a nabob you're getting to be, son, everyone bowing and scraping over you as if you were an earl on the way to becoming a duke," Lincoln said, hiding dismay behind facetiousness. Robert, who understood him very well without agreeing with him in the slightest, gave him a sharp look. Lincoln sighed; he hadn't really intended to provoke his son. He tried to smooth it over: "As I told you, it *is* good to see you—better than setting eyes on anyone else I've seen lately, and that is a fact."

"Unless I'm much mistaken, it's also faint praise." But Robert, fortunately, sounded amused, not angry. He went on, "Being held superior to John Pope, whom I suspect you have in mind, is closely similar to being reckoned taller than a snake, lighter than an elephant, or more in favor of abolition than an Alabama planter." His tone grew more sympathetic: "It was very unlucky for you, Father, that you had to fall foul of a man who bore you a grudge from the War of Secession."

"Few U.S. soldiers from the War of Secession bear me no grudge." Lincoln spoke with sadness but without resentment. "They have their reasons: whom better to resent than a man who led them into a losing war? Suffering in war is hard enough in victory, but ten times harder in defeat."

"Few of them are so resentful as to want to put a rope around your neck," Robert said.

Lincoln thought of Pope. He thought of Colonel—now Brigadier General—Custer. He thought of the bloodthirsty guard he'd been assigned, who would still have been soiling his drawers when the War of Secession ended. He didn't answer.

Robert said, "Now that you're here, Father, how do you aim to amuse yourself and stay out of mischief?"

"Amusing myself should be simple enough," Lincoln replied, "for I intend to get myself into as much mischief as I can: which is to say, I intend to struggle for the soul of the Republican Party. Our main plank can no longer be permanent, unyielding hostility toward the Confederate States. We have tried that twice now, and Blaine is failing with it as badly as I failed. The people will never give us a third chance, and I see no way to blame them for their reluctance. Fighting the Confederate States, England, and France, we are simply overmatched."

"A conclusion I reached myself some time ago," Robert said as they rolled into the fashionable North Side neighborhood he called home. He paused to get his pipe going, then asked the inevitable question: "And what plank would you put in its place?"

"Justice for the working man, and freeing him from oppression at the hands of the capitalist who owns the factory in which he labors," Lincoln said. "We have lost sight of the fact that capital is only the fruit of labor, and could never have existed if labor had not first existed."

"You intend to convene a meeting of Republican leaders and convince them of this doctrine?" Robert said.

"I do," Lincoln answered simply.

"They will eat you up, Father, the way savages in the South Sea Islands eat up missionaries who are sent to convert them to a new faith they do not want."

"Perhaps they will," Lincoln said. "I aim to make the effort regardless. For I tell you this, son: if the Republican Party *will not* build on this plank, some other party *will*, and *will* make a go of it."

General Orlando Willcox held out his hand. "Good-bye, Colonel. I have enjoyed your presence here, and I shall miss you."

"I thank you," Alfred von Schlieffen said.

"And I shall miss you as well," Frederick Douglass said, his voice as deep and pure as a tone from the lower register of an organ. "You always treat me as a man first, and as a black man after that if at all."

"You are a man: so I have seen," Schlieffen said, as he might have to a soldier who had fought well. Captain Oliver Richardson scowled at him. He took no notice of Willcox's adjutant, but climbed up behind the private who would take him to the train on which he'd return to Philadelphia.

South of the Ohio, cannon still bellowed and rifles still rattled. Schlieffen's driver let out a wistful sigh. "Colonel, you reckon the president's going to take the Rebs up on that call for peace this time?"

"I am not the man to ask," Schlieffen told him. "Your own officers will a better idea have of what your president wills— *wants*—to do." Had he worn Blaine's shoes, he would have made peace on the instant, and then got down on his knees to thank the Lord for letting him off on such easy terms. But that was not the question the soldier had asked him.

After spitting a brown stream of what the Americans called tobacco juice into the road, the driver said, "My officers won't give me the time of day. Hellfire, they won't tell me whether it's day or night. I was hopin' you might be different."

A German officer would not give one of his common soldiers the time of day, either. A German common soldier would not expect to get the time of day from one of his officers. The American private sounded aggrieved that he was not made privy to all his superiors' opinions and secrets. Americans, Schlieffen thought, sometimes let the notion of equality run away with them.

He and a couple of U.S. officers—one with his arm in a sling, the other walking with the aid of a crutch—had a first-class car to themselves. One of the Americans produced a bottle. They were both drunk by the time the train left Indiana for Ohio.

They offered to share the whiskey with Schlieffen, and seemed surprised when he said no. Once they'd passed it back and forth a few times, they forgot he was there. That suited him fine till they started to sing. From them on, work got much harder.

He persevered. Minister von Schlözer would need a full report on the Battle of Louisville to send to Bismarck. Schlieffen himself would need an even fuller one to send to the General Staff. The report did not go so well as he would have liked, and the music—for lack of a suitably malodorous word—was not the only reason. Parts flowed smoothly; as long as he was talking about matters tactical—the effects of breech-loading rifles and breech-loading artillery on the battlefield—he wrote with confidence. That was part of what the Chancellery and the General Staff had to have. But it was only part.

He sighed. He wished the strategic implications of the Louisville campaign were as easy to grasp as those pertaining to tactics. That breechloaders and improved artillery gave the defensive a great advantage was obvious. So strategists had been sure before the outbreak of the war, and so it proved, perhaps to a degree even greater than they had envisioned.

What remained unclear, while at the same time remaining vitally important, was what, if anything, an army taking the offensive could do to reduce the defenders' advantages. *Unfortunately,* he wrote, *the U.S. forces did not conduct the campaign in such a way as to make such analysis easy, as they took little notice of the principles of surprise and misdirection. Based on what I observed, I can state with authority that headlong assaults against previously readied positions, even with artillery preparation by no means to be despised, is foredoomed to failure, regardless of the quality of the attacking troops, which was also high.*

He sighed again. Every U.S. campaign he had studied, both here and in the War of Secession, had a ponderous obviousness to it. Like McClellan before him, Willcox seemed to have taken the elephant as his model. If he smashed to pieces everything between him and his goal, he could knock down the tree, reach out with his trunk, and pluck off the sweet fruit.

No U.S. general seemed to have figured out that, if he went around the tree instead of straight at it, the terrain might be easier than that right in front of it, and the fruit might fall of its own accord. The Confederates understood as much, even if their opponents didn't. Robert E. Lee hadn't gone straight for Washington, D.C., in 1862. No, he'd moved up into Pennsylvania and forced the USA to respond to his moves in a fluid situation. Lee seemed to have been blessed with an imagination. The only hint of such a feature U.S. commanders displayed was in their fond belief that they *could* batter their way through anything, and that had proved more nearly a madman's delusion than healthy imagination.

Schlieffen wrestled with his reports till evening, and then after dark by gaslight. By that time, the American officers had stopped singing. Having drunk themselves into a stupor, they were snoring instead. That racket was, if anything, even worse than the other had been, which Schlieffen hadn't reckoned possible.

They were monstrously hung over the next morning, an indication to Schlieffen that God did indeed mete out justice in the world. In short order, they put his faith to the test. One of them pulled a new bottle of whiskey from his carpetbag, and they got drunk all over again. This time, Schlieffen was tempted to get drunk with them, if for no other reason than to blot out their raucous voices. Satan sent temptations to be mastered. He mastered this one.

He sent up a hearty prayer of thanksgiving when, late that second night, the train pulled into Philadelphia. Gloating at the sad state of the two U.S. officers was something less than perfectly Christian. No man, he told himself, was perfect. Gloat he did.

A driver waited to take him back to the sausage manufacturer's establishment. When the fellow greeted him in German, he automatically replied in English. Then, feeling foolish, he thumped his forehead with the heel of his hand. "Please excuse me," he said in his native tongue. "Not only have I used nothing but English lately, I am so tired I can hardly put one foot in front of the other."

"Ich verstehe, Herr Oberst," the driver answered reassuringly. *"Bitte, kommen Sie mit mir."*

Schlieffen did come with the driver. He fell asleep in the carriage, and then, once back in a proper bed for the first time since his departure, did as good an imitation of a dead man as was likely to be found this side of the grave. When he awoke, a glance at his pocket watch sent him leaping from that soft, inviting bed in something close to horror: it was nearly eleven.

Kurd von Schlözer waved aside his mortified apologies. "Think nothing of it, Colonel," the German minister to the United States said. "I understand that a man returning from arduous service on his country's behalf is entitled to a night in which to recover himself."

Reminding Schlieffen he had done his duty was the best way to restore him to good humor. "Thank you for your patience with me, Your Excellency," he said. "Now I have been away from newspapers and the telegraph for two days. Has President Blaine yet answered the new Confederate call for peace?"

Schlözer shook his head, a slow, mournful motion. "He has not said yes; he has not said no. I spoke with him yesterday, urging him—as I have urged him before—to accept these terms before he finds himself forced to accept terms far worse."

"And what did he say? What could he say?" Schlieffen asked.

"He actually said little," the German minister replied. "I do not think he believes any longer he can win this war. But I do not think he believes he and his party can afford the embarrassment of admitting they are defeated in a war they began, either."

"Their coasts are bombarded and sacked. Their lakeside cities are shelled. They are beaten on the border of the provinces whose annexation they are trying to prevent. They are invaded from the north. Their own invasion of the enemy's territory is one of the bloodiest failures in all the history of war. If this is not defeat, God keep me from it!"

"Colonel, did I think you mistaken, be sure I would say as much," Schlözer answered.

"What does Blaine say? How does he justify going on with a war he cannot win?" Schlieffen asked.

"He says the United States, because they are still standing, are not beaten," Kurd von Schlözer said. "How to turn this into anything anyone might recognize as a victory is beyond me. It is also beyond him, although he will not admit as much."

"What can be done to make him see what is so?" Schlieffen asked. "The only reason he has not had to pay fully for his folly is that the United States are too large to be devoured at a gulp."

"I understand this, believe me," Schlözer said. "Blaine understands it, too; he is not altogether a fool. But he reckons that size is an advantage and a reason to keep fighting. And he is so full of hate for Great Britain and for France for aiding his enemies that he has let his hatred cloud his mind and keep him from thinking clearly."

"Being so large has helped Russia many times," Schlieffen said. "It is indeed a factor to be reckoned with. But the Russians use it by letting invaders plunge deep into their land, and by fighting them only when and where they choose: thus did Napoleon come to grief, and the Swedes before him. It is our own greatest concern, should we ever have to fight the Russian Empire."

"But invasion here is no more than a minor issue, and was undertaken only after the United States rejected President Longstreet's peace offer the first time he made it," Schlözer said.

"Yes, the Confederates have adopted a strategy of the defensive, which suits what the new weapons can do," Schlieffen agreed. "Full details will appear in my report. Longstreet is clever, to hold to this strategy even when he could gain more for the moment by abandoning it."

"Longstreet is clever," the German minister to the USA repeated. "I have heard—you need not ask where—that some Confederate generals strongly advocate imposing a more punishing peace on the United States, and a large invasion of the USA to force its acceptance. Longstreet resists this proposal, and imposes his policy on government and Army both."

"This is what the head of a government is supposed to do," Schlieffen said. "For that matter, Your Excellency, President Blaine has imposed his policy on the government and Army of the United States."

"So he has, Colonel," Kurd von Schlözer said. "So he has. The other thing a head of government is supposed to do, however, is choose a wise policy to impose. Both concerns are important, for, if the policy itself is misconceived, it will fail no matter how vigorously it is imposed. Sometimes, in fact, a misconceived policy will fail more spectacularly the more vigorously it is imposed."

Schlieffen considered that. His main concern was devising policy, not seeing that it was carried out. After a bit of thought, he inclined his head to the German minister to the United States. "Your Excellency, I think you may be right."

On one side of Jeb Stuart stood *Señor* Salazar, the *alcalde* of Cananea. He had forgotten his English, and was screaming at the commander of the Department of the Trans-Mississippi in rapid-fire Spanish. At Stuart's other side stood Geronimo and Chappo. Geronimo was shouting in the Apache language, far too fast for Chappo to hope to translate. Every so often, the old Indian, who understood and spoke Spanish, would break into that language to respond to something Salazar had said.

Surrounded by unintelligible cacophony, Stuart turned to Major Horatio Sellers and said, "Good God—I think I'd sooner deal with camels." After his wild ride in the direction of Janos and back again, that was a statement of profound distress indeed.

His aide-de-camp nodded. "At least camels don't form factions, sir. Nice to think there's something you can say for the brutes."

Stuart raised a hand. "Gentlemen, please—" he began. Neither the Apaches nor the *alcalde* paid any attention to him. He drew his pistol and fired it into the air. While the report still echoed, he shouted "Shut up, all of you!" at the top of his lungs.

That did the trick, at least for the moment. Into the sudden silence, Major Sellers said, "We've been trying to sort out just what the devil happened here since the day you rode out of town, sir. The only thing I can tell you, even now, is that the Indians and the Mexicans would have had a battle of their own if our own boys hadn't been keeping 'em apart ever since." He shook his head. "You listen to one story and then you listen to the other story and it's as though they're talking about gunpowder and grits—you wouldn't believe both yarns started from the same place."

"You try to listen to both stories at the same time and all you get is a headache worse than the one *mescal* gives you," Stuart said.

Salazar followed that. He nodded. After Chappo translated it for Geronimo, the ghost of a smile appeared on the medicine man's face—but only the ghost, and only for a moment.

Stuart went on, "The people of Cananea—all the people of Sonora and Chihuahua—are now the subjects of the Confederate States of America. We will protect them from anyone who troubles them in any way." *Señor* Salazar looked smug. Before he could say anything, though, Stuart continued, "The Apaches are our allies, who have fought alongside us and bled alongside us. We will also protect them from anyone who troubles them in any way."

"How in blazes we're going to do both those things at once—" Major Sellers muttered under his breath.

Resolutely, Stuart pretended not to hear that. At the moment, he didn't know how the Confederate States were going to do both those things at once, either. He did know they would have to do both of them if they were going to administer Chihuahua and Sonora. Feeling rather like King Solomon listening to the two women claiming the same baby, he said, "Let's see if we can sort this out and keep the peace here. I want to hear these stories one at a time." Digging in his pocket, he produced a fifty-cent piece, tossed it in the air, and caught it. "It's tails. *Señor* Salazar, you go first."

The *alcalde* glared venomously at Geronimo and Chappo. He

was bolder around them than he had been when they and the Confederates first came to Cananea, no doubt because he'd seen that the Confederates would not let the Apaches harm him or his people. "They are animals," he hissed. "Why should we live at peace with them? They do not know what peace means."

"You are the ones who break oaths," Chappo shouted, not waiting for any response from his father.

"One at a time." Stuart held up his hand again. "No insults from either side. Just tell me what you say happened. *Señor* Salazar, go on."

"*Gracias,*" Salazar said with dignity. "Here, I will tell you the precise truth, so you will know the lies of the *Indios* when you hear them." Jeb Stuart coughed. The *alcalde* sent him a look almost as venomous as the one he was aiming at the Apaches, but then went on, "These . . . *Indios*"—he visibly swallowed something harsher—"invaded my village drunk on *mescal*, stole away three of its finest and loveliest virgins, and ravaged them over and over, like the—" He checked himself again. "One is now dead of what they did to her, and the other two have both tried to hang themselves since. Is it any wonder we are outraged?"

"If that's what happened, no." Stuart turned to Chappo and Geronimo. "That is a hard charge against you. What have you got to say about it?"

Chappo had been translating the *alcalde*'s remarks for his father. Now, when Geronimo spoke, he did the same for Stuart: "My father says Cananea has never had three virgins in it, not here, not *here*, and not *here*, either." He pointed in turn to his crotch, his mouth, and his backside.

Señor Salazar gobbled in fury, and looked about ready to explode. "No insults," Stuart said sternly. If he felt like guffawing, his face never found out about it. "Go on."

Geronimo spoke again. Again, Chappo translated: "My father says three *putas* came to our tents. I do not know how to say *putas* in English: women who give you their bodies if you give them something."

"Whores," Major Sellers said succinctly.

"Whores—thank you," Chappo said. He collected English words the way his cousin Batsinas collected artisans' tricks. Batsinas had made himself a pretty fair blacksmith in a few months' time, and was always trying to trade for new tools. Stuart took that as a good sign, a sign that the Apaches could, with patience, be civilized. *Perhaps with the patience of Job,* he thought.

Before Chappo could apply his new vocabulary, Salazar erupted again, shouting, "Lies! Lies! All lies!"

"He let you speak," Stuart told him. "You will let him speak, or I will decide this case for him on the spot. Do you understand?" Ever so reluctantly, the *alcalde* composed himself. Stuart nodded to Chappo and Geronimo again.

Through his son, Geronimo said, "Like I say, these three whores"—Chappo pronounced the word with care it did not usually get—"came to our tents. They had *mescal* with them. Some of my warriors enjoyed them, yes, and gave them silver, it could be even gold, for their bodies and for the *mescal.*" After a bit, the old medicine man added, "Our women do not make free of themselves like this, and, if they do, we cut off the tip of their nose."

"Ought to do that in New York City," Major Sellers said with a coarse laugh. "Sure would be a lot of ugly women there, in that case." The biggest city in the USA had in the Confederate States the name of being the world's chiefest center of depravity.

However much Stuart agreed with his aide-de-camp, he waved him to silence. Then he asked Geronimo, "How did the woman of Cananea come to die during all this?"

"She is not dead," the Apache leader answered. "She fell in love with one of my men, and they ran off together."

"Bring them back," Stuart said. "Send men after them. If you can prove this, you had better do it."

Chappo translated for Geronimo but then, sounding worried, spoke for himself: "The woman will say the man took her away by force, whether it is true or not. She will try to take the blame off herself."

"It could be," Stuart said in neutral tones. In fact, he thought it likely. No one—Confederate, Yankee, Mexican, Indian—was fond of accepting blame. He turned to *Señor* Salazar. "Who are the two women who did come back to Cananea, and where do they live?"

"One is Guadalupe Lopez; her family's house is by the plaza," the *alcalde* answered. "The other poor victim of the *Indios'* desires is Carmelita Fuentes. She lives on the edge of the town, by the road toward Janos."

"Thank you, sir." Stuart tugged at his beard as he thought. After a few seconds, he said to Major Sellers, "Send men to both these houses. See if there are any unusual amounts of U.S. gold and silver coins in them. The Apaches have been doing a lot of looting up in New Mexico Territory. If they have silver and gold to spend on women, that's the money they'll be spending."

"Yes, sir." His aide-de-camp beamed. "That's very clever, sir."

Now Salazar was the one who spoke in tones of alarm: "I must remind you, General, Cananea has since a long time traded with *los Estados Unidos*. Much money of that country is in this town. You must not be surprised to find it in many homes."

"It could be," Stuart said, as neutrally as he had toward Chappo. "We'll find out any which way, the same as we'll find out whether the Apaches bring in this other girl of yours and what she says when they do."

The *alcalde* bowed. "I will go with your soldiers to the houses of these two poor women and aid them in any way I have the power to do."

"You will do nothing of the sort. You will stay here with me." Stuart put the snap of command in his voice. The last thing he wanted was Salazar telling the women and their families what to do and what to say. He let the *alcalde* save face by adding, "I have men who speak Spanish. Doing this will be good practice for them."

Under the circumstances, Salazar could only acquiesce. He looked very unhappy doing it. Geronimo and Chappo looked unhappy, too. Seeing that, Stuart realized nobody knew exactly what had passed between the women of Cananea and the Apaches, and Indians and Mexicans both feared finding out exactly what had passed would show them in a bad light.

Horatio Sellers had been thinking along the same lines. When he came back from sending soldiers into Cananea, he spoke to Stuart in a low voice: "What do you want to bet we find out the greasers *were* whores and the redskins *did* ravage 'em?"

"Wouldn't surprise me one bit," Stuart answered, also almost whispering. "They aren't sure who did what, but they were sure they were ready to kill each other on account of it. We're going to need more Regulars in the Army than we used to, just because of these two provinces. We'll need to patrol the border with the Yankees, we'll need to patrol the new border with the Empire of Mexico, and we'll need to patrol every foot of ground in between unless we want fights like this one almost was to break out three times a week."

"God help the secretary of war when he tries to explain that to Congress," Sellers said.

"God help Congress if they don't listen," Stuart returned. Whether the congressmen in distant Richmond would listen was anyone's guess. If they didn't, the noise would get louder soon. Stuart was sure of that.

After a couple of hours, the soldiers who had searched the Lopez and Fuentes houses reported to Stuart. "We found five U.S. silver dollars at one place, sir, and two U.S. quarter-eagles at the other, sir," said the lieutenant who'd led them. "Five dollars at each place—"

"More than those Mexican sluts are worth," Major Sellers muttered.

As if by accident, Stuart trod on his toe. "Doesn't prove anything, not really," the commander of the Trans-Mississippi said. "We *are* close to the U.S. border. The women still insist they were violated?" At the lieutenant's nod, Stuart sighed. "All right. Let's see if the other one turns up. If she doesn't, then I reckon we have to believe the *alcalde*."

But she—Maria Guerrero was her name—did indeed turn up, four days later. Once back in Cananea, she loudly proclaimed the outrages the Apache in whose company she was found had inflicted on her. The warrior in question, a stalwart brave named Yahnozha, as loudly insisted on her willingness. She wasn't bruised and battered and beaten, but she declared she'd been too terrified to resist. Yahnozha said she hadn't wanted to resist.

Impasse. Stuart hated impasses. He hated ambiguity of any kind. The older he got, the more ambiguity he saw in the world. He hated that, too. "In a battle, by God, you know who's won and who's lost," he complained to his aide-de-camp. "That's what war is good for."

"Yes, sir," Sellers agreed. "But what do we do now, since nobody here knows anything and nobody much wants to find out?"

"Convince the Apaches and the Mexicans to forget this time, since nobody *is* sure about it," Stuart said. "That's all I can think of now. Next time they quarrel, maybe who did what to whom will be a little clearer. I hope to heaven it is, I tell you that."

He did his best to keep the peace between allies and subjects. Time helped, too. When they hadn't flown at each other's throats for a while, he decided they probably wouldn't, not over this. He wished he could believe either side would really forget it. Try as he would, he had no luck with that.

☆ **XVI** ☆

Frederick Douglass' train pulled into Chicago at the South Side Depot, on the corner of State and Twelfth Streets. Looking out the window at the hurly-burly on the platform, Douglass was forcibly reminded that, while the Army of the Ohio butted heads with the Confederates at Louisville, most of the United States kept right on with the business on which they had been engaged before the war began.

After seeing nothing but blue uniforms for so long (save only during that brief, appalling interlude when he saw gray and butternut uniforms instead), Douglass blinked at the spectacle of checked and houndstooth and herringbone sack suits and brightly striped shirts on men, and at the fantastic, unfunctional cut and bright colors of women's clothes. Truly this was a different world from the one he'd just left.

Carrying his suitcases, he made his way to the waiting line of Parmelee's omnibuses. The driver, who was taking a feed bag off a horse's head, looked at him with something less than delight. "What would you be wanting?" he asked, brogue and carroty head of hair alike proclaiming him an Irishman.

"To go to the Palmer House," Douglass replied evenly.

As they often did, his deep, rolling voice and educated accent went some way toward making up for the color of his skin. So did his destination, one of the two best hotels in Chicago. Instead of snarling at him to take himself elsewhere, the omnibus driver, after a visible pause for thought, said nothing more than, "Fare is fifty cents."

Have you got fifty cents? lurked behind the words, as it would not have were the driver addressing a white man. With practiced carelessness, Douglass tossed him a half-dollar. "I've been there before," he said.

458

The driver plucked the coin out of the air, as if it would vanish if he let it touch the ground. Douglass boarded the half-full omnibus. The driver stared at him, as if wondering how much he could get away with. Douglass looked back with imperturbability as practiced as the carelessness. The Irishman's shoulders slumped. He picked up Douglass' bags and heaved them, a little harder than he might have, into the boot at the rear of the omnibus.

Before long, all the seats on the conveyance were taken—except the one next to Frederick Douglass. He wondered how many times he'd seen that over the years. More than he could count, certainly. The driver evidently reckoned that last seat would not be filled, for he climbed up into his own place, flicked the reins, and got the omnibus rolling. Above the streets, telegraph wires were as thick as vines in the jungle.

"Palmer House!" the driver shouted when he got to the hotel, which occupied the block on Monroe between State and Wabash, the entrance lying on the latter street. Douglass, a couple of other men, and a woman got off the omnibus. Douglass tipped the driver a dime for getting his bags out of the boot, then went inside. The lobby was a huge hall with a floor of multicolored marble tiles. Spittoons rang to well-aimed expectorations; poorer shots gave the marble new, less pleasant, hues. Western Union boys and letter carriers hurried through the hall in all directions.

To Douglass' relief, he had no trouble with his reservation. "Room 211," the desk clerk said, and handed him a key with that number stamped on it. The fellow looked back at the great grid of pigeonholes behind the front desk. "Yes, I thought so—there's a letter waiting for you."

"Thank you." Douglass took the envelope, which bore his name in a script long familiar. The note inside was to the point. *If you are not too tired,* it read, *meet me for supper at seven tonight in the hotel restaurant. We were in at the birth; let us pray we are not to be in at the death.* As usual, the signature ran the cross stroke of the initial of the Christian name into the beginning of the first letter of the surname: *A. Lincoln.*

"Help you with anything?" the desk clerk asked.

"Only in reminding me whether I remember correctly that the entrance to your restaurant is on the State Street side of the building," Douglass replied.

"Yes, that's right." The clerk nodded. He wasn't calling Douglass *sir*, but in all other respects seemed polite enough. The Negro discounted slights far worse than that.

He went upstairs, unpacked, and took a bath in the tin tub down at the end of the hall. Refreshed, he went back to his room, relighted the gas lamp above the desk, and wrote letters and worked on a newspaper story till it was time to join the former president for supper.

At the Palmer House restaurant, the maître d' gave him a fishy stare. "I am to dine with Mr. Lincoln," he said, and the ice began to break up. A discreetly passed silver dollar made the fellow as obsequious as any Confederate planter could have wanted in a slave.

Lincoln was already seated when Douglass came up. He unfolded to his full angular height like a carpenter's jointed ruler. "Good to see you, Fred," he said, and held out his big, bony hand.

Douglass took it. "It's been too long," he said. "But neither of us is in fashion these days, and so we both have to work harder just to make our voices heard. That leaves too little time for sociability."

"Ain't it the truth?" Lincoln said in the rustic accents of his youth. "Well, sit yourself down, we'll get outside some supper, and then we'll hash this out and see what we come up with."

"An excellent proposal." Douglass did sit, then examined the menu. He spoke with firm decision: "I shall have a beefsteak. If I can't get a good one in Chicago, they have vanished off the face of the earth."

"I had beef last night, so I believe I'll order the roast chicken," Lincoln said. "Considering what we shall be about over the next few days, though, I wonder whether cooked goose wouldn't be a better choice."

"Surely things have not come to such a pass," Douglass said.

Lincoln looked at him. Lincoln, in fact, looked through him. The ex-president said not a word. Douglass, feeling himself flush, was glad his brown skin kept that from showing. When the waiter came round to see what the two men wanted, he reckoned the interruption not far from providential.

His beefsteak, when in due course it arrived, occasioned another interruption, a rapturous one. Across the table from him, Lincoln methodically demolished half a chicken. Both men drank whiskey with their meals.

"How you stay so lean with such an appetite is beyond me," Douglass said, patting his own considerable girth.

Lincoln shrugged. "I eat—and I am eaten." He had not drunk to excess, any more than Douglass had, but perhaps it was the spirits that let his frustration with the world in which he found himself come forth to a degree he did not usually permit. Or perhaps it was something else. After one of his self-deprecating chuckles, he said, "I bear up well in the presence of mine enemies; only with my friends do I let my sorrows show. Having so few friends these days, I am most often quite the jolly gentleman."

He looked as jolly as an undertaker. He usually looked that way, regardless of how he felt. Douglass said, "Surely the state of the Republican Party cannot be so bad as you implied in your invitation to this supper."

"Can't it? Why not?" Lincoln asked, and Douglass had no answer. The former president went on, "This may be the last supper of the Republican Party."

"With the way the war has gone, I fear you're likely right," Douglass said. "I had such hopes when we began it, and now . . ." His voice trailed away.

"Now we've both come closer than we would have liked to making the acquaintance of the hangman," Lincoln said, and Douglass winced and nodded. Lincoln continued, "But that is not what I meant. Our party would face hard sledding, and face it soon, even had the war gone as we should have liked."

"You are, I believe, too much the pessimist," Douglass said. "Had we succeeded in forcing the Confederate States to disgorge Chihuahua and Sonora, Republican strength would have been assured for years to come."

But Lincoln shook his head. "Try as I will, I cannot make myself believe it, for we have abandoned the principles upon which we—you and I and others—founded the party in the first place. When was the last time you heard a Republican speak up for a fair shake for the working man or for justice and equality for all men? Those are the ideals we espoused when we were young. Have they changed from boons to evils as we grew old?"

Douglass frowned and looked down into his glass of whiskey. In those charged, heady days before the War of Secession, everything had seemed possible. He spoke carefully: "Since the war, we may perhaps have grown too concerned with giving the country back its spine and allowing it to stand tall in the world, and—"

"What about caring what it stands for when it stands tall?" Lincoln broke in. "We have forgotten the working man as the capitalist ground him into the dirt. We have looked outward too *much*, and at ourselves too *little*, and so a pit yawns beneath the party. Unless the mass of men believe we represent them and can better their lot, they will cast their ballots elsewhere, and I for one shall not blame them. In their shoes—when they have shoes—I should cast my vote elsewhere, too."

"I look outward," Douglass said. "I look south, to my brethren yet in bondage."

"I know you do, old friend," Lincoln said. "Nor do I presume to condemn you, for there your heart lies. But do you not see that the factory owners in the United States abuse the working classes in much the same way as the slaveowners in the Confederate States abuse the Negro?"

"It might seem so, to a white man," Douglass snapped. But then he softened: "We have disagreed here for years, you and I. I ask you, Abraham: where is the factory owner who, when a pretty woman in his employ strikes his fancy, can abuse her chastity as he wishes?" His mouth tightened. The color of his skin, the shape of his features, testified that he was the product of such a union.

Lincoln replied, "Where is the slaveowner who, when times are slack or when a hand grows old, can turn him out to starve without a backwards glance, as if he were discarding a torn glove? The evils are not identical, but both spring from superiors enjoying untrammeled power over those they call inferiors, which is, as I have long maintained, destructive of democracy."

"The plight of the Negro is worse, and more deserving of attention," Douglass insisted.

"The plight of the Negro in the United States is not far different from the plight of other proletarians in the United States, and grows less different day by day," Lincoln said. "In looking toward the Negro in the Confederate States, for whom we can do little, you ignore both the Negro and the white man in the United States, for whom we can do a great deal."

"I look to amend the worst evil I see," Douglass said stiffly.

"Which is also the one least susceptible to amendment." Then

Lincoln laughed, which irked the Negro orator and journalist, who found nothing amusing in the discussion. Seeing his expression, the ex-president explained: "I went through what they call the Lincoln-Douglas debates more than twenty years ago, and now I find myself in the midst of the Lincoln-Douglass debate."

"After some of the things the Little Giant said about the colored man, I'll thank you not to compare me to him," Douglass said, but he was smiling now, too. "You lost that election, but those debates made you a force to be reckoned with."

"And all that reckoning with me got the country was a lost war and a new, unfriendly neighbor on our southern border," Lincoln answered. "All that electing me got the party was the assurance it would not elect another Republican president for the next generation."

Yes, Douglass thought, Lincoln was letting his bitterness show tonight, more than he normally did. The Negro said, "Cheer up, old friend. You yourself spoke of the king who charged his wise men to come up with a saying that would be true and fitting in all times and situations. They gave him the words, 'And this, too, shall pass away.'"

"Yes, and do you know what those wise men were talking about?" Lincoln asked. Douglass shook his head. "The Republican Party," Abraham Lincoln said.

Captain Saul Berryman looked neither so bright nor so young as he had before the war against the many foes of the United States. "Good morning, Colonel Schlieffen," he said wearily. He did not bother speaking German, as he had before, but waved Schlieffen to a seat in the outer office. "General Rosecrans will be with you shortly."

"Thank you," Alfred von Schlieffen told Rosecrans' adjutant. Captain Berryman only grunted by way of reply. He had already immersed himself once more in the paperwork that had engrossed him when Schlieffen walked into the office.

The closed door to Rosecrans' inner sanctum did little to muffle the phrases he was, presumably, bellowing into the telephone: "Yes, Mr. President . . . No, Mr. President . . . No, no, no . . . I'm sorry, Your Excellency, but I don't think we can manage that. . . . What? What? I'm sorry, I can't hear you." That last was followed a moment later by a sharp little crash, as of the newfangled machine's earpiece being slammed back into the bracket on which it rested when not in use.

Major General William Rosecrans opened the door to the inner office and peered out, a hunted look in his deep-set eyes. "Ah, Schlieffen," the general-in-chief of the United States said, suddenly genial. "I'd sure as hell sooner talk with you than with James G."—his beard swallowed a word or two—"Blaine."

"Thank you, General," Schlieffen said, rising and going into Rosecrans' office. What he thought of an officer who would curse his commander-in-chief he kept to himself. Instead, pointing to the box on the wall, he said, "I am sorry it did not let you hear well."

"What?" Rosecrans stared. Then he laughed. "I could hear just fine, Colonel. What happened was, I got sick of listening. Any time a man asks you to do what isn't possible, you're a damned sight better off pretending you can't make him out."

Schlieffen thought of the British admiral, Nelson, deliberately raising a telescope to his blind eye so he could keep from officially seeing an order he did not like. With as much sympathy as he could put in his voice, the German military attaché asked, "What does the president ask of you that you cannot do?"

He wondered if Rosecrans would answer him. He wouldn't have answered a question like that from a foreign attaché, were he back in Berlin. But the American soldier did not hesitate. "What does he ask?" Rosecrans echoed. "What does he ask? He asks me to win the goddamn war for him, that's what. Not so much at this stage of things, is it?"

His breath stank of whiskey. Even a sober man, though, would have been hard pressed to be optimistic at the moment. "How does he want you do do this?" Schlieffen inquired.

"How?" Rosecrans howled, stretching the word out into a cry of pain. "He hasn't the faintest idea how. I'm the soldier, so that's supposed to be my affair. Have you got a won war concealed anywhere about your person, Colonel Schlieffen? *I* haven't, sure as the devil."

"If President Blaine still wants you this war to win, I do not know how to tell you to do this," Schlieffen said. "The only question I have is why he does not take the peace the Confederates say they will give him and thank God for it. When we France beat, we from them took two provinces and made them pay five milliards of francs."

"What's a milliard?" Rosecrans asked. Schlieffen took a pen from its inkwell and wrote the number on a scrap of paper: 5,000,000,000. Rosecrans looked at it. "Oh. Five billion francs, you mean." He whistled softly. "That's a lot of money."

"*Ja,*" Schlieffen answered laconically.

"That's a hell of a lot of money," Rosecrans said, as if the German had not spoken.

"*Ja,*" Schlieffen said again, and then, "and Longstreet wants to take no provinces—no, no states, you would say—from the United States. He wants to take no money from the United States. He wants to take only the two provinces he bought from the Empire of Mexico, and to have the United States say they are his. With what he could do, these are good terms, *nicht wahr?*"

"Oh, they're good terms, all right," Rosecrans said. "You ask me, they're *too* damn good. It's as though Longstreet is saying, 'We can lick you any old time we please, and we don't have to take anything away from you to make that so.' It's—humiliating, that's what it is."

Schlieffen essayed a rare joke: "If President Blaine does not for these terms care, President Longstreet will them harder make. Of this I am sure. Do you not think that I . . . am right?" He nodded to himself, pleased he'd again remembered the English idiom.

"In a red-hot minute," Rosecrans said, which the German military attaché, judging by the tone, took for agreement. Sighing, scowling, Rosecrans went on, "But he can't do that now, because that would be humiliating, too. Do you understand what I'm saying, Colonel?"

"Oh, yes, I understand," Schlieffen said. "But in war, the way not to be humiliated is to win. If you lose a war, how can you keep this from happening to you? The enemy to be stronger himself has shown."

"Hasn't he, though?" But then Rosecrans violently shook his head. "No, Goddamn it, the Confederates haven't shown that they're stronger than we are. As strong as we are, maybe, but not stronger. It's only after England and France jumped on our back that everything went into the privy."

"But we of this spoke down in Washington before the war began," Schlieffen said. "Britain and France have been friends to the Confederate States since before the War of Secession. The

United States should have had ready a plan to fight at the same time all three countries."

"I remember you saying that," Rosecrans replied. "I have to tell you, I didn't take it seriously then. Do you really mean to tell me that back in Berlin you've got a plan for war against France and one for war against France and England and one for war against France and England and Russia and one for—"

"Aber natürlich," Schlieffen broke in. "And we think of also Austria-Hungary and Italy, though they are now our friend. And we remember Holland and Belgium and Denmark and Sweden and Turkey and—"

The general-in-chief of the United States stared at him. "Jesus Christ, you do mean it," Rosecrans said slowly. "What do they do in that General Staff of yours, Colonel, sit around all day studying maps and timetables and lists of regiments and I don't know what all else?"

"Yes," Schlieffen answered, surprised yet again that Rosecrans should be surprised at the idea of military planning. "We believe that, if war comes, we should as little to chance leave as we can."

"A lot of chance in war," Rosecrans insisted. "Can't help it." Yes, he was an American, looking for nothing more than the chance to go out in the field of uncertainty and snatch what he could from it.

"Yes, this is so," Schlieffen said. "A lot, there is. As little as there can be, there should be." What the United States had snatched from the field of uncertainty was a thumping defeat.

"Maybe," Rosecrans said, like a man admitting Limburger cheese might possibly taste good in spite of the way it smelled. "Maybe." He brushed a pale speck from the dark blue wool of his tunic. "The more you talk about it, Colonel, the more I do think the United States should send some of our officers to your country after this blamed war is finally over—if it's ever over— so we can take a long look at how you go about things."

"They would be welcome," Schlieffen said. "Your neighbors who do not love you are allied to the French, who do not love us. Since we have one enemy who is the same, it might for us be good to be with each other friends." He held up a hasty hand. "You must understand, I speak here only for myself, not for Chancellor Bismarck."

"Yes, yes." General Rosecrans nodded impatiently. "I can't

speak for the secretary of state, either. Speaking for nobody but William S. Rosecrans, though, Colonel, I'll tell you I like the idea pretty goddamn well."

Alfred von Schlieffen sat very still, contemplating what he had just said. *The enemy of my enemy is a friend* was an ancient truth. France, so far as he could see, would never be anything but Germany's enemy. France was the Confederate States' friend; the Confederate States were an enemy to the United States, also unlikely to be anything else.

So far as he could see, real, close friendship between Germany and the United States made good strategic sense. He wondered what Minister von Schlözer would think of the idea. Up till now, German relations with both the USA and the CSA had been polite, even cordial, but not particularly close. Would Chancellor Bismarck want to continue what had been working well enough, or would he be interested in changing things? If he was, a U.S. military mission to Berlin might be one tooth of the key in the lock.

Schlözer will have a better idea of the chancellor's mind than I do, Schlieffen thought. Then he realized Rosecrans had just spoken, and he had no idea what the general had said. "I am sorry," he said. "You must please excuse me. I was thinking of something else."

"I guess you were," Rosecrans said with a chuckle. "The Judgment Trump could have sounded right then, and you never would have noticed. What I said was, I'll take the notion of sending officers to Berlin over to the secretary of state to see what he thinks of it."

"That is good. I am glad to hear it," Schlieffen said.

"Damned if I know what will come of it, though." Rosecrans' good humor vanished. "Ever since Washington warned us against entangling alliances, we've held apart from 'em. Of course, in Washington's day we didn't have nasty neighbors tangled up with foreigners themselves. But he's like the Good Book to a lot of people here, even if he was from Virginia."

That Rosecrans was himself talking with a foreigner never seemed to enter his mind. Schlieffen had seen in other Americans the same interesting inability to judge the effects of their own words. It did not offend him, not here; he would not let it offend him. "You will do what you can do, General, with the officials of your country, and I will do what I can with the officials of mine, and we will see what from this comes."

Before Rosecrans could answer, the box on the wall clanged to let him know someone wished to speak with him. He grimaced and swore fiercely under his breath. But then, like a hound summoned to the dinner bowl by the ring of a bell, he got up and went to the telephone. "Rosecrans here," he shouted into it. "Yes, Mr. President, I hear you pretty well right now. What were you saying before, Your Excellency?" A pause. "But, Mr. President . . ."

Schlieffen quickly realized the conversation with President Blaine was liable to go on for some time. He half rose. General Rosecrans nodded permission for him to go. He respectfully dipped his head to the American general-in-chief, then left the inner office.

"Auf wiedersehen, Herr Oberst," Captain Berryman said when he emerged; Rosecrans' adjutant had regained enough spirit to try German again. *"Ich hoffe alles is mit,* uh, *bei Ihnen gut?"*

"Yes, everything is well with me, thank you," Schlieffen answered. "How is everything with you?"

Before Berryman could answer, Rosecrans' bellow of frustrated fury did the job for him: "God damn it to hell, Mr. President, I can't give you a victory when the sons of bitches are coming at us five ways at once. . . . Yes, well, maybe you should have thought about that more before you dragged us into this miserable war. . . . Maybe you should think about making peace, too, while you've still got the chance." The sharp click that followed was, again, the earpiece slamming down onto its rest.

Schlieffen and Berryman looked at each other. Neither found anything to say. After a polite, sympathetic nod, Schlieffen let himself out of the antechamber.

Abraham Lincoln appreciated—indeed, savored—the irony of meeting in the Florence Hotel to do battle for the soul of the Republican Party. Here he was, doing his best to make the party remember the laborers who had helped bring it to power, and doing it in a hotel erected by the Pullman Company on part of the city within a city they owned: factories, houses, blocks of flats, all in the holy name of Pullman.

Robert had arranged it, of course. His Chicago connections were far better than his father's, these days. The room, Lincoln could not deny, was splendid: magnificent walnut paneling, table with legs even more elaborately carved than that paneling, chairs upholstered in maroon velvet and soft enough to swallow a man, gaslights overhead so ornate, they resembled a forest frozen in beaten bronze.

"I think we are all here," Lincoln said, looking around the room. Fewer were here than he had hoped. Some of his telegrams had gone unanswered; some men he had hoped would accept had declined. He wondered whether he had enough strength at hand, even if everything went as he wanted, to turn the party into the path he had in mind. The only way to find out would be the event.

Around the table, heads nodded. There sat Frederick Douglass, with his big frame and white mane and beard as solid and impressive as a snow-topped mountain. There was John Hay, a lighter presence, once Lincoln's secretary, then minister to the CSA in Blaine's administration till war broke out. There sat Benjamin Butler, a clever mind concealed within a bald, bloated, sagging walrus of a body: before the War of Secession a Democrat who thought Jefferson Davis might make a good president of the United States, at its end a U.S. general who'd had to flee New Orleans in a Navy frigate to keep the returning Confederates from hanging him without trial.

Next to Butler, rotund Hannibal Hamlin fiddled with his spectacles. He had been Lincoln's vice president, and had gone down to defeat with him in 1864. But he was a Maine man, and secretary of state to boot, and as such more likely than others to gain the ear of President Blaine. Senator James Garfield of Ohio sat farthest from Lincoln. An officer during the War of Secession, he had risen to prominence as a member of the military courts that purged the Army of defeatists after the fighting ended. But for Hay, he was the youngest man in the room.

"I think two questions stand before the house today," Lincoln said, as if he were addressing the Illinois Assembly. "The first is, where does our party stand now? The second, and more urgent, is, where do we go from here?"

"Where we are, is in trouble," Ben Butler declared in his flat Massachusetts accent. "How do we get out of it?" He shook his big, round head; the gray hair that fringed his bald pate flew this way and that. "Damned if I know. Hanging Blaine from the Washington Monument might be one place to start."

"He did what he was elected to do." Hannibal Hamlin spoke up in defense of the president.

"So he did, and did it damned badly, too," Butler sneered.

"Fighting the Confederate States, opposing their tyranny, is not and cannot be a sin," Frederick Douglass declared.

But Butler had an answer for him, too: "Fighting them and losing is."

"As you will know from the invitations I sent you, I was speaking in more general terms," Lincoln said. "The question I wish to address is, assuming the war lost, as it seems to be, how is the Republican Party once more to recover its status with the American people?"

"By doing as it was meant to do from the outset: by championing freedom over all this continent," Douglass said.

"In aid of that," John Hay said, his voice light and thin after the Negro's, "I have heard that Longstreet will formally free the Negroes in the CSA once this war ends. His allies are said to have extracted such a promise from him as the price of their aid against us."

"One more reason for Blaine to come to terms, then," Douglass exclaimed, his leonine features lighting with hope. A moment later, though, he spoke more cautiously: "If it be true, of course. You, John, will be the best judge of us all as to that."

"With my few months in Richmond before the fighting started?" Hay said with a laugh full of self-mockery. "I believe it to be true, having heard it from sources I reckon trustworthy, but I can offer no guarantee. Nor, even if it is true, can I guess how much *de facto*, as opposed to *de jure*, freedom the Negroes in the Confederate States are to have."

"Giving them any at all goes dead against the Confederate Constitution," Garfield pointed out.

"That doesn't always stop us," Butler said. "I don't see any reason the Rebs will lose a whole lot of sleep over it."

"Your cynicism, Mr. Butler, has truly astonishing breadth and scope," John Hay murmured. Butler gave him an oleaginous smile, as at a compliment. Maybe he thought it was one.

Lincoln said, "When a man has *no* freedom, *any* increase looms large. I hope you are indeed correct, John. The Negro unchained will grow in ways the men now his masters do not expect." Frederick Douglass nodded vigorous agreement to that. Lincoln continued, "Even as the chains may fall from the limbs of the slave in the Confederate States, so they are being fitted to those of the laborer in the United States. Standing firm against this, we can and shall become the party of the majority once more, after the misfortune of the war sinks below the surface of public recollection."

James Garfield frowned. "I don't see how sounding like radicals will take us anywhere we want to go."

"Justice for the working man is not a radical notion," Lincoln said, "or, if it is, that stands as a judgment against the United States."

"But what do you mean by justice, Lincoln?" Garfield demanded. "If you call raising a Red rebellion, the way you tried to do in Montana Territory—if you call that justice, I want no part of it."

"I make two points in response to that, sir," Lincoln said. "The first is that I raised no rebellion, Red or otherwise. I made a speech, similar to many other speeches I have made over the years. If the miners in Helena were forcefully of the opinion that it fit the circumstances under which they lived, I cannot help it. Second and more basic is the fact that the people do retain the right of revolution against a government they find tyrannical."

"Now you do sound like a Red," Ben Butler rumbled. His jowls shook with the weight of his disapproval.

"Without the right of revolution, we should to this day be British subjects, revering Queen Victoria," Lincoln said. "We might make discontented British subjects, but British subjects we should be. If we were still British colonies, we would retain the right of revolution against the Crown. How can we not retain it, then, against the government in Washington?"

"In Philadelphia, you mean," Butler said. "On this theory, you should have let the Confederate States go without firing a shot."

"By no means," Lincoln said. "They sought to break, and, sadly, succeeded in breaking, a union; they did not aim to establish a more perfect one for the nation as a whole."

"A subtle distinction," said Butler, an admirer of subtle distinctions.

"My view," Frederick Douglass said, "is that, while Mr. Lincoln exaggerates the likenesses between the position of the Confederate slave and that of the U.S. laborer, we may, if we so desire, use such exaggerations to good effect on the stump."

"That is what I meant to say, yes," Lincoln said, "save that I purpose making this principle the rock on which our platform stands, not just a net with which to sweep up votes when the next election comes."

Hannibal Hamlin said, "If we take this line, the Democrats will call us a pack of Communards, and that alongside all the other low things they are in the habit of calling us."

"The Democrats lined up in support of property when that included property in Negro slaves. They have not changed since." Lincoln did not try to hide his scorn. "If they start flinging brickbats, they'll have to duck a good many, too."

"How much good will any of this do, gentlemen, when we are tarred with the brush of two losing wars in the space of twenty years?" John Hay asked.

"Exactly my point," Lincoln said. "If we go on as we have been, we are surely ruined. If, on the other hand, we make the changes in our course I have suggested, we offer the entire nation a new birth of liberty. Otherwise, I fear, government of the people, by the people, and for the people shall perish from this earth, replaced by government of the rich, by the rich, and for the rich. The free men who made the United States a beacon to the nations of the world shall be reduced to gearing in the vast capitalist engine of profit."

"I just don't see it," Senator Garfield said. "I wish I did, but I don't. No room for compromise in any of this. Without compromise, you can't have politics. The brickbats will be flying, all right, but they'll be real brickbats with real bricks. That's the direction whence class warfare comes."

"Yes, it is," Lincoln said softly. "Do you think we can avoid it by pretending the seeds from which it springs are not already planted and growing?"

"Whether we can avoid it is one question," Hay said. "Whether we should embrace it is another question altogether."

"You mean that, John." Lincoln's voice was full of wonder, full of grief. Hay was his protégé. Hay was nearly as much his son as was Robert. As far as Lincoln could see, his own course of thought had followed over the years a perfectly logical, perfectly inevitable path. And yet, the handsome young man who was now an even more handsome middle-aged man had not gone in the same direction. For that matter, neither had Robert Lincoln.

Hay said, "I think everyone here, with the possible exception of Mr. Douglass, feels the same as I do." He sounded sad, too, the way a doctor sounded sad when he had to tell a family the situation for a sick man was hopeless, and that he would soon die.

Lincoln looked around the table, silently polling the men he had asked to join him in Chicago. With him, they could have swung many in the Republican Party to his views. If they were against him, reform along the lines he desired would not come, not through the Republicans. "Gentlemen, think again, please," he said. "Can you not see that this country needs a new birth of freedom if it is to go on being the wonder and the envy of the world?" He knew he was pleading. The last man with whom he'd pleaded was Lord Lyons, the British minister to the United States during the War of Secession.

He'd failed then. After Lee's victories in Pennsylvania, the British government had recognized the Confederate States as a nation among nations and, with France, had forced the USA to do likewise. He was failing now, too. He saw that by the way his comrades would not meet his eyes.

Garfield said, "Lincoln, if we Republicans tried to go down your road, I think you would split the party not in two but in three. Some would go with you, and I expect you would gain a few among the Socialists and others who believe in notions even more radical than yours."

"Thank you so much," Lincoln murmured.

"I mean no offense. I speak the truth as I see it, as you do." Garfield was earnest, sensible, in the middle of the road. He proved as much, continuing, "Some would probably try to hold the party on the course it has now. I lean that way myself, truth to tell. And some would bolt to the Democrats."

"And," Hannibal Hamlin added, "the devil would come down with chilblains before we won another election."

Benjamin Butler said, "It occurs to me that what we may need is not more freedom but a little less. Compared to any European country, this is a land full of bomb-flinging anarchists. We're so damned free, we've thrown two wars away because we did not properly prepare for either of them. Take Germany, now— nothing in Germany but coal and potatoes, far as the eye can see. But they've got discipline there, by God, and they're the strongest power on the continent."

"I wouldn't go so far as Mr. Butler," Hay said, "but I am

compelled to believe there is some truth in what he says." Hamlin nodded. So did Garfield.

Lincoln discovered he'd only thought he knew despair. He turned to Frederick Douglass. "What of you, Fred?" he asked.

Douglass had less political clout than any of the others, but more moral authority. After staring for a while at something only he could see, he answered, "My own people, both in the Confederate States and in the United States, need more freedom, not less. I must believe the same also holds true for white men." Had he stopped there, he would have aided Lincoln. But he went on, "Neither am I convinced that taking the Republican Party into the streets, so to speak, is the way to gain a majority for it."

"Let me ask the question another way," Lincoln said: "Other than taking the Republican Party into the streets, how is it to gain a majority? Only sixteen years of accumulated disgust at Democratic fecklessness let us win this latest election. Things being as they are now, when do you gentlemen foresee our winning another one, and by what means?"

For close to two minutes, no one answered. Then James Garfield said, "Whatever the means may be, they shall not include riots and rebellion, which would only raise enmity against us."

"Like pressure from steam in an engine, pressure for change *will* rise in the United States," Lincoln said. "Whether it rises *through* the Republican Party or *outside* the party remains to be seen. I would sooner see it rise through the party, that we may channel it for the nation's good and for our own."

He looked around the table again. Not even Douglass looked as if he agreed with him. Ben Butler said, "If workers go into the streets, soldiers go into the streets, too. Soldiers carry more rifles. They always have. They always will."

"Unless and until they turn those rifles against the men who give them orders they cannot in good conscience obey," Lincoln said, which produced another long silence. Into it, he continued, "Gentlemen, I say this with a heavy heart, but I say it nonetheless: if, as this meeting makes it appear likely, the Republican Party cannot find room to encourage change, I shall work outside the confines of the party to encourage it. For change, sure as I live and breathe, is coming. And, though they may not be here today, there are those calling themselves Republicans who will follow me."

"You would deliberately split the party?" It was half a gasp from Hannibal Hamlin, half a wheeze.

"No, I *would* not," Lincoln answered. "But I *will*."

"If you try, we shall read you out and pretend you were never in," Butler said. "The way the Democrats have campaigned against you ever since the War of Secession, we might be better off reading you out."

"An ostrich may bury its head in the sand and pretend the lion is not there," Lincoln said. "Will that keep the lion from enjoying a supper of ostrich?"

Butler got to his feet. Since he was short and squat, drawing himself up to his full height was less impressive than it might have been otherwise, but he did his best. "I think we have heard enough," he said. "Thank you for inviting us here, Mr. Lincoln. I expect each of us can find his own way out, his own way back to his hotel, and his own way home."

One by one, the Republican leaders filed past Lincoln and toward the door. As John Hay went by, the ex-president softly asked, "*Et tu*, John?"

"*Et ego,* Mr. Lincoln." Hay's voice was sad, but it was firm. Like the others, even Frederick Douglass, he left without a backwards glance.

Lincoln stood all alone in the room poor men had built so rich men might confer in it. "Labor first," he said, as he had so many times. "Labor first, *then* capital. If they cannot remember that on their own, I shall make certain they are reminded of it." And he left, too, his back straight, his stride determined. He had been a Whig. He was—no, he had been—a Republican. Now . . .

"They have lost the war," General Thomas Jackson told Major General E. Porter Alexander. "If they cannot realize that on their own, I shall make certain they are reminded of it."

"Yes, sir." Alexander was not a young man, but retained a large measure of boyish enthusiasm. "President Longstreet's tried to make 'em take their medicine. If they won't open their mouth, we'll just have to yank it open and shove the pill down their throats whether they like it or not."

"Well put." Jackson studied the dispositions on the map. "Everything appears to be in readiness."

"Everything on my end is, sir," his chief artillerist answered. "The guns await only your order to begin."

"Tomorrow morning at half past five," Jackson said. "The end of the day, if God grant victory on our arms, should see the removal from our soil of more than half the Yankees now infesting it."

"Here's hoping you're right, sir," General Alexander said. "And if you are, I'm damned if I can see how they'll be able to go on fighting after that."

"Do not speak so lightly of damnation." Jackson put a rumble of reproof in his voice. "To tell the truth, though, I cannot see how they have gone on fighting so long when so little has gone right for them. Much as I hate to say it, they are braver than I reckoned."

"Hasn't done 'em much good, and that's what counts," Alexander answered.

Absently, Jackson nodded. "Courage and the goodness of one's cause, unfortunately, do not always go hand in hand."

"Yes, sir, that's a fact." His artillery chief nodded, too. "If Douglass taught us anything, he taught us that." Alexander's chuckle had a slight nervous edge. "And, looking out of the other side of the mirror, he learned the same thing from us, I reckon."

"Goodness does not depend on the position from which one observes it," Jackson said sternly. "Goodness *is*." He sounded very certain. He *was* very certain. Even so, he did his best not to think about Frederick Douglass. He also noticed that E. Porter Alexander didn't reply, which might well have meant Alexander, too, carefully wasn't thinking about the Negro.

He went to bed that night with the rattle and bang of rifle fire from the trenches in Louisville and to the east of the city and the occasional rumble of artillery in his ears. Everything sounded as it had since the U.S. flank attack bogged down. Thus lulled, he fell asleep almost as soon as he finished his prayers. Neither too much noise nor too little would give the Yankees anything out of the ordinary with which to concern themselves.

An orderly shook him awake with the words, "Half past three, sir, like you ordered."

Yawning, Jackson got into his boots and stuck his hat on his head. The orderly gave him a big tin cup full of coffee strong enough to try to climb over the rim. The handle burned his fingers. The coffee burned his mouth when he gulped it down.

"Ahh," he said—a gasp of approval. "I'm ready. Now off to meet up with General Alexander."

He reached the artillerist, at batteries east of Louisville that had come to Kentucky gun by gun from all over the CSA, about half an hour before the show was scheduled to begin. "Good to see you, sir," Alexander said, saluting. In the dim gray of early dawn, he seemed as much a ghost as a man. "Everything is ready. We await only the hour."

"As it should be," Jackson said. Every so often, he would hold his watch next to a lantern. Time moved more slowly than it had any business doing. He'd seen that before. It always bemused him. At last, a little after he could see the time without putting the watch up to the light, he said, "The hour is come."

As if his words had been a signal, a great bellow of artillery rose west of him: all the guns that had defended Louisville against the flanking attack now sent their full fury against the line upon which they had halted the U.S. forces. The flashes from their muzzles lit up the horizon, as if the sun were rising from the wrong direction.

E. Porter Alexander beamed. "Isn't it bully, sir?"

In searching for a description, Jackson would sooner have found one in the Book of Revelations. Even so, he did not reprove his gayer subordinate. "It will do, General. It will do."

U.S. artillery, both in the salient east of Louisville and on the far side of the Ohio, was quick to respond. All through the fight for Louisville, the U.S. cannon had given Jackson more worry than anything else. The United States had brought a lot of guns into the fight, and handled them well. Their artillerymen might lack Porter's imagination, but they were solid professionals. Their shells would punish the Confederate entrenchments.

In spite of that counterfire, the C.S. soldiers in those entrenchments opened up on the Yankees in front of them with their Tredegars: a hailstone-on-tin-roof accompaniment to the big guns' thunder. Jackson was sure Rebel yells rang out all along the line as the Confederates there went over to the attack, but the roar of the guns drowned them.

"I pity those poor fellows," Alexander said. "They can't possibly break through, and they'll pay a stiff price for trying."

"It is the price of victory," Jackson said in a voice like iron. His chief artillerist grimaced, but finally nodded.

The sun rose. Jackson waited, still as a statue, while messengers brought word of the fighting to the west. As General Alexander had predicted, the U.S. position facing Louisville was more than strong enough to keep the attacking Confederates from doing much past getting into the first couple of lines of trenches. Jackson had hoped for more, but he had not really expected it.

An hour passed. Turning to Alexander, he asked, "Do you think they are fully engaged, reserves coming up, all their eyes turned on the fight right in front of them?"

"Sir, if they're not, they never will be," Alexander replied. With a faint hint of scorn, he added, "They have so much trouble seeing what's right in front of their noses, they sure as the devil aren't going to look any further."

Jackson considered. From the outset, he had held this moment in his hands and his hands alone. He stared eastward. His nostrils flared, like a wolf's when it takes a scent. He nodded, a sharp, almost involuntary motion. "Let it begin," he said.

E. Porter Alexander shouted an order. All the guns within the sound of his voice let loose. That roar signaled the eruption of all the guns the Confederates had assembled along the southern flank of the Yankees' salient. Up till now, nothing much had happened along that flank. Jackson had kept it strong enough to discourage U.S. forces from trying to shift direction and move against it, which hadn't been hard: the enemy's aim remained focused on Louisville alone.

Along with guns, he'd been quietly bringing men forward over the past few days. Now, as they burst from their trenches and dashed toward those of the Yankees, he did hear Rebel yells through the gunfire, a great catamount chorus of them.

"The men must go forward at all hazard, so long as any hope of success presents itself," he said aloud, as he had in the orders he'd sent to the brigade commanders south of the U.S. salient. "If we are to roll up the Yankees' strong fortified west-facing line, we can only do so by an unexpected assault from the flank and rear."

"Pour it on, boys!" Porter Alexander was yelling. "Pour it on!" Jackson tried to inspire his men to the same clear, cold despisal of the foe and certainty God was on their side as he felt himself. Alexander was warmer and earthier at the same time. "Give 'em a good boot in the ass!" he shouted. "Come on, you mangy bastards, *work* those guns!"

He got louder and coarser from there. Jackson started to rebuke him, then noticed how splendidly the sweating, smoke-stained artillerymen were handling their cannon. He held his peace. After the battle was over, perhaps he would reprove Alexander for some of his more blasphemous suggestions and ask that he refrain from using them in the future. Meanwhile, the artillery commander was getting results. That counted for more.

Streams of Yankee prisoners began shambling past what had for so long been the dividing point between their army and that of the CSA. One of them, a man old enough to have fought in the War of Secession, recognized Jackson. "God damn you, Stonewall, you sneaky son of a bitch!" he shouted. Jackson tipped his hat—to him, that was praise. The Confederates guarding the U.S. soldiers laughed. So did a few of the Yankees.

Some of the U.S. guns north of the Ohio shifted their fire to oppose the Confederate breakthrough. Jackson used a telescope to watch shells bursting among his advancing soldiers. But, for once, the U.S. artillerymen were slower than they should have been in responding to changing conditions on the field. As an old artillerist, Jackson also realized the smoke and dust his own bombardment was kicking up hampered the foe in his choice of targets.

More prisoners came back, some of them carried on makeshift litters by their comrades. Messengers came back, too. One young man, his voice cracking with excitement, exclaimed, "General Jackson, sir, them damnyankees is unraveling faster'n the sleeve off a two-bit shirt. They would run, only they ain't got nowheres to run to."

"God having delivered them into our hands, let us make certain we do not fail to achieve His great purpose by permitting them to slip through our fingers," Jackson said, and ordered more reinforcements forward.

General Alexander was also sending some of his guns forward so they could bear on the retreating U.S. soldiers. "You know something, sir?" he said. "This business is a lot more fun when you're moving ahead than when you're falling back."

"I believe I may have made a similar observation myself, at one time or another in my career," Jackson said.

"Yankees aren't having much fun right now," Alexander said.

Jackson smiled. It was the sort of smile that made blue-tuniced prisoners shiver as they stumbled into captivity.

A messenger ran up. "Sir," he panted, "we-uns just ran over the biggest damn Yankee supply dump you ever did see."

"Put guards around it," Jackson ordered. "Let no one go into it. Arrest any who try. If they resist even in the least, shoot them. Do you understand me, Private?"

"Y-Y-Yes, sir," the messenger stammered, and fled.

To E. Porter Alexander, Jackson said, "During the War of Secession, we lived off Yankee plunder because we had so few goods of our own. Sometimes we foraged when we should have been fighting. Now, with a sufficiency of our own supplies, fighting shall come first, as it should."

"Telling soldiers not to plunder is like telling roosters not to tread hens," Alexander said.

"Sooner or later, the philandering rooster ends up in a stew," Jackson replied. "The plundering soldier is also likely to end up stewing, especially if he pauses to plunder when he should advance."

Before long, disarmed Confederates started coming past him: only a trickle compared to the number of Yankee prisoners, but too many to suit Jackson. Some of them called out to him in appeal. He turned his back, the better to remind them they had jeopardized his victory with their greed.

Messengers also kept coming back. They were far more welcome, since almost all the news they brought was good. Here and there, by squads and companies, the Yankees kept fighting grimly. More often, though, they gave way to the alarm that could jolt through even experienced troops when flanked, and tumbled back toward the Ohio in headlong retreat.

Slyly, Porter Alexander asked, "What do we do if we go and catch Frederick Douglass again?"

"Dear God in heaven!" Jackson clapped a hand to his forehead. "I forgot to issue any orders about him. We give him back to the United States, exactly as we did before. President Longstreet, I must say, convinced me of the urgent necessity for following that course and no other."

He shouted for runners and sent orders for the good treatment of any captured elderly Negro agitator up to the front along with orders for continued advances. No news of any such prisoner's being taken got back to him. No news of any such Negro's being conveniently found dead on the field got back to him, either. But then, such news wouldn't. If Douglass had been killed by bullet or shell or hasty noose, his body either lay unnoticed where it had fallen or had been flung into a ditch to make sure it stayed unnoticed.

"Maybe he was back in U.S. territory when the attack began," Jackson said hopefully. "For our sake, I pray he was. For his sake, I pray he was, too."

"You say that about Frederick Douglass, sir?" E. Porter Alexander gave him a quizzical look.

"I do," Jackson answered. "He has, I would say, already done as much damage to our cause as he is likely to do." He did not mention President Longstreet's plan for manumitting Negroes in the CSA after the close of the war. General Alexander did not need to know about that, not yet. Jackson wished he didn't need to know about it, either.

Over the months since Longstreet had broached his intentions to him, he'd reluctantly decided the president knew what he was doing. Longstreet, as far as Jackson was concerned, made a better politician than a soldier; he was full of the deviousness politics required. If he said manumitting the Negro would redound to the advantage of the Confederate States, odds were he knew whereof he spoke.

"Sir!" A messenger shattered Jackson's reverie. "Sir, we have men on the Ohio!"

"Praise God, from Whom all blessings flow," Jackson murmured.

"We won't keep 'em there," Alexander predicted. "The damn-yankees can send too many shells down on 'em from across the river."

"You're likely right," Jackson said. "But that they are there spells the ruin of this salient, and all done in the space of a couple of hours."

"Uh, sir, look to the sky," Alexander said. "The sun'll be going down in an hour or so."

Jackson looked, and blinked in astonishment. Where had the time gone? "Very well, General: in the space of a day. I hope you are satisfied." He used words that seldom passed his lips: "I certainly am."

* * *

"Brother Sam," Vernon Perkins said severely over breakfast, "I must tell you that I am most vexed at the way your dog gobbles everything in his bowl and then steals from the portion allotted to Rover."

"You have to remember, Vern," Sam Clemens answered, "Sutro is named for a politician, so it's in his nature to steal whatever he can grab."

"And stop calling me Vern!" His brother-in-law's voice went shrill. "Vernon is a perfectly good name, and the one by which I prefer to be known."

"All right . . ." Sam was on the point of calling him *Vern* again, as if absentmindedly, but Alexandra's warning glance persuaded him that wouldn't be a good idea. He ate the rest of his insipid, lumpy oatmeal, grabbed his hat, and fled the regimented boredom of his brother-in-law's house for the genial, congenial chaos prevailing at the *San Francisco Morning Call.*

Wrecking crews were still tearing down buildings the British bombardment and invasion had ruined. Already, on some sites that had been cleared, new construction was going up: pine frames of a yellow bright enough to hurt the eye. On lots still empty, signs promised resurrection almost as fervently as did the Bible. THE OTTO V. JONES INSTITUTE OF PHRENOLOGY SHALL REOCCUPY THESE PREMISES, one declared. "Too bad," Sam said, and walked on.

Half a block farther south, another sign in the middle of a vacant stretch of ground said, WHEN COHAN'S OPENS UP AGAIN, WE'LL HAVE A BETTER FREE LUNCH TABLE THAN EVER. Always a man to prefer five-cent beer and free lunch to phrenology, Clemens beamed at that. Two lots farther on again, yet another sign offered a simple promise: WE'LL BE BACK.

Once Sam got down to the *Morning Call* offices on Market Street, he forgot about signs. "What's the story on Kentucky?" he called, walking in the door.

"U.S. troops still in the city of Louisville," Clay Herndon said. "General Willcox says he pulled back from the salient east of town to consolidate for another push somewhere else. New York quotes Berlin quoting London quoting Richmond quoting Stonewall Jackson saying we pulled back on account of he licked the stuffing out of us."

"That sounds about right, even if it did go through more hands than a streetwalker when the fleet sails into port," Clemens said. "And what's the latest out of Philadelphia, or don't I want to know?"

Herndon spoke in a monotonous drone: "President Blaine is reported to be studying the situation and will comment further when more is known." He went back to his normal voice: "He's probably hiding under the bed, waiting for the Rebs to walk in and cart him off."

"Why would they want to cart him off?" Sam asked with a bitter snort. "He does them more good right where he is. I don't suppose he's said anything more about Longstreet's call for peace since yesterday?"

"Nary a word," Herndon answered.

Clemens snorted again. "Well, I don't reckon we ought to be surprised. Since the last time Longstreet said he could have peace if he wanted it, we've been licked up and down both coasts, in New Mexico, and on the Great Lakes. If that wasn't enough to give the man a clue, why the devil should he take any notice of throwing away half of what's supposed to be the best army we've got?"

"Damned if I know." Herndon paused to light a cigar, then added, "You forgot about Montana."

"Oh? Have we been licked there, too?" Sam asked. "You didn't say anything about that."

"Don't know if we have or we haven't," his friend replied. "Not enough telegraph lines up where the soldiers are for anyone to know anything. Word goes from Louisville to Richmond to London to Berlin to New York to here a hell of a lot faster than it leaks out of a place like that."

"They've kicked us around everywhere else," Sam said, "*they* being whoever's gone up against us. No reason to expect anything different out in the middle of nowhere, is there?"

"Can't think of any," Herndon said. "Wish I could."

"Don't we both?" Sam walked over to his desk and sat down. All unbidden, he saw in his mind the grimy face of the Royal Marine who could have killed him out in front of the newspaper offices. Even though he was sitting, his knees quivered. "We were at their mercy," he muttered, more than half to himself. "They could do anything they wanted with us—and they did."

The telegraph clicker started delivering a new message. "Let's see what's gone wrong now," Herndon said. Out came the message, a word at a time. "London by way of Berlin by way of New York City—the British and Canadians are saying they've reached the line in Maine that was the British claim line before the Webster-Ashburton Treaty, and they'll stop there and annex it to Canada."

"Is that what they're saying?" Clemens raised a bushy eyebrow. "How does that square with what Longstreet's been saying about peace without losing pieces of the USA?"

"Damned if I know," Herndon said again. "Of course, Longstreet only speaks for the Confederate States. Not likely the limeys would let him tie their hands. They do as they please, not as Old Pete pleases."

"You're right about that," Sam agreed. "The British Empire is the biggest dog around, which is why Englishmen can act like sons of bitches all over the world. But good God, Clay, now they've given Blaine a reason to keep fighting, and one that makes some kind of sense. This damned war is liable to drag on forever."

"Congressional elections next year," Herndon said reassuringly. "With the House of Representatives Blaine'll get after this fiasco, he won't see two bits of money for the Army. He'd have to give up then."

"He should have given up weeks ago," Clemens snapped. "He shouldn't have started the blamed war in the first place." He shook his fist in the direction of Philadelphia. "I told you so, Mr. President! Now if only you'd gone and listened to me. But what the hell: no one else does, so why should you be any different?"

Herndon didn't answer that. Sam fired up a cigar and filled the space around him with noxious fumes. Thus fortified, he attacked the pile of stories on his desk. Colonel Sherman was proclaiming that more fortifications could make San Francisco invulnerable to attack from the sea. Sam scribbled a note at the bottom of the article: *Comments about stolen horses and locked barn doors would seem to fit here.*

Edgar Leary had covered Mayor Sutro's latest *pronunciamento* about the urgency of rebuilding what the Royal Navy and Marines had devastated. Sam devastated Leary's prose, shelling adjectives and bayoneting adverbs. He had a scrawled suggestion for a further line of development on this piece, too: *The faster we rebuild, the less anyone checks on how much money gets spent and on who spends it. It will stick in somebody's pockets, odds are those of some of His Honor's chums. Whose? Find out, and we'll shake this city harder than any earthquake ever did.*

He didn't think Leary could or would find out; Adolph Sutro had proved adept at covering his tracks and those of his henchmen. But it would give the kid something to do and keep Leary out of his hair for a while, which wasn't the worst bargain in the world. And Leary, even if he couldn't write for beans, was pretty good at getting to the bottom of things.

The rest of the pieces were routine: a looter caught in the act and shot dead, the usual rash of robberies and burglaries and assaults, and praise for the entertainments offered in those theaters to which the Royal Marines had not applied the most incendiary form of dramatic criticism. Having covered both the police-court circuit and the theaters in his time, Clemens knew how hard it was to breathe life into reports concerning them. After marking the copy with a relatively gentle hand, he passed it on to the typesetters.

That done, he pulled out a blank sheet of paper, inked his pen anew, and . . . did not write. He knew what he wanted to say. He knew what he needed to say. He'd been saying it ever since the war broke out, and suggesting it before the war broke out. What point to doing it again? If your editorials sounded the same day after day after day, how did that differ from touring the police courts and recording the never-ending human folly and viciousness they memorialized?

At last, he found a way. "No wife-beater ever born," he muttered, "no wife-beater with the worst will in the world, does a millionth part of the harm James G. Blaine caused with only good intentions."

That scornful grumble gave him a title for the editorial that would not write itself. GOOD INTENTIONS, he printed in block capitals at the top of the page. The title gave him an opening sentence.

We know what road is paved with good intentions. What we need to do now is take a long, hard look at how the United States found themselves on that road, and how they will be able to get off it again without becoming too badly scorched in the doing. Heaven and the infernal regions both know there is blame and to spare to go around.

Ever since the voters in their wisdom threw Abe Lincoln out on his ear—after in their wisdom electing him four years earlier and thus proving what a remarkably changeable commodity wisdom can be; quicksilver won't touch it, and not a single, nor even a married, woman in the electorate to blame it on—after heaving Lincoln over the side, I say, we spent the next many years electing Democrats whose notion of statecraft, as best anyone can tell, was to bow down to Richmond as the pious Mussulman bows in the direction of Mecca. And the voters saw this, and said that it was good.

And Richmond said it was pretty good, too, and gobbled down Cuba without so much as calling for a toothpick, and sent redskins into Kansas until any old run-of-the-mill bald man was reckoned to have had his coiffure lifted by the Kiowas. And the Democrats in the White House sighed and wrung their hands and likely knocked back a beaker or three of whiskey on the sly, since they had hardly more use for the Kansas Jayhawkers than they did for the niggers of Cuba.

Kick a country or any other dog long enough, though, and it will turn and try to bite you. As we had coughed up Abe Lincoln, so in the fullness of time—if last November will do duty for that article—we coughed up James G. Blaine. And Blaine snarled, and Blaine growled, and, like a fierce old bulldog tormented past endurance, Blaine bit.

Like an old old bulldog, though, Blaine unfortunately neglected to equip the said bite with anything in the least resembling teeth. And so, having closed his gums round the leg of the Confederate States, he has hung on like grim death while they and England and France all belabor him with a fine assortment of clubs and switches and bludgeons. He will gnaw off the Rebels' leg or die trying—so his mumbled growls proclaim.

That he *will* die trying—that *we* will die while he tries—has long since become obvious to everyone save him alone; he is evidently an old blind bulldog as well as an old toothless one. Our own fair city has already paid the price for his bullheaded bulldoggery. If he persists, how long will it be before we once more play the *rôle* of a china shop?

What will it take to make him come to his senses, if by some accident he should have any left? He—

Sam hadn't noticed the telegraph clicking away. In a voice filled with excitement, Clay Herndon cried, "Blaine's calling for an unconditional cease-fire on all fronts. He's thrown in the sponge, Sam!"

Clemens stared at the editorial he'd been writing. He picked up the sheet, tore it to shreds, and flung them into the waste-paper basket. He was grinning from ear to ear as he did it, too.

☆ **XVII** ☆

"Come on, men!" George Custer shouted. "Are we going to let a pack of damned Volunteers get the better of us?"

That made his men ride harder, which was what he'd had in mind. It also made Colonel Theodore Roosevelt, who was trotting along beside him, display a mouthful of very large teeth in a grin the Cheshire Cat might have envied. "I'm glad you think well of my regiment, General Custer," Roosevelt said.

"I've seen worse," Custer allowed, which only made Roosevelt's grin wider. After coughing a couple of times, Custer went on, "Colonel Welton, who is an old friend of mine, spoke highly of them, and I do begin to understand why. He spoke highly of you, too, Colonel."

"He's very kind," Roosevelt said. The grin did not diminish. Roosevelt knew others had a good opinion of him. He had a good opinion of himself, too.

Custer wondered if he'd been such an arrogant puppy at the same age. He probably had; as Henry Welton had said, he never would have bulled his way onto General McClellan's staff otherwise. Now, observing the phenomenon from the outside, as it were, he wondered why no one had taken a gun and shot him for the way he'd carried on.

Roosevelt said, "General, didn't I hear that you brought a good many Gatling guns up with you from Utah Territory?"

"I brought them," Custer admitted. "I left them behind with the Seventh Infantry. They slowed down my riders to an intolerable degree." He felt nothing but relief at finally having got rid of the contraptions.

But Roosevelt frowned. "We haven't enough horse here, even with your regiment and mine combined, to halt the damned Englishmen. The mechanized firepower the Gatlings represent would have been most welcome. Don't you agree that war is increasingly a business where the side with more and better weapons holds an advantage mere courage is hard pressed to overcome?"

"I most assuredly do not," Custer snapped. "Put brave men in one army and a rabble of clerks and tinkers in another, and I know which I would favor. Why do you suppose the dashed Rebels licked us in the War of Secession?"

Roosevelt was not one to back down, any more than Custer was. "How do you think Lee's men would have fared, General, had they gone up against today's rifles and artillery with their muzzle-loaders and Napoleons?"

That question had never crossed Custer's mind. He was not much given to abstract thought. Before he could answer, the need for him to answer went away: a scout came riding up, calling, "General Custer! General Custer! The British are coming!"

Colonel Roosevelt whooped. "Tell me your name's not Paul Revere, soldier."

The scout ignored him. "Sir, their infantry is drawn up in line of battle, they've got cavalry in front and on both wings, and I spotted a couple of field pieces with 'em, too. If we don't get out of their way, they're going to try and bull right through us, you mark my words, sir."

"If they want a fight, they shall have it," Custer declared.

"Sir, I've been dogging that army for a while now," Roosevelt said. "As I told you before, they badly outnumber us: your regiment and mine together, I mean. Should we not find a defensible position and let them move upon us?"

"Colonel, if you wish to withdraw, you have my permission," Custer said icily. "Perhaps you will permit some of your braver soldiers to remain?"

"Sir, I resent that." Roosevelt scowled and went red. "My men, begging your pardon, have done a damn sight more fighting in this war than yours have. You'll not find us backward now."

"Very well, then," Custer said, having insulted the younger man into doing what he wanted. Roosevelt, if he was any judge, would fight his men with no thought for tomorrow to prove his courage and theirs. "I will want your troopers on either flank, to oppose the enemy's cavalry while we Regulars discuss matters with his foot soldiers."

"Yes, sir." Roosevelt's salute was so precise, Custer wondered if his arm would break. After a moment, he added, "I understand that General Gordon, the British commander, is very much a straight-ahead fighter, too."

"Is he?" Custer shrugged. It mattered little to him. He knew what he was going to do. Past that, he didn't much care. "I intend to send him straight to a warmer clime than this." Roosevelt liked that. The grin came back to his face. He saluted again, this time as if he meant it rather than as a gesture of reproof, and rode off shouting orders for the Unauthorized Regiment.

Custer started shouting orders, too. "Sounds like a big fight brewing, Autie," his brother said.

"I reckon so, Tom," Custer agreed. "Not quite the enemy I wanted—I still owe the Rebs a couple of good licks—but this will do. This will do, by jingo."

"I'll say it will." Tom Custer beamed. "Did I hear right? Have they got a lot more men than we do?"

"That's what Roosevelt says." Custer shrugged. "He's the one who's been skirmishing with the limeys ever since they came down out of Canada. If anybody knows what they've got, he's the man."

"Fair enough." The prospect of going up against long odds didn't bother Tom—quite the reverse. "They won't expect us to hit 'em, then. They'll be looking to have everything their own way. Let's lick 'em, Autie."

"I sure aim to try." Custer reached out and slapped his brother on the back. They grinned at each other. Tom was the only man in the whole U.S. Army who might have relished a good scrap more than he did.

The Regulars deployed from column to line with a nonchalant ease that came from not just weeks but years of endless repetition on the practice field. Roosevelt's Unauthorized Regiment was nowhere near so smooth. But the Volunteer cavalrymen weren't slow, either. Custer found nothing to complain about on that score. From the right flank, Roosevelt waved his hat to show he was ready to go forward.

Custer waved, too, so Roosevelt would know he'd seen him. The brevet brigadier general turned to the trumpeter beside him. "Signal the advance," he said. As the horn call rang out, the men of the Fifth Cavalry cheered loudly. Not to be outdone, so did the regiment Roosevelt had raised.

When Custer reached the top of a low swell of ground, he

pointed ahead and cried out, "There is the enemy. Let us sweep him from our sacred soil, as our forefathers did a hundred years ago in the Revolution." The forefathers of a lot of his troopers had been grubbing potatoes out of the ground of Ireland a hundred years before, but no one complained about the rhetoric. The men raised another cheer.

General Gordon had ordered his army as the scout described: cavalry right and left, a screen of horsemen in front of the infantry, and the thin red line of foot soldiers stretching across the prairie. Off to the right of Custer, Roosevelt's men shouted. Idly, Custer wondered what their colonel had told them.

The British army disappeared from sight for a while when Custer rode down the far slope of the rise. He wished the Englishmen would vanish as easily when the time for fighting came, as it would in mere minutes. Up another swell of ground he trotted, his men close behind. Thin over a couple of miles of ground, the enemy's cheer reached his hear.

"They've seen us!" he called. A moment later, he spied a flash, and then another one, from behind the line of British infantry. A couple of hundred yards ahead of him, dirt fountained up into the air as two shells landed. Custer laughed out loud. "They can't hit the side of a barn, boys!"

Calmly, methodically, the British artillerymen served their field guns. The cannons flashed and roared again. One of the shells fell short. The other landed behind Custer. Glancing back over his shoulder, he saw a horse down and kicking. His troopers cheered once more.

"This is nothing," Tom called to him.

"You're right," he said. "During the War of Secession, a couple of miserable little popguns banging away like this wouldn't even have been enough to wake us up." He pointed toward the British cavalry ahead. "By God, they *do* still have lancers! I wouldn't have believed it if I hadn't seen it with my own eyes."

His own men rode in loose formation. The lancers, mounted on horses that might have carried knights of the Round Table, formed lines that were real lines. All their lances came down at once; sunlight glittered off steel. As one, those big horses began to trot.

"What a bully show!" Custer cried, nothing but admiration in him for his enemies' horsemanship.

"Yes, and now we're going to smash it all to pieces," Tom

replied. Custer nodded, and then felt his face grow hot. What they would smash it with were breech-loading carbines—modern industry set against medieval courage. Maybe Colonel Roosevelt had known what he was talking about after all.

Custer gauged the range. "Fire at will!" he shouted. Behind him and to either side, the Springfields began to bark. He raised his own carbine to his shoulder, picked one of those lancers, and fired at him.

The man did not go down. Custer had not particularly expected him to, though he'd hoped he would. But a lot of troopers were blazing away at the Englishmen. All along the line of lancers, those big horses crashed to the ground. Men slid from the saddle or threw down their steel-shod spears to clutch at wounds. The ones who were not hit kept coming. Riders moved up from the second rank to take the places of those in the first who had fallen.

As the lancers drew nearer, Custer felt . . . not fear, for he had never known fear on a battlefield, but a certain amount of intimidation. The big, tough men looked ready to ride over the Fifth Cavalry and trample them into the grass and dirt of the prairie as if they had never been.

Then he shot at an Englishman and hit him square in the chest. The luckless fellow dropped his lance, threw up his hands, and slumped dead over his horse's neck. More and more Englishmen were falling as the range narrowed, and they could do nothing to hit back. None of them wavered, though.

"Christ, they're brave!" he shouted.

"Christ, they're stupid," his brother shouted back, reloading his Springfield.

A lancer thundered toward Custer. He fired at the fellow and missed. The lancehead pointed straight at his breastbone. In another couple of seconds, the British soldier would spit him as if he were a prairie chicken roasting over a campfire. He yanked out his Colt revolver and fired three quick rounds. One of them missed, too, but one hit the horse and one the rider. Custer didn't think any of the wounds would kill, but the lancer lost interest in skewering him.

Here and there, British lancers did spear his men out of the saddle. Here and there, too, the Englishmen drew their own revolvers and blazed away at his troopers. But a lot of the horsemen in red tunics were down, and more of them fell every minute. Flesh and blood, even the bravest flesh and blood, could take only so much. After some minutes of desperate, overmatched fighting at close quarters, the lancers broke away from the Fifth Cavalry and galloped for their lives back toward their infantry or away to the wings to shelter among horsemen whose rifles could protect them.

Custer cheered and waved his hat. "Forward, men!" he shouted—the order he always loved best. "Follow me! We've given their horse a good lesson. Now to deal with the foot."

He galloped past a dead redcoat, then past a British horse with a broken back trying to drag itself along with its forelegs. Then he and his troopers thundered toward the British infantry, who waited in a two-deep firing line to receive them. A shell chewed up the prairie off to his right. Fragments of the casing hissed past his head. He shrugged and kept riding.

Every so often, along that firing line, a red-coated soldier would go down. The British held their positions as steadily—indeed, as stolidly—as any troops Custer had seen during the War of Secession. As he rode toward the British line, doubt tried to rise in his bosom. Cavalry had had a devil of a time shifting steady infantry during the last war. True, his men carried breech-loaders now, but so did their foes. The British lancers had been as brave as any men he'd ever seen. Would the foot soldiers be any different?

He did what he always did with doubt—he stifled it. "Here we go!" he shouted. "For the United States of America! Chaaarge!"

As if held by a single man, all the rifles along the British firing line leveled on the Fifth. As if held by a single man, all those rifles fired at the same instant. A great cloud of black-powder smoke rose above and around the enemy. Through it, flames thrust like bayonets from the muzzles of the Englishmen's Martini-Henrys.

Three balls snapped past Custer. Not all his men were so lucky as to have bullets miss them. The charge broke up almost as if the troopers had slammed into a wall. Men screamed. Horses screamed—louder, shriller, more terrible cries than could have burst from a human throat.

The British infantry fed more cartridges into their rifles. Precise as so many steam-driven machines, they gave the Fifth Cavalry another volley, and another, and another. The horsemen replied as best they could. Their best was not enough, not nearly. The redcoats not only outnumbered them but were also firing on foot rather than from the bounding backs of beasts. Englishmen, many Englishmen, toppled and writhed and cursed and shrieked. The Americans, though, melted away like snow on a warm spring afternoon.

"We can't do it, Autie!" Tom Custer shouted.

If Tom said a piece of fighting could not be done, no man on earth could do it. "We'll have to fall back," Custer said, and then, to the bugler, "Blow Retreat." But no call rang out. The bugler was dead. "Retreat!" Custer yelled at the top of his lungs. "Fall back!" The words were as bitter as the alkali dust of Utah in his mouth. So far as he could remember, he'd never used them before.

Fewer of his men heard him than would have heard the horn. But they would have fallen back whether he ordered it or not. They now made the same discovery the British lancers had not long before: some fires were too galling to bear.

Then Tom shouted again, wordlessly this time. The shout ended in a choking gurgle. Custer stared at his brother. Blood poured from Tom's mouth, and from a great wound in his chest. Ever so slowly, or so it seemed to Custer, Tom crumpled from his horse. When he hit the ground, he didn't move.

Custer let out one long howl of pain. The worst of it was, that was all he had time for. Even without Tom—and Tom, surely, would never rise again till Judgment Day—he had to save his force. His head swiveled wildly to east and west. Did the Volunteer cavalry know he couldn't maintain the fight? If they didn't, they would have to face the weight of the whole British army by themselves.

But no—they were breaking away from combat, too, falling back to screen the retreat of the Regulars. That was humiliating. Even more humiliating was that the British cavalry showed no great inclination to pursue. Roosevelt's Unauthorized Regiment had given the limeys all they wanted and then some.

The boy colonel rode over to Custer. "What now, sir?" he asked, as if his superior hadn't just finished feeding his own prized regiment into the meat grinder.

What now, indeed? Custer wondered. Without Tom, he hardly cared. But he had to answer. He knew he had to answer. "We fall back on our infantry and await the British attack as the enemy awaited ours," he mumbled. It was a poor solution—even with Welton's infantry, he didn't have the manpower General Gordon did. But, battered and dazed as he was, it was the only solution he could find.

"Yes, sir!" Roosevelt, by his tone, thought it brilliant. "Don't worry, sir—we'll lick 'em yet."

"Come on, men!" Theodore Roosevelt shouted. "We've got to keep the damn limeys off the Regulars' backs a little bit longer."

First Lieutenant Karl Jobst gave him a reproachful look. "Sir, I wish you would have found a politer way to put that."

"Why?" Roosevelt said. "It's the truth, isn't it? Right now, General Custer's men couldn't fight off a Sunday-school class, let alone the British army. You know it, I know it, and Custer knows it, too."

His adjutant still looked unhappy. "They fought General Gordon's men most valiantly—smashed the lancers all to bits and hurt the infantry, too."

"That they did. They charged home as bravely as you'd like," Roosevelt said. "So did the six hundred at Balaclava. They paid for it, and so did the Regulars. Custer's brother's down, I heard, among too many others. We won our part of the fight. Unfortunately, the result is measured by the whole, which here proves less than the sum of its parts."

Off from behind him came a brief crackle of rifle fire. The British cavalry, confident he would not turn on it with the whole Unauthorized Regiment, was dogging the tracks of the U.S. force, keeping an eye on it as it retreated. Every so often, British scouts and his own rear guard would exchange pleasantries.

"Sir, do you happen to know where Colonel Welton has positioned the Seventh Infantry?" This was not the first time Jobst had asked the question. Though normally a cold-blooded fellow, he could not keep concern from his voice. The Seventh Infantry was his regiment, Henry Welton his commander, to whose rule he would return when Roosevelt went back to civilian life.

Now, though, Roosevelt had to shake his head. "I wish I did, but General Custer has not seen fit to entrust that information to me." He rode on for another few strides, then asked a question of his own: "You being a professional at this business, Lieutenant, what is your view of Custer the soldier?"

"I told you before he came up to Montana, sir, that he had a name for impetuous boldness." Karl Jobst started to say something else, stopped, and then began again: "The reputation appears to be well founded."

After a while, Roosevelt realized that was all he'd get from his adjutant. If Jobst said anything more—something on the order of, *He took a perfectly good regiment and chopped it into catmeat,* for instance—and word of that got back to Custer, it would blight the lieutenant's career. No one could possibly doubt Custer's courage. He'd done everything he could, going straight into the British. But that hadn't been enough, and hadn't come close to being enough, to turn them back.

Roosevelt sighed. "Well, in his shoes I might well have done the same thing. With the enemy in front of him, he could think of nothing but driving them off."

"I do believe, sir, that you might have handled the engagement with rather more finesse," Jobst said. Roosevelt needed a moment to realize that was praise, and another moment to realize how much. If a Regular Army officer felt a colonel of Volunteers could have done better than a Regular brevet brigadier general, that spoke well of the Volunteer indeed—and not so well of George Custer.

A few minutes later, Custer rode back to confer with Roosevelt. Even if Custer had been overeager in the attack, even if the loss of his brother left his face raw with anguish, he was handling the retreat about as well as any man could. He kept a firm rein on both his unit and the Unauthorized Regiment, and made sure he found out whatever Roosevelt's riders could learn about British dispositions and intentions.

Roosevelt found a moment to say, "I'm sorry about your loss, sir."

"Yes, yes," Custer said impatiently—he was surely doing his poor best not to think of that. "Now we have to see to it that our country's loss does not include the whole of this force."

"Yes, sir. I wish I could tell you more," Roosevelt said. "Their cavalry screen keeps us from finding out as much as we'd like, just as ours does to them."

Custer gnawed at his mustache. "I wish I knew how far ahead of their infantry the cavalry's got. Not far enough to suit me, unless I miss my guess. Infantry pushed hard can almost keep up with horsemen. Once we've joined with Colonel Welton, odds are we shan't have to wait long before they attack us."

"You don't think they'll simply ignore us and go on down

toward the mines around Helena, which I presume to be their goal?" Roosevelt said.

"Not a chance of it, Colonel." Custer spoke with decision. "We shall be far too large a force for them to dare to leave us in their flank and rear. We could and would work all sorts of mischief on them."

"That does make sense," Roosevelt said. "And, from what I've heard, their General Gordon is a headlong brawler, as I believe I've mentioned once before."

"Yes, yes," Custer said again. Roosevelt bristled at the tone, even if Custer was not, could not be, quite himself. Had the general commanding U.S. forces in Montana Territory done so well, he could afford to ignore what anyone told him? The answer was only too obvious. Had the general done as well as all that, he and Roosevelt would have been riding north, not south. But then Custer showed he'd heard after all: "If he's so very headlong, maybe he'll run onto our sword, the way bulls do in the arena."

"I do hope so, sir," Roosevelt said. Custer's response let him ask the question in whose answer both he and Karl Jobst were keenly interested: "Where has Colonel Welton set up the position that awaits us?"

"Not far from the Teton River," Custer replied, which told Roosevelt less than he would have liked but more than he'd already known. The brevet brigadier general went on, "He has orders to pick the best possible defensive position. We should be in it, wherever it proves to be, by nightfall."

There *was* information worth having. "If we are, we'll fight in the morning," Roosevelt said.

"I expect we will," Custer said. He hesitated, gnawing at his mustache once more. That was unlike him. After a moment, he went on, "I am thinking of dismounting my men and having them fight on foot. That would leave your regiment, Colonel, as our sole force on horseback. I shall rely on you to keep the British cavalry off our flanks."

"We'll do it, sir," Roosevelt promised. "That's the sort of job Winchesters were made for." The Unauthorized Regiment would never have got close enough to the British infantry to engage them with the repeating rifles, whose effective range was not great. With Springfields, Custer and the Fifth Cavalry had slugged it out with the foot soldiers in red—and had come out on the short end of the fight.

"I shall rely on you, as I did in the engagement farther north," Custer said. Roosevelt didn't mention that his part of the force had driven back their opponents. Custer already knew that. He nodded absently to Roosevelt and then trotted south, to the regiment he had long commanded.

No sooner had he gone than Karl Jobst rode over to Roosevelt, a questioning look on his face. Roosevelt repeated what Custer had said. Jobst brightened. "Colonel Welton knows how to read a field as well as anyone I've ever seen," he said. "He'll pick the best place he can find for us to make a stand."

"Good," Roosevelt said. A moment later, he wished his adjutant had put it a different way. Making a stand implied that defeat carried disaster in its wake. That was probably true here, but he would sooner not have been reminded of it.

As Brigadier General Custer had said, they met Henry Welton about four that afternoon. And, as Lieutenant Jobst had said, Welton did indeed know how to read a field. He'd chosen to defend the forward slope of a low, gentle rise. No one could possibly approach without being seen and fired upon from as far out as rifles could reach.

And not only had he picked a good position, he'd improved on what nature provided. His men had dug three long trenches and heaped up in front of them the dirt they'd shoveled out. The trenches and breastworks didn't look like much from the front. Roosevelt wondered if they were worth the labor they'd cost.

So did Custer, who was arguing with Welton as Roosevelt rode up. Welton looked stubborn. "Sir," he was saying, "from everything I saw in the War of Secession, any protection is a lot better than just standing out in the open and blazing away at the bastards on the other side."

"All right, all right." Custer threw his hands in the air. "Have it your way, Henry. The dashed things are dug, and you can't very well undig them. But while you've been building like beavers, we've been fighting like fiends."

"Yes, sir, I know that," Henry Welton said. He nodded to Roosevelt. "And was I right about the Unauthorized Regiment?"

"They fought well, I'll not deny it," Custer replied. Theodore Roosevelt drew himself up straight at the praise. He thought his troopers deserved even better than that; they'd outfought the Regulars seven ways from Sunday. But, whatever else Custer might have been about to say, he didn't say it. Instead, he stared and pointed. "Colonel, you've posted all my damned"—he didn't bother with *dashed*; he was exercised—"coffee mills in the forward trench? Don't you think we'd be better off with riflemen there?"

"Sir, I thought we might as well use the Gatling guns, since we've got them," Welton answered. Roosevelt stared at them with interest; he'd never seen one before. They did look rather like a cross between a cannon and a coffee mill. Welton went on, "If they perform as advertised, they should be well forward, I think. If they don't, we can always bring riflemen in alongside them."

"They're the only artillery we've got," Custer said worriedly. "That means they belong in the rear." He looked around—probably for his brother, Roosevelt thought. He did not see Tom Custer. He would never see Tom Custer again. Not seeing him, the brevet brigadier general settled for Roosevelt. "What's your opinion in this matter, Colonel?"

"They're already emplaced," Roosevelt answered, "and they're not quite like artillery, are they, sir? If you're asking me, I say we leave them."

Custer yielded, as he likely would not have done with Tom to back him: "Have it your way, then. If they don't work, it doesn't matter where in creation they are. I reckon that likely, myself. As you say, though, Colonel Welton, we can always bring up riflemen."

"Sir, with your permission, I'm going to throw out a wide net of cavalry pickets, to make sure the British don't try anything in the night," Roosevelt said. "When the real fight comes, I'll keep them off your flanks."

"That's what you're here for," Custer agreed. "Go do it." It wasn't quite a summary dismissal, but it was close. Roosevelt saluted and stomped off.

Occasional rifle shots punctuated the night, as American and British scouting parties collided in the darkness. The British weren't trying a night attack; their pickets rode out ahead of their main force to keep the Americans from unexpectedly descending on them. Roosevelt snatched a few hours of fitful sleep, interrupted time and again by riders coming in to report.

He drank hot, strong, vile coffee before sunup as he deployed his men. He commanded the right, as he had in the earlier fight against General Gordon's army. The left wing was largely on its own; he knew he wouldn't be able to keep in touch with it once the fighting started.

And it would start soon. When men found targets they could actually see, cavalry skirmishing picked up in a hurry. On came the British infantry, deployed in line of battle, rolling straight toward the position Custer and Welton were defending. Roosevelt's men tried without much luck to delay them; their British counterparts held them off.

Behind the British line, the field guns accompanying the men in red opened up on the U.S. entrenchments. Custer and Welton had nothing with which they could reply; the Gatlings couldn't come close to reaching those cannon. In the trenches, the Regulars, infantry and dismounted cavalry alike, took what the enemy dished out. Roosevelt's respect for them grew. That had to be harder than fighting in a battle where they could strike back at what was tormenting them.

"Once General Gordon has us properly softened up, or thinks he has, he'll send in the infantry," Karl Jobst said.

Gordon let the two field guns pound away at the entrenchments for half an hour, his foot soldiers pausing just outside rifle range. Then the cannon fell silent. Thin in the distance, a bugle rang out. The British infantry lowered their bayoneted rifles, as the cavalry had lowered their lances. The bugle resounded once more. The Englishmen let out a great, wordless shout and marched forward.

"What a bully show!" Roosevelt exclaimed. "Enemies they may be, but they are splendid men." He raised his Winchester to his shoulder and tried at very long range to pot some of those splendid men.

Unlike the luckless lancers, the British infantry fired as they advanced; their breechloaders made reloading on the move, which had been next to impossible during the War of Secession, quick and easy. A cloud of smoke rose above them, thicker and thicker with every forward stride they took.

Smoke rose from the trenches where the bluecoats crouched, too. Englishmen began falling. Their comrades filled their places. No doubt Americans were falling, too, but Roosevelt couldn't see that. What he could see was the red British wave flowing forward, steady and resistless as the tide. The redcoats drew within four hundred yards of the frontmost entrenchment, within three hundred . . .

"They're going to break in!" Roosevelt cried in bitter pain.

And then, through the din of the rifles, he heard a sound like none he'd ever known before, a fierce, explosive snarl that might have been a giant clearing his throat, and clearing it, and clearing it. . . . Amazing puffs of smoke blossomed in the center of the U.S. front line. "The Gatlings!" Karl Jobst yelled, somewhere between astonishment and ecstasy.

Roosevelt had no words, only awe. In what seemed the twinkling of an eye and was perhaps two or three minutes of actual time, those steadfast British lines abruptly ceased to exist, in much the same way as a slab of ice will rot when hot water pours over it. For the first half of that time, the infantry kept trying to go forward in the face of fire unlike anything they'd ever met or imagined. They dropped and dropped and dropped. Not one of them got within a hundred yards of the trench. After that, the foot soldiers, those of them still on their feet, realized the thing could not be done. They also realized they were dead men if they didn't get out of range of the terrible stream of bullets pouring from the Gatling guns.

It was not a retreat. Custer had led a retreat. It was a rout, a panic-stricken flight, a stampede. The British, surely, were as steady in the face of familiar danger as any men ever born. In the face of the snarling unknown, they broke. Some of them—Roosevelt took off his spectacles and rubbed his eyes to be sure he was seeing straight—threw away their rifles to run the faster.

He spent only a little while luxuriating in amazement. Then he started thinking like a soldier again. "After them!" he shouted. "After them, by jingo! They thought they'd run over us like a train, did they? Well, they've just been train-wrecked, boys. Now we haul away the rubbish."

Now his men, cheering as if their throats would burst, pressed hard upon the fleeing foe. The British horse, which had been screening an advance, suddenly had to try to screen a broken army falling back. The enemy's field guns fired a few rounds of canister before the men of the Unauthorized Regiment, coming at them from three directions at once, overran them and killed their crews.

"Captured guns," Lieutenant Jobst said cheerfully. "That's the true measure of victory. Has been as long as cannons have gone to war."

"After them!" Roosevelt shouted. "We don't want to let even a single one get away. No, maybe one, to tell his pals up in Canada what it means to invade the United States." He fired at an English cavalryman and knocked him out of the saddle. "Easy as shooting pronghorns!" he exulted.

North over the prairie went the pursuit, as it had gone south the day before. The troopers of the Unauthorized Regiment took rifles away from slightly wounded or exhausted Englishmen they passed and rode on after the main body. Roosevelt didn't think he had enough men to beat them, but they were so shaken he intended to try if he got the chance. They might all throw down their guns and give up at a show of force.

And then, from behind, he heard not one but several buglers blowing Halt. His men looked at one another in surprise, but most, obedient to the training he'd drilled into them, reined in. "No!" he raged. "God damn it, no! I didn't order that! I'll kill the idiot who ordered that. We've got 'em licked to a faretheewell."

"Halt!" a great voice shouted: George Custer, who must have almost killed his horse catching up to Roosevelt's men. To Roosevelt's amazement, tears streaked Custer's cheeks, not just tears of grief but tears of fury. To his further amazement, Custer reeked of whiskey from twenty feet away. "Halt, damn it to fucking hell!" he shouted again.

"What's wrong, sir?" Roosevelt demanded.

"Wrong? I'll show you what's wrong!" Custer waved a sheet of paper. "What's wrong is, a cease-fire with the English sons of bitches went into effect yesterday, only we didn't know it. We just licked the boots off the shitty limeys, we just got my brother killed, in a battle we never should have fought, and now we have to let what's left of the bastards go home. I haven't had a drink of liquor, save for medicinal purposes, in almost twenty years—not since before I married Libbie. Do you wonder, Roosevelt, do you wonder that I got myself lit up riding after you?"

"No, sir," Roosevelt said, and then, "Hell, no, sir." After a moment, he added, "Is anything left in your bottle, sir?"

"Not a drop," Custer answered. "Not a single fucking drop."

"Too bad," Roosevelt said. "In that case, I'll just have to find my own."

Frederick Douglass got off the train in Rochester. His wife and son were the only black faces on the platform. Anna Douglass burst into tears when she saw him. Lewis folded him into a hard, muscular embrace. "Good to have you home, Father," he said. "Let me take your bag there."

"Thank you, my boy," Douglass said. "Believe you me, it is very, very good to be home again." He gave Anna a gentle kiss, then stood up tall and straight before her. "As you see, my dear, I have come through all of it unscathed."

"Don't sound so proud of yourself," she said sharply. "I reckon that was the Lord's doin', a whole lot more'n it was yours."

He looked down at the planks of the platform floor. "Since I cannot possibly argue with you, I shall not even try. The Lord took me through the valley of the shadow of death, but He chose to let me walk out the other side safe. For that, I can only praise His name."

Anna nodded, satisfied. Lewis Douglass asked the question his father had known he would ask: "What was it like, sir, coming up before Stonewall Jackson?" A frown twisted his strong features; he laughed ruefully. "If working with you on the newspaper hasn't yet taught me the futility of asking what something is like and then expecting to feel the answer as did the man who had the experience, I don't suppose it ever will."

"If it hasn't yet taught me that futility, why should it have done so with you?" Douglass returned. "What was it like? It was frightening." He held up a hand before his son or wife could speak. "Not in the way you think, either. It was frightening because I found myself in the presence of a man both formidable and, I judge, good, but one who believes deep in his heart in things utterly antithetical to those in which I believe, and who reasons with unfailing logic from his false premises." He shivered. "It was, in every sense of the word, alarming."

They all walked out toward the carriage, Anna on Frederick's arm. As Lewis put the last suitcase behind the seat, he remarked, "You have said before that it is possible for a slaveholder to be a good man."

"Yes." Douglass helped his wife up, then climbed aboard himself and sat beside her. "It is possible," he went on as Lewis took the reins. "It is possible, but it is not easy. Jackson . . . surprised me."

"I reckon you surprised him, too." Anna patted her husband's arm.

"I hope I did. I rather think I did," Douglass said. "And I have what may be great news: in Chicago, I heard that the Confederates are—no, may be—planning to manumit their bondsmen once the war, now suspended, is truly ended, this being a *quid pro quo* in return for their allies' assistance against the United States."

"Wonderful news, if true," Lewis said. "We've heard the like now and again down through the years, though, and nothing ever came of it. Who told you this time, Father? Lincoln?"

"No, John Hay," Douglass answered. "Since he was minister to the Confederate States, he should know whereof he speaks. Lincoln had other concerns." He let out a bitter sigh. "Lincoln has had other concerns than the Negro before, which I say though he is and has always been my friend. In the summer of 1862, he drafted a proclamation emancipating all slaves within the territory of the Confederate States, then waited for a U.S. victory to issue it, lest it be seen as a measure of desperation rather than one of policy. The victory never came, and, when our straits indeed grew desperate, he let that paper languish, having been convinced it was by then too late to do any good. I shall go to my grave convinced he was mistaken."

"Of course he was, Father," Lewis said angrily. He looked back over his shoulder. "In all the years since, you have never spoken of this, nor has anyone else I ever heard."

"The proclamation was never widely known, for obvious reasons," Douglass answered. "Once the Confederate States succeeded in breaking away, it became moot, and what would have been the point to mentioning it? As you'll remember, the fight to emancipate the Negro slaves remaining within U.S. territory after the War of Secession was quite hard enough."

"That is so, and you may be right about the rest, too," Lewis said, "but it galls me to think the United States went down to defeat when we still had a weapon we could loose against the enemy."

Frederick Douglass let out a hoarse whoop of laughter. "You say that, after the ignominious cease-fire to which President Blaine has agreed? We have an army's worth—no, a nation's worth—of weapons we have not loosed against our enemies in this fight, and now we shall not loose them."

"And that's a right good thing, too," Anna Douglass said, "on account of the only thing we would do with 'em is shoot our own selves in the leg."

Lewis pointed north, toward Lake Ontario. "Two ironclads flying the Union Jack steam back and forth out there. We are under their guns, as we have been since they first bombarded us.

We are helpless against them. The problem is not only poor use of the weapons we have, but also weapons we lack."

"We have now twice gone unprepared to war," Douglass said. "May God grant that, where we did not learn our lesson the first time, we shall do so the second. I hope that, in years to come, smoke will billow from the stacks of the factories producing every manner of gun and munition so that, should another war ever come, we shall at last be ready for it."

When the carriage reached the street on which Douglass lived, Lewis had to rein in sharply to keep the horses from running down Daniel, who was pedaling his bicycle along without the slightest care for where he was going. The boy handled the high-wheeled ordinary with far more confidence than he'd shown before Douglass left for Louisville: too much confidence, perhaps.

Seeing Douglass, he whizzed close to the carriage. "Welcome back!" he shouted. "Welcome home!"

"Thank you, son," Douglass answered. By then, Daniel was speeding away again. Douglass wondered whether he heard. Even so, the journalist softly repeated the words: "Thank you." To Daniel, he wasn't a Negro, or, at least, wasn't first and foremost a Negro. Before that, he was a neighbor and a man. To Douglass, that was as it should be.

Lewis reined in again, in front of the house where Douglass and Anna had lived so long. "Here we are, Father." He grinned and tipped his cap. "Cab fare, fifty cents."

Douglass gave him two quarters, and a dime tip to boot. He would not let Lewis return the money, either, saying, "It's the best ride I've had since I left home, and one of the cheaper ones, too."

"All right, since you put it that way." Lewis shoved the coins into his pocket. "Good to know I have a trade I can fall back on at need. Heaven knows the newspaper business isn't so steady as I wish it were."

"See what you get for not pandering to the most popular opinions?" Frederick Douglass kept his tone light, but the words were serious, and he and his son both knew it. He got down, then helped Anna. She felt fragile, bony, in his arms. Anxious, he asked, "My dear, how are you?"

"As the good Lord meant me to be," she answered, to which he found no response. She went on, "Pretty soon I'll see Him face-to-face, and I intend to have a good long talk with Him about the way things do go on in this here world."

"Good," Douglass said. "I'm sure He could have made a much better job of things had He had you to advise Him."

Anna glared, then poked him in the ribs. They both laughed. Together, they walked into the house. Douglass stopped in the front hall. The feel of the throw rug under his feet, the rows of framed pictures on the walls, the infinitely familiar view of the parlor on one side and the dining room on the other, the faint smell of paper and tobacco and food—all told him he was home, and nowhere else. A long, happy sigh escaped him.

"Are you glad to be back?" Anna asked slyly.

"Oh, maybe just a bit," he answered. They laughed again.

Lewis came downstairs, brisk and quick and sure of himself. "I've put your bags in the bedroom, Father. That's settled for you." He was a young man still, and certain that things were easily settled. A small problem solved, he moved on to a greater one: "Where do we go from here?"

"How do you mean that?" Frederick Douglass asked. "I myself am going upstairs before long, to find out if I still remember what sleeping in my own bed feels like. If, however you mean *Where does the colored man go from here?* or *Where do the United States go from here?*—well, those questions require a little more thought. Only a little, you understand."

"I had suspected they might." Lewis chuckled without much mirth. "Any quick answers, before I see to the horses and the carriage?"

"You let your father rest," Anna said with a touch of asperity. "He hasn't had hisself an easy time of it."

Nothing could have been better calculated to make Douglass say, "I will answer—a horseback guess, before Lewis goes back to the horses. As I said before, the lot of the colored man in the Confederate States may improve, though to what degree I cannot now guess. The lot of the colored man in our own country? I see no great change on the horizon, though I wish I did. We shall have to go on working state by state for laws asserting our rights, for the national government, having finally broken our chains, can go no further without another Constitutional amendment, and you know as well as I how likely that is."

"Un-," Lewis said wryly. "All right, that's not a bad summation for us. Can you do as well for the country?"

"No one can guess where the country goes from here," Douglass said, shaking his massive head. "We shall have to see what the full effect upon us is of this defeat. Lincoln believes the white laborer will be pressed down until he is no better off than the Negro—but Lincoln, being white, cannot fully grasp all the vicissitudes of being black. Ben Butler, if I understand him rightly, feels the national government needs to organize us down to our shoelaces, to make certain we are never again caught short by our enemies. Whether the national government can do that, whether it will do that, whether it should do that—if I could read a crystal ball, I would wear a turban on my head, not a derby."

"What does President Blaine think?" Lewis asked. "Did you get any hint of that in Chicago?"

"No," Douglass answered. "Surprisingly little was said of him at that meeting. Perhaps that was because he is sure to fail of reelection when his term is up, perhaps because he has not clearly shown he has any thoughts to speak of past unwavering hostility toward the Confederate States, and he has bought only disrepute on that policy."

"More Democrats," Lewis said with a sigh.

"More Democrats," Frederick Douglass agreed, as mournfully.

Anna said, "You was right the first time, Frederick. Now go on upstairs and get yourself some rest. You can do that your own self, and do it this here minute. The rest of it'll still be here when you get up."

"She's right, Father," Lewis said.

"She generally is," Douglass answered. He headed for the stairway.

Under flag of truce, General Thomas Jackson approached the line where his men had halted the Army of Ohio's push into Louisville. His guards looked jumpy, even though no guns had barked for several days. "Do you really trust the damnyankees, sir?" one of them asked.

"They fought honorably," Jackson answered. "If I was not afraid to come up here while the fighting raged, why should I fear doing so with the cease-fire in place?"

"I don't like it," the guard said, stubborn still. His eyes flicked now here, now there. "Lordy, they made a hell of a mess out of this here place, didn't they?" He paused a moment in thought. " 'Course, we helped, I reckon."

A call came from within the U.S. lines: "That you, General Jackson?"

"Yes, it is I," Jackson replied. To his ear, the U.S. accent was sharp and harsh and unpleasant.

"Come ahead, General," the Yankee said. "General Willcox is here waiting for you."

"Come I shall," Jackson said. He picked his way over broken bricks and charred boards. Here in the center of Louisville, nothing but rubble remained. The only walls to be seen were those U.S. and C.S. soldiers had erected from bits of that rubble. None of the graceful architecture that had made Louisville such a pleasant place before the war survived.

And President Longstreet, Jackson thought, *is willing to let the United States off without a half-dime's indemnity.* His mouth tightened. Christian charity was all very well, but what point to charity toward those who deserved it not?

A couple of men in blue uniforms showed themselves. They stood up a little warily; for a long time, showing any part of your body was an invitation to a sharpshooter to drive a hole through it. One of them said, "If you'd been here a few days ago, Stonewall—"

"No doubt my men would say the same to you, young fellow," Jackson answered. He wasn't so severe as he might have been; that was soldier's banter from the Yankee, not out-and-out hatred.

A trim young captain in tunic and trousers far too clean and neat for him to have served at the front line came up out of a trench and nodded. "I'm Oliver Richardson, General Jackson— General Willcox's adjutant. If you'll be so good as to come with me, sir . . ."

When Jackson saw Willcox, he stabbed out a forefinger at him. "I remember you, sir!" he exclaimed. "Unless I'm much mistaken, you were in the West Point class of the year following mine—class of '47, are you not?"

"That's it, sure enough," Orlando Willcox answered. "And I went into the Artillery, just as you did." He let out a rheumy chuckle. "We were all on the same side once, we old-timers. Another few years, sir, and no men in your country or mine who served with one another before the War of Secession will be left."

"You're right, General," Jackson said. "We are now separate, and grow more separate every day—despite, I might add, the ill-advised efforts of the United States to exert a nonexistent influence upon our peaceful domestic affairs." Remembering the cease-fire, he held up a hand. "But let that go. It is behind us, God grant forever. Your men here fought most valiantly. You have every reason to be proud of them."

"The same holds of yours," Willcox said.

He paused, perhaps waiting for Jackson to praise his generalship so he could again return the compliment. Jackson had not so much diplomacy in him. "To business," he said. "I am charged by President Longstreet to inquire of you when you intend to abandon these lines and withdraw all forces of the Army of the Ohio from the soil of the Confederate States."

"I cannot answer that at the present time, General Jackson," Willcox replied. "I have as yet been given no orders on the subject. Absent such orders, what choice have I but to hold the men in place?"

"Sir, I mean no disrespect to you or to your government, but this is not entirely satisfactory." If that wasn't an understatement, Jackson had never uttered one. "The United States requested the present cease-fire, presumably because you felt yourselves to be at a disadvantage. This being so, I must tell you that we shall not indefinitely tolerate your occupying territory that has belonged to our nation since the close of the War of Secession."

"Come with me, General," Orlando Willcox said, and began to walk away from the gathered men of both sides. When his adjutant started to come, too, he waved the young captain back.

Taking that as a hint, Jackson also motioned for the soldiers who had accompanied him inside the U.S. lines to hold their places. He followed the commander of the Army of the Ohio till they were out of earshot of their subordinates. Willcox stopped then, his boots scrunching on broken bricks. Jackson halted beside him. Quietly, the Confederate general-in-chief asked, "How now, sir?"

"How now?" Willcox said, also in a low voice but with unmistakable anger. "How now? I shall tell you how now, General. Getting any orders out of Washington City—excuse me, out of Philadelphia; I spoke from force of habit—is a miracle comparable to that which our Savior worked with the loaves and fishes. Getting orders in a timely fashion would be a miracle comparable to the Resurrection. I say *would be* rather than *is*, for I have seen no timely orders."

"This is not as it should be," Jackson said, and tried to decide whether that was a bigger understatement than the one he'd made a moment before.

"Some such conception had already formed in my mind, yes," Willcox said. Jackson did not remember any sardonic streak in him, but they'd had little to do with each other for more than thirty years, and nothing to do with each other for more than twenty. Maybe Willcox had changed. Maybe, on the other hand, he'd just been tried beyond endurance.

"What am I to tell my president, then?" Jackson asked. "He will suspect your government of having asked for this cease-fire so you could strengthen your position here, not as a prelude to abandoning it." Longstreet would certainly suspect that. Longstreet and suspicion were made for each other.

General Willcox spread his hands. "This is not the case. The cease-fire requested was on all fronts, against all enemies. What point to making such a request for the purpose of fortifying one relatively small position from which, you must be able to see as well as I, we have no prospect for large or rapid advance?"

"That is so," Jackson admitted. But then he felt he had to qualify his words: "I say it is so in my own person, you understand. How the president will view the matter when I report to him remains to be seen."

"Of course, General." Willcox's laughter was bitter. "The responsibility for war and peace and, in the broad sense, for the conduct of the war lies with the civilian branches of government. Who, though, who takes the blame when their plans go awry? Do they blame themselves? Have you ever seen them blame themselves?"

Jackson did not answer. In the main, he agreed with Willcox. Most professional soldiers, in the USA and CSA both, would have agreed with Willcox. But not all the blunders in the U.S. campaign in Kentucky lay with the civilians. Willcox could not have more plainly advertised what he purposed doing had he telegraphed Jackson ahead of time, and his flanking attack had been woefully late.

Willcox went on, "I do not desire any more fighting here. Not a man in my command wants any more fighting here. If, however, we are ordered to resume the struggle"—he spread his hands again—"we shall do so. What is the soldier's lot but to obey?"

"What do you judge President Blaine's likely response would be to an ultimatum demanding withdrawal from Louisville on pain of renewed war?" Jackson asked.

"I cannot answer that question," Willcox said. It was the proper response, but disappointed Jackson all the same; he had hoped Willcox's anger might lead him into a revealing indiscretion. The commander of the Army of the Ohio went on, "The only one who knows Blaine's mind for certain is Blaine, and, by all we've seen, he is none too sure of it, either."

That was indiscreet. It might have been revealing, had recent events not shown it to be a simple statement of fact. Jackson said, "President Longstreet is not pleased that you remain here, and will grow less pleased by the day."

"I wish I could tell you more," Willcox answered. "I am, however, not a free agent, any more than you are, sir. Probably less than you are, for I doubt the apron strings holding you to your government are as tight as the ones I am compelled to wear."

"I doubt that—but then, I would, wouldn't I?" Jackson said. He and Willcox looked at each other with wry sympathy. Soldiers from one side often had more in common with soldiers from the other than with the civilians who told them what to do. "You have no better word to give me, General? Nothing I can send to Richmond to help ensure that we remain untroubled here?"

"If I had it, I would gladly give it: I assure you of that," Willcox said. "But I cannot give what I do not have."

"Very well." Jackson's nod was almost a bow. "I thank you for your time, sir, and I thank you for your courtesy. Please do take it as given that, should you at any time desire to visit me at my headquarters, you shall have no difficulty in passing through the lines and you will be most welcome there."

"You are very kind, sir." Willcox did bow. After further protestations of mutual esteem, the two men parted. Jackson made his way back into Confederate-held territory. He got aboard his horse there; entering the U.S. lines mounted might have made him seem like a man who judged himself a conqueror, and so he had refrained (even if he did so judge himself).

As he rode south, devastation gradually diminished. Single buildings and then whole blocks appeared, as if they were growing out of the rubble. His headquarters, being beyond the range of U.S. artillery, were set among unharmed trees and houses on the outskirts of town, and were quite pleasant. Taken as a whole, though, Louisville would be a long time recovering.

He wired Longstreet the results, or rather lack of results, of his meeting with General Willcox. The answer came back within a few minutes: WILL ANOTHER BLOW AID IN SHIFTING THE YANKEES? IF SO, CAN YOU LAY IT ON?

I CAN, he replied by telegraph. WILLCOX JUDGES BLAINE DOES NOT KNOW HIS OWN MIND. A BLOW MAY RESTART THE WAR.

He paced back and forth, awaiting the president's judgment. Longstreet was right; telegraphic conferences were not all they might be. After a while, the clicker brought the president's response. HAMMERING FULMINATE OF MERCURY UNWISE, Longstreet said. WE CAN WAIT. WAITING HURTS USA WORSE.

ALL IN READINESS HERE AT NEED, Jackson wired.

I ASSUMED NOTHING LESS, Longstreet eventually answered. I RELY ON YOU. KEEP ME APPRISED OF YOUR SITUATION.

That last wire made Jackson feel good. He knew Longstreet had sent it for no other reason than making him feel good. Knowing why Longstreet had sent it should have lessened the effect. Somehow, it didn't. Jackson took that to mean Longstreet was a formidable politician indeed.

He chuckled, which made the telegrapher waiting for his reply give him a startled look. "Never mind, son," Jackson told him. "It's nothing I didn't already know."

Alfred von Schlieffen's office in Philadelphia was neither so comfortable nor so quiet as the one he had enjoyed down in Washington. Nor did the German military attaché have here the reference volumes he'd used there. That Philadelphia did not lie under Confederate guns was at the moment, in his view, less of an advantage than the other factors were annoyances.

He had—he hoped he had—the books he needed here. He looked from an account of Lee's advance up into Pennsylvania, the advance that had won the War of Secession for the CSA, to an atlas of the world. Tracing Lee's movements day by day, fight by fight, gave him a fresh appreciation not only of what Lee had accomplished but also of precisely how he had accomplished it.

Indirect approach, Schlieffen scribbled on a sheet of foolscap. He had been studying Lee's campaigns since he came to the United States; they were not so well known to the General Staff as they should have been. When he traced on the map the Army of Northern Virginia's movements, he saw strategic insight of the highest order. He had seen some of that all along. Now he saw more. He also saw, or thought he saw, how to apply that insight to his own country's situation. Up till now, he had been blind to that.

Had Beethoven had this inspired feeling, this dazzling burst of insight, when the theme for a symphony struck him? For his sake, Schlieffen hoped so. The German military attaché felt like a god, noting the movements on the map as if he were looking down on a world he had just made and finding it good.

He underlined *indirect approach.* Then he underlined the words again—for him, an almost unprecedented show of emotion. Lee's goal all along had been Washington, D.C., yet he'd never once moved on the capital of the United States. He'd swung up past it and then around behind it, smashing McClellan's army and ending up here in Philadelphia before Britain and France forced mediation on the USA.

But Washington had been the *Schwerpunkt* of the entire campaign. Not only had Lee taken advantage of the U.S. government's urgent need to protect its capital, he had also used the great wheel around the city to gain the Confederacy the largest possible moral and political advantages.

Schlieffen flipped pages in the atlas. Since it was printed in the USA, the states of the United States and Confederate States came before the nations of Europe, and were shown in more detail. *Provincialism,* Schlieffen thought scornfully. But the maps he needed were there, even if toward the back of the book.

"Ach, gut," he muttered: the map of France also showed the Low Countries and a fair-sized chunk of the western part of the German Empire. In the Franco-Prussian War, the armies of Prussia and her lesser allies had moved straight into France and, after smashing French forces near the border, straight toward Paris. That coup would not be so easy to repeat in a new war; he had seen for himself how stubborn good artillery and good rifles could make a defense.

As if of itself, the index finger of his right hand moved in a wide arc, from Germany around behind Paris. He smiled and scribbled more notes. That sort of maneuver would make the French come out and fight in places they had never intended to defend and hadn't spent years fortifying. And what Frenchman, even in his wildest nightmares, could imagine Paris attacked from the rear?

The finger traced that arc again. Schlieffen noticed it ran through not only France but also through Luxembourg, Belgium, and perhaps Holland as well. In case of war between Germany and France, all three of the Low Countries were likely to be neutral. Would this maneuver be valuable enough to justify violating that neutrality and bringing opprobrium down on Germany's head?

"*Ja,*" Schlieffen said decisively. Whether the General Staff would agree with him, he did not know. He did know his colleagues back in Berlin had to see this notion, and had to see it soon. Even if they did not accept it, it would give them a new point of departure for their own thinking.

He was writing furiously, moving back and forth between the maps of France and Pennsylvania, when he noticed someone knocking on the door. The knocking was loud and insistent. He wondered how long it had been going on before he noticed it.

"How is a man to get any work done?" he muttered, and gave the door a resentful stare. When that failed to stop the knocking, he sighed, rose, and opened the door. Kurd von Schlözer stood in the hallway, looking less than happy himself. "Oh. Your Excellency. Excuse me," Schlieffen said. "How may I serve you?"

Seeing Schlieffen contrite, the German minister to the United States made his own frown vanish. "You must come with me to President Blaine's residence," he said. "Perhaps between the two of us, we can convince him not to resume this idiotic war."

"Must I?" Schlieffen asked, casting a longing glance back toward the maps and papers.

"You must," Schlözer said. Sighing again, Schlieffen obeyed.

While in Philadelphia, President Blaine resided at the Powel House, a three-story red brick building on Third Street, about halfway between Washington Square and the Delaware River. The reception hall was full of rich, ruddy mahogany. Schlieffen noticed it only peripherally. He paid closer attention to James G. Blaine, whom he had never before met.

Blaine was about fifty, with graying brown hair and beard, and would have been most handsome had his nose not borne some small resemblance to a potato. He gave an impression of strength and vigor. Married to good sense, those were valuable traits in a leader. A vigorous leader without good sense was liable to be more dangerous to his country than an indolent one similarly constituted.

"Minister Schlözer, Colonel Schlieffen—say your say." Blaine sounded abrupt, as if nothing the two Germans might say had any hope of changing his mind.

Kurd von Schlözer affected not to notice. "I thank you, Mr. President," he answered in English more fluent than Schlieffen's. "My attaché and I are here to try to persuade you that, since you have wisely chosen peace, you would do your country a disservice if you allowed the talks between your representatives and those of your opponents to fail."

"I would do my country a worse disservice if I let my enemies ride roughshod over the United States," Blaine growled.

"But, Your Excellency, how by weapons can you keep them from doing this?" Schlieffen asked. "They have on every front defeated you."

"Not in Montana, by jingo!" Blaine exclaimed with savage pleasure.

"Oh, yes—the battle after the cease-fire," Schlieffen said. The U.S. press shouted that fight to the skies. Putting what the U.S. papers said together with what came from Canada and London by way of Berlin, the military attaché gathered that the U.S. and British had tried to impale themselves on each other's guns, and the British had succeeded.

"That shows what we can do when we set our minds to it," Blaine declared.

"Yes, Your Excellency—but what of all the fights before the cease-fire? What of all the fights that made you for the cease-fire ask?" Schlieffen said.

Blaine looked as if he hated him. He probably did. Schlieffen bore the hatred of an American with indifference only slightly tinged by regret; it was not as if that could matter to him in any important way. The president of the United States said, "I did what I had to do to still public outcry. That having been accomplished, I am now obliged to seek the best possible peace for my country."

Schlieffen thought of Talleyrand, battling for France at the Congress of Vienna after Napoleon's overthrow—and gaining concessions, too, despite the weakness of his position. Then he thought again. Talleyrand was a gifted diplomat, something the Americans, despite their many abilities, had yet to produce.

"If only we were not so alone in the world," Blaine said querulously. "If only every nation's hand were not raised against us."

"That is not so," Kurd von Schlözer said. "Throughout this unfortunate time, Mr. President, the hand of Germany has been outstretched in friendship and in the search for peace."

"Sir, you are right about that, and I beg your pardon," Blaine replied. "Germany has done everything a good neighbor can do. But Germany, though she is a good neighbor, is not a near neighbor. All the nearest neighbors of the United States have joined together in oppressing us."

As you should have anticipated, Schlieffen thought. *As you should have prepared for.* But that was water over the dam now. Aloud, he said, "Your Excellency, General Rosecrans and I have about this talked. Germany is not your near neighbor, no. But Germany is to France a near neighbor, a nearest neighbor. France is now your enemy. France has our enemy been, and is likely our enemy again to be. Two lands with the same enemy can find it good to be friends."

He watched Blaine. Slowly, the president of the United States nodded. "Rosecrans has mentioned these conversations to me," he said. "For all their history, the United States have steered clear of entangling foreign alliances." Rosecrans had used that phrase, too; it seemed deeply engrained in the minds of all U.S. leaders. Blaine might almost have been quoting Scripture.

"Your Excellency, the Confederate States have had foreign allies," Kurd von Schlözer said. "The United States have not. When you and they have quarreled, who has had the better of it?"

Blaine's mouth puckered. His cheeks tautened against the bone on which they lay. "I do take the point, Your Excellency." And then, instead of merely saying he took it, he looked to take it in truth. "When you fought the French, you beat them like a drum. The last time we beat anyone like a drum, it was the Mexicans: not much of a foe, and a long time ago."

"Perhaps, then, you will to Berlin send officers to learn our ways," Schlieffen said. "Perhaps also your minister to my country will speak with Chancellor Bismarck to see in what other ways we can work together to help us both."

"Perhaps we will," Blaine said. "Perhaps he can. It might be worth exploring, at any rate. If nothing comes of it, we are no worse off."

Schlieffen and Schlözer glanced at each other. Schlieffen knew fellow officers who were avid fishermen. They would go on at endless, boring length about the feel of a trout or a pike nibbling the hook as it decided whether to take the bait. There sat James G. Blaine, closely examining a wiggling worm.

"The enemy of my enemy is—or can be—my friend," Schlieffen murmured. Blaine nodded again. He might not bite here and now, but Schlieffen thought he would bite. Nothing else in the pool in which the United States swam looked like food, that was certain.

"May we now return to the matter of the cease-fire and the peace which is to come after it?" Schlözer said. Schlieffen wished the German minister had not been so direct; he was liable to make Blaine swim away.

And, sure enough, the president of the United States scowled. "The Confederates hold us in contempt," he said sullenly, "and the British aim to rob us of land they yielded by treaty forty years ago. How can I surrender part of my own home state to those arrogant robbers and pirates?"

"Your Excellency, I feel your pain," Schlözer said. "But, for now, what choice have you?"

"Even Prussia, for a time, yielded against Napoleon," Schlieffen added.

Blaine did not answer. After a couple of silent minutes, the two Germans rose and left the reception hall.

☆ **XVIII** ☆

The cab drew to a halt by the edge of the sidewalk. The Chicago street was so narrow, it still blocked traffic. Behind it, the fellow atop a four-horse wagon full of sacks of cement bellowed angrily. So did a man in a houndstooth sack suit whizzing past on an ordinary. The cab driver said, "That's sixty-five cents, pal. Pay up, so I can get the hell out of here."

Abraham Lincoln gave him a half dollar and a quarter and descended without waiting for change. No sooner had his feet touched the ground than the cab rolled off, escaping the abuse that had been raining down on it.

This was a Chicago very different from the elegant, spacious North Side neighborhood in which Robert lived. People packed the streets. Lincoln had the feeling that, were those streets three times wider, they would still have been packed. One shop built from cheap bricks stood jammed by another. All of them were gaudily painted, advertising the cloth or shoes or hats or cheese or dry goods or sausages or pocket watches or eyeglasses sold within. Most had signs in the window proclaiming enormous savings if only the customer laid down his money now. FIRE SALE! GOING OUT OF BUSINESS! SHOP EARLY FOR CHRISTMAS!

Capitalism at its rawest, Lincoln thought unhappily. The weather was raw, too, a wind with winter in it. Hannibal Hamlin, who, being from Maine, knew all about winter, had called a wind like this a lazy wind, because it blew right through you instead of bothering to go around. Lincoln pulled his overcoat tighter about him; he felt the cold more now than he had in his younger days. The wind blew through the coat, too.

He looked around. There, a couple of doors down, advertising itself like all its neighbors, stood the frowzy, soot-stained office of the *Chicago Weekly Worker*. Lincoln hurried to the doorway and went inside. A blast of heat greeted him. Because the winters in Chicago were so ferocious, the means deployed against them were likewise powerful. He hastily unbuttoned his coat. Sweat started on his forehead.

A bald man in an apron and a visor who was carrying a case of type looked up at the jangle of the bell over the door. "What do you wan—" he began, his English German-accented. Then he recognized who was visiting the newspaper, and came within an inch of dropping the case and scattering thousands of pieces of type all over the floor. "What do you want, Mr. Lincoln?" he managed on his second try. The type metal rattled in its squares, but did not escape.

"I would like to see Mr. Sorge, if you would be so kind," Lincoln answered, as politely as if he were addressing one of his son's clients rather than a typesetter who hadn't had a bath in several days. "I do understand correctly, do I not, that he heads the Chicago Socialist Alliance?"

"Yes, that is right," the man in the apron said. "Please, you wait here, uh—" He looked confused and angry at himself. He'd probably been about to say *sir*, and then caught himself because *sir* was not the sort of thing a Socialist was supposed to say. He set down the type case, grunted in relief at being rid of the weight, and hurried into a back room.

A couple of printers and a fellow who, though he was surely a Socialist, too, looked like most of the other reporters Lincoln had seen over the years stopped what they were doing to gape at him. Then the typesetter came out of the back room with a lean man in his fifties, a fellow whose wary, hunted eyes said he'd made a lot of moves one step ahead of the police in the course of his lifetime.

"You *are* Abraham Lincoln," he said in some surprise. "I wondered if Ludwig knew what he was talking about." Like the typesetter's, his speech had a guttural undertone to it. "And I, I am Friedrich Sorge. I have had to flee Germany. I have had to flee New York City—Democrats can be as fierce in their reactions as Prussian *Junkers*. But I will not flee Chicago. '*Hier steh' ich, ich kann nicht anders.*' "

"I don't follow that," Lincoln said. "I'm sorry."

"Here I stand, I cannot do otherwise," Sorge translated. "Martin Luther. A progressive in his day, aiding the rising bourgeoisie against the church and the feudal aristocracy that supported it. Now, Mr. Lincoln—why do you stand here?"

"Because it has been made painfully clear to me that the Republican Party is not and cannot be the party that represents the laboring class in the United States," Lincoln answered. "I believe that class deserves representation. I believe this democracy will fail unless that class has representation. If the Republican Party is not up to the job, then the Socialists will have to be."

Friedrich Sorge and Ludwig the typesetter exchanged several excited comments in German. After a minute or so, Sorge returned to English: "This is what we have been doing since founding the party ten years ago."

"I know," Lincoln said. "I've watched you. I've watched your progress with no small interest. I would have watched it with even greater interest had there been more progress to watch."

"Too many American workers are in love with the *status quo* to make progress quick," Sorge said with a grimace. "It is the same as it is in Europe. No, it is worse than it is in Europe. In the United States, a man who despairs of factory labor will go and start a farm or prospect for gold in the hope of becoming rich at a stroke. This can never be an answer, but it can look like one, and it gives the capitalists a safety valve to drain off revolutionary energy."

"The safety valve will not stay open much longer," Lincoln said. "The prairies are filling up. Failed miners become proletarians in Western towns instead of Eastern cities, or they stay on as miners for the lucky handful who do grow rich, and serve as labor in the mines of the big companies."

"Yes." Sorge nodded emphatically. "So, as I say, though progress is slow, the revolution will come, and will throw down the capitalists and their minions."

"You believe the engine *is* broken and *will* explode," Lincoln said. Sorge nodded again. So did Ludwig. The ex-president went on, "I believe the engine *is* broken but *may perhaps* be repaired. The Republicans would not hear me because I dared to say something was wrong with the engine. Will you now cast me forth because I dare to say it may be set to rights?"

For a moment, he thought Sorge would tell him yes, and that would be that. Then the Socialist newspaperman said, "Come back into my office, Mr. Lincoln. We do not need to speak of these things standing here at the counter like men choosing pickles from the barrel."

The office was small and cramped and dark and full of bookshelves. Most of the books on them were in German, the rest in English and French. The word *Socialist* looked much alike in all three languages. Sorge had to clear more books off the chair in front of his desk to give Lincoln room to sit down. The desk itself was a disorderly snarl of papers.

Seeing Lincoln take the measure of the little room, Sorge chuckled wryly. "I, you see, will never be a wealthy capitalist. Luckily for me, I never wanted to be a wealthy capitalist."

"Had you wanted to be one, I should be here, or perhaps somewhere else close by, speaking of this with someone else," Lincoln answered, "for the Socialists in Chicago would have a leader, regardless of whether or not you were he. Now to come back to the question I asked out front: will you condemn me for not being revolutionary enough, as the Republicans condemned me for being too revolutionary?"

"Socialist thought is divided on whether the proletarian revolution is inevitable," Sorge said. "The Marxian Socialists, now, believe it is, and—"

"I am familiar with the division," Lincoln broke in. "Not long ago, in Montana Territory, Colonel Theodore Roosevelt accused me of being a Marxian Socialist, and I told him I had to decline the honor. This was before he became a national hero, you understand." His laugh was as wry as Sorge's. "Now, of course, I could deny him nothing."

"Of course," the Socialist answered, his voice curdled with irony. "The only confusion the papers have had is whether to fawn more on Roosevelt or on Custer. If something is before their eyes, they will never look farther. Pah!"

"This digression is my fault," Lincoln said. "I do apologize for it. Let me ask my question a third time: am I too soft for you, as I am too hard for the men of what had been my party?"

Sorge frowned in thought. "I have seen little in the behavior of capitalists to cause me to believe they will not create so much outrage among the proletariat as to make revolution inevitable."

"You have never seen the behavior of capitalists reined in by government regulation, either," Lincoln replied.

"No, I have not," Sorge said. "I have not seen the second

coming of Jesus Christ, either. I do not expect to see the one thing or the other while I live, and which is less likely I would not even guess."

"Here in the United States, the power of the ballot box gives the laboring classes a power, or the potential for a power, that they lacked in the days when Marx wrote the *Communist Manifesto*, and in the places he knew best," Lincoln said.

"Marx yet lives. Marx yet writes," Sorge answered in tones of reproof.

"But he does not live here. He does not write here," Lincoln said. "By what I have read of his writings, he does not understand the United States well. You have lived in New York, you say. Now you live in Chicago. Can you tell me I am mistaken?"

He gave Friedrich Sorge credit: the Socialist gave the question serious thought before answering. At last, Sorge said, "No, Marx does not understand this country as well as he might."

"Good. We can go on from there. Will you also agree this is true of many Socialists in the United States?" Lincoln asked, pressing the newspaperman as if he still were a lawyer questioning an opposing witness. "With the labor problems this country has, would you not have enjoyed greater success if you could have figured out how to make the voting man see things your way?"

"It could be. It is not certain, but it could be," Sorge said cautiously. "I think you are now coming to say what it is your aim to say. Say it, then."

"I will say it," Lincoln replied. "Leaving revolution out of the bargain save as a last resort, I feel the Socialists offer the laborers of this country their best chance to reclaim it from the wealthy. If and when I bolt the Republican Party, I can bring some large fraction of its membership—a third, maybe half if I'm lucky—with me into the fold here. That is not enough to elect a president or senators, not yet, but it is enough to elect congressmen, state legislators, mayors, and it is a base from which to build. When Blaine goes down in '84, as you know he will, more people will see the Republicans are doomed and join our ranks. Now, how does that look to you?"

Sorge licked his lips. He was tempted; Lincoln could see as much. The prospect of some actual power hit the newspaperman like a big slug of raw rotgut whiskey. Playing to win was a game very different from playing to agitate. Slowly, Sorge said, "This is not something I can decide at once. Also, this is not something I can decide alone. I shall have to talk with some men here and wire others what you propose." He dug through the rubbish on his desk till he found a pencil. After licking the point, he scribbled for a minute. Then he said, "If I understand you, what you have in mind is . . ."

"Yes, that's right, nor near enough," Lincoln said when the Socialist had finished reading back his notes. "Off the record, Mr. Sorge, how does it strike you?"

"I am more revolutionary than you; you are right about that," Sorge answered. "But you are also right in saying we have not done as much as we might have. Maybe—maybe, I say—this will show us the way."

"This is how the Republican Party was born, more than a generation ago," Lincoln said. "Antislavery Whigs, Free-Soilers, Know-Nothings, even a few Northern Democrats who couldn't stomach the extension of slavery—we all joined together to work for a common goal. I think this new coalition may do the same in regard to wage slavery."

"I hope you are right." Sorge gave him a keen look. "President Blaine will call you a traitor, and, when he loses the next election, he will say it is for no other reason than that you and your followers left the party."

"President Blaine is not in the habit of listening to what I say, no matter how hard a time I have convincing people that that is so," Lincoln said, sadly remembering John Taylor's miscalculation. "I see no reason why I should be obliged to take notice of what President Blaine says, especially when, from this day forth, we shall no longer be members of the same party."

Friedrich Sorge pulled open a file cabinet behind his desk. When his hand came out of the drawer, it was clutching a whiskey bottle. More rummaging in the cabinet and in his desk produced two tumblers, mismatched and none too clean. He poured a couple of hefty dollops, handed one glass to Lincoln, and raised the other high. "To Socialism!" he said, and drank.

Lincoln drank, too. The whiskey was bad, but it was strong. "To Socialism," he said.

Brigadier General George Custer rode along bare yards south of the forty-ninth parallel of latitude, the border separating

Montana Territory from Canada, along with a troop from the Fifth Cavalry. Bare yards north of the border, not quite in rifle range but not far out of it, a troop of red-coated British cavalrymen rode along dogging his trail. Neither side had fired a shot since General Gordon took his mutilated army of invasion back over the border. Both sides were ready. For his part, Custer was eager.

Several reporters rode along with the Fifth Cavalry. One of them, an eager young fellow named Worth, asked, "How does it feel, General, to have your brevet rank made permanent?"

"Well, I'll tell you, Charlie, it beats the hell out of going to the dentist to get a tooth yanked," Custer quipped. Charlie Worth and the rest of the reporters laughed appreciatively. Custer held up a hand to show he wasn't through. The newspapermen fell silent, to hear what other pearls of wisdom might fall from his lips. He went on in a serious, even a bombastic, vein: "My only regret is that the promotion comes as the result of a battle from which we could not seize the full fruits of victory because of the cease-fire's having gone into effect. Absent that, we should have pursued to destruction the ruffians who dared desecrate our sacred soil."

Awkwardly, the reporters scribbled as they rode. "God damn, but he gives good copy," one of them muttered to another in admiring tones. The second man nodded. Custer didn't think he was supposed to hear. His chest swelled with pride. Truly he was the hero of the hour.

He waved to Charlie Worth. The reporter, honored at being shown such a confidence, rode up close to him. Custer said, "Do you mind if I make another foraging run amongst your cigars, Charlie?"

"Why, not at all, General." Worth held out a leather cigar case. Custer took a fat stogie from it and reined in so he could strike a match. He coughed a couple of times after he got the cigar going and sucked smoke into his mouth. Before the battle by the Teton River, the only tobacco he'd smoked had been in a few peace pipes handed him by the leaders of Indian tribes he'd smashed.

A reporter asked, "What is your view of the cease-fire, General?"

"I regret that it came when it did, as it prevented us from punishing the British as they so richly deserved," Custer replied. "I also regret it even more on general principles, for it has humiliated us before the nations of the world for the second time in a space of less than twenty years."

His stomach knotted at the thought. He had loved his country longer and more faithfully than he had loved his wife. Now, as in 1862, the United States were going down to mortifying defeat, and that despite his victory, a victory which, had he learned of the cease-fire in time, would never have happened. When he'd married Libbie after the War of Secession, he'd promised to stop cursing and stop drinking. He'd held to the promise till he learned his victory counted for nothing. He'd stayed drunk for days after that, and let out all the oaths he had in him. He was still drinking, he was still swearing, and he'd taken up smoking for good measure.

Camp that evening brought everybody up close to everybody else; men stayed near the greasewood fires for warmth. To the north, the campfires of the troop of British cavalry were a constellation of brightly twinkling stars on the horizon.

Custer and his troopers wolfed down salt pork and hardtack. Some of them crumbled the biscuits and fried them in the grease from the pork, of which there was always an adequate supply. "How do you people eat this stuff day after day, week after week, and live to tell the tale?" one of the reporters asked.

"So sorry, boys," Custer said. "Next time you ride along with us, we'll make sure we cater the affair from Denver."

That got a round of laughter, as he'd hoped it would. Then one of the reporters—it was Charlie Worth, damn him—asked, "How did Colonel Roosevelt and the Unauthorized Regiment take to Army rations?"

"I'm afraid I really don't know," Custer answered, his voice all at once as cool as the breeze hissing down from the north. "I never discussed that with Mr. Roosevelt." He laid the tiniest bit of stress on the civilian title.

The reporters, of course, made their living noticing tiny stresses. "Come on, General," one of them said. "What do you really think of Colonel Roosevelt"—he laid the tiniest bit of stress on the military title—"as a soldier? What do you think of the men of the Unauthorized Regiment as soldiers?"

"Have mercy, gentlemen," Custer said. "I've answered those same questions a lot of times over the past weeks." *And I'd like it a lot better if you asked them a damned sight less often.* Having to share the limelight with the boy colonel gave him worse dyspepsia than salt pork and hardtack gave the reporters.

They wouldn't leave him alone. He might have known they wouldn't leave him alone. "Come on, General," Charlie Worth coaxed. "Give it to us straight. You can do that."

"I can only repeat what I've said a great number of times," Custer answered: "Colonel Roosevelt and his volunteers were gifted, patriotic amateur soldiers, and fought as well as men of that sort could be expected to fight." Every word of that was true. If the reporters judged the tone to be ever so little on the slighting side, was that his fault?

One of the newspapermen said, "General, isn't it a fact that the Unauthorized Regiment performed better against the limeys than the Fifth Cavalry did?"

"Like hell it's a fact," Custer snarled, "and if Roosevelt has been saying that, he's a damned glory-sniffing liar."

"No, General, I never heard it from him," the reporter said hastily. "But didn't the Unauthorized Regiment fight Gordon's cavalry to a draw and then chase the redcoats halfway back to Canada after the what-do-you-call-'ems—the Gatling guns—chewed them to smithereens?"

"The Unauthorized Regiment," Custer said, as if lecturing on strategy at West Point to a class of idiots, "engaged the enemy forces pursuant to my orders. Had I placed them in the center and us on the wings, we would have done as well against the British cavalry, but they would have fared far worse against Gordon's foot. Since my men were fighting dismounted at the battle by the Teton, they were not so well positioned to pursue as were the Volunteers."

All that was true, too. Had Theodore Roosevelt been sitting by the campfire, Custer was sure he would have agreed with every word. (Custer was also sure he would have tried to aggrandize himself one way or another, though; that trait being acutely developed in him, he had an eagle eye for spotting it in others.) But reporters were not after agreement. Agreement didn't sell papers. Argument did. "What about the—Gatterling?—guns, General?" another news hawk asked.

"Gatling guns," Custer corrected. "Gatling." *Idiots indeed,* he thought. "Well, what about them? Even if we hadn't had a one of them, Gordon's men hadn't a prayer of carrying our position."

He thought that was true, too, but he wasn't quite so sure. Bold as he was, he wouldn't have cared to mount an infantry assault on men in earthworks. Even in the War of Secession, that sort of business had proved hideously expensive. With the right troops, though—good American boys, not those limey bastards—he might have had a go of it.

Charlie Worth said, "I hear tell Roosevelt says those Gatling guns saved your bacon in that fight—chewed the Englishmen up and spit 'em out again."

"This being a free country, Mr. Roosevelt may say whatever he likes," Custer answered. "If you prefer the word of a man who became a soldier only because he was rich enough to buy himself a regiment over that of one who has devoted his entire life to the service of his country, you may do so, but I daresay no one will take you seriously afterwards."

That flattened young Worth, who gulped his coffee down in a hurry so he could get a big tin cup in front of his red face. But one of the other men asked, "Colonel Welton, down at Fort Benton, tells it pretty much the same way, doesn't he?"

"I haven't heard what Henry has to say," Custer replied. "I will note that, while I and many of the officers of my regiment were promoted for our work by the Teton, Colonel Welton remains a colonel. In this you have the War Department's judgment on the value of our respective contributions."

The reporters scrawled furiously. One of them muttered, "When the devil are we going to be able to get to a telegraph clicker?"

Charlie Worth came up with a question no one else had asked Custer: "Andrew Jackson licked the British after the War of 1812 was over, and he ended up president of the United States. Now that you've done the same thing in this war, would you like to end up the same way?"

"Why, Charlie, the notion never entered my mind till this moment," Custer answered truthfully. Also truthfully, he went on, "Now that it is in there, I have to tell you I like it." The reporters laughed.

"You're a Democrat, aren't you, General?" somebody asked.

"What sensible man isn't?" Custer returned. "Did I hear rightly that Lincoln has shown the Republicans' true colors by going Communard?" Several reporters assured him he had heard rightly. Sadly, he shook his head. "If Blaine weren't in the White House, General Pope could have done the country a good turn by hanging old Honest Abe. He'll cause more trouble now, mark my words."

"Lots of Democratic politicians who could run for president," Charlie Worth observed. "We don't have so many soldiers who know how to win battles. What if they want you to stay in the Army?"

"I shall serve the United States wherever that service can lend the greatest aid," Custer declared, his tone grandiloquent and, on the whole, sincere.

Winter was on the way to Sonora and Chihuahua. That was obvious to Jeb Stuart: instead of being hotter than blazes, the weather was all the way down to warm. As for Stuart himself, he was on the way to El Paso, which suited him down to the ground.

He turned in the saddle and spoke to Major Horatio Sellers: "Won't it be fine, getting to spend Christmas somewhere near the edge of civilization?"

"Yes, sir," his aide-de-camp agreed enthusiastically. "If El Paso isn't civilization, at least it's on the railroad line to it."

"I like that," Stuart said. "It's true both literally and metaphorically. We are going to have to build a line through to the Pacific just as fast as we can scrape together the capital. Until we have one, and the feeder lines down to the city of Chihuahua and to Hermosillo, we aren't going to be able to control these provinces . . . Territories . . . states . . . whatever we finally call them."

"That's true, sir." Major Sellers nodded. "I expect we'll end up with a Pacific Squadron in the Navy, too, and we'll also need the railroad to keep that supplied." He chuckled. "The damnyankees will love having us for neighbors, too; you can just bet on it."

"One of the reasons they fought this war was to keep our frontier from touching the Pacific; no doubt about that," Stuart said. "But they lost, and now they'll have to make the best of it."

"Serves them right for starting the fight in the first place," Sellers said. "You ask me, sir, President Longstreet ought to squeeze an indemnity out of them that would make their eyes pop. Paying for a railroad would be a lot easier then."

"Old Pete knows what he's doing—you can doubt a lot of things, Major, but you'd better think twice before you doubt that," Stuart said. "My guess is, he reckons the United States hate us plenty now that we've licked them twice. Piling on an indemnity would be adding insult to injury: that's how he'd see it, I think."

Before Major Sellers could reply, a commotion to the rear made him and Stuart both look over their shoulders. Stuart soon heard men calling out his name. He waved his hat and shouted to show where he was.

A grimy, sweaty rider on a lathered horse came pounding up to him. "General Stuart, sir," the Confederate trooper gasped, "everything's gone to hell back in Cananea, sir."

"Oh, Lord." Stuart did not look at his aide-de-camp. Horatio Sellers had been sure nothing good would come of cooperating with the Apaches, and maybe he'd turned out to be right after all. "I left a troop of cavalry behind there to make sure the Mexicans and the Indians didn't go at each other."

"Yes, sir," the trooper said. "Wasn't enough, sir. You remember that Yahnozha who ran away with the Mexican gal, and she says he drug her off and he says she was beggin' for more?"

"Oh, yes. I remember," Stuart said, a sinking feeling in his midsection. "What about him? Did he steal another woman?"

"No, sir," the soldier answered. "The gal's father and her brother, they was layin' for him, and one of 'em put about three bullets in his belly, and the other one, he put two, three more in his head. Then they cut off his privates, sir, and left 'em sittin' by the carcass for the Indians to find. That started the fightin', and it's been a regular war ever since—you'd best believe it has."

"Christ," Stuart said, an exclamation that had nothing to do with the approach of the holiday season. "What the devil have you men been doing to put the lid back on the place?"

The look the trooper sent his way reminded him how insubordinate so many Confederate soldiers had been during the War of Secession. They were men accustomed to speaking their minds regardless of the niceties of rank. This cavalryman was stamped from the same mold. He said, "What we've been doing, sir, is trying to keep from gettin' ourselves killed. Hell of a lot more Apaches down by Cananea than we-uns, an' every one of 'em totes a Tredegar just like the ones we've got. Hell of a lot more Mexicans than we-uns, too. They got every damn kind of rifle you ever did see. We try and get between the greasers and the red-skins, only means we get shot at from both sides at once."

"Who's winning?" Major Sellers asked. His voice was exuberant, almost gleeful. "Whoever gets killed off, long as it isn't our own soldiers, we're well shut of 'em." Stuart glared at him. He stared right back, not so noisily insubordinate as the man who'd ridden in from Cananea, but not backing away from his opinion by even an inch, either.

"Well, sir, that's right hard to say," the Confederate trooper answered. "The Mexicans, they don't get to go out of their houses a whole lot, but they've got plenty of vittles, and any Injun sticks his head up inside of rifle range, he's liable to end up with his brains rearranged, you know what I mean? Every now and again, some of the greasers, the ones with the best guns and the most balls, they'll sneak out of a night and shoot at the Apaches' camp."

"We can't have that," Stuart said. "We can't have any of that sort of nonsense. If we let it go on there, it'll go on all over these two provinces." He heaved a deep, regretful sigh. "So much for Christmas on the edge of civilization. Bugler!"

"Yes, sir!" The trooper produced his polished brass horn.

"Blow Halt," Stuart said. He sighed again. "Then blow About-face. We're going to have to go back there and stamp out that foolishness."

"The whole army, sir?" Major Sellers sounded appalled. He'd been looking forward to Christmas in Texas, too, perhaps even to taking leave and traveling back to Virginia for Christmas with his family.

But Stuart answered, "Yes, the whole army. The Apaches and the Cananeans are going to think they were strolling along the railroad tracks when a train ran over them. If we smash both sides now, it will save the Confederate States a lot of trouble for years and years to come."

"All right, sir; we'll do that, then." Sellers' laugh held a gravelly rumble of doom. "I've been saying all along that we ought to clean out those Indians. The faster and harder we do it, the better off these provinces will be."

"I knew you'd say, 'I told you so,' Major," Stuart said, and his aide-de-camp grinned, altogether unabashed. The commander of the Department of the Trans-Mississippi stroked his beard, working through the orders he would have to give to make the army reverse its course. "First thing we need to do is send a wire to El Paso, letting people know what's happened. Next thing—" He glowered his discontent at the desert all around. "We're already the other side of Janos, better than two days away from Cananea no matter how hard we push." He shook his head, annoyed at his wits for working slower than they should have. "No, most of us are better than two days away from Cananea. Colonel Ruggles!"

"Sir!" At that shout, the commanding officer of the Fifth Confederate Cavalry rode up on his camel. Stuart's horse snorted at the other beast's stink and tried to rear. He didn't let it. Calhoun Ruggles went on, "What can I—what can we—do for you, sir?"

Briefly, Stuart explained what had gone wrong in Cananea. He finished, "I want the Fifth Camelry to ride out ahead of the rest of the army and hit the Indians and the Mexicans before either side expects you. If you can, smash 'em up by yourselves. If you can't manage that, do everything you can. You know we won't be far behind you."

"All right, sir, we'll handle it," Colonel Ruggles said. "And if the redskins light out for the mountains, I reckon we'll chase 'em down before they can get there. They say they can go faster on foot than troopers can on horseback. I'd like to see 'em try and outrun my critters." He leaned forward in his peculiar saddle and set an affectionate hand on the side of his mount's neck. The camel twisted and tried to bite. Ruggles laughed as if he'd expected nothing else.

As Stuart had seen for himself, the Camelry was not in the habit of wasting time. Aboard their moaning, snorting, hideously homely mounts, Ruggles' troopers soon headed west. Stuart would have sworn his horse let out a sigh of relief when the camels trotted away.

Major Horatio Sellers gave Stuart a sly look. "I notice you're not riding with the Fifth this time, sir," he said.

"That's right, I'm not, and I'll give you two good reasons why," Stuart answered. "The first one is that anybody who gets on a camel more than once proves to the world he's a damned fool." He waited for his aide-de-camp to grunt laughter, then went on, "And the second one is that Colonel Ruggles and his regiment are perfectly able to handle the size of the trouble they've got in Cananea without me, and I don't want them thinking that I think they can't."

"Ah." Sellers nodded. "Yes, sir; that makes good sense."

The men grumbled as they headed back toward Cananea.

Some of them had wives in El Paso. Some had sweethearts. All of them, by now, had had a bellyful of Chihuahua and Sonora. But, aside from that grumbling, without which they would hardly have been soldiers, they went where they were ordered.

When they came into Janos just before sundown, they found the town in an uproar. The camels of the Fifth Cavalry had gone through and past the town two or three hours earlier. A couple of companies of Confederate soldiers occupied the adobe fortress that was Janos' principal reason for being, and from which Mexican troops had withdrawn when Maximilian sold his northern provinces to the CSA. They were as indignant and almost as upset as everyone else in town; the Camelry had passed by so swiftly, the men of the garrison had hardly had the chance to learn why they were on the move.

"Something in Cananea, ain't it?" one of the Confederates asked as the force Stuart led got ready to camp for the night.

Bugles roused the soldiers well before dawn. Stuart drank cup after cup of strong black coffee, and was still yawning when he swung aboard his horse. His bones ached. He wondered if he was getting too old for much more campaigning. If he was, he wouldn't admit it, not even to himself—perhaps especially not to himself.

He and his troopers kept to a moderate pace on the road between Janos and Cananea, the road they were getting to know altogether too well. Not much water lay between the two towns, and pushing too hard would have killed horses even at this season of the year. Major Sellers remarked, "The Apaches aren't worth a single good cavalry horse, you ask me, and the same goes for the Mexicans."

"We wouldn't have had nearly so much fun up in New Mexico Territory if it hadn't been for the Apaches," Stuart remarked. Since Sellers could hardly disagree with that, he grunted and did his best to pretend he hadn't heard it.

Stuart waited to see if he would get more reports from Confederate troopers forced out of Cananea, but none came back to him. "Either they aren't coming," he said to Major Sellers, "or Colonel Ruggles is keeping them for himself. If I had to bet, I'd go the second way."

His aide-de-camp nodded. "I think so, too. He's ahead of us, so he needs to know worse than we do."

"Which doesn't mean we don't have to know at all," Stuart said fretfully.

A couple of hours later, a camel rider did come back to Stuart's force with news that fighting in and around Cananea still was going on, or still had been going on when the troopers who brought word to Colonel Ruggles left the town. "By what everybody says, sir," the messenger reported, "they're going at it hammer and tongs." He paused to spit a stream of dark brown tobacco juice into the light brown dirt. "Reckon they purely don't like each other."

Stuart got another short night and woke too soon to the blare of the horns. Walk, canter, trot—instead of the ambling pace they'd set on the way east, when they saw no need to hurry, his troopers used the alternating gaits that kept their horses freshest while eating up the ground. As morning passed into afternoon, he heard one of the men say to another, "I hope the damn camel boys kill all the lousy sons of bitches on both sides, so when we get there tomorrow we've got nothin' to do but spit on their graves."

Toward evening, a thick column of smoke rose in the west, silhouetted against the light sky there. The troopers cheered. "I expect that's the Camelry, cleaning up the fight," Horatio Sellers said.

"Hope you're right," Stuart said, and rolled himself in a blanket on his folding cot as soon as he had seen to his horse.

Some time in the middle of the night, a sentry shook him awake. "Sorry to bother you, sir," the man said, "but Colonel Ruggles just rode in."

That was plenty to make Stuart open his eyes. He pulled on his boots and ducked out of the tent. Calhoun Ruggles stood by the embers of a campfire perhaps twenty feet away. "I saw the smoke, Colonel," Stuart said around a yawn. "Was that us, putting down Apaches and Mexicans alike?"

He expected Ruggles to nod, but the commander of the Fifth Confederate Cavalry shook his head. "No, sir. That was the damned Apaches, burning damn near all of Cananea to hell and gone just before we got there. Not much of the place left standing, and a hell of a lot of Mexicans dead."

"Jesus," Stuart said, yawning again. Ruggles joined him. He went on, "How in blazes did that happen?"

"In blazes is right," Colonel Ruggles answered. "A couple of the Mexicans who lived—Salazar the *alcalde* is one of 'em—says the Indians got hold of some kerosene some kind of way, and that clever one called Batsinas poured it in front of doors and such. Then they shot fire arrows into it, and the wind did the rest of the job for 'em."

"Jesus," Stuart said again. "I bet it was Batsinas' scheme, too." The Apache had been so eager to learn from the white man, and had figured out a way to use some of the white man's products to deadly effect, too. Stuart went on, "I hope you licked the redskins once you got to Cananea, anyway."

Glumly, Calhoun Ruggles shook his head again. "No, sir. Time we got there, they'd all hightailed it toward the mountains." Even more glumly, he pointed southwards. "I put men to chasing 'em, but they had a better than decent start on us—and they can move, too. I tell you, sir, they can really move, a hell of a lot faster than I ever thought they could. I reckon they're holed up in the Sierra Madre somewheres, and I'll be damned if I look forward to digging 'em out."

Rain pattered down on San Francisco. Having grown up and lived for much of his life in a place where rain was liable to fall any old time, Sam Clemens took it in stride. His wife, a native San Franciscan, did not approve. "It has no business doing this," she said. "It's nothing but a nuisance, especially on a day when you have to go to work."

"Not that big a nuisance," Clemens answered. "If there's one thing about your brother we can count on, it's that he has more than one umbrella. He may even be willing to let me borrow one, provided I post a bond not to stab anyone with it or use it as a swimming hole for seagulls."

Sure enough, from an ugly ceramic vase in the front hall sprouted the handles of four or five umbrellas. And, sure enough, Vernon Perkins did not complain about Sam's borrowing one—nor did he ask for the bond Sam had predicted. He was so glad to see his brother-in-law leave his house, he would help in any way he could.

Clemens strode carefully along wet sidewalks and picked his way through puddles in the streets. No matter how careful he was, his feet were wet by the time he got to the *Morning Call* offices. If he'd been a reporter, he wouldn't have been too proud to take off his shoes and put his stockinged feet close by the fire till they dried out. As an editor, he felt that beneath his dignity. That left him with dignity unimpaired and wet feet.

"Thank God for good coffee," he said, pulling the pot off the stove and filling a cup. "I never knew this horrible muddy slop *was* good coffee till my sister-in-law broadened my horizons. Bath water with cream is what she makes." He sipped and nodded. "This, now, this'll grow hair on a man's chest—maybe even on my brother-in-law's. If it weren't that Vern's daughters look like him, poor things, I'd say he was the likeliest man in this town to make his next position harem guard for the Turkish sultan." His voice rose to a screechy falsetto.

"For some reason or other, Sam, I get the feeling you don't *like* your brother-in-law," Clay Herndon drawled. "Why on earth is that?"

"Why on earth is which?" Clemens asked. "Why do you get that feeling, or why don't I like the whey-faced, self-righteous, prissy, tight-fisted little horse's ass? I swear to Jesus, Clay, if brains were steam pressure, he couldn't blow his own nose."

"I'll bet he loves you, too," Herndon said, laughing.

"Doesn't everyone?" Sam said blandly, which made Herndon and all the other newspapermen in earshot laugh even louder. Sam took another sip of snarling coffee, then asked, "Has anyone got a Christmas present for me?"

"More sandpaper to keep your tongue sharp, maybe?" Herndon suggested.

"And it's coal in the stocking for the distinguished correspondent of the *Morning Call*," Clemens said, at which Herndon made as if to throw his cup at the editor. Sam went on, "What I'd really like is something closer to peace than this miserable cease-fire we've been enduring. Sooner or later, the CSA will get tired of it, or England will, and then some poor town on the border will catch hell—or maybe catch hell again, depending."

Edgar Leary spoke up: "If you look at things the right way, San Francisco is a town on the border."

"No, Edgar," Sam said gently. "If you look at things the *wrong* way, San Francisco is a town on the border. That's what worries me more than anything else: I can see some British admiral down in the Sandwich Islands making sure his fleet has enough coal to get from yon to hither, so he can leave a calling card in President

Blame's—uh, Blaine's—front hall, just to remind him that England doesn't care to leave her business lying around unfinished."

"Trouble is, the calling card would be aimed at Blaine, but it would land on us," Clay Herndon said.

"That's what war is about," Clemens agreed. "The people on top are stupid—you have to be stupid, to want to be on top—so you have to kill a lot of ordinary folks before you get their notice. Till you've done that, they keep on the way they always have. Why not? They aren't the ones who are bleeding."

He finished the coffee, poured more into the cup—not quite so much this time, to leave room in case he felt like fortifying it from the whiskey bottle in his desk drawer—and carried it away to get some work done. Edgar Leary followed him. He didn't look on that as a good sign; Leary sometimes put him in mind of a puppy slobbering on his shoes—which, he thought, were damp enough already. Hoping to forestall the young reporter, he made a production out of getting one of his nasty cigars going.

Leary showed no signs of disappearing, not even when Sam (close enough to accidentally, he could say it was and sound as if he meant it) blew smoke in his face. Sighing, Clemens gave up and asked, "Well, what have you got for me today, Edgar?"

"Sir, you remember how you told me to nose around and see what I could come up with about where the rebuilding money here was going?" the youngster asked.

"Oh, yes, I remember that," Clemens agreed. *It's kept you out of my hair for weeks. I'd hoped for longer, but this isn't bad.*

"I've found a few interesting things," Leary said. "May I show them to you? I hope you're not too busy."

Sam's desk was disappointingly uncluttered. If he claimed excessive work, he'd make himself a liar so blatant, even Leary could see right through him. "Yes, show me what you've got, Edgar," he said, doing his best to sound enthusiastic about whatever trivial nonsense the cub would lay before him.

Beaming, Leary hurried away. He unlocked a drawer in his desk, took from it a fat manila envelope, and hurried back to Clemens, who manfully suppressed a groan: if Leary was going to show him nonsense, why did there have to be so blasted much of it? The young reporter pulled a stack of papers about half an inch thick from the envelope. "Here you are," he said. "Why don't you start with these? They'll give you a general idea of what I've dug up. I've arranged them chronologically, so you can start at the beginning and work right through."

"Thanks," Sam said tightly. He started flipping sheets of paper. The first few were invoices: construction firms billing their patrons for amounts that didn't seem too far out of line, considering how urgent all the repairs were and how far a lot of things had to be freighted to San Francisco. Sam was about to start asking rude and pointed questions when the invoices gave way to letters. With an editor's eye, he first noted the bad grammar in the topmost one. Then he saw it was about sharing the profits on a substandard piece of construction. Once he'd spotted that, his eyes flew down to the signature. They widened.

"My God!" he breathed. "Crocker is one of Sutro's right-hand men." He shook his head. "No, that's not right. Sutro is a finger or two on Crocker's right hand." He looked up at Edgar Leary. "Where in blazes did you come up with this?"

"Which one are you talking about?" Leary looked over his shoulder. "Oh, that. That's not even a good one." He waved his hand in disparaging fashion. "Why don't you keep going a little longer?"

"I don't know. Why don't I?" Sam murmured. Keep going he did, now with interest kindled. By the time he was halfway through the stack of papers, he kept pausing every so often to stare at Leary. When he was all the way through, he let out a long, shrill whistle. "You realize what you've got here means the penitentiary for about half the city government of San Francisco?"

"Only if the other half has the best lawyers in the country," Leary answered, and patted the manila envelope. "There's still a lot in here you haven't seen, don't forget. The only thing missing"—he looked disappointed—"is anything directly tying His Honor to the graft."

"It doesn't matter," Clemens answered. "I never thought I'd say that, but it's true. It doesn't matter. The only question left about our magnificent Mayor Sutro is whether he'll poll even fewer votes in San Francisco in his next election than Blaine will in his. I wouldn't have figured such a prodigy possible, but now I see I may be wrong."

"Oh, I don't know," Leary answered. "If all the building-firm bosses and all their laborers vote for Sutro, he's liable to be reelected."

Sam shuddered. "That's a horrible thought, Edgar." He paused to light another cigar, then pointed at Leary with it. "I want you to write this all up for me. I think you've got a week's worth of stories here, and every one of them on the front page—hell, every one of them the lead story of the day, unless we get a peace or go back to war or Blaine drops dead or does something else useful. All under your byline, of course."

Leary's eyes glowed. "Thanks," he whispered. He might be young, but he wasn't a cub any more, or he wouldn't be after these stories ran. He'd just put his name on the map in big letters.

"You've earned it," Clemens answered. He could think of editors who would have taken Leary's work and written their own stories from it. He knew what he thought of those editors, too. "Now—before you go and write it up, where in heaven's name did you get your hands on all these papers?"

Edgar Leary's face tightened. Clemens knew what that meant. Sure enough, the youngster said, "From people who don't want their names in the newspaper. When you look at what they've passed to me, can you blame them?"

"Edgar, after this business breaks, you're going to wonder why you ever wanted *your* name in the newspaper." Sam held up a hand to show Leary he wasn't through. "I mean it. These stories will yank the tails of some of the richest, most important people in San Francisco. They'll come gunning for you, and that's liable not to be a figure of speech."

"If the Royal Marines couldn't get me, I don't reckon the nobs on Nob Hill are up to the job, either," Leary said.

"Ah, the blithe confidence of youth," Sam murmured. It was the same sort of confidence that made soldiers charge enemy lines, sure the bullets would miss them. Youth also had another type of confidence, though. "You're certain—absolutely certain—all your toys here are the genuine article?"

"Could anybody put together a sheaf that thick just to set us up for a fall?" Leary demanded.

"I wouldn't think so, but I was surprised the day I found out babies didn't come from the cabbage patch, too," Clemens said.

Leary blushed bright pink. He said, "Besides, I've compared the handwriting on some of these papers to ones I know are genuine, and I haven't seen a one that doesn't match."

"Now you're talking!" Sam exclaimed. "That's what I wanted

to hear from you. One day a year from now, a lot of rich men's lawyers are going to call you every sort of liar in the book, and they'll stick in a few new pages and draw your face on every one of 'em. Radicals hire bomb-throwing maniacs. Rich men hire lawyers. They're more expensive, but they ought to be, because they do more damage."

"Does that make you a Socialist, then?" Leary asked, his voice sly. "Are you going to follow Abe Lincoln under the red flag?"

"Edgar, if you'll recollect, I didn't follow Abe Lincoln twenty years ago." For the first time since his brief affiliation with the Marion Rangers landed him in hot water, Sam spoke of it without self-consciousness. "I haven't seen any reason to change my mind since. Bomb-throwing maniacs aren't *good* for a country, for heaven's sake—they're not as bad as lawyers, that's all. And talk about damning with faint praise; it's about like saying prettier than camels or wetter than the Sahara or more interesting than my wife's brother."

Still sly, Leary asked, "And what would he say about you?"

"I haven't the foggiest notion," Clemens answered. "I always nod off before I get the chance to find out." Leary laughed. "Think I'm joking, do you?" Sam said severely. "Only shows you've never met dear Vern—or maybe just that you don't re-member it. Here." He handed the papers back to the young reporter. "Get to work. Don't waste another minute. You've got a whole city government waiting to be embarrassed."

Leary went back to his own desk and began to write. Sam rose, stretched, and walked to the doorway. It was still raining, the sky gray as cement. "What a beautiful day," he said.

A church bell in the town of Fort Benton solemnly intoned the hour. A moment later, a much smaller clock in the office of Colonel Henry Welton also began to chime. Theodore Roosevelt counted with it: ". . . ten, eleven, twelve." He looked around the office in blurry surprise. "Midnight already. Doesn't—*hic!*—seem like midnight. Merry Christmas to you, Colonel."

"And a merry Christmas to you, Colonel." Henry Welton's voice wasn't so clear as it might have been, either. The bottle on the desk between the two men was nearly full. It was not, how-ever, the bottle with which they had begun the evening. Welton poured whiskey first into his glass, then into Roosevelt's. "And what shall we drink to now?"

Roosevelt answered without hesitation: "To the true hero of the battle by the Teton!" He drank. The whiskey hardly burned as it slid down his gullet. He'd had a lot already.

Welton drank, too. "You're kind to an old man," he said. "The reporters don't reckon you're right. The War Department doesn't reckon you're right. And you're just a damned officer of Volunteers, the nearest thing to an honorary colonel as makes no difference. So what the devil do you know? What the devil can you know?"

"I know that if you hadn't posted those Gatling guns in the front trench line, General Gordon's men probably would have overrun the position," Roosevelt answered. "I know that General Custer tried his damnedest to talk you into moving them, and you wouldn't do it. I know that Custer's taken all the credit for winning the battle, and left you not a crumb."

"No, Custer hasn't got all the credit," Welton said. "You've managed to lay your hands on a good-sized chunk yourself. And do you know what, Colonel? I don't think Brigadier General Custer likes that for hell. And do you know what else? I don't give a copper-plated damn what Brigadier General Custer likes or doesn't like." He sipped more whiskey.

"You've known him a long time," Roosevelt said, to which Welton nodded without saying anything. Roosevelt took another drink, too. As if to be fair, he said, "He is a brave man."

"I've seen very few braver," Welton agreed. "But I'll tell you something else, too: I've seen very few who love themselves more, or who work harder to make sure other people love them. There's an old saying that if you don't toot your own horn, nobody will toot it for you. Custer's got himself bigger cheeks than a chipmunk coming out of a corncrib."

Roosevelt would have found that funny had he been sober. Drunk, he laughed till the tears rolled down his own cheeks. "I'll miss you, Colonel, by God I will," he said with the deep sentiment of the whiskey bottle. "They can't hold off much longer on releasing the Unauthorized Regiment from service, and then I go back to being a rancher outside of Helena."

Welton yawned against the hour and the liquor. "Won't be the same, will it, Teddy?" He'd never before called Roosevelt that. "You're not only an old man of twenty-three now, you're a real live hero to boot."

"I'm—I'm—" Roosevelt yawned, too. Suddenly, figuring out what he was seemed like too much trouble. "I'm going to bed, Colonel."

"Good night," Welton said vaguely. By the look of things, he was going to fall asleep where he sat. Roosevelt rose and went outside. It had snowed the day before; the cold slapped Roosevelt in the face, sobering him a little. No snow now—the night was brilliantly clear. The moon had set a couple of hours before. Jupiter and Saturn shone in the southwest; Mars was brilliant, and red as blood, high in the south.

Slowly, methodically, Roosevelt made his way out to the gate. The camp of the Unauthorized Regiment was only a few yards away. "Here's the old man back," his own sentries called, one to another. He found his tent, wrapped himself in a blanket and a buffalo robe, and either passed out or fell asleep very, very quickly.

Come morning, his head pounded like a locomotive going up a steep grade. The dazzle of sun off snow only made him hurt worse. Every one of his soldiers who spotted him greeted him with "Merry Christmas, Colonel!"—greeted him loudly and piercingly, or so he thought in his fragile state. He had to answer the men, too, which meant he had to listen to his own voice. It sounded as loud and unpleasant as anyone else's.

After a breakfast of coffee, two raw eggs, and half a tumbler of brandy begged from the regimental physician on the grounds that easing a hangover was surely a medicinal use for the stuff, he felt like a human being, although perhaps one whose parts were not perfectly interchangeable. A cigar helped steady him further. He smoked it down to a tiny butt, flipped that into the snow, lighted another, and headed into town.

The saloons were open. As far as he could tell, the saloons in Fort Benton never closed. Somebody was playing a piano, not very well, in the first one past which he walked. Several people were singing. The words had nothing to do with the holiday season. Even so, the saloon boasted a Christmas tree, with candles gaily burning on all the branches and a red glass star at the top. Why the tree didn't catch fire and burn down the saloon and half the town was beyond him, but it didn't.

Two doors down stood another saloon, also tricked out with a Christmas tree full of candles. Inside, people were singing carols in the same loud, drunken tones the folks in the first place had used for their bawdy song. Would God be happy to hear carols sung like that? Roosevelt chewed on the question as he made his way toward church.

Before he got to the white clapboard building, a man came out, spotted him, and extended a forefinger in his direction. "Colonel Roosevelt!" the fellow called. "Merry Christmas! May I speak with you for a moment?"

"And a merry Christmas to you, Zeke," Roosevelt replied. Zeke Preston wasn't the preacher. He was a reporter. Most of the men who had swarmed into Montana Territory to cover the British invasion were gone now. Of the handful still in Fort Benton, Preston was probably the best. Not only that, a lot of papers back in New York State printed what he wrote. Thus Roosevelt knew it behooved him to stay on the reporter's good side. "What can I do for you today?"

Preston came down the steps and kicked his way through the snow. "Can I trouble you with a couple of questions before you go in?" He was a lean man in his thirties who wore a walrus mustache that didn't go with his pale, narrow face; Roosevelt wondered if he was consumptive.

"Go ahead," Roosevelt said. "You've caught me fair and square."

"Good." The reporter reached into an overcoat pocket and drew out a notebook and pencil. "Lucky I don't have a pen," he remarked. "Weather like this, the ink'd freeze solid as Blaine's head." He waited for Roosevelt's chuckle, then said, "The more time passes after the battle by the Teton, the more credit General Custer takes for himself. What do you think of that?"

He'd told Colonel Henry Welton exactly what he thought of it. Welton was his friend. He knew reporters well enough to know they had their own axes to grind. "He was the overall commander, Zeke. If we'd lost, who would have ended up with the blame?"

"He says your men fought well—for Volunteers." Sure as hell, Preston was trying to goad him into saying something that would make a lively story.

"It's Christmas. I'm not going to pick a quarrel on Christmas." But Roosevelt couldn't quite leave that one alone. "I will say that the Unauthorized Regiment was the force running Gordon and his men back toward Canada when word of the cease-fire reached us and made us hold in place."

Preston scribbled, coughed, scribbled again. "What's your opinion of Gatling guns, Colonel?"

Roosevelt had been over that one with Henry Welton, too. For the reporter, he put on a toothy grin and answered, "My opinion is that I would much rather be behind them than in front of them. If you ask General Gordon, I expect you will find his opinion the same."

"I've heard some argument about how those guns should have been positioned," Preston remarked after an appreciative chuckle at Roosevelt's comment. "Where do you stand on that?"

"They did well where they were," Roosevelt said. "I saw no point to moving them from the front line and they were not moved, if you'll recall. General Custer was persuaded they belonged there."

He waited for Zeke Preston to ask him about that persuading. Maybe, belatedly, Colonel Welton wouldn't be an unsung hero after all. But Preston flipped the notebook shut and stuck it and the pencil back in his pocket. "Thanks very much, Colonel. I won't bother you any more, not today I won't. Merry Christmas to you." Off he went, breath smoking in the chilly air.

Roosevelt sighed and went up into the church. It was Methodist, which would have to do; that faith certainly came closer to his own than the one preached in the two Catholic churches Fort Benton also boasted. When he walked in, the congregation was singing "Away in the Manger," a good deal more tunefully than the same carol would have been managed in the saloon.

He added his own booming baritone to the song. His voice, his uniform, and his upright carriage drew the notice of the folk who crowded the little church, almost all of them in their holiday best. Roosevelt gave notice as well as drawing it; some of the women were worth noticing. A blonde in a deep blue princess dress with a satin jabot and laced, pleated cuffs—it would have been the height of style in New York City five years earlier—caught his eye and held it.

When he'd had enough of caroling—and more than enough of the prune-faced Methodist preacher—he made his way toward the door. The pretty young woman contrived to leave the church at the same time. They walked down the narrow stairway side by side. She smelled of rosewater.

"Merry Christmas to you, miss," Roosevelt said when they were down on the tracked, snowy ground once more.

"The same to you, Colonel." She kept walking along beside him. His hopes rose. In a casual tone of voice, she went on, "If you care for some mince pie, I baked one yesterday. I'd be days and days eating it all by my lonesome."

"Why, that's very kind of you—very kind of you indeed." He smiled. "If your family won't mind sharing, I'd be delighted."

"I am a widow," she answered.

Sometimes that was a euphemism for a streetwalker. Sometimes it wasn't. If she was a woman of easy virtue, she was cleaner and, by all appearances, better-natured than most of her fallen sisters. "Mince pie, then," Roosevelt said—and if she felt like giving him more than mince pie, that would be fine, too.

She lived in a tiny, astringently neat cabin next door to a saloon—not that anything in Fort Benton was far from a saloon. Sure enough, a mince pie sat on the table. She cut Roosevelt a slice. It was good. He said so, loudly, adding, "Thank you for making a soldier far from home happy."

"How happy would you like to be?" she asked, and walked around the table and sat down on his lap.

The bed was close to the stove. Everything in the cabin was close to the stove, which helped keep the place tolerably warm. Roosevelt had had a couple of other women throw themselves at him since he rode down to Fort Benton a hero, or as much of a hero as this hash of a war offered. The experience had been both new and delightful. He wasn't sure whether this was another hero's reward or a business transaction. As he fumbled with the buttons of his trousers, he resolved to worry about it later.

"Oh," she said when, presently, he went into her. She was quiet after that, working intently beneath him, till she stiffened again and quivered and cried out, "Oh, Joe! Oh, God, Joe!" He didn't think she knew what she was saying; he hardly knew what she was saying himself then. His own ecstasy came less than a minute later. Afterwards, he decided she probably was a widow after all.

Being twenty-three, he would have been ready for a second round in short order, but she got off the bed and started dressing again, so he did, too. He was left with a puzzling problem in etiquette after that. If she was a streetwalker as well as a widow, he'd anger her if he didn't offer to pay. If she wasn't, he'd offend her if he did.

He stood irresolute, a rare posture for him. Without answering the question behind it, she solved the problem for him: "Merry Christmas, Colonel Roosevelt."

"Thank you very much," he said, and kissed her. "I don't think I've ever had a nicer present, or one more charmingly wrapped." She smiled at that. He opened the door, and grunted at the cold outside. He'd gone several steps back toward the Unauthorized Regiment's encampment before he realized he'd never learned her name.

XIX

The clock in Frederick Douglass' parlor chimed twelve. All over Rochester, clocks were striking twelve. Douglass raised a glass of wine to his wife and son. "Happy New Year," he said solemnly.

"Happy New Year, Frederick," Anna Douglass said, and drank. "When I was young, I never reckoned I'd live to see such a big number as 1882."

"May you see many more new years, Mother," Lewis Douglass said.

"You're not drinking, son." Frederick Douglass had emptied his own glass, and was reaching for the decanter to refill it.

"No, I'm not," Lewis said, "for the year ahead looks none too happy to me."

"Compare it to the year just past," Douglass said. "When seen from that perspective, how can it fail of being a happy year?"

Lewis gravely considered that. He showed the result of the consideration not by words but by downing the wine in front of him in a couple of quick gulps. When Douglass held out the decanter, he poured his glass full again, too. "Compared to the year just past, any year save perhaps 1862 would seem happy."

Anna cocked her head to one side, listening to bells ringing unconstrainedly and to firecrackers and pistols and rifles going off in the street, some quite close by. "It don't sound the way it ought to," she said.

"It doesn't, does it?" Douglass said. "Something's missing."

Lewis supplied the deficiency: "No cannon this year. No cannon, by order of the mayor and the governor and whichever soldier makes the most noise around these parts. They all fear the British gunboats out on the lake will mistake the celebration for an attack on themselves and use it as a pretext for bombarding the city. A happy new year indeed, is it not?"

"They might do it, too," Douglass said gloomily. "They might enjoy doing it, the better to coerce the president into yielding to their demands."

"He might as well," Anna said. "Things ain't gwine get no better on account of he don't. They done licked us, so they gets to tell us what to do."

Anna's grammar was not all it should have been. That did not make what she said any less true. Lewis must have thought as much, for he said, "Mother, we ought to send you to Washington, because you see these things a lot more plainly than President Blaine is able to."

"What Blaine can see and what he can do are liable to be two different propositions," Douglass said, regretting every word of defense he spent on the man who had had the best chance since the presidency of Abraham Lincoln to do something about the Confederate States—had it and squandered it. "He's made his bed, and now—"

"And now the whole country has to lie in it," Lewis broke in. He reached for the wine decanter once more, then yanked his hand away. Bitterness filled his voice as he went on, "I'd get drunk, but what's the use? Things wouldn't be any better when I sobered up again."

"Well, I don't aim to get myself drunk any which way," Anna Douglass said. "It's a sinful thing to go and do. What I aim to do is go to bed." She struggled to her feet. "Frederick, you'll help me up the stairs."

"Of course I will, my dear." Douglass rose, too. His body still responded readily to his will. He helped his wife up to the bedroom, helped her out of her dress and corset, and made sure she was comfortable before he went back down to talk with his son a while longer.

Lewis was taking short, quick, furious puffs on a cigar when Frederick Douglass came back to the parlor. "What's the use, Father?" he asked as Douglass sat down once more. "What in God's name is the use? Why don't we all pack up and move to Liberia? We might accomplish something there."

"You may, if you like," Douglass answered evenly. "I've thought about it once or twice—maybe more than once or twice." His son stared at him. He nodded, his face grave. "Oh, yes, I've thought about it. In Liberia, the pond is so small as to make me— or you, should you ever choose to go—a very large fish indeed, which cannot help but feed a man's pride. But if I left, I should be giving up the fight here, and as much as proving the Confederates right when they say the black man cannot compete equally against the white. Every column I write here shows the CSA to be founded on a lie. How could I do the same in Africa?"

Lewis did not answer right away. He took the cigar from his mouth and sat for some time staring at the glowing coal. Then, savagely, he stubbed out the cigar. "Well, you're right," he said. "I wish to heaven you weren't, but you are." He got up and clapped Douglass on the shoulder. "Happy New Year, Father. You were right about that, too. Set next to the one we've escaped, the year ahead can't be so bad. Good night. You needn't get up—rest easy."

Douglass rested easy. He heard his son take his overcoat off the tree in the front hall, put it on, open the door, and close it after him. Bells on the carriage jingled as Lewis drove home. Douglass looked at the decanter of wine. Like a voyage to Liberia, it tempted him. But, ever since his escape from slavery, he had seldom run away, and he had never been a man who drank alone. Picking up the cut-glass stopper, he set it in its place. Then, with a grunt, he rose once more and went off to bed. He listened to clocks striking one. He expected he would also listen to them striking two, but drifted off before they did.

Other than having a new calendar, 1882 seemed little different from the vanished 1881. Warships flying the Union Jack remained outside Rochester harbor, as they did outside other U.S. harbors along the Great Lakes. No warships flying the Stars and Stripes came out to challenge them. That sprang in part from the cease-fire, but only in part. The rest was that the U.S. Navy's Great Lakes flotilla was incapable of challenging its British counterpart.

One day in the middle of January, the War Department announced that the troops of the Army of the Ohio were returning to U.S. soil. By the way the announcement sounded, no one would have guessed it meant the U.S. Army was abandoning the last foothold it held in Kentucky. The telegram made the move sound like a triumph.

"Look at this!" Douglass waved the announcement in his son's face. "*Look* at this. How many dead men in Louisville? *They* won't be coming back to Indiana. And for what did they die? For what, I ask you?"

"For President Blaine's ambition," Lewis answered. "Nothing

else." The abject failure of the U.S. war effort had left him even more estranged from and cynical about the society in which he lived than he had been before the fighting started.

But Douglass shook his head. "The cause for which we fought was noble," he insisted, as he had insisted all along. "The power of the Confederate States should have been kept from growing. The tragedy was not that we fought, but that we fought while so manifestly unprepared to fight hard. Blaine gets some of the blame for that, but the Democrats who kept us so weak for so long must share it with him. If we are to have a return engagement with the Confederacy, we must be more ready in all respects. I see no other remedy."

"I never thought I'd live to see the day when you and Ben Butler were proposing the same cure for our disease," Lewis said. "The Democrats like him, too."

That brought Douglass up short. Butler had no more kept silent about the proposals he had made in the meeting at the Florence Hotel outside Chicago than Abraham Lincoln had about his. Both men were stirring up turmoil all through the battered country, and each one's followers violently opposed the other's. As Lincoln had joined with the Socialists, so Butler was indeed drifting back toward the Democrats, from whose ranks he had deserted during the War of Secession.

Reluctantly, Douglass said, "An idea may be a good one no matter who propounds it."

"Nero fiddled while Rome burned," Lewis retorted. "You temporize while the Republican Party goes up in flames."

"I am not temporizing," Douglass said with dignity. "I have done all I could to hold the party together. I am still doing all I can. It may not suffice—I am only one man. But I am doing my best."

"You'd have a better chance if your skin were white," Lewis said. Douglass stared at him. Negroes in the U.S. seldom spoke so openly of the handicap they suffered by being black. Lewis glared back in furious defiance. "It's true, and you damn well know it's true."

But Douglass shook his head. "Not for me. Had I been born white—had I been born *all* white"—he corrected himself, to remind his son they both had white blood in their veins—"I suspect I would have drifted into some easy, profitable trade, never giving a second thought, or even a first, to politics. Being the color I am, I have been compelled to face concerns I should otherwise have ignored. It has not been an easy road, but I am a better man for it."

"I do not have your detachment, Father, nor, frankly, do I want it," Lewis said. "I wish you a good morning." He departed Douglass' home without much ceremony and with a good deal of anger.

Douglass had to go out himself a couple of days later, when his wife developed a nasty cough. The new cough syrups, infused with the juice of the opium poppy, really could stop the hacking and barking that seemed such a characteristic sound of winter. Thanking heaven for modern medicine, Douglass bundled himself up and trudged off to the nearest drugstore, a few blocks away.

He thanked heaven for the day, too. As January days in Rochester went, it was good enough—better than good enough. It was bright and clear and, he guessed, a little above freezing. Not too much snow lay on the ground. Even so, he planted his feet with care; the sidewalks had their share of icy patches.

"Half a dollar," the druggist said, setting on the counter a glass bottle with the label in typography so rococo as to be almost unreadable. His voice was polite and suspicious at the same time. Douglass' fur-collared overcoat argued that he had the money to pay for the medicine. His being a Negro argued, to far too many white men, that he was likely to be shiftless and liable to be a thief.

He reached into his pocket and found a couple of quarters, which he set beside the bottle of cough elixir. Only after the druggist had scooped the coins into the cash box did his other hand come off the bottle. That care made Douglass want to laugh. He was stout, black, and well past sixty. Even if he did abscond with the medicine, how could he possibly hope to get more than a couple of blocks without being recognized or, more likely, tackled with no ceremony whatever?

He was carrying the bottle of cough syrup out of the store when three middle-aged white men started to come in. He stood aside to let them use the narrow doorway ahead of him. Instead of going on past, though, the fellow in the lead stopped, rocked back on his heels, and looked at him with an expression of mingled contempt and insult.

"Well, looky here, Jim. Looky here, Bill," he drawled. "Ain't this a fine buck nigger we got?" His friends laughed at what they and he thought to be wit.

Douglass stiffened. "If you gentlemen will excuse me—" he said, his voice chillier than the weather outside.

"Listen to him, Josh," either Jim or Bill exclaimed. "Talks just like a white man, he does. Probably got a white man inside him, that he ate up for breakfast." All three of them found that a very funny sally, too.

"If you gentlemen will excuse me—" Douglass repeated, bottling up the fury he felt. He took a step forward. More often than not, his sheer physical presence was enough to let him ease through confrontations like this.

It didn't work today. Instead of giving way before him, the white man in the lead—Josh—deliberately blocked his path. "No, we don't excuse you, Sambo," he said, and looked back over his shoulder. "Do we, boys?"

"No," one of Jim and Bill said, while the other was saying, "Hell, no."

Josh stuck a finger in Douglass' face. "And do you know why we don't excuse you, boy? I don't excuse you because it's all your goddamn fault."

"I have no idea what you are talking about," Douglass said, now alarmed as well as furious. This sort of thing hadn't happened to him in Rochester for many years. He knew too well how ugly it could get, and how fast it could get that way. Carefully, he said, "I do not know what you believe to be my fault, but I do know I have never set eyes on any of you before in my life." *And, if God be kind, I shall never see you again.*

"Not you, you—you niggers," Josh said. "Hadn't been for you niggers, this here'd still be one country. We wouldn't have fought two wars against the lousy Rebels, and they wouldn't have licked us twice, neither."

"Yeah," said Jim or Bill.

"That's right," Bill or Jim agreed.

They weren't drunk. Douglass took some small comfort in that. It might make them a little less likely to pound him into the boards of the floor. He said, "Black men did not ask to be brought to these shores, nor did we come willingly. The difficulty lies not in our being here but in the way we have been used. I myself bear on my back the scars of the overseer's lash."

"Ooh, don't he talk fancy," one of the men behind Josh said.

"Reckon that's why the overseer whupped him," Josh replied, which was a disturbingly accurate guess. He didn't attack, he didn't make a fist, but he didn't get out of Douglass' way, either. "Ought to all go back to Africa, every stinking one of you. Then we'd set things to rights here."

"No." Now Douglass let his anger show. "For better and for worse, I am an American, too—every bit as much as you. This is my country, as it is yours."

"Liar!" Josh shouted. His friends echoed him. Now he did fold his hand into a fist. Had the bottle Douglass held been thicker, he would have used it to add strength to his own blow. As things were, he feared it would break and cut his palms and fingers. He got ready to throw it in Josh's face instead.

From behind him came a short, sharp click. It was not a loud noise, but it was one to command immediate, complete, and respectful attention from Douglass and from the three white men of whom he'd fallen foul. Very slowly, Douglass turned his head and peered over his shoulder. The druggist's right hand held a revolver, the hammer cocked and ready to fall.

"That's enough, you men," he said sharply. "I've got no great use for niggers myself, but this fellow wasn't doing you any harm. Let him alone, and get the hell out of here while you're at it."

Josh and Jim and Bill tumbled over one another leaving the drugstore. The druggist carefully uncocked the pistol and set it down out of sight. Frederick Douglass inclined his head. "I thank you very much indeed, sir."

"Didn't do it for you so much as to keep the place from getting torn up," the druggist replied in matter-of-fact tones. "Like I said, I don't much care for niggers, especially niggers like you that put on airs, but that ain't the same as saying you deserved a licking when you hadn't done anything to deserve one. Now take your cough elixir and go on home."

"I'll do that," Douglass said. "A man who, for whatever reason, will not let another be beaten unjustly has in himself the seeds of justice." He tipped his hat and walked out of the store.

Once on the sidewalk, he looked around warily to see whether the white ruffians might want another try at him. But they were nowhere around. They must have had enough. His sigh of relief put a fair-sized frosty cloud in the air.

When he got home, Anna was sitting in the parlor, coughing

like a consumptive. "Hold on, my dear," he said. "A tablespoon of this will bring relief."

"Fetch me a glass o' water with it, on account of it's gwine taste nasty," she answered. She sighed when he brought the medicine and the water. "I ain't been out of the house in a good while now. Anything much interestin' happen while you was at the drugstore?"

Douglass gravely considered that. After a moment, he shook his head. "No," he said. "Nothing much."

Snow blew into Friedrich Sorge's face. As it had a way of doing in Chicago, the wind howled. Sorge clutched at his hat. The Socialist newspaperman had an exalted expression on his face. Turning to Abraham Lincoln, he shouted, "Will you look at the size of this crowd? Have you ever in all your life seen anything like it?"

"Why, yes, a great many times, as a matter of fact," Lincoln answered, and hid a smile when Sorge looked dumbfounded. He set a gloved hand on his new ally's shoulder. "You have to remember, my friend, that you have been in politics as an agitator, a gadfly. From now on, we will be playing the game to win, which is a different proposition altogether."

"Yes." Sorge still sounded dazed. "I see that. I knew our joining would bring new strength to the movement, but I must say I did not imagine it would bring so much." He laughed. The wind did its best to blow the laughter away. "Until now, I did not imagine how weak we were, nor how strong we might become. It is . . . amazing. Not since I left the old country have I been part of anything to compare to this—and in the old country, we were put down with guns."

Lincoln had different standards of comparison. To him, it was just another political rally, and not a particularly large one at that. Muffled against the cold and the wind, men and women trudged south along Cottage Grove Avenue toward Washington Park. Considering the weather, it wasn't a bad crowd at all. It was also, without a doubt, the most energetic crowd Lincoln had seen since the War of Secession.

Red flags whipped in the wind. It had already torn some of them into streamers. Men had to wrestle to keep the signs they held from flying away. JUSTICE FOR THE WORKING MAN, some said. TAX CAPITALISTS' INCOME, others urged. REVOLUTION IS A RIGHT, still others warned.

Some of the people on the sidewalks cheered as the marchers walked past. Others hurried along, intent on their own business or on finding someplace to get out of the cold. Policemen in overcoats of military blue were out in force. They had clubs in their hands and pistols on their belts. If peaceable protest turned to uprising—or, perhaps, if the police thought it might, this gathering too could be put down with guns.

Trees in Washington Park were skeletally bare. What little grass snow did not cover was yellow and dead. It was as bleak and forbidding a place as Lincoln could imagine. But it also struck him as the perfect place to hold a rally for the new fusion of the Socialists and his wing of the Republican Party.

"In the summer, you know, and when the weather is fine, the rich promenade through here, showing off their fancy carriages and matched teams and expensive clothes," he said to Friedrich Sorge.

Sorge nodded. "Yes, I have seen this." He scowled. "It is not enough for them that they have. They must be seen to have. Their fellow plutocrats must know they, too, are part of the elite, and the proletariat must be reminded that they are too rich and powerful to be trifled with."

"Thanks to their money, they think it is summer in the United States the year around," Lincoln said. "To the people coming into Washington Park now, blizzards blow in January and July alike."

"This is true," Sorge agreed emphatically. He hesitated. "It is also very well said, though with my English imperfect you will not, perhaps, find in this much praise. But I think you have in yourself the makings of a poet."

"Interesting you should say so," Lincoln replied. "I tried verse a few times, many years ago—half a lifetime ago, now that I think about it. I don't reckon the results were altogether unfortunate, at least the best of them, but they were not of the quality to which I aspired, and so I gave up the effort and turned back to politics and the law, which better suited my bent."

"You may have given up too soon," Sorge said. "Even more than other kinds of writing, poetry repays steady effort."

"Even if you are right, as you may well be, far too many years have passed for it to matter now," Lincoln said. "If, by lucky chance, some phrase in a speech or in an article should strike the ear or mind as happily phrased, maybe it is the poet, still struggling after so long to break free."

More miserably cold-looking policemen directed the throng to an open area in front of a wooden platform from which more red banners flew. The wind was methodically ripping them to shreds. "Say your say and then go home," a policeman told Lincoln. The former president judged that likelier to be a plea from the heart than a political statement; the fellow's teeth were chattering so loudly, he was hard to understand.

Friedrich Sorge said, "Not too hard, is it, to know which of our followers came from your camp and which from mine?"

"No, not hard," Lincoln said. The difference interested him and amused Sorge. About four out of five people in the crowd obeyed without question the police who herded them where they were supposed to go. The fifth, the odd man out, called the Chicago policemen every name in the book, sometimes angrily, sometimes with a jaunty air that said it was all a game. The fifth man, the odd man, was far more likely to be carrying a red flag than the other four.

"Some people, Lincoln, you see, truly do believe in the revolution of the proletariat," Sorge said.

"I do recollect that, believe me," Lincoln answered. "What *you* have to remember is that some people don't. Looking over the crowd here, I'd judge that most of the people in it don't. What we have to do to build this party is to make the people who don't believe in revolution want to join so they can reform the country, and at the same time keep the ones who are revolutionaries in the fold."

Sorge's mouth puckered as if he'd bitten into an unripe persimmon. "You are saying—you have been saying since we first spoke—that we must water down the doctrines of the party the way a dishonest distiller will water down the whiskey he sells."

"Look at the crowd we have here today," Lincoln said patiently. "With a crowd like this, we can make the bosses think twice before they throw workers out in the streets or cut their pay. With a crowd like this, we can elect men who see things our way. Wouldn't you like to see a dozen, or two dozen, Socialist congressmen on the train for Washington after the elections this fall?"

"I do not know," Sorge said. "I truly do not know. If they call themselves Socialists but hold positions that are not Socialist positions—"

"If they're not pure enough to satisfy you, you mean," Lincoln said, and Sorge nodded. Lincoln's sigh swirled him in fog. "You can stand against the wall and shout 'Revolution!' as loud as you like, but you won't have many people standing by you if you do. If you want to get on the floor and dance, you have to know the tunes the folks out there are dancing to."

Another policeman made his way over to Lincoln and Sorge. He was swinging his arms back and forth and beating his hands together, and still looked miserably cold. He wore a bushy mustache full of ice crystals. "If you ducks have to go speechifying, why the hell don't you do it and get it over with?" he said. "More time you waste, the better the chance somebody's going to freeze to death waiting for you to get on with it. Me, for instance."

"That's a good idea," Lincoln said, and Sorge did not disagree.

They ascended to the platform together. A hum of anticipation ran through the crowd. The hard-line Socialist minority began shouting slogans: "Workers of the world, unite!" "Down with the capitalist oppressors!" "Revolution!" They tried to turn that last into a rhythmic chant.

Abraham Lincoln held up his hands for quiet. Slowly, he gained it. Friedrich Sorge had agreed, with some reluctance, that he should speak first. Lincoln's logic was that a fiery call for revolution would frighten off the more moderate members of the crowd if they heard it before they heard anything else: they would think the party had no room for them. Lincoln hoped to show them otherwise. Once he'd done that, Sorge could be as fiery as he liked.

"My friends," Lincoln said, "let me begin by speaking to you of religion." That intrigued some of the crowd and, no doubt, horrified the rest, including the men waving red flags. Intrigued or horrified, they listened. He went on, "Some men think God has given them the right to eat *their* bread in the sweat of *other* men's faces. That is not the sort of religion upon which people can get to heaven."

Silence persisted for another few seconds. Then a great roar rose up from the crowd, not only from the ordinary, respectable folks who had been Republicans and were trying to find out why Lincoln was abandoning the party he had led to the White House but also from the hard cases waving red flags. Friedrich Sorge clapped his gloved hands together again and again.

"Here," Lincoln said, and now the crowd hushed at once to hear him. "I am a poor hand to quote Scripture, but I will try it. It is said in one of the admonitions of the Lord, 'As your Father in heaven is perfect, be ye also perfect.' He set that up as a standard, and he who did most toward reaching that standard, attained the highest degree of moral perfection. So I say in relation to the principle that all men are created equal. If we cannot give perfect freedom to every man, let us do nothing that will impose slavery on any man." He had to pause again, for no one could have heard him through the cheers.

When he could speak once more, he went on, "Let us turn this government back into the channel in which the framers of the Constitution originally placed it. Let us stand firmly by each other. And let us discard all quibbling about this class and that class and the other class." Now Sorge looked less ecstatic. Lincoln did not care. He forged ahead: "Let us hear no more how this man is only a laborer, and so counts for nothing. Let us hear no more how that man is a great and wealthy capitalist, and so his will must be obeyed. Let us discard all these things, and unite as one people throughout this land, until we shall once again stand up declaring that all men are created equal."

Again he drew cheers from both factions in the crowd. When they washed over him, he felt neither chilled nor old. As they ebbed, he resumed: "I think this new Socialist Party is and shall be made up of those who, peaceably as far as they can, will oppose the extension of capitalist exploitation, and who will hope for its ultimate extinction—who will believe, if it ceases to spread, that it is in the course of ultimate extinction.

"We have to fight this battle upon principle, and upon principle alone. So I hope those with whom I am surrounded here have principle enough to nerve themselves for the task and leave nothing undone that can be fairly done, to bring about the right result. It is altogether fitting and proper that we should do this. I shall not keep you here much longer, my friends. Our purpose should be, must be, and is simple: to do all which may achieve and cherish a just and lasting peace among ourselves, and with all nations."

He stepped back. For a moment, no applause came, and he wondered if he had somehow lost his audience as he ended. But no: when the cheers and clapping thundered out, he realized the crowd had granted him that moment of enchanted silence every speaker dreams of and few ever get. He bowed his head. In that brief stretch of time, some of the bitterness of almost twenty years' wandering in the wilderness left him at last, and, when he stood straight again, he stood very straight indeed.

Friedrich Sorge tugged at the sleeve of his coat. He bent down to listen to his colleague through the ongoing roar of the crowd. Half angrily, half admiringly, Sorge demanded, "What am I supposed to say, after you have said all this?"

"What you were going to say—what else?" Lincoln answered. "I spread oil on the waters where I could. Now you go on and stir them up to a storm again."

And Sorge did his best. It was a speech that would have set a torch under one of the small crowds of dedicated men he was used to addressing, and it did set a torch under some of the crowd in Washington Park. When he spoke of Marx, when he spoke of 1848, when he decried the brutal suppression of the Paris Commune, he struck chords in many of them. To many who heard him, though, those were foreign things of little meaning, and he did nothing to relate them to the experience of the working man in the United States.

Listening to him, Lincoln understood why Socialism had remained so small a movement for so long: it simply was not, or had not been, aimed at the common American laborer. He aimed to change that. He thought he'd made a good start.

On and on Sorge went, considerably longer than Lincoln had done. People began drifting out of the park. When the Socialist finished—"Join with us! You have nothing to lose but your chains!"—some of the applause he got seemed more relieved than inspired.

Policemen began shouting: "Now you've heard 'em! Now get the hell out of here! Show's over. Go on home." Near the platform, one of those policemen turned to his pal and said, "Anybody wants to know, we ought to take all these crazy bomb-throwing fanatics and string 'em up. That'd go a long way toward setting the country to rights."

He made no effort to keep his voice down; if anything, he wanted the men on the platform to hear. Sorge turned to Lincoln and said, "You see how the oppressors' lackeys have learned their masters' language. You also see how they ape their masters' thoughts. When we go to the barricades—"

But Lincoln shook his head. "You notice he does not do anything about it. The first amendment to the Constitution protects our right to speak freely." He let out a chuckle the wind flung away. "The first amendment also protects his right to speak freely, however distasteful I find his opinion."

Sorge made a sour face. "Bah! You Americans, I sometimes think, suffer from an excess of this freedom."

"If you feel that way, you should have allied yourself with Benjamin Butler or with the Democrats, not with me," Lincoln answered. "And when you say *you Americans*, you show why the Socialists have not made a better showing up until now. You must remember, you are not looking at the United States and their citizens from some external perspective. You are—we are—a part of them."

Had he spoken angrily, the union between his wing of the Republican Party and the Socialists might have broken down then and there. As it was, the look Sorge sent him was thoughtful rather than irate. "Perhaps you touch here on something important. Perhaps you do indeed," the newspaperman said. In musing tones, he went on, "Socialism from France is different from Socialism in Germany. Perhaps Socialism in the United States will prove different from both."

"Come on down from there, you damned crazy loons," said the policeman who'd called a moment earlier for hanging them, "before you both freeze to death, and before I do, too."

Sorge might not have heard him. "When the time comes for it to grow, as the dialectic proves that time will come, I wonder what face Socialism will wear in the Confederate States."

Lincoln paused halfway down the steps. "A black one," he predicted. "If ever there was a proletariat ruthlessly oppressed and valued only for its labor, it is the Negro population of the CSA."

"An interesting notion," Sorge said. "It is for now a *lumpenproletariat*, one without an intelligentsia through which to vent its rage. But, in the fullness of time, this too may change." He suddenly seemed to realize he was alone on the platform. He also suddenly seemed to realize how cold he was. "Brr! Let us be off."

Surrounded by their supporters, Sorge and Lincoln made their way out of Washington Park. Cabs waited to take them back into Chicago. Friedrich Sorge jumped into one. He waved to Lincoln.

"Today the city, tomorrow the world," he said gaily, then gave the driver his address. The cab clattered off.

Ducking his head to fit through the short, narrow doorway, Lincoln climbed into another cab. "Where to?" the driver asked him. He gave his son's address. The driver said nothing, but flicked the reins and got rolling.

Friedrich Sorge lived in a cramped, cluttered, dingy South Side flat. Lincoln had visited him there. He had not visited Lincoln in turn; Robert had made it very plain that, while his father was welcome at his luxurious home, his father's political associates were not. Lincoln sighed. He would, sometime soon, have to find a place of his own. The idea of a Socialist leader operating out of a mansion struck him as too absurd for words.

The cab made its slow way through the bustle of Chicago. The deeper into the city it got, the more streaked with soot the snow on the ground was. Lincoln peered out through the smeary window at bustle and filth alike. "Tomorrow the world," he said softly. "Tomorrow—the world."

Jeb Stuart surveyed the magnificent terrain surrounding him with an emotion closer to despair than admiration. The Sierra Madre Mountains, the extension of the Rockies south of the U.S. border, were steep and treacherous and full of endless trails not wide enough for two men to ride abreast—often barely wide enough for one man on camel- or horseback—and full of endless valleys where endless numbers of Indians could camp and elude his men. And moving guns was even harder than moving men.

Colonel Calhoun Ruggles rode only a couple of men ahead of him. "I wish the Camelry had been able to run down the damned Apaches," Stuart said. He regretted the words as soon as they were out of his mouth; he knew Ruggles had done everything he could to run the red-skinned warriors to earth.

The commander of the Fifth Confederate Cavalry looked back over his shoulder. "Sir, I honest to God thought we'd run 'em the way hounds run a coon. They made fools out of me and my troopers, and I'm not ashamed to admit it. Any men who can make fools out of my troopers—well, they're men in my book."

"They made fools of the Yankees for a lot of years," Stuart said, doing his best to encourage Ruggles after tearing him down. "They helped us make fools of the Yankees, too, remember. Maybe they decided it was our turn now."

Colonel Ruggles shook his head. "That's not it, or not all of it, anyway. After they burned Cananea, they knew damn well we couldn't let them get by with it, and so they lit out for the mountains." His head went this way and that, too, with no sign whatever that he was enjoying the scenery. "And now we're supposed to dig them out. Rrr." The noise he made was very unhappy.

From behind Stuart, Major Horatio Sellers spoke up: "There is one good thing about this whole business."

"What? About wandering through the mountains for more than a month, with damn near the only times the Apaches show themselves the times when they bushwhack some of our scouts?" Stuart exclaimed. Calhoun Ruggles also shook his head in disbelief.

But, sure enough, Sellers came up with one, saying, "If we do flush the Apaches out of their hiding places here, there's not a chance they'll ever come up with new ones, because there can't be any better in the whole wide world."

"By God, Major, you're right about that," Ruggles said. Stuart found himself nodding, too. In an odd sort of way, Sellers' words offered consolation. The aide-de-camp was right: ground just didn't come any worse than this.

Slowly, tortuously, the troopers descended into a valley where they'd camp for the night. Stuart did not have nearly so big a force with him as had set out from Cananea in pursuit of the Apaches. For one thing, supplying a large force in this cut-up land was impossible. For another, guarding the supplies that did come in required a lot of soldiers. Some of those supplies, inadequately guarded, were now in the Apaches' hands.

Something small and bright and colorful as a jewel hovered in front of Stuart for a moment. It stared at him for a moment out of beady black eyes, then shot off impossibly fast at an equally impossibly angle.

"Hummingbird!" he said, startled. He'd seen hummingbirds back in Virginia, of course, the familiar ruby-throats; El Paso had others, occasionally glimpsed as they buzzed from flower to flower like oversized bees. But he'd never seen one with a purple crown and brilliant green throat before. He wondered what other strange creatures the mountains harbored.

He must have said that aloud, for Major Sellers grunted laughter. "Well, there's the Apaches, for starters," he said. He took the saddle off his horse and set it down on a round brown rock, then started currying the animal. As with any good trooper, his horse came first.

A scout came up to Stuart. "Sir," he said, "there's a trail up ahead, looks like one the Apaches used once upon a time, anyway. Got Mexican plunder all along it: dresses, saddles, flour sacks, things like that. None of it's what you'd call fresh, though. Reckon they came that way some other time when they was raidin' through these parts. Might mean we're gettin' closer to 'em, though."

"So it might." Stuart scanned the peaks ahead. The sun still shone on some of them, though shadow filled the valley. Somewhere up there, along those ridge lines, Apaches were spying on his encampment, even if he had not the slightest hope of spotting them. Almost to a man, the Indians had sharp eyes. They also had, and knew how to use, telescopes looted from the U.S. Army. They were liable to know what he was up to better than he did himself.

That thought had hardly crossed Stuart's mind before Horatio Sellers burst out in a storm of angry curses. Stuart spun around. "What's the matter, Major?" he asked.

"My blasted saddle's disappeared," Sellers answered. "I set the stupid thing on a rock right there"—he pointed—"and now it's gone."

Gone it was. "You *did* put it there," Stuart said. "I saw you do it. It isn't there now." That was pointing out the obvious.

"The son of a bitch goddamn well didn't up and walk off by itself," Sellers said. "If I find the bastard who lifted it, I'll make him sorry he was ever born." He glared around at the amused soldiers who were watching and listening to him. Stuart would have suspected—Stuart did suspect—them, too. The next soldier who didn't relish a practical joke on a superior would be the first.

One of the men pointed toward a patch of waist-high scrub oak near the edge of the light the campfire cast. "Sir, ain't that your gear?"

Sellers' gaze followed the trooper's outthrust finger. "It is, by Jesus!" he rumbled. "How in the damnation did it get way the hell over there?" He rounded on the nearby cavalrymen. "All right, 'fess up. Which one of you blackguards went and shifted it?"

Instead of confessing, the soldiers denied everything, each more vehemently than the last. Stuart had heard a great many soldiers tell a great many lies in his day. As with anything else, some were good, some bad, some indifferent. Either these men were all inspired liars, or— "Major, I think they may perhaps be telling you the truth."

"Yes, sir!" Major Sellers came to attention stiff as rigor mortis: respect exaggerated to the point of parody. He performed a precise about-face and stomped over to the saddle. When he picked it up, he let out an oath that was startled rather than furious: "Son of a bitch! Did you see that?"

Several people, Stuart included, said, "No." Most of them added "What was it?" or words to that effect.

"An armadillo." Sellers stood there holding the saddle, an extraordinarily foolish expression on his face. "I must have put this thing"—he hefted it—"on top of a big goddamn armadillo instead of a rock. It just ran off into the bushes."

With a certain amount of relish, Stuart said, "The saddle didn't up and walk off by itself, eh? This time, it damn well did."

Sellers carried it back over by his horse and set it down, with ostentatious care, on a piece of flat, level ground. That care didn't keep him from getting ragged unmercifully by the Confederate troopers the rest of the night. Stuart did his share of the ragging, or maybe a little more. If the lurking Apaches, wherever they were, had been able to figure out what the fuss and feathers were all about, they were probably laughing, too.

When morning came, though, the time for laughter was gone. Stuart's army swung into motion once more, advancing along the trail the scouts had found the evening before. It was broad and easy at first, but soon narrowed and climbed steeply. A pack mule went over the side and rolled to the bottom of a gully. It scrambled up onto its feet, none the worse for wear except for a patch of hide scraped off its flank. A few minutes later, another mule missed a step. Its bray of terror cut off abruptly halfway down the rocky slope. It did not get up when it stopped rolling, and would not get up again. Its head twisted at an unnatural angle.

A little past noon, a scout came back to Stuart with a prize: a Tredegar cartridge an Apache must have dropped. "Has to be one of the redskins we're after, sir," the fellow said. "Means we're on the right trail."

"Yes." Stuart's head came up. "Can't mean anything else." Tredegars were mighty thin on the ground south of the border— back when this had been south of the border. "Maybe we'll catch up with them yet." He frowned. "And maybe they left it there for you to find so they could draw us into a trap." He ordered more scouts forward, and sent men to scrambling along the ridge line to smell out any ambush on either flank.

In the next valley they came to, they found the remains of a Mexican army camp. The camp looked to have been abandoned in great haste a couple of years before, and then plundered by the Indians. "They did try to put them down," Colonel Calhoun Ruggles said.

"Yes, and look what it got them." Major Sellers spoke like a man passing judgment.

"We'll do better," Stuart said. "The Empire of Mexico hasn't been what anyone would call vigorous about fighting the Indians. We *will* do it, because they haven't got any place to run to from here."

"They could go up into the USA, sir," Sellers said.

Stuart shook his head. "Not after they made common cause with us against the Yankees. The USA would sooner kill 'em than look at 'em after that, you mark my words. We'd be the same. If a Comanche band comes out of New Mexico and wants to take our side against the damnyankees, do we let 'em?"

Ruggles was best qualified to speak to that, and did: "No, sir. It happened once or twice, not long after the War of Secession: some of the Comanches reckoned they could play us and the United States off against each other." His smile was thoroughly grim. "Buzzards ate well for a few days afterwards."

Two valleys deeper into the mountains, the Confederates came upon an abandoned Apache encampment, and not an old one, either: some of the ashes in the fire pits were still warm, while flies buzzed around the bones of butchered beeves. "Now we're getting somewhere," Stuart said with more satisfaction than he'd shown since the army plunged into the divinely beautiful, hellishly rugged terrain of the Sierra Madre. "If we can get them on the run, they'll start making mistakes, and they can't afford that."

He snapped orders. Three trails led out of the valley. Mounted scouts trotted rapidly down all of them. Within half a minute of one another, three explosions shattered the quiet. All told, they cost four men killed and half a dozen wounded. One of those wounded, one of the luckier ones, told Stuart, "It was a charge buried in the ground, sir, with a trip line for a horse or a man to set it off." Blood was soaking through the rag wrapped around his forearm. "I didn't think those Apache bastards knew about little tricks like that."

Stuart and Major Horatio Sellers looked at each other. Both spoke the same name at the same time: "Batsinas." Stuart went on, "What's the name of that Yankee who comes up with a new invention every day before breakfast? Tom Edison, that's who I mean. The Apaches have got themselves a regular Tom Edison in that fellow."

"If they're going to start planting torpedoes in the road, we won't be able to rush after them," Sellers said.

"We can't rush after them in this country, anyway," Stuart answered. "So long as we get them, that's what counts."

Unhappily, Sellers said, "Damned redskins didn't even give us a clue about which way they went. If they'd put a torpedo on one trail and left the other two alone, we'd have a pretty fair notion which one to follow."

"Not necessarily," Stuart said. "A torpedo on one trail could as easily lure us into an ambush or a false path as to show the way the Indians did go. They're more than clever enough to do something like that. We've seen as much."

Major Sellers looked unhappier still before at last nodding. "I said before, we should have slaughtered them," he muttered.

"We got good use out of them up in New Mexico Territory," Stuart said. "If they hadn't quarreled with the Mexicans, we'd still be on good terms with them." He craned his neck to look around. Which of the crags ahead held Apaches with Tredegars? Behind which bushes were they crouching? He couldn't begin to guess, and that worried him. He did some muttering of his own: "Now we have to make sure they don't slaughter us."

With some misgivings, he pushed his force down the trail the scouts reported to be most used. The column had not got far when boulders thundered down the mountainside above them. The avalanche scraped several men and horses and camels and mules off the paths into a ravine below. For a moment, Stuart spied men up above him, looking at what their handiwork had done. When Confederate troopers opened fire on them, they disappeared. He hoped his men had hit some of them, but he wouldn't have bet on it.

"Come on," he called to the soldiers. "We just keep after 'em, that's all."

Perhaps half a mile farther down the trail, another landslide took its toll. Doggedly, the Confederates pressed on. "This is the difference between us and the Empire of Mexico," Major Sellers said. "If the Apaches gave the Mexicans a little licking, they'd leave. The redskins must reckon we'll do the same." He shook his head. "Won't happen."

"No, indeed," Stuart said. "We shall teach them a new reckoning."

Maybe his army's persistence started giving the Indians that new reckoning. Or maybe he had chosen the right trail after all, and was nearing whatever encampment Geronimo's men had set up after abandoning the shelters his troopers had already found. Whatever the reason, the Apaches started shooting at the Confederates from the slopes above them and from in back of rocks and bushes ahead.

Soldiers who were hit screamed. Soldiers who were not, though, went into action with a fierce joy. If the Apaches would stand and fight, they could fight back. At Stuart's shouted orders, they went forward dismounted, so they could advance over ground their mounts could not cross. Gray and butternut uniforms were hard to see against rock and dirt as they moved ahead.

Stuart shouted other orders, too, to a runner. The man dashed back along the trail, breasting the tide of troopers going forward. He did his job better—which meant faster—than Stuart had dared hope. Only a few minutes passed before first one and then another of the army's field guns began landing shells on the positions from which the Apaches were fighting. Getting those guns over what passed for trails in the Sierra Madre had been back-breaking labor—luckily, not man-killing labor—but it paid dividends now.

The Apaches did not care for coming under shellfire—or perhaps it unnerved them where bullets whipping past did not because it was less familiar. It made some of them break cover, a mistake often fatal. Yelling and whooping, the Confederates on foot went forward.

U.S. soldiers in a position like the one the Apaches held would have slugged it out with their Confederate opponents and made them pay a high price for every foot they gained. Had Stuart been defending that position against the Yankees, he would have done the same. The Apaches, though, did not fight to spend men. He'd seen that before. When they were under pressure, they saw nothing shameful about escaping from danger.

Firing slowly died away as the C.S. troopers found no more targets, real or imaginary: for Stuart was sure his men had frequently fired at bushes and rocks and even—he glanced over at Major Sellers—armadillos. "Forward!" he shouted, and forward the column went.

A few hundred yards beyond the place where the Apaches had made their stand, the trail led into another wide, fertile valley. Water trickled down from springs on the hillsides. Even in winter, everything was green. Birds chirped and warbled. Flies buzzed. The Apaches had had a camp there. It was far more hastily abandoned than the one Stuart's army had overrun early in the morning. A couple of beef cattle the Indians hadn't been able to take with them lowed mournfully.

Major Horatio Sellers rubbed his hands together. "We've got 'em on the run now, by God!"

Jeb Stuart looked around, as he had at the other abandoned camp. He saw no one but his own men. That did not mean no one but his own men saw him, and he knew it. "They've got enough places to run to," he said, not so delighted with having driven the Indians from their refuge as he'd thought he would be.

"Sooner or later, we'll get 'em," his aide-de-camp said.

"Yes, I figure we will, too," Stuart agreed. "As you said, Major, we're a lot more stubborn than the Mexicans. But I hadn't realized how many hiding places this country offers till I traveled it. We'll be a good long while at the job, I fear—years, most likely."

Sellers' mouth twisted. "I don't like that notion so very much."

"Neither do I, not even a little." Stuart drew himself up straighter. "It's got to be done, though, and I expect we'll do it . . . eventually." After that last word was out of his mouth, he wished he hadn't said it. Then he looked around at the Sierra Madre again. He sighed. *Eventually* had needed saying.

From a bush so small no white man would ever have imagined using it for a hiding place, a rifle barked. Something hit Stuart a heavy blow in the belly. He grunted, as if at acute indigestion. "My God!" Horatio Sellers cried. "The general's shot!"

Next thing Stuart knew, he was lying in the dirt. Someone was making a noise like a fox with its leg in a trap. He realized it was he. The pain had started. It was very bad. It was worse than very bad. It was tremendous, appalling, all-consuming. He writhed and moaned and then shrieked, unashamed. None of it did any good.

Leaning over him, Sellers shouted, "Fetch the surgeon, dammit!"

Blood poured between Stuart's fingers as he clutched at himself. The surgeon wouldn't do any good, either. Wishing he could lose consciousness again, Stuart was only too sure of that. He shrieked again. He couldn't help himself. However long *eventually* was, he wouldn't be here to see it.

Brigadier General George Custer threw more coal into the stove in his quarters at Fort Benton. The fire in the stove glowed a cheery red. Despite that, he was anything but warm. A blizzard howled outside.

He scraped a match against the sole of his boot and lighted a cigar. Libbie gave him a disapproving look. "*Must* you do that?" she demanded.

"Dashed right I must," Custer said, and sucked in smoke. He didn't cough at all now. Sometimes the smoke even tasted good.

"*Dashed?*" Libbie set her hands on her hips. Her eyes sparked. She was a very determined person. "Autie, you didn't just promise not to swear where I could hear. You promised not to swear at all."

Another nice thing about a cigar, Custer had discovered, was that it gave him an excuse not to talk for a little while. Libbie wasn't just determined; she was tenacious as a terrier. Tom would have known how disapproving of his new vices she'd be. Tom had loved her, too, loved her like a sister. Poor Tom. Custer wondered if the empty place inside him would ever disappear. He didn't think so. When he couldn't use the cigar to keep quiet any more, he said, "Times have changed, and not for the better, either."

"And," Libbie went on implacably, "you promised your sister you would never again drink liquor, and I know you have violated that pledge as well."

"When I promised her, I never dreamt my beloved country would go down to humiliating defeat at the hands of the Black Republicans not once but twice," Custer said. "Can you blame me if I seek consolation?"

"I might not blame you had you sought consolation *once*, though even that would be a violation of your promise," Libbie said. "But, having reacquired the habit you abandoned so long ago, you have indulged it not once but repeatedly."

The reason for that was simple: after twenty years, Custer had rediscovered how much he enjoyed the feel of whiskey coursing through him. Coming right out and saying so, however, struck him as impolitic. What he did say was "I am far more moderate than in the old days."

"If you mean you aren't staggering down the street puking every few steps, well, yes, that is true." Such acid filled Libbie's voice, Custer flinched from it as he never had from enemy fire. Inexorably, she went on, "But if you think you are fulfilling your promise, I cannot agree."

Custer did not answer. He felt trapped. Not only did the blizzard keep him from escaping his wife, it also kept him from escaping Colonel Henry Welton. Welton was a model of military punctilio; nothing he did, nothing he said, could possibly be construed as offensive toward the newly promoted superior now residing in what had been his fort for so long. All the same, Custer felt about as welcome as a man in the last stages of cholera.

Libbie might have picked the thought out of his head. She said, "That foolish infantry colonel thinks he should have more of the credit for winning the battle by the Teton, Autie. I can't imagine why, but he plainly does. Everyone wants some of the glory that should rightly attach to you."

Whatever she thought of Custer's shortcomings—and she was seldom reticent in telling him what she thought—she was as determined as he to wring the greatest possible advantage out of his virtues. He said, "I still maintain, and shall continue to maintain, that we should have done as well against the British without the Gatling guns as we did with them. Tom would back me, I know it. Dear Lord, if only he could have then! I wish the stupid things had not been on the field at all; in that case, no occasion for argument would have or could have arisen."

"Of course not," Libbie said soothingly. Then her brow, which she prided herself on keeping smooth, furrowed. "I wish that that Colonel Roosevelt had not been on the field, either. He has stolen much of the approbation that would otherwise have gone to you."

"I've thought about that," Custer said, "and I have decided it does not matter."

"It certainly does," Libbie exclaimed indignantly. He nodded, ever so slightly; he'd succeeded in diverting her from his flaws. She continued, "How can you possibly say it does not matter when he has what should be yours?"

"Because whether he has it or not, what can he do with it?"

Custer said. "He is a colonel of Volunteers whose regiment has been mustered out of U.S. service, so he cannot harm my Army career. And he is a puppy of twenty-three, so he cannot be my rival for any political office, the Constitution disqualifying him from such a pursuit on account of his age. Q.E.D., as my instructors in the mysteries of geometry were given to saying."

"All that may be so," Libbie said, and then, grudgingly, "I suppose all that is so. Nonetheless, I am ever so glad he has left Fort Benton. Say what you will about him, enough ambition burns in that man for a hundred Henry Weltons. Deny it if you can." Her chin jutted defiance.

"Let him be as ambitious as he likes," Custer said. "His desires cannot impinge on mine."

Her voice dropped almost to a whisper: "Do you think you can be nominated for the presidency? Do you think you will be nominated for the presidency?"

"I *can* be," he answered. "Jackson was. Harrison was. Taylor was. Winfield Scott was, too, though he failed of election."

"Whoever faces Blaine year after next will not lose," Libbie said.

"No, I shouldn't think so," Custer agreed. "Whether I *will* be nominated depends on whether I can keep my name in the public's eye between now and then, and also on whether the leaders of the party decide I am the man whose name they want to put forward at the convention."

"And whatever fame this Roosevelt gained at your expense will make both of those things less likely," Libbie pointed out. "There. Do you see? You have contradicted yourself." She looked as triumphant as if she had just driven back an invading British army.

Before Custer could reply, someone knocked on the door to his quarters. Through the yowling wind, a soldier called, "Colonel Welton's compliments, General, and would you and your lady care to join him for supper?"

"Yes, we'll come," Custer said, and then, to Libbie, "Wrap yourself up warm, my dear, and we'll see what the cooks have done with—or to—supper." Her coat was of Angora sheep, and warm. His own, of buffalo hide, had served him well in the field.

Even so, that first dreadful breath of air once he left his quarters almost froze him from the lungs outwards. His teeth chattered. A moment later, he heard Libbie's clicking away, too.

Snow swirled around him, making even the short walk to the officers' dining room an adventure. The way was made more uncertain because the dining-room shutters, like most of the rest at Fort Benton, were closed to help hold in heat. Custer had to grope for the latch. Only when he opened the door did yellow lamplight spill out and illuminate the endlessly blowing snow—and no sooner had he opened the door than shouts of "Close it!" rang out from within.

He waved Libbie in ahead of him, then went into the dining room and shut the door after himself. The first breath of warm air inside was nearly as stunning as the first frigid breath outside had been. Sweat sprang out on his forehead. He got out of his overcoat in a hurry. So did Libbie.

"Good evening, General Custer, ma'am," Henry Welton said. He rose and saluted.

Custer returned the salute. "Good evening, Colonel," he said. Yes, everything was perfectly proper, perfectly correct, and colder than the blizzard outside. Everything had been that way since he'd brought the Fifth Cavalry down to Fort Benton after the first of the year. He sniffed and smiled. "What's for supper?" he asked. "Whatever it is, it sure smells good."

Sometimes his pretense broke the ice for a little while. Today was one of those times. Henry Welton actually smiled back and answered in civil tones: "Fried potatoes from our own garden, boiled beans and salt pork, and roast prairie chickens." He even essayed a small joke: "Not too hard keeping meat fresh, this season of the year."

"No, indeed." Custer tried to joke back: "Not too hard keeping meat *hard*, either, this season of the year."

Welton smiled again. So did a couple of his junior officers. So did Custer, with some effort. It didn't help much. He and the officers of Welton's Seventh Infantry were smiling past one another, like carriages going by on opposite sides of the road.

Custer was fond of fried potatoes, though he would have liked fried onions—or onions of any sort—even more. The beans and pork were beans and pork; he'd been eating them for so many years, he hardly noticed them on his plate except insofar as they helped fill his belly. He enjoyed the prairie chickens. They were all dark meat, and full of flavor.

A couple of whiskey bottles and a pitcher of lemonade from concentrate went around the table. Most of the officers drank whiskey. Libbie filled her tin cup with lemonade and pointedly passed the pitcher to Custer. "Wouldn't you like some, Autie?"

That would have sounded harmless to anyone who didn't know her well. To Custer, it was anything but. "With the weather like this, I do believe I'd sooner have something to help keep me warm," he said. One of the whiskey bottles sat within reach. He poured some—not an enormous tot, by any means—into his cup, then raised it high. "Confusion to our enemies!"

Not even Welton and his officers could find fault with that toast. They drank with Custer. As the liquor ran down his throat, Libbie gave him a look that should have completely counteracted its warming effect, but somehow didn't quite. She did no more than that. In public, she stood foursquare behind Custer, for behaving in any other way might have harmed his chances. What she was liable to say when they went back to their quarters was another matter. Custer didn't care to think about that. To help keep him from thinking about it, he poured more whiskey into the cup. Libbie sent him another glacial glance.

"Confusion to our enemies indeed," Henry Welton said. He was drinking whiskey, too, and making no bones about it. "It's the best thing that could strike them, from our point of view, and the only thing that could bring them down to our level."

When it came to politics—with, no doubt, the exception of Custer's political ambitions—Custer and the officers of the Seventh Infantry were not so far apart. Almost to a man, they loathed the administration currently in Washington, or rather in Philadelphia, having been shelled out of Washington. Only the presence of Libbie Custer and some of the other officers' wives kept them from expressing their opinion in terms even more forceful than the ones they used.

Custer said, "We didn't know what the devil we were doing when we made war, and we don't know what the devil we're doing now that we're trying to make peace, either."

"Blaine can't stomach giving away half of Maine," Welton said scornfully. "If he does, it'll make the state we ship him back to smaller."

"We should have hanged Lincoln—look at the rabble-rousing he's doing now—and we should hang that dashed idiot Blaine, too," Custer said. Even with whiskey in him, he would not curse in the presence of women.

"That's what comes of electing Republicans," Libbie said. There her opinions marched with her husband's.

"Once we finally do have peace—if we finally do have

peace—that'll be a sham, too, nothing but a hoax and a humbug," Custer said. "It always has been. Sooner or later, the Fifth will go back to Kansas, and we'll ride along the border with the CSA, and sure as the devil the Kiowas and the Comanches will ride up and burn a farm and kill the men and do worse to the women, and then they'll go back down into Indian Territory where we can't follow 'em. It's been going on ever since the War of Secession, and what can we do about it? Not a blasted thing I can see." A considerable silence followed. Into it, Custer added, "That's the way it's always been, and I don't see it changing any time soon. I wish I did, but I don't."

Not quite quietly enough, one of Henry Welton's officers muttered, "I wish to Jesus the Fifth *would* go back to Kansas, and get the devil out of *our* hair."

Another considerable silence filled the room, this one not nearly so sympathetic nor companionable as the first. Custer might have blown up. Instead (and he saw Libbie looking at him in surprise), he sipped his whiskey and affected not to hear. When the Fifth did go back to Kansas, he would not be going back with it, at least not as regimental commander. That was too small a position for a brigadier general to hold. Maybe, as John Pope had been doing before being sent to Utah, he would take charge of several regiments. Maybe the War Department would send him back to Washington, to help clean up the mess there. Whether or not he did that, someone would have to take care of it.

And maybe, when 1884 rolled around, he would lay down his commission, take off his uniform, put on a civilian sack suit and top hat, and campaign not against the British or the Confederates or the Indians but against the manifest and manifold iniquities of the Republican Party. That, though, was not entirely up to him. He would have to see what—and whom—the leaders of the Democrats had in mind.

Henry Welton said, "General, when you do go back to Kansas, would you arrange to leave behind some of your Gatling-gun crews as a defense against another British invasion?"

"Why, certainly," Custer said. "As a matter of fact . . ." He was about to say, *You're welcome to every blasted one of them.* Before he could, he saw Libbie looking intently at him. That look reminded him of the slaughter the Gatlings had wreaked on the Kiowas. They might do the same again. Tom would surely have thought so. He softened his words: "As a matter of fact, you can have several of them."

"Thank you, sir." By Welton's tone, he'd expected Custer to give him all the contraptions.

Maybe the whiskey helped fuel Custer's chuckle. Being too predictable didn't do. "See me tomorrow, Colonel, and we'll see if we can't settle on how many can stay here and how many will go with us."

"Yes, sir, I'll do that," Welton answered. "I do wish you all the best on your return to Kansas." That was more polite than the way his junior officer had phrased it, but meant the same thing. Henry Welton did not care for having a bigger chief in the teepee with him.

When supper was over, Custer and Libbie made their way back to their quarters. It was cold outside, and had got colder since they'd come to the dining room. Inside, it was nice and warm. Libbie spoke one word: "Whiskey." All at once, it was chillier in there than out in the snow. Custer wanted another drink.

☆ **XX** ☆

"Is it then agreed, General?" Alfred von Schlieffen asked. "You will send officers to Berlin to study the methods of the German Empire?" *You will send officers to Berlin to learn how to do things right?* was what he meant, but, although no diplomat, he knew better than to phrase it so.

Major General William S. Rosecrans scratched the end of his long nose, then nodded. "It is agreed, Colonel," he told the German military attaché, "or rather, the president, the secretary of state, and I agree to it. The Royal Navy, unfortunately, has other ideas."

Schlieffen said, "Had President Blaine made peace some time ago, the British would not have found it necessary the blockade of your coast to resume."

"I am painfully aware of that," Rosecrans said, and his voice did indeed hold pain. "The entire country, I would say, is painfully aware of that—the entire country, less one man."

"What can be done to persuade him?" Schlieffen asked. "Even if he would for more war make ready, he cannot fight more now. He needs to win time in which the United States can get over this fight. So it has always been. So, I think, it will always be."

"Do you know the fable about the goddamn donkey dithering between two bales of hay, Colonel?" Rosecrans asked. After Schlieffen had nodded, the U.S. general-in-chief went on, "Well, sir, James G. Blaine is that donkey, except both bales are poisoned. If you were one of my colonels instead of one of the Kaiser's colonels, I'd say he was a prize horse's ass, too. But you aren't, so I won't."

"But you just—" Schlieffen broke off, realizing exactly what Rosecrans had done. The military attaché sniffed, as if he had a cold. He'd smelled liquor on Rosecrans' breath before. He didn't smell it now. Anger and frustration could also drive a man into indiscretion.

Rosecrans went on, "One bale of hay is making peace with the bastards who beat us. But that means admitting they beat us, and he can't stomach it. The other bale is going back to war with 'em. But if we do, the only thing that'll happen is that they'll lick us some more. He knows as much, but he keeps trying to sick it up, too. And that leaves him nothing to do but dither. Stupid fool's got pretty good at it, too, wouldn't you say? He's had practice enough lately, anyway."

"This dithering, though—" Schlieffen liked the sound of the word, and repeated it: "This dithering cannot last. President Blaine must remember, he is not the only one who can begin again the war. Come soon or come late, your enemies will force you to fight if you do not obey now. This blockade is only a small thing. Much more could come. Much more would come."

Rosecrans' wrinkles got deeper. "I know that, damn it. You'll have a friend in Richmond—your attaché to the Confederate States, I mean."

"*Aber natürlich,* a colleague." Schlieffen made the correction without noticing he'd done it. Since his wife's death—to a large degree before his wife's death, too—he'd so immersed himself in work that he had no time for friends.

"Then you'll have got word from him, one way or another, that the Confederate States are moving troops toward the Potomac," Rosecrans said.

"I had heard this, yes," Schlieffen said, nodding. "I was not going to speak of it if you did not; such is not my place."

"They're moving a good many troops." Rosecrans' voice was sour, heavy. "The railroad makes it easy to move a lot of troops in a hurry—hell of a lot easier than moving 'em on roads knee-deep in mud would be. They aren't coming up toward the border for their amusement, or for ours."

"You are also moving troops, I know," Schlieffen said.

"Oh, yes." The U.S. general-in-chief bobbed his head up and down. "If they hit us, we'll give 'em the best damn fight we can—don't doubt it for a minute, Colonel, the best fight we can. But what you may not have heard"—he was almost whispering now, like a boy talking about some bugbear or hobgoblin—"is that General Jackson is back in Richmond."

"No, I had not heard that," Schlieffen said. On hearing it, he heard also that Rosecrans was a beaten man. No matter how many men the USA moved down to the Potomac, Jackson would find a way to beat them, because Rosecrans thought Jackson would find a way to beat them. Someone—Schlieffen annoyed himself by not recalling whether it was Napoleon or Clausewitz—had wisely said that the moral was to the physical in war as three was to one. As Austrian and Prussian armies had for so long gone into battle against Bonaparte convinced before the fighting started that they would lose, so Rosecrans faced the prospect of confronting Jackson.

"Well, it's true; God damn it to hell, it's true," Rosecrans said.

Schlieffen listened with half an ear, trying to remember which military genius had come up with the maxim. He couldn't. Like a bit of gristle stuck between two back teeth, it would bother him till he did. He became aware that Rosecrans had said something else, something he'd missed entirely. "Excuse me, please?" he said, embarrassed at piling one professional failure on another.

"I said, a few friends in the world sure would come in handy about now," Rosecrans repeated.

"For this war, you have no friends who can give you help," Schlieffen said. "This was, I hear from every American, the idea of your President Washington. This man has not been your president for many years. Maybe it is time to think that matters have perhaps changed since his day."

"I'll tell you what I'm starting to think," Rosecrans said savagely. "I'm starting to think Washington was nothing but a stinking Virginian, and the Rebs can damn well keep him and his ideas both."

Schlieffen did not smile. He made a point of not smiling. Not only would smiling have been against his interest and his country's, he was such a resolutely moderate man that smiling did not come easy to him anyhow. In his usual careful way, he said, "I hope you will also say this to your president and to your foreign minister—no, secretary of state you call him."

"I've been saying it since things started going downhill without any brakes," Rosecrans answered. "I've been saying it to anyone who will listen. Colonel, if you think President Blaine is inclined to listen to me, you had better think again. If you think he's inclined to listen to anybody, you had better think again."

"This is not good," Schlieffen said.

The telephone jangled. Rosecrans jerked as if a horsefly had bitten him. "Guess who that is," he said with a martyred sigh. "He may not listen, but by Jesus he likes to talk."

Schlieffen left the office of the general-in-chief. Behind him, Rosecrans bellowed into the newfangled instrument. As Schlieffen came out into the outer office, Captain Saul Berryman looked up from his paperwork with a martyred expression. *"Auf Wiedersehen, Herr Oberst,"* he said.

"Good-bye, Captain," Schlieffen answered. He had more than a little sympathy for Rosecrans' adjutant, a capable young man trapped in a position where his ability did his nation less good than it might have in the field.

The calendar said spring was only a few days away. Freezing rain pelted down in spite of what the calendar said. Schlieffen hardly noticed as he walked to the carriage waiting for him and climbed in. His mind was elsewhere. *Napoleon or Clausewitz? Clausewitz or Napoleon?* That he could not make a fact he knew spring up and stand to attention infuriated him.

"Back to the consul's establishment, Colonel?" the driver asked.

"Yes," Schlieffen snapped. He paid no more attention to the driver's chattering teeth than he had to the weather that caused them. The wheels of the carriage slipped a little on the icy paving stones, but then the toe calks on the horse's shoes bit and the carriage began to roll.

Despite the weather, some sort of political demonstration was going on not far from the War Department building. *Socialists,* Schlieffen thought, seeing the red flags that hung sodden from their staffs. He'd seen more Socialist demonstrations than he liked back in Germany, but never till now one of this size in the United States.

When he reported what he had seen to Kurd von Schlözer, the German minister to the USA nodded. "One faction of Blaine's own party has made common cause with the Socialists," Schlözer said.

"Really? I had not heard." Save as they affected military affairs, Schlieffen paid little attention to politics.

Schlözer gave him a look that said he should have heeded them more closely. "If we have no peace, soon we shall have fighting in the streets. With the Socialists now stronger, we may have revolution, Red revolution," he said. "This is a land of revolution, and the Socialists—the new Socialists, I mean—know it and exploit it."

"God forbid," Schlieffen said. "If they try to raise a revolution, may they be met with iron and blood." After using Bismarck's famous phrase, he nodded to Schlözer. "You know I feel the same about the Socialist movement in the Fatherland."

"Oh, yes, my dear Colonel, of course," Schlözer said. "No man of property, no man of sense, could possibly say otherwise. But too many Americans, like too many Germans, have neither property nor sense. And the leaders of the Socialists here, like the leaders there, have an oversupply of cunning, if not of sense."

"This has not been true in the United States," Schlieffen said. "So much I know—otherwise, the Socialists here would have stirred up far more trouble than they have."

"Now, though, men who really know something of politics have started waving red flags for purposes of their own," the German minister said. "In matters of politics, Blaine is now as dead as a salt·herring. Even if he could have been reelected before—which would have taken an act of God—he has no hope whatever with a large part of his party going over to the radicals. He must understand as much."

"This is not good," Schlieffen said, as he had to Rosecrans. "A man without hope will do irrational things. Since Blaine did irrational things even when the situation for himself and his country looked better, who knows how crazy and wild he might become now?"

"We shall see." Kurd von Schlözer sounded less gloomy than Schlieffen would have. Schlieffen wondered if his superior was deluding himself about how sensible President Blaine could be. From what the German military attaché had seen, expecting common sense from Americans was like looking for water in a desert: you might find some, but, even if you did, it would be only an oasis in a vast stretch of hot, dry, burning sand.

"Napoleon!" he exclaimed suddenly, and felt much better about the world. Hot sand had made him think of Egypt, which had made him think of Bonaparte's campaign there, which in turn had reminded him of whose adage had crossed his mind during his conversation with Rosecrans.

Kurd von Schlözer gave him a curious look.

A couple of days later, after a cable from Berlin, Schlözer requested an audience with Blaine. When the request was granted, the German minister asked Schlieffen to accompany him. "Of course, Your Excellency," Schlieffen said, "if you think my being there will do some good. If not, I have other matters to occupy my time." He was still refining the plan for movement against France whose basic idea he'd borrowed from Lee's campaign in Pennsylvania. He'd had wires of his own from Berlin; the General Staff was enthusiastic about the outline he'd sent.

But Schlözer said, "Military affairs are likely to be discussed, so your place is with me." However much Schlieffen would have liked to go on burrowing through his books—inadequate though his research tools here in Philadelphia were—he could only obey. Hiding a sigh, he set down his pen and, carefully locking the door to his office behind him, followed Schlözer downstairs to the carriage.

Bright sunshine made him blink. The bad weather had blown past Philadelphia the day before; now he could believe spring was at hand. Soon—all too soon—summer would grip the eastern seaboard of the United States in its hot, sweaty fist.

Down from Germantown the carriage made its way, dodging among others like it, rumbling wagons, men on horseback, men on bicycles with improbably high front wheels, and swarms of men and women on foot. And then, as had happened to Schlieffen coming back from the War Department, a political rally snarled traffic that would have been bad without it. Now red flags rippled in a friendly breeze; now not only the most dedicated Socialists, those fearing neither catarrh nor pneumonia, assembled under the flags. Now nervous-looking soldiers helped police route buggies and horses and pedestrians around the streets the demonstrators clogged.

Schlieffen and Schlözer never came within two blocks of the rally. Even so, the Socialists' shouts rose above the clatter of horses' hooves, the rattle of iron tires on paving, and the squeals and groans of axles needing grease. "Can you make out what they are saying, Your Excellency?" Schlieffen asked.

"I believe the cry is, 'Justice!'" Schlözer clicked his tongue between his teeth. "If I were petitioning the Almighty, or even my government, I would sooner ask for mercy. But then, I am an old man, and well aware of how much I need it. Waving flags in the street is not an old man's sport."

Because of the rally, they got to the Powel House fifteen minutes late. President Blaine brushed aside Kurd von Schlözer's apologies. "Don't trouble yourself about it, Your Excellency," Blaine said. "I want to tell you that I received yesterday a telegram from the U.S. minister in Berlin informing me that his talks with Chancellor Bismarck continue to go well, and that prospects look bright for increased cooperation in all spheres between our two great countries."

"I am delighted to hear this, Mr. President," Schlözer said, and Schlieffen nodded, knowing *all spheres* included the military. But the German minister looked grim as he continued, "I also received yesterday a telegram from Berlin, whose contents I wish to discuss with you now. I must tell you that the governments of Britain, France, and the Confederate States are most dissatisfied with the dilatory pace of negotiations with your government. Since Germany is neutral in this conflict, they have united in asking Chancellor Bismarck to make me the channel through which they express to you their dissatisfaction. If you refuse to meet their demands, I cannot answer for the consequences."

Blaine flushed. His large, bulbous nose went redder than the rest of his face. "Their demands are outrageous, impossible!" he shouted, as if he were on the rostrum rather than sitting in his office. "How am I to yield so large a portion of my home state to the invaders? How am I to acquiesce in the Confederacy's acquisition of lands to which that nation has no right?"

"If you had yielded Sonora and Chihuahua before, you would not now the loss of part of Maine face," Schlieffen said. "You have lost the war. *'Vae victis,'* as Brennus the Gaul said to the Romans he had beaten."

Blaine glared at him. "The Romans ended up whipping the Gauls, so that 'Woe to the conquered' applied to the conquerors. We can fight on, too."

Sadly, Schlieffen shook his head. "No, Your Excellency, not in this war. You are defeated."

Kurd von Schlözer said, "The reason we were tardy, Mr. President, was the large Socialists demonstration that forced traffic to make a detour around it."

Blaine's complexion darkened once more. "Socialists!" he said, as if pronouncing an obscenity. "Most of them are traitors to the Republican Party, nothing else."

"As may be," Schlözer said. "Would you not agree, though, that they leave your own political future more . . . uncertain than it was before the schism in your party took place?"

Now Blaine had heard blunt talk from both the German attaché and the German minister. "You tread close to the edge, sir," he growled. Schlözer sat impassive, waiting for a more responsive answer. At last, obviously hating every word, Blaine said, "You may be right."

That was the response for which Schlözer had waited. "Being now without hope and so without fear, Your Excellency, can you not act as a disinterested statesman and serve with a whole heart the needs of your country? You have the chance, Mr. President, and a rare chance it is for an elected official, to do just that without considering your own future political advantage, for you can have none."

Had Blaine not been in the room, Schlieffen might have smiled. Schlözer could not have urged a more sensible, more logical course on the president of the United States. The only question remaining was whether sense and logic could still reach James G. Blaine.

Schlieffen added a few words of his own: "If you do not do this, Your Excellency, your country will only suffer more. In your heart, you must know this is so."

Again, Blaine stayed silent a long time. At last, very low, he repeated, "You may be right." He let out a long, shuddering sigh. "Making peace with the enemies of my country is like looking into my open grave. But, as you say, I am already dead, so what does it matter how I am buried?"

"Think of your country," Schlözer said.

"Think of the future, and what your country and mine may do there," Schlieffen said. Slowly, Blaine nodded.

Philander Snow spat a brown stream into a drift of the stuff whose name he bore. Theodore Roosevelt had changed the calendar from March to April a couple of days before. He'd seen spring snow in New York State; seeing it in Montana Territory did not delight him, but it did not surprise him, either.

His mind had a way of running toward what would be. "We've got to plant as soon as we can, Phil," he said. "We shan't have a long growing season—we never do, not here, but it will be even shorter this year. Everything must be in readiness to move the moment conditions permit."

Snow spat again. "It will be, Colonel." He'd taken to calling Roosevelt that since his boss' return from commanding the Unauthorized Regiment. Having been mustered out of the U.S. Army,

Roosevelt no longer had any formal right to the title. The next time he corrected the ranch hand about it would be the first.

"That's good, Phil. That's what I want to hear," he said, now, adding, for about the hundredth time, "I know I can rely on you. If I'd ever had any doubts—which I haven't—the way you and the rest of the hands who didn't join my regiment brought in the harvest last fall would have shot them right between the eyes."

"That's white of you, Colonel. We reckoned it was the least we could do, seein' how you and the Unauthorized Regiment was doin' everything you could to keep them goddamn English bastards from comin' down and burnin' us out." Snow loosed yet another stream of tobacco juice. "Ask you somethin'?"

"You may ask," Roosevelt said. "I don't promise to answer."

"Fair enough." Snow nodded. "All kinds of talk been goin' around about how you'll up and sell this here ranch and go back to New York to do some politicking there. Is it so, or is it a pile of humbug?"

"I'd love to go back to New York and politic there," Roosevelt answered. "The only trouble with the notion is that, in order to run for the State Assembly, I must have attained the twenty-fifth year of my age. I am old enough to have fought for my country and to have commanded men in battle, but not old enough to help legislate for my state."

"Plumb crazy, you ask me," Philander Snow opined. " 'Course, nobody asked me."

"Crazy it may be," Roosevelt said. "The law of the state it is. And so I shall stay here in Montana Territory, here on the ranch, a while longer, at any rate." He did his best to speak lightly, as if that mattered to him only a little. Inside, he seethed with worry lest the fickle populace forget him before he reached the age where he could offer himself for approval.

"Well, I'm powerful glad to hear that," Snow said. "Powerful glad. I've been pleased with my situation here, and I'd hate to have to go looking for another one on account of you was sellin' the place for no better reason than to go back East and tell lies to people the rest of your days."

"Is that what politics means to you?" Roosevelt demanded. The ranch hand nodded without hesitation. Roosevelt's sigh loosed a cloud of steam into the chilly air. "I give you my solemn word: I shall always tell the truth to the people."

"I've heard a lot of people say that." Snow spoke in ruminative tones. "Maybe you're telling the truth, Colonel. I hope to Jesus you are, matter of fact. But it wouldn't startle me out of my stockings if I found out you wasn't."

"I shall always tell the truth to the people," Roosevelt repeated. "Always. Do not doubt me on this, Phil; I mean every word I say. You are right when you assert that the American people have already heard too many lies."

Snow cocked his head to one side and studied Roosevelt for a while before saying, "It's a young man's promise, Colonel. Maybe there's a reason a fellow has got to be twenty-five before he can run after all. You get older, you figure out there's a deal of gray between black and white."

"A man who will see gray once will see gray all the time." Theodore Roosevelt scornfully tossed his head. "A man who sees gray will never see black, nor white either, even when they are there. That, I think, defines your run-of-the-mill politician to a T. I may be a politician one day—I *would* be lying if I said I didn't fancy the notion—but, whatever else history may record of me, it shall never say I was run-of-the-mill."

Philander Snow gave him another measuring appraisal, punctuating it by putting another brown spot in the white by his feet. "I don't reckon anyone will call you that. Some other things, maybe, but not that one there."

"I hope no one does," Roosevelt said. "Even those who were great in their time are so easily forgotten. Who now recalls the deeds of Lysander the Spartan or Frederick Barbarossa?"

"Not me, that's for damn sure," Snow said at once.

"Just so," Roosevelt said. "Just so. I want my name to *live*, to be a possession for all time." Phil wouldn't have heard of Thucydides, either, so Roosevelt didn't bother explaining where he'd got that last phrase. But, even if the ranch hand hadn't heard of him, a lot of what the Greek historian had to say about the war between Athens and Sparta in the fifth century before Christ could as readily have been written about the modern struggles between the USA and the CSA. Just as Sparta had got aid from rich Persia against Athens, which otherwise was probably the stronger, so the Confederate States had used help from England and France to put down the United States, which alone was the larger, richer, and more populous of the two.

Snow said, "Good shootin' the breeze with you, boss. I'm headin' off to check on the stock." He trudged down toward the barn, his boots crunching as each step broke the crust on the latest snowfall.

Roosevelt went inside to catch up on the bookkeeping. No sooner had he got to work than dark clouds rolled across the sun. He lighted a lamp in the study. A few minutes later, it went dry, filling the room with the stink of kerosene. When he went to put more into it, he discovered the ranch house was almost out.

He went to the door and shouted for Philander Snow. Eventually, Snow stuck his head out of the barn. When Roosevelt asked him if there was any kerosene in there, the ranch hand answered, "Sure as hell ain't. We should have bought some the last time the Handbasket went down to Helena, only we forgot."

"Damnation," Roosevelt muttered. "None in the hands' quarter, either?"

"Sure as hell ain't," Snow repeated. "Oh, maybe enough for a day or two, you spread it out amongst there and the barn and the ranch house. But maybe not even that much, neither."

"Damnation," Roosevelt said again. Then he brightened. "Well, hitch up the horses to the Handbasket. We'll just have to go down to Helena again and get some." Any excuse to get into town, even his own absentmindedness, was a good one as far as he was concerned. Here on the ranch, he was feeling isolated again. The year before, he'd been part of great events. Now, unless he went down to Helena, he didn't even know about them till long after they happened—not till someone chanced to bring word up to the ranch.

Thinking along with him, Snow said, "We got the chance to find out what in hell's gone wrong the past few days. Swear to Jesus, sometimes I laugh till I'm like to bust, listenin' to you cuss old Blaine and the Socialists and whoever else you ain't feelin' happy about of a mornin'."

"I'm so glad I amuse you," Roosevelt said. "I wish I amused myself. You do know that what you're laughing about is the humiliation of the United States?"

"Oh, no, Colonel—what I'm laughin' about is you cussin' the humiliation of the United States," Snow said, a distinction a Jesuit might have envied. Before Roosevelt could remark on it, the hand went back into the barn, presumably to hitch the horses to the farm wagon. When he brought the wagon out, he gave Roosevelt a wistful look. "Don't suppose you'd want some company on the way down to Helena?"

"I alone committed the sin of omission," Roosevelt answered. "I alone shall atone for it." Philander Snow let out a gusty sigh. He'd done his best to get out of several hours' work: done his best and failed, in which he resembled his country. Having failed, he went back to the unending chores that bulked so large in farm life.

Roosevelt rattled down the road by himself. In the back of the wagon, the five-gallon milk cans in which he'd bring back the lamp oil did considerable rattling of their own. They had KEROSENE painted on them in big red letters, to make sure no milk went into them by mistake.

With snow on it, the ground was still hard. Before long, the snow would melt, and everything would turn to mud. Getting to Helena through the resulting morass was liable to be an all-day job, as opposed to a couple of hours each way.

A horseman came up the road toward Roosevelt. As the fellow trotted past, he took off his hat and waved it, saying, "Good day to you, Colonel."

"And to you, Magnussen," Roosevelt answered. "You look well. How's that leg of yours feeling? I remember your captain saying you fought bravely."

"Oh, thank you, Colonel." The former trooper of the Unauthorized Regiment blushed like a girl. "The leg is good. How do you recall all your men, and who got hit in the leg, and who in the arm, and so on?"

"How? You just do it." Roosevelt saw nothing out of the ordinary in carrying a flock of details in his head. "It's no harder than memorizing the multiplication table—easier, for men have faces and voices, and numbers don't."

Magnussen laughed. "Easier for you, maybe, Colonel, but not for the likes of me." He lifted his hat again, then rode on.

"A man can do anything he sets his mind on doing," Roosevelt called after him. Magnussen gave no sign that he'd heard, though he wasn't out of earshot. Roosevelt shrugged. Too many men would not set their minds on anything worth doing. That, to him, was why they did not succeed. He loosed an angry snort at the absurdity of Abraham Lincoln's Socialist notions.

When he got to Helena, he took some little while reaching the general store. Men who'd served in the Unauthorized Regiment were thick on the ground in the territorial capital. If Roosevelt had taken all of them up on the drinks they wanted to buy him, he would have forgotten his name, let alone such minutiae as where he lived and what he'd come into town to buy.

He filled the milk cans from the big wooden barrel behind the counter at the store. The proprietor, a big redhead named McNamara, said, "I reckoned you was runnin' low last time you was in, Colonel, but you always know your own business so good, figured I was crazy myself."

"Even Jove nods," Roosevelt said, which meant nothing to the storekeeper. Grunting, Roosevelt carried the full milk cans out to the wagon. He turned down another drink while he was doing that.

Virtue unalloyed would have sent him straight back to the ranch. His virtue turned out not to be quite free of admixture. Instead of riding out of town with the kerosene, he went over to the offices of the *Helena Gazette*. As usual, a crowd had gathered in front of the building to read the newspaper on display under glass.

Roosevelt hitched the wagon and started working his way through the crowd toward the paper. He didn't worry about the kerosene; nobody could inconspicuously amble off with a five-gallon milk can full of the stuff. Men made way for him, so he got to the *Gazette* far sooner than he would have before he'd recruited the Unauthorized Regiment. They reached out to shake his hand or slap him on the back. If Helena had anything to say about it, he could have been elected president tomorrow.

What he read, though, made him grind his teeth. "The arrogance of our enemies!" he burst out. "But for Maine, they hold not a single square inch of our sacred soil, yet they presume to order us around as if we were beasts of burden."

"What are we going to do to them?" somebody asked. "What *can* we do to them? We're too busy squabbling among ourselves to hurt anybody else." He pointed to a story about a Socialist parade in Boston that had got out of hand. The police had opened fire, and four were dead, including one policeman. *Red is the color of the blood of martyrs,* a Socialist spokesman was quoted as saying.

"To hell with Abraham Lincoln," Roosevelt ground out. "Custer was right—Pope should have hanged him while he had him under lock and key in Utah Territory. He's ten times as much trouble as all the Mormons and all their wives put together." He heard himself in some surprise; he hadn't thought he might agree with Custer on anything.

About half the crowd in front of the copy of the *Gazette* loudly approved his words. The other half—miners, mostly—as loudly told him where to go and how to get there. Helena, he remembered, had broken out in riots after one of Lincoln's speeches, while Great Falls had stayed calm. To a man who had nothing to offer but the sweat of his brow, class warfare was a seductive strumpet indeed.

"I don't think Lincoln's is the best way for the working men of this country to get a square deal," he said, sticking out his chin. "And besides, if we fight one another, who wins? Do the capitalists win? Do the workers win? Not a chance in hell, either way. I'll tell you who wins: the British and the French and the Confederates. Nobody else."

That got him a thoughtful silence. He was happy enough to gain even so much; he'd been wondering whether Helena would erupt again on account of him. He knew where the Gatling guns were. Colonel Welton had kept most of them even after Custer returned to Kansas. They were the most telling argument yet prepared against the rise of Socialism.

But then a miner said, "Colonel, you can talk about winners and losers as much as you like—when you're one of the winners. When you're putting in twelve, fourteen hours underground six days a week and you don't make enough to feed yourself, let alone your wife and children, well, hell, you've already lost. How are you worse off then if you try and do something different? What can you throw away that ain't already gone?"

The miner drew applause from people who had booed Roosevelt; those who had agreed with him stood silent, waiting to hear what he would say. He picked his words with care: "Do you want to burn down the timbers that are holding up the roof of the tunnel? That's what Red revolution means. If you want to shore up the roof so it doesn't come down on your head, peaceably petition the government for redress of grievances."

"And a hell of a lot of good that'll do," the miner said. "They only listen to the bastards with money."

"No," Roosevelt said. "They listen to the bastards with votes. And you mark my words, sir: they will go a hell of a long way to keep the revolution from coming. A man will do a great many startling things if all his other choices look worse. On that you may rely."

"Lincoln said the same damn thing, and you were going on about hanging him," the miner said.

"Lincoln pays lip service to peaceable redress, but he doesn't believe in it," Roosevelt said. "I do."

The miner looked him up and down. "You don't mind me saying so, there's a hell of a lot of difference between what some pup who was a cavalry colonel for a little while thinks and what goes through the head of a fellow who was president of the United States and who's been trying to help the little fellow, the laboring man, his whole life long."

Some little pup who was a cavalry colonel for a little while. A flush heated Roosevelt's cheeks and turned his ears to fire. Now he knew what came after hero: has-been. Savagely, he said, "Lincoln is the past. I am the future. And Socialism, sir, Socialism is the road to ruin."

If he impressed the miner, the man—who had to be at least twice his age—did not show it. "Talk is cheap," he said. "You get to be as old as Lincoln is nowadays, you look back and see what you've done, see if you measure up. You ask me, it ain't likely."

"I will take that wager, and I will take that chance," Theodore Roosevelt said. "And there is one thing Lincoln has done that I swear before almighty God I shall never do."

"Yeah?" The miner laughed. "What is it?"

"If the chance should come my way to fight the Confederate States of America, I shall never lose a war to them," Roosevelt promised. The miner laughed again. Roosevelt didn't care.

General Thomas Jackson had just finished the last piece of fried chicken on his plate and was wiping his fingers when someone knocked on the door of his Richmond house. "Who could that be?" his wife said in some annoyance. "I had looked for a quiet evening at home. Since the war took you away from your family for so long, I think I am entitled to look for a few quiet evenings at home with you."

"Let us hope it is some traveler who has lost his way and seeks directions, then," Jackson said. "But if it is not, Mary, that too is as God wills."

Cyrus, the butler, came into the dining room. "General Jackson, suh, Senator Hampton say he wish to have a word with you," the slave reported.

"Hampton?" Jackson's eyebrows rose. So did he. "Of course I'll see him. You've put him in the parlor?" Cyrus nodded. Jackson headed in that direction. "I wonder what on earth he can want with me, though."

When he went into the parlor, Wade Hampton III rose from a sofa to shake his hand. The senator from South Carolina was five or six years older than Jackson, portly but erect, balding, with a neat beard once brown but now mostly gray and splendid mustachios. He and Jackson had known each other for twenty years, since the days when the former planter commanded a cavalry brigade under Jeb Stuart.

After the greetings were done, after Hampton had declined food and drink, the South Carolinian closed both doors into the parlor, having first looked up and down each hallway to ensure that no one lurked nearby. That bit of melodrama accomplished, he said, "I must have your word, General, that, come what may, what we say and do here tonight shall remain solely between the two of us."

"Well, sir, that depends," Jackson said. "If you are contemplating treason against the government of the Confederate States, I'm afraid I cannot help you."

He'd meant it for a joke, a piece of light badinage. The last thing he expected was for Wade Hampton to look as if he'd just taken a gunshot wound. Slowly, Hampton said, "Treason against the government of the Confederate States is not the same as treason against the Confederate States. Of this I am convinced down to the bottom of my soul. If you disagree, tell me at once, and I shall bid you a good evening and beg your pardon for having disturbed you."

"You had better tell me more," Jackson said, also slowly. "I must confess, I have not the faintest idea of what you are talking about. Do you believe that I, in my recent conversation with General Rosecrans and Mr. Hay, am somehow betraying our country? If so, sir, we would be wiser to continue this conversation through our friends." Dueling had been illegal in Virginia for many years. From time to time, though, gentlemen still traded fire on the field of honor.

But Hampton hastily held up a hand. "By no means!" he exclaimed. "You do not tarnish the honor of the Confederacy;

your every action brightens it. Would to God others might say the same instead of trampling our beloved Constitution in the dust."

"Take a seat, sir; take a seat," Jackson urged. After Hampton sat, so did the Confederate general-in-chief, on a cane-backed chair well suited to his rigid posture. "You still have the advantage of me, for I know of no plots brewing against our government."

"You have a sizable army in northern Virginia, ready to compel the Yankees to obedience," Hampton said. After Jackson nodded, the senator went on, "I trust the men would also obey you if you called on them to preserve our republic from those who would destroy the principles on which it was founded."

"Speak your mind, if that is what you came for," Jackson said. Wade Hampton did nothing of the sort, but sat mute. Jackson's bushy eyebrows came down low over his eyes. The scowl that made soldiers quail had no effect on the senator. Sighing, Jackson did something out of the ordinary for him: he gave ground. "Very well—you have my promise."

"I knew you were a true patriot," Hampton breathed. "Here, then: I shall ask my question, which is this—if you order your men to defend the Constitution of the Confederate States, will they move against the men here in Richmond who set it at naught?"

When Hampton spoke of setting an army in motion against Richmond, that *was* liable to be treason, though Jackson could not imagine his old comrade-in-arms disloyal to the CSA. "From whom, in your view, does the Constitution want defending?" he asked.

And, at last, the senator from South Carolina brought his fear and anger out into the light: "From President Longstreet, General, and from any other man who would tamper with the structure of society we have so long maintained in our beloved nation."

"Ahh." Jackson let out a long exhalation. "You oppose him because he intends to manumit the Negro."

"Of course I do," Hampton said. "What right-thinking white man in this country does not? My home state was first to leave the USA because of the federal government's continued interference with slavery, as our ordinance of secession clearly shows. Shall we tolerate from Richmond the tyranny that led us to break with Washington?"

Jackson sighed again, this time with deep regret. "I am afraid we shall, Senator," he said. Hampton stared at him. He went on, "The president has persuaded me that his policy is in the best interest of our country. If not for the intervention of Britain and France, we might well have failed in the War of Secession. If not for their intervention, we should have had a far more difficult time in this war. If we forfeit their support by maintaining an institution they despise, how shall we fare against the Yankees the next time we have to face them?"

"We'll lick 'em, of course," Wade Hampton III replied at once. "We always have. We always will."

"I wish I shared your certainty," Jackson said. "From the bottom of my heart, I wish I shared your certainty. But I do not. I cannot. Since I do not and cannot, and since I know the president purposes giving the Negro the name of freedom but not much of the thing itself, I am willing to suspend my disagreement with him on this matter and to believe him better acquainted with what will best serve us than I am myself."

Hampton's countenance darkened. "General, you are making a mistake if you choose to side with a man who would cast down our peculiar institution."

"Senator, you are making a mistake if you seek to suborn me into treason against the duly elected head of my government," Jackson answered evenly. "The Army *will* stand behind the president, sir; you may take that to be as much a given as one of Euclid's axioms of geometry. This being so, have we anything further to say to each other?"

"I think not." Senator Hampton headed for the door. "You need not accompany me, General; I can find my own way out." He opened the door from the parlor to the front hall, then slammed it shut. Another window-rattling slam marked his departure from Jackson's home.

"Good heavens!" his wife exclaimed when he returned to the table. "You sent the senator away unhappy, Tom." She took a longer look at Jackson. "And you are unhappy, most unhappy, yourself. What happened between the two of you?"

"Nothing I much care to discuss," Jackson answered. "Least said, soonest mended." He hoped with all his heart that his flat rejection of Hampton's overtures would persuade the senator any attempt at a *coup d'état* was foredoomed to failure. If it didn't, force of arms would persuade Hampton and whoever backed him of the same thing. "We had a disagreement, that's all, and the senator from South Carolina is and has always been a man of somewhat hasty temper."

His son's eyes glowed. "Hampton's red-hot for holding the nigger down and putting a foot on his neck," Jonathan said. "I'll bet he was trying to talk Father into going against manumission."

Jackson rolled his eyes up to the heavens. "Senator Hampton is a fool," he growled. Jonathan grinned an enormous grin, convinced his father's words meant he was right. So they did, though not quite for the reason he thought. Jackson himself paid as little attention to politics as he could. Hampton's appeal had taken him by surprise. But if his purpose was so obvious that even a youth—a youth more politically alert than the Confederate general-in-chief—could see it, people of greater prominence than that youth also would see it.

And, sure enough, when Jackson went to the War Department the next morning to continue discussion with General Rosecrans and Minister Hay, he was not altogether astonished to have a young lieutenant take him aside and lead him down the hall to a small room where President Longstreet sat waiting. Without preamble, Longstreet said, "You had a visit from Wade Hampton last night."

"Yes, Your Excellency, I did," Jackson said.

"He asked you to help overthrow the government if I persist in moving us toward manumission." Longstreet did not phrase it as a question.

"By his request, Mr. President, what passed between us last night is a private matter," Jackson said.

"You need not tell me—I know Hampton's mind," Longstreet said. "I also know you sent him away with a flea in his ear."

"How do you know—?" Jackson paused. "You are having him watched." Spoken so baldly, it sounded like a transgression.

But Longstreet nodded, unembarrassed. "I most certainly am. If he were actor enough to simulate the fury he showed outside your home, he would do better before the footlights than in the Senate. I assure you, General, I do not intend our nation to be torn asunder in the hour of our greatest triumph."

"Our greatest triumph." Jackson sighed. "A great pity General Stuart cannot now enjoy it with us."

"That it is," Longstreet agreed. "Still, he fell in action, as he no doubt would have wished to do, and we have avenged and shall avenge ourselves upon the Apaches manyfold for his assassination." But nothing, not even the death of a friend of many years, could derail Longstreet's train of thought for long. "Believe me, General, I am glad you share my views on the integrity of our nation."

"I do indeed," Jackson said. On the other hand, Abraham Lincoln had not intended the United States to be torn asunder, either.

But Longstreet, almost as if in response to Jackson's thought, went on, "And I shall not allow Hampton and his fellows any opportunity to do us mischief, either. I shall steal their thunder. Easter has come and gone; the end of April approaches. Still Blaine delays and delays and delays. He shall delay no more. Is the army gathered by the Potomac in readiness?"

"You know it is, Your Excellency," Jackson replied, as if he had been insulted.

"Of course I do," the president said soothingly. "Still, the question had to be asked. At today's session with the Yankees, you and Minister Benjamin are to tell them the war will resume in forty-eight hours unless we, the British Empire, and France have the full acquiescence of the United States to all demands made against them before that time shall have expired."

"Yes, sir!" Jackson's voice bubbled with enthusiasm. "We shall punish them as they deserve." He thought for a moment. "And, in so doing, we make Hampton and his complaints into smaller matters than they would be otherwise."

"Just so," James Longstreet said. "I have told you before, I believe, that you are, or you can be, more astute in matters political than one might suppose."

"You flatter me beyond my deserts, sir," Jackson said. "Like you, my son had no trouble ciphering out the reason on account of which Senator Hampton paid me a call, though I did not realize what it was until he made himself unmistakably plain."

"Jonathan's a clever lad," Longstreet said, smiling. "Remember, the United States are to have forty-eight hours from the moment you deliver the ultimatum. Make careful note of the time, that we may not unduly delay their punishment should its infliction prove necessary."

"I shall carry out your orders in every particular, Mr. President," Jackson said. "You may rest assured on that score."

"I do, General, believe me." Longstreet got to his feet. "And now Lieutenant Latham will take you to Mr. Benjamin. I leave to the two of you the manner in which you present the ultimatum to the United States. I am confident that, between your ingenuity and his, you will devise a plan more likely to meet our needs than any my poor wits might conceive."

"*I* am confident I know a man hiding his light under a bushel when I see one," Jackson said. Ignoring Longstreet's modest little wave, he went on, "I also have great faith in Mr. Benjamin's ingenuity." He rose and followed the young officer to the room where the Confederate minister to the USA waited.

"Ah, General Jackson!" Judah P. Benjamin exclaimed in delight, or an artful counterfeit thereof. "The president has told you of his intention?"

"He has." Jackson knew how abrupt his nod was. Benjamin's round, smiling, Semitic face, framed by hair and beard dyed a black that defied and denied his years, never failed to make the Confederate general-in-chief nervous. The statesman was too openly successful, too openly clever a Jew to suit Jackson's stern Christianity.

"My view, General, is that you should be the one to deliver the ultimatum," Benjamin said now. "Coming from your lips, it will possess an aura of authority I could never give it. Were I to present it to Hay and Rosecrans, they would the more readily assume it to be negotiable."

"So they would," Jackson agreed. Benjamin's smile never wavered. Jackson did not think to wonder if he had insulted the Jew by assuming him to be flexible in all circumstances. Drawing out his pocket watch, he said, "The Yankees should be here in a few minutes."

Another young Confederate lieutenant escorted the U.S. representatives into the room. After polite greetings, John Hay said, "I should like to bring to your attention a new proposal President Blaine has authorized me to—"

"No," Jackson interrupted.

"I beg your pardon?" the U.S. minister to the Confederate States said.

"No," Jackson repeated. "The time for proposals from President Blaine has passed. He is in no position to offer them. He has, in fact, but one choice left: peace on our terms or war." He delivered Longstreet's ultimatum in tones as fierce as he could muster. Having done so, he noted down the time on a scrap of paper: twenty-seven minutes past ten in the morning.

Hay and Rosecrans both stared at him, the one with something like horror on his handsome face, the other in a sort of weary resignation. Rosecrans found his tongue first: "And what happens if President Blaine makes no reply, saying neither yes nor no?"

"That is a well he has drunk dry: it will be construed as rejecting the ultimatum," Jackson replied. "If we do not hear that he has accepted our terms within the space of forty-eight hours, now less"—he looked at the watch again—"two minutes, the war shall begin again, and where it shall end is known but to God."

"General, this is a brutal and most unreasonable way of forcing your will upon us," John Hay said.

"Yes, it is, isn't it?" Jackson agreed placidly. He said no more than that, leaving the U.S. minister to the Confederate States nothing on which he could hang a further protest.

Judah P. Benjamin spoke for the first time: "Gentlemen, I would suggest that, in view of the present circumstances, you might be well advised to communicate this ultimatum to President Blaine as soon as is practicable, to give him the greatest possible amount of time in which he can decide."

Under his breath, General Rosecrans muttered, "Blaine's had months to decide. What the devil difference will two more days make?"

Jackson and Benjamin both started to speak at the same time. The Confederate minister to the USA caught Jackson's eye. Benjamin's own eyes, dark and all but fathomless, glinted. Jackson inclined his head, allowing his clever companion to say whatever he intended. Turning another of his woundingly bland smiles on the U.S. representatives, Benjamin remarked, "I believe it was Samuel Johnson, gentlemen, who observed, 'When a man knows he is to be hanged in a fortnight, it concentrates his mind wonderfully.' "

Hay winced. Rosecrans muttered again, this time unintelligibly. Gathering himself, Hay said, "I hope you will permit us an adjournment, then, to wire your demands to our president."

Now Judah Benjamin nodded to Jackson. "I not only permit it," the Confederate general-in-chief said, "I require it."

Rosecrans' comments to himself sounded sulfurous, even if Jackson could not make them out in detail. With a sigh, Hay asked, "May we have a written copy of the ultimatum, to be sure it is communicated accurately to President Blaine?"

Jackson shook his head. "No, for I have not got one. The terms are of the simplest, however: either your government shall yield within forty-eight hours less ... thirteen minutes now, or there will be renewed war."

"War *à l'outrance*," Benjamin added. Rosecrans, who plainly did not understand the French phrase, glared at him. Hay, who plainly did, also glared, in a different, more nearly desperate way. The two U.S. representatives rose, shook hands again with their Confederate counterparts, and took their leave.

"From now on, sir, these talks will be in your hands alone, I expect," Jackson said to Benjamin. "I shall shortly travel north to the Potomac, to take charge of operations against the United States in that region."

"In my opinion, General, you need not be overhasty," the minister to the United States replied.

"I dare not take the chance of your being mistaken," Jackson said.

"However you like." Benjamin habitually looked amused. At the moment, he looked more amused than usual. "Whether we do go to war or not, though, the president has effectively spiked Senator Hampton's guns, would you not agree?"

"You know about Senator Hampton?" Jackson blurted, and then felt extraordinarily foolish: whatever went on in the Confederate States without Judah P. Benjamin's knowledge could not be worth knowing.

Benjamin's laugh made his big belly shake. "Oh, yes, General, I know about Senator Hampton. A great many people know about Senator Hampton. That you did not until last night speaks well of your devotion to duty."

The Jew was indeed a statesman, Jackson thought; he had never been called blind more politely. In musing tones, he asked, "Could he have raised a revolution with my help?"

"With your help, General, anything would be possible," Judah Benjamin answered. "Without it, he is bound to fail." Benjamin hesitated, then went on, "Had President Longstreet reckoned your help likely to be forthcoming, the distinguished senator from South Carolina would have found himself unfortunately unable to call on you yesterday."

"Would he?" Jackson murmured. Benjamin gave him a solemn nod. He nodded back, unsurprised. After a moment's consideration, he nodded again, this time in firm decision. "Good."

* * *

Samuel Clemens woke with the bed shaking. He sat bolt up-right, ready to run if it was an earthquake. By the way Alexandra smiled at him, it wasn't. He could barely see her smile; the sun hadn't risen yet. "What time is it?" he asked around a yawn.

"A little before five," his wife answered. "You wanted me to get you up early, though—remember? Philadelphia sun time is more than three hours ahead of us here."

Clemens grimaced and nodded. "Which means that, whatever Blaine aims to do, he'll do it too early in the morning." He got out of bed with a martyred sigh. "Light the lamp, will you, my dear?" Gas hissed. Alexandra struck a match. Yellow light filled the bed-room. Sam sighed again as he walked to the closet. "We're finally back in a home of our own—in a bed of our own, by God—and Blaine routs me out of it on a Saturday morning. There is no jus-tice in the world—and no clean trousers, either, by the look of things."

"There are so," Alexandra declared. By then, Sam was getting into a pair of them. She gave him a dirty look.

He affected to ignore it, but from then on aimed his barbs at the administration rather than his wardrobe: "He shouldn't have started the war in the first place. Once he'd botched it, he should have quit when Longstreet gave him the chance. That would have saved San Francisco, and saved us the torture of living with your brother."

"You can't blame the president for that," Alexandra said.

"Who says I can't? I just did." Clemens warmed to his theme: "He dithered till he lost half of Maine, too. And now that the ulti-matum's landed on him, he still can't make up his blasted mind. If he doesn't give in before half past seven or so, we're going to take *another* licking, and for what? For what, I ask you?"

His wife said, "Why don't you finish dressing? I'll go down-stairs and make some coffee for you." It was not a responsive answer, but Sam doubted James G. Blaine could have given him a better one. *And heaven only knows what sort of coffee Blaine makes,* he thought, rummaging in a drawer for a cravat.

Fortified with coffee, bread and butter, and a slab of ham left over from supper the night before, he headed east along Turk Street toward the *Morning Call.* Not all the houses in the neigh-borhood had yet been rebuilt; empty lots gave the street the aspect of a barroom brawler who led with his teeth instead of his left.

Every few paces, Clemens looked back over his shoulder. Hills hid the Pacific from his eyes. Whether he could see it or not, though, he knew it was there. Somewhere on it, probably somewhere not far from San Francisco, sailed a Royal Navy flotilla. He was sure of that. The Pacific Squadron of the U.S. Navy, or what was left of it, was out there, too, but he had no faith in its ability to halt the British warships, or even to slow them much. When a fast steamer from the Sandwich Islands gave them the word to move . . .

Since the British attack on San Francisco, Colonel Sherman had brought in many more guns to defend the coast. Clemens didn't think they would do much good, either: they were small-caliber field pieces, which had the twin advantages of being common and mobile but were hardly a match for the huge cannon the ironclads of the Royal Navy mounted. Still, Sherman was making an effort, which put him ahead of most of the U.S. government.

Market Street was quiet as Sam turned onto it. Not only was Saturday a half day for most people, he was earlier than usual getting to the office. He walked in just before a quarter to seven. He wasn't the first man there, either, not by a long chalk. Reporters clustered round the telegraph clicker like relatives round the bed of a sick man who was not expected to live.

"No news yet, eh?" Clemens asked.

"Not a word," Clay Herndon answered, before anyone else could speak. "The only question left is whether the wire comes from Philadelphia or the Potomac. Will Blaine see sense, or will he throw away Washington City and Maryland to go along with Maine?"

"Blaine will let the war go on." Edgar Leary spoke with great assurances. His whole manner had changed since his stories on corruption in the rebuilding of San Francisco ran in the *Morning Call*. Now he seemed to reckon himself a man among men, a pup no longer. He had reason for that newfound confidence, too; thanks to those stories, several prominent men were presently occupying small rooms with poor accommodations and unpleasant views. He went on, "He's dragged his heels all the way through this mess. Why would he change now?"

No one argued with him. Clocks in the office and outside struck seven. "Less than half an hour to go," Herndon muttered. "Big story coming, one way or the other."

"Bastards," somebody said softly. Clemens wondered whether the fellow meant the enemies of the United States or the Blaine administration. After a moment, he realized the curse could be inclusive.

At nineteen minutes past seven, the telegraph receiver began to click. "It's early," Edgar Leary noted. "Have the Rebs jumped the gun, or has Blaine thrown in the sponge? My bet's on the Rebs."

But the telegram came out of Philadelphia. Clay Herndon, who happened to be closest to the machine, read the Morse characters emerging word by word on the tape as readily as if they were set in fourteen-point Garamond. "President Blaine accedes to Confederate ultimatum," he said, and then, through a burst of startled exclamations and cheers, "President Blaine's complete statement follows."

"Read it out, Clay," Sam said. "Read it on out. Let's see how he puts it in the best light he can."

He promptly regretted that, for Blaine went on at greater length than he'd expected. But neither he nor anyone else in the offices of the *Morning Call* interrupted the reporter as he gave voice to the words flowing from the clicking receiver: "Finding no hope for the successful employment of our arms against the enemies who ring us round and who have unjustly combined against us, I am compelled at this hour to yield to the demands imposed upon the United States by the Confederate States, Great Britain, and France. I do this with the heaviest of hearts, and only in the certain knowledge that all other courses are worse.

"This surrender offers a fitting occasion to present ourselves in humiliation and prayer before that God Who has ordained that it be so. We had hoped that the year just past would close upon a scene of victory for our righteous cause, but it has pleased the Supreme Disposer of events to order it otherwise. We are not permitted to furnish an exception to the rule of Divine government, which has prescribed affliction as the rule of nations as well as of individuals. Our faith and perseverance must be tested, and the chastening which seems grievous will, if rightly received, bring forth its appropriate fruit.

"It is meet, therefore, that we should repair to the only Giver of all victory, and, humbling ourselves before Him, should pray that He may strengthen our confidence in His mighty power and righteous judgment. Then we may surely trust in Him that He will perform His promise and encompass us as with a shield.

"In this trust and to this end, I, James G. Blaine, president of the United States, do hereby set apart today, Saturday, the twenty-second day of April, as a day of fasting, humiliation, prayer, and remembrance, and I do hereby invite the reverend clergy and people of the United States to repair to their respective places of worship and to humble themselves before almighty God, and pray for His protection and favor to our beloved country, and that we may be saved from our enemies, and from the hand of all that hate us.

"And I do further urge and direct the citizens of the United States to observe the twenty-second day of April in each succeeding year as a day of humiliation and remembrance, so that the infamous defeat we have suffered on this date shall never be lost from the minds of the said citizens until such time as it may, by the grace of God, be avenged a hundredfold."

The clicker fell silent. Several men sighed. Sam realized he wasn't the only one who'd been holding his breath toward the end. Clay Herndon said, "Well, well, who would have thought it? Even James G. Blaine can read the writing on the wall, provided only that you make the letters big enough."

"The writing on the wall, eh?" Sam said. "That must be why he blamed God for our losing, or one reason for it, anyhow. The other two that spring to mind are that God doesn't vote, and He hardly ever stands up on His hind legs and calls someone a damned liar."

Outside, church bells began to ring out. Noise on the street swiftly swelled: shouts and cheers and snatches of song. Here and there, gunshots rang out. One of them sounded as if it came from right outside the offices. Somebody yelled, "That's the boy, Reuben! Shoot 'em all off—we ain't gonna need 'em no more." Another shot shattered the morning, presumably from Reuben's gun.

"We aren't the only ones with the news," Herndon observed. "That one would have gone to a whole raft of telegraph instruments."

"Everybody who has it likes it, too," Edgar Leary said.

Samuel Clemens made himself stop thinking like an American delighted the war had indeed ended—regardless of the terms on which it had ended—and start thinking like a newspaperman again. "Half the people who've got the word print papers of their own," he growled. "Out of that bunch, we're going to be the ones who put the news on the street first, or I'll know the reason why."

That blunt announcement sent people flying away from the telegraph clicker as if it had suddenly become red-hot. One of the typesetters yelled, "We'll need a transcript of what Blaine had to say. If somebody writes it out, it'll be a hell of a lot faster to set than if we've got to do it from the Morse."

"Clay, you take care of that," Sam said. "You've already read it through once, so you've got a head start on everybody else. Headline above it will be 'War Ends'—screamer type, of course."

"You want seventy-two point?" the typesetter asked.

"No, ninety-six, Charlie," Clemens answered. "Hell, 108 if you've got it. That's not a headline we get to use every day. If only we could write *Blaine Tarred, Feathered, and Ridden Out of Philadelphia on a Rail* underneath it, everything would be perfect." He hesitated. "Well, almost perfect: we'd have to drop the type size a good deal to fit that on one line."

"Boss, you'll give us an editorial to run alongside of Blaine's statement?" Leary said.

"What?" Sam frowned. "Oh. Yes, I suppose I'd better, hadn't I?"

He went back to his desk, swept a snowdrift of papers out of the way so he'd have room to write, and set a fresh sheet down in the middle of the space he'd cleared. After he'd inked a pen, he stared at the blank paper. For a man who wrote for a living, getting started was always the hardest part of the job.

Words did not want to come. He'd set everybody else on the *Morning Call* running like a dog with a tin can tied to its tail, and the words did not want to come. He glared at the paper. He glared at the pen. The fault was not in them. He knew where the fault was. He did not have a mirror at his desk, so he could not glare at himself.

He took out a cigar, scraped a match afire, and lighted the malodorous stogie. Neither the harsh smoke he held in his mouth nor the stinking fogbank with which he surrounded himself helped concentrate his mind on the business at hand, as they often did. He smoked the cigar down to a dank, soggy butt with quick, angry puffs, then lighted another. Nothing even vaguely resembling inspiration struck.

Setting the second cigar in the grimy brass ashtray that held the corpse of the first, he opened a desk drawer. If inspiration wasn't lurking in tobacco today, maybe it was hiding somewhere else.

He pulled the cork from the bottle with his teeth and took a long swig. Whiskey ran molten down his throat. His eyes opened very wide. He took another drink. It exploded in his stomach like a ten-inch shell from a British ironclad. He felt ready to whip his weight in wildcats.

He picked up the pen and poised it above the paper. No words came out. He was as silent and frustrated as a veteran actor—say, one of the Booth brothers, whose careers went back before the War of Secession, and whose tours had crisscrossed the USA and the CSA ever since—inexplicably stricken with stage fright in front of a packed house.

Clay Herndon trotted up to him, carrying a sheet full of words from edge to edge and top to bottom. Sam ground his teeth, even though he knew the words were Blaine's and not Herndon's. "Here's the transcription of the statement," Herndon said, waving it about. "I'll give it to the typesetters. What are you going to say in your—?" Most of a sentence too late, his eye fell on the still-blank page in front of Clemens.

Sam's eye fell on it, too . . . balefully. "Damned if I know," he ground out.

"Even if it's only 'Mary had a little lamb,' you'd better say it fast," Herndon said. "You were right—we can't be the only paper getting a new edition to press as fast as we can set the type."

"I know, God damn it, but I'm dry," Sam said. "I haven't been this dry since the stagecoach ride through the desert from Salt Lake to Virginia City."

"You've got to say *something*," Herndon insisted.

"Yes, but what?" Clemens said. "What the devil can I say that Blaine didn't already? The war's done. We lost. Any fool can see that, and even a fool can see it now, or Blaine wouldn't have given up. The thing is so obvious, it's impossible to write about without sounding like an idiot." Herndon didn't say anything. Sam caught him not saying anything. "When has that ever stopped me before, eh?"

"You can't prove that's what I was thinking," the reporter answered with a grin.

"And a damned lucky thing for you I can't, too," Sam said. "Go on, get that set. I'll come up with something in the next few minutes, or else we just have to go on without me." He didn't like that. It was embarrassing. But getting the news out on the street third would be a lot more embarrassing. Herndon dashed away to the typesetters.

It's over. Almost of its own will, Clemens' pen set down two words. He stared at them. They came close to serving as an editorial by themselves. What else did he need to say? He thought about that for a few seconds, then wrote one more sentence: *Thank heaven!* He nodded, picked up the paper, and hurried after Clay Herndon.

AUTHOR'S NOTE

This is a novel about the aftermath of a Confederate victory in the Civil War. It is not in any sense a sequel to my earlier novel about a Confederate victory in the Civil War, *The Guns of the South.* Here, the Confederacy is imagined to have won by natural causes, so to speak, rather than by intervention from time-travelers with an agenda of their own, and to have done so in 1862 rather than 1864.

The differences are crucial. The Civil War is, and deserves to be, perhaps the most intensely examined period of American history. For better and for worse, all that the United States is today (even that we say *The United States is*, not *The United States are*), it is because of what happened in and immediately after the Civil War. Change anything there, and subsequent history changes drastically.

Take the three cigars around which Lee's Special Order 191 was wrapped. In real history, two Union soldiers, Corporal Barton Mitchell and First Sergeant John Bloss, discovered them after a Confederate courier lost them. Learning Lee's battle plan and how widely Lee had divided his army while invading U.S. territory let General McClellan win the battle of Antietam. That victory, in turn, let Lincoln issue the Emancipation Proclamation, which changed the moral character of the war. It effectively made sure that Britain and France, which were at the time trembling on the brink of recognizing the Confederate States and forcing mediation on the United States, did not do so.

Had those cigars and that order not been lost ... the world would be a different place today.

I need to make a couple of remarks about my handling of the characters in this novel. All speeches and writings attributed to

Samuel Clemens, in particular, are of my own devising. The same does not apply to the political speeches I have put in the mouth of Abraham Lincoln. In them, I have frequently used his own words on the relationship between labor and capital and between employee and employer, sometimes verbatim, sometimes adapting his thought on slaves and owners to apply to workers and owners. I have done this not only for dramatic effect but also to show the plausibility (and what more can one demand of a novelist?) of the views I have ascribed to him in the changed circumstances I have envisioned here.

THE GREAT WAR: AMERICAN FRONT

The stunning sequel to *How Few Remain*
by Harry Turtledove

1914. As Europe is engulfed in the fires of World War I, the United States and the Confederacy, bitter enemies for five decades, enter the fray on opposite sides. The USA, led by President Theodore Roosevelt, aligns with the newly powerful Germany, while the Confederates, under Woodrow Wilson, join forces with their longtime allies, Britain and France.

For both sides, this fight will be different from any other—a war fraught with global consequences, and waged with the chilling innovations brought about by the dawning modern age: the machine gun, the airplane, and poison gas. The terrible bloodshed will take place all across the North American continent.

The events of *How Few Remain*—the Confederate victory and the subsequent division of America—set the stage for this extraordinary epic of the first World War as it might have been. THE GREAT WAR: AMERICAN FRONT begins a chronicle in which Harry Turtledove will create a vast, vibrant canvas, blending actual events and players with a brilliantly reinvented history. This unforgettable, deeply moving, and superbly original novel is a masterpiece of imagination and another triumph for its acclaimed creator, the recognized Master of Alternate History.

Published by Del Rey ® Books.
Available soon in bookstores everywhere.
Visit us at www.randomhouse.com/delrey/althist

DEL REY® ONLINE!

The Del Rey Internet Newsletter...

A monthly electronic publication, posted on the Internet, GEnie, CompuServe, BIX, various BBSs, and the Panix gopher (gopher.panix.com). It features hype-free descriptions of books that are new in the stores, a list of our upcoming books, special announcements, a signing/reading/convention-attendance schedule for Del Rey authors, "In Depth" essays in which professionals in the field (authors, artists, designers, salespeople, etc.) talk about their jobs in science fiction, a question-and-answer section, behind-the-scenes looks at sf publishing, and more!

Internet information source!

A lot of Del Rey material is available to the Internet on our Web site and on a gopher server: all back issues and the current issue of the Del Rey Internet Newsletter, sample chapters of upcoming or current books (readable or downloadable for free), submission requirements, mail-order information, and much more. We will be adding more items of all sorts (mostly new DRINs and sample chapters) regularly. The Web site is http://www.randomhouse.com/delrey/ and the address of the gopher is gopher.panix.com

Why?
We at Del Rey realize that the networks are the medium of the future. That's where you'll find us promoting our books, socializing with others in the sf field, and—most important—making contact and sharing information with sf readers.

Online editorial presence:
Many of the Del Rey editors are online, on the Internet, GEnie, CompuServe, America Online, and Delphi. There is a Del Rey topic on GEnie and a Del Rey folder on America Online.

Our official e-mail address
for Del Rey Books is delrey@randomhouse.com (though it sometimes takes us a while to answer).

✎ FREE DRINKS ✎

Take the Del Rey® survey and get a free newsletter! Answer the questions below and we will send you complimentary copies of the DRINK (Del Rey® Ink) newsletter free for one year. Here's where you will find out all about upcoming books, read articles by top authors, artists, and editors, and get the inside scoop on your favorite books.

Age _____ Sex ❏ M ❏ F

Highest education level: ❏ high school ❏ college ❏ graduate degree

Annual income: ❏ $0-30,000 ❏ $30,001-60,000 ❏ over $60,000

Number of books you read per month: ❏ 0-2 ❏ 3-5 ❏ 6 or more

Preference: ❏ fantasy ❏ science fiction ❏ horror ❏ other fiction ❏ nonfiction

I buy books in hardcover: ❏ frequently ❏ sometimes ❏ rarely

I buy books at: ❏ superstores ❏ mall bookstores ❏ independent bookstores
     ❏ mail order

I read books by new authors: ❏ frequently ❏ sometimes ❏ rarely

I read comic books: ❏ frequently ❏ sometimes ❏ rarely

I watch the Sci-Fi cable TV channel: ❏ frequently ❏ sometimes ❏ rarely

I am interested in collector editions (signed by the author or illustrated):
     ❏ yes ❏ no ❏ maybe

I read Star Wars novels: ❏ frequently ❏ sometimes ❏ rarely

I read Star Trek novels: ❏ frequently ❏ sometimes ❏ rarely

I read the following newspapers and magazines:
     ❏ *Analog*   ❏ *Locus*   ❏ *Popular Science*
     ❏ *Asimov*   ❏ *Wired*   ❏ *USA Today*
     ❏ *SF Universe*   ❏ *Realms of Fantas*y ❏ *The New York Times*

Check the box if you do not want your name and address shared with qualified vendors ❏

Name _____

Address _____

City/State/Zip _____

E-mail _____

turtledove

PLEASE SEND TO: DEL REY®/The DRINK
201 EAST 50TH STREET NEW YORK NY 10022

HARRY
TURTLEDOVE

Published by Del Rey® Books.
Available in your local bookstore.

Call toll free 1-800-793-BOOK (2665) to order by phone and use your
major credit card. Or use this coupon to order by mail.

__DEPARTURES	345-38011-8	$5.99
__THE GUNS OF THE SOUTH	345-38468-7	$6.99
__HOW FEW REMAIN	345-40614-1	$7.99
__A WORLD OF DIFFERENCE	345-36076-1	$5.99

The Worldwar Series:

__WORLDWAR: IN THE BALANCE	345-38852-6	$5.99
__WORLDWAR: TILTING THE BALANCE	345-38998-0	$6.99
__WORLDWAR: UPSETTING THE BALANCE	345-40240-5	$6.99
__WORLDWAR: STRIKING THE BALANCE	345-41208-7	$6.99

The Videssos Cycle:

__THE MISPLACED LEGION	345-33067-6	$5.99
__AN EMPEROR FOR THE LEGION	345-33068-4	$5.99
__THE LEGION OF VIDESSOS	345-33069-2	$5.99
__SWORDS OF THE LEGION	345-33070-6	$5.99

The Tale of Krispos:

__KRISPOS RISING	345-36118-0	$5.99
__KRISPOS OF VIDESSOS	345-36119-9	$5.95
__KRISPOS THE EMPEROR	345-38046-0	$5.99

The Time of Troubles:

__THE STOLEN THRONE	345-38047-9	$5.99
__HAMMER AND ANVIL	345-38048-7	$5.99
__THE THOUSAND CITIES	345-38049-5	$6.99

Name_____

Address_____

City_____State_____Zip_____

Please send me the DEL REY BOOKS I have checked above.

I am enclosing	$_____
plus	
Postage & handling*	$_____
Sales tax (where applicable)	$_____
Total amount enclosed	$_____

*Add $4 for the first book and $1 for each additional book.

Send check or money order (no cash or CODs) to:
Del Rey Mail Sales, 400 Hahn Road, Westminster, MD 21157.

Prices and numbers subject to change without notice.
Valid in the U.S. only.
All orders subject to availability.   TURTLEDOVE